THE
RAGGED MAN

Also by Tom Lloyd from Gollancz:

The Stormcaller
The Twilight Herald
The Grave Thief

THE
RAGGED MAN

THE TWILIGHT REIGN: BOOK 4

Tom Lloyd

GOLLANCZ

LONDON

The right of Tom Lloyd-Williams to be identified as the author
of this work has been asserted by him in accordance
with the Copyright, Designs and Patents Act 1988.

First published in Great Britain in 2010
by Gollancz
An imprint of the Orion Publishing Group
Orion House, 5 Upper St Martin's Lane,
London WC2H 9EA
An Hachette Livre UK Company

A CIP catalogue record for this book
is available from the British Library

ISBN 978 0 575 08558 9 (Cased)
ISBN 978 0 575 08559 6 (Trade Paperback)

1 3 5 7 9 10 8 6 4 2

Typeset by Input Data Services Ltd, Bridgwater, Somerset

Printed and bound in the UK by CPI Mackays, Chatham ME5 8TD

The Orion Publishing Group's policy is to use papers that
are natural, renewable and recyclable products and made
from wood grown in sustainable forests. The logging and
manufacturing processes are expected to conform to the
environmental regulations of the country of origin.

www.tomlloyd.co.uk
www.orionbooks.co.uk

For Fiona, with all my love

Acknowledgements

The biggest thank you must be said to all those who handled the real life side of things so those of us less capable didn't have to – most particularly to my wife, Fiona, and my wonderful in-laws, David and Elizabeth, who worked so hard on the wedding. On top of that, Fi, you're a star for putting up with me day after day – cheerfully living with oddness, forgetfulness, geekery and prog metal. If that doesn't deserve being bought a puppy, I don't know what could.

Many thanks also to Nat, for talking through so much over so many drinks, along with his powers of speed reading that I've happily abused. Also to Lou Anders for advice, support and braving some rather rough first chapters, my brother Richard, David Devereux and Sara Mulryan for more of the same, and all the happy nutters on the Tom Lloyd forum for their enthusiasm, encouragement, reminders and *some* of the suggestions. The cannon-mounted flying carpets I'm still not convinced about, however, and the shower-scene definitely isn't going to happen.

Robin Morero also deserves recognition for everything he's done on the website, in between nappy changes, as do everyone at Pyr and Gollancz – in particular Jo Fletcher for ~~supurb~~, ~~surperb~~, ~~supp~~ … decent editing, Gillian for all sorts, and Charlie for putting up with me being repeatedly stupid. But not Simon. He knows why.

THE LAND

Xomejx
Merlat
Perlir
White Isle
Canar Thrit
Vanach
Tirah
Lomin
ELVEN WASTE
Tor Milist
Scree
Helrect
Mantil
Narkang
Raland
Canar Fell
Aroth
THE Circle City
Embere
Tor Salan
Denei
Castle Keriabral
Ter Nol
Mustet
Thotel
Sautin
ELVEN WASTE
Vijgen
Lochet
Mekray
Verech
Cholos
Tserol
Tiotte
Lenei

N

DS'05

WHAT HAS GONE BEFORE

The Grave Thief

In the aftermath of the firestorm that consumed the city of Scree, it soon becomes clear that Rojak's magic has left a legacy beyond death and destruction. While the followers of Azaer scatter and Isak leads the Farlan Army home, a strange mood takes hold of those remaining outside the city. The city's six principal Gods – Death, Karkarn, Nartis, Vasle, Belarannar and Vellern – are furious at having been driven out of Scree during the city's last days, and their rage badly affects those most closely aligned to them, including the Knights of the Temples and King Emin himself – he had been ordained a priest years before. In their temporary madness, they turn on the civilian survivors and butcher them.

When King Emin returns home to Narkang he is not only guilty about the slaughter he participated in, but distressed by the continuing echoes of Lord Death's rage, which is still affecting his judgement. He responds to intelligence about Venn, Azaer's follower, and the manipulation of Scree's population by Rojak's plays, by ordering a mass assassination of the Harlequin clans, only too aware of their potential influence in the Land. Even as he is doing this, Venn is returning home to the clans with the mage Jackdaw bound to his shadow, about to do exactly as Emin fears: to twist the Harlequins' purpose and deliver to Azaer a small army of unparalleled warrior-preachers who can erode the authority of the Gods on a Land-wide scale.

King Emin's agent, Doranei, discovers the Crystal Skull they recovered from Scree might not have been Azaer's goal there, after all – worse still, they might even have done Azaer a favour by killing the Skull's owner, for they left the path clear for Azaer's followers to retrieve the journal of Vorizh Vukotic.

In Tirah, as Isak's thoughts grow increasingly morbid, the Yee-tatchen white-eye Xeliath arrives in the city, and the trial of Duke Certinse looms. On the first day of the trial a squad of mercenaries break in to the Temple of Law. Although the duke fails to escape, he is able to die fighting, instead of being executed. More worryingly for Isak, when Certinse's mother releases a huge daemon, two of Death's violent Aspects appear from Isak's shadow to kill it before Isak himself can, confirming his fears that he has somehow managed to tear the five Aspects known as the Reapers from Death's control.

In Byora, Ilumene and Aracnan engineer a meeting between the ruler, Duchess Escral, and a newborn baby, Ruhen, whose body is now inhabited by Azaer. The duchess adopts Ruhen as, far to the north, Venn begins preaching about such a child to the now-susceptible Harlequins, matching his words to Ruhen's actions.

Elsewhere in Byora, while the Farlan agent Legana is waiting for Zhia Vukotic to arrive in the city, the Goddess Fate – the Lady – appears to her and makes an unprecedented offer: that Legana should become Fate's Mortal-Aspect. After Legana accepts, her first mission is to murder a high priest with undue influence over Duchess Escral – but the mercenary Aracnan beats her to it. He attacks her, trying to hide his crime, and Fate steps in – only to discover, too late, that he owns a Crystal Skull. The Goddess cannot save herself, but she can save her new Mortal-Aspect, and before Aracnan kills her, she throws Legana from the building.

Further south, Lord Styrax, the Menin ruler, crushes the renowned defences of Tor Salan in a single blow and heads north towards the Circle City, determined to bring the trading heart of the West into his empire, whether the rulers of Byora, Akell, Ismess and Fortinn, the quarters that make up the Circle City, want to or not.

Back in Tirah, Isak has called all of the Farlan nobility to his official investiture as Lord of the Farlan. Each must swear allegiance to him. To keep the tribe's increasingly troublesome clerics in check he makes a bargain with Cardinal Certinse. Isak has revealed he is dreaming of death at Styrax's hands, so after the ceremony, Mihn goes to question the witch of Llehden. Their conversation results in the witch tattooing magical charms over Mihn's body, linking him directly with both Xeliath and Isak.

While Mihn is learning of the afterlife, Vesna is ambushed by fanatics. After he has killed them all, he discovers the 'ambush' was in fact a test, engineered by Karkarn, the God of War, to see if he is indeed the right man for the high honour the God wishes to bestow upon Vesna: to become his own Mortal-Aspect. Vesna, shocked, finds himself unable to make an instant decision.

In Byora, the Lady's death has sparked an increase in the tensions between the ruling nobles and city's clerics. An assassination attempt on Duchess Escral fails, thanks to Ilumene's help, but her husband is killed. The clerics follow this personal attack with a full-scale assault on the Ruby Tower, which Ilumene uses to massacre the city's mage-priests – and as another demonstration of Ruhen's supernatural powers.

Legana is being slowly nursed to health by a priest. When she is well enough, he helps her escape from the Temple District, just as Duchess Escral orders the symbolic barring of the door to Death's temple and Ilumene leads a crackdown in her name on the city's clerics. Outside the Temple District Legana encounters Doranei, and they exchange information before Doranei goes in search of his lover, Zhia Vukotic. Now they know who's pulling the strings in Byora. Legana reports that to Isak.

Religious fanaticism and active reaction against it are both on the increase, and violence is breaking out in all the Land's cities. To avoid outright civil war led by a white-eye as powerful as he is, Isak is forced to persuade one of his most loyal subjects to start a crusade against the Menin. Legana's report makes him realise he is being drawn inexorably towards the man he believes will kill him – but he refuses to shy away from his destiny any longer, and he adds his forces to the crusade.

As Isak heads south, Lord Styrax reaches the Circle City and his decisive action forces the surrender of its most powerful quarter. Once in control of the city, he begins to investigate the secret at its very centre, the Library of Seasons, which sits in a valley between the city's four domains. By the time Isak's army reaches them, he has solved the mystery, and just as the crusade attacks his forces he retrieves a Crystal Skull from the library and wakes the dragon set to guard it. Isak is intent on disrupting Azaer's plans by attacking Byora, but he is drawn into battle with the Menin and becomes the dragon's target, just as the Menin Army springs a trap.

Isak, realising the danger they're in, accepts that he is going to die. He has been dreaming of this for too long. He orders Vesna to lead the army out of danger, while he delays the Menin and attacking dragon. When he is unable to persuade Isak to change his mind, Vesna finally accepts Karkarn's offer and leads the Farlan Army away as Mortal-Aspect of the God of War, while Isak advances on the Menin alone, but with the full power of his Crystal Skulls unleashed. He knows he cannot defeat Lord Styrax, so he takes the only choice remaining to him: the manner of his death. He kills Kohrad, Styrax's white-eye son, and even as he himself is being cut down, he boasts about Kohrad's death to Styrax. The grief-stricken Menin lord retaliates by using his own vast power to send Isak direct to Ghenna, the dark place of eternal torment, instead of just killing Isak and ushering him to the final judgement of Lord Death. As Isak is cast down to the realm of daemons, far away in Llehden, Mihn realises his last desperate gamble must now be played.

PROLOGUE – PART 1

Death stalked the field. As the last of the sun's rays winked out of the sky, a heavy shroud settled over the fields beyond Byora. It was followed by an unnatural hush that rolled in like sea-fog. Bird calls became distant before gradually fading into nothing, but as the gloom deepened there came other sounds: whispers and low, mournful cries from the torpid fens. Uncertain lights winked in the misty distance in cold imitation of life, but then even the voices of spirits and daemons quietened in the presence of something more terrifying yet. In the broken silence the darkness on the edge of the fens slowly deepened and took form.

A hooded head surveyed the still battlefield. The scarce fauna of the fens kept quieter than ever while the baleful creatures that roamed it nightly fled. The newcomer did not notice. They were not what He sought.

The night-robed figure strode forward, pausing a while to look left and right, as though scenting the air. The stink of decay was unmistakable: the rot of butchery that lingers on a killing ground long after the last corpse is buried. He saw the freshly dug heaps all around, unmarked barrows that would soon be beaten from the Land's memory by wind and rain. Around them hung pale shapes, the shades of those robbed of life and senses, unaware of everything but the emptiness within. In a fit of generosity He gestured towards them and watched the handful of lost fade to nothing, ushered towards the Herald's Hall and their Last Judgment.

In the centre of the mounds was a crude monument: upraised spears set in a circle, within which fresh skulls were piled. Above them all flapped a flag of black and red depicting a stylised skull with long, curved canines.

Buried beneath was a corpse, a young man killed before his time, but that was not why He lingered. There was a scent on the air, one unsuited to a cold, muddy field where the promise of rain hung in the air. It spoke of fire and pain: an echo of horror etched into the earth.

The stench of daemons was strongest at a fissure barely twenty paces from the monument. The jagged tear in the ground was no more than a few yards deep, and stained by their corrupt touch. He stood over the rent, unmindful of the distant shrieks that shuddered up through the ground. It took one as strong as He to notice them at all; no mortal would ever be so attuned to the Land, not even the strongest of witches.

He did not speak. He had no words for the dead, or the deed – it was done now, and He was all too aware of the damage done by revenge. Instead He reached out His bone-white arms out into the night. In His left was a double-headed spear studded with glinting gems; the right was empty. The air seemed to contract and reel around Him, though His robe was barely ruffled by the assault, and when the spear cut an arc through the air the darkness was beaten back.

He grabbed with His free hand, which closed about a spitting thread of light. The night boiled off the thread like black smoke, but He ignored it, and twice more grabbed at thin air, each time capturing a new thread, a slightly different tint, in His fist. The empty black cowl regarded the three threads for a while as He stared intently at His catch.

Then, with shocking speed, He spun about and swung with the flat of the spear at the darkness behind. A momentary burst of light tore through the gloom and a fourth thread appeared. This too was scrutinised, but no further violence was required. He jerked the threads closer, and as he tugged, almost carelessly, four figures from the empty night air appeared to cower and stagger before Him.

A hump-backed wolf cringed from His presence, squirming on its belly over the blood-soaked ground until it reached His side. The others came less easily, but by the force of His will He dragged them close and wrapped the threads around the spear shaft. He ran a long, bony finger over each, and the newcomers flinched as though they had been struck, then stood still, finally resigned to their fates.

'One is missing,' Death said.

The Headsman raised his head, his poise subservient though his

2

voice betrayed no emotion. 'She has grown stronger. Our sister has made bargains to keep herself from you. She is gone far from this place.'

'Broken from my grip and teased away,' He said, looking to the northeast, 'but we all shall pay the price of such a bargain.'

He turned abruptly, heading back towards the fens. The others could not help but follow, and within a few steps all five had faded from sight. The night returned and the breeze dared sweep over the battlefield once more, the chill air empty of all now but the voices of the lost.

PROLOGUE – PART 2

As the light began to fade in the Great Forest, miles east of the closest Farlan outpost, bloodlust broke the silence and an old woman ran through the rising shadows, then vanished. They pursued with eager abandon, spreading left and right to sight their prey once more and run her down. Orders were called; sharp and ugly syllables barked in an alien tongue. She crouched low behind a tangled briar for a while longer, hands pressed flat on the damp carpet of leaves, and listened to their confusion. Not waiting for one to chance upon her the woman broke cover, her feet kicking up a flurry of debris as she raced through the trees.

She plunged downslope, her ragged dress billowing in the wind as she skidded down a channel cut by the rain, then slewed left to drop over a rise flanked by a pair of tall beech trees. With a howl the rider in front recklessly followed, only to find the ground fall sharply away. Horse and rider pitched forward and dropped ten feet down the vertical bank. The creature's desperate kicks twisted it around and as it fell on its rider a brief scream pierced the air.

Their voices changed in an instant. The game had become serious and now they drove forward with mounting anger. Again the woman disappeared, melting into the shadows like a will o' the wisp, while they cursed and screamed threats at the empty forest. The flanking riders wheeled in a circle, furiously searching for a flash of movement until, finally, they were rewarded. Fifty yards downslope she broke from cover again and the chase was on again, the riders crouching low over the necks of their horses as they closed the gap.

They grinned when she darted over another rise and scrabbled down the slope on the other side, trying the same lure again, only to find herself penned in on three sides. The old woman lunged for the only escape route but one rider was quicker and cut her off.

She headed in the opposite direction, but floundered in the soft, sodden earth that sank beneath her feet. She slithered down on her belly to the floor of the gully, ending up behind a long stone protruding from the bank, and there she cowered.

The riders approached at leisure, two with arrows nocked on the off-chance she might find the strength to try the slope again. Teeth bared and weapons raised, they formed a half-circle as the woman cringed behind the stone. Her face was covered by a tattered shawl and her fingers tapped the stone's surface, as if seeking reassurance in its strength.

At a guttural command from the leader one rider awkwardly dismounted and lurched towards her.

The Elf was more deformed than most of his kind, his shoulders twisted so that his shield almost dragged along the ground, but his spear was swept back, ready to stab. She flinched and peered up at him through a long tear in her shawl. Her fingers were still dancing over the stone. As he neared he heard a frantic whisper, too quiet and hurried to make sense of, but he guessed what it was.

'She prays,' he announced to his comrades, sharing a grin with the nearest. 'Do they hear, human?' he called out to her in poor Farlan, his malformed throat mangling the flowing sounds of each word. He switched back to Elvish. 'Where are your fucking Gods now?'

Abruptly she stopped.

He cocked his head at her, suddenly aware of eyes like pale blue ice shining up at him through the twilight gloom. Her hands flat against the stone, she pushed herself up with a strange, crab-like movement, stopping only when he levelled his spear and held it inches from her face.

'Where are my Gods?' she repeated softly, peering out through fronds of matted grey hair. 'I am more interested in your Gods now.'

He took a step back; she had replied in perfect Elvish, something he had never heard from a human before. The Elf glanced back at his commanders, the warleader and his sister, the mage. Sensing danger the mage wasted no time in summoning the spirits bound to her; three wispy forms like puffs of smoke, one black, two white, appeared in the air near her.

'And there they are,' the old woman announced with a smile. She offered the spirits a bent-backed bow.

'Kill her,' ordered the mage.

The soldier turned and lunged, but the old woman dodged his spear somehow. As the shaft slipped past she caught it and tugged it, jerking the soldier off-balance and within reach of a backhand slap that sent him crashing to the ground.

'We are not so different,' the crone mused as she turned to the others.

The two archers drew back their strings as she edged forward, grinning toothily. One bow shattered in the hands of its owner. The other managed to fire before his did likewise, but he snatched at the shot, and it skewed a yard wide. A spear was thrown, but she twitched it aside with a flick of her long fingers and it buried itself deep into the soft earth. When no more were thrown she took a step forward and grinned down at the dazed Elf at her feet.

'Not so different indeed,' she continued. 'Both once tied to the Gods, both now free to learn a new way.'

She hesitated, her tongue flicking out like a snake catching a scent on the breeze. The fallen Elf touched a grimy hand to his face then held it up for inspection. His eyes widened as a discoloration on the skin deepened before his eyes and swelled in an instant to become a bleeding sore.

'And how well have you learned!' she cackled, gesturing towards the spirits circling the mage. 'You have found new Gods, ones weak enough to be controlled and enslaved – and so you become the thing you hate most.'

The Elf at her feet began to keen in fear, pawing at his face as the disease spread, ravaging the skin faster than the eye could follow. He tried to howl, but his throat was already ruined and in moments he was unable to even whimper like a dying puppy.

None of the rest noticed; they were transfixed by the sight of the old woman shaking out her ragged clothes and straightening. Her appearance changed in seconds as she grew taller before their eyes. A thick stink of putrefaction filled the air and her skin paled to the chalk-white colouring of a corpse as her body juddered like a plague victim. Then the transformation was over and she looked up, her blue lips twisted into an uneven smile. A tarnished crown appeared in the tangled thicket of her hair.

'So I shall learn from you all,' the Wither Queen announced to the terrified Elves. The quickest-witted of them wrenched his horse around to flee, but the Wither Queen was faster. She raked her nails through the air in his direction and was rewarded with a scream from his horse. She followed it with a flurry of slashes directed at the remaining soldiers and in a heartbeat they were all lying on the ground, some crushed, others merely dazed. The Wither Queen spat on her palms and flung the spit out with an incantation and riders and horses alike coughed bloody foam. The horses reeled, sinking jerkily to their knees.

Only the mage was left, almost paralysed with terror as she cringed in her saddle. She was oblivious to the bound spirits darting frantically around her head. The Wither Queen stepped forward, a terrible hunger in her face. The mage's horse collapsed and she was tipped forward to sprawl flat in the dark forest mud, senseless for a moment. When she came to, she tried to scrabble away from the advancing Goddess, knowing it was far too late. Convulsions began to wrack her body.

Above her the spirits raced around in frenzied fear until the Wither Queen reached out a hand, fingers splayed as though to pluck them like fruit. The spirits stopped and hung in the air above the mage's corpse, their shapeless forms coalescing into vague shapes of smoke. They sank to the ground and submitted without a fight, offering obeisance until they were mere puddles of mist.

'They find themselves new Gods and bind them like slaves,' the Wither Queen whispered with cold tenderness to the spirits. 'That shall be their undoing. The dead one sought to use me, then leash me. I could smell his betrayal even as I could see Death's hand reaching for his shoulder, but I will be a slave no longer. He freed me. He forced me to learn new ways and now he is not there to limit me.'

She reached down and stroked her fingers through each of the spirits in turn, bringing a piece of each to her mouth to suck down eagerly.

'There are more of you, so many more – enough to carry my plagues to every corner of the Land,' she said to her new Aspects. With them following at her heel, the Wither Queen began to drift forward on an unseen breeze, her body fading like mist until it was barely an outline in the shadows. By nightfall the first Elven encampment had been scoured of life.

PROLOGUE – PART 3

Doranei watched as shadows stole through the streets below, slipping through the alleys and coalescing into darkness. He blinked, and the curved avenues of Byora faded from his perception as the stepped city was swallowed by the dark.

Been taught my whole life to look for shadows, he thought. *Now they're all I see.* 'I saw another prophet today,' he said aloud, the sound feeling out of place in the high, silent room.

'I'm sorry? You saw what?' Zhia Vukotic came closer, her sapphire eyes shining in the light of a single candle.

'A prophet, didn't you hear?'

She ignored the edge in his voice. These past two weeks there had been an ever-present air of anger and antagonism about the Narkang man, even in bed. The scent of violence would have frightened any normal woman, but Zhia feared only for him. She tried to remember how long it had been since grief had consumed her every thought.

'I was watching your face,' the vampire admitted; 'I wasn't paying attention to the words. Tell me about the prophet.'

Doranei remained silent for a time, his face twitching slightly, as though words were fighting to get out but couldn't quite force their way through. Tsatach's eye had only just sunk behind Blackfang and the striated clouds over the mountain were tinged a startling burnished orange. It was a beautiful sight but Zhia realised he saw nothing, barely noticing even the bulky silhouette of a dragon, rising to circle on the high thermals like a hunting hawk.

There was a black need for destruction fizzing through Doranei's blood, not unlike that in the maddened beast Kastan Styrax had awakened and left to devastate the Circle City. Zhia and her brother, Koezh, had caused its slumber; the spell they used had corroded

8

what had already been an unknowable, unpredictable intellect. Now hatred filled its mind, arbitrary and unquenchable.

'A man this time. It struck him in the middle of the street,' Doranei said abruptly, no louder than a whisper. 'No warning. I thought he was drunk when he staggered into a wall.' Unconsciously he raised his goblet and drank. She saw his lips twitch just before the rim touched, a name spoken silently.

They stood alone in the high room on the topmost level of a whorehouse known as the Velvet Cup. Doranei had pulled open the shutters on one side of the room to watch the sun set – at least, that was what he would claim. Zhia knew it was the sight of the Ruby Tower wreathed in shadow that obsessed him; that and watching the junction where his friend Sebe had died. The choice of vantage point had been pure chance, as was the direction Ilumene and Aracnan had taken as they went to lead Byora's soldiers against the Farlan. When you were angry at chance, and Fate had been murdered mere miles away, who could you take it out on?

'That's something I have never witnessed, not in all my years,' Zhia said, 'but I do not envy you it.'

'He didn't hurt anyone,' Doranei continued, more to himself than in response. 'There was a detachment of Ruby Tower Guards at the crossroads; one of them laid him out as he made for a beggar. They manacled him to a pillar while they sent for orders, he stood there for an hour snarling like a rabid dog before they worked out what to do with him.'

'Did he say anything?'

Doranei turned to face his vampire lover. Zhia frowned under his scrutiny as Doranei appeared to search for something in her face. Her black hair was tied up in a way he'd not seen before, braids woven together and bound by a thin copper band on the top of her head. It wasn't quite the style many mercenaries used, but it was similar.

'It was fast, too fast to follow properly. I only heard one scrap.' He gestured at the Ruby Tower, now just an outline in the evening gloom. 'What your friend will have to say about it I don't know.'

Zhia didn't rise to the bait, knowing he was looking for an excuse to rage, to vent the grief he felt over Sebe's death. He didn't want

9

to hurt her, she knew that, and anyway, any confrontation between them would leave Doranei injured, not her, but she suspected he'd prefer a beating to the pain of grief.

'Ruhen is not my friend; you know that's not the reason I cannot join your assault.'

Lord Isak's death had resonated throughout the Land with enough force to turn a dozen men and women in Byora alone into prophets, but it was a death less than an hour before Isak's that had cast this veil of anguish over the King's Man. Zhia had seen the destruction of the junction of roads not long after; she could easily picture the wild storm of magic unleashed there by a maddened Demi-God. Buildings had shattered at Aracnan's touch; the cobbles were torn up as though fifty-foot claws had ripped through the street.

Sebe's body was buried in the devastation, and the wrecked houses were still burning fiercely when she returned to the city and found Doranei, filthy and soot-stained, tearing his hands on the rubble, alongside dozens of others. Only fifty bodies were recovered in the end; hundreds more, Sebe amongst them, had been lost to the ferocity of the flames.

Zhia had dragged Doranei to safety, all but imprisoning him in the tavern's cellar to keep him off the streets, but he had barely slept since. He would lie in the bed they shared, his eyes wide; staring at nothing, while she lay powerless to help. At times he looked almost frantic, bewildered, as the tears refused to come, undone by a lifetime of stoicism and detachment.

From his own position three streets away Doranei had heard Aracnan's crashing response to Sebe's poisoned arrow, increasing in violence as the seadiamond venom burned ever hotter in the Demi-God's veins. It was a weak poison compared to most, but Aracnan had made the mistake they had been counting on. When he'd been struck in the shoulder he'd realised the bolt might be poisoned, and had used magic to counter the effects – but this particular venom was magnified by the presence of magic.

Witnesses had reported the stones cracking under Aracnan's feet as he screamed in agony – the flesh of the nearest bystanders had blackened and burned even before he started lashing out with arcs of fire. The house where Sebe was positioned, most likely levelling a second crossbow at Ilumene, had exploded under the magical assault. Only Aracnan's collapse into unconsciousness from the mounting pain had saved the district.

Zhia's voice forced its way into his thoughts. 'Doranei, what did the prophet say?'

The King's Man looked down, knuckles white as his hand tightened on the window sill. 'A great lord falls, a new God rises.'

CHAPTER 1

A whisper of evening breeze off the lake brushed Mihn's face as he bent over the small boat. He hesitated and looked up over the water. The sun was about to set, its orange rays pushing through the tall pine trees on the far eastern shore. His sharp eyes caught movement at the tree-line: the gentry moving cautiously into the open. They were normally to be found at twilight, watching the sun sink below the horizon from atop great boulders, but today at least two family packs had come to the lake instead.

'They smell change in the air,' the witch of Llehden commented from beside him. 'What we attempt has never been tried before.'

Mihn had noticed that here in Llehden no one called her Ehla, the name she had permitted Lord Isak to use; that she was the witch was good enough for the locals. It was for Mihn too, however much it had confused the Farlan.

Mihn shrugged. 'We are yet to manage it,' he pointed out, 'but if they sense change, perhaps that is a good sign.'

His words provoked a small sound of disapproval from Xeliath, the third person in their group. She stood awkwardly, leaning on the witch for support. Though a white-eye, the stroke that had damaged her left side meant the brown-skinned girl was weaker than normal humans in some ways, and glimpses of the Dark Place hovered at the edges of her sight; a shred of her soul in the place of dark torment because of her link to Isak. Her balance and coordination were further diminished by exhaustion: Xeliath was unable to sleep without enduring dreams terrible enough to destroy the sanity of a weaker mind.

Mihn had been spared that at least; the link between them was weaker, and he lacked a mage's sensitivity.

Together they helped Xeliath into the boat. The witch got in beside her and Mihn pushed it out onto the water, leaping aboard once it was clear of the shore. He sat facing the two women, who were both wrapped in thick woollen cloaks against the night chill. Mihn, in contrast, wore only a thin leather tunic and trousers, and the bottom of each leg was bound tight with twine, leaving no loose material to snag or tear.

Mihn caught sight of an elderly woman perched on a stool at the lakeside and felt a flicker of annoyance. The woman, another witch, had arrived a few days earlier. She was decades older than Ehla, but she was careful to call herself *a* witch of Llehden – as though her presence in the shire was on Ehla's sufferance alone. She had told Mihn to call her Daima – *knowledge* – should there be a need to differentiate between them. For almost fifty years Daima had laid out the dead and sat with them until dawn, facing down the host of spirits that are attracted by death in all its forms. She had a special affinity for that side of the Land, and had ushered ghosts and other lost souls even to the Halls of Death, going as far within as any living mortal Ehla knew of.

The old woman had reiterated again and again the dangers of what they were about to attempt, particularly marking the solemnity and respect Mihn would need to display. That she was presently puffing away on a pipe as she fished from the lakeshore did not exactly impart the level of gravity she had warned them was imperative to their success.

With swift strokes he rowed to the approximate centre of the lake and dropped a rusty plough-blade over the edge to serve as anchor. Once the oars were stowed the failed Harlequin took a moment to inspect the tattoos on his palms and soles of his feet, but they remained undamaged, the circles of incantation unbroken.

'Ready?' the witch asked.

'As ready as I ever will be.'

'The coins?'

He could feel the weight of the two silver coins strung on a cord around his neck. Mihn's extensive knowledge of folklore was serving him in good stead as he prepared for this venture. It was common practice for dying sinners to request a silver coin between their lips, to catch a part of their soul. Whoever sat with them until dawn would afterwards drop the coin in a river, so the cool water could ease any torments that might await them. Daima had provided this service often enough to know where to find two such coins easily enough.

'They are secure,' he assured them.

'Then it is time,' Xeliath rasped, pushing herself forward so that Mihn was within reach. The young woman squinted at him with her good right eye, her head wavering a moment until she managed to focus. She placed her right hand on his chest. 'Let my mark guide you,' she said, stiffly raising her left hand too. That, as always, was half-closed in a fist around the Crystal Skull given to her by the patron Goddess of her tribe. 'Let my strength be yours to call upon.'

Ehla echoed her gesture before tying a length of rope around his waist. 'Let my light keep back the shadows of the Dark Place.'

Mihn took two deep breaths, trying to control the fear beginning to churn inside him. 'And now—'

Without warning Xeliath lurched forward and punched Mihn in the face. A sudden flash of white light burst around them as the magic humming through her body added power to the blow. The small man toppled over the edge of the boat, dropping down into the still depths. Ehla grabbed at the coil of rope fast disappearing after Mihn.

'I've been looking forward to that bit,' Xeliath said, wincing at the effect the punch had had on her twisted body.

The witch didn't reply. She peered over the edge of the boat for a moment, then looked back towards the shore. The sun was a smear of orange on the horizon but it wasn't the advancing evening that made her shiver unexpectedly. In the distance she saw Daima set her fishing rod down while barely a dozen yards from the old woman, a pair of gentry crept forward to drink from the lake.

Ehla pulled the hood of her cloak over her head and did the same for Xeliath before helping the girl to sit down in the curved hull of the boat. Above, the sky slowly darkened while they made themselves as comfortable as they could.

'Now it is up to Mihn,' she said quietly.

Legana felt the touch of Alterr's light on her face and drew back a fraction until her face was again shadowed from the moon. With her half-divine senses open to the Land she could feel her surroundings in a way that almost made up for her damaged eyesight.

14

The woman she was stalking was no more than two hundred yards off and coming closer. Like a snake tasting the air Legana breathed in the faint scents carried on the breeze. The spread of trees and the slight camber of ground unfolded in her mind: a complex map of taste, touch and other senses she had no names for. Within it the other woman shone, illuminated by a faint spark within her that tugged at Legana's weary heart.

She replaced the blindfold and waited for the right moment to step out from the shadows. The blindfold hampered little, and it made her appear less of a threat; it did Legana no harm to remain cautious and look feeble. Her voice had been ruined by the mercenary Aracnan's assault and normally she would be forced to communicate by means of the piece of slate that hung from a cord around her neck – but the woman had the spark within her, as Legana herself did. It was faint – she had clearly strayed far from the Lady – but Legana hoped it would be enough for her divine side to exploit.

When the woman was only a dozen yards away Legana moved out from behind a tree. The woman gave a yelp of surprise and drew an axe and a shortsword in one smooth movement. In response Legana leaned a little more heavily on her staff and pushed back the hood of her cloak so the woman could see the blindfold clearly.

'*Not a good night to be walking alone,*' Legana said directly into the woman's mind.

The other glanced behind her, wary of an ambush. As she did so the scarf over her head slipped, showing her head was nearly bald. 'How did you do that? Who says I'm on my own?'

'*I know you are.*'

'You're a mage without any fucking eyes, what do you know?' the stranger snapped. She was shorter than Legana by some way, and more powerfully built. The lack of hair made her look strange and foreign, but as soon as she spoke her accent labelled her as native Farlan.

'*I know more than you might realise,*' Legana replied, taking no offence. A small smile appeared on her face: before Aracnan's attack she had been just as prickly as this woman. It had taken an incurable injury to teach her the value of calm. The quick temper of her youth would do a blind woman no good, whether or not she was stronger than before.

15

'For example,' Legana continued, '*I know you strayed from your path a long time ago – and I know I can help you find it again.*'

'Really? That's what you know, is it?' The woman shook her head, confused by the fact that someone was talking thought to thought, but anger was her default state, as it had once been for Legana, and it presently overrode her questions. 'Looks to me like you're the one who's lost the path, and being blind I'd say you're in a lot more trouble than I am out here.'

'*What is your name?*'

For a moment she was silent, staring at Legana as though trying to work out what threat she might pose. 'Why do you want to know?' she asked eventually.

Legana smiled. '*We're sisters, surely you can tell that? Why would I not want to know the name of a sister?*'

'The Lady's fucking dead,' the woman spat with sudden anger, 'and the sisterhood died with her. If you were really one of us you'd have felt it too, mad, blind hermit or not.'

Legana's head dipped for a moment. What the woman said was true. Legana had been there when the Lady, the Goddess Fate, had been killed. The pain, both of that loss and her own injuries that day, were still fresh in Legana's mind.

'*She's dead,*' she said quietly, '*but sisters we remain, and we need each other more than ever. My name is Legana.*'

'Legana?' the woman said sharply. 'I know that name – from the temple in Tirah. But I don't recognise you.'

'*I've changed a little,*' Legana agreed. '*I couldn't speak into another sister's mind before.*'

'You were the scholar?' the woman asked sceptically. 'The one they thought would become High Priestess?'

Legana gave a sudden cough of laughter. '*If that's what you remember we were at different temples! I was the one she beat for insolence every day for a year – I was the one who excelled only at killing. I was sold off to Chief Steward Lesarl as soon as I was of age.*'

The woman let her shoulders relax. Grudgingly she returned her weapons to her belt. 'Okay, then. You were a few years younger, but we all heard about the trouble you caused. I'm Ardela. What happened to your voice?'

Legana's hand involuntarily went to her throat. Her skin was paler even than most Farlan – as white as bone, except for Aracnan's shadowy handprint around her neck. Underneath were some barely perceptible bumps: an emerald necklace had sealed her bargain with Fate when Legana had agreed to be her Mortal-Aspect, but the violence done subsequently had somehow pushed the jewels deep into her flesh.

'*That I will tell you when I tell you my story,*' Legana said. '*First, I want to ask you, where are you going by yourself in a hostile land? You don't strike me as the sort to be left behind by the army.*'

Ardela scowled. 'The army wouldn't have noticed if half the Palace Guard had deserted; they're in chaos after Lord Isak's death.'

'*So why are you here?*'

'I think my time with the Farlan is done,' Ardela said after a long pause. 'Doubt it would be too safe for me to return to Tirah; a few grudges might come back to haunt me.'

'*Then where are you going?*'

'Where in the Dark Place are you going?' she snapped back. 'What's your story? You're a sister, but a mage too! You're crippled, but wandering out in the wilds all by yourself? There are Menin patrols out this far, and Farlan Penitents who've deserted, and Fate knows what else lurking—'

Legana held up a hand to stop Ardela. '*I'll tell you everything; I just want to know whether you are looking for renewed purpose, or just a job in some city far away from your "grudges". I want to know whether you still care for the daughters of Fate.*'

Ardela didn't answer immediately; for a moment her gaze lowered, as though she were ashamed. 'Whatever I care for, I cannot return to Tirah,' she said at last.

'*Could you stand to meet a temple-mistress, if it were somewhere other than Tirah?*'

'You asking whether they'd accept me, or I'd accept them?'

'*Their opinion will be my concern, not yours. We must all start afresh if we're to survive this new age.*'

'Yes, then – but it don't matter, the Lady's dead.' A spark of her former fierceness returned to Ardela's voice. 'Whatever you think you can do, the Daughters of Fate are broken.'

'*But perhaps I can remake them,*' Legana said. '*I don't know how yet, but I'm the only one who can draw them back together. They're the only real family I've ever had and I won't just stand back and watch them drift away. Without the Lady we've lost the anchor in our hearts; we're bereft. Who knows what our sisters will do if the ache of her loss stops them caring about anything?'*

'I do,' Ardela said in a small voice. 'I've lived that way for years now.'

'*Then let's do something more with ourselves,*' Legana suggested, holding a hand out to the woman.

Ardela took it, and allowed herself to be led by a half-blind woman into the darkest part of the wood, where Legana had sited her small camp. On the way Legana told Ardela what had happened to her throat, how she had become the Lady's Mortal-Aspect, and then witnessed her death a few days later.

When Legana mentioned Aracnan, and the one whose orders he must have been following – the shadow, Azaer – Ardela flinched, and her own story began to pour out of her. She cried, ashamed for her employment by Cardinal Certinse, whose entire family had served a daemon-prince, and sorrowed by the savagery and depravity of her life during those years. In the darkness the women held each other and wept for what they had lost. Long before dawn broke they knew they shared an enemy.

He fell through a silent storm, tossed carelessly like a discarded plaything. Tumbling and turning, he dropped too quickly even to scream. Unable to see, unable to speak, he tried to curl into a ball and protect his face from the thrashing storm, but the effort proved too much. There was no energy in his limbs to fight the wild tumult, nor breath in his lungs to give him strength. But as he fell deeper into darkness, the panic began to recede and some measure of clarity started to return to his thoughts.

The storm, he realised eventually, was chaotic, assailing him from all directions, and though every part of his body told him he was falling, as the blind terror began to fade he realised he was in a void, a place where up and down held no meaning. He was apart from the Land, tumbling through chaos itself – until Death reached out to claim him.

All of a sudden the air changed. Mihn felt himself arrive somewhere with a jolt that wrenched him right around. His toes brushed a surface beneath him and gravity suddenly reasserted itself. He collapsed in a heap on a cold stone floor, a sharp pain running through his elbows and knees as they took the impact. Instinctively he rolled sideways, curling up, his hands covering his face.

Once his mind stopped spinning Mihn took a tentative breath and opened his eyes. For a moment his vision swam and he moaned with pain. Then his surroundings came into focus. A high vaulted ceiling loomed somewhere in the distance, so vast, so impossibly far that his mind rebelled against the sight. Before Mihn could understand where he was he had rolled over again and was vomiting on the stone floor.

Almost instantly he felt a change within himself as sight of something mundane became a lodestone for his thoughts. Underneath him were flagstones, as grey as thunderclouds, pitted with age. He struggled to his feet and lurched for a few drunken steps before regaining his balance. Once he had done so he looked at his surroundings – and Mihn found himself falling to his knees again.

He was in the Halls of Death – the Herald's Hall itself. All the stories he had told, all the accounts he had read: none of them could do justice to the sight before him. The human mind could barely comprehend a place of magic where allegory was alive enough to kill. The hall stretched for miles in all directions, and was so high he felt a wave of dizziness as soon as he looked up. Gigantic pillars stood all around him, miles apart and higher than mountains, all made of the same ancient granite as the roof and floor.

There was no one else there, Mihn realised. He was quite alone, and the silence was profound. The vastness of the hall stupefied him. Mihn found himself unable to fully comprehend so unreal a space, made more unworldly by the silence, and the stillness in the air. Only when that stillness was broken – by a distant flutter from above – did he find himself able to move again. He turned, trying to follow the sound, only to yelp with shock as he saw a figure behind him where there had been no one before.

He retreated a few steps, but the figure didn't move. Mihn didn't need the accounts he'd heard about the last days of Scree to recognise the figure: with skin as black as midnight, robes of scarlet and a silver standard, it could only be the Herald of Death, the gatekeeper of His throne room and marshal of these halls.

The Herald was far taller than Mihn, bigger even than the tallest of white-eyes. Prominent ears were the only feature of the hairless black head. Eyes, nose and mouth were indentations only, token shapes to hint at humanity which served only to make the Herald more terrifying.

Behind the Herald, away in the distance, Mihn saw a great door of white bones. Now, in the shadows of the hall's vaulted roof, there was faint movement: indistinct dark coils wrapped around the upper reaches of the pillars, then dissipated as others flourished, coming into being from where, he could not tell.

Death's winged attendants. In Death's halls, other than Gods, only bats, servants of the Chief of the Gods Himself, could linger. Bats were Death's spies and messengers, as well as guides through the other lands. If a soul's sins were forgiven, bats would carry the soul from the desolate slopes of Ghain, sparing it the torments of Ghenna.

The Herald of Death broke Mihn's train of thoughts abruptly by hammering the butt of the standard on the flagstone floor. The blow shook the entire hall, throwing Mihn to the ground. Somewhere in the dim distance a boiling mass stirred: vast flocks of bats swirled around the pillars before settling again.

When Mihn recovered his senses the Herald was staring down at him, impassive, but he wasn't fooled into thinking he would be allowed to tarry. He struggled to his feet and took a few hesitant steps towards the huge gates in the distance. The rasp of his feet across the floor was strangely loud, the sound seeming to spread out across the miles, until Mihn had recovered his balance and could walk properly. Obligingly the Herald fell in beside him, matching his uneven pace. It walked tall and proud at his side, but otherwise paid him no regard whatsoever.

After a moment Mihn, recovering his wits, realised some subtle compulsion was drawing him towards the ivory doors of Death's throne room. The doors themselves were, like the rest of the hall, of a vastness beyond human comprehension or need.

As he walked he became aware of a sound, at the edge of hearing, and so quiet it was almost drowned out by the pad of his footsteps and the clink of the Herald's standard on the flagstones. In the moments between he strained to hear it, and as he did so he detected some slow rhythm drifting through his body. It made him think of distant voices raised in song, but nothing human; like a wordless reverence that rang out from the very stone of the hall.

It intensified the awe in his heart and he felt his knees wobble, weakening as the weight of Death's majesty resonated out from all around. His fingers went to the scar on his chest. It had healed soon after he and the witch left Tirah, but the tissue remained tender, an angry red.

He kept his eyes on his feet for a while, focused on the regular movement and the task at hand, until the moment had passed and he felt able to once more look up towards the ivory doors. They appeared no closer yet, several miles still to walk, by Mihn's judgment.

He suddenly remembered an ancient play: the ghost of a king is granted a boon by Death, to speak to his son before passing on to the land of no time.

"'The journey is long, my heir,'" Mihn whispered to himself, "'the gates sometimes within reach and at others hidden in the mists of afar. They open for you when they are ready to – until then hold your head high and remember: you are a man who walks with Gods.'"

After a few more minutes of silence he began to sing softly; a song of praise he had been taught as a child. The familiar, ancient melody immediately reminded him of his home in the cold north of the Land, of the caves the clans built their homes around and the cavern where they worshipped.

When he reached the end of the song he moved straight on to another, preferring that to the unnatural hush. This one was a long and mournful deathbed lament, where pleas of atonement were interspersed with praise of Death's wisdom. Considering where he was going it seemed only sensible.

21

CHAPTER 2

In the silence of the ghost hour two figures walked through the fens beyond Byora. The expanse stretched for miles; few knew the safe paths and still several of those fell victim each year to the sucking mud or malign spirits. Marsh alder and ghost willows studded the watery landscape, either solitary trees looming in the mist like spectres or small copses huddled and hunched like bitter old men.

The brother and sister walked side by side, neither carrying a lantern, despite the deepening gloom. They were several miles from Byora, at the very heart of the fens. Though the air was cold, the vapour of their breath was barely visible even once the sister stopped and pushed back the hood of her cape to speak.

'This will serve,' Zhia said.

The sun had sunk below the eastern horizon and its light had faded from all but a sliver of the clear evening sky. A low mist surrounded them and everything beyond ten yards in any direction was tinted white and indistinct. In the distance a light flickered, pale blue and cold. From another direction came the cough of a fox and a wordless mutter that faded to nothing when she turned her sapphire eyes that way. The light she ignored. No will o' the wisp would come closer unless someone were floundering in the water, and only then when their struggles had weakened considerably – and that was not going to happen tonight.

Koezh looked at the ground around them. A hump of earth less than a dozen yards across, but firm underfoot thanks to the roots of an ancient marsh alder that bore the scars of a lightning strike. One branch had fallen; grass was already growing up around the wood. Its furthermost twigs were draped in the still water like the fingers of a corpse. The tree was old and with an open break running down the main trunk wouldn't last many more winters, so it was perfect for their purposes.

'And to guard it?'

Zhia drew her long-handled sword and used the tip to cut a circle in the sodden ground around the tree. At her murmured command the circle glowed briefly, a pale blue light similar to the will o' the wisp. That done, she sheathed the sword and drew another from her back, this one wrapped in cloth. She freed her gloved left hand from the folds of her cloak and raised her hood before unwrapping the cloth. Both turned side-on, hiding as much of their faces as possible, as a bright white light shone out and dissipated the surrounding curtain of mist.

Without waiting Zhia pushed the shining crystal sword into the split part of the marsh alder and muttered a few more words. The trunk of the tree closed up over Aenaris and the light winked out. Zhia turned away, fingers touched to her face, hissing with discomfort. The Key of Life shone with light as pure as the sun's; the vampire's cheek now bore a blackened scorch-mark.

Koezh gave a polite cough and drew a dagger from his belt. 'The Key of Life will make the tree stand out if someone passes this way,' he said as he cut a band of bark away from all around the tree's base. A touch of his broadsword made the exposed wood blacken and decay. A little mud covered the damage and made it barely noticeable. 'I doubt that will kill the tree, but it might slow it up a while.'

'I'm rather more concerned some daemon will discover it,' Zhia said pointedly. 'The Devil Stair Lord Styrax created is only a few miles away and who knows how many places in these fens reach down to Ghenna? No human will find their way here, even if we were followed, not once I'm finished.'

'All the same, caution is rarely without worth,' he replied. 'It will take any daemon time to work out how to handle the sword of the Queen of the Gods. Perhaps we should save our concern for finding a new resting place for Aenaris.'

'A permanent one? That won't be necessary.'

Koezh looked askance at his sister. 'My sister the convert? Once more you have faith in a cause?'

'I have faith in my own senses,' Zhia replied, not bothering to rise to his insinuation. 'Players remain in this game who can give us what we want. One of them will win out.'

'Which?'

'Perhaps the shadow after all. Few of the power players consider it any real threat; it seems to be content to wait and let them exhaust themselves fighting each other.'

'And this is the side you wish to support?'

Zhia looked surprised. 'What do you mean, "wish to support"? You'd prefer to do nothing? Prefer the Land to continue as it has for the last seven millennia?'

'I am just one man. I cannot choose a fate for the entire Land.'

She laughed. 'Compassion? Just another part of our Gods-imposed curse – and yet another thing we might be freed of.'

'At what price?'

'Let consequences be someone else's problem, we've had enough of them.'

He regarded her as he used to when they were children and he the reticent elder brother. 'So you are decided?'

'Not at all, that time is yet to come.' Zhia's voice became more insistent. 'Don't you feel it though? Can't you sense change on the horizon? That our time has finally come?'

'I do.' Koezh gave a sigh and looked to the western horizon. The sky was black, and the first stars of night had appeared. 'Yet still I think of the price others might bear.'

At last Mihn came to the ivory doors of Death's chamber and there he stopped. Something inside told him he would be permitted a moment to wonder at the sight – to tremble at the judgment that lay beyond. The doors to the throne room appeared to be more than three hundred feet high, but Mihn guessed measurements meant little in the Herald's Halls. The walk there had taken hours; the ghost of fatigue fluttered through his body, but he was cool and his breath was calm.

The huge doors that dominated the miles-high Herald's Hall were somehow brighter and more real than the hard, cold stone underfoot. The wall they were set into was indistinct, slanted away from Mihn and stretching into the murky distance, with no corners in sight. The doors themselves were composed of a chaotic network of bones, ranging from the smallest finger-bone to thigh-bones broader and longer even than the biggest of white-eyes; bigger than Mihn imagined a dragon's bones would be. White marble formed a peaked frame around them, through which ran threads of faintly glittering silver.

The tangle of interlinked bones was bleached a uniform white. There were gaps Mihn would have been able to slip himself into, perhaps even make his way all the way through, but some fearful part of him pictured the bones closing around him, including him in the structure. He stepped back and looked up and a moment of renewed dizziness washed over him as his mind struggled to accept the sight. When that passed Mihn began to see a purpose to the chaotic structure; a pattern that absorbed the jumble of linked bones to impose a rigid grandeur upon the whole.

Somehow that realisation made him feel better, easing the feeling of being lost amidst chaos. The time had come, so without even his staff to hand – the witch Daima had sternly forbidden him to carry anything, he could take only what could be worn – Mihn touched his finger to the nearest bone. It was freezing cold, and a chill ran up the underside of his arm while a great creak rang out through the hall. The doors yielded smoothly, beginning to swing inwards. They moved silently once they had cleared each other, barely disturbing the air.

He felt his breath catch as a vast, dark room was revealed. Torches flickered distantly on the walls, enough only to trace the bare lines of Death's throne room. As he walked forward he looked around, the Herald keeping pace at his side. The throne room was hexagonal, maybe not as staggeringly vast as the Herald's Hall, but still bigger than any human construction – as big as the entire Temple Plain in Thotel. The Hall of Judgment had two doorways in it. On Mihn's right was the second of those, two pillars supporting a portico above a door of profound and featureless blackness.

Atop the portico were statues, distant enough to appear small to Mihn, but illuminated by huge flickering torches on either side. On one end stood a group he recognised all too well from his lord's shadow – worryingly, the largest of the five was the Wither Queen. On the other were daemons of various shapes, only one of which he recognised: a minotaur-like figure with a gigantic hammer known as Getan of the Punishment. Carved into the jutting portico itself was an image of a dragon, wings outstretched in a way that reminded him of the entrance to the Tower of Semar in Tirah Palace.

A faint breeze touched his skin as the doors closed behind and Mihn's gaze was dragged inexorably away to the other side. The sudden weight of terror and awe mingling drove him to one knee. Through the darkness, set against the centre of the wall, he could make out an enormous throne, part of the very fabric of the hall itself.

The throne was two hundred feet high, of sculpted stone that needed no finery or adornment to convey its power, and it was occupied by a gigantic cowled figure that slowly appeared from the gloom. Mihn could feel Death's presence like a raging wind blowing through the room, power incarnate that made his bones judder and his hands tremble. The cold of the grave was tangible on Mihn's skin, a biting chill that worked its way into his veins as he stared in horror at the emaciated white fingers curled around the end of one armrest. A golden sceptre rested in the crook of His left arm, decorated with spirals of ruby and diamond. Of His face there was no sign – even here in the Hall of Judgment the face of Death was hidden – but Mihn could feel His eyes, white-hot on his skin.

The throne had iron braces hammered into its side, which held hundreds of sceptres, orbs and other royal accoutrements. Carelessly scattered on the stone floor below was a carpet of skulls and weapons, some shining with unnatural power, others ancient and corroded.

Offerings for the dead, Mihn realised, *tributes for the Final Judgment of those lost.* He paused. *Weapons thrown into lakes to find their way here, just as I was.*

All around the edge of the room were statues, some the size of a white-eye, others half again as large. The smaller appeared to be powerful men, lords and ladies, while the larger were Gods and their many Aspects – but so huge was the room that it still looked desolate despite the hundreds of figures. The interior was empty, adorned only by a massive square flagstone in the very centre of the floor, as black as Death's own robe and echoed in every formal courtroom throughout the Land.

He looked past the statues and noticed rounded protrusions jutting out from the wall. Distantly he could make out a low hum, deep and threatening. As he looked closer a shape moved at the top of one, darting out from an opening to rise up and disappear from sight – a black-winged bee, Death's chosen creature.

Now indistinct grey shapes moved slowly around the room. As Mihn tried to observe them, to make out a face or form, he realised they were being drawn inward towards the square in the centre: the spirits of the dead, making their reluctant way towards judgment.

Mihn struggled to his feet, his balance again failing momentarily as he glanced up to the apex of the room and his senses failed to comprehend the room's unreal proportions. The slap of his palm against the stone cut through the quiet and made him wince, but not even the Herald at his side appeared to notice. The eyeless, expressionless Herald stood tall beside him, giving the impression of watching over the entire room. Mihn wondered whether each drifting shade also felt the Herald at their side, or whether his not-quite-extinguished mortality made him a curiosity.

No time to waste, Mihn reminded himself. Daima's words of wisdom echoed in his mind: *'Don't tarry – don't think about what you're doing. The Gods love a bold man and this isn't a place for second thoughts.'*

He set off towards the black square, the Herald at his side still walking in perfect time. As he reached it Mihn caught a slight movement in his peripheral vision, a flutter of wings arcing down from the dark reaches of the hall's roof: a stream of bats attending their master. Mihn had been to many places where the bat was sacred to the locals, considered the keepers of history and guardians of secrets. The bats were his messengers, the black bees his fearless warriors. The bees were impossible to fight, driven by a selfless will. They appeared only rarely in myth, but they were known to be remorseless when they attacked.

As Mihn entered the black square a great weight fell upon his shoulders, dragging him, head bowed, to his knees. The presence of Death surged all around him, like black flames leaping from the stone. Dread filled Mihn's stomach as the touch of that power drove the breath from his lungs. An excited chatter and click of bat-song raced all around him, assailing his ears before suddenly breaking off. He recoiled from the oppressive silence that replaced it, realising what would come next.

'Mihn ab Netren ab Felith,' Death intoned, His voice as deep and penetrating as the greatest of temple bells. 'For what purpose do you come here? You stand between the lands of the living and the dead. A witch and one of the Chosen stand in your shadow, yet you kneel for judgment.'

Mihn opened his mouth to reply, but the words would not come. He forced himself to swallow and breathe, ignoring the cold taste of ashes in the air. With an effort he managed to raise his head and look at the cowled darkness that hid Death's face, but it was only when he reminded himself of his mission that he found the courage to speak.

'Lord Death, I do not seek your judgment, not yet. Instead I beg a boon.'

'Are you so certain? Etched in your face I see a life lived only reluctantly. Come, receive my judgment – embrace the peace you crave.'

Mihn felt his hand begin to tremble and his vision swam. Death's words spoke to the very core of him, their deep tones reverberating through his soul and shaking the strongest of defences.

'I ... I cannot,' he gasped even as he felt tears spill down his cheeks.

'No mortal is denied my judgment,' Death replied. 'No obligation you bear will hold you from it. You learned the tales of the Harlequins; you know it is both the wicked and the good who receive judgment. It is a blessing for as many as it is punishment.'

'This I know,' choked Mihn, unable to stop shaking as part of him cried out to receive the oblivion it would bring, 'but as long as I have a choice I must keep to my word—'

'Do not decide in haste,' Death commanded before Mihn could fully finish. 'No God can see the future, but immortals do not sense time as you do. History is not a map to be read, nor a path to be followed. It is a landscape of contours and textures, of colours and sounds. What lies ahead of you is duty beyond the call of most mortals – that much I can see. The burden is great. Too great, even.'

'This I know,' Mihn repeated in a small voice.

He remembered what the witch of Llehden had said the night she burned Xeliath's rune into his chest, the third favour he had asked of her. '*It is said that to ask of a witch a third time is to give away a piece of your soul ... That claim I offer to another; to the grave, to the wild wind, to the called storm.*'

For his sins – for his *failures* – Mihn had agreed, but even then the full import of his words had sickened him to his core. He had not felt the weight of the obligation as heavily as when Lord Death spoke to him now.

His voice fell to a whisper. 'Whatever is asked shall be done. Whatever cannot be asked of another will be done. Whatever should not be asked of another, it will be done.'

The God regarded him for a long, unbearable time. At last Death inclined His head slightly. 'As you wish.'

Silence reigned once more. Even the circling, spiralling bats were hushed. Mihn found his head bowed again. A movement in the corner of his eye prompted him to glance to the right and there, instead of the Herald he saw the faint grey face of a woman peering down at him from the edge of the black square.

Too astonished to react, too drained and awed to fear the presence of a ghost, Mihn simply stared back. He couldn't make out much; it was like a darker, fogged version of when Seliasei, one of the spirits inhabiting Morghien, stepped out of the aged wanderer's body. The spirit's jaw was moving and it took Mihn a moment to realise it was trying to speak to him. What chilled him, and made him look away, was the pity in the ghost's eyes.

Pitied by the dead. Oh Gods, what have I done?

'Mihn ab Netren ab Felith,' Death declared in a voice that rattled Mihn's teeth, 'speak the boon you crave.'

'I— Your blessing,' Mihn said hesitantly, rather more hurriedly adding, 'Lord Death, my duty leads me beyond your doors. I beg permission to leave this room without receiving your judgment, to ascend the slopes of Ghain and pass through the ivory gates of Ghenna.'

'Such permission is not mine to give,' Death replied in an emotionless voice. 'The slopes of Ghain are mine to rule and all may walk them as they wish, but beyond the River Maram the rule is only of chaos.'

'I understand. I ask only permission to leave this hall and re-enter it again without your judgment being pronounced.'

Death leaned forward. 'So granted, but entry through those doors will not be without peril. The guardian heeds neither God nor mortal. The bones of those who have turned from Ghain's ascent litter the first step on your journey.'

Mihn bowed his head in acknowledgment. 'I thank you, my Lord.'

'You do not fear it?'

'My fear is reserved for others,' Mihn said, trying to keep his voice from breaking as his throat dried at the thought. Daima had warned him about the journey he would have to take; the Jailer of the Dark was only the most certain of the many horrors he would have to face. But there was no choice.

'Very well. Your have my favour.' Death gestured to the objects adorning his throne. 'I offer you the pick of my trophies. Each one bears my blessing, and will keep you safe on the slopes of Ghain. A thousand torments await the judged there, but the taste of the living will be all the sweeter for them.'

Mihn opened his mouth to speak, then stopped and thought. Of Daima's many warnings, the first had been to take neither staff nor weapon with him. '*Carry nothing but what you wear. A weapon is an invitation to war, and they will smell the blood on it.*'

'I thank you, Lord Death, but I do not go to war on Ghenna. I must trust myself alone.'

He felt the weight on his shoulders lessen as Death sat back in his throne. 'Good. I had thought to have the Mercies teach you that lesson, but it is one you have already learned.'

Death raised a bone-white finger and pointed towards the door beneath the great stone dragon. 'Go then. Find what you seek.'

Mihn stood and backed out of the black square, bowing all the while. As soon as he was out he saw the woman's ghost drift within and Death's gaze lifted as the Herald stepped beside Mihn once more. The small man looked first at Death, then His Herald before rubbing a hand roughly over his face and blinking hard.

'Strange,' Mihn commented to the expressionless Aspect of Death. 'I never really thought I'd even get this far.'

There was no reply, or even a sign the Herald had heard him. Mihn gestured towards the door and set off towards it, the Herald beside him.

'Now I just have to break into the Dark Place itself.'

As he walked, he felt the weight on his shoulders returning with every step.

Venn moved with the painful care of an old man whose next fall would be his last. Walking across the floor of the shrine cavern and up the gently sloped tunnel that led to the Land outside, even so

30

short a distance, left the renegade Harlequin fatigued and huffing for breath in the cold air. He found the steps up to the tunnel particularly difficult; the priestess, Paen, was at his side and had to help him balance as he lifted one foot after the other.

She seemed taller now than when he'd first returned, when her pride had been the key Venn had used to unlock the Harlequin clans – she was standing tall and strong and proud while Venn grew steadily weaker. His unnatural grace was a distant memory now, his speed as absent as the whipcord strength he'd once boasted.

Paen tried to dissuade him from this daily pilgrimage, but Venn knew he had to do it. With two heartbeats hammering in his ears and the breath of two men forcing its way through his lips, Venn knew he had to force himself to move each day, no matter how hard, otherwise he would slowly succumb to the fatigue that was deep in his bones. It was bitterly cold outside, where the snow still lay thick on the ground, but that was still preferable to an interminable tramp around the vast cavern, past the shrines and open temples that littered it.

Jackdaw was silent, even after Venn had dismissed the priestess and two apprentice Harlequins who watched over him with possessive reverence. The black-clad Harlequin was the herald of a new dawn in their eyes; something between an oracle of the Gods and a prophet. They feared and worshipped him in equal measure.

Jackdaw remained a secret from all the others, but while the former monk of Vellern was the secret of Venn's success, as his magery slowly turned the Harlequins to Azaer's service, he was slowly killing Venn. His presence in Venn's shadow was taking a toll the Harlequin would not be able to bear much longer.

I am failing you, master, Venn thought distantly, knowing Azaer could most likely not hear his prayers; not while the shadow inhabited a mortal body. *I had thought this was how I would deliver the Harlequin clans to you, but I do not have the strength. These spells you taught Jackdaw did everything I asked, but I am failing nonetheless.*

He began to shuffle through the snow, barely noticing the cold at first. The evening was clear and sharp, the stars bright and the hunter's moon free of cloud. In Kasi's light the cloud-oaks studding the forest below glowed a dull white against the miles of dark pine. He stopped and looked up at the sky above the forest: Kasi lay low against the horizon while the greater moon, Alterr, was a yellowed lump at its zenith.

Kasi: this monument to a dull, unthinking thug, and Alterr: a spiteful bitch whose icy heart is displayed for the whole Land to pity. Neither of you deserve the magnificence of the night.

He hunched over, coughing, as the cold air began to tickle his throat, the effort causing his whole chest to ache.

Perhaps I shall ask to be the one to change that.

Venn smiled to himself at the thought. In the fullness of time there would be nothing beyond Azaer's ability to grant.

He continued on, taking careful steps alongside last night's trampled path, which had already compacted into treacherous ice. His bearskin was a leaden weight on his shoulders, but without it he would freeze so he bore it, and fought his body to keep the signs of hardship from his face. As he made his slow progress he watched carefully for discarded branches or stones that might trip him. Slowly an ache built in his chest, dull but insistent, wrapped around his ribcage like a serpent's embrace. He let out a grunt. His foot scuffed along the snow-covered ground and hit something, a yielding mass that rolled under his foot and pitched Venn to the ground. A tearing sensation raced through his chest, driving the wind from his lungs.

He cried out again, unable to bear the pain as purple stars burst before his eyes. The apprentice Harlequins were quick to run to his side. One feeble arm, unable to break his fall, was pinned under his body.

They were about to roll him onto his back when the priestess' stern voice cut the air. 'No, fetch a stretcher!'

Without thinking Venn pushed himself over with his free arm. The weight on his body had lifted without warning, the sapping ache of exhaustion that gripped his body vanishing into numbness.

Spirits below, am I dying?

The pain in his chest was gone; whatever had happened in the fall, now he felt nothing.

'Sweet Prince,' exclaimed the priestess as she hurried over. The apprentices stepped back from Venn.

She crouched at his feet and Venn lifted his head to look at her, puzzled. She appeared to be inspecting his boots – no, she was looking at the lump he had tripped on.

'It's a man,' she breathed.

Venn struggled into a sitting position, then looked down with wonder as he realised the ease with which he had moved. The apprentices stared at him with even greater astonishment and fear than they had before.

'A man?' he rasped.

She looked up, the face behind her half-mask of obsidian shards betraying even greater shock than the others. 'Master— Your face—? You look—'

'Reborn,' Venn muttered, realisation stealing over him. 'My faith has restored my youth.'

'A miracle,' one of the apprentices breathed. 'That fall should have killed you in your weakened state!'

Venn inclined his head. 'And yet my weakness has become strength.'

Paen turned to the figure on the ground, rolling the body over so they could see his face.

'He's not of the tribes,' she announced with alarm. These parts were remote and the Harlequin clans did not welcome travellers eager to discover their secrets. She turned the head to one side. 'These are feather tattoos; he was a priest of Vellern?'

'*What?*' screamed a voice in Venn's mind. '*What is happening?*'

'He must have travelled a long way to reach us, but he died at the very entrance to the cavern,' Venn said softly. '*Hush your mouth, Jackdaw, let me think.*'

'Is he Farlan?'

Venn peered at the dead body. There was no mistaking the face; it was the former Prior Corci, the monk dubbed Jackdaw by his new master, Azaer. The puckered scars where Azaer had ripped a handful of tattooed feathers from his cheek were clearly visible. Venn restrained the urge to laugh long and loudly.

'It appears so,' he ventured, thinking madly. 'Please, help me up.'

He allowed the apprentices to slip their hands under his arms and bear him upright, tottering a little for good measure before adopting the same hunched posture imposed on him for months. Acting was part of a Harlequin's training, and Venn shuffled over to the corpse as like the man who had ventured outside a few minutes earlier as possible. The strain might have been lifted from his face, but he'd quickly realised a more gradual return to his former strength would be safer. Jackdaw's magic had not dampened their ability to question.

'What was he doing here?' one of the apprentices asked in a whisper.

'*What's happening? What has happened to me?*' Jackdaw wailed in Venn's mind.

'Seeking me,' Venn said finally. 'The Land has sickened and men seek a cure to its ills. This man has followed his faith and given his life to call us forth.'

'Should we leave sooner than the Equinox Festival?' Paen asked.

Venn bowed his head. 'We will leave within the week. My time of testing is over; I will soon be strong enough to travel again.'

'*Venn, I'm lying dead on the ground!*' Jackdaw shrieked hysterically, unheard by the others.

'So you are,' Venn said softly once the others were out of earshot, trying to hide the quick grin that stole over his face. '*Our master has quite a sense of humour.*'

'*Humour?*' Jackdaw screamed, '*my body is dead! Merciful Gods, I'm trapped inside your shadow, and I cannot feel anything! I'm a ghost, a living ghost!*'

'*Living? Oh, I don't think so, my friend,*' Venn replied.

'*Far from it,*' purred a third voice inside him.

Venn froze, an icy twitch of fear running down his spine.

'*Morghien will so relish having competition for his title.*'

'Spirits below,' Venn breathed, stumbling in shock. The priestess gave him a puzzled look but Venn ignored it, as he ignored Jackdaw's sobs of terror. On the wind there was a faint smell, one Venn recognised all too well: the scent of peach blossom . . . despite the winter snow.

'*Indeed,*' said Rojak.

Mihn stepped through the black doors and for a gut-clenching moment everything went dark. There was a distant boom as the enormous doors closed again. After a while he realised there was some faint light on the other side. At first he could see little, though he could feel the oppressive presence of a vast slope, stretching up ahead. The incline was shallow, and more or less regular, but it continued endlessly into the distance with nothing beyond. A hot, sour-smelling wind drifted over him, and Mihn felt very vulnerable and exposed as he took in the boundlessness of the place.

Behind him came a great rasping noise, accompanied by a stench so foul he found himself gagging even as he ran blindly for several hundred yards, not daring to look back. Ancient, brittle bones crackled underfoot, and an awful whispery sound was interspersed with faint sighs and occasional groans. Daima had warned him not to linger there, nor to look back, but there was little need for her caution: Mihn knew full well the rotting corpse of a dragon was bound to this side of the doors and he had no desire to look upon it. Bad enough that he would have to if he returned.

As he reached a chunk of rock twice his height that was protruding awkwardly from the slope Mihn stopped, realising the bones underfoot had given way to grit and dirt. As he paused to catch his breath he felt the heat radiate out from the rock. Now he dared to look at his surroundings and take in the sight of Ghain, the great slope which all souls must walk before they reached either the land of no time or the punishments of Ghenna.

The darkness was not so complete as he'd first thought, more a ghastly red tint, and little by little he started to see some detail of the immeasurable mountain slope. Nothing was clear, but at least he could discern where the bigger stones lay, and the cant of the ground. Here and there boulders punctuated the jagged, stony slope. He crouched and ran his fingers through the dirt at his feet. It felt gritty, almost greasy on his skin, quite unlike the sands of a desert.

There were a few stunted trees but Mihn knew this was not a place where any real life could be sustained. Up above was a roiling mess of smoke-clouds that looked positively poisonous, far from the sort that might provide rain. He started out towards the nearest tree, but after a few hundred yards he began to make out shapes around its base and as he got closer he could see something writhing in its crooked, dead branches ... He turned away at once, giving the strange sight a wide berth.

When he was safely clear, Mihn stopped and looked up the slope. He felt terribly alone, as fearful as an abandoned child, and part of him wanted to curl up in a hollow and hide from the dread that pervaded the slope. The quiet was broken only by tremors running through the ground and the distant moans of the damned drifting on the air, which was uncomfortably hot, irritating his eyes and throat. At last Mihn shook himself and started off again, trudging up the slope. He kept a wary eye open, checking in all directions every few minutes, but Ghain remained empty until he came to a hollow in the ground, a dozen yards across, below a level stone. From Mihn's angle it looked like a door lintel set into the slope and while there was nothing but the position of the stone to differentiate it, something made Mihn stop.

He checked his feet and palms, brushing the dirt from his bare soles and ensuring the tattoos put there by the witch of Llehden remained unbroken. Reassured, he skirted the hollow and checked around. Some faint dragging sound seemed to accompany a tiny movement in the distance, but it was miles away and Mihn discounted the threat, at least for the present. He bent and picked up a large stone, hefting it to feel the weight for a moment, then hurled it into the hollow.

The dead soil exploded into movement, a grey cloud of dust erupting up as some hidden creature snapped at the stone. It clawed at the place where the stone had landed, then shook violently to bury itself once more in the ground.

Mihn gaped. Years ago a friend had shown him an ant-lion's lair, and whilst he had seen only the claw of whatever lay in hidden in Ghain's slope, it had to be several hundred times larger than the savage insect they'd teased out of the ground all those years ago. He shivered, and continued even more warily on his way.

Death was not a God prone to exaggeration. He had said there were a thousand torments lurking on the slopes of Ghain, and as he walked, Mihn began to wonder whether these were neither daemon nor Aspect: *What if they are the mischief and cruelty of mortals given flesh? Or is all I see born of my own fears?*

He shivered and chanced a look behind. He felt like he'd walked several miles already and as he turned he saw, far away, the pitted stone construction that housed the door to Death's throne room, standing alone like a forgotten monument, forever overshadowed by the enormous, torn wings of a shape perched above it. The wings reflected no light, throwing off even Ghain's lambent glow.

Behind the gate a featureless wasteland stretched out into the distance: endless flat miles of red dust and rock. There was no escape from Ghain, this empty place that sat between the domain of daemons, Ghenna, and the implacable Jailer of the Dark. In the Age of Myths, the dragon had been too proud and too powerful to accept death, so the Gods had chained it there, to prevent it from ever returning to the Land.

Mihn felt it watching him, its presence like acid on the breeze. Above his head something invisible flapped past with slow, heavy strokes. He shrank down instinctively but the sound of tattered leather wings soon passed and he was left alone once more, feeling increasingly bleak.

He rubbed his palms together and looked at the stylised owl's head on each. While he hadn't seen what had flown past, it had been close enough to see him. Clearly the magic imbued into his skin by the witch was still working here.

Please let that continue, he prayed fervently. *Without it I don't stand a chance.*

How much the tattoos could protect him he didn't know, but he had no wish to find out what would happen if the magic failed. As he lingered, chilling howls rolled over the dusty slopes, provoking renewed fear. Mihn wondered how he ever thought what he was attempting was even possible . . .

But he walked on, glad to turn his back on the dragon. He focused on picking his way up the slopes rather than thinking too hard about the sounds that echoed across Ghain. Still he saw no others, neither torments nor trudging souls, until the slope suddenly levelled out for a stretch and he saw a silver pavilion emerge from the gloom.

Not far away was a figure, a man in rags, slightly transparent, who wore around his neck a collar with a dozen or more long chains attached; they were twenty or thirty feet in length, of all sorts of thicknesses and materials, and they dragged behind the soul along the ground. The soul was looking up the slope as he plodded slowly on, but he made no progress because one of the multitudes of chains had snagged on a stone.

Mihn looked around. He could see nothing else nearby, neither spirit nor daemon. As he neared the tormented soul he checked again, but there was no visible cover that some creature might lurk behind. The soul himself paid Mihn no attention as he tried in vain to march forward. The ground was flat and featureless, with no indication of lurking torment, despite the easiness of the prey –

and Mihn suddenly realised why: they would not come within sight of Mercy's pavilion, for fear of the only Aspects that trod Ghain's slope.

Mihn had spent the last few days before his journey trawling his remarkable memory for stories of this place, anything that might help him survive his sojourn here. So it was apparently true that following Death's judgment, the Herald would affix a collar around each soul's neck, so they would proceed up Ghain's slopes dragging their sins behind them. There was copper for avarice, jade for envy, pitted iron for murder; a different material for each sin. Death had built seven pavilions on Ghain, and some of the sins could be forgiven at each. This was a journey all mortals made; some ascended only part of the way before they were borne off to the land of no time, while others were forced to travel untold miles to the fiery River Maram and across to the gates of Ghenna itself, before which the last of the pavilions stood. Even then, some sins were unforgivable, and the dead would be forced to continue onwards.

He crept closer to the chain, watching the soul carefully, but he appeared not to notice the not-dead traveller at all, not even when Mihn nudged the chain – ivory for malice of deed – off the stone. Once freed the soul continued to plod onwards, and as he began to approach the empty pavilion Mihn followed at a cautious distance, wanting to witness what would happen, despite his fear of being observed.

The pavilion was hexagonal, with a pillar at every corner supporting the scrolled roof, and an iron lantern hanging from each pillar. There were bee-shapes cut into the lantern sides, indicating that this was Death's province still, though only a few rays of light escaped.

The soul walked up the steps of the pavilion and across the centre, oblivious of his surroundings. In a flash of light a woman appeared at the spirit's side. She was robed in gold and white and carried an enormous golden hammer, which she smashed down on the trailing chains as they passed her. One shattered in a brief blaze of light and faded to nothing. The rest remained unbroken, continuing to drag after the soul, who made no reaction. The woman lowered her hammer and turned towards Mihn as he approached.

'You should not have freed him. It is not your place to judge the dead,' she called to him.

'I did not judge,' he replied, bowing to her as he approached the steps. 'I merely showed mercy. There are many chains around his neck; he will not be escaping Ghain's slopes too quickly.'

The woman nodded approvingly. 'You bear no chains. Have you led a blameless life?' She stretched out her hand and a long curved horn chased with silver appeared in it. 'Few come to me this way; usually only children have no chains. Rarely do I have the pleasure of calling Death's attendants for a grown man.'

Mihn shook his head. 'My judgment is not yet at hand, Lady. You must not call them but must let me pass.'

'*Must* let you pass?' the woman said. 'You walk these slopes out of choice, and the folly is your own – but I am a Mercy. Lord Death alone commands me.'

Mihn ducked his head in humility. 'That is so, but it is written that all those who name you may ask a boon of you. This I so do, Kenanai the Mother, to pass uncalled and unharmed.'

The Mercy was silent for a while as she stared at him. She betrayed no emotion but he assumed she was confused by his presence; such a thing had never happened before for those asking a boon of the Mercies in myth had always been immortals.

Eventually Kenanai lowered her hand and the horn vanished. She gestured after the spirit, indicating that he could pass.

'It is granted.'

A low rumble echoed across Ghain's slopes and she too disappeared, leaving the pavilion empty and still but for the flickering light of the lanterns. Mihn climbed the steps and as he crossed the pavilion he whispered an ancient prayer to the Mercies. When he reached the other side he stopped and looked around. The soul he had helped was nowhere in sight, though he could see the trail in the dust left by the chains. Other than that, Mihn could see only the empty landscape – broken boulders, dust and dead trees – for miles in all directions.

'"This journey I walk alone,"' he quoted grimly. 'And how alone I feel now.' He continued his ascent, choosing his path as carefully as he could, keeping a look-out all the time. Occasionally creatures flew or scampered across his path – many-limbed beings like horrific spiders the size of small dogs and crawling bat-winged monstrosities – and once he saw a daemon marching grimly across Ghain's jagged landscape: a fat figure as tall as he, with four spindly arms, each dragging an ancient weapon behind it. His heart jumped as the daemon paused and looked up, as though sniffing the air, but whatever it had noticed, it wasn't enough to make it linger there for long.

Each time he saw movement he would stop and crouch, trusting the witch's magic to keep him safe. Each time, he was passed by without note. Distance proved meaningless in this blasted place, where a dozen steps felt like a mile. All Mihn was certain of in this strange domain was that no time was passing as he walked. After a score or more miles he was no less exhausted by the journey than he had been when he started. Though the neverending heat and the fear Ghain itself engendered sapped his strength, the exertion of walking had no discernible effect, he was glad to discover.

Another of the Mercies' pavilions was passed, then another, and another. After some indeterminate period of time he had counted off six, and he knew he was close to his goal – though before he could reach the one that remained, Mihn would have to cross the river of fire called Maram – the barrier that kept the daemons of Ghenna within the Dark Place. A new fear started up within him: worry that a bargain the witch of Llehden had made had in fact not been kept and the next step of his journey would be all the more risky. It was a gamble he hated to have been forced into, and while he knew it had been necessary, Mihn couldn't help but wonder what sort of chain it might add to his own burden of sins.

At last he came to a peak, where indistinct clouds raced close overhead. His human senses saw it as a great crater at the peak of Ghain, within which the ivory gates of Ghenna's entrance were to be found, but he knew it was not so simple – not even by digging down through the rocky slope of Ghain could one break into the Dark Place; it took an immortal's eyes to fully behold the mountain and the Dark Place within.

He stood at the peak of the slope and looked back over the empty miles he had walked, then down at the swift, churning river of orange flames no more than a hundred yards off. As Mihn tried to follow Maram's twisty path, he found the effort hurt, and his vision became blurred. Maram obviously didn't like to be stared at.

He gave up and concentrated on the two constructed features he could see: a silver pavilion, bigger and more magnificent than the rest, stood just the other side of a thin bridge that crossed Maram. Mihn knew from the myths he'd studied that the bridge was only a hand-width wide, and covered in nails to tear the feet of sinners. Aside from the pavilion, the other bank was hidden by impenetrable shadows, though Mihn felt a subconscious horror at what lay beyond.

The scene was exactly as the stories described, but nothing could prepare a man, not even a Harlequin, for the sight of it. For a moment he forgot his mission and simply stared: at Maram, at the nail bridge, at the Dark Place beyond ... until a soft moan broke the silence and awakened him from his reverie, enough to stir him into movement. He scrambled down the slope towards to the edge of the river, where a figure stood, ghostly of form and clad in tattered rags, the soul of a woman. The chains she was dragging were far longer and heavier than those carried by the first soul Mihn had met – despite the Mercies, there remained dozens of sins unforgiven by Lord Death. Mihn could see half-a-dozen were the pitted iron of murder.

The soul was walking towards the bridge, compelled, as all souls were. Mihn watched, shaken, as she ground to a halt, turning about in confusion, as a shapeless but unmistakably malevolent black mist swirled about her feet.

He saw her walk a few yards back the way she had come, head bowed and feet dragging with exhaustion, before being turned again, and again.

After a while Mihn approached, with great caution, watching the black mist in particular. He knew the threat it posed, but he was far more afraid that the scent of the soul's many sins would attract Ghain's many torments.

He opened his mouth to speak, but he felt the words catch in his throat, the bile rising, for all that he knew how necessary this was. The soul's journey up Ghain's slopes must have been long and hard, attracting each of the thousand torments like moths to a flame, and it was impossible to tell how many years it had felt like to her.

The passage of time in the afterlife bore little relation to that of the Land, and Ehla's bargain, suggested by Daima – who knew the lay of Ghain better than most mortals – might have kept the soul walking for centuries more, especially given the weight of her sins. That she was a grievous sinner, one ineluctably bound for the Dark Place, made Mihn feel no better about inflicting further cruelty – even more since the first Mercy had told him judgment was not his to mete out.

Mihn reminded himself of the choices involved and called out, 'Duchess, turn around and close your eyes to it.'

The soul turned, as though waking from a dream.

'It—It is everywhere,' she sobbed eventually. 'I cannot . . .'

'Close your eyes,' Mihn commanded, 'and walk.'

After more wails of protest he repeated himself, and this time the soul did as he ordered. Almost instantly the swirling blackness around her stopped its darting movements and rose up angrily. For a moment Mihn thought it was about to take form and attack him, but instead it raced away, disappearing into the distance.

'Now cross the bridge,' Mihn told the soul.

The soul that had once been Duchess Lomin, quietly executed for heresy and treason, began to trudge wearily towards the bridge. She stopped as she reached it. The bridge was roughly built and insubstantial, just a thin, nail-studded walkway, with a single hand-rail on the left-hand side. She started to gather the chains dragging behind her, intent on draping them over the rail, until Mihn called out again to stop her.

'You must carry your sins; you must bear them, or risk the boatman dragging you from the bridge.'

On cue a scow appeared from nothing, racing towards them on the fiery tumult below. Standing at the prow was a single figure swathed in red robes. Its face was hidden by a veil and a jewelled pouch hung from its waist: the Maram boatman, neither daemon nor God, but a being of power whose true name was hidden to mortals. The Maram boatman was one of the few beings in existence that bowed to no authority. To see behind its veil was to see horror itself, so the legends said, and to be dragged into the river by the pole with which it propelled the scow was to become fuel for the flames.

The figure raised its pole as it reached them and swiped at the handrail where the duchess had been about to heap her chains. The pole caught only air, and the boatman flashed on underneath, a deep laughter echoing all around.

Reluctantly the soul started across the bridge, her chains heaped in her arms. Mihn watching as she laboured across, blood from her torn feet and arms dripping into the river below. He was horrified when he saw the trapped souls in the flames, leaping and fighting to lap up the falling droplets of blood. He looked away, at the pavilion at the other end of the bridge, only to see a shifting mass of darkness that was just as terrible.

This close Mihn could hear the screams ringing out from Ghenna's ivory gates, the hoarse voices of the damned, the yammer of the Dark Place's foul denizens. Jagged metallic sounds echoed discordantly over the river of flame, heavy thumps like huge hammers and screeching like the scrape of knives. He suppressed a shiver and walked to the end of the bridge.

The ghostly soul of Duchess Lomin had reached halfway, wailing piteously as she walked, but he willed the sound into the background, just another cry of the damned. The bridge of nails was nothing to what awaited her in Ghenna, and the time for pity was gone. Once her soul was near the end of the bridge Mihn readied himself and checked for the boatman again. It was nowhere in sight, but that meant little.

He took a deep breath and leaped up onto the single handrail, and as he did so, the boatman appeared again, poling the scow along with deceptive lethargy. Mihn wasn't fooled; he had seen how quickly it could move, but he forced himself to ignore it. He looked down at the rail beneath his feet. It wasn't wide, but at almost the width of his foot it was thicker than the cable every Harlequin learned on.

'A shame I was only passable at wire tumbling,' Mihn muttered to himself, 'but this will be easier – and it did teach me to be good at grabbing the rope before I fell.'

He took a pace forward, testing his bare feet on the wood. It bore him easily enough, so before he could think any more about the consequences he set off at a brisk trot, his arms held wide for balance. The boatman underneath carved a path through the fire as it brought the scow sharply around. Mihn kept his eyes on the rail under his feet and the dark shape of the Maram boatman in his peripheral vision. The scow darted forward, racing to intercept him before he reached the other side, and Mihn slowed his pace a fraction, measuring out his steps as the little boat reached the bridge and the boatman raised his pole like a lance to snag Mihn's legs.

At the last moment Mihn flipped his body forward, tucking his head down and throwing his legs over. Distantly he heard a screech as the pole caught only the wood underneath and then his feet were over, landing safely on the rail again as he dropped into a crouch. The boatman shot past underneath and jerked hard back around. Mihn stayed where he was, watching it come back on-path with unnatural speed to try the tilt again.

The end of the bridge was still a distance away.

'I'm not going to make it in time,' he murmured.

The boatman turned again, running alongside the far bank of the river behind him.

Damn, it is learning from its mistakes. He didn't wait to watch any more but broke into as fast a run as he dared. He guessed the boatman could cover the distance in a matter of seconds.

Something different then, he thought, picking a spot ahead. He scampered forward until, without warning, he dropped onto his belly and wrapped arms and legs around the rail. He felt the pole whip over his head and dip as fast as the boatman could manage, but it was quick enough only to skim Mihn's cropped head and then it was gone.

Out of the corner of his eye he saw the scow turn again to avoid colliding with the bank, but now there was no time to waste. He jumped up and raced for the end of the bridge – until, in his haste Mihn misjudged the last footstep and slipped sideways, crashing to the ground at the steps of the silver pavilion. He lay on his back a moment, panting, staring up at the darkly boiling sky above before a bright flash of light prompted him to scramble up again.

In the centre of the pavilion stood the soul of Duchess Lomin, still laden with the massive chains of her sins, while beside her was the last of the Mercies, a tall, bearded man wearing a crown. His hammer was pitch-black, but no less ornate than those of the other Mercies Mihn had passed. With a solemn flourish the man brought the hammer on the ground behind the soul, not apparently caring that its sins were still held tightly to its chest.

That done, he reached out his right hand, but instead of a silver-chased horn, a twisted spiral of carnelian appeared in the Mercy's hand and he sounded a deep, forbidding note. Mihn felt his breath catch as an answering note came from within the darkness beyond.

He crouched at the foot of the stair to watch. This close to the pavilion he saw the roof and pillars were not pristine but scored and scratched: it was so close to Ghenna that even Death's authority was not untouchable.

At first nothing happened, then a great hot wind began to whip up all around. Mihn screwed his eyes as tight as he could against the dusty whirlwind. With mounting dread he felt the swirling darkness being driven up and away, and he opened his eyes in time to see for the first time the entrance to Ghenna.

No more than fifty yards away stood several enormous barred gates, each apparently carved from a single piece of ivory, and set into bare rock. The entrance to Ghenna was a humped peak in the centre of the crater, curved around the level plain that stood between the gates and the Mercy's pavilion. Each gate was hinged at the top and opened outwards, but they opened only for those who'd sold their soul to one of Ghenna's inhabitants. The bars were slightly curved, the smooth flow to the design suggesting an organic creation rather than the rigid regularity of a human construction.

The journals of Malich Cordein had named the three main gates for him: Jaishen Gate, the smallest, was on the left; the largest of them all, Gheshen, was in the centre, with Coroshen on the right. There were three other gates, each around fifty feet tall – less than half the size of Jaishen's – that Malich had called the borderland gates, opening to the parts of Ghenna where no master ruled and the daemons fought a never-ending war of attrition.

Mihn scanned each of the main gates in turn. He had no idea which would open to admit the soul. Malich himself had dealt with a prince of Coroshen, the domain that existed nearest to the surface, but Duchess Lomin was of the Certinse family and he guessed the Certinses would have sought help elsewhere – if ever there was a family to play two sides it was theirs.

'Mihn, you must move,' Mihn growled to himself as the soul walked out of the pavilion and stopped. He urged it on until at last the soul began to stumble towards the gates. 'They are creatures of darkness; they turn away from the light. You need to go closer to them.'

Against every natural instinct, against the terror that was welling up in his gut, Mihn followed his own advice and forced himself forward. The ground was hot now, enough to scorch his feet, and the air was growing foetid and sulphurous, but he ignored the increasing discomfort, intent only on the gates ahead. One began to open, and Mihn threw himself forward, just in time to grab the bottom rung of the Jaishen Gate before it lifted away. He swung his leg over the smooth ivory and hauled himself up until he was sitting on the lower bar.

As he looked around he noted to his relief there were no sounds of alarm, no hungry calls of delight at the sight of an undamned soul. It looked like the old myths had once more come to his aid: the denizens of Ghenna did indeed turn their faces away from the light of the last pavilion. Mihn wasted no time as the gate continued to rise; he could see patrols of minion daemons, armed with harpoons or huge barbed fishing lines – the sort of weapons that had damaged the pavilion, he now realised. The daemons were only at ground level; a skilled climber like Mihn might be able to make his way up, and avoid the guards and hunters entirely – or so he hoped.

A condemned soul would stumble around in the darkness beyond the pavilion until it was snagged by one of those patrolling daemons and hauled through one of the gates into Ghenna, to the domain of whichever master the daemon served. There, the damned soul would have to face horrors unnumbered and untold, until the end of time or the fires of torment forged them into a new shape.

There were gaps in the gates easily large enough for souls to be dragged through, big enough even for daemons to step out from Ghenna – but they would not, not whilst the last of the Mercies stood, forever watchful, in his pavilion.

As the Jaishen Gate lifted, Mihn found it easy to climb the massive ivory bars. The biggest were easily twice as thick as his own body and bore his weight easily. When he reached the side he looked down and saw two massive, squat beasts standing below the gate, one end of a long iron bar strapped to their backs that lifted the bottom edge of the gate as they walked forward. From the way their heads swayed he guessed the beasts were blind – that was how they were able to face the light of the Mercy's pavilion. They sniffed at the stinking air, snuffling their way towards the soul of Duchess Lomin, limping onwards to its eternal damnation. The beasts lunged at her, displaying rows of jagged teeth in huge mouths, but they could move no more than a foot before being stopped by the pivot mechanism they were harnessed to.

Excited howls emanated from deep within Jaishen as the gate began to close and darkness started to return. A pair of spindly figures quested out, advancing on the soul with hands covering their eyes. When they found her they ran exploratory hands all over the soul's ghostly body before grasping it firmly and dragging it further within. Somewhere in the depths Mihn heard a heavy booming, a steady rhythm that prompted high-pitched squeals from the long dark tunnel below him. The horn sounded again and the beasts turned to pull the gate closed. It was only when the darkness had descended fully that Mihn heard the soul's wailing renew.

Mihn clung tight to his perch, too focused on the task in hand to feel pity now. He had been studying the paintings of Elshaim, a necromancer-turned-prophet – the same painter whose works Malich Cordein himself had spent several years poring over – and it looked like he was right: the gate's gigantic hinges *did* protrude, and as the gate closed, so a wide gap began to appear in between the ivory frame and the rock.

Mihn slipped quickly into the gap as it opened up before him. He felt a fleeting flush of relief as he reached towards the rock roof and found it jagged and uneven, providing plenty of hand-holds for him to pull himself inside. Moving carefully, he advanced inside the tunnel, and he was several yards from the gate when Jaishen ground shut once more. As it closed, a bone-numbing tremor rumbled through the rock.

Mihn braced himself on the unnatural honeycombed rock and rested for a moment, focusing all his strength into calming the fear now burning inside him. That great grinding closure hit him like the kick of a mule, driving the wind from his lungs, leaving him shaking and gasping for breath.

Mihn had made it to Ghenna, and here he was, all alone in the Dark Place. Not even the Gods could help him now.

CHAPTER 3

As he woke, Major Amber twitched his head, which was enough to send a spasm of pain racing down his neck. He whimpered, but a moment later panic overshadowed everything and wakefulness hit him like a deluge.

Cold fear enveloped his mind; all he could feel was searing agony, a rod of iron where his spine should be. Every other sense was numb. He tried to lift his arm and felt nothing, nothing at all. When he tried to open his eyes all he managed was a facial twitch, and another wrenching spasm. At last he edged them open, only to immediately close them against the searing light.

'Hush now,' said a woman's voice beside him as Amber began to hyperventilate in terror, wincing at every gasp. 'Hey, settle down – you're injured, but you will recover.'

He felt a weight on his chest, a palm pressing down to hold him still, and he moaned in relief. For a while all he could remember was stars bursting in his head, the crunch of bones breaking and the death-cry of the man he'd killed. The details eluded him for the moment as his thoughts floundered, lost in a world of hurt.

'That's better,' the woman continued, her voice soothing. Her fingers found his, and this he could feel, a comforting sensation. 'You're bound to the bed,' she told him, 'you broke a few bones and the surgeons wanted to keep you still.'

He tried to respond, but all that came out was a wheeze.

'Don't speak; you're too weak. I'll fetch a healer. We'll talk later.'

Her hand moved away and Amber felt himself slide back into the cool arms of sleep. When he awoke a second time it was better; as he opened his eyes he felt the return of some part of him that before had been trapped in the darkness. He still hurt all over, but now he was aware enough to feel the bed underneath him, and he could tally the individual injuries. His neck was now a dull throb, and he found he could lift his left arm, although moving his right caused him to hiss in pain.

'Ah, awake at last,' came the same woman's voice. 'I was beginning to worry they'd given you too much there.'

He turned his head gingerly to the left and took a moment as Horsemistress Kirl came into focus. She smiled down at him from a campaign chair and leaned forward. Behind her he saw a white plastered wall and a shuttered window, the only light in the room provided by a small fire and two large pillar candles standing iron lamp-stands.

'Don't try to move. Our best healers have been working on you, but there's only so much a mage can do.'

'How long?' Amber croaked.

'Since the battle?' She thought for a moment. 'You woke the first time two weeks back. Another day and a half since then.'

Amber opened his mouth to say something else, but this time the effort defeated him. Instead he bathed in the warmth of the Horsemistress' lopsided smile. She'd cut her dark hair shorter since he'd last seen her and it hung loose to the raised collar of her unbuttoned tunic.

Amber started: that wasn't her uniform – he didn't recognise it at all. Kirl was an auxiliary attached to Amber's legion, the Cheme Third – so why was she wearing a fitted cavalryman's tunic? The scarlet adorned with blue and white slashes and gold buttons was more along the lines of Amber's formal Menin officer's uniform than Kirl's usual plain grey outfit.

'You like it?' Kirl asked with a coquettish smile. 'I found it in the Farlan baggage. The Penitent Army left everything and ran; Hain reckons it was made for an officer of the Cardinal Paladins.'

Amber didn't respond immediately, then he realised he was staring, his mouth open, and he looked away.

'That good, eh?' Kirl laughed, 'I'm glad to hear it!'

He coughed. 'Aye, not bad,' he said hoarsely.

His throat was dry and sore, but he ignored the pain. Kirl's lovely crooked smile was enough to make his breath catch when she wore drab riding leathers; dressed in a fine, narrow-waisted tunic ... As she bent over him to help him lie back he breathed in her scent and prayed she wouldn't notice any stirrings under the blanket.

'You tending to me?' he rasped. 'What's happened since the battle?'

She scowled. 'Not much that needs my attention. I've got all my horses pastured for the moment and I'm just trying to keep my head low. It's all ... *tense* out there right now, but you're a fucking hero and you've got a nice warm room, so I might possibly have stretched the truth a little so I could hide out in here till everyone calms down.'

She gestured around her and Amber realised for the first time that he was in a bedroom large and luxurious enough for a duke, even though it was mostly empty. A wooden partition was drawn up to one side of him to keep the fire's heat close. He could see nothing around him to tell him who the room normally belonged to, but someone had dragged his kit in – and even managed to retrieve his scimitars from the battlefield! The career soldier in him prayed to Karkarn that same someone would have seen fit to clean the swords and hammer out the nicks before they got rusty.

'Colonel Uresh knows where I am if he needs me, so do my men. I'm doing as much good tending to you as anywhere else – more, probably.'

'"Stretched the truth"?'

The lovely smile returned. 'You don't need to worry about that right now,' she said with a soft laugh, 'but I think Hain's reached a whole new level of admiration for you now.'

Amber couldn't help but cough at the thought. He knew full-well what was pretty much always on Captain Hain's mind when he wasn't fighting. The sight of Kirl in that tunic really wouldn't have helped.

'Well, look at that,' Kirl said with a purr of interest. 'That thought's put some colour in your cheeks! For now, Major Amber, you might want to hear what's been happening since you fainted on the battlefield.'

'Fainted!' Amber gasped as the memory of the battle finally appeared in his mind: Lord Chalat, Chosen of the Fire God Tsatach, wading through the Menin ranks wreathed in flame; Amber fighting his way through the ranks to slam a spiked axe into Chalat's chest—

'So one witness, who'll remain nameless, is telling everyone he can,' Kirl continued, 'and by the way, Captain Hain's treating that axe like it's a holy relic now.' She paused and cocked her head, then added, 'Which I s'pose it might be. Anyway, Lord Isak's dead, but not before he killed Scion Styrax – and for that our lord sent him straight to the Dark Place!'

She shivered at the thought and fell silent, all traces of her smile gone.

Amber felt the strength drain from his body. He'd not been close to Kohrad Styrax, but he had known the hot-tempered youth for years, and had fought beside him more than once. The idea of Kohrad dead was too much for him to grasp immediately. It felt unreal, even to a man used to the loss of comrades.

'You can tell where it happened too,' Kirl said in a hushed voice. 'There's a point out on the field where the ground's as hot as new-fired clay, so folk've been saying. We routed the Farlan, killed a large part of the Penitent Army and chased the rest most o' the way to Helrect. Lord Styrax's overcome with grief so General Gaur's been giving the orders – you can image how close he is to dis-embowelling anyone who comes near.'

Amber nodded, wincing, all too easily able to imagine General Gaur's current state of mind. The beastman's overriding sense of duty would not allow him to withdraw into grief when there was an army to manage, but Gaur had been as much of a father to Kohrad as Styrax himself.

'And then there's the small matter of the dragon,' Kirl said after a pause.

'Dragon?' Amber coughed.

'Aye, our lord woke it up about the time you fainted and broke half-a-dozen bones on your way to the ground. The beast is just a bit fucking angry at the situation. No one knows what's left of the Library of Seasons, but a large part of Ismess has been levelled and the Fortinn quarter has taken quite a battering too. So's Byora, but some folk are saying that's because some Raylin mercenary went mad during the battle.'

'And Lord Styrax isn't doing anything about it?'

She reached for a waterskin and helped him to drink. 'Ah, well now, Lord Styrax ain't doing much of anything at the moment, and as long as that continues, the chaos outside is just going to go on getting worse.'

Amber took a minute or two to drink, then announced, 'I need to be out of this room.'

'Don't be bloody stupid, you can't even stand up.' Kirl enumerated his injuries: 'Three bones in your foot are broken, and your shin snapped when a horse trod on you. On top of that you've managed to break your wrist, your arm in two places, your collarbone and three ribs – for pity's sake, Amber, you even managed to break your nose when you smacked yourself into that mad white-eye! You're staying here until the priests o' Shotir tell me you're healed enough to move and that's that.' She gave him a small pat on the head. 'Don't worry. I reckon the Menin Army will manage to survive a few more days without their newest hero.'

Mihn worked his way further into Ghenna, moving quietly, hand over hand along the roof until he found a ledge where he could rest. Once there he took stock, listening to the sounds of the Dark Place. The main tunnel to Jaishen, the lowest domain of Ghenna – so far as such things could be placed – fell away sharply at a right-hand bend, after which were dozens of smaller tunnels branching off in all directions.

Now he was inside, the old myths weren't going to be much help to him; those poor troubled mortals who had been afforded visions of the Dark Place had never learned much of use. Malich Cordein had been told more than most by the daemons he bargained with, thanks to the fact that he was an unusually powerful necromancer. Those who sold their souls for power were received with all ceremony into whichever of the chaotic domains their master dwelled, but the three greater domains were made up of many hundreds of others that were in a constant state of shifting allegiances. All Malich had confirmed was that Coroshen was the most ordered, Gheshen the most prone to open war, and Jaishen – Jaishen hung over an endless void from which even Gods would never return.

And it was here that Mihn intended to go, to the very depths of Jaishen, where the fissures in the rock opened onto nothingness. Lord Isak had left him a letter detailing his dreams since Scree. It was written in a shaky hand, and described being bound to the rock above an endless emptiness. It was not something he had ever managed to tell anyone out loud, but for an unlettered young man brought up in a world far from books or school learning, the disjointed sentences had conveyed a sense of horror that had made Mihn's skin prickle.

The clamour surrounding the soul's arrival had long died down, and away from the preternatural blackness that shrouded the gates, Ghenna was only as dark as a moonless night – if the stars had been tinted with blood. Not far down the tunnel Mihn came to a crossroads of sorts, where another, flatter, tunnel crossed the main one before splitting into two. The crossroads was marked by a blazing wheel hanging from the rocky roof. Mihn approached cautiously, but though he saw movement there, he thought the scampering daemons had vanished long before he got near—

—until a drawn-out scream pierced the air. It took Mihn a moment to realise the sound had come from the wheel itself, from a figure bound to it, writhing in the flames. He picked his way carefully down the tunnel wall, moving as quickly as he could, but still he could hear the figure wailing, until at last it fell into silence. He turned to look back – just as a dark shape shook free of the shadows and leapt towards the wheel, a long fan-like tail thrashing. The daemon's jaw latched onto the figure's leg and dangled there for a second before its weight caused the flesh to tear and it fell away. As the daemon fell, the figure's screams were renewed.

Mihn turned his back on the terrible sight. The rune burned into his chest was hot to the touch now; concentrating, he thought he could feel it drawing him, so he followed it to the smallest downward-leading tunnel he could see. He moved as quickly as he dared, listening all the while for footsteps, or any other movement. There were plenty of shadows to keep him concealed while the faint red light of Ghenna shone from the rock walls.

To his relief Mihn didn't find himself tiring as much as he'd feared as he made his way from handhold to foothold. Up and down seemed to have less meaning here; despite the clear path on the ground, he found he could keep to the walls with ease. There was a light from somewhere down the tunnel, and though he kept turning corners and discovered nothing, nonetheless the light illuminating the path continued, remaining steadfastly sourceless.

It took him a while to realise the light was not natural – as if anything could be, in a place such as this. The side tunnels he passed were almost pitch-black, and while the light ahead was barely enough to see by, without it he would have been lost. A cold finger of horror ran down Mihn's spine as he imagined trying to find his way through Ghenna without it.

It had to be the witch of Llehden's contribution. *Thank you, Ehla,* Mihn thought. Ehla meant Light in the Elvish language, and a light in dark places was what she had called herself. Maybe, in giving Isak that name by which to address her, she had helped shape the role she would play in Isak's future.

After what felt like hours of slow, cautious progress Mihn's path levelled. He had had to hide once or twice as daemons dragged their heavy, slug-like bodies past, but other than that he'd seen little – until he caught a glimpse of something, a flickering light, emanating from a circular tunnel some three feet wide. He slipped inside, curious to see what lay on the other side of the rock. He needed a sign that he was heading in the right direction; maybe this would be it.

Mihn edged his way down the tunnel's slight slope until he reached the end, where he found a fissure in the rock wall. He peered through – and had to stop himself screaming as he caught sight of a torture chamber out of his worst nightmares. The flickering light came from a great lake of flame in the centre of an enormous cavern. Surrounding the fire lake were daemons, hundreds, even thousands of them, and to Mihn it looked as if they were engaged in the most cruel punishments daemonkind could devise. Others stood around tables heaped high with food, gorging themselves, while their fellows operated complicated machines of torture.

All around the cavern Mihn could see bodies impaled on the spiky branches of gnarled old trees. Great iron chains were hammered into the rock, forming a criss-crossed network from which more of the damned hung, some limp, some flailing madly. In the fire he saw thrashing limbs, with darting black shapes moving between them.

He looked up: the roof of the great cave was a sagging dome, rising to a peak in the centre, far beyond his sight—

—and his heart stopped for a moment as a noise came from near his feet, a questing snuffle, sounding as if it was moving towards him. It stopped, and without hesitating, Mihn dived towards the thing, and managed to use his body to drive the daemon into the side of the tunnel. He reached down, and when he felt something thin whip against his hands he instinctively grabbed it, catching the daemon by a forelimb and pulling it close.

In the fiery light he tried to make sense of what he had caught. He yanked it towards him, and discovered something a little smaller than he, with a flattened head like a monkfish, a bulbous throat and the body of a salamander. The snarling daemon began to buck wildly, until Mihn caught the other forelimb and pulled both arms back, stopping the thing from twisting and biting him.

The daemon tried to roll, but Mihn was ready for it and let go of one arm before it slammed him face-first into the rock. It wrenched around, but succeeded only in trapping its free limb underneath it. Mihn ended up astride the daemon. He put one knee on the demon's throat and heaved with all his might on the other forelimb.

For a moment he feared he wasn't strong enough, but finally he was rewarded with a *crunching* sound, then a *snap!*, the one from beneath the daemon's body, the other from the socket of the limb he was pulling on.

The daemon gave a muted wail, all it could manage with Mihn's knee in its throat. Mihn turned and grabbed its tail, pulling it as hard as he could, effectively rolling the daemon up, until the daemon's spine snapped under the strain and it went still, dead at last.

At first Mihn didn't dare let go. After twenty heartbeats listening out for anything that might have been attracted by the scuffle he breathed again, and dropped the tail, letting the corpse uncurl on the ground.

Gods, that was lucky, Mihn thought, *anything larger and I'd have not stood a chance.*

He inspected his hands. They didn't appear damaged. The tattoos remained intact, but there was daemon blood on them now. There were several scratches on his arms and fingers, but as he watched they healed up, leaving only the faintest of marks.

So that's another true story: the torments of Ghenna really are unending. Wounds heal at an unnatural pace – so they can be inflicted again. He shook his head. *But now is really not the time for me to start cataloguing the truths in the old myths. I need to move fast, get away from this corpse before something smells it or stumbles over it.*

He scrabbled back to the main tunnel and looked about cautiously. There was nothing there that he could see, only the same dull glow somewhere down the end that picked out the jagged lines of the rock walls. He didn't dare to breathe a sigh of relief, but he pulled himself out of the side tunnel, lowered himself to the floor and set off towards the very depths of Jaishen.

It was impossible to tell how long he travelled. He passed huge dark chambers resonating with the sound of great hammers crashing down, and small alcoves where forgotten souls were chained or nailed to the bare rock. When the tunnel opened up again he scaled the wall, keeping near to the roof and freezing whenever sounds of movement came from below. Several times he found himself watching ragged processions of daemons pass by underneath: some marched to war, others bore trappings of state rich enough to put any mortal king to shame, and all were surrounded by crowds of nightmarish minions.

Twice he had to backtrack to find another route that avoided the enormous caverns. The first cave of torture had been horrific to look at even from afar, and the sounds that he heard echoing out from them left him trembling. Several times distant footsteps forced him to sit motionless in the darkness, trusting to the witch's tattoos to keep him hidden – and he *did* trust them; the daemon he had killed by the torture cave had not smelled him until it was very close, and it hadn't seen him at all until he moved.

For long periods Ghenna appeared empty, as he passed through desolate tunnels bigger than any lord's halls, trying to ignore the loneliness and misery that suffused the air, then he would hear something stop and sniff around, as though guessing he was near – but each time the daemon would move on eventually, leaving him able to breath Ghenna's foul air freely again.

Suddenly the sound of hammering hooves drove him to seek a hiding place further up the wall. As he clung, pulse pounding loud enough to disturb even the tormented, dozens of daemons poured into the tunnel, racing swiftly towards him and he found himself watching a gruesome running battle between enemies he couldn't differentiate.

The daemons were appallingly violent in battle, ripping limbs off as if for sport, then Mihn had to swallow his nausea as the victors settled down to feast on the dead. Eventually the last warriors had eaten their fill and dragged off the remaining bodies, leaving in their wake only a handful of broken weapons and a carpet of black, viscous blood.

Mihn waited, shuddering, until the last sounds of the retreating daemons had faded into silence, but this time, when he resumed his journey, he felt a sudden glimmer of hope, like the first rays of dawn breaking across the sky. He started to pass fissures in the rock, and for the first time he felt a slight breeze stirring the stifling air. It stank like a charnel house, and did nothing to cool his sweat-soaked body, but it was more than welcome after so many hours of the choking still air.

Mihn realised the breeze must be coming from the abyss beneath Ghenna – and since even a gale would not penetrate far in this unnatural place, he must be getting close. Hope gave him renewed strength, and the next few miles passed quickly, punctuated only by solitary screams and moans that made him wonder whether the tormented down here had been left all alone. He saw no more great caverns of punishment or halls of the infernal, and almost without meaning to, he found himself searching the side-tunnel entrances for markings. The deepest pit of Ghenna was supposed to be reserved for Aryn Bwr, the last king of the Elves, called the Great Heretic by the Knights of the Temples.

It was said his name was inscribed above the place where he would be imprisoned for eternity – his *true* name, excised from history by the remaining Gods of the Upper Circle when he had been cursed, and condemned to the Dark Place, before his final defeat. His true name remained in Ghenna for it was a place outside the power of the Gods. Mihn wasn't sure he believed that, and he certainly didn't intend to waste time looking for it, but he expected to be heading there or somewhere close. Whatever path Lord Styrax had created into Ghenna, there would have been one waiting for seven thousand years to open up for Aryn Bwr's soul.

Now the wind was blowing harder, and Mihn had to force himself to continue in the face of what was turning into a full-on gale. Ehla's light was fading too, and increasingly Mihn was traversing tunnels with only his ears to protect him and his hands to guide him. Then the red tint would return and the coils around his heart would relax again, but he was reminded that the witch's magic was no guard against the daemons of Ghenna. If they detected his presence, he would be there for eternity – there would be no last judgment for him, no Mercies to absolve him of his sins, only the unending horrors of the torture pits.

He slipped around another corner – and this time he felt an

immediate change as the immense presence of rock all around him unexpectedly opened out, altering even the small sounds his hands and feet made.

The going was harder now, as Mihn found himself almost slipping down the rockface. A dull ache permeated his body, and the thought of the return journey started to sap his will, until he found himself at an entrance conspicuously edged in Ehla's dull red light, glowing like a fire's embers. Mihn touched the rock gingerly, but it felt quite normal. He checked around carefully – this was not the time to be surprised – and went through . . .

His hand closed on instinct, as if reaching for the staff he'd left behind. The chamber itself was small, anonymous, lacking the immensity he expected of Aryn Bwr's prison. it was no more than fifteen yards long and only a few arm-widths across, no fitting prison for a soul that called storms and left its mark on Gods and nations – even though most of the floor was open to dizzying emptiness.

Mihn peered down the length of the cave and felt his breath catch. At the far end a figure was hanging. He was chained to the wall, his broken, inward-bent toes barely brushing the floor. He was naked save for the tattered remains of a cape he'd favoured in life. Though he was slick with filth and gore, still Mihn could see the terrible network of scars that covered most of the skin, testament to the horrors that had been inflicted upon him, and open wounds, some with implements of torture still protruding from the gashes, that dripped black blood. Even the left arm was patterned with shadowy scars, all the more obvious for the unnatural pallor of the skin, which had been burned white by the storm in Narkang. Isak's face was hidden by hair grown long and matted, as though he had been here years.

Mihn looked around. There were a few thin paths snaking across the room, but he realised the daemon possessing Isak's soul had little need of them, for there it was, clinging to the roof near its prize. Each of the six limbs ended in a splayed foot. Most were hooked into crevices; one was raised, covering its eyes from Ehla's light. It had a sinuous, scaled body, and a frill of spines protruded from its neck. Other than a mass of raised, pointed scales and a pair of very pointed lower canines, Mihn couldn't make out much of the face.

'Jailer,' Mihn called softly.

The daemon whipped around with frightening speed, but Mihn had not moved and it couldn't get a fix on him.

'I smell a soul,' it said, its voice an oily, bubbling sound. It used Mihn's own dialect fluently.

'But no inmate of this place,' Mihn said firmly.

The daemon moved a step towards him, one leg still up to protect its eyes. 'That matters not. Soon your soul will be mine. This light will not hide you.'

'I have other light to employ,' Mihn warned it.

As he spoke the rune on his chest lit up, a sudden white shaft that stabbed at the shadows. The daemon stopped its advance. It faced him as best it could, but made no further movement forward.

After a moment Mihn looked down. The rune no longer shone so brightly, but even through his tunic he could see its outline. 'I seek the release of the soul you have imprisoned here,' he said boldly.

'No! It is mine, my prize!'

'Release it to me,' Mihn ordered, 'or there will be more light than all of Ghenna has ever seen. Release the soul, or I will blind you, and when others come, drawn by your cries, you will be helpless against them and you will lose both this soul and your life to them.'

'It is my prize,' the daemon insisted, sounding rather pitiful, 'and of no use to you. You will never escape Ghenna with it. You will die a thousand deaths if you bring light to the Dark Place.'

Mihn recognised bluster, and realised his threat really was frightening the daemon, however much truth lay in what it said. Losing the soul to another daemon would hurt it, no matter what happened to Mihn. This way the creature would be grateful enough for anything it got in return . . .

'You underestimate me,' he said 'I made it here without being detected.'

'You cannot carry my soul all the way up to the ivory gates, little mortal,' the daemon hissed, looking at him properly for the first time. 'Better you leave it here than risk the hordes tearing it apart—'

'I have a better solution,' Mihn interrupted. He looked at the

59

white-eye chained to the wall, but Isak had not moved. He hung from his chains like meat on a hook.

'This place does not obey the rules of the Land but the commands of its inhabitants. With your help the path to the ivory gates can be level enough to walk rather than climb.'

'I cannot keep the others from finding you,' the daemon snarled; 'they will scent his blood long before you reach the gates.'

'That is my problem. Will you help me?'

'What do you offer?'

Mihn took a deep breath. 'I offer my soul. To release this one and aid my path to the River Maram I offer my soul. I will be your prize once I am dead.'

'You are not so great as this one!' the daemon protested, but Mihn saw it edge forward and sniff the air hungrily.

'Not so great, no, but you smell power on me nonetheless. My name is Mihn ab Netren ab Felith; I am the Grave Thief, slayer of a white-eye queen, the bondsman of Nartis' Chosen. What claim I have on my soul I offer to you, and when my deeds here are known by the Land my soul shall be a worthy prize.'

He saw the daemon shiver in anticipation, and he knew he had won; it could barely contain its pleasure at the prospect. Finding a sharp edge on the wall Mihn scraped a finger down it, breaking the skin. He squeezed his finger, letting the blood well up for a while before flicking it in the direction of the daemon. It scuttled forward, snuffling at the ground until it found a droplet and delicately touched its tongue to it.

'A bargain is made,' the daemon gurgled, sounding like a drowned man in its eagerness.

It gave a twitch of the head and the cave twisted a quarter-turn around Mihn, so that Isak was now chained to the floor. Mihn, still gripping the rock himself, barely avoided falling himself. Isak's head snapped back and for the first time Mihn saw a sign of life as the white-eye's mouth opened and a weak moan of pain came out.

He hurried to Isak's side, slipping a hand into his pocket to retrieve the leather gloves he had brought for this purpose. All of Elshaim's paintings of Ghenna had included chains that were covered in biting mouths, and Mihn could not risk his tattoos being ripped from his skin, now of all times. The chains binding Isak were sharp-edged, shredding Isak's skin where they touched, but as Mihn ripped them off him he saw the flow of blood quickly slow and the wounds start to scab over. Mihn looked at the palms of his gloves and was not surprised to see them already badly scratched.

'Isak,' he whispered as he freed the white-eye, 'can you hear me?'

Mihn could sense the daemon's evil delight as Isak did not respond. Though it kept its distance, watching them, its forked tongue tasted the air as though lapping up the last few scraps of Isak's torment.

Isak's white eyes were open, but staring at nothing. Mihn gripped one of the shards of iron protruding from Isak's body and yanked it out, eliciting a low howl of pain. That wound continued to bleed as Mihn worked on removing the other bits piercing his skin, adding to the covering gore on Isak's skin.

'More use to me than you,' the daemon cackled. 'Leave it here and I shall grant you a long lifetime before you return to me.'

'The span of my life is in the hands of another,' Mihn said sharply, 'and she carries a Crystal Skull. If you cheat her of it, her vengeance will be terrible.'

Once Isak was free of the daemon's implements Mihn cradled his lord's massive head in his hands and peered into his eyes.

'Isak,' he said piercingly, 'hear me, Isak.' The rune on his chest pulsed briefly. The daemon felt it too and whimpered, scrabbling at the rock in an effort to retreat from the light.

Isak's eyelids flickered and Mihn saw even they bore the scars of damage.

'Gods, how long have you been here?' Mihn asked softly, wondering whether Isak would ever be able to stand long enough to be helped out.

'An age!' crowed the daemon from the other side of the prison, 'ten thousand days pass in a heartbeat here, empires fall in a day!'

The figure at Mihn's feet mumbled something in a ruined voice, still staring into nothingness. He couldn't make out the words.

'Then ten thousand days is long enough,' Mihn declared. He held out a hand to Isak and commanded, 'Get on your feet, soldier; this is the long walk home.'

Isak's fingers twitched, but other than that there was no sign he had even heard the words.

'*Brace yourself,*' came Xeliath's voice in Mihn's ear.

Before he had time to realise what she was going to do a flood of magic surged through his body. The rune flared white, the daemon screamed and Isak convulsed as though caught in the teeth of the storm.

'Get up!' Mihn roared, buoyed by the energising rush of raw power in his veins. He stood and gripped Isak's arm, pulling with all his strength. 'Isak Stormcaller, on your feet!'

Somehow he managed to yank Isak to a seating position while crackling sparks of magic raced over the white-eye's body. At last Isak moved by himself, his limbs wobbling as, with Mihn's help, he raised his body until he was close enough to upright. The white-eye, swaying, towered over Mihn, but it was only the smaller man's efforts that stopped him toppling face-first into the void.

As Mihn struggled to steady him, using both hands, he suddenly felt droplets spatter onto his face and he flinched away, thinking it was blood. Then Isak's head turned and he saw it was tears, streaming from the man's agony-wracked face.

'Give me Eolis,' Mihn demanded, taking Isak's chin and angling his head so the white-eye was looking him in the face. Behind him the daemon screamed and cursed them both, but he ignored it and put his fist inside Isak's clawed hand.

'Give me Eolis,' he repeated, placing his other hand on the rune on his chest.

Xeliath obliged with another burst of magic, but it was only when he repeated the order again that a spark ignited Isak's eyes and the prison shook with a sudden crash of light. When Mihn blinked away the dazzling flares dancing before his eyes there was Eolis, lying in his hand: the long single-edged sword with an emerald pommel that had been bound to Isak's soul.

Carefully, he unpicked Isak's fingers which had automatically closed about Eolis, trapping his own, and took the weapon.

'Leave,' the daemon hissed frantically, 'you must leave now!'

It darted one way then the other before stopping and waving a limb towards the prison's exit. The rock groaned and began to move, widening until it was big enough for the two of them to leave side by side.

'Get out, others have sensed you! Go that way; it will lead you to the gates.'

Mihn took a firm grip of Isak's hand, leading the huge white-eye forward like a child. He held Eolis held out before them. The tunnel was empty, and there was a far shallower incline than the sheer slope he'd climbed down to reach the prison. He felt no warnings from Ehla or Xeliath, and though he hated the very idea, he realised he would have to trust the daemon – it appeared to have kept its word.

If any do come this way, he thought grimly, *Eolis will ensure they keep clear. I intend to keep my vow, even here, but they do not need to know that.*

Mihn walked as quickly as he could, with Isak stumbling along beside him and crying out occasionally – but still he matched Mihn's steps. Mihn knew a white-eye would fight on with mortal injuries that would stop any normal man, the instinct to fight and survive overriding everything else, but these grievous wounds had to be sorely testing the limits.

The tunnel spiralled slowly upward, a long and regular path that Mihn became increasingly certain would bring them to the surface, but as they walked, he could hear daemonic voices coming from all directions. At first they were distant, echoing, but now they were getting closer. At last Mihn realised they were walking parallel to another main tunnel, and through gashes in the rock wall he caught glimpses of a savage battle, like that he'd passed on the way in, lit by dancing flames.

He thought they had managed to get past, free and clear, when an oval eye appeared at one of the larger holes, and in the next moment a daemon had slipped through. It was smaller than the one he had killed, but far more solid, brandishing foot-long claws at the end of its arms.

Mihn raised Eolis and the creature hesitated, but it did not back off. It screeched defiantly at him and the sound provoked a flurry of movement; within moments the tunnel had ripped and distended to accommodate the bulk of a dozen demons, some even bigger than the white-eye Mihn was supporting.

Mihn's heart sank. He couldn't hope to fight them all, even if he did break his vow never to use a sword again, but before any of the daemons summoned the courage to face Eolis a distant crack of thunder reverberated through the rock.

The daemons glanced nervously around; that wasn't the usual booming that echoed through Ghenna but a sharper, more immediate sound. It came again, this time accompanied by a crack of lightning that left them all reeling from the light. In the afterglow stood the image of a brown-skinned girl clad in brilliant crystal armour. At the sight of her, the daemons started squealing and fled as if running for their lives. Mihn started walking again, realising Xeliath was readying herself to step over into the Dark Place. Now daemons melted away into the adjoining tunnels as he approached, content to hiss and glare at him from the dark corners while leaving his path unimpeded.

Every hundred paces or so Xeliath reappeared for an instant, filling the tunnel with searing light, ensuring the denizens of Jaishen were aware of her presence. Without these regular visitations they would have been attacked and overpowered within minutes, but even the most gigantic of the fanged monstrosities kept clear of the savage force at Xeliath's command. Mihn found himself whispering a short prayer to Cerrun, God of Gamblers: a desperate plea, that not even the princes of the Dark Place would risk fighting someone with such strength. A Crystal Skull was powerful enough to kill Gods and daemon-princes – who, even in victory, might be devoured by their cannibalistic minions if they were badly injured.

Exhaustion started to bite as Mihn felt his legs grow increasingly heavy. The air became denser and hotter the further they walked, and though the daemons made no forays against them, they afforded them only minimal room to pass. When he looked behind his lord he saw those trailing were lapping up the blood that dripped from Isak's wounds, their impossibly long tongues seeking out the tiniest drop.

At last they arrived at the crossroad where the burning wheel hung up above. Mihn started to press on, ignoring the tortured soul, but he was dragged to a halt by Isak, who stopped suddenly and stared directly up at the shrieking figure, the first time he had properly engaged with his surroundings since the chains had been dragged from his body.

Mihn felt the bile rise in his throat at the cruelties that must have been inflicted on Isak to produce so many scars. The only part of his body untouched was the rune burned into his chest; otherwise the torturer had been indiscriminate. His nipples, genitals and lips all bore signs of vicious abuse, his teeth were twisted and broken, his finger- and toenails torn out. The wider expanses of flesh were carved with a jagged script, one Mihn had never seen before, and scars caused by the spiked chains that had bound his body overlaid everything else like bloody shadows.

'Come,' Mihn said softly, urging Isak to keep moving.

Now the white-eye needed little encouragement. His eyes started to focus and his mouth was part-open, as though on the point of a sob that never came. As his great limbs started to shake Mihn tightened his grip on his lord.

Escaping the gate itself proved easier than he had expected. The chained beasts might not have been able to see Eolis, but they could sense the power of the sword and as they instinctively backed away, the gate started to lift. Mihn walked Isak carefully between the beasts, quickening his pace to clear the gate as they retreated again, pulling the gate shut behind them.

But there was no time for Mihn to pause and congratulate himself. From the steps of the Mercy's silver pavilion Mihn could see daemons of all sizes lining the three gates, staring after them with unreserved hatred. A flash of lightning raced across the gates and Xeliath appeared for a second or two, standing halfway between the gates and the pavilion.

She was dressed for battle in glittering crystal armour, and as she surveyed the arrayed armies of the Dark Place she gave a short laugh and spat in the dirt at her feet. The daemons began to clamour and howl furiously, beating at the ivory gates and stamping their feet so hard Mihn felt the ground shaking.

'Fuck all of you!' she yelled, directing an obscene gesture towards the largest of the daemons with her left hand, the one that had a Crystal Skull fused to the palm in the real world.

The cacophony increased tenfold, but the Yeetatchen white-eye turned her back and vanished into the darkness. Mihn didn't wait to see what response this elicited but hurried to the river, where flames were lapping against the bank. Instantly the boatman appeared before him, veiled and silent.

'Bear us across,' Mihn commanded.

'Each must pay with a soul. Will you give your own?' the boatman asked in a deep, inhuman voice.

Mihn reached into the neck of his tunic, pulled out the two silver coins strung on a chain and held it out to the boatman.

'I offer two souls.'

65

The association of souls with silver coins in Ghenna had come from the practice of laying the dead out with a silver coin in their mouth to draw up part of the soul. Daima had assured Mihn that the two men these coins belonged to were already in Ghenna; they would leave the question of ownership to the boatman and whichever daemon held them.

The boatman stared at Mihn for a while, then at Isak. At last it snatched the chain from Mihn's hand and drew the skiff up to the bank, stepping back to make room. Mihn helped Isak in first, making him kneel for safety before stepping swiftly into the remaining space himself. His caution was well justified as the boatman pushed off the moment one foot had touched the seat; only his superb balance and a firm grip on Isak's shoulder stopped Mihn from pitching over backwards into the fiery river.

The boatman laughed loudly as Mihn crouched at his feet but he poled the barge around and to the other bank with a dozen languid strokes. As soon as they touched land Mihn leapt out and dragged Isak with him. They set off up the short path to Ghain's summit, enduring the boatman's callous laughter until it faded on the wind.

With every step Mihn found himself weakening, the strength seeping out of his muscles as he gradually submitted to the terror inside him. Freed of his chains, Isak had regained a measure of his former strength and at the summit it was he who drove the pair over it. Though he had not spoken, nor really registered Mihn's presence, the white-eye survival instinct was a force in itself.

Once over the crest, Mihn dragged Isak to a halt. He leaned on the larger man and forced himself to stand upright as he gasped for breath. His hands were shaking, with fear and fatigue. The air was thin up there and it took a minute or more before his heart slowed its frantic beat and his lungs stopped aching. Isak stood motionless beside him, looking down on the desolate slopes of Ghain. He said nothing; Mihn couldn't tell if the white-eye even saw the empty miles ahead of them. Only the occasional spasm running through his body made Isak look more than a reanimated corpse, but Mihn had hardly expected cheerfulness or laughter.

I walked into the Dark Place and I lived, Mihn thought, using his sleeve to wipe the sweat from his face. He looked back. There was no daemonic army pursuing them; not even the boatman was visible, but he didn't want to wait around. A daemon-prince might fear Xeliath's Crystal Skull as much as the rest of its kind, but it wouldn't be afraid to send others in its stead.

'Come, my lord,' he said with a sigh, forcing his legs to take the first few steps down the empty slope. 'We are not home yet.'

The journey downslope was far easier than the ascent, and the further they got from the gates of Ghenna the faster they moved, ignoring the dead landscape around them The silver pavilions were empty, though Mihn thought he could sense some presence in the air that he assumed was the Mercies. Isak, feeling it too, lowered his head and tightened his grip on Mihn's arm, but they passed freely, finding themselves a step closer to the Land. Ghain itself appeared abandoned, for they walked a different path to that of the dead, and if there was pursuit, it was far enough behind to leave no trace.

They stopped once, after all of the pavilions were behind them, when Isak began to huff and whimper like a frightened dog. He kept his head down, staring blindly at the ground, but a swirl of wind wrapped around them and he looked increasingly pained and fearful.

Mihn hauled him onward, until he saw the reason for Isak's terror and dread descended over him too: there, on the horizon, stood the vast black doors of Death's chamber, set in a huge, weathered stone frame attached to nothing. A great darkness hung above it, black as pitch.

What if I open that door and there is nothing but Ghain's wilderness on the other side? He shook the thought from his head and upped their pace, his own sheer determination overriding Isak's shaking reluctance. As he neared the gate Mihn saw the darkness above it start to shift and a loud clanking of chains rolled out across Ghain like discordant temple bells.

'Now would be a good time,' Mihn muttered under his breath, 'assuming you aren't too tired after insulting every daemon in existence.'

A clap of thunder came as response and Xeliath flashed into existence, appearing at their side and walking in perfect time, as though she had been with them the whole journey.

'They needed a reminder of how things are,' Xeliath commented lightly, spinning an ivory glaive in her hand before letting the weapon rest upon her shoulder.

Mihn looked at her. The chestnut-skinned girl was as heart-stoppingly beautiful as when she'd spoken to him in his dreams. The visor on her crystal helm was raised enough for Mihn to see a contented little smile on her face.

'Grandiose insults and the prospect of violence,' Mihn commented. 'Bloody white-eyes.'

Xeliath's grin widened, but any further conversation was cut off as an enormous shape fell to the ground in front of the gate with a crash. They all staggered as the earth quaked underfoot, but not even the cloud of dust was enough to hide the huge dragon now blocking their way.

Mihn faltered, stunned by the monstrous size of the beast. He had never seen a dragon up close before – they were rare creatures in the Land; he'd only ever seen the beasts flying high in the sky. In the Elven Waste he had seen war wyverns go into battle, but they were lesser cousins; this dragon was as powerful, as terrifying, as any that had ever existed.

Measuring more than fifty yards from tail to snarling nose, the dragon was a sooty-black colour. Its torn, ragged wings looked as much smoke as membrane. The wings were crookedly raised, as though shading its body from the sun, and Mihn, remembering the stories of its enslavement, realised the beast could no longer furl its wings properly. Death himself had shattered the bones, and the deep scoring on the stone doorframe indicated it was forced to climb to its perch.

A curved horn rose from its long snout, and grey tusks swept back from the lower corners of its mouth, past its eyes and over its head. The dragon's muscular body was ungainly, its limbs twisted and misshapen, and its thin tail, curled like a scorpion's, finished in a long crescent blade.

The chained beast roared its defiance and Mihn clapped his hands over his ears even as he gagged at the foul stench on the wind: the stink of decay that emanated from the dragon.

Xeliath kept on walking, her arms raised to ensure the dragon's attention was on her alone. Her hand burst into spitting green swirls of magic and white light flooded the plain. The dragon reared, spreading its torn wings as best it could and beating at the air as though trying to retreat – causing the light to falter until Xeliath snarled and intensified the surging coils of magic around her hands.

She began to speak quickly in Elvish, the air around her shuddering at each syllable, but the dragon, fearless and full of rage, ignored her, advancing until the pitted chain that tethered it to the doorframe was stretched taut. The wind swirled up around Xeliath until she was partially hidden from view by shadows glinting with gold and emerald. As the pressure on Mihn's ears began to build Xeliath stamped one foot, and long coils of light lanced forward to lash the dragon's body.

The magic carved furrows through its flesh but the dragon just roared louder, refusing to retreat. It snapped at the glimmering coils with its huge mouth, somehow finding purchase on one, and wrenched its head from side to side like a shark feeding.

As the dragon pulled Xeliath off-balance, her concentration broke and the magic dispelled. It raised its forelimbs, claws extended, and raked through the air towards them. Mihn saw the trails of magic in the air and dropped to the ground, pulling Isak with him, as Xeliath made a sweeping gesture through the air with her glaive and a blistering white shield appeared in front of them all.

In the next moment black slashes tore through its surface and even Xeliath flinched away.

'Give me Eolis,' she yelled, reached back towards Mihn with one hand.

'I thought you would be able to force a path through!' he shouted as an ear-splitting roar of fury deafened them.

'It must be a bloody male,' Xeliath shouted back, a mixture of bloodlust and elation on her face. 'The bastard thing is too proud to back down!'

'Can you kill it?'

'Who knows?' she laughed. 'The Gods failed, but I'll give it a damn good try! Get Isak to the side and wait for your chance.' She grabbed Eolis from Mihn's unresisting grip and hefted it appreciatively.

'What about you?' he began, but she was already moving.

'Go!' Xeliath yelled, breaking into a run directly towards the dragon and shrieking a Yeetatchen warcry.

Mihn tore his attention from the shining figure and looked to

Isak, who was staring at the dragon as though physically pained by it. With Mihn's support he moved to the right of the black doors and stood, trembling, watching as Xeliath charged with wild abandon, cutting and hacking with all a white-eye's force. A white band of energy thrashed around her, protecting her from the dragon's raking claws. She forced the beast back, then feinted left, and the dragon followed.

That was the opening Mihn had been waiting for and he pulled Isak towards the door with all his strength as Xeliath screamed in furious delight.

They were a foot away when the dragon whipped its tail along the ground and slipped the horn-blade underneath Xeliath's protective ring. She screamed in pain, and the sound of shattering crystal rang across the plain, swiftly followed by a roar from the dragon as the spitting band of light slanted around and pinned the tail to the ground.

As Xeliath stabbed Eolis right through it Mihn pushed Isak forward, not stopping even when he saw the dragon pounce: once they were through, then Xeliath could retreat. Light exploded up from the ground as the creature smashed its claws down, but Xeliath knocked its head aside, tearing a chunk of decaying flesh from its face. That wasn't enough to stop the creature biting down, to the sound of more shattering crystal. As he laid his hand on the black door itself Mihn heard Xeliath's bellow.

Though he hated to leave Xeliath he couldn't wait. He put his shoulder to the door and drove forward as hard as he could. Isak stood for a moment, then added his own weight. The black door resisted a moment, and then something gave and the two men collapsed forward. Darkness enveloped them, a rushing cold that hit Mihn with all the shock of a kick to the gut.

He tumbled forward in panic, freezing cold all around him, and a moment later he felt some force dragging him up until he broke the surface of the lake. Mihn's first breath was a howl of agony, and his remaining strength failed him. It was only a strong hand grabbing him by the scruff of the neck that stopped him dropping back in the water and sinking like a stone. He fell roughly against the side of the boat, and instinct was strong enough to make him grab on for all he was worth.

An animal yowl shocked him so badly he almost let go entirely, but as he flailed in alarm he realised the agonised sob came from Isak. The white-eye's huge bulk had risen to the surface too, and like Mihn he was gripping the side of the boat for all he was worth. His cries were shaking the entire boat.

'What happened to Xeliath?' demanded the witch of Llehden, standing in the prow of the boat, a rare look of concern on her face.

Mihn was summoning the strength to reply when he saw Xeliath slumped in the bottom of the boat, still and apparently unbreathing.

'How——?' he began, as Xeliath gave a sudden, violent jerk, but his immense relief was short-lived as the girl lifted her shoulders and coughed up gouts of blood over her stomach. She started to convulse and her eyes opened, reflecting not victory but agony.

He threw himself into the boat to hold her, but she twisted out of his grip and screamed in pain before vomiting more blood.

'Mihn, see to Isak,' the witch commanded, though there was little he could do for the white-eye, who remained clinging to the side of the boat with all his Gods-granted strength, keening piteously.

'No!' shouted the witch, who lifted the girl's head as Xeliath's struggles lessened. She held Xeliath close and began to mutter an invocation, but as far as Mihn could see the only effect she was having was to make the blood flow faster.

Xeliath twisted her head towards Isak and at last she seemed to focus, the pain receding in her eyes for a moment. Her damaged features twisted into a small smile.

'Free,' she whispered, almost too feebly for Mihn to hear. She coughed again and the smile vanished, followed a moment later by the bright spark in her white eyes,

'Xeliath,' the witch cried, but quietly now, the voice of mourning. Mihn felt a familiar presence suddenly descend, shrouding the boat to darken the night even further. Something hard clattered on the bottom of the boat and Mihn's heart sank. The cold of the lake filled his bones as Mihn watched the Crystal Skull roll to a stop in front of him, freed at last from her grip.

CHAPTER 4

The biting wind gusted through Byora's streets. The sky had been a uniform grey for days now, but there had been little more than a smattering of rain this morning and as midday approached Luerce decided it would stay dry and settled down for the day on the cobbled ground. The disciple of Azaer arranged a white blanket around his shoulders like a tent, keeping out the chilly air, and set to playing the mystic.

He didn't mind; it was easy enough to sit there motionless all day, watching his flock, though he saw no reason to endure a soaking too. From all around him came the keening of the faithful. The cant of liturgy had devolved into meaningless sounds, but interspersed within the drone were new prayers that Luerce had instilled in the minds of the weakest. It was a modest start, but fear would provide fertile soil, especially with him there to tend it and a dragon's shadow cast over the quarter.

Luerce looked around. The crowd had grown again today; hundreds were clustered around the gates to the Ruby Tower compound. Many were beggars but already there were others, lurking on the fringes, seeking something, though they did not yet realise that. He saw grief in their eyes, and loneliness. Some were consumed by petty hatreds or avarice, and Luerce took especial note of those: the bullies and the cowards, those with a lifetime of identifying the vulnerable, they'd be ideal to swell the ranks of Ruhen's preachers.

Luerce occupied an honoured position within the crowd of devotees, and even the newcomers could see he was special. Most of the disciples sat in tight circles of five or six, with Luerce alone in the middle of them all, with his back against the compound wall. From there the Litse could survey his small kingdom: the desperate and the mad, all huddled pathetically in the shadow of the Ruby

Tower where Ruhen lived, hoping for salvation from the Circle City's latest terror.

On Luerce's left a craftsman, still wearing his tool-belt, approached the wall, a reverent look on his face. He picked his way carefully past the mumbling, white-swathed bundles, hunched over as though apologetic about being upright while everyone else was sitting. The man sank to his knees as soon as he was within reach of the wall and looked up at the fluttering strips of prayer-inscribed cloth adorning it.

He raised his own contribution, fixed to an iron nail like the others, and hammered it in. He was large and powerfully built, his brown hair tangled and his beard unkempt, giving him the appearance of a barbarian from the Waste, but the expression on his face was piteous. A muddy thumb-print adorned his cheek as though in mockery of a Harlequin's bloody teardrop, and his face was streaked by tears that flowed once again as he prayed.

A child could look fiercer than this bear of a man, Luerce thought as he gazed past him and noted with satisfaction that the guards on the gate were paying no attention. The watchful gaze of a Harlequin ensured that: while the storyteller had not spoken one word except in song, its demeanour was unmistakable, even to the witless thugs who comprised the duchess' personal regiments. It stood over the crowds day and night, a sentinel for the faithful as they awaited Ruhen's benediction.

Slowly we go, oh so slowly. Luerce's attention drifted from the motionless Harlequin to a white-clad disciple who was handing out black-crusted bread to the crowd. The man was speaking urgently as they jammed the bread into their mouths, bending right over them as he whispered.

Keep on with the good works, my friend, but any more of your religious nonsense and you'll find an accident coming your way. We cannot bully the people into following Ruhen; they must beg it of him. He rubbed his thin fingers over his bald head, feeling the unfamiliar shape of his skull once covered by luxuriant blond hair. The beggar beside him looked up at the movement, awaiting his next command. He could see in her hollow eyes the awe she still felt, the otherworldly image he now presented to the Land. Once she had been beautiful, but hunger had taken its toll – for which Luerce was profoundly thankful. He had no wish to discover how his master would react if he discovered Luerce submitting to temptation whilst playing the holy man – and Ruhen *would* find out, no matter how he tried to cover his tracks. He had no doubt of that.

'Go and read the latest prayer,' he said softly. She scrambled to obey, almost barging the bear-like man out of the way in her haste.

'A prayer for salvation,' she announced with what she clearly thought was grandeur, 'salvation from the dragon that killed his family yesterday.'

The wordless prayers increased in volume at her words, and drained what was left of the man's remaining strength. He huddled over his knees, doubled up by the pain inside.

Luerce smiled inwardly. *About bloody time. I was wondering if I was going to have to do it myself.*

He looked around, searching for a picture of misery amidst a sea of it. The mercenary Grisat was difficult to pick out now that he'd shed his penitent's uniform, but Bolla, Grisat's brother-in-arms, was far easier to spot. The tall shaven-headed man sat bolt-upright, staring into nothing as he chewed numbroot day and night.

Ah, numbroot addicts, the most amenable of fools. Luerce smiled inwardly, remember his former life of petty theft and fraud. Numbroot was as benign a drug as one could find, and it took real commitment to wind up an addict, as Bolla clearly was. Aracnan, the Demi-God who served Azaer, had used Grisat to engineer a campaign of resistance after the failure of the clerics' rebellion. Bolla had played his part in that without questioning his orders, using numbroot to dull the pain of his injuries along with his ability to care about the rest of the Land.

'Our brother asks for salvation,' Luerce called out, causing a small commotion as the huddled mass turned to look at him. 'Byora's children cry out for salvation! Pray, pray with me for intercession!'

As he finished his eyes came to rest on Bolla and Grisat. More voices joined in the chant, the volume increased and Bolla began to sway in an unconscious response to the sound. Grisat, a solid-looking man, contrived to look even more miserable. Though he looked as if he had entirely gone to seed, the mercenary was still strong, well worth his pay – but Luerce only had one use for him. Finally, reluctantly, Grisat lifted his grey eyes to meet the Litse's. The order was understood.

The mercenary flinched and tugged his filthy coat tighter around his body, but he wasted no time in using the magical link Aracnan had created between them to contact the Demi-God. In a few moments Luerce saw Grisat shudder and knew the mercenary had found Aracnan. The Demi-God had been wounded as he went to join the battle against the Farlan, shot with a poisoned crossbow bolt by a Narkang agent. It was taking all of Aracnan's considerable skill just to stay alive, and the pain had left him unhinged. This would not be a comfortable experience for Grisat.

Satisfied the bond was active, Luerce bowed his head and added his own voice to the wordless anthem ringing out down the street. The beggars squatting in the street as though protesting the state of the Land were the broken and the lost; their mournful song was almost primal, and their many hurts the most basic a human could feel. Luerce felt himself enveloped in the building dirge. Swept up by the fervour, by the desperation of those around him who had lost everything, he found tears spilling down his cheek as his voice rose above the rest.

Spurred on by the Litse's fervour the howls increased until he was lost in a bubble of mourning, voicing their fears and their grief, their rage against the Land and the inaction of the Gods. Some were mad, driven by what they had seen. Some were ill. Some were sickened by the actions of priests and lords alike.

The great towers of Byora's noble district echoed with their pain, pain that could not be exhausted even by hours of song, and as evening began to close in and the ghost-hour spread shadowy fingers over the streets, their prayer was answered.

The delegation was small, no more than fifty-strong, including the squads of Ruby Tower Guards ahead and behind. Natai Escral, Duchess of Byora, rode side-saddle at the head of the nobles, the child Ruhen perched in her lap and Hener Kayel, her bodyguard, riding alongside. The duchess was a middle-aged woman, though she looked older than her years, however immaculately turned out she was. She couldn't hide the crow's-feet or the shadows of broken sleep under her eyes, and she was stooped with fatigue, riding without her customary grace.

From time to time the duchess would shake herself, as though pushing herself to stay awake. When she turned her face to the cool breeze those around her would be afforded a glimpse of the proud elegance that had dominated the largest and most disparate quarter of the Circle City for so many years. Even in black mourning, with only her ruby circlet for adornment, she stood out from the Litse nobles and ministers following.

Every few minutes her thoughts would turn back to the child nestled in her lap: the little boy she called a prince as often as her son but who was, in truth, none of those things. Shadows danced in Ruhen's eyes, and she hungered for the soothing sight of his face like an opium addict for the next fix. It was Sergeant Kayel who directed her horse then, when her attention wandered from real life.

Sergeant Kayel wore the uniform of a Ruby Tower officer, but the buttons were gold, the cloth finer and the tailoring far better than any normal soldier's garb. A big man by Narkang standards, and massive next to the slender Litse locals, Sergeant Kayel – Ilumene, to give him his real name – remained unchallenged by other Ruby Tower men because of the fear he engendered. He had been first among King Emin's élite troops as much because of his presence as his ability, and his regal demeanour remained a useful tool now.

Behind the duchess and her bodyguard rode an even stranger pair: a white-masked figure in black and a dark-haired Byoran noblewoman dressed sombrely but festooned with gems, quite unable to resist showing off her jewels to the city. The masked man, Koteer, had skin and long hair the colour of funeral ashes. He was as tall as a white-eye, and dressed like a wandering duellist. He paid his companion, Lady Kinna, no attention whatsoever. Koteer was the eldest of the Raylin sons of Death, known as the Jesters; he spoke for all four of them. The Demi-God had said nothing about why he had joined them that day; he had not needed to. Sergeant Kayel had appeared to be expecting the grey-skinned giant, and the duchess had been lost in Ruhen's eyes, leaving only Lady Kinna in a position to challenge them – and in the end she had said nothing for fear of the Demi-God. That fear was echoed by the soldiers escorting them.

They rode past the crossroad where Aracnan had been nearly killed. One beam protruded up from the blackened mess that was all that remained of the shattered buildings, and people had braved the rickety remains to nail scraps of white cloth prayers to it.

As soon as they were out of the city all eyes turned to the churned ground where the Menin and Farlan armies had fought, where lords and commoners alike had fallen to Karkarn's hands. The Menin had dug great pits and burned Farlan corpses in their hundreds, and even now the unmistakable smell lingered. As the delegation turned north, not even Kayel's vicious reputation stopped most of the soldiers ignoring unit discipline and looking behind them at the battlefield, playground of the God of War, where one patch of ground remained burning hot, blistered and scourged of all life. Next to it stood the gruesome memorial to Scion Kohrad Styrax: thousands of skulls boiled clean and bound within a circle of spears. There were already rumours running wild throughout the city of a ghostly figure seen in the torchlight, and of people disappearing nearby.

Before long the group rounded the black spur of rock that marked the boundary between Akell quarter and Byora. Blackfang, the vast broken stub of a mountain onto which both cities backed, was wreathed in low, sullen clouds. The approach to Akell was uncomfortable as the road twisted past deep dykes intended to channel attackers down the single central road, allowing the defenders to take them out more easily.

At last they found themselves picking their way through the stinking army encampment that surrounded the Fist, Akell's huge forward defence. The square fortress could house thousands of soldiers, and there were still three legion flags flying over the rows of tents outside it. Positioned on top of the Fist's jutting gatehouse was Lord Styrax's enormous personal standard: a stylised, blood-red fanged skull on a black field.

The Byoran delegation rode uneasily up to the gatehouse between rows of grim-faced Menin. Shaven-headed foot soldiers stood side-by-side with cavalrymen sporting wild black curls, and all stared with undisguised curiosity. No one moved, however, until they reached the gatehouse itself, when a grey-clad official emerged and bowed low to the duchess.

'I beg an audience with Lord Styrax,' the duchess announced loudly as Ruhen turned his hypnotic gaze on the Menin official.

'I—Ah, your Grace,' the man started in hesitant Byoran, trying not to be thrown by Ruhen's stare, 'your request is not possible. I apologise.'

Sergeant Kayel slipped from his horse and gave the man an inadvisable look, considering the watching soldiers. He lifted Ruhen gently from the duchess' lap and dropped to one knee to allow the duchess to dismount easily.

The official, a rake-thin man of around sixty summers with the heavy brow and prominent jaw so common among the Menin, waited patiently while Natai Escral arranged her dress and took Ruhen's hand. Then he said, 'Your Grace, I apologise, but Lord Styrax is not receiving visitors and General Gaur is occupied in Fortinn quarter. If you have a written petition for him, you may give it to me – or I would be happy to summon a lord to hear you.'

'I will speak to Lord Styrax,' the duchess declared firmly.

The official frowned, his eyes flitting down to the little boy at her side. 'Your Grace, he is not receiving visitors. My lord is in mourning; he is in no mood for civil affairs.'

'Then we will talk of uncivil things,' she insisted, 'of the beloved lost and the dangers that remain in this Land.'

The official could not help but glance up into the sky, watching for the black shape that had been inflicting devastation on the Circle City ever since being awakened. 'Your Grace, madam, I am sorry, but he will not see you.'

'Then I will wait here until he changes his mind. If I am to be his vassal I must be permitted his audience.' She turned to her bodyguard. 'Kayel, perhaps you would fetch me a stool?' She gestured at the ground where she stood, on the centre of the road leading out of the Fist's main gate.

'Your Grace,' the official urged, a slight note of panic entering his voice, 'my instructions were most specific: no one is to be permitted into Lord Styrax's presence. I dare not disturb him.'

'Have courage,' came a small voice that sent an electric twitch down the official's spine. Ruhen looked at him.

The man quivered a moment, then turned back to the gate.

Duchess Escral called out to him again, 'Tell your lord I would speak to him of sons – of princes cherished.'

The man glanced back, an expression of horror on his face, but he bobbed his head again and disappeared behind the flame-scarred door.

*

The creak of the door opening was enough to jolt Amber from a confused dream, a chaotic memory of his childhood home that faded as he opened his eyes. In the doorway stood Horsemistress Kirl, looking concerned. It was dark in his room, and Amber guessed he'd slept past nightfall.

'What's happened?' Amber croaked.

Kirl looked at him, then walked to his bedside. 'I'm not really sure. I just heard that bloody Duchess Natai's staging some sort of protest at the gate – says she isn't moving until Lord Styrax grants her an audience.'

'She wants to speak to a grieving white-eye?' Amber sounded aghast.

Kirl gave a humourless snort. 'I know – daft bitch! Colonel Uresh tried to speak to her and she just ignored him and kept repeating her demand.'

'Where's General Gaur?'

'Fortinn; Uresh doesn't want to send a rider though. Every time Gaur turns his back in Fortinn the gangs start fighting each other again. Duke Vrill's scouting the northeast towards Raland and all the other nobles are just plain scared, I think.'

'What about Gaur's huntsmen?'

While General Gaur had never been ennobled, the beastman Lord Styrax had hauled from the fighting-pits was now a powerful landowner in his own right. Much of that land he kept for private hunting, and instead of hurscals he had a band of huntsmen as his staff. Like irregulars they occupied a position outside of the Menin Army structure, and Lord Styrax used them for a range of unortho-dox activities. Amber guessed a few of Gaur's commanders would be on first-name terms with the Lord of the Menin.

'Probably in Fortinn,' Kirl said, 'with General Gaur – they are his bodyguards, after all, and it's not a happy place at the moment.'

'Let's see how much my luck rides then,' Amber muttered, raising his good left arm and beckoning Kirl over. 'Help me up.'

'Are you mad? You're staying right there,' she said sharply.

He gave her a level look. 'No, I'm getting up and you're going to help me. Look at my face and tell me whether you think I'm in the mood to argue.'

'Are you pulling rank on me?' Kirl asked after a moment's hesitation.

'Hoping I don't have to.'

She wrinkled her nose. 'Fine. Let's get you sitting on the side of the bed. If you can do that without passing out, I'll fetch some crutches and find out exactly what the duchess wants.'

Amber gritted his teeth. His right arm was wrapped in wooden splints and bandages, and in spite of the magical healing it wasn't yet ready to take any weight. Kirl was tiny next to him and she needed to haul at his good arm with all her strength to help him raise his shoulders off the bed. Once he started to move, he found his left leg was similarly useless, and though Kirl was manoeuvring him as carefully as she could, he was biting down so hard he thought he was going to shatter his teeth.

After several excruciating minutes he opened his eyes and found himself perched on the side of the bed, his right foot pressed hard against the floor as he tried to balance.

'Maybe with that crutch I'll fetch a Priest of Shotir to take the edge off the pain?' Kirl asked, watching his expression.

Amber nodded as gently as he could, not wanting to jerk anything else now he had been reminded of the joys of broken ribs.

'Right, stay there and try not to cry,' she said, heading back out. 'You're meant to be a hero, remember?'

Before long Amber was making slow and painful progress past two separate rings of security to Lord Styrax's chambers. At both security checkpoints Amber was recognised, and admitted with a mixture of awe and pity, which bolstered his strength a little. Outside his lord's door the adrenalin wore off and he started to waver. Kirl had to prompt him twice before he raised his hand to knock.

There was no response. Amber waited a long while before hesitantly knocking again, but when he was greeted with silence he turned the latch himself, his hand shaking with the strain, and eased the door open.

Still nothing.

He shuffled forward, Kirl taking as much of his weight as she could bear. Inside, a single lamp on the right-hand wall gave dim illumination, but as Amber looked around, two more lamps sputtered into life, then the fire ignited, apparently of its own volition.

'Do you often walk into your commanding officer's room uninvited?' asked a deep voice. Amber turned towards it and visibly winced at the jolt of pain from the brutalised muscles in his neck.

'No, my Lord,' he replied, shuffling around until he could face Lord Styrax. The huge white-eye wore a black tunic, uniform of the Bloodsworn cavalry, and boots to his knees, but for once the tunic was in disarray, the boots scuffed. He sat in a solid armchair backed up against the wall, supporting his great head in one hand.

'Yet you do so now.' Styrax's voice was as deep as one might expect from a white-eye of his size, but now it was a ragged growl, one Amber had rarely heard. It didn't bode well, and the major was further discouraged when he saw Kobra, Lord Styrax's sword, embedded a foot deep into the stone wall. Kobra was a prize plucked from his dead predecessor's fingers, a powerful artefact, but Amber didn't think anything but a white-eye's rage would have the strength to drive it into solid stone.

'I apologise, my Lord,' Amber said with a slow bob of the head that was about all he could manage by way of a bow. Beside him Kirl did a better job of offering respect, but all that achieved was to only make Styrax focus on her instead.

'Why are you being nursed by a Farlan Cardinal Paladin?' he asked.

'Ah, Horsemistress Kirl is attached to the Cheme Third, my Lord; she just helped herself to some knight's baggage.'

He grunted.

'An . . . an honour to be in your presence, my Lord,' Kirl managed to say at last, bowing again.

'I'm sure it is. Tell me, Horsemistress, do you have children of your own? With Major Amber, perhaps?'

Kirl coloured and looked down. 'No, my Lord.'

Styrax didn't speak again for a while.

Gods, has Kohrad's death broken him? Amber felt a chill on the back of his neck. *Have we come all this way only to be stopped by this?*

'Why not?' Styrax asked, all of a sudden. They both blinked. Neither could think of anything helpful to say in response. 'Well?' he asked again. 'Man might not look much, but he's minor nobility, a hero of the army. You could do worse.'

'I—I'm sure I could,' Kirl mumbled.

'Well then?'

'He—Ah, he has n-never asked such a thing of me,' Kirl stammered. The question had thrown her completely, but she dared not look to Amber for help. Lord Styrax stared straight at her, his piercing eyes fierce, his tone threatening.

'Amber, get her with child. I command it,' Styrax growled.

The major guessed his lord was making an effort at levity, but everything the white-eye said was laden with anger. Amber was not a man of subtlety, but he knew white-eyes well enough to know that treating the command as a joke would have been foolish.

'What are you waiting for?' The hostility in his voice increased a notch and Amber felt Kirl's supporting hand begin to tremble.

'I fear I'm in no condition at present, my Lord,' Amber said at last.

'You think killing white-eyes is a good-enough excuse?' Another notch.

Amber fought the urge to take a step back as the air grew close and hot around him.

'Kirl, could you wait outside?' he croaked, taking his eyes off Lord Styrax for a moment. She tried to hide her gasp of relief, slipped out from under his arm and offered the Menin lord a hurried bow before backing out.

A few seconds of silence stretched into ten. When Amber could stand it no longer he took one of the biggest risks of his life. 'My Lord, I cannot begin to imagine your grief. I mourn your Scion also.' His voice wavered slightly. Men dealt with grief in different ways, but among soldiers great sensitivity was impossible. This was uncharted territory for Amber.

What could he say about Kohrad? 'He wasn't as mad as some' probably wasn't appropriate, but it was all Amber could think of. The impetuous youth had shown potential, but he had always been a young white-eye for ever in the shadow of one greater than he would ever be.

'I was proud to have fought alongside him,' he said at last.

Styrax raised a hand. 'Spare me the platitudes, I have heard them already.'

Amber swallowed nervously. 'I apologise, my Lord, I had not intended it to sound that way.'

'How had you intended it then?' Styrax snapped, straightening up. He gripped the armrests of his chair as though poised to leap up and attack the major.

'I did not know your son well enough to say anything else,'

Amber said in a meek voice. 'Kohrad inherited more from you than he ever realised. He was unknowable to a man like me, but he was Menin, and a soldier, too; little more than a boy making a good account of himself in a man's world.

'My father always told me that battle forged a bond between men – I might not have known Kohrad well, but I shared that with him at least, and I'm glad to have done so.' As he finished, Amber realised that he was shaking so much he could barely keep his balance.

'Those are your words of sympathy?' Styrax sat back, his anger dissipated suddenly. 'While this cancer eats away at my gut you tell me that?'

'I am sorry, Lord. Death and duty is all I know.'

'Why don't you lecture me on duty too?'

'I am yours to command, Lord.' *Bugger, that was more rude than meek.*

His words prompted a momentary change in the air as Styrax eyed him gravely. 'Do so and I'll put your head through the wall.'

'Yes, my Lord.'

Another long pause. Amber tried to stand as close to attention as he could manage, while a thousand emotions flashed across Lord Styrax's normally still face.

'Why are you here?' the white-eye asked at last.

'Duchess Natai Escral of Byora is requesting an audience of you.'

'And you think I care?' roared Styrax.

He propelled himself up, and sprang forward so quickly Amber, wobbling precariously on his crutch, edged back to the wall.

'The Gods themselves could be waiting at my door and I would not give a shit!' he shouted, making the heavy chair shiver and the dust motes dance in the lamp light. 'You disturb me for this? Get out of here while you still can, and pray I only strip you of your rank! You think killing Tsatach's Chosen gives you the right to irritate me with impunity?'

Amber blinked and found Styrax's hand at his throat.

The white-eye forced Amber's head up so he was looking him in the eye. His face was tight with barely restrained fury.

'All I have is my duty, Lord,' Amber repeated hoarsely. His muscles were screaming out in agony. He felt on the edge, as if he would fall into unconsciousness, so bad was the pain.

'Don't think that will save you.'

'I do not.'

'Then choose your next words carefully.'

'I—I cannot, Lord. What must be said is foolish. Even your commanders know what must be said, and they fear to say it.'

'Then make your last words good,' Styrax snarled, his grip tightening a fraction.

'We need you.'

'Don't take me for a fool! That is *not* what you came to say!'

'No, Lord.'

'So talk while you still can.'

'Kohrad was only a part of what you are trying to achieve here, Lord. You cannot stop now,' Amber whispered.

'*Now* it hardly matters!'

'That is grief talking, nothing more.'

'Grief is all I have.'

'No, Lord.' Somehow, Amber managed to bite back the pain. He rallied himself and tried again. 'There are more Crystal Skulls to track down. There are more monuments to build.'

Styrax shook him, like a lion subduing its prey. 'Who have you been talking to?' he snarled.

'Talking to? No one, Lord, but I walk in your shadow and you taught me to see the Land with open eyes. There is more to the monuments you build than celebrating victory; of that I am certain. They are too few to be of use yet – whatever use you intend to put them to. Your empire must continue to expand; the campaign is not over.'

'And so?'

The major gasped for breath, but he managed to croak out, 'And so . . . So your vassal begs an audience, my lord, and those you rule need your intervention. A dragon ravages the Circle City, at a time when you need it to be strong and whole. Your work is not done; your grief must be put aside.'

Styrax's grip on Amber's neck lessened.

Amber tried to relax. 'Only then will there be time for mourning, once the Library of Seasons is safe to walk again.'

The hand slipped away and Amber fell to the floor.

CHAPTER 5

'My Lord,' the servant called in a quavering voice, 'the Duchess of Byora and her retinue.' He stepped aside, making room for the duchess. This wasn't the sort of grand hall which would normally accommodate such a meeting, but the Fist was a fortress and lacked such amenities.

The duchess entered the dark room slowly, taking a moment to grow accustomed to the light before she curtseyed stiffly. She was not used to paying obeisance to others, and sitting for an hour at the gates of the Fist hadn't helped her disposition, but the white-eye seemed neither to notice nor to care.

'Lord Styrax,' she said while her retinue filed into the gloom behind her, 'I thank you for granting this audience. I can only imagine—'

'Correct,' Styrax growled, 'you can only imagine it. Do not waste my time with sentiments you do not understand.'

'My Lord,' the duchess exclaimed in genuine shock, 'my robes of mourning are no mere affectation! I myself lost my husband in the clerics' rebellion.'

Styrax made a dismissive gesture and she bit her tongue as her still-raw grief raged at his arrogance. She gave the room a cursory inspection and guessed it was an officers' mess, with doors on each wall and a fireplace in front of her big enough to heat the entire room. Lord Styrax sat with his back to it, wearing a black uniform emblazoned with his Fanged Skull emblem. He was unshaven and looked exhausted, and in the dim light the Menin lord looked old, as though his unnaturally long span was at last catching up with him.

'Major Amber,' the duchess said, inclining her head graciously to the soldier at Styrax's right hand. She noted how he winced as he acknowledged her greeting. He was not in full uniform. One leg was splinted and stretched out on a stool; one arm was cradled in a sling. His bruised and bloodied face and the broken line of his nose put her in mind of Sergeant Kayel.

There were two other Menin, a man and a woman, in the room and she felt her breath catch at the sight of them. They sat to one side and were clearly not going to be part of the discussion, but they were priests of the War God and their presence made Natai's hands tighten.

The bastard priests were at the very heart of Byora's problems, from the murder of her husband to the fear that permeated its very streets. The religious district in Byora remained closed since the failed coup, and Natai had not been in the same room as a priest since the Gods had struck down two who tried to murder her and Ruhen. Even the sight of their robes made her want to order Kayel to draw his sword—Though that pair looked like no priests she had ever met, with their weatherworn faces freshly scrubbed, their boots—

She stopped.

No priests wear boots like those.

The duchess looked at the Lord of the Menin. *You bastard, dressing up your troops as priests to see how I would react ... Did you think perhaps I would not notice?*

'My Lord, let me make known to you my advisors,' Natai said softly as she gestured towards Lady Kinna and the Demi-God Koteer.

'One of them looks a little young,' Styrax said. In the weak light his white eyes were even more apparent. She felt their heat on her skin.

'My ward, Ruhen.' She looked around and realised there was no seat for her. This was a studied insult, a major breach of protocol.

'You will not be staying long enough,' Styrax said, seeing her reaction.

Ruhen took a sudden step forward, slipping from Kayel's unresisting hands to grasp the duchess' skirt. He tugged it and she looked down at him, smiling.

'I'm tired,' he complained. He shook his head and his carefully brushed hair fell over his eyes, deepening the shadows in them.

'There are no seats, sweetheart,' Natai said, ushering him back to Kayel.

'But he has one,' Ruhen protested in rare annoyance, pointing a little finger at Lord Styrax. There was a collective intake of breath even as Natai shushed the boy and pushed him back into Kayel's charge.

'I apologise, Lord Styrax,' she said, trying not to show her fear. 'He is only a child.'

'An allowance can be made,' Styrax said in an oddly hollow voice. 'Ruhen, come over here. You may sit on my knee.'

Before Natai could react Ruhen had again slipped Kayel's grasp and trotted across the room. He was the size of a six-year-old, and he looked tiny in comparison with the seven-foot-tall white-eye. Though his head was no higher than Styrax's knee, he did not appear in the least daunted. When he was close enough he reached up his arms to be picked up and with the gentleness of a father the mighty Styrax obeyed the unspoken order, sitting the little boy on his thigh, supporting his back with one huge hand.

Finally, Styrax looked at Natai. 'Now, duchess, present your petition,' he said.

Natai blinked for a moment at Ruhen, who gave her a little wave, then she hurriedly gathered her thoughts. 'My Lord, the Circle City is plagued by the dragon you released. It is killing my own citizens, and the destruction in Ismess is extensive.'

'Are you asking me to clear up after myself?'

'I ... I would not have put it so, my Lord—'

'Then I am mistaken?'

A pause. 'No, my Lord, you are not, but I would not wish you to feel that I had spoken to you as I would to Ruhen.'

Styrax glanced at Amber, but the soldier said nothing.

Nai, the strange mage who had been appointed Natai's Menin liaison, had claimed Amber had killed the Chosen of Tsatach during the battle with the Farlan. That Styrax had looked to the man during this meeting showed he was probably telling the truth, and Major Amber's star was indeed in the ascendancy.

'You want me to do something about this dragon,' Styrax said at last. 'Isn't it traditional to invite adventurers and wandering knights to kill it? You could offer them half of Lord Celao's kingdom instead of your own, since Ismess is the most affected.'

'I fear more than a few soldiers have already died at its claws,' Natai said, not rising to his sarcasm. 'More do so every day, trying to protect the innocents of the quarter. Who, because of the rules you yourself have imposed, are unable to travel from the city, and thus cannot flee the creature's predations.'

'Ah, my fault yet again.' He gestured towards Amber. 'Unfortunately, my champion managed to hurt himself while out giant-killing. It'll be a while before he's back at work.'

'So you will not act?' the duchess asked with a hint of anger.

'Dangerous words, duchess,' Styrax snapped. 'Hinting at cowardice is a poor way to win me round; you would not live long enough to see whether pricking my pride has the desired effect!'

'I apologise if I gave such an impression, my Lord.' The duchess curtseyed again, lower this time than when she had she entered the room.

'Do not take me for a fool, madam! You want me to react angrily, to claim I've never backed down from a fight – to remind you that since I became an adult I've never lost a battle?' Styrax leaned forward. 'But I don't need to tell you that, do I? And you bring your pet Jester with you too, to flatter my martial prowess by such a champion begging for my help.'

The duchess looked discomforted by that, and was for a moment unable to remember why she had invited the Demi-God to accompany her.

'Well, Koteer? Are you going to stand there like a fool, or will you get on your fucking knees and beg?' Styrax demanded loudly.

Whatever the son of Death intended was forestalled when Ruhen tapped the Menin Lord on his thigh. 'You shouldn't use that word,' he said, shaking his head.

Styrax looked down. 'You think not? Is that what your nurse has taught you?'

Ruhen pointed towards Kayel, who made a good show of colouring and studying his own boots. 'He does sometimes.'

'I bet he does, the scamp,' Styrax said, making a visible effort to get a grip on his rage. 'You must tell your nurse that *some* people can say what they like.'

'Do you let your little boy say it?' Ruhen asked with disarming directness. The boy looked up through his tousled hair at the huge face above him.

Natai didn't know whether to grab the child and run, to try to save them both from the lash of the white-eye's unbridled fury, or if she should wait, and see if the child's innocence would calm the savage beast.

Styrax looked into the swirls of shadow in the child's eyes and felt his boiling rage subside. 'I—My son knew who he had to respect,' he replied in a choked voice.

Ruhen patted the thigh he was sitting on with the exaggerated solemnity of a child. 'Don't be sad. He isn't hurting now.'

Natai watched Styrax's face with bated breath. The effect of Ruhen's words was clearly visible and she felt a surge of jealousy that the child was bonding with him, not her. If it had been any other child, Styrax would dismissed them all, maybe even violently, but she knew herself how difficult it was to tear oneself from the warm embrace of Ruhen's eyes.

'I can't be sure of that,' Styrax said.

Ruhen gave him a guileless smile. 'He isn't hurting any more,' the little boy said again, firmly.

It looked as though a weight had lifted from his shoulders, the lines softening on the huge lord's face. Then he remembered himself and carefully lifted Ruhen off his knee again, nudging him towards Natai.

'Duchess, I have heard your plea,' he said in a calmer voice. 'You are correct that the Circle City is under my control and my subjects deserve my protection. I will find a way to kill or drive off this dragon, you have my word. For now, however, I will be left to my mourning.'

Mihn jammed his spade into the freshly turned earth and wiped the sweat from his face. The day was unusually bright for the time of year, but the brisk breeze that skipped off the glinting lake kept it cool. No birdsong cut the air, only the wind through the leaves and the rushes over at the water's edge. The smell of wet earth surrounded him.

'The day smells of hollow victories,' he said to the Land in general, finding solace in the words of others, 'a grave freshly dug, the rain on my cheek and a prayer in the air.'

'But who is it you pray to?' asked the witch of Llehden. He turned to see her standing behind him, her face shadowed from the late morning sun by a white mourning shawl. 'Myself, I find I do have not the strength for it.'

She carried an oak sapling in both hands, one recently pulled from the ground, to be planted over Xeliath's body in the Yee-tatchen fashion.

'Yet you wear the devices of Gods on your mourning shawl,' Mihn pointed out, though he didn't recognise the images.

Her hand automatically went to the old brass brooches pinned to the shawl.

'They are Kanasis and Ashar, the local Gods of Llehden.'

'Aspects of Amavoq?'

She shook her head. 'Kanasis is a stag Aspect of Vrest and Ashar's the Lady of Hidden Paths, an Aspect of Anviss. The God of Woods is more welcome here than his queen and mistress. We prefer not to fear the creatures of the forest.'

Mihn snorted and looked around at the dark trees of Llehden. 'That's something of a surprise; these woods are as unfriendly after nightfall as the Farlan eastern forests.'

'Llehden is a place of power, it attracts all kinds of creature, but that doesn't mean we should live in fear. Enter a gentry den and you'll be torn limb from limb; see one in the wood and your luck will hold all day, I'm told.'

'You're told? Surely you see them more than most?'

She shrugged. 'A witch makes her own luck. Even a drunk on a winning streak wouldn't be so foolish as to gamble against a witch.'

Mihn turned back to the grave he'd dug. 'Even a drunk knows luck will eventually run out,' he said with a heavy heart. 'Only I failed to see it coming.'

'Don't be a fool. You knew it was coming; you just assumed the price would be one you could bear to pay.'

'So what do I do now then?' he snapped. 'Just accept it?'

'Unless you are about to place yourself above the Gods, yes.'

The witch's calm voice angered Mihn, but as he scowled at her the trees nearby shuddered under a breeze he couldn't feel on his face.

'Death's a part of life, had you forgotten that? Don't start getting above yourself, Grave Thief.'

His head dropped as the dull ache in his gut intensified and eclipsed the anger of grief. 'How can you be so accepting?'

'Because there is no other choice. Xeliath was one of the Chosen; and she died in the boat with us, not on Ghain. She isn't bound for Ghenna – and what more can we ask of Lord Death? To choose the time and manner of one's death? She died to save Isak when he could not protect himself – a charge given to her by the Gods themselves when she was Chosen – and she died fighting, strong and fierce. Do you think Xeliath would have had it any other way?'

Mihn reluctantly shook his head. 'I know you're right, but—Is there nothing I can do?'

'You can remember her fondly, and thank her for her sacrifice. I suggest you keep away from the afterlife for as long as possible – you pledged your soul to a daemon, remember.'

He nodded, not wanting to get into that argument again. Offering his soul had not been part of the plan.

'It's time. Go and fetch Isak, if you can shift him.'

'And if I can't?'

'Bring Xeliath by yourself.'

He set off along the lake shore towards the small house. Daima was keeping watch inside, a grim expression on her face and a thin pipe clamped between her teeth. The only table in the main room was taken up by Xeliath's body, wrapped in a length of green canvas.

'It's time,' Daima said, grimacing as she pulled on her pipe, as if the tobacco had soured. It took her a while to get up; she had been sitting with the body for hours while he dug the grave.

Mihn looked at Isak, who was lying on a makeshift bed, his back against the far wall, staring at the floor. His arms and legs were drawn into his body and his lips moved slightly, as though he was whispering to himself, though Mihn could hear no sound. Every once in a while Isak's eyes would widen, then he would take a heaving breath, almost as if he was surprised at the need to breathe once more. He was oblivious to anyone else's presence.

'Did you expect anything different?' Daima asked. 'It most probably felt like years to him.'

'Have you checked his bandages?'

'Aye, and he's healing even quicker than you'd expect of his kind. Still hasn't spoken, though.'

'Not at all?'

'Hasn't even noticed I'm here. Give him time; some things don't heal as fast as others.'

Mihn walked over to Isak, and his body tensed a little more as Mihn's shadow fell over him. His scars seemed to darken, even more than they should in the shadow, and Mihn heard the faintest of whimpers break the silence.

'Isak,' Mihn whispered, crouching down beside him, 'Isak, can you hear me?'

There was no response, but when Mihn tried to take Isak's hand he felt the massive muscles tense and it was drawn in protectively. Mihn applied a touch more pressure, but he got nowhere. However gaunt he now looked, the white-eye was more than double Mihn's body-weight; it would be impossible to move him if he decided to resist.

Mihn gave up for now and went to gather Xeliath in his arms.

'Isak, we have to bury Xeliath,' he said, trying one last time, but there was no response. With a sigh Mihn headed for the door, leaving Isak to shiver and whisper alone.

'A wounded animal takes time to coax round,' Daima said as they rounded the house and headed for the grave. 'Let it happen at its own pace.'

At the tree-line Mihn could see the pale faces of the gentry watching them. The forest spirits wouldn't help or hinder, but they often watched funerals from afar – the one act of reverence they appeared to approve of. Mihn was startled when the caw of a solitary raven overhead prompted low mutters and growls from the watching gentry.

'That is what worries me,' Mihn replied after a while. 'The animal inside Isak is a dangerous one. What if that is all that is left?'

It was night by the time General Gaur returned to the Akell quarter of the Circle City. With his right arm bandaged he rode awkwardly, accompanied by a disordered group of his huntsmen. It was only the quality of his armour that distinguished him from the ragged champion Lord Styrax had extended a hand to in the fighting pits of Kravern, the great city at the entrance to the Ring of Fire. The decades since had not touched the beastman other than the faintest of silvering around his dark muzzle.

He passed Lord Styrax's guards without being challenged; a grey-haired huntsman at his side. They entered the dark officers' mess without knocking and sank to their knees.

'My Lord,' the men said in unison, their heads bowed.

'The Duchess of Byora came to see me,' Styrax said, his voice sounding tired. 'She came to remind me of my duties as her liege lord.'

When Gaur saw the fatigue in his lord's eyes he felt a flicker of alarm. Never before had he seen the white-eye appear so weak, so exhausted. The room smelled of old smoke and sweat, and whatever was burning in the fireplace hadn't been stored properly; though it took the edge off the chill in the room, it smelled sour, and smoked badly.

'In that case she's got more balls than the rest of the Circle City,' Gaur said.

'We knew that before the invasion.' Styrax rubbed his hands over his face, trying to massage away the ache behind his eyes. 'Nonetheless, it's a timely reminder. Our schedule does not allow for grief.'

'The dragon? I've heard it's battered Ismess into submission as effectively as Lord Larim was going to.'

Styrax nodded. 'I hadn't expected that, a dragon staying so close to human habitation. The spell that kept it sleeping must not have been as accomplished as its creator intended – unless she's more of a vicious bitch than we had heard. Its mind must be permanently damaged.'

'Wouldn't be the only one,' Gaur added with a twitch of his black mane. 'Word from Byora says the mercenary, Aracnan, has lost his mind; the poison's driven him mad. Chade suspects it's seadiamond venom.'

The huntsman bowed to Styrax when his name was mentioned. He was a small man, and his pinched, battered face made his age difficult to gauge. A hard life had left its mark: his teeth were yellowed, misaligned, and several were missing, and his cheeks were pitted with smallpox scars. On such a face the eager expression he was displaying looked far from natural.

'Don' know it well misself o'course, but I remember hearin' about it years back. Damn stuff's easy t'cure, so they say; supposedly alcohol kills it, so prob'ly all you'd need is to get yersel' blind drunk – but magic, that excites the stuff, makes it work faster—'

'So it's perfect for killing mages,' Styrax finished. 'How very like King Emin. His inventiveness is not to be underestimated; something to bear in mind when we march west.'

'West? You mean after we've dealt with the Devoted?' Gaur asked.

'After several things,' Styrax agreed. 'Chade, there's wine over there, pour us all a cup.' When the man was out of immediate earshot, Styrax asked, 'Apotheosis?' He gave Gaur a meaningful look.

'Yes, my Lord,' the general replied. 'He knows a little – not all – and I believe he's the man to run it.'

'Good. I don't have the energy to speak in code.'

The huntsman returned balancing three goblets. General Gaur took one and Chade handed the second to Lord Styrax. He waited for the Menin lord's nod before raising the goblet to his lips.

'It's time for the next phase of our conquest,' Styrax said after a moment. 'Duke Vrill is scouting the northeast, sounding out the remaining Knights of the Temples. Embere is the weaker of their two cities there, so Vrill is focused on Raland and General Telith Vener. The Knight-Cardinal is confined to quarters, and I doubt the general will be over-eager to liberate the only man to outrank him in the Order.'

'Not if Vrill offers him the right deal,' Gaur agreed. Vener would most likely accept a title; he'd rule over both cities as the Menin vassal happily enough. Duke Chaist, the ruler of Embere, wouldn't be so happy, but his army had been mauled pretty comprehensively by Vener's men the previous summer. The Menin's recently recruited Chetse legions would help solve any future argument there.

'In the meantime, a little confusion among the Devoted here would be a good idea. Start Apotheosis in Akell, then send word back to your men in the Chetse cities. The north is going to be more of a challenge, but it's important they head there too – it's the body-count that matters, and there are a lot of targets in the Farlan cities.'

Chade, aware of the significance of drinking with his lord, ventured to ask, 'We holdin' off in Tor Salan for the time bein'?' He didn't know much about Apotheosis, but he was aware that this secret undertaking was the principal driving force behind the Menin lord's invasion of the West, and the rewards for those involved would be commensurately great.

'There's been enough bloodshed there, for the present at least,' Styrax said. 'The city's unstable right now, and this is a long-term operation. There will be time enough for Tor Salan next year, if it's needed – our final phase will not take place before next summer, at the earliest. Send your agents to Sautin and Mustet to continue Apotheosis there, then have them work their way further west.' Styrax paused. 'I hope I don't need to remind you that you must be careful about whom you select for this operation.'

Chade nodded hard. 'All in hand, my Lord. At the general's orders I've bin pickin' soldiers out've the stockade all this last year. They's an evil bunch; half of 'em would cut a man's throat for lookin' funny at him, so they'll bloody jump at the bounty you're offerin'. Piety'll be the least o' my problems.'

'Good. Keep them in close teams and have them led by men with sense, preferably your huntsmen. We want this done properly, and that means covering your tracks and ensuring any suspicion is directed elsewhere. If you need to kill rival priests, the bounty will be paid on them too.'

Styrax raised a warning finger to Chade. 'I want it made damned clear: they follow orders and be careful, and they'll be rewarded the rest of their days. If they're sloppy or lazy there'll be a bounty on their heads big enough that even the mothers who bore them will be eager to claim it.'

'What about the Mortal-Aspect?' Gaur said. 'He can't be ignored.'

'Agreed. We need a Raylin to deal with the problem, and a powerful one at that. Aracnan would have been my first choice, but it appears he's no longer an option.'

'Aye, he's dead, that'un,' said Chade eagerly, 'or leastways as far as our use goes, and if he survives, he won't be the man he once were. Smart money is on a slow an' painful march to the Herald's hall for that'un.'

'Then the Poisonblade is our best alternative, don't you agree?'

General Gaur's tusks rasped through the bristles on his cheeks. He hated all Elves, instinctively, down at the very basest level, for no reason he could explain. Styrax had told him his own private theory: that Gaur's ancestry included some of the warrior races created to fight in the Great War. 'What will be his price?' the general said at last.

'I think we can safely assume it will be high. Offer him Lord Chalat's sword. It's one of his race's ancient relics, after all. I'm sure Major Amber will understand; I will provide compensation for the loss of his spoils.'

'I will instruct Larim to begin negotiations.' Gaur finished his wine before adding, 'So: our goal is to have severely diminished numbers in the Circle City, the Chetse lands, the southwestern states and the Farlan lands by the coming winter.'

'By which point,' Styrax went on, 'we should be getting established in Narkang territory, with the aim of implementing Apotheosis there some time the following summer. '

'But we do nothing about the Farlan Army?' Gaur asked. 'We gave them a mauling, but they're a long way from beaten, and not pressing the advantage for a whole year gives them time to regroup, recover and rebuild numbers – more than we can deal with if Narkang isn't beaten by winter.'

'We can stir trouble up there with minimal effort. They're currently leaderless; that's means they're likely to be arguing amongst themselves all the time we're hunting in the west. We'll buy some suzerains and that'll help to further undermine Farlan unity. But you do have a point; perhaps we should send a peace envoy now, to give them one more thing to disagree about, and stall them further? I've a long way to go before I complete my collection; there's no rush here.' His hand went to a pouch hanging from his sword belt. It held something the size of a man's fist.

'Is that why we're going west?' Gaur asked, surprised. 'All because of dodgy intelligence provided by some low-grade necromancer that King Emin has the Skull of Ruling?'

Styrax shook his head. 'The conquest comes first, although it won't hurt to see if we can prise it from him. When we do move, ensure a messenger has gone to speak to the king in advance – perhaps he'll barter it away since he's no mage himself.'

Gaur felt sceptical, but it would cost them nothing to try. 'There's one more for the taking, much closer,' he pointed out.

'Aracnan, yes,' Styrax said, 'but let's not move yet. Zhia and Koezh will doubtless be watching him carefully. They know I have several Skulls already, and if I look too keen to kill Aracnan they will feel threatened for their own.' He gave a humourless snort. 'Besides, right now I have a dragon to kill. Aracnan can be next week's problem.'

Knight-Cardinal Horel Certinse, head of the Knights of the Temples, glowered and paced restlessly as he demanded, 'What news of the other quarters, Captain?' He'd been unable to concentrate or sit still all day.

Captain Perforren reported, 'Nothing of great interest, sir. Akell has seen more of note than anywhere else today.' The tall soldier glanced nervously at the door whenever he heard a sound elsewhere in the townhouse. It was a modest building for the Knight-Cardinal and his staff to be confined to, and the attendant priests installed as his 'spiritual advisors' to monitor Certinse's activities made it even more cramped.

The Knight-Cardinal stopped dead and frowned. 'What do you mean?' His house-arrest was making him feel powerless and frustrated, emotions he was quite unused to.

'The duchess came to petition Lord Styrax, so I've heard. He made her wait several hours, but he did eventually admit her to his august presence.'

'Yet I am ignored by even Styrax's subordinates?' Certinse scowled. 'This cannot just be grief, or Styrax showing me my place. That I am so cut off must be of more significance. Does he not care at all about going to war with Raland and Embere? Could he have secured an alliance with that worm Vener without me knowing?' He looked at Perforren and shook his head. 'No, the Serian still reports to me, however gutted the Devout Congress has left it.'

He walked to the window and looked out for a moment. The captain could see his commander muttering silently; he glanced suspiciously at Perforren for a moment before resuming his pacing.

Perforren wasn't worried by the look; the Knights of the Temples were in chaos and his lord was right to be fearful of everyone. He'd just reminded himself that Perforren could be trusted absolutely – one of the few of his men who could. They were both Farlan originally, and Perforren was the son of a loyal family retainer who had been with the Knight-Cardinal since before Lord Bahl had banned the Order from Farlan lands.

Every officer of the Knights of the Temples had to be ordained as a priest – to the God of their choice – before being allowed to command troops, a time-honoured tradition that had served them well over the centuries. It didn't necessarily mean a lifetime of study and prayer, but it did ensure no one joined the Order lightly, and there was responsibility on both sacred and secular levels. The majority of the officers lived relatively secular lives, but the Gods' influence was there nonetheless. Unfortunately for Certinse, the specific God to whom they made their commitment was not made public, and the records were nowhere to hand.

Each of those turned into rabid fanatics by the rage of the Gods were aligned to one of the six principal Gods of Scree, that much he had deduced. How to tell who among his officers was secretly aligned to the various factions of fanatics was something he had yet not worked out, but he knew Perforren was, like him, a devotee of Anviss, and thus unaffected.

'Six more men were executed by High Priest Garash,' the captain said grimly after minute's silence. 'Three for whoring, two for gambling, one for some non-specified reason.'

'Damn the man,' Certinse said. 'He's not even bothering to follow the Codex of Ordinance any more. I'd hoped I could use its rules to curtail his excesses.' He threw up his hands in disgust. 'Karkarn's tears, what am I reduced to? I must ask you to hide in here when I retire so that bastard priest doesn't have to insist on being present; I'm surprised they're not whispering we are . . .' His voice tailed off as he sank down onto the side of his bed.

'By the Dark Place, we cannot continue this way. The Order will tear itself apart if we do.'

'I've been speaking to those sergeants I trust, sir' – he broke off and raised a hand at Certinse's alarmed expression – 'only those I know well, I assure you, and asking in only the most general of terms. The enlisted men are unhappy with what's going on, but they're Godsfearing, and it's going to take more than Garash's harsh punishments before they even think of rising up against the priests. There's talk of informers being recruited into every squad, men who will only take orders from priests—'

'Gods, has it come to this, when we must murder our own?' Certinse shook his head in despair.

'I . . . I may have a solution, sir,' Perforren said hesitantly.

Certinse looked at him, but the captain looked down at his

hands, saying nothing. After a few moments, Certinse said softly, 'Well, Captain? What is it?'

The anxiety was plain on his long face. His bloodshot eyes moved towards the door and back again.

Certinse got up and moved closed to his aide. 'Captain?'

'Sir—' He swallowed, and started again, 'You probably haven't heard, but there are beggars and the like gathering outside the gates of the Ruby Tower. They believe the child, Ruhen, has been sent to intercede for them with the Gods. Since the clerics' revolt, and then the duchess locking down Hale district, the numbers outside the tower have increased every day.'

'Ruhen? The child taken in by the duchess?' Certinse's hand fell to his sword hilt and a look of suspicion crossed his face. 'Are we to replace one mortal power over us for another?'

'No, sir, but perhaps the men might be more willing to act if they have a figure to inspire them?' Perforren suggested. 'They say the child gives men heart with a mere look. Right now our men are feeling frightened, and abandoned by the Gods. They are men in search of salvation.'

From the look on Certinse's face Perforren saw his words had had the right effect. The Order's self-appointed mission was to provide the prophesied Saviour with an army. For more than a century, this is what it had been working towards. Normally soldiers were resistant to change, but if the dogma was already built into the Order's rituals, it would be accepted more easily.

'It would explain why the duchess and her bodyguard fussed so over the child,' he said after a while. 'To Ghenna with them all! I will not let a rabble of clerics take the Order from me, not while I still draw breath.'

Perforren inclined his head in agreement but before he could speak there was a soft knock at the door. The two men exchanged looks, and Perforren shook his head, indicating that he knew nothing of the arrival.

At his commander's gesture he went to open the door to a Litse man with a thin, washed-out face and long white robes too rough and badly cut to belong to a priest.

'Good evening, Knight-Cardinal,' the man said with a small smile and a bow.

'Who in Ghenna's name are you?' Certinse exclaimed. He looked

99

at Perforren, but his captain still looked blank. His expression turned fearful as he took in the long white robes.

'My name is Luerce, Knight-Cardinal,' said the visitor. 'I am blessed to number among Ruhen's Children.'

Certinse grabbed Perforren roughly by the shoulder. 'What did you do, you fool?' he demanded.

Perforren gaped in helpless astonishment.

It was Luerce who answered for him. 'He did nothing – at least as far as I am aware, anyway,' said the Litse. 'I heard the Knights of the Temples were making enquiries and I decided it was time to pay you a visit.'

'This is all coincidence? I do not believe in coincidence!' Certinse snapped.

'Ah, but a fortuitous one, by the looks on your faces.'

'We were just discussing the child,' Certinse said, determined to give no more away.

Luerce's face blossomed into happiness. 'He does so love new friends. However, I doubt that had I come yesterday instead, our conversation would have been any different—'

'Wait a moment,' Perforren interrupted, finding his voice at last. 'How did you even get inside the building? We're under house arrest, and we are watched by both Menin troops and clerical spies.'

Luerce stepped into the room and closed the door behind him. He looked sly and he answered, 'How? Let us just say that shadows are kind to me.'

CHAPTER 6

Camatayl Castle stood south of the eastern end of the Blue Hills, which stretched between Narkang and Aroth. Camatayl, an unlovely and unloved structure that looked increasingly grim with every passing year, had been built by one of the more effective warlords in that area, but it now occupied a part of Emin Thonal's kingdom that had no need of such a fortress. By contrast Kamfer's Ford, a prosperous market town, flourished half a mile to the north, on the lower ground, where the King's Highway met the river.

The castle comprised a main square tower, built on the highest point for miles around, with walls as thick as one might expect of a castle that had survived two hundred years in troubled parts, and a much smaller tower beside the single gate. The steward lived in the smaller tower with his family and a handful of retainers. While useless for defending King Emin's new nation, he recognised that Camatayl would be a fine base for anyone plotting insurrection, so the royal warrant had been given to a loyal knight rather than the local suzerain. However proud the man was of his new appointment as Steward of Camatayl, he knew the king expected of him first and foremost a visible lack of ambition, and he was careful to ensure he had nothing to fear from the King's Men who regularly passed through Kamfer's Ford. The main tower was used only by the royal couple on their travels; the rest of the time it remained a brooding reminder of unhappy times past.

Legana and her two companions arrived at Kamfer's Ford just as evening settled in, and their first thought was to find the inn recommended by another traveller along the way. They were an unusual trio to be travelling alone, but it didn't take them long to realise the odd looks they were receiving were not just curiosity: there was a strange air in the town's streets.

At the door of the inn, Ardela laid a hand on Legana's arm to catch her attention. 'Wait; let me check the bar first,' she said quietly.

Legana looked at her, then past Ardela and up the street, head tilted. Ardela was beginning to recognise that pose – she had as fine a nose for trouble as any devotee of the Lady, but Legana possessed some sixth sense now, a divine form of a dog's ability to smell fear.

'*I'm not sure the bar will be any different to the street,*' Legana said into the mind of her companions.

'There'll be more drunks there, that's for damn sure,' Ardela replied. Cardinal Certinse's former agent was trying hard to change her ways, but she was still a belligerent young woman, and muscular, too. If there was any fighting to be done, Ardela intended to do it herself rather than allow Legana to put herself at risk.

'*But they'll be locals and I like a good bar fight as much as the next girl.*' Legana looked at Ardela and smiled in her otherworldly way.

That smile always made the newer of her followers, a young devotee called Shanas, shiver slightly.

'*When the next girl's you, at any rate. We'd hear if there were soldiers inside looking to cause trouble – all we'll find in here is farmers and traders and if any of them need a lesson about bothering strange blind women, so be it.*'

Legana had put her blindfold on again, deciding it was better to look like a helpless blind and dumb woman than making everyone nervous by appearing to stare into their souls. She wore a scarf tied around her throat to cover the shadowy handprint there but she was otherwise dressed just like her companions, a long cloak covering manly tunics and breeches and a variety of weapons. She was about to reach for the door handle when she suddenly stopped. She cocked her head, looking slightly to one side of the door, and gave a small smile.

'*Perhaps you should go first,*' she said, patting Ardela's forearm and urging her forward. Ardela shrugged and gave the door a push just as it was opened fully by a fat man sporting a greasy moustache and an entirely false expression of surprise.

'Ah, good evening!' he said in the overly slow voice of a man talking to a foreigner. He wasn't quite able to hide the nervousness on his face.

'He was waiting behind the door,' Legana explained. 'Someone must have seen us coming. He doesn't want us inside.'

'Hello,' Ardela said awkwardly in the local dialect, 'ah, speak Farlan?'

'Of course, mistress,' he replied, not moving from the doorway but looking from one woman to the other, as though unsure who he was really addressing. 'You go to the tower?'

Ardela gave Legana a puzzled glance. 'Eh, the tower? No, why?'

Relief flooded over the innkeeper's face. 'My apology, you are strangers; that is all.'

'Do all strangers go to the tower?'

'No one,' he said with curious finality, 'no one goes to the tower, but now . . .'

He tailed off and pointed to Camatayl Castle, where the tower was barely visible against the dark sky. Light shone from half a dozen of the windows. Just looking at the tower brought back the innkeeper's apprehension. 'I have a man, inside. He drinks and asks of the castle.'

'We wanted a room for the night,' Ardela explained with an impatient sniff. 'We were recommended.'

'*But now I want a drink*,' Legana announced firmly in Ardela's mind.

Ardela's shoulders slumped momentarily, but she knew Legana would not be swayed. It was a similar whim that had led them to find the meek Shanas. She was no more than seventeen summers of age, and she had been taken in by a farmer after collapsing as the Lady was killed. When she had recovered enough to start the journey back to her temple there'd seemed little point. Legana and Ardela had found her, still in shock, and with no idea what she should be doing.

'But a drink first,' Ardela added, at which the man stepped back and ushered them in.

Ardela led the way, followed by Legana, who was ostensibly being helped by Shanas – though a careful observer would have noticed little actual assistance being given or taken. The bar was low-ceilinged, and all three women had to walk carefully, to avoid catching their heads on the bowed beams crossing the room. A pleasantly pungent wood burned in the central fireplace, giving the room a welcoming feel, but despite that the place was less than half-full. The patrons – who looked to be locals – were all, with the exception of one man, squeezed around the tables on the far side of the fire.

That single drinker sat at the near end of the bar with his back to them. It was immediately obvious that he was the reason they were all keeping their distance: the man was massive, as broad as a Chetse, even without the bulky sheepskin coat he wore. What grabbed Ardela's attention even more than the large man was the huge crescent-bladed axe propped up against the bar within easy reach. It looked to be made of black-iron, with a brass-capped, forward-curved handle, and it had spikes on the reverse and top. This was neither a forester's axe, nor even that of a professional soldier.

'*If we're lucky he's a mercenary, and one who takes his trade seriously,*' she thought, catching Legana's attention.

As the Mortal-Aspect of the Lady looked around the bar through her blindfold, the mercenary stiffened. He turned to face them, one hand slipping to his axe handle.

'Here to start a fight?' he called, using Farlan but in a rough accent Ardela couldn't place. 'If so, that's your hard luck.' His cropped hair was shot through with grey, and his face was weatherbeaten and wrinkled. He bore a distinctive curved scar on his cheek. And he was a white-eye.

'*Bugger, a Raylin.*'

'Just passing through,' Ardela replied in what she hoped was a placatory voice, 'but I hear the tower's the place to be tonight.'

'Mebbe,' he said, curious now. 'Doubt you'll be welcome without an invite.' He reached behind him and grabbed his mug, and downed the rest of his beer, his eyes never leaving Legana. 'About time I headed off there. Can tag along if you want.'

He plucked the huge axe from the floor like it was a twig and slipped from his stool, giving the three women a wide grin. The innkeeper rushed out of a door at the end of the bar, presumably to have the man's horse fetched.

Adding to Ardela's confusion, the white-eye carefully fished out a copper coin and deposited it on the bar before heading towards them. Men who looked like him rarely paid for their drinks – they knew full well they wouldn't be challenged over a single pint. Innkeepers were normally pleased to see them leaving without blood being spilled; a pint was a small price to pay for peace.

'What's your name?' Ardela found herself asking without thinking.

He stopped and looked her up and down, grinning. 'I got lots o' names.' He pointed at Legana. 'You tell me her story and I'll give you one.'

Without waiting for a reply he continued to the door.

Shanas had to hop out of the way rather than be knocked over. Ardela stared after him, until she realised Legana still wore her small smile.

'*Luck is a choice taken*,' Legana said to her companions, a phrase each had heard often as novices of the Lady.

Ardela sighed, recognising from Legana's expression that, once again, chance favoured Fate's Mortal-Aspect, and followed him out.

Outside they were greeted by the sound of hooves as a stablehand brought over the mercenary's horse. Again the Raylin image didn't quite fit. The horse, though an ugly-looking beast, looked impeccably cared for, and yellow and blue ribbons were threaded through its braided mane.

The white-eye set off in the direction of the castle, leading his horse, giving no sign that he was even aware of the three women trailing along behind until they reached the edge of the town, where he turned and called out, 'Whole town's shitting themselves. No lord of the castle, just a steward who don't use the tower, and all the townsfolk are scared of the place.' He gave a loud laugh. 'When the tower's all lit up, men like me come – the stories they tell of it might be right.'

And having said his piece, he moved on, making no effort to slow his pace for the blind woman's comfort.

The road to the castle led off from the highway some fifty yards after the last house on that side of the river. It was overgrown, clearly seldom used, and led to a bare, windswept hill, but Ardela hardly noticed; a woman who'd travelled the wilds up and down the Land wasn't bothered by this sort of thing.

Unbidden, a memory rose in her mind, of one castle that had truly frightened her – or at least, would have, had she not swallowed down a concoction brewed specifically to numb such thoughts. The great fortress deep in the forests northeast of Lomin had been abandoned until Cordein Malich discovered it. More than once she'd found herself waking screaming when she'd dreamed of the place and the horrors it contained. *That* was a castle to fear.

As though she could sense what was going through Ardela's mind, Legana shifted her grip, slipping her arm through Ardela's and wrapping her hand around the woman's closed fist. Ardela felt a pang of gratitude for the comforting gesture and relaxed her fist, interlocking her fingers with Legana's and giving a squeeze of thanks.

When they were close enough to be seen from the castle walls someone hailed them all from above the gate, shouting, 'Come no further, identify yourselves.'

The white-eye spat on the ground. 'I got invited here an' I don't like to be kept waiting. Open that sally-port window and I'll show you,' he said, pointing with his axe towards an iron grille set into the main gate.

'And the rest?'

Them?' the white-eye said before Ardela could respond, 'dunno, but they're interesting enough to let in.'

He walked up to the gate as a small hatch opened at head-height behind the grille. He raised the butt of his axe and pushed the brass cap of the handle between the bars for the man to look at. Whatever was embossed seemed to do the trick and seconds later they heard the bolts being pulled back.

As the four of them entered the castle, Ardela and Shanas looked around the courtyard in curiosity while Legana stared straight at the great tower opposite them. The small tower was a good size in its own right, big enough for a decent household and staff, with a large barracks and a long wooden stable – the latter currently full to bursting, judging from the restless clatter of hooves coming from it.

'Stable my horse,' the white-eye called to one of the men who'd opened the gates, carelessly tossing him the reins and heading on across the courtyard. He glanced back at Legana and laughed cruelly. 'Good luck persuadin' these boys they should let you in!'

The gatekeeper looked more like a knight on campaign to Ardela, dressed in functional fighting clothes with a crest on his collars and a sword on his hips, but the man just gave a wolfish grin and led the horse away to the stable. One of the remaining men nodded to his companion and headed back up the ladder to the lookout position; the other walked over to face the three women.

'So, who are you?' he asked in Farlan, the dialect the white-eye had used. 'There's no open invite to this party and anyone he thinks interesting means trouble to my mind.'

'Who the buggery was he?' Ardela demanded.

The soldier laughed. 'You don't know? Piss and daemons! And you still followed him here?' He paused and stepped closer to Legana, prompting Ardela to close in protectively, until Legana raised a hand, calming her.

'You look familiar,' the man mused, stepping back a few seconds later. 'I've seen you before.' His voice was less than friendly.

Legana shrugged and tugged the blindfold down from her eyes. The only men from these parts she'd met, mercenaries aside, were King Emin's bodyguards in Scree. Either he was one of those, or she'd be fighting her way out soon enough.

'Fate's eyes,' the man breathed, peering at her, 'you've changed a lot since then.'

Legana ignored the fact that his hand had moved to his hilt and lifted her slate to write on it. – *When?*

'When? Just the summer, and considering the company you kept back then I'm not sure I like the fact you're changed.'

—*Your Brother.*

The man shook his head. 'He weren't the one I was thinking of.' He stepped back again, aware Ardela was poised to draw her sword. 'But I heard some strange things in recent times; sounds like you deserve condolences for more than one reason.'

Legana dipped her head in acknowledgment. There was a moment's silence before the soldier cleared his throat.

'Right, well . . . Best get you inside with the others and fed.'

He set off without waiting and after a brief hesitation the three devotees followed along, Legana voicing for their benefit the question they were all thinking. '*Others?*'

The 'others' turned out to be two women and a mismatched collection of men. The majority were like the soldiers manning the gate – Ardela realised there were too many for them all to be titled. When she got close enough to one to inspect the crest they all bore on their collars, she realised she was looking at King Emin's bee symbol.

King's Men then, she thought, returning the stares she was getting from all around.

Ardela hadn't come into contact with King Emin's personal agents before, but she'd heard enough to respect them, and she guessed that the two dozen men assembled here comprised a significant proportion of the force. They had been ushered into a large square hall on the ground floor of the tower. The room itself lacked any decoration beyond the flags of the nation. The most significant feature was a huge cauldron, smelling of stew, simmering away at the far end in a massive fireplace. A balcony jutted out over the hall and a wide stone staircase ran up the left-hand wall.

Two King's Men got up without a word and abandoned their table to make space for Legana. She didn't need to be guided towards it, but sat with the caution of the blind. Once comfortable, Legana looked slowly around the room, pausing at each knot of people in the big hall. More than one man flinched under her gaze and Ardela couldn't help but wonder what Legana was seeing with her shining emerald eyes.

Devotees were trained to assess people at a glance; even someone like Ardela, who had strayed from the path, did so by instinct. The King's Men occupied the left-hand wall, and sitting with them were two mages who seemed together to average each other out: one was a shrunken little worm of a man, the other oversized, like a white-eye who'd done nothing but eat for months on end.

Sitting close by, but not quite included, were the only other women present. They sat together, and were obviously wary of everyone, despite the fact one was most likely a battle-mage. She wore her dark hair as short as a boy's, and her leaf-brown padded tunic was adorned with a crisscrossed network of silver chain and crystal shards.

The other's trade was harder to discern. A long scar down her right cheek showed she hadn't spent her life closeted away, but she carried no obvious weapons and she was dressed in normal travelling clothes, which made her stand out in this crowd.

The rest were an ugly bunch. Four dark-skinned, tattoo-covered mercenaries from the south were sitting with a shaven-headed man who sported bronze earrings in his left ear and had a sheathed pair of scimitars slung over his shoulder. A second battle-mage, who looked, judging by his clothes, as if he'd fallen on hard time, loitered in the corner. He was biting his nails and eying his more reputable colleagues across the room.

Their white-eye was busy downing a jug of wine and ignoring his hunched table companion, whose face was hidden by a raised hood. Sitting furthest from everyone was a broken-nosed man of thirty-odd summers who bore the scars of many a kicking, if Ardela was any judge. He looked like a vagrant they'd picked up off the street rather than a mercenary, his hair and beard tangled and as filthy as his clothes, but she guessed it wasn't just the smell that kept the rest away. From the way several of the mercenaries were eying each other she guessed they had met before, most likely not always on the same side.

Finishing his wine the white-eye slipped off his sheepskin coat to reveal well-muscled arms that rivalled the southerners' for tattoos. He obviously startled one or two of the King's Men, who whispered to their companions and checked their weapons were at the ready, but the white-eye seemed to be enjoying the reaction he was getting. He made an obscene gesture at the nearest, all the while chuckling mightily.

'*A room I seem to belong in,*' Legana commented to her sisters. '*I smell Gods and daemons in the room, and mages of all sorts.*'

'Daemons?' Ardela said out loud in surprise. The man with his hood still raised flinched as she spoke and turned slightly to look at them askance. Whatever he saw he didn't like and curled even further in on himself, but they caught sight of metal on his chest before he turned away. A soldier most likely.

'*Cursed. There's a God and daemon inside him, fighting for control.*' Legana tilted her head and continued to stare at him. '*Once a priest, I think. There's something of Vrest about him.*'

'Most likely he's Devoted then,' Ardela murmured, 'or leastways once was. Lots of them take Vrest's orders when they get made up to officer rank, and they do like questing after daemons.'

Any further conjecture was prevented by the sound of boots coming down the staircase. The three women turned as more King's Men descended, one a scowling white-eye carrying a long mace who Ardela guessed to be Coran, King Emin's bodyguard. He was as big as any white-eye of the Palace Guard and just as brutal-looking. She doubted the man had ever been handsome, but his face was not so much scarred as battered, like that of an ageing prizefighter.

Coran's expression darkened as he looked around the room. He had the sort of permanent scowl of a man vicious to the bone, no matter what company he kept. Ardela wondered if he saw his own face as a legitimate weapon, if he could hurt the other man with it; she'd met some – a few – like that, when the fight wasn't fun if they both didn't end up bruised and bloody.

As though to confirm Coran's identity, a man came out onto the balcony a few seconds later beamed down at the assembled crowd. He wore a rusty-red hat adorned with peacock feathers and a black brigandine that echoed the peacock feather pattern. Ardela couldn't see his much-described piercing blue eyes from the other side of the room, but since the second thing every report of the man mentioned was his infuriating, mocking smile, that she noticed easily enough.

'Ladies and gentlemen, thank you for coming,' he said in a clear, aristocratic voice. 'As for my uninvited guests, this is a particular pleasure,' he added with a slight bow.

'I don't like surprises,' growled the dishevelled battle-mage, standing up. He spoke Farlan with a clipped accent that chopped up the rhythm of the words and made them ugly in the ears of a native speaker. 'Uninvited guests ain't a welcome one – and don't get me started on him,' he added vehemently, pointed an accusatory finger at the vagrant standing on one side.

'Piss on you,' the white-eye with the axe interjected, reaching for another jug of wine. 'Stop your whining, Wentersorn, 'fore I cut your other one off.' He jabbed a thumb behind him towards Legana. 'Before anything, tell me about her. Who gets in without an invite?'

King Emin leaned forward on the balcony rail. 'It is a fair question, but I doubt there's much I could tell you of any accuracy – the Land is a different place since last we met. She is, however, welcome here as my guest so I would appreciate a little courtesy from all of you.' He looked at Legana. 'Lady, would you and your companions help yourselves to food? You will, I hope, forgive me if you have already heard any of this.'

When Legana had indicated her assent and Shanas had fetched them some stew, King Emin cleared his throat and started, 'You all know what you're good at, and what sort of job I generally have for you. Those who don't know their companions can worry about that afterwards – you can all swap reputations, delightful nicknames and tales of adventure after I've finished. I need men I can trust to take orders, and if any of you have a problem with that, then best you say so now. After tonight, if you continue with us I'll consider you part of the Narkang Army. Should you choose not to join us, I'll have to insist you stay a while to ensure you can't betray our plans, but you will be afforded every measure of hospitality and comfort, of course.'

The white-eye raised a hand to attract the king's attention, making Ardela feel for a moment like she was back at her lessons in the temple. 'Hope that don't apply to me,' he said with a grin that didn't reach his white eyes. 'Ain't taking fucking orders from any o' them.'

King Emin gave the man an indulgent smile. 'Then it is fortunate that I'm putting you in charge of part of the unit.'

'Hah! You'll be making me nobility next!' the white-eye said with a laugh.

Half the men in the room realised the king hadn't been joking and began to object, but Emin hushed his troops and waited for the mercenaries to quieten down.

'Enough of the bravado,' he said. 'If there's any man among you who wants to test himself against Daken you can take it out into the courtyard now – no, that's excepting you, Coran!' he snapped as his bodyguard hefted his mace. 'Daken leads one half of the unit, Coran the other. You each will be responsible for getting them to the Circle City by whatever unobtrusive method is necessary—'

'That means secret-like,' Daken interjected, looking directly at the rogue mage, Wentersorn, 'for the dumbshits among you.'

'Yes, Daken, yes it does,' Emin said with exaggerated patience. 'For preference it would also include not starting a fight with your own men too. Once in Byora you will liaise with my man in the quarter, who will give you your final orders.'

'What about him?' Wentersorn demanded in a whining voice, pointing at the vagrant standing all alone. 'You can't expect any of us to travel with Shim the Bastard!'

Considering Daken's naked hostility towards him, Ardela guessed Wentersorn had to be genuinely afraid to speak up again and she turned her attention to Shim. The man kept his eyes low.

'Several of the Brotherhood will be part of your group. Some will be filling you in on necessary details of how they work, and two will be escorting Shim separately.'

Shim said something in response that Ardela couldn't understand, but the mage did. He shrank back for a moment, then found his courage and replied in the Narkang dialect, drawing his knife. It was quite clear what he meant, whatever language.

'*Curious,*' Legana said, '*it seems he's a mage-killer of some sort. Not a mystery I want to investigate too closely, I think.*'

'What are we doing here?' Ardela whispered back.

'*Waiting for our turn,*' Legana replied. '*King Emin may be the patron we're looking for – his agents and officials may be able to find our sisters faster than we ever could alone.*'

'You're going to ask him outright?'

'*He's a politician; when have you ever heard a politician say something plainly? But look at who we're sharing a room with – this is part of an ongoing campaign and the man is having to recruit Raylin mercenaries to bolster his numbers.*'

'So he might need us more than we need him?'

'*Luck's a chance taken.*' Legana repeated. '*Let's wait and see what chances the King of Narkang has to offer us.*'

While they spoke, Daken had stirred himself to take control of his new troops. He wasn't as tall as the king's bodyguard, Coran, but he was nonetheless a white-eye, and not even the battle-mage looked keen to face him down. Once all was quiet again King Emin wound the briefing up.

'If you've quite finished, I suggest you eat and drink your fill and be ready for an early start. Daken, I want them ready to leave at dawn so hangovers are your problem. Veil, make yourself and the other four known to your unit commander. Gentlemen, ladies, you've all been offered a good price for your services and continuing allegiance afterwards.' King Emin paused, then his voice hardened. 'Don't test my patience by trying to renegotiate now.'

With that he disappeared from view. The room was silent for a moment before one of the King's Men rose and headed for Daken, which became the cue for the rest to start their conversations again. For a moment Ardela thought they had been forgotten, but then she realised Coran was staring at her. Once he realised he had her attention he indicated up the stairs with a twitch of his head.

Ardela whispered to Legana, who scribbled something on her slate and climbed to her feet.

There were fewer eyes on them than Ardela had expected. The odd couple of mages were watching Legana with puzzled expressions, but the others were more concerned with Shim the Bastard, whoever he was. The normal troops were sizing up their new comrades, trying to keep an eye on the more obvious threats – all except Daken, who appeared to be basking happily in their unhappy attention. Now she knew his name, Ardela recognised him; his reputation wasn't one to necessarily be proud of – he was known as Daken the Mad Axe, not so much a delightful nickname as an accurate one, if even half the stories were to be believed.

As the three reached Coran he reached out to take Legana's arm, but she kept back and raised the slate. Reading whatever she'd written on it brought the colour darkening in Coran's cheeks. Ardela saw his fist tighten, but the man had a good enough hold on his temper to turn away and lead them up the stair without a word.

Ardela coughed to smother her laugh as she caught sight of what Legana had written – *Touch me and you'll be missing a ball too*. The white-eye's reputation was not a pleasant one, especially where women were concerned.

Legana followed Coran unaided up the single flight of stairs, running her fingers along the bare wall to help her balance. Ardela and Shanas kept close behind and they found themselves entering a cold, almost-bare study. A dozen unopened wooden crates stood on the floor. The only furniture was a dusty desk and a tall shelved cabinet, which occupied much of one wall. King Emin perched on one corner of the desk and inclined his head courteously as each woman entered.

'Normally I wouldn't believe your presence here could be merely fortuitous, but after Doranei's reports I have to accept the possibility,' he said to Legana.

Legana hesitated for a moment, and just when Ardela was expecting to be told to relay her words to the king, Legana erased the message on her slate and scribbled quickly.

Interesting, Ardela thought as she watched Legana hold up the slate. *She doesn't want him to know about that yet.*

'"Chance, nothing more,"' King Emin read aloud. He shrugged. 'Certainly it was not *fate*, and for that you have my condolences.

Doranei has told me something of your situation. I can surmise a little more, and I believe my help might prove valuable. As it happens I have a task that your sisterhood would be most suitable for.'

Legana gave him her most radiant smile. Faced with that, Emin's own faltered a fraction.

'Damn,' he said. 'This looks like it's going to cost me.'

CHAPTER 7

Grey ghosts of mist hung over the valley floor, sheltered from the listless breeze by the cliffs of Blackfang. Nothing moved inside the valley; no creature or spirit heard the silence shrouding the Library of Seasons broken by a small sound coming from the northern cliff. Set into the rock was a solid doorway, securely barred on the outside. The sound came again, tiny, even amidst the fearful hush: the muffled click of a leather-wrapped hook catching a bolt, the slow scrape of the bolt being dragged open. It was followed by a long, patient pause of several minutes – long enough, perhaps, to ensure anything hearing the rasp of metal would have investigated by then.

The valley floor was gradually being brought into life by the faint brightness spreading across the sky and by the time one of the doors eased open and Captain Hain of the Cheme Third Legion peered out, the murk of dawn was starting to dissipate. Directly in front of him Hain could see a small stretch of grass that extended for twenty yards, dropped away gently on the left, and ending more abruptly on the right at the white stone walls of the animal pens.

Debris was scattered all around the sloped roofs, and a single furrow, a large one, had been carved into the turf. Beyond the pens was the shell of a large, low building; the roof that had once covered one end had been ripped off and through a hole in the outer wall Hain could see the interior was equally wrecked.

To the left, around the base of Blackfang's peak jutting out into the bowl of the valley, he could make out half of the Fearen House, the largest building in the valley. The great dome looked intact, but one wing had been ripped clean away. Lord Styrax's beastmasters thought the dragon would most likely have chosen the Fearen House to sleep because of the amount of power in the place – most of the books were preserved by magic. No magic had worked in the valley itself until the spell had been broken; the attendants had ensured any ageing works were moved to a library annex outside the valley, where the protection spells would reactivate and slowly restore the book until it was fit for another fifty years in the library.

He began to mouth a prayer to Karkarn before catching himself – he wasn't going into battle, he had only a knife on his belt, and rumour was the Menin were no longer favoured by Karkarn: the priests travelling with the army and in Akell, where most of the Menin were billeted, had been troublesome for months. Demanding greater involvement in political and military matters had apparently been only the start and factions were now developing.

Ritual and combat training mixed easily for the War God's chosen tribe. Many of the officers, including as Major Amber, had learned weaponscraft at a training temple dedicated to minor Aspects of Karkarn. Now there were divided loyalties, and like many, Hain wasn't sure what side he was on in the argument between Gods and tribe. Loyalty to the Gods was something he had always taken as a given, but it was the priests themselves who were pushing men into taking sides and declaring what authority they bowed to – nation, lord or priesthood.

He shook the matter from his head. Now was not the time for such things; he had a dragon to worry about. His task was to scout the valley without getting eaten, and lay the snares.

Captain Hain took a deep breath and stepped out into the weak light of dawn, moving as silently as he could to the animal pens. When he glanced behind at the doorway he could just make out the eyes of one of Gaur's huntsmen, lurking at the edge of the tunnel that led back to the Akell quarter. The man gave him an unnecessarily cheerful thumbs-up that made Hain shake his head in bemusement.

Bunch of madmen, the lot of them, he mused. *So why is it I'm the one playing rat-mazes with a damn dragon?*

He reached the animal pens and, trying not to breath in the pungent odour, crouched down to check his route. Then he set off at a crawl towards the shattered building. Guessing stealth would serve him better than haste, he kept an eye on the distant Fearen House, ready to sprint for the tunnel entrance at the first sign of movement. It was only a hundred yards of ground, but for Hain it felt like it took an age to cross. He could smell the charred wood before he reached the building, but when he got there the thick stone walls appeared sound enough for his purposes.

Hain made his way around the edge and surveyed the rest of the valley. The Scholars' Palace had been almost entirely destroyed, with what was left of the lower floors scorched and blackened. Great chunks had been ripped from the building and thrown down onto the valley floor. There was a lot of debris lying around, but other than the one wing which had been torn open the Fearen House didn't appear to be much damaged, and as far as Hain could see, it was empty. His breathing came a little more easily at that, but only until he began to imagine the creature perched on the cliffs, watching him like a hawk watches a mouse. The dread returned.

A little surprisingly, the huge gate that led to Ilit's Stair, the two-hundred-yard-long slope leading down into Ismess, was untouched. The dragon had destroyed large sections of the quarter, but it obviously preferred to fly over the cliffs of Blackfang rather than waddle out through the gate. Of the remaining large buildings inside the valley, two had been completely destroyed while the rest appeared whole.

There was no sign of the beast anywhere right now so Hain took one last look up at the cliffs and made his way back to the other corner of the ruined palace and gestured to the waiting huntsman. He emerged from the tunnel, carrying a pair of shovels, with a long cable looped over his shoulder.

Hain pointed at a patch of ground between them and the animal pens. 'That's the spot,' he whispered.

'Don't believe we're even tryin' this,' the huntsman moaned with a shake of the head. 'You're goin' t'get us killed, settin' snares for a damn dragon!'

'Shut up and get back there for the rest,' Hain hissed, trying to keep from raising his voice. 'We know they're not going to hold it.'

The huntsman said nothing more as he handed over the cables and made his way back to the doors. Hain watched him for a moment, wondering if the man was right, then he shook himself. It didn't matter if the huntsman was right or not; he had orders to carry out. He bent to the task of separating out the cables on the grass, trying to put to one side the ridiculousness of the idea – even though it was partly of his devising.

'Let's hope the beastmasters are right about dragons being similar enough to wyverns,' he muttered, 'otherwise looking stupid's going to be the least of our problems.'

He peered up at the sky, which was lightening with every passing minute, though dawn was still a way off. The beastmasters had said there was no way of predicting when the dragon would be active and away from its lair, but darkness would prove no barrier to its eyesight. Hain's best bet was to work alone and quietly, as soon as it was light enough for him to be able to see the dragon approaching.

So get a bloody move on, he ordered himself, and started to cut the turf. *Whether it works is someone else's problem.*

A knock came at the door of the orphans' chamber. The Duchess of Byora looked up from her breakfast and watched blearily as Sergeant Kayel crossed over to the door and opened it a fraction. Mornings had always been precious to Natai. Whether or not her husband, Ganas, had risen with her, she had cherished these precious few hours before official duties took over. It was a fair indulgence, she thought; no matter the problems the day might bring, she was always better prepared, both in temper and per-spective, having spent some time with her young wards first.

Natai looked around. The orphans' chamber was conspicuously lacking in one detail: orphans. Only Ruhen was present, together with his painfully thin nurse, Eliane, who was sitting in the furthest corner of the room. The rest were absent, as were the nurses who tended to them, and Natai felt a flicker of anger – until her gaze returned to Ruhen, sitting happily at her side. This morning he was playing with an old quill, drawing elegant spirals on a battered piece of parchment. She tilted her head to look at the page; the shapes looked almost like writing from a far-distant place.

'Ruhen, dear, would you draw something for me?' she asked on a whim.

'Yes, Mother,' the boy replied solemnly, looking up at her through his long lashes. The ache in her head softened as he smiled, and the shadows wove patterns in his eyes.

So beautiful, she thought dreamily, *so beautiful, and so clever.*

She moved her hand to stroke the line of his jaw and tuck an errant lock of long brown hair behind his ear to stop it falling over his face. Ruhen's cheek dimpled a fraction and Natai felt a flutter of pleasure in her belly.

How foolish I was to think him so young when he first came to me—No, he has been here for years, of course. I am his mother, I gave birth to him. I remember the pain, the first clench of labour as Ganas and I went on our Prayerday trip . . .

Her thoughts tailed away into nothing. Remembering was hard, so hard, and so painful. She was Ruhen's mother, and that was all that mattered. He gave her joy by his mere presence, and in time she would be proud to watch him grow into a prince, to rule all of the Circle City.

'Your Grace?' A deep voice interrupted her reverie, making her flinch. She looked around vaguely until she realised it was Sergeant Kayel who was talking.

'Yes? Yes, what is it?' She frowned. 'Did someone bring a message?'

'They did, your Grace,' Kayel replied. He heaved his large frame into a chair and dropped his elbows heavily on the table.

Natai pursed her lips. Her bodyguard should not eat with his mistress, should he? She wished for a moment she could remember . . . She watched him drop a handful of letters on the table and pick up several hardboiled eggs in his scarred hands.

'Strangely enough,' Kayel continued after filling his mouth with one egg, 'the letters ain't for you, your Grace. One is for me.'

'Who would write to you? Who are the others for?' She caught sight of Ruhen, holding out his hand for the one of the eggs Kayel had.

'You want one?' Kayel offered an egg to the little boy, but not close enough for Ruhen to take it. 'What do you say, then?'

'Now,' Ruhen said with a firmness that made Natai tense. Kayel chuckled and leant over, extending his reach until the boy could take it from him.

Natai relaxed again. *A boy must have a father,* she reminded herself. *Ganas was a sweet man, but he was weak. Kayel is a better influence for my little prince.*

'Anyways,' Kayel continued, one cheek bulging, 'the other letters are for Aracnan and the Jesters. The seal is Menin, General Gaur's own.'

'What does he want with you?'

Kayel smiled and a knife seemed to magically appear in his fingers. He picked up the letter and ran the blade under its seal. He unfolded the letter, held it up to the light and read it out loud.

'Sergeant Kayel, you are cordially invited to join Lord Styrax the morning after tomorrow at dawn for a hunt. Attendance is mandatory for all subjects loyal to the new ruler of the Circle City.'

'Well, you must not refuse him then,' Natai said suddenly. 'To do so would give grave offence.'

'Hunting though? You invite noblemen hunting, not men like Raylin mercenaries, men like me!' Kayel thought for a moment before giving a cough of laughter. 'Hah, damn it, of course! Can't really refuse him now can I? Not when it was your idea for the hunt in the first place. You take noblemen if you're hunting for deer. You take Raylin and the like if you're going after larger game.'

'My idea?'

'Yes, your Grace. You were the one who asked him to free us from the beast preying on the folk of Ismess. He's gathering warriors and adventurers together to hunt a dragon; Piss and daemons, but I wouldn't miss that fun for all the money in Coin. And when nobles go hunting, there's always business to be talked over afterwards. So I wonder what it is he wants – and who else is invited? ' His face fell slightly. 'Giving Aracnan the good news might not be a bundle of fun.'

'His wound still ails him?'

Kayel gave her a contemptuous look. 'He's an immortal who is slowly dying, driven mad by pain while the rot in his shoulder goes deeper into the bone. Ailing don't really cover it.'

'Library,' Ruhen said, putting his pen down.

'That's right dear, soon you'll be able to go to the Library of Seasons again and see the funny men with wings,' Natai said.

'Aye,' Kayel agreed pensively, brushing the back of one thumb with the edge of his dagger. 'A prince needs a suitable education now, don't he?'

A small drop of blood fell onto the letter, but only Ruhen paid it any attention. He watched the bright spot run down the paper, his eyes dancing with delight.

*

'This Menin occupation has become tiresome,' Zhia announced, slipping her arms from the sleeves of her dress and letting it fall about her ankles. 'There are altogether too many curious faces on the streets, even at night.'

The naked vampire ignored the bedroom's chilly air and carefully unwound her plait to leave her hair falling freely about her shoulders. Doranei turned slightly so he could see her slim body silhouetted in the faint daylight creeping around the door. He felt a familiar stirring of lust banish the fog of sleep and for a while he just enjoyed the sight of her, every movement graceful and neat.

'Where did you go?' he asked eventually, propping himself up on one elbow. 'I didn't hear you leave.'

Zhia's sharp teeth flashed white in the twilight. 'I didn't want to wake you.' With a twitch of her fingers the blanket lifted off Doranei's body and the cold air rushed in. As Doranei instinctively curled up Zhia slid sinuously into his arms. By the time the blanket dropped down again his body was tightly wrapped around hers, his lips on the nape of her neck as Zhia pushed against his chest.

'You went to feed?' Doranei said softly in her ear, breathing in the delicate perfume she wore.

'I did. A girl has needs even you cannot satisfy,' Zhia purred, reaching back around his waist to pull him tighter against her. As he kissed her again she took his hand and pressed it against her chest, hard enough to make him wince.

Doranei didn't say anything more. He might not like it, but he was a professional killer; what right had he to pass judgment on her Gods-imposed curse?

'How are you going to spend the day?' she asked eventually.

He sighed. 'I have the usual errands to run. I can't afford to let our agent here out of the safe house, he's too easily recognised and Ilumene *will* have people looking for him.'

'Then an evening of drinking in Coin? That disguise would suit you better if you had a beautiful lady to accompany you.'

Doranei gave a noncommittal grunt. Even washed, shaved and dressed in fine clothes he hadn't managed to attract the right friends in the cardhouse; bringing Zhia in would complicate matters in other ways. His usual method of intelligence-gathering – befriending soldiers, cooks and servants – had been precluded now a traitor comrade was overseeing security at the Ruby Tower.

He was hoping the merchants of Coin and the minor nobility of Eight Towers would tell him enough instead, but it was hard to lay the groundwork in fraught times like these, when he didn't look like he belonged. Zhia did, but she wore a dark allure like a mantle, and Doranei was noticeable enough already.

'Ashamed to be seen in public with me?'

'Don't be foolish.' He kissed her, and added, 'If you could make yourself look a little less beautiful, confident and terrifying all in one go, then I'd have no argument. But I already attract too much attention, and you, my love, you dominate any room you enter.'

She pulled his hand up to her lips and kissed his fingertips as gently as a butterfly. 'You grieve for Sebe. When you drink, you glower, and frighten those around you. However delicate your touch, you still resemble a white-eye looking for something to kill; that's what they notice in Coin.'

'It isn't so easy to throw off,' he growled.

'I know that, pretty one,' Zhia continued in a conciliatory tone, 'but it is a detail you must address. There's enough grief around that folk will understand it. Wear something to explain your mood and their suspicion will be allayed.'

'You think that'll be enough?'

'I don't know; you won't tell me what information you are seeking.' There was an edge of hurt in her voice that made Doranei want to immediately apologise, but he suppressed the feeling.

'Do we need to have this conversation again? I'm not your pet to be indulged, and we're not on the same side in this war.'

'Those are not sufficient reasons to mistrust me. I can provide you with a plan of the Ruby Tower, of the duchess' security arrangements – whatever you want. Lady Kinna is still under my control, and her access is unrestricted.'

'They are all the reasons I have,' Doranei said, knowing he sounded petulant, 'and besides, my orders are clear enough.'

'Your king does not trust my motives; I understand that, but do you honestly believe I would give you false information or betray your plans to the shadow? Do you believe I would ever put you in danger?'

'Zhia—Of course I don't, but this is how things must be. Can we—' he broke off to stroke her back, and whispered, 'Zhia, can we please talk of inconsequential things instead?'

She heard the tired edge in his voice and, knowing how exhausting an emotion grief was, she didn't push matters further. Zhia gently kissed each of his callused knuckles before using his hand to cup her face. 'As you wish, pretty one. We will talk of the children we will never have instead; of the life we will never lead. I require a minimum of two girls – I remember having a sister most fondly.'

'At least two?' Doranei winced at the thought. 'Just one with her mother's smile would be trouble enough for me.'

'You would rule them without ever realising it,' Zhia said with laughter in her voice, 'as their father, the proud merchant, comes home after a long day to a great clatter of feet as his adoring women rush to greet him.'

'Merchant? What would I sell?' Doranei asked in surprise, unable to imagine himself doing anything so safe – or so legal. 'My entire life's been in the king's service.'

'This is the life we will not lead,' Zhia reminded him. 'Your father was a soldier in King Emin's conquest, but he wanted a better life for his son and so he apprenticed him to a wine trader. You, in turn, are so filled with pride when young Manayaz announces he intends to join the Kingsguard, you cannot resist giving him your blessing.'

He frowned. 'Manayaz? Even in your homeland, boys can't have been called that since the Great War. Your father rather coloured most folk against the name.'

'Manayaz,' Zhia said with finality. 'He will have his father's size and his mother's speed. No bully will take exception to his name more than once.' She pulled Doranei's hand tighter against his chest. 'He will be a fine older brother to little Sebetin, the one whose smile melts the hearts of even his fierce gaggle of sisters.'

'Sebe,' Doranei whispered, 'named for their favourite uncle, who still manages to get me into daft scrapes when we're both old, rich and fat.'

'The very same; who wakes early when he comes to visit and drags the children out with the dawn so we can have these few quiet moments together. These moments that mean as much to me as anything – these moments that last as we grow old together and watch our children make all the same mistakes we did when we were young.' Zhia smiled and squeezed his hand. 'Except the ones involving jumping off buildings or petting guard dogs; they'll have the sense not to do those.'

'What fools we are,' Doranei said bitterly. 'You, who doesn't grow old; I, who'll not survive to do so.'

'It is not too late for you,' Zhia said with a shake of the head. When she tried to continue, however, she felt the words catch in her throat. Neither of them could believe that; it wouldn't matter what she said.

They lay together in silence until sounds began to emanate from elsewhere in the building and the tavern servants started their day. With the quiet broken Doranei eased himself away from Zhia, who let him go and watched while he dressed. Her eyes were closed when he bent to kiss her forehead and only opened again when the door clicked shut behind him.

CHAPTER 8

Low shafts of sunlight pushed between the trees as the witch of Llehden walked towards the lake. It was early enough to be crisp and cold still – two hours after dawn, and the sun hadn't yet warmed the frost off the rusty bracken. The witch wore a wolfskin cloak, fastened at the throat by a bronze stag's head clasp that looked incongruous with the rest of her clothes, and in her arms was a large, awkward-shaped bundle. Occasionally the bundle would wriggle, prompting the witch to shift her hold a little and whisper soothing words.

At the end of the path the trees opened up and afforded her a view across the still water. The other side of the lake was punctuated by rampant clumps of reeds standing higher than a man, beyond which stretched the long, undulating expanse of Tairen Moor. Several villages bordered the moor, but the only people you would ever find on the moor were travellers using the single road and the few peat-diggers and herdsmen who lived there.

The witch headed for the cottage on the lake's shore. The sound of chopping wood rang out from the trees behind as she left the path, but stopped when she called loudly, 'Grave Thief!'

As she reached the cottage door Mihn appeared from around the corner, sweat-slicked and red-cheeked from his exertions in the cold morning air.

'Good morning,' he called, wiping the sweat from his forehead with the back of his hand. 'You have something for us?' he added, when he noticed the bundle in her arms.

'For your patient.'

Mihn smiled faintly and came around to open the door for the witch. 'I am glad to hear it. He is not much better since you last visited. The man is still there, but he is hiding deep inside.'

They entered, and the witch lost no time in crossing to where Isak was lying. He was not so tightly curled up as before, and it looked as if he had reacted slightly to the sunlight shining through the door, but he was a far cry from the arrogant, ebullient youth she had first met.

'Is he biddable?' she asked.

'Just about.' Mihn went to the square brick stove in the centre of the room and lifted the lid of a pot that was bubbling away on top of it. He stirred the contents, sniffing appreciatively, and replaced the lid before adding, 'I have managed to get him up off the bed – I even got him outside once, but he went and fell into the water not long after so I do not know if that counts as a success.'

The witch frowned at him a moment, then crouched at Isak's bedside. Her lips moved silently, and one hand reached out towards him. After a while she glanced back at Mihn.

'I fear to take any more of his memories. The holes I've put in his mind will never heal.'

'Then it will have to be enough,' Mihn replied. 'You did not promise anything more than that. If you have removed the worst of his experiences in Ghenna, then I am satisfied the risk was worthwhile. Some things no one should remember.'

The witch nodded and turned back to her patient. 'Isak, can you hear me?'

The big white-eye turned his head fractionally at the sound of his name, but his eyes didn't focus on the witch and after a moment he looked down again. If she was disappointed, the witch didn't show it. Instead she pushed the bundle onto the bed beside him and carefully peeled the folds of the blanket open. Within was a bundle of floppy limbs and soft, greyish fur. She gently took Isak's hand and put it down beside the bundle, and his touch was rewarded with a muffled squeak before the puppy lifted its head from the blanket and tentatively licked his fingers.

Isak recoiled. The witch could feel his body tense as he drew his hand back – but not all the way. His fingers remained outstretched, as though ready to reach again, waiting only for a cue. The witch stepped back and joined Mihn, who was watching.

The puppy, finding itself lacking the warmth of the witch's body, lifted its head and looked at its new surroundings. Isak's huge, heavy breaths made its flop-ears twitch and it started to snuffle its way around until it found the big man behind it.

Still Isak didn't move, but both of them could tell he was more alert now than he had been since Xeliath had died.

The puppy took a while to get its folded limbs into some sort of order, then it bumbled its way forward towards Isak's face, wriggling into the white-eye's warm lee. It gave him a tentative wag, the tip of its tail brushing Isak's fingers. After a moment they saw his fingers close a little, not grabbing at the tail, but letting the fur brush his flesh. The puppy edged closer to Isak's face and pushed its nose against his shirt, snorting softly to itself as it breathed in his scent. Now Mihn could see it was a gangly bundle of grey-black fluff, all big paws and belly, with a ruff of dark fur around its neck. He couldn't recall seeing any of its kind in Llehden before but he resisted the temptation to ask where it had come from.

'Are you sure about this?' Mihn whispered.

'No,' the witch admitted, 'but Daima is. Before we can speak to the man we must remind his body of more basic things. The sensation of being alive is strange enough to him, but there are inbuilt needs – for warmth and comfort – that a pack animal might be able to coax out.'

Jerkily, Isak slid his hand forward on the bed and the puppy caught the movement and gently batted at his scarred fingers with a paw. Its ears pricked up. The hand didn't recoil this time, and Mihn saw Isak had closed his fingers a little further again, as though reaching for the sensation of soft fur once again. The puppy flopped its head down beside his fingers and gave the nearest another lick.

Still not looking at the puppy, Isak drifted towards it, sliding his head off the makeshift pillow and laying it flat on the bed. The puppy twitched its ears in response, but didn't raise its head again.

'I spoke a charm over it as I walked,' the witch explained. 'It will be sleepy for a while longer – dogs need little encouragement there. I thought it best their first hours together were slow, rather than boisterous.'

Mihn nodded slowly. 'I'm not chewing his food for him,' was all he said before leaving to return to his wood chopping.

The witch gave a half-smile as she noted the flicker of hope on Mihn's face as he left. 'Which one?' she called after him.

*

'How much longer?' Count Vesna growled, pacing around the mage and flexing his fingers impatiently. The scrape of steel-covered fingers sounded like knives being readied for murder.

'Not long, I hope,' the mage's attendant replied in a hesitant voice. 'Your presence will, ah, be a complicating factor. A distraction to his trace.'

The attendant was a man of forty summers, but he had been reduced to a nervous child in Vesna's presence.

Can't blame him now, can I? Vesna thought, halting to concentrate on getting a grip on his emotions. *I'm not human now – this is how men act in the presence of the Chosen.*

He looked down at his left hand and waggled his fingers. They moved more easily than they ever had in armour before, but that was small consolation for the fact the metal had fused to his skin from fingertip to shoulder. Vesna had expected the teardrop-shaped ruby attached to his cheek to remain, but not this too. Now he was just as noticeable as a white-eye, except amidst soldiers, and even then, Vesna had discovered all eyes turned towards him. He could see the fear in their eyes, and the awe at the presence of the Mortal-Aspect of Karkarn, the God of War's chosen general. Every soldier could feel him like the heat of a furnace on their skin.

There were four of them in the guest bedroom of Perolain Manor, in the southernmost reaches of Helrect's borders. The countess who owned it had, Vesna suspected, once been a member of the White Circle. As a result she couldn't have been more helpful to the retreating Farlan Army in an effort to avoid possible reprisals.

Outside, a gale howled and battered the walls of the manor. He had been able to smell the cold emanating off those aides who'd come in from the camp to report. It was a freezing night once again, and more than one had had to gasp for breath as they stood as near as they could to the small fire.

Suzerain Torl stood at Vesna's side: a tall, stern man, and the tribe's most devoted soldier. Neither looked at his best; having lost most of the army's baggage in their retreat the Farlan troops could hardly now be described as the peacocks their enemies nicknamed them.

The strain of the past weeks was clear to see on Torl's lined face. The suzerain looked exhausted, as if he had aged ten winters in one, but Vesna would have traded with him in a heartbeat. He looked at his left arm and flexed his fingers. The armour covering it was far less unwieldy that it had previously been, but still … Once made to measure for him, the black-iron was now a horrifying parody of Lord Isak's lightning-marked arm.

The divine air surrounding Vesna hadn't been enough for Karkarn, it appeared, nor had turning the scars of past injuries blood-red, so they stood out on his pale Farlan skin. Now Vesna was a clear statement to the entire Land: *Gods walk among mortals once more.*

'Count Vesna?' the mage said in an abrupt, emotionless voice. He knelt on the stone floor, swaying rhythmically as though listening to a song in his head. Despite the privations they were all suffering, the mage's head was freshly shaved and his skin scrubbed clean as he was ritually purified.

'Yes,' Vesna barked, moving back around the mage with such speed the attendant's eyes widened in surprise.

'This is Fernal,' the mage replied after a pause in which he had mouthed Vesna's reply. The ritual matched his thoughts to those of his twin, allowing them to relay a conversation across hundreds of miles. 'I am here with Chief Steward Lesarl, Lady Tila and High Cardinal Certinse.'

Vesna and Torl exchanged puzzled looks. Only one person could speak through the mage; why would that be Fernal? Vesna imagined the huge Demi-God sitting in the now-vacant ducal throne in Tirah, and something about that image made him pause. As big as the Chosen, with midnight-blue skin and a mane of shaggy hair falling from his fierce, lupine face; Fernal presented a savage visage that belied his quiet nature. He was a bastard son of Nartis, the Farlan's patron God, but he remained an outsider to the tribe.

'I have been named Lord of the Farlan,' the mage said after a longer pause. 'Lord Isak appointed me as his successor and the Synod has reluctantly confirmed it.'

Vesna gasped. Isak had discussed nothing of the kind with him, and he was one of the dead lord's closest friends. 'I—I had no idea,' he stammered, seeing Torl was as shocked as he was. 'I congratulate you, my Lord.'

Isak's death hung like a black cloud at the back of Vesna's mind, but he refused to allow himself to mourn yet – not while his grip on the battered Farlan Army remained so tenuous. His new-found divine emotions had allowed him to dissociate himself from the ball of loss that appeared in his stomach whenever he remembered the moment when he had sensed Isak die, as he was cutting a path through the small Byoran Army, but he knew he could not keep it away forever.

The power now surging in his veins had not removed his humanity, though he had feared it might, but other than that, Vesna found himself not so different to a God. His strength was increased, his speed was unnatural, but his mind was still that of the flawed man he had been before.

The awe he saw in every soldier's face was unnerving in its intensity, but it was just that – intensified, rather than new. Vesna has been a hero of the army for ten years or more, and he had seen it before.

'Thank you,' said the mage dully, 'I am told your circumstances have also changed.'

Vesna looked at the black steel plates attached to his left arm and touched the ruby lodged in the skin of his cheek.

'I am changed, but I remain a servant of the Farlan,' he said carefully. *Gods, what is Tila going to think when she sees what I've become?* he wondered privately. *No, she will know to expect changes. Thank the Gods I told her about Lord Karkarn's offer before I left.*

'You're welcome,' said a voice inside his mind, prompting Vesna to flinch. *'I'm happy to claim the credit on behalf of us all.'* Karkarn chuckled. *'Still skittish about communion with your God, I see? Never mind, it will pass. Just be thankful I don't have Larat's appetites.'*

The Mortal-Aspect of Karkarn shook his head to try and get the sensation of being ridden like a horse out of his mind. The God of War had shown no compunction about appearing without warning, seeing through his eyes as though he was just an instrument.

And for my sins, maybe I am.

'That is good to hear,' the mage repeated, eyes closed, rocking backwards and forwards on his knees. 'We have need of you here more than ever. Lord Isak's death has been widely reported, and there have been a dozen new prophets in Tirah alone. The clerics are using it as an excuse to demand greater control over the running of the tribe.'

'Has there been bloodshed?' Vesna asked.

'Only a few small incidents. The clerics are trying to get the population on their side before pressing the matter. High Cardinal Certinse may buy us some time but the fanatics grow restless. It appears the worst did not all travel with the army.'

'What are your orders?' Vesna asked, remembering to add, 'Lord Fernal,' after a moment.

'Pull the army back to Farlan territory; have the Quartermaster-General set up camps for them, one on the border, a second near to Tirah. Return to the city yourself with a legion of Ghosts.'

'Yes, my Lord. Ah, Lord Fernal? The clerical troops were scattered after the battle, those that survived, anyway. I have about seven thousand men under my command; of those only about a division's worth are clerics.'

'You think the rest will return here?'

'Possibly. The Penitent troops took the worst of the casualties, but some escaped the killing ground. There is no way of predicting how they will act now.'

For a while the mage was silent and Vesna assumed Fernal and his companions were discussing matters amongst themselves. He turned to Torl for a wiser man's thoughts, but he had nothing to offer. The suzerain looked troubled and distracted, presumably at the thought of a non-Farlan as lord of the tribe.

White-eyes were difficult masters, but they were sanctioned by the Gods, and they were predictable to a certain degree. Fernal did not fit into the rigid Farlan structure. He had been presented as the protector of the Witch of Llehden, and had been assumed to be just another Raylin mercenary by the Farlan nobility. That he was a bastard son of their patron God had mattered little to them. The title Demi-God meant Fernal was more mortal than divine, but for the Farlan it made him nothing more than a wandering fighter to be employed or killed.

'The Penitent armies are a problem for another day. Have your scouts keep a weather eye, but travel for speed, not safety. I need your presence in Tirah, both you and your troops. The clerics will hesitate in the presence of the Mortal-Aspect of Karkarn, and Lady Tila has guaranteed your continuing loyalty.'

That stopped Vesna in his tracks. It had never occurred to him that he might be considered a threat to the nation now. He and Torl hadn't thought to discuss allegiance yet.

'*Consider your new lord,*' Karkarn reminded him, '*so new to his* position that they are most likely still deciding whether it a legal claim.'

'He cannot afford to assume,' Vesna agreed, 'so Tila has offered herself as hostage to my actions. But what do I do when I return?'

'Be the good servant. Lord Fernal knows nothing of war; suggest he needs a general in supreme command. You are now the best choice, General Lahk and Suzerain Torl would both agree.'

'What are you planning?'

'You expect me to demand a coup? No, nothing so dramatic, but you are my Mortal-Aspect now and I dub you the Iron General. A general is nothing without an army behind him – to serve all of the Gods, you must ensure the armies of the Farlan are mobilised and ready to fight.'

'How do I go about that?'

'You will find a way.'

'Count Vesna,' the mage interrupted in his dead tone. Vesna assumed it was meant in a questioning way.

'Yes, Lord Fernal,' he said, gathering his wits.

'Will you serve me?'

'I will, my Lord. Do you have any further orders?'

'Yes. Lord Isak's directions included orders to send his Personal Guard to King Emin's service. I do not know why, but I intend to respect his wishes.'

'As you command, sir.'

'Good. Can you tell me how Lord Isak died?'

'I . . .' The words caught in Vesna's throat and he felt his armoured hand tighten into a fist. 'He died in battle with Lord Styrax. While fending off a dragon, he advanced alone on the Menin Army.'

'Why would he do that?'

'To save us.' Vesna felt his hand start to shake and realised it was because he was clenching his hand so tightly. 'The army was in danger of being obliterated, so he sacrificed himself.'

'I understand,' came the maddeningly level response. 'It must—'

Before he could finish the sentence the mage's eyes flew open, an expression of pain crossing his face, and he fainted into the waiting arms of his attendant.

Vesna cursed under his breath; he would learn nothing more now for a week at least. As soon as the attendant had confirmed the mage was still breathing Vesna bowed to Torl and stalked out.

With the weight of the Land on his shoulders, he went to find

Major Jachen, commander of Isak's Personal Guard.

It seems I have much to learn about being a God. I can't even enjoy the thought of ruining Jachen's day.

Lord Fernal looked up at the three humans anxiously watching him. 'One of you should speak.'

Tila looked at the other two and cleared her throat. 'If the Penitent troops took such a beating, the cults will have to recruit before they can challenge your authority.'

'Not necessarily,' Lesarl said gloomily. 'The cults have done themselves no favours, but – with your pardon, my Lord – the clerics are at least human, and Farlan. Son of Nartis or no, there'll be plenty of folk who will see you just as a monster.'

Fernal nodded, absentmindedly scratching the fur on his cheek with a long hooked talon. He wore as little as ever, despite the cold vestiges of winter lingering in the Spiderweb Mountains. Only his cloak had changed; upon Lesarl's advice he had replaced it with a fine white cape edged in gold and emblazoned with the snake emblem of Nartis.

Quitin Amanas, Keymaster of the Heraldic Library, was due later that morning to draw up a crest and colours for Fernal. The new Duke of Tirah might not have pale skin or wear clothes like the rest, but his position in society was set and Lesarl was keen to have every possible custom adhered to.

'My Lord,' High Cardinal Certinse began hesitantly, nervously pinching the scarlet hem of his robes, 'may we return to the matter of a confessor for you? I know it is unpalatable—'

'Unless you find one young and plump, yes, they probably would be,' Fernal interrupted. The three Farlan stared at him in shock until the huge Demi-God shook his head and gave a soft growl. 'Just a joke! That is something I am still allowed to do – despite Cardinal Veck's best efforts.'

From their expressions, the humour was lost on them, so Fernal quickly moved on, 'If you can find an advisor not acting under orders of fanatics I would agree. However, the nature of your tribe is that every man has a master, so I doubt you will.'

Lesarl was quick to agree. 'Cardinal Disten is about the only one who I would trust right now to withstand pressure from his superiors, and suggesting him would negate the point of agreeing to a confessor in the first place!'

'Then keep looking,' Certinse insisted. 'The factions within the cults are becoming increasingly restless – if I can't give them something of substance soon my position will become an irrelevance.'

'How many factions?' Fernal asked.

Certinse grimaced. 'It changes from week to week, but they're beginning to coalesce. Broadly speaking; the Council for Piety is populated by the priests of Vellern, some of Vasle's, and the priests and chaplains of Nartis. The God of the Birds may have only a minor temple here, but Vellern was more hurt by the abomination in Scree than any other and these days, it's zealotry that counts, not seniority.

'The Adherents are driven by my own cardinal branch and some of Death's priests; the Warriors of the Pantheon are comprised of priests of Karkarn and Vasle, with Lady Amavoq's bitch-priestesses weighing in because they're determined not to be out-done in matters of spite.' Certinse wearily shook his head. 'Amavoq was not even one of those affronted in Scree.'

Fernal's brow crumpled even more as he counted the Gods that had been mentioned. There had been six affected by the minstrel's spell in Scree, six Gods whose cults had been taken over by fanatics. 'There is one more God to account for?'

'Aye, Belarannar's followers have allied with the remainder of Death's. What they call themselves now I couldn't tell you; it changes on a weekly basis.' Certinse held up his hand before Fernal could speak again. 'That is only a most simplistic view; there are schisms, rogue elements and the Gods only know what else going on right now, but I think most of the rest will only cause trouble for each other. I know of at least a dozen deaths of ordained men and women at the hands of their own.'

'Aside from those you yourself ordered killed?' Lesarl asked acidly, waving away the High Cardinal's indignation. 'Enough. I will find some concession we can give you. Your clerk is a handy man with a knife and Senior Penitent Yeren should be able to handle anyone they send now the Temple of the Lady is not accepting commissions.'

Certinse rose and bowed to Lord Fernal. 'Tell that to Unmen Telles,' he muttered in a resigned voice. 'She had her head ripped off by an Aspect of Vellern, so I heard.' Not waiting for a response he headed for the door.

He paused to straighten his robes and to stand a little more upright. Waiting in the corridor was his staff, six priests of different cults, all with sharp eyes and even sharper tongues.

A good thing I renounced my bond with Nartis years ago, Certinse thought as he glared at the first man to blurt out a question. *I have so many masters now; I don't think I could serve a God as well.*

The High Cardinal – with his attending party of priests and penitents – travelled by carriage back to the Domon Enclave in the east district of Tirah. The compound of beautiful, grand old buildings constructed around three large quadrangles served as the administrative hub of the cult of Nartis. At its heart was a temple to Nartis as fine as any in the Land, but restricted for use by clerics and the nobility. The stone temple spire and its surrounding framework of wrought iron dwarfed the entire eastern half of the city. It had been designed to attract the arrows of their patron God during Tirah's regular storms.

Not even the sight of the enclave in all its glory was able to lift Certinse's gloom. Normally the sight of the manicured lawns, soaring architecture and myriad Aspect shrines never failed to inspire him; he had walked these stone cloisters as a young man, marvelling at the wealth and power on display, dreaming of the day his family would secure the very post that he had, perversely, been given in the end by his enemies.

'Stop the carriage,' he ordered suddenly as they passed through into the enclave.

Ignoring the questions from his shepherding priests he stepped down and shut the door firmly behind him. The driveway between the main gate and the warden's office where all guests were received was no more than forty yards. Certinse waved the carriage on and stood alone for a while in the cold, watching the sun momentarily break through the clouds and cast its light over the rooftops.

'What am I doing?' he muttered to himself, waiting until the sun had disappeared once again before setting off down the driveway. There were few people about in the outer grounds today, and none willing to pay too close attention to the High Cardinal.

'For the first time in years, perhaps in my entire life, I feel like praying,' he murmured to himself with a wry smile. 'Has that ever happened before? Before I was old enough to understand it I knew my family were different, that Nartis was not our lord. Did I ever make that choice, or did I just do what I was told?'

He shook his head, knowing he was well past questions such as that. 'And now I have an urge to pray. And what holds me back?' He paused, considering. 'I suppose it is the fear of what might happen. However weak my link to Nartis might be these days, he might respond to the office I hold, even if the man himself is nothing to him.'

Reaching the central quadrangle he looked up to the windows of his private rooms and saw his aide, Brother Kerek, looking down from the chapel window.

What's he doing in there? Certinse wondered, and stepped up his pace a little.

Nodding absentmindedly to priests on the way, he made his way to his rooms, ignoring the salutes of his guards as they opened the doors for him. As he walked through the austere audience hall used for greeting chaplains and low priests he realised a monk holding a letter was waiting on him ... and the letter in his hand reminded Certinse that he had written to several abbots recently and had no response ... but that was something that could wait.

'Brother, I have an urgent matter to attend to. Please wait here and I will have my aide summon you presently,' he said, barely pausing.

The monk bowed his assent as a second pair of guards admitted Certinse to his formal reception room, used for more notable guests but presently containing only Senior Penitent Yeren, who was sleeping off his latest hangover.

Certinse scowled, ignoring the guards chuckling at their commander's state, but he didn't bother to start another argument. Most likely Kerek had news for him; one of the few places they could talk without other priests listening in was in the High Cardinal's private chapel, which was forbidden to those of other cults.

As he walked through his private study to the chapel he called softly, 'Kerek?' The vicious little clerk turned, an enquiring look on his face. 'Yes, your Eminence?'

'Well? What is it?' Certinse asked gruffly. 'I assume you're in here for a reason and I don't believe it's a love of Nartis.'

His aide frowned. 'Your Eminence, you ordered me to wait for you here.'

Certinse opened his mouth to deny doing any such thing when he heard the door open behind him and the Senior Penitent strode in. Before Certinse could protest, the mercenary had his left arm out wide and was hugging Certinse to his chest.

A white-hot pain flared in Certinse's back and wrapped its way around his body. He felt as though his ribs were on fire. Yeren kept on moving, his powerful arm keeping the High Cardinal upright as he bore him backwards.

Kerek started to move, but he faltered at the sight of Yeren storming towards him, so shocked that he didn't even raise his arms to defend himself as Yeren hacked his broadsword into his scrawny neck.

The aide dropped like a stone, blood spraying out over the highly polished wooden floor. His legs kicked once and fell still, but Certinse, himself paralysed with pain, saw none of it. He stared up at Yeren as the mercenary surveyed the room, then checked back the way he'd come. Certinse's body spasmed and he wheezed in pain, but as much as he wanted to, he couldn't find the strength to scream. His body rigid in agony, he watched Yeren's expression change from grimly professional to calculating wariness, until, finally, he allowed himself a small smile of relief.

'That went well, don't you think?' Yeren said quietly to Certinse. 'Weren't sure how quick Kerek was going to be there. Still, he were just a priest in the end, however much he liked his knife.'

All Certinse could manage was a small 'gah' of wordless pain, which served only to increase Yeren's smile.

'Aye, hurts like a bastard, don't it? My advice is to try not to scream, not when you got a knife in yer lung. You'll just make it worse, and you already pissed yerself, which ain't fitting for a man o' the cloth.'

Yeren peered over Certinse at Kerek's corpse. 'Good thing you lot ain't priests of Death,' he said brightly, 'I hear some o' them dabble in a bit of necromancy on the side. Wouldn't want anyone callin' up yer spirit and askin' who did this.'

Certinse felt a chill start to seep into his legs. He tried to push Yeren away, but the slightest movement sent a spike of pain down his back and he could do nothing to fight the man.

'Yeah, I know,' Yeren continued in an almost sympathetic voice, 'but I can't be dealin' with any o' that "last dying breath" crap. We'll stand here 'til you pass out, which shouldn't be long now, and I'm sure yer beyond savin' – better that than I stick you a dozen times to make sure.'

Certinse listened dumbly to the sequence of his death, unable to respond or even move. Suddenly words from his childhood appeared in his memory, prayers of repentance he hadn't spoken in earnest for decades. Yeren watched his lips move fractionally and nodded, as though his concerns had been confirmed.

'Close yer eyes now, Old Bones hisself won't be long.'

CHAPTER 9

Ilumene couldn't stop himself grinning. Despite the early hour and the dew seeping into his breeches, he found himself waiting with a handful of others to ambush a deranged dragon – it was so daft, it was hilarious. They lurked under a damaged roof in the ruined building nearest to the Byoran tunnel in the Library of Seasons. Next to him stood the immortal mercenary, Aracnan, who was by contrast, still and entirely emotionless. He looked asleep but Ilumene knew that sleep eluded him, no matter how tired or how hard he tried.

Aracnan was meditating as a way to deal with the pain the King's Man had inflicted upon him, using his millennia of experience to block out the fire in his veins. His hairless skin looked different now, greying and stale where once it had been ivory and full of unnatural vitality. He had lost none of his bulk, but the toll of his shoulder injury was evident to all. Ilumene had fought with the King's Men long enough to know the poison they had used – and the festering hole that would have opened up when Aracnan tried to heal himself with magic.

The stink of Aracnan's flesh was revolting, but Ilumene had spent the summer months in Rojak's company, while the minstrel decayed from the inside out as Scree slowly collapsed. After that he could endure any stink.

'This is crazy,' whispered one of the soldiers for the fourth time that morning. 'Styrax has gone mad with grief.'

His taciturn companion, a white-eye with a mass of scars on his face and throat, grunted in agreement. It was the most noise the man made, and Ilumene was starting to wonder if that was all he could say.

Ilumene's grin widened even more. 'You think?'

He looked over at the valley wall, twenty yards to the left of the Akell tunnel entrance. Tethered to the rock was a thick-shouldered fighting dog. It had been unmuzzled ten minutes ago, but instead of barking to draw the dragon's attention it had settled down and contentedly gone to sleep.

'Foot-traps?' the soldier hissed. 'Ballistae to pin its wings? Soldiers on foot? That's no way to hunt a fucking dragon!'

Ilumene shrugged and patted the crowbill axe he'd brought from the Ruby Tower's armoury. There was a second strapped to his back and a normal axe on the ground behind him; the crowbills were the best thing a man on foot had to pierce a dragon's scales, but if he did, the weapon would most likely lodge there and he'd best have a back-up ready.

'Something of a speciality of yours, is it?' Ilumene asked lightly.

Major Fenter Jarrage, of the Knights of the Temples, was in full battle armour, which told Ilumene that the man hadn't thought too hard about what they were about to do. The white-eye was too, but he looked far stronger and quicker. Despite being the poorest fighter of the four Jarrage nodded emphatically, as though he were a veteran leading a squad of recruits. Just around the cover were four more noblemen from Akell and Fortinn – they were all past forty summers and they were dressed in gaudy hunting leathers, so Ilumene hadn't bothered with their names.

'Done a bit in my time,' the Major went on, 'not dragons, but sand wyverns are close enough, I reckon. Was stationed in Tserol for a time and they would come in from the desert.'

'How would you do it then?'

Jarrage slapped the crossbow slung over his shoulder. 'Bloody regiment with these would be a good start, lined up where we are. They punch through armour well enough; reckon they'll manage dragon scales too, and they're easier to aim than ballistae. Biggest problem is stopping it flying away, you put a hole in its wing, you ain't stopping it, and if it can choose when and how it's going to fight you're lost.'

Ilumene didn't bother to ask how one got a hundred cross-bowmen out of those tunnels without making a sound, nor point out the bolts wouldn't go deep enough to do much more than irritate a gigantic, deranged, fire-breathing dragon.

Nice to know someone's probably going to die before me though. He was well aware that they were all most likely a distraction when it came to the actual killing. They might get a lucky blow in, but it would be someone rather more than human who did the real damage.

No, we're not just a distraction, Ilumene reminded himself. *Styrax is building himself a legend and he needs witnesses. They say he killed a daemon-prince in Thotel and won over the Tachrenn of the Ten Thousand – now he's going to add a dragon to the tally of his kills.*

Even Ilumene had to admit it was an impressive list; killing Lord Isak was nowhere near the greatest feat Styrax had achieved, notable though it was.

Show the priests you can face down and kill a daemon-prince. Show the commoners you're a dragonslayer. Remind the soldiers like me you cut down Koezh Vukotic, one of the greatest swordsmen in history. If my loyalty were up for grabs I'd be persuaded.

'Bugger this for a game of soldiers,' Ilumene announced suddenly. 'I'm bored now.'

He picked up a broken stone the length of his thumb and threw it with unerring accuracy at the dog. The stone thwacked into its flank, causing the dog to wake and yelp. It looked up and Ilumene waved to attract its attention, swearing at it under his breath. The fighting dog jumped to its feet and began barking as loudly as it could, straining at the chain tethering it to the cliff. The sound echoed around the still valley, strangely loud as it reverberated back off the cliffs.

'Piss and daemons, Kayel!' Jarrage exclaimed, hurriedly winding back the mechanism of his crossbow and slotting a bolt into place. He did have a halberd as back-up for the slow-loading crossbow and Ilumene was keen to see how that fared, albeit from a suitable distance.

'I've got a busy afternoon planned,' Ilumene said with a cruel grin and turned to Aracnan to attract the Demi-God's attention. His eyes were open and Ilumene saw a moment's confusion before Aracnan focused on the barking dog and remembered where he was.

'It is time,' Aracnan said, and he rose to one knee with a wince.

His right arm was bound to his chest to keep the wound from working further open, but Ilumene knew he was as capable with his left arm. Aracnan drew his black sword and Ilumene saw the

Crystal Skull he possessed moulded around the guard – the Skull called Knowledge that Aracnan had taken from the original owner, though he had claimed it had been destroyed. Although any use of magic would cause Aracnan unbelievable pain, the Skull's power could still augment that of his sword. The blade's surface was swirling and surging with pinpricks and trails of faint light, like a meteor shower in the sky.

Ilumene reminded himself of the plan, such as it was. Ballistae were hidden inside the two tunnels. Behind one were three Litse white-eyes, the Jesters and a Ruby Tower captain, while Lord Styrax, General Gaur and four more Menin were positioned behind the other.

The dragon would be attracted by the noisy snack, then snagged by the foot-traps that, with luck, would keep it distracted long enough for the ballistae to wound it and keep the beast on the ground. After that Ilumene had stopped listening to the briefing. He was confident Styrax would be the one to kill it; all he had to do was concentrate on staying alive.

On cue a low sound rumbled across the valley like distant thunder. The fighting dog hesitated and stared into the distance, then started to bark a challenge. Ilumene kept his eyes on it, moving to one knee and working his muscles to loosen them up after the wait.

The only real armour he was wearing were the long steel-backed gloves he used to cover the scars on his arms. The rest of his outfit was tailored black linen, like he'd worn when still a member of the Narkang Brotherhood, and a stiffened brigandine. It wouldn't stop the dragon's claws, but it might protect his ribs if he was knocked flying.

A second rumbling growl was followed by a single whoosh of wings against the air. The dog faltered, turning in a circle, trying to run and bark, while keeping its eyes on the dragon. Ilumene followed the beast's approach by watching the dog, gauging distance by the increasingly frantic barks.

Two more wing-beats, then a thump as the dragon landed. From the sound it was just around the corner of the building. For a moment it didn't move, then there was a loud hissing rasp, like a snake moving through leaves, and the dog yelped in fear as the creature advanced into view.

Ilumene gaped for a moment; it was vast, bigger than any living creature he'd ever seen. The dragon's body was long and lithe with a bulky knot of muscle at the base of its wings, a deep emerald colour that shone in the pale winter light. It had three sets of black horns; one shorter pair swept low and forward to protect its throat, a long recurved pair above those and a third set pointing back to complete the protection of its head. The dragon's muzzle was thick and snub-nosed, sporting a large pair of upper canines – inelegant but powerful.

Ilumene glanced over at the tunnel doors. They remained closed, ready to jerk back the moment the order came.

'Now's our chance,' he breathed, looking back at the dragon. Its wings were half-furled, doubled over, but standing high on its back like a butterfly's. 'Gods, it's a perfect target.'

He jumped to his feet, waving frantically towards the tunnel doors. 'Now! Now, you bastards!' Ilumene screamed as loud as he could, 'Fire!'

The dragon snarled and jerked its head around. Seeing them it half-turned, pushing up from the ground with its powerful fore-limbs, but dropping back with a jolt as one snagged. The beast roared with fury and lunged forward but the movement was awkward as a second cable on the ground hooked its rear talons.

'Fire, you bastards!' Ilumene roared again, waving his axe madly to keep the dragon concentrating on him.

For a moment nothing happened and he felt a cold trickle of terror run down his spine, from the left a black bolt flashed across the valley and sped past the dragon, causing it to rear up in surprise and rage. Now it was facing the doorway where the shot had come from. It roared at the new threat, a deep bellow magnified by the cliff-walls that Ilumene felt like a blow to the head.

He clapped his hands over his ears, taking a step back as the dragon moved and the cables hidden under the turf whipped up like striking snakes. Before the creature could take the strain and rip the cables from the ruined building they were anchored to, a black spot appeared in the centre of one of the pale green wings and caused it to billow like a sail.

The dragon reeled from the blow, its right wing pitching over its back before it caught its balance. It roared again, and tried to leap up into the air to gain some advantage, but only one wing opened and the powerful jump became an ungainly fall as its right wing remained folded, pinned by the fish-hooked ballistae bolt caught in it.

'Come on!' Ilumene yelled to his companions, feeling the familiar sense of bloodlust welling up inside.

The others jumped up and Aracnan moved alongside Ilumene. Out of the corner of his eye Ilumene saw a flash of white and realised the winged Litse white-eyes had emerged, but he didn't slow his charge. The dragon had its back to him, concerned only with the source of the bolt. With an ear-splitting roar the dragon spat a gout of flame towards the door. Ilumene couldn't see what it hit, but he took the opportunity to close the ground, crow-bill axe raised above his head.

He and Aracnan reached the dragon together. Ilumene ran up the beast's planted hind leg and jumped off it, throwing himself up onto the body of the beast so he could put his entire weight behind the blow Aracnan headed for its belly. While its wing was still outstretched Ilumene slammed the axe below the muscles at the wing's base.

The axe bit in, and was torn from his grip, and Ilumene rolled clear as the dragon bellowed again, recoiling from the blow and rearing, just as Aracnan struck. The Demi-God dropped at the last minute and let his momentum carry him right underneath the creature's body, slashing its belly as he passed.

Ilumene fought his way upright. As he scrambled away he glimpsed two Litse in the sky above him, hurling javelins at the dragon's armoured head. A moment later he ducked as he heard the thwack of a crossbow bolt strike the dragon's scales and glance off, followed by the deeper thunk of the tail against an armoured body. Ilumene threw himself to the ground and crawled out of range as fast as he could.

Once back he saw figures surrounding the dragon, all looking pathetically small against it. One of the Litse swooped too low, trying to get close enough to hit its eyes, and the dragon bit like a striking snake. The Litse howled as his leg was caught and he was dragged from the sky, tossed up and bitten again before being thrown away and crashing in a broken heap against the cliff. One of the hunting noblemen tried to exploit its distraction, but while the dragon snapped at another Litse it crushed him with a foot.

Ilumene pulled his dagger and cut the ties that affixed his second axe to his back, catching it as it dropped. The dragon's head swung past him, focusing on the noblemen running at it. With a flick of its tail the dragon bowled the pair over, swatting them with ease. As that happened the Jesters ran forward with long easy strides, their weapons drawn but in no apparent rush. Captain Latiar of the Ruby Tower was behind them, carrying a boar-spear, but they all leapt away when the dragon spat a ball of flame at them.

The nearest Jester wasn't quick enough. His leg was caught by the unnatural flames and in a moment the fire had caught on his clothes and it had swept up to consume his entire body before anyone could attempt to help him. The Demi-God's grey-skinned brothers watched the thrashing figure for a moment, all emotion hidden by their leather masks, then charged again. The dragon raked at the air with its dextrous forelimb, forcing both to stop, or be eviscerated.

And a black-armoured figure leaped from the cliff-face onto the creature's back.

The dragon reared again, roaring furiously as Lord Styrax hacked down at the shining green scales underfoot. The impact of sword and scales produced an explosion of light that momentarily blinded Ilumene, and when his eyes cleared he saw the dragon had reached around to gore Styrax, only to have one of its long horns chopped in half by his fanged broadsword. The dragon snarled and shook Styrax off its back. The white-eye seemed to be expecting the move, leaping clear and rolling to his feet in one smooth movement. The dragon clawed at him with a forelimb and he threw himself aside, rolling again as it furrowed the ground.

The dragon turned to follow him, swinging its tail around in a wide arc to keep the remaining Jesters clear. Its head dipped again and Ilumene saw a blast of red sparks from Styrax's sword as he warded off the blow. The white-eye struck back, two swift blows that missed, but gave him enough time to leap left again and avoid being gored. A green haze suddenly filled the air around the dragon and the Jesters cried out, covering their faces as though a sudden inferno had flared up.

Darting streams of emerald light began to race through the air like hunting swallows, arrowing down at Styrax and forcing him to parry strike after strike. A heartbeat later and his sword flared red, and the streams started to explode as Styrax struck them. Once the majority had been destroyed Styrax chanced another blow at the dragon, the light of his sword extending from the tip like a whip to slash across its broad chest again and again. The dragon spat fire at him, but a white shield appeared between the two and the fire was absorbed. It tried to turn and bring its tail to bear, hammering it down towards Styrax's head, but he battered it aside.

The white-eye reached forward with his scarred left hand and grabbed at the air, drawing the white shield back to his body. As it reached him the magic expanded and became a swirling ball of blistering energy. He planted his feet and threw the ball forward, where it exploded on the dragon's chest. The impact drove it upright, its one good wing spreading to steady it. It was the opportunity Styrax had been waiting for, and he was already moving.

He threw himself forward in a blaze of magic and lunged with his fanged sword. The points bit and drove deep between the scales of the dragon's forelimbs. The dragon howled and raked down, an explosion of emerald fire and sparks obscuring them for a moment before it cleared.

Styrax was still standing. He cut left and right, severing one clawed toe entirely, and the dragon slammed its head down, unmindful of the risk, and sideswiped Styrax before he could reverse his sword, knocking the Menin lord from his feet.

General Gaur saw the danger and tried to buy Styrax time, throwing his huge axe so the dragon had to dodge instead of ready-ing itself for the killing blow. The beast warrior hurled himself aside to avoid the dragon's lashing tail that crashed down a moment later.

Ilumene blinked. Styrax was up again, rising higher than any normal man could and hacking at the dragon's neck. Through a mist of blood and magic Styrax struck again, then cut upwards with a reverse-blow. The injury didn't seem to slow the dragon, but this time its attempt to gore Styrax was parried and he caught it a glancing blow on the jaw before it pulled back.

Shapes appeared around Styrax's head, too fast for Ilumene to make out before they exploded in white sparks. In response Styrax cut a circle in the air, a trail of golden light spinning and coalescing in its wake. The dragon lashed down, gripping the ring with its claws to rip it away. Somehow it held long enough for Styrax to duck underneath and cut upwards at the dragon's stunted dew-claw.

The dragon jerked back immediately, forelimb curling protectively inwards, and Styrax moved closer, sword swinging across his body to fend off its other set of claws. It lunged down at him again with its horns, only to be smashed aside with a sudden flare of magic that opened up its defences. Styrax immediately hacked deep into its massive jaw, putting his full weight into the blow.

The beast reeled and as it pulled back Styrax swung up in another long loop. A golden arc appeared above the dragon's head, yanking it down as he tugged at the air with his left hand. The head came back into range and Styrax roared with triumph as he hacked into its throat with all his unnatural strength.

Not trusting that to be the killing blow he struck again and again while the golden tether held it, but still somehow the beast strained and burst through the restraint. Styrax grabbed a handful of empty air and pulled himself higher off the ground to chop again at the dragon's long neck. He was forced to twist in midair and barely avoided the lunging jaws.

He grabbed the dragon's horns for leverage and somehow hauled himself up so he could slam Kobra's double-tip into its throat, thrusting up with the huge broadsword as he dragged down on the horn. Surrounded by a glittering corona of magic Styrax forced the head down below his body and hacked into the wound as hard as he could.

Dragon head and white-eye fell to the ground together. Styrax was up in a flash to cut again at the beast, but Ilumene could see it was unnecessary. The dragon's huge body convulsed and spasmed briefly, then slumped still.

It was dead, but Styrax didn't stop, slashing at the corpse with all the fury of an enraged white-eye, with all the passion of a man grieving. When finally he realised it was over the beast's head was attached only by a few sinews. He let his sword fall from his hands, forgotten, and slumped to his knees. The echoes faded and a sudden silence fell over the scene.

Ilumene looked around. Even the Jesters looked stunned by the battle they had witnessed. It had been mere moments since Styrax had leaped into the battle. Neither of the surviving Demi-Gods had managed to take a step closer. Their sword-tips rested on the grass. The dispassionate Ilumene had to remind himself to breathe again as he stared at the figure in black armour.

Styrax knelt with his head bowed, a foot away from a horn almost as long as his own body, staring at the corpse but not making a sound. Slowly, carefully, he got to his feet and retrieved his sword, wiping it and sheathing the weapon before he turned his back on them all.

And you thought to fight him, Lord Isak? Ilumene thought with wonder and scorn. *As a pawn of Azaer's machinations you were a fool. As a boy trying to choose his own destiny, you were even worse. It's a shame you were so keen to run towards your own death. I'd have enjoyed that moment when you realised you never stood a chance against us.*

CHAPTER 10

For once King Emin slept late, only waking mid-morning at the hysterical chatter of a blackbird somewhere close to his bedroom window. Camatayl Castle was quiet despite the hour. He got out of bed and pulled on the nearest clothes before pushing open the shutters to look out of the window.

The fields beyond were largely empty, just a few dozen shaggy goats and a herder perched on a drystone wall. The tower walls were so thick that he had to lean right out before he could see the nearest of Kamfer's Ford's buildings. A gust of cold air chased him back inside the room and he pulled the shutter with him. He'd need another layer before he headed outside.

In the next room he found Sir Creyl, Commander of the Brotherhood, and one of their newer recruits, Kap Daratin. Sir Creyl, a former gangster, sat in the furthest corner so he could watch both entrances to the room. Despite there not being enough room at the small table, Daratin was trying to do the same, his bowl of rice porridge perched on the corner of the table. The room itself was plain, whitewashed plaster adorned only by a trio of tiny gold-inlaid icons and a simple woven rug on the floor.

The young man flinched when King Emin entered, new enough as a King's Man to have to fight the urge to stand when his monarch entered the room. He came a hair's breadth from tipping the whole bowl into his lap, but like all members of the Brotherhood he had lightning reactions.

'Your Majesty,' the two men said together, with Daratin continuing, 'Shall I fetch you some breakfast?'

Emin nodded. There were servants in the tower, but this wasn't an official trip. Away from the eyes of polite society the Brotherhood usually waited on him; it avoided the requirements of ceremony and protocol. When Daratin had left King Emin took his seat at the table. Sir Creyl gestured towards a clay bottle but Emin shook his head.

'Even watered down I've never had a taste for beer at breakfast.'

Sir Creyl smiled, his ice-blue eyes sparkling. 'It's so weak you can hardly call it beer; best way to start a day.'

'I think I'll start with red tea, thank you. My head feels heavy enough this morning without help.'

'That's not like you; you're usually insufferable from dawn onwards. Why do you think I drink?'

Emin ignored the quip. 'I know, but I don't even feel like I slept. Must have though, I remember dreaming of my son as a toddler, trying to run from a Menin Army.'

'Ah, a new father's fears; I remember them well!' Creyl laughed. 'Why do you think I *started* drinking?'

'It's guilt at leaving so soon. Once things are set up here maybe I'll be able to return to Narkang for a while.'

'Once that old bastard Aladorn is signed on, you'll be well covered here,' Sir Creyl declared. 'He won't refuse you, no matter how old he's got.'

Emin pictured the man who'd helped mastermind his conquest of the kingdom, twenty years previously. General Dall Aladorn had been a cantankerous and belligerent drunk of fifty summers then. Sir Creyl was right that he'd be keen to prove he still had what it took to win a war. Emin's only concern was that the general had pickled his brain out of sheer boredom; he wanted to see the man himself before asking him to prepare for invasion.

'We'll find out when he gets here,' Emin said eventually. 'For the moment, could you give me a moment's peace? Perhaps go and see to our guests' needs?'

Sir Creyl left without a word, recognising the order easily enough. When Daratin returned with a stack of honeyed flat-breads he set the plate on the table and exited quickly himself. Emin picked at the food, his appetite pretty nonexistent. He was just about to give up and ring for his tea when there was a knock at the door.

'What now?' he sighed before calling for the person to enter.

He frowned, not immediately recognising the woman in the long dress with a green scarf half-covering her face. When he did he almost fell off his chair as he scrambled up, reaching for a sword he'd forgotten to buckle to his hip.

'Oh, that's not very friendly,' said the young woman, pointing a slender finger at him and making a sharp downward motion. 'Sit.'

Emin felt an irresistible weight appear on his shoulders and drive him back down into his seat. She stepped forward and gave him a fond smile, one he recognised all too well.

'This can't be,' he muttered. 'It's impossible! What sort of trick is this?'

'Aren't you pleased to see me?' she asked, shutting the door behind her and walking to the centre of the room. Her dress was elegant but old-fashioned, twenty years out of date. She was no more than twenty-five summers old, with bright yellow eyes and auburn hair hanging in a plait over her left shoulder.

'If you really were my sister,' Emin growled with mounting anger, 'then yes, I would be delighted. But she's dead. If you're looking to make an enemy of me you're going about it in the right way.'

The woman sat at the table, still smiling. 'You have a life-size painting of her in your throne room and one of the finest buildings in Narkang bears her name, yet you're not glad to see her in all her beauty before you. You humans are fickle.'

Emin didn't reply. His mind was racing, frantically trying to work out who or what would be so casually callous as to wear Gennay's face. After a moment he realised the impersonation was not perfect; Gennay Thonal's eyes had been a glittering ice-blue, like her younger brother's.

It's a God, it must be – and if my guess is right, one not usually clothed in female flesh.

'Another wager won,' Emin said grimly. 'Morghien told me I was being arrogant when I suggested one of you would make me an offer.'

'But did you expect me?' asked the yellow-eyed God, unperturbed that its guessing game was already over.

'The list of suspects wasn't long. Few of the Pantheon would deign to visit me nowadays.' Emin took a breath to regain his composure. 'If you want a Mortal-Aspect, your best bet is the man who was here a few nights past.'

'Daken?' she said, laughing. 'Oh please; the man is useful for getting rid of inconveniences, but you insult me by suggesting it.'

She tilted her head in thought. 'At any rate the man bears something of a grudge. I don't believe he's suitably grateful for the gifts bestowed upon him.'

Emin gaped. 'He's aligned to your Trickster Aspect, Larat! I can't believe Litania has an agreeable influence on anyone's life, but to be her plaything . . . ?'

The God of Magic and Manipulation shrugged. 'He thrives, what more does a white-eye wish for? It smacks of ingratitude. Nevertheless, to link myself to that oaf? I would prefer a Mortal-Aspect to complement my intellect, not muddy the waters.'

'He's no fool,' Emin countered, 'and if you think to win me by flattering my intelligence—'

Larat raised a hand to cut him off. 'Your intelligence is what it is; your ego equally so. Concerning Mortal-Aspects, let us say I remain unconvinced. A bold move, perhaps, but as I see it, one yet to bear fruit.'

'Then why are you here?' asked Emin, mystified. 'Your Lord has made His feelings towards me most clear. You could find few breakfast companions more out of favour with Lord Death. I am barred from His temples; I will not receive any aid from Him or His followers . . .'

'How you must be weeping into your pillow,' Larat broke in. 'Are your feelings stung? Let me offer this salve; Death is lord of us all and as we are assailed, so He bears the brunt of it. He has lost many followers and Aspects – one of whom has bloomed in the meantime – so do not imagine you are so special in His treatment of you.'

'Why are you here?' Emin repeated. He didn't really expect a straight answer – that was not in Larat's nature – but he'd had an uneasy night and his patience was worn thin.

'Can I not enjoy the company of mortals? As you can imagine, Lord Tsatach's sense of humour is somewhat limited. After a few centuries one has heard them all.'

Despite his ill temper Emin pictured the few Chetse he'd known in his life and almost smiled at the image. Then he caught himself and realised it was the God's attempt to manipulate his mood. He dug his thumbnail into his finger as hard as he could, something Morghien had taught him. Pain sharpened the mind, just as the glamour of the Gods dulled it.

'Might I suggest you pay your social calls on someone with a little less to do? I have guests I must speak to.'

'Ah yes, the intriguing Legana, that shadow of herself. One of many interesting new flavours to this Land. Still, when things get desperate and down to the bone I find it is ancient methods that serve us best.'

Emin's eyes narrowed, sensing the significance of what he was being told, without understanding it. 'The ancient isn't really my domain; I leave that to others.'

The God wearing his sister's face smiled indulgently. 'Time you paid it a little more attention. This kingdom of yours isn't what we planned for humanity, but some of us appreciate that change comes to all things. Mild impieties and direct threats to the greatest of Gods aside, it stands as a better future for the Land than others.'

'Please, enough of the flattery,' Emin said. 'My queen would be upset if I started getting a high opinion of myself.'

'I can remind you of your inadequacies easily enough,' Larat said, 'but I see no profit in doing so at present.'

Larat leaned forward and put one elbow on the table, resting her chin on one hand with a fluid motion that no mortal beyond a Harlequin could achieve.

Emin recognised the pose, from the painting of Gennay, but the gesture only hardened his resolve.

'The Farlan are in chaos,' Larat continued, 'something that will only increase in the years to come. Lord Styrax is building himself an empire and collecting artefacts powerful enough to kill Gods. It is only a matter of time before he crosses your borders.'

'That I know. I'm already making preparations.'

'But have you yet realised why he is collecting these artefacts?'

'I don't know enough about them to deduce that.'

Larat's young face was now stern and serious. 'The Skulls are objects from the dawn of time. Aryn Bwr found them and reforged them to their present form, but they are far older, and the last king's changes were not extensive, however ingenious.'

'But what is their significance? Did Aryn Bwr upset the balance of the Land by reforging them?'

'In unison there is very little they cannot do. It is no coincidence that they number twelve.'

'Twelve?' Emin hesitated. 'The Upper Circle of the Pantheon?

That little detail has been omitted from every scripture I've ever read. And does it go further than that? Are you aligned to a specific Skull, bound to it, even?'

'The bearer of each is permitted to ask a question of the one aligned to it. Some knowledge should not be shared – the very act *would* upset the balance of the Land.'

'I don't understand what you are telling me, what you're asking of me.'

'There are forces in this Land that would like the balance to be upset, things to come undone.'

'Who? The Vukotic family?'

'Among others. What I am telling you is to survive – to keep the Land a place where the Gods are still welcome. It is the natural order of things; without it you will find this world far less of a paradise than it is at present.

'Lord Styrax was a mistake of ours – when Aryn Bwr's soul did not find its way to Ghenna we knew he had prepared some sort of contingency plan.'

'If you're so concerned,' Emin broke in, 'why not take a stand? Damned by Death or not, I'm not as powerful as a God of the Upper Circle. And somehow I suspect you're not here to announce the Gods will march with me against Lord Styrax.'

Emin felt the room grow cold as Larat stiffened in her seat. 'We have learned that lesson already.'

'To let others do the killing for you?'

'To not allow others to murder the divine,' Larat said, a warning look in her eyes. 'One of our kin has already died in this war; we do not intend others to run that risk.'

'You would run such risks to avoid even one of your kin dying? This is a war you could win – if you were willing to accept losses.'

'Losses are unacceptable,' Larat snapped, 'as are too many of the Upper Circle being weakened. None of our own will ally against the Upper Circle, but do not think we are so united that the victors in any war wouldn't risk being turned on by their own kind. The majority rule of the Upper Circle prevents lesser Gods falling like jackals upon each other, but with losses – or more weakened, as Ilit was at the Last Battle – a new war might be sparked.'

Emin was silent a while as he tried to digest what Larat had told him. These were truths unacknowledged in the mortal Land. Just as kings kept secrets from their own people, some things even a king should not know too much about. The fact that a God was sharing secrets was a worrying development.

The king nodded, having to clear his throat before he could speak. 'I understand – it is safer to use mortals than to walk the Land and become a target for your own kind – and daemons too, perhaps?'

So completely was his last comment ignored that Emin guessed he had scored a hit.

'Kastan Styrax was intended to be the Saviour of the tribes of man, the leader to defeat Aryn Bwr when he returned. Our mistake was to make the man too powerful, too skilled, and he turned against us.' For a moment Larat's expression fell blank, further reminding Emin that the God only wore his sister's image. Gennay had been an animated, passionate girl. Her face had never been so blank until death.

'Aryn Bwr was only defeated when we forced a decisive confrontation; until then he had avoided large-scale battle because he knew Death and Karkarn in particular were too powerful for him. Follow his example; history's lessons should be learned well.'

Larat stood. 'And now it is time for you to wake up,' the God said with a snap of the fingers.

Emin's head jerked up from the table. He looked around, bleary-eyed and dizzy, his senses trying to resolve the conflict as he moved into a position he thought he was already occupying. He was at the small table where Daratin's porridge was still cooling, a waxy film on its surface. He pushed himself to his feet, groaning at a building ache in his head. It felt like he had a hangover as bad as any he remembered, a crown of thorns within his skull that scratched and scraped.

'Damn Gods,' he muttered, heading for his bedroom to find appropriate clothes for the rest of the castle, 'like frisky old spinsters. The more you run from them, the more interested they are in you.'

She waited all day, barely moving from her concealed hollow, while the Elves fussed and prepared at the stream below. Unused to feelings of any kind, the Wither Queen found time to savour what ran through her now: a strange sense of anticipation and excitement, coupled with an innate apprehension.

They are inventive, these mortals. How their hatred has driven them!

The small camp had been at the stream for weeks preparing the ground, but now a team of slaves had arrived and were readying the ground upstream for the final stage. It was fascinating – and horrifying. When the Wither Queen had come across the camp, deep in the empty forest and far from prying Farlan eyes, she had been about to scour it clean when her spirits had noticed a strange shrine.

She had probed the ground with infinite patience and care, careful to avoid the notice of the two mages who were there so she could watch them at her leisure. They would all die soon enough, that was beyond doubt, but their actions had intrigued her. The shrine had awakened some sense of curiosity she had not known she possessed. That flicker had grown stronger when she found a second shrine not far downstream.

Two shrines? But Elves do not pray.

The entire race had been cursed, cast out after the Great War, so what were they doing playing with shrines? She sent her darting spirits out to watch and listen, before some innocuous comment had allowed the truth to flower in her mind.

They were farming.

Astonishingly – born of desperation, and a hunger for any small measure of revenge – the Elves were farming Gods.

The Wither Queen fought to control the screaming rage inside her when she realised, but it hadn't taken long for her fury to be eclipsed by something else: the desire for power, the recognition of an opportunity there for the taking.

The spirits the mages had enslaved were, in some fashion, local Gods. The difference was power, the quintessence of Godhood: they were made of magic, and changed by it, moulded by the elements they were associated with and the worship they received.

Like some insects had different stages of growth which bore no resemblance to the others, except at their core, so the spirits the Elves had found were unlike the Gods ... they were at an early stage, and they could be controlled, and cultivated, and developed into weapons.

She could not imagine how many such shrines there might be

hidden in the forest. Their prophets must have given them warning of Aryn Bwr's impending rebirth, and while the Elven race was broken and scattered, some semblance of order must have remained for them to maintain their systems of nobility and slavery.

Her lips widened into a sliver of a smile at the thought of this practice extended throughout the Great Forest. Little shrines beside each river, lake, hill or copse – anywhere spirits might gather. It was remarkably simple: the mage's acolytes would find a likely spot and prepare the ground, somewhere they had fished, or simply been so thirsty they were sufficiently appreciative of the water to give thanks. They built a small shrine of stones and left an offering. That would be enough to gather the wandering, formless spirits found throughout the Land, restlessly searching for purpose, for belief, for praise.

While keeping the mages well away the prayers would continue, the offerings too, until one spirit had latched onto the shrine and made the place its home. A shape would start to develop, a presence or image, the more worship that took place. This stream had two shrines with different characteristics: the upper stretch was deep and fast and the lower was shallower and slower, so two spirits could be attracted to a relatively small stretch of water.

Given time the two would come into conflict and one would be absorbed by the victor; the Wither Queen knew that all too well. When a God reached a certain power, it was impossible to entirely be subsumed by another God – that was how Aspects were created: linked and subservient, but able to retain some measure of the self. A God strove for power, it was part of their very being, and it might well be that several competing spirits had come across the shrine and tried to make some connection with the acolyte before the strongest won out.

The Wither Queen watched the slaves. They had a great pile of sacks filled with earth and boulders and they were waiting for the order to begin. She thought it might happen during twilight, when the Gods withdrew slightly from the Land; a basic precaution whenever the work was heretical. As the sun dropped the Wither Queen waited with a growing hunger, determined to gather these two more spirits to her. She had already taken more than a score – every Elven mage she had encountered had possessed at least one –

and while they were all very weak, they would grow stronger as she did.

At last the sun began to fall below the horizon and with a clipped command the slaves were set to work damming the stream. They worked quickly, fast enough to panic the spirits inhabiting each stretch. The Wither Queen could imagine them experiencing a new sensation: fear at the prospect of being just a voice on the wind again. They would reach out in whatever direction they could, begging their new followers for help as the flow of water began to dwindle. By some great fortune their followers were mages too, barely children, but with a flicker of talent that was enough to make it an option to those with none.

As the gloaming descended the Wither Queen sensed movement, a sparkle of life and energies. The spirit from the upper section had grown strong enough to have a corporeal self and now it appeared like a ghost before the kneeling acolyte: the outline of a child with wild flowing hair, looking around at the camp but unable to see the others waiting on its fringes. After a while it entered the acolyte and not long after the weaker spirit did the same, but with less hesitation. Once that was done, the inhabited acolyte walked away from the stream while the guards moved in to destroy the shrines, leaving the spirits with no place to return to.

They had started to cart away the stones to dump in the forest when the Wither Queen rose from her hiding place. Her own slaves, some like pale pinpricks of light, the strongest scampering like spectral rats, had encircled the camp by the time she was spotted and the alarm raised. The mages put up a fight, but it was a poor one. Every touch brought their twisted, malformed bodies out in boils and blisters, plague spreading so fast that the last few cut their own throats rather than suffer such horrors.

She didn't care what they did, as long as they were dead. Only the mages mattered; the imperative to scour the forest of Elves was fading from her mind and she felt Lord Isak's compulsion to murder them all gradually wither. She would still do so because of what she was, but once her strength grew beyond a certain point she would be able to kill any mortal, bargain or no bargain. They worshipped her in Lomin, and at the two other shrines set up for that purpose, but it was a feeble thing now that the boy was dead. No bargain lasted beyond death and that meant it would not bind her as soon as worshippers stopped going to the temples.

Once her bargain was broken, then . . . then the more she killed, the more they would flock to praise her – the more they would beg her to spare them. The Wither Queen tasted the fear on the air and smiled. Her time was coming.

CHAPTER 11

Mihn felt that familiar ache of guilt as he set the bowl of food on the bed near Isak's head. It was irrational, he knew, but seeing his friend so changed, his body so battered and abused, was hard to bear. No part of him had been spared; even his eyeballs bore signs of torture. It was not hard to see why the white-eye had retreated deep into himself: the only way to save what scrap of sanity he could.

The daemons had torn and ripped and burned and shredded his flesh, endlessly, feeding on the fear and pain from every new attack – small wonder Isak had cringed when Mihn had sharpened a knife a few days back. He was more careful now, not to do anything that might evoke memories best forgotten.

The witch had delved into Isak's mind to find the blackest knots of horror, and had used her magic to rip them free – but she couldn't get them all. Only the worst had been taken, the memories that could not remain if Isak was ever to speak again, rather than spend any waking minutes shrieking aloud, his sleeping moments sobbing as he relived each horror in his nightmares. Other memories might be lost alongside them; they did not know, but it was a risk they had to take.

Mihn saw Isak's nostrils flare slightly at the scent of food: that faint recognition hadn't yet gone so far as to prompt Isak to action, but it was a start. The puppy lying outstretched next to Isak was more receptive: he stirred and looked up. Mihn wasn't sure what sort of dog it was – though young, it showed the promise of powerful body and legs, and he guessed it was bred for guarding, maybe even fighting, rather than hunting. Right now it tired easily, growing too fast to be boisterous for long, but that would change soon.

The dog yawned wide, its tongue lolling, and thumped its tail against Isak's thigh. It licked Mihn's wrist and started to move towards the bowl, but Mihn moved it out of the puppy's reach and opened Isak's shirt to check on his injuries. He gently removed the witch's poultices, wiped the skin clean and examined the scabs underneath. There was no sign of infection, and the deep cuts were closing nicely – though Mihn had expected Isak to heal unnaturally quickly, he was still a little surprised to see even the broken skull was knitting together well, and where the skin had been ripped away new tissue was growing.

He shuddered. Even with that degree of healing, the injuries were so wide-ranging that from some angles it was almost impossible to recognise the youth he'd first met. The shape of Isak's head had changed with those depressions; patches of scalp had been cut away, along with chunks of his ears. Half his teeth were missing, or had subsequently fallen out, and the line of his jaw indicated at least two breaks ... the litany of damage continued all over his body and Mihn guessed it was only the hours they had spent escaping Ghenna that had allowed the healing to start before they reached the Land.

The puppy gave an excited squeak and began stalking Isak's bowl. Mihn sat back, to watch Isak and see whether he would notice or react. Isak remained staring into space, unfocused, but as the puppy wriggled its way towards the bowl he did at last move an arm to impede it.

Mihn held his breath, hoping this was not coincidence. The puppy tried to squirm out from under Isak's arm and he twisted his body a little – maybe not properly, as if he had noticed the prospective thief, but enough to shield his food.

'Good,' Mihn said lightly, 'you are going to have to keep an eye on that dog, or he'll snaffle every meal I make the moment your back is turned.'

Isak didn't respond, but Mihn hadn't expected him to. His goal was to keep talking normally to Isak, waiting for the words to filter in and remind him of human interaction; he knew it would work eventually.

'Come on, you,' he said to the puppy, who gave an excited little bark. Mihn scooped up the dog up and set him on the ground. The bowl of scraps was devoured in half a minute and once it had finished Mihn played with the puppy, all the while keeping one eye on Isak.

After a while Mihn noticed Isak beginning to move – he was feeling around himself on the bed. His eyes remained unfocused as he stared at the flames in the stove, but his hand was definitely moving with some purpose, albeit in an uncertain, jerky manner, as though he was searching for the puppy. Mihn was sure he had grown used to have it sleeping pressed up against his body; missing its presence was a good step forward ...

Eventually Isak's searching fingers reached the soup and ended up planted firmly in the bowl. Mihn felt a flicker of disappointment. The soup wasn't hot enough to scald, but it wasn't the result he had hoped for. As he watched, Isak slowly withdrew his fingers and, oblivious to the soup dripping onto his blanket, held them up in front of his face, as though trying to work out what to do with them. Tentatively, he brought the fingers up to his mouth and pressed them to his lips.

Mihn scarcely dared breathe as Isak licked the soup from his fingers. For the first time, his gaze left the flames and he looked at the bowl. He still looked glazed, but there were signs of effort in Isak's face, a small spark of animation that gave Mihn heart.

'That's it, Isak, the bowl is just there if you want to eat,' he called softly, rising and going to the bed. He gently guided Isak's hand to the bowl and cupped his fingers around it before helping him to draw it towards his face. Isak was still lying on his side. When the edge of the wooden bowl bumped against his lips his tongue flicked out, as though expecting more soup.

'Just lift yourself up and drink from the bowl,' Mihn encouraged him.

Whether or not Isak heard the words, he did start to move, turning his body until he was almost face-down in the bowl. He started lapping awkwardly at the soup like a dog.

'Well, that is not ideal,' Mihn continued brightly, 'but however you want to start, my Lord. A week with a puppy has taught you something at least – and your table manners were never that impressive anyway.'

Isak positioned his elbows more comfortably under his body and continued to lap at the soup, hands curled protectively around the bowl until it was all finished. Mihn replaced it with the one he had been about to eat himself, and that too was devoured.

'That is more than you have eaten since' – he hesitated for a moment – 'since you came back. How about we try for the privy tonight as well? Wiping you down is not my favourite activity.'

Isak was wearing only a long, open-fronted robe and a knotted piece of cloth that served as a nappy more than preserving his dignity. Mihn's experience with babies was extremely limited, but he assumed they had no regard for when they messed themselves. Luckily, the lessons of childhood were still embedded somewhere in Isak's mind, and he was exhibiting a little more control than a baby. Mihn had resorted to treating white-eye and dog alike: after eating, the two of them were taken outside. It had taken some persistence to get Isak standing up so Mihn could lead him outside, but the alternative was much less palatable to contemplate.

This evening the lake was hushed and still, with few birds disturbing the silence. Mihn looked around as the puppy bounced forward, holding its nose high as it suddenly caught a scent. He felt a little disquieted; it was early for such quiet, but as he turned he caught sight of movement on the water's surface.

With Isak in tow he walked down to the water's edge and peered through the faint moonlit mist. As his eyes adjusted he saw two specks of pale light drifting just above the still surface, and as he watched, one suddenly darted across the other, causing it to hop up in the air. Eventually he realised they were not specks of light, but white creatures catching the moonlight.

'Moondancers,' he whispered to Isak.

The white-eye was standing very still and tense, looking out over the water with his arms wrapped about himself and his body stooped, as though he was cold – though his skin was hot to the touch, as though some part of him resided still in Ghenna and warmed him by it.

Moondancers were not ghosts or spirits, but a rare bird that lived on water. Mihn had found a nest once; they were tiny little things with large webbed feet that allowed them to move across the water's surface as they hunted insects. He smiled as he recalled how, in the daylight, they had been an unimpressive dull grey, but here in the moonlight their feathers caught the light, shimmering weirdly—

Mihn's moment of wonder was abruptly cut off as something

black rose up from the surface and grabbed one of the moon-dancers, dragging it under the water with a loud splash. Mihn frowned. He hadn't realised there was a pike in the lake, or any other sort of predator that would hunt like that. The remaining moondancer had already disappeared into the rushes and a heart-beat later the lake surface was once again as still as glass.

As he scanned the water to see if there was any further sign of movement a low growl came from beside him – not the puppy, it was too deep. When he turned, Isak was still hunched over, with one arm pulled into his chest, but he had lowered his right arm and his hand was balled into a fist. A second splash came from the lake, and the moonlight caught a ring of ripples out on the water, a little closer this time.

Isak gave another growl, his damaged throat giving it an unearthly quality, and Mihn jumped as a light suddenly shone from beside him: Eolis had appeared from thin air in Isak's hand, as though they were still in Ghenna. The sword was shining alarmingly brightly in the moonlight, invitation as much as threat.

Isak did not appear to have noticed its appearance, but he was more alert, poised as though expecting to be attacked. The puppy at his feet was silent, looking at the lake with an air of expectation.

'Time to go back inside,' Mihn said firmly. 'Isak, back into the house.' He tried to push the white-eye in the right direction, and after a few moments Isak allowed himself to be shoved back inside the house, the puppy close beside him. Mihn stood at the threshold and looked back at the lake. There were more ripples on the surface now, and they were barely ten yards from the shore. Quickly he kicked off his boots and shrugged off his coat before picking up the steel-shod staff beside the door. Thus armed he shut the door behind him and stood on one side, keeping in the shadows.

Mihn watched as the ripples drifted closer. He checked the tattoos on his hands in the moonlight, to reassure himself the circles had not been broken by scratches, or anything else. When he turned his hands over the other way, the tips of the leaves tattooed from shoulder to wrist on each arm were revealed, hazel on the left and rowan on the right. A moment later and Mihn felt a slight change descend over him, a warmth that made him sigh with relief. The now-familiar sense of detachment from his surroundings was a welcome indication that the witch's magic still worked. He just had to hope it would be enough to keep him hidden from whatever was stalking them.

A dark shape – a long black head – broke the surface of the lake, followed by forelegs that delicately tested the mud back at the water's edge. After a moment the creature heaved itself forward and Mihn saw a sinuous body with a flattened, abrupt muzzle and four powerful legs. The hind legs were significantly larger, and once the creature had left the water and was standing on firm ground Mihn saw its chin dipped so low it nearly brushed the ground. It moved like an animal hunting

A second one broke the surface just behind it – and Mihn caught sight of something on its back. The creature had a whip-like tail curled forward like a scorpion's but lying almost flat along its back. What chilled him more was the wet gleam of pitted iron chains running from the tail's barb and all along its bony back to trail on the ground behind it.

When it turned slightly and its legs caught the moonlight Mihn saw chains running down its legs to its claws. When the tail rose slightly, the chains clinked as they were lifted. The chains were part of its tail, Mihn realised, like a flail that could be whipped forward at its prey, and this was no natural creature, but a daemon rising from the Dark Place itself, dragging chains of sin after it.

Enkin, Mihn realised with a start, *and seeking a trail they cannot find*. He remembered the stories about the Enkin, but even as a Harlequin he had never truly believed them.

The hounds of Jaishen, they were called, daemons that had hunted Aryn Bwr, the last king of the Elves, for seven millennia, and brought horror in their wake. Many referred to Aryn Bwr as the Great Heretic because he had led the rebellion against the Gods and forged the weapons that had killed many of the Pantheon. No mortal's damnation had been more assured despite the last king's best efforts to be reborn in Isak's mind. Now the last king's soul had been sent to Ghenna, they were without purpose – but it appeared Mihn's harrowing journey had brought at least a taste of Aryn Bwr back to the Land. The witches were sure Aryn Bwr's soul had been torn from Isak as he fell to Ghenna, and Mihn could not doubt it – he would not have been left like forgotten scraps after a kill had the two not been separated completely.

Mindless hunters without prey, he guessed, watching the first lift its body high and taste the air with its tongue. *Unless that prey is Isak now? Do hounds care if they find a different prey to the one whose scent they hunt?*

The daemon turned its head towards the cottage and Mihn felt his hand tighten on his staff. His tattoos wouldn't mask Isak's scent on the ground, nor that of the puppy. It looked directly at him for a long while, then jerked around to the right, to the tree-line, upwind of them. As Mihn watched, the daemon and his hounds moved swiftly away.

Mihn let out a sigh of relief. He'd found the bi-toed tracks of a gentry pack that way – daemons or no, they wouldn't enjoy it if they did track down a score or more of the fierce forest spirits.

As though to confirm his notion, when the Enkin disappeared into the trees Mihn heard a warning hiss, the sound clear and unmistakable in the silent night air, first from the trees where they were heading, then closer to Mihn. Then an inhuman chatter came from deeper in the woods. He scanned the shadows but he could not see the gentry anywhere; they were perfectly hidden, and not about to reveal their location yet.

The Enkin shuffled through the undergrowth, pausing at every warning hiss, but continuing until they had reached the tree-line – when the whole gentry pack began growling, sounding far more threatening now. Mihn tried to follow the sounds, but they came from different directions and he guessed the full pack was there, two dozen males and females, each stronger by far than a human.

Whether they could count or not, the Enkin appeared to come to the conclusion that they were outnumbered. Mihn glimpsed the angled body of one turn and head out back towards the lake, but now they moved so quietly that once the bushes again concealed them only the warning growls of the gentry moving further away told Mihn they were leaving the area.

It took almost a quarter of an hour before there was quiet again, long enough for him to feel the chill settling in his bones. He headed back inside at last, intending to bar the door as soon as he was in, but he stopped short at the sight of Isak, sitting on the edge of his bed. His long legs were stretched out and Eolis rested across his knees. The right knee had been the last of his injuries to heal. Considering the damage, Mihn was expecting Isak to walk with a limp. In spite of the remarkable healing that had taken place, ridges of scarring had changed the shape of the knee entirely.

Mihn stared at the silver sword a while, musing on how it had just appeared from nowhere – from Ghenna. He knew Eolis was bound to Isak's soul even more than the gifts of the Chosen normally were, but the last time he saw it Xeliath had been attacking the Jailor of the Dark with it. Though it was not now needed, the weapon showed no sign of disappearing again. It looked as real, as solid as anything else in the room, however out of place it might be.

Isak suddenly looked up at Mihn, his face so mournful and anguished that Mihn felt the guilt strike him like a kick to the chest.

'It hurts,' the white-eye whispered in a hoarse voice.

Mihn was too stunned to speak for a moment. 'What hurts?' he said eventually.

'Everything,' Isak replied. 'The echo is everywhere.'

Mihn opened his mouth to reply, but Isak turned away and lay down on his bed, Eolis still clutched in his hand. The puppy trotted over, unconcerned, and clambered up too, settling himself on Isak's feet.

Oh Gods, Mihn thought with a heavy heart, *does he remember the pain of the Dark Place? How could any man live with that echo in his bones?*

Mihn slept badly and woke with the dawn. From the taut stillness of Isak's body he guessed the white-eye was also awake, but he still faced the wall, and he did not respond when addressed. Mihn left him alone and wrapped himself in his heavy coat to attend the stove. The sky was overcast and a cold, whipping wind stung his cheeks, but as he watched the puppy bound out to the shore, nose pressed against the ground, Mihn feel the gladness of life again.

He left the dog to his explorations and used the outhouse, then went to check his rabbit snares in the trees. He hadn't caught anything – something had knocked the snare aside without being snagged – so he reset it and returned to drop a line in the lake.

When he reached the cottage he found Isak standing at the water's edge, his robe fluttering in the wind. Without speaking, Mihn went to stand by his side. For a long while they stood and stared down at the rippling water. Despite his desperate desire to hear Isak speak again, Mihn knew the man couldn't be rushed: his mind might not have been broken in Ghenna, but that didn't mean Isak was quite the same man as the one Lord Styrax had killed.

'How long?' Isak said at last in a croaking voice.

'For me or you?'

There was no reply. Mihn continued to watch the steady movement of the water at his feet. The wind was blowing from behind them, and it carried the whisper of leaves.

'Am I alive?'

'Yes, Isak,' Mihn said firmly, 'you are.'

'I don't feel alive.'

Mihn turned and saw puzzlement and pain on Isak's face, the sort of disbelief Mihn had seen on the faces of the mortally wounded as they stared at the haft of the spear or blade that had killed them.

'It will take time, that much is certain,' he said softly. 'Do not expect too much of yourself. What you have experienced would have broken a lesser man.'

'I am not broken?' Isak replied in a whisper that struck at Mihn's heart, but before he could respond there was a gasp from behind them.

Mihn turned quickly, stepping in front of Isak protectively until he saw Chera, a girl who lived in the nearest village, standing by the tree-line. She had several times brought supplies from the witch, though she had never entered the cottage. Now she stared aghast at the two of them, not noticing when Mihn waved her forward.

Pulling his coat tight around his body, Mihn hurried over. Chera had barely twelve summers, but she was a sensible girl, and the witch had entrusted her with a number of tasks. Though she had been wary of the newcomer in their midst, she had never looked terrified, as she did now, staring at Isak.

'Chera, what is wrong?'

'It's the ragged man,' she whispered, eyes wide with fear. 'Don't you see 'im?'

'Of course I see him; he is a friend of mine.'

As soon as he said that Chera dropped her bundle and began to back away. 'Friend?' she gasped. 'The ragged man's a stealer o' souls!'

Mihn shook his head. Llehden had its own folklore; the region was one well-known for its particular spirits and ghouls. The stories weren't entertainment to the locals but rules to live by, otherwise their babies would be stolen by the Coldhand folk, and travellers snared by the gifts of the Finntrail or hunted down by Eyeless Sarr.

'He is no spirit,' Mihn gently chided, realising she was on the point of fleeing, 'just an injured man who needs my help remembering who he is.'

Chera shuddered and her mouth fell open as she began to cry. With a start Mihn realised she had wet herself in fear. 'The ragged man's king o' the Finntrail,' she sobbed, 'and 'is soul got swept off by a storm – he can't remember who he is so he has t' steal the souls of others!'

Mihn blinked. He hadn't expected his words to fuel her terror. 'Chera—' he began, reaching out towards her.

The movement shattered the remains of her resolve and the girl fled, running hell-for-leather down the path away from him without a look back. Mihn watched her disappear into the woods until he couldn't hear the sound of her feet any longer. He looked back at the lake. Isak hadn't moved the whole time.

'The ragged man, eh?' he said wearily as he picked up the bundle of food. 'And here I am: the Grave Thief. What a cheerful pair we make.'

CHAPTER 12

Major Amber looked up from his meal when a horn sounded in the distance: a single note that carried from the edge of the camp. It was all he needed to hear. With the help of crutches he got to his feet and made his way to the window.

'What's that about?' Horsemistress Kirl asked through a mouthful of mutton. Food in the Fist was far better than what was being served to the troops outside.

'Nothing to concern you,' Amber said distantly.

After another week of daily ministrations from the mages of Larat and the Priest of Shotir, his injuries had healed enough for him to get up and move about without help, if not without pain. His entire body still hurt, and he'd not be fighting any time soon, but it was a blessing to be out of his bed again nonetheless.

Kirl shrugged and went back to her food. In the darkness outside there was little to see, but Amber remained looking out of the window. He could just about make out the shapes of soldiers moving on the ground below and after a minute he caught sight of the one he was looking for.

The road to the Fist was marked with torches, clear lines in the evening gloom that stood out amidst the campfires. A pair of horsemen approached through the bustle of an army yet to settle down to sleep. Amber couldn't make out any detail, but guessed the smaller of the two would be Gaur's man, Chade. Lord Larim had told them to expect the Poisonblade at nightfall. When the riders were a hundred paces from the main gate Amber turned and headed for the door, grabbing a large sheathed sword as he did so and swinging the baldric over his shoulder.

Kirl watched him struggle to open the door without letting either crutch or sword fall, but she did nothing, just helped herself to the food he'd left. Amber glanced back just before he closed the door as she scraped the last of his rice into her bowl. The horsemistress had surprised him by showing a greater piety than he'd expected from her. From his sick bed it had been hard to miss her quietly saying the morning devotionals, or the prayer to Grepel of the Hearths when she lit the fire. Though she'd never given the impression of being a great supporter of dogma, or the priesthood in general, Amber was keen to avoid her discovering anything about the meeting he was heading off to. She caught him looking and flashed a brief smile; the major felt himself colour and retreated.

He made his way to the apartments General Gaur had made his own. Gaur's huntsmen stood guard rather than Menin soldiers, but they allowed him through with nothing more than a suspicious glance. They were an ugly lot, criminal-looking, but under the tattoos, ritual scarring and bone piercings, there were some educated minds as sharp as the long knives they carried.

Inside he was greeted by General Gaur, who relieved Amber of the sword and directed him to an armchair. Unusually, the beast-man was out of uniform, dressed instead in a formal robe of red, edged in white fur and detailed with black insignias of the Menin and Chetse legions under his command. Amber looked at his own uniform and felt a flush of embarrassment when he realised how in need of cleaning it was. Convalescence and renown were making him forget the officers' code.

'How are you, major?' Gaur asked abruptly.

'Well enough, sir,' Amber confirmed. 'No strength for much more than walking from room to room yet, but at least I can do that. I've recovered some of my senses since I stopped taking the pain medicine.'

Gaur gave an approving nod. 'Good. Lord Styrax wants you in Byora as soon as possible – we're going to lift the restrictions on travel throughout the Circle City so you need to be in place there.'

'Lifting restrictions so soon?'

'Trade is the Circle City's lifeblood; if that isn't allowed to continue the resentment will only grow, and that's no way to build an empire.'

Gaur settled himself into another armchair and turned to face Amber. He rested the sword in the crook of his arm. 'Ismess has been shattered; that is nothing more than a minor problem. We occupy Akell to keep the Devoted on a short leash, and Fortinn is mainly at war with itself. Meanwhile, Byora's ruler is caught up in something altogether more complicated; I know Lord Styrax has told you this, that we believe her to be under Azaer's control. Azaer's disciples will keep down any insurrection, so as long as normal life is allowed to continue, the entire Circle City will quickly come to accept its new circumstances.'

'What resources will I have to monitor Duchess Escral and Byora?' Amber asked.

'Just a few troops, and some of my huntsmen – but there will be a standing garrison in Byora, of course, so that might as well be the Cheme Third until we march again. For the time being they will be kept close to the armoury and leave policing the city to the duchess' troops – she's not so foolish as to try anything, and a bit of normality will do the quarter good. You should set up operations away from your legion, remain on injury leave and relax a little. Have your men observe these "children" gathering outside the Ruby Tower in particular, but ... Well, it is possible you will gather the best intelligence yourself. As yet we don't know Azaer's intention, and before we assume its plan is hostile to our own, we should allow its people the opportunity to approach us.'

'And Zhia Vukotic?'

Gaur nodded. 'Yes indeed. Lord Styrax believes she will want to clarify her position as far as we are concerned, so you should expect her too.'

The discussion was cut off by a sharp rap on the door and before waiting for invitation Chade had entered, ushering in a companion and closing the door swiftly behind them both before he'd even bowed to his lord. The other was tall enough that he had to duck his head a little as he entered, but having done so he then stood motionless while Chade bustled around him.

The newcomer was almost entirely hidden under a long cloak; what part of his face not shadowed by the hood was covered by a dull green scarf. Over one shoulder was a thin, rectangular weapons-bag that reached almost to the ground. To Amber's eyes he was oddly slim – most men of that height were white-eyes, and bulky with heavy muscle. Despite having the advantage of several inches' height over Amber, the newcomer looked like he weighed several stone less.

After a long moment the newcomer pulled his scarf away from

his face with deliberate slowness, then slipped back his hood. Amber blinked in surprise; there was nothing unusual about his face at all. It was unremarkably in every way; it was the face of a typical Menin.

'Your true face please,' Gaur growled.

The man's mouth curled into a slight smile. He peeled his gloves off to reveal long, delicate fingers and unfastened his cloak. Underneath he wore a black tunic patterned with sinuous green dragons, overlaid by crossed baldrics. A bronze gorget at his neck was engraved with what looked like writing and studded with small gems.

He unhooked it, and Amber gave a start that sent a fresh twinge of pain around his ribcage.

The man's face seemed to fall away from his head and vanish for a fraction of a second. As Amber's eyes refocused he saw no man's face at all: a sharper, curved jaw line, a thinner skull and more prominent cheekbones. Though Amber had been expecting it, he could not quite stop a moment of shock.

As beautiful as a woman, with an unknowable air and a cruel glitter in his eyes, the true Elf slipped back his hood and gave a mocking half-bow. By some freak of birth he had been untouched by the curse and was one of only a handful of true Elves born to each generation. In that instant their eyes met, Amber realised Arlal Poisonblade knew exactly how rare he was.

'Drink?' Gaur asked, indicating a tall silver jug to Arlal's left.

'No,' he said, his voice little more than a whisper. With fastidious care the Elf tucked his gloves into his belt and slipped the weapons-bag from his shoulder. The only adornment he wore other than the gorget was a silver belt-buckle in the shape of a dragon's head. Everything else was as plain and practical as one might expect of an assassin in the land of his ancient enemies.

'Will you sit?'

'No.'

'To business then.' If Gaur took offence at the Elf's demeanour he gave no sign of it. He patted the sheathed sword meaningfully. 'We have another job for you. More difficult this time.'

'Who?'

'A Farlan general. By now we assume he will have returned to Tirah.'

'A general more difficult than the Krann of the Chetse?' Arlal said contemptuously. His Menin was imperfect, as though he was reluctant to sully his mouth with a human dialect, but it was understandable.

Amber was careful not to react. He'd known a Raylin mercenary had wounded Krann Charr with a magical arrow, but he hadn't been part of Lord Styrax's inner circle before the invasion and the name of the assassin had remained a secret. Even with the heretical direction their plans were now going in it was a shock to hear a true Elf had struck the first blow of their conquest – the arrow had allowed Charr to be possessed by a daemon, which had then usurped Lord Chalat's position.

Without Arlal's first blow the Menin advance force would never have been able to defeat the Chetse in one sudden strike, and Amber himself would never have had the opportunity to meet the Chosen of Tsatach in battle barely a month past, let alone kill him; more likely he'd have died assaulting Thotel.

'He is no longer just a general; he is also the Mortal-Aspect of Karkarn,' the general said.

The Elf laughed. 'Your Gods are so weak now they need mortals?'

Gaur didn't respond. No good could come from discussing the Gods with an Elf, one cursed or not.

'The spirits are stirred up. I hear their whispers in the dark,' Arlal continued, a sudden intensity crossing his face. 'They tell me the Farlan thief is dead.' The Elf's eyes glittered with avarice and Amber realised the thievery he meant was Lord Isak's possession of Siulents and Eolis – the greatest of Elven weapons.

'That is true,' Gaur confirmed. 'He was foolish enough to face Lord Styrax in battle.'

'Then my price is what is rightfully mine,' the Elf spat.

Gaur cocked his head and Amber realised he had been expecting that. 'His gifts? We do not have them to offer; all but his helm were sent to the Dark Place with him.'

As Arlal hesitated, Amber understood: they knew almost nothing of the Elven race, or its prophecies, with the exception of the prophet, Shalstik, who foretold Aryn Bwr's rebirth, but Eolis and Siulents would be more than just weapons to them. They were symbols of their greatest king – it might be that possession of them alone would be enough to confer the authority to rule, even without using them to claim he was Aryn Bwr reborn.

'What do you offer?' Arlal said at last.

'This sword,' Gaur said, holding out the weapon Amber had won. 'Taken from Lord Chalat's dead fingers, it is Elven-made – I believe in your tongue it is named Golaeth.'

Amber could see Arlal's shoulders stiffen, but the Elf made no effort to reach for the weapon.

'It is perhaps a relic of my people, but it is a poor thing compared to Eolis. It is not enough to kill a God.'

'He is no God, only one touched by the divine,' Gaur pointed out. 'It will be no different to killing one of the Chosen.'

'I need more.'

Gaur looked over at Amber briefly, who had nothing to contribute beyond meeting Gaur's look and looking stern, and hoping his slight nod would add to the impression of compromise. 'What do you need?' the beastman asked.

'Arrows to kill him, Golaeth if they fail to. The helm and its weight in rubies as final payment.'

'Rubies?'

The Elf gave a curt nod, but no explanation, and Amber realised suddenly he did have a contribution to the conversation.

'For making bloodrose amulets,' the major said, his eyes on Arlal. 'It's said they're composed of rubies.' One of the mages healing him had mentioned it – Lord Chalat had been thought to wear such an amulet, though nothing had been found on his body. They were created by the Elven warrior orders and used instead of physical armour. Clearly some such orders remained.

'Our friend here has plans of his own back home,' Amber went on, watching as Arlal's eyes narrowed enough to prove him right. 'With Golaeth, enough rubies to make several bloodrose amulets and Aryn Bwr's helm, he may find power and supporters enough for a coup.'

'That, human,' Arlal spat, 'is not your concern.'

'It is not,' Gaur agreed, 'but the price is acceptable. Inform Lord Larim of your requirements and he shall ensure the arrows are made.'

He held the sword out and this time Arlal took it and slipped the ancient copper-bladed weapon from the sheath to inspect it.

Like many magical weapons it was oversized, too big to be of any real use without its imbued power. It would have looked comical in the hands of the slender Arlal but for the ease with which he moved it through the air. It was a straight, double-edged blade coming to a short point, and as Arlal ran reverential fingers down the flat Amber saw four complex swirling runes briefly glow orange.

'Agreed,' Arlal said finally, sheathing it again. He flicked the clasp of his cloak so that it fell from his right shoulder and he could attach the scabbard to his baldric; in a few moments the sword had disappeared, the cloak returned to position, and gorget and scarf restored. 'You require method or time?' he asked.

'As long as it happens before the end of summer, dead will do.'

Arlal murmured agreement and left with Chade hard on his heels.

When the sound of footsteps had receded, Amber turned to the general. 'How heavy is the helm then?'

'Not heavy.'

'Light as a bloody feather, I'd guess,' the major said, his amber eyes flashing with laughter.

'Close,' Gaur admitted with a twitch of a furred cheek that could have been a smile, although with tusks protruding up to his nose it was hard to tell. 'He may get one small amulet from them.'

'Pretty and stupid,' Amber commented as he eased himself upright again, 'just how I like 'em.'

'Thank you, Major,' the beastman replied gravely. 'Time for you to get back to your duties, I think.'

Daken reached out and grabbed the nearest King's Man by the scruff of the neck. 'What d'ya mean, they lifted the restrictions on entry? I've just spent a fucking hour in that there damned barrel! And with Telasin bloody-Daemon-Touch with me!' he added, pointing at the man now clambering out of the same smuggler's barrel. 'When he farts, it smells like the bastard Dark Place – and I had to put up with that for *nuthin*?'

'Could've been worse,' Coran called, clambering out of his own and gesturing to the woman behind him, 'Sparks kept comin' off Ebarn the whole bloody journey.'

Daken released the man and turned to watch Ebarn, the Brotherhood's dark-haired battle-mage, who was clambering her way out with a scowl on her face. She was a few winters older than Doranei, and a veteran of King Emin's war against Azaer.

'You learn to keep your fucking hands to yourself,' she growled, 'and that'll stop happening.' Once she was standing upright again Ebarn groaned and flexed her muscles before running her finger through her cropped hair.

Coran didn't smile with the rest of the Brotherhood, the more unusual of whom were still being helped out of the barrels used to smuggle them into Byora.

They were being unpacked in the storeroom of Lell Derager, the Farlan's agent and pet wine merchant. The cheerful middle-aged merchant and his two most trusted men were releasing them one by one from the half-dozen fake barrels they had escorted into the city.

Once she'd stretched, Ebarn noticed that Coran was still staring at her, and she turned away with a slight sneer on her face. The white-eye had never been popular with women, not even the whores on whom he spent most of his money. He'd never acquired the skill of treating one as a colleague.

Coran rubbed his hands together as though warming them up. 'My fingers have gone numb with all those sparks – didn't know what I was touching.'

'We've heard you say that before,' called Ebarn, 'and not even the goat-herder believed you then!'

While the rest of the Brotherhood smirked, Doranei's face remained set and stony. Coran ignored the taunting and made his way over to Doranei. He gripped his shoulder and looked him straight in the eye, his expression grave. They all knew Sebe and Doranei had been as close as birth-brothers, and his loss wasn't just that of a comrade. Doranei gave a glum nod of thanks and thumped Coran on the back in reply before pushing past him.

'You must be Daken,' he said to the other white-eye, who was eying him appraisingly.

The mercenary nodded as he tugged his enormous axe from the barrel and swung it up onto his shoulder.

'The answer to your question is this: you didn't put up with Telasin for nothing. While the restrictions have been lifted, there'll have been half-a-dozen folk watching the gate and taking note of anyone unusual coming in.'

'Well, we're in now,' said the mercenary battle-mage, Wentersorn, as he emerged from his own barrel and immediately sidestepped away from Daken. The white-eye hadn't had the opportunity yet to live up to his reputation, but the Mad Axe still clouted Wentersorn around the head every time he came within reach. 'I take that as a good sign, so how's about we find us some whores to celebrate my homecoming?'

'Fucking mercenaries,' Doranei sighed. 'Does keeping a low profile mean nothing to you?'

Wentersorn scowled and pointed at Daken. 'He's my commander, not you.' He gave Daken a hopeful look, not a kindred spirit, but at least a common interest. The white-eye's appetite for women was said to surpass even Coran's.

'Much as I'd love to agree with the ugly little shit and go get me some,' Daken said, 'we don't need the trouble.'

He lifted his shirt to reveal a mass of blue tattoos and pointed to the largest, a woman's head and upper torso in profile. Her mouth was twisted into a cruel smile and her fingers ended in sharp claws. As Doranei watched the smile widened a shade and her fingers briefly stroked the line of Daken's pectoral muscle.

'Litania does love to join in,' Daken said. He pointed to a series of scars just below his navel, adding, 'And she's a biter.'

Doranei coughed to cover his surprise and forced himself to tear his gaze from the Aspect of Larat inhabiting a man's skin. 'Well, if that's settled, have your men find bunks in there.' He pointed to a wide door on his left. 'That storeroom's been cleared; it's cramped, but it'll serve for tonight. Food and beer will be provided. Daken, do you have a second-in-command?'

The white-eye jabbed a thumb towards a bald man with bronze earrings and a pair of scimitars. 'Brother Penitence there.'

'Brother Penitence?' Doranei and Derager gasped in unison, both sounding dismayed.

'Aye, he's a cleric – Mystic o' Karkarn to be exact!' Daken gave a laugh at their expressions. 'Hah, look at the pair of ya; we ain't completely dumb, I just wanted to see your faces at his name.'

'I realise the name would be unwise in these troubled times,' the Mystic of Karkarn said in a surprisingly cultured voice. Many of their number were former soldiers, and most barely educated. 'Considering the way so many cults have abused the office of the Penitency in recent months I am willing to give it up for the time being. My birth name was Hambalay Osh; that is what you may use instead.'

'What's a mystic's involvement here?' Doranei demanded. 'I can't believe you're being paid like a mercenary.'

Osh dipped his head to acknowledge the point. 'I am an old acquaintance of the king's; one who owes him a considerable favour and whose skills are the only way of addressing the balance.'

Doranei grunted. This was neither the time nor place to pursue the matter. 'Follow me,' he said, and led them up to a staircase. Coran, Daken and Osh followed him two floors up to an attic room that had two small beds and a table at the window. One of the beds was neatly made up, a man's possessions arranged with military precision on top. As Coran passed it he kissed the knuckles of his right hand and touched them to the maker's mark on the guard of the dagger that lay there. The little-known but much admired weaponsmith provided most of what the Brotherhood carried.

Doranei headed for a seat at the window and took a moment to gaze out at the view across Breakale district to Eight Towers.

'What's the latest then?' Coran asked after a minute or two, interrupting Doranei's reverie.

'Apart from the lifting of restrictions?' he said. 'Only Lord Styrax killing a dragon.'

The white-eye whistled. 'Must've taken some doing.'

'Smacks of showin' off if you ask me,' Daken commented, perching carefully on one of the beds until he was sure it could take the weight of a white-eye.

'Maybe,' Doranei said. 'Whatever the truth, it sounds like he's won over more than a few by it. Folk here have never had such a powerful ruler and they're beginning to think it's better to be inside his empire reaping the benefits than outside trying to fight it.'

'Might have a point there,' Daken said with a grin. 'So we're goin' to be the ones fightin' it – folk call me mad; what's your excuse?'

'It's not our concern at the moment; we've only got one target in Byora.'

'Why? If not this season, then one comin' soon, Lord Styrax is goin' to want to add Narkang to his empire. Why not throw a few sails in the pond?'

Seeing both Doranei and Coran looking puzzled by the expression Daken explained, 'Sail-raptors? No? Ah well, type o' lizard; swims, eats ducks, scares the shit out of 'em. Anyways, why not try slow him up a bit?'

'You don't get to question the king's decisions,' Doranei replied, 'and we don't have the time or resources to set up something that'll catch a big-enough duck to make our lives worthwhile. The Menin can't move much further, they must be badly stretched as it is. If they don't stop to consolidate they'll lose the city-states they've taken and while they're doing that, we'll be invoking our agreements with the Farlan. Now, if you don't mind, let's return to the reason why we're here.'

'Killing Ilumene,' Coran said, savouring the words.

'Not only,' Doranei corrected sharply. 'As you'll see tomorrow – well, not you two, I guess, just Osh and me – there's more than just Ilumene in Byora.'

'Such as?'

'A child, Ruhen, and the rest of Duchess Escral's inner circle, a man called Luerce, even Aracnan, if he's still alive after Sebe winged him with a poisoned bolt.'

'Who's this Luerce?'

Doranei scratched the stubble on his cheek. 'I don't know if I've quite worked out his place in things yet. This is what I've got so far: there's a crowd of beggars camped right outside the gates to the Ruby Tower, writing prayers and fixing them to the wall and gates, asking Ruhen to intercede with the Gods on their behalf. Ruhen is—well, we'll come to him. The beggars are being organised by Luerce and his followers – they're calling themselves something like Ruhen's Children, though I've heard a few other names mentioned.'

'So what's the game?'

'I don't know yet,' Doranei admitted. 'The duchess has been turned against the cults; Hale district is still almost entirely shut off. The goal appears to be cutting the population off from the Gods, removing the priesthood from daily life. By having them call to Ruhen they're weakening the Gods, but to what end I can't say. This would have to go on for decades – and spread throughout most of the Land – before the Gods were weak enough for Azaer to be any sort of rival.'

'Could someone else be a rival instead?'

Doranei sighed. 'Perhaps – certainly someone with a Skull could kill a God, and the weaker they got, the easier it would be.'

'Remember that trip you got sent on after Scree?' Coran asked pointedly, 'to the monastery on the lake? You're looking for mad and strong enough to kill Gods – there's your answer.'

Doranei considered Coran's point. While King Emin had left the ruins of Scree with the Skull of Ruling, Azaer's disciples had been intent on getting something else the island-monastery's abbot had in his possession. The journal of Prince Vorizh Vukotic had been Azaer's prize, and its contents remained a worrying mystery.

'You could be right,' Doranei mused, 'but it doesn't explain why – unless it's revenge for something that happened in the Age of Myths, there's not a good enough reason. Just to cause chaos and misery can't be all there is to it: there has to be a plan, and that's what we're missing.'

'What if this is a game of the heavens?' Osh asked unexpectedly. 'I don't pretend to understand much of what is going on, but I suspect my theology is better than any of you. There is clear precedent of insurrection there – Lliot, the God of All Waters, rebelled against the rule of Death and His queen. That failed, so perhaps another God has chosen a different line of attack and found a daemon cunning enough to lay the way for it. If successful, the rewards would be commensurate.'

'The king doesn't believe so,' Doranei said. 'It's the best explanation we have, but investigations say it ain't right. No God of any significance has been spared the effects of the backlash, and the king's mages have consulted a host of daemons – there would be some sort of a whisper about it if such a thing were happening. Anyway, Azaer's no true daemon—'

'And too fucking arrogant to be a hired hand,' Coran broke in.

Doranei nodded. 'Even with the collusion of a God it doesn't fit with what we know of the shadow. If it sparks a war within the Pantheon it will be solely for its own purposes.' He raised a hand to stop any further conversation. 'We can discuss this later, but right now we have an assault to plan. Surviving that is my only concern at this time.'

'So what's the bet?' Coran asked automatically.

Doranei glowered and glanced at Sebe's belongings on the bed.

'You kill Ilumene or Ruhen, or you finish off Aracnan, you can name your fucking price. I'll pay it gladly.'

The next day was one of unexpected sunshine, long shafts of light cutting through clumps of drifting cloud to shine down upon Byora's streets. It felt to Doranei like the entire population had been ushered outside, flocking to the recently replenished markets or just making the most of the weather after the months of grim, lingering cold. He had left the wine merchant's not long after dawn, taking with him the Mystic of Karkarn, Hambalay Osh, and Veil, one of the Brotherhood.

The trio took a long, winding route through the quarter. They were in no hurry to get to the Ruby Tower; it was the perfect day to get a feel for the city again – they'd be more inconspicuous than usual with so many people out and about. The streets of Wheel and Burn were hives of activity now the Menin had reinstated free passage and carts of all sizes had clogged the streets in their eagerness to deliver the raw materials Byora so desperately needed. The few Menin patrols they saw were carefully keeping out of the way of everyday life; many were sitting outside taverns and eateries, behaving themselves like soldiers under orders.

Heading into Breakale, the central district where more than half of Byora's citizens lived, they found the streets no less busy. Doranei led them past the Three Inns crossroad, where their Brother Sebe had died, to an eatery that faced east, towards Black-fang. The wedge-shaped building had been built to divert the floodwaters that occasionally swept off the mountain slopes, and from the tip of the wedge on the upper floor they had a good view of the surrounding area. Since it was well before midday, they had it to themselves.

They sat in silence, sharing a jug of weak wine and watching gangs of labourers work through the rubble of the buildings that had once stood to the right of them; the place where Sebe had been holed up with his poison-tipped arrows, from where he shot Aracnan. And it was there he had died, when the immortal mercenary had indiscriminately unleashed the power of his Crystal Skull, killing hundreds in a storm of raging magic.

'Here's to you, Sebe,' Veil said at last, raising his goblet in salute, 'you monkey-faced little bugger. We'll miss you.'

Doranei kept quiet, he'd said his goodbyes already, but he downed the rest of his wine with the other two. When a girl brought them a plate of bread and white crumbly cheese he ignored it and picked up the wine jug, his eyes still on the workmen below.

'Something I thought I'd never see,' he said eventually, more to himself than the others. 'You see those men with white scarves tied round their necks?'

Veil looked up from his food a moment. 'Look like they're in charge of the work. Some sort of labourers' guild? I saw a few on the way here like that.'

Veil was a wiry man a few winters younger than Doranei. He wore his dark hair long, tied back with twine. Unlike Doranei he'd been late coming into the care of the Brotherhood; he'd been twelve winters when his parents died of the white plague. He'd been marked as someone worth watching from his very first night, when he'd blackened Ilumene's eye before the older boy had managed to land a blow, a very rare occurrence.

'I've been asking about that building. The owner was killed when it collapsed, but someone bought the plot and is rebuilding. Word is that it's going to be some sort of sanctuary.'

'And?'

'And that sanctuary will be for anyone in need, run by followers of the child Ruhen – that's what the white scarves signify. They're the ones camped outside the Ruby Tower.'

Veil took a closer look at the men Doranei was talking about. One wore a tattered leather jerkin that looked like padding to go underneath mail; the rest looked in even worse condition. 'It's no sense of civic duty. The fucker's pissing on Sebe's grave.'

'The ones you saw in the other districts have been preaching a bit too, mainly anti-cult talk. There's no one in Byora going to defend any of the cults nowadays, not since the clerics' rebellion when they tried to assassinate the duchess. Sebe and I started listening when we realised there's a whole bunch of them spreading the word. Those who're receptive to the message are taken aside and told about a prophecy, a prophecy of the Saviour that's known to only the Harlequins.'

'Let me guess,' Osh said grimly, 'this prophecy sees no need for the cults at all?'

'They're keeping it close to their chests at the moment, only telling those willing to believe anything: the desperate, the poor, those with a grudge against the Gods or the cults. There have been stories running through the city for weeks now about Ruhen performing miracles – breaking a curse, protecting the duchess from the clerics trying to kill her – that's what the crowd outside the compound are there for. They're praying to this child to intercede on their behalf with the Gods.'

'So those who know the secret put two and two together and get a new God for their pains.'

Veil grimaced, imagining what sort of God Azaer would make.

Osh paused mid-bite. 'There's a crowd of beggars outside the Ruby Tower gates? How big?'

'Few hundred at least,' Doranei said.

'Are we talking fanatics here?'

'Not for the most part, mostly folk broken by the Land they're living in and desperate for something better.'

'Thank the Gods,' Osh said with relief. 'We already know we're going to have to deal with guards and distract any Menin soldiers – I don't much fancy cutting my way through a crowd of men and women willing to die to protect the child.'

'Speaking of which,' Doranei said, 'what tricks do we have on that front? The crowd should be easy enough to frighten out of the way, but that's the easy part. We need a diversion to give us a chance, and I guess we'll need every mage we've got inside the compound.'

'The king has assembled a box of tricks for you to play with,' Veil said with a half-smile. 'For fighters we got the Brotherhood. We've got four thieves from Tio He who're bloody covered in charms of Cerdin, and we've got Osh here. Plus two high mages in the forms of our favourite bickering old women – Masters Shile Cetarn and Tomal Endine – plus two battle-mages. And then we've the more unusual members of our team: Camba Firnin is an illusionist by trade, but she's from the College of Magic and her bag of powders and chemicals'll do more than just make you think you're dead. Telasin Daemon-Touch you must'a heard of, and Shim the Bastard is a mage-killer, probably our best chance to deal with Aracnan. Daken plans on tying him to a stick and keeping him out front.'

Doranei sighed. 'And then there's Daken, the Mad Axe,' he added.

'Aye, and her that comes with him,' Veil said darkly.

'Daken and I have been speaking about that,' Osh interjected. 'Litania is a fickle bitch, to use Daken's term. She comes out to play when she feels like it, and she causes havoc whenever she does. We cannot have her with us in the Ruby Tower; it's just as likely she'll be the death of us as she will any sort of help.'

'So your suggestion is?' Doranei asked, knowing he wasn't going to like the answer.

'Daken asks her to provide the diversion.' Osh raised a hand, seeing Doranei open his mouth to argue. 'We keep one of the king's mages back in case all she does is swamp the district in butterflies or something of the like – you'll want one in reserve anyway, to cover your retreat.'

'But to willingly let the Trickster loose in a city?' Veil asked, aghast. 'You've no idea what destruction she could wreak!'

'Do we have a choice?'

Neither of the Brothers replied. Doranei looked towards the upper levels of the Ruby Tower, visible above the rooflines. Veil continued to stare at Osh, trying to think of an argument against the proposal. He closed his mouth again when Doranei gave him a slap on the arm and pointed at the street opposite.

'Look, what's that all about?'

The cobbled street had a smoother patch just as it reached the crossroads, where Aracnan's magic had somehow fused the cobbles together. It led from Eight Towers district, the widest and quickest route from the Ruby Tower through the city, and walking down it now was a group of a dozen men and women, some wearing white, some dressed entirely in white. Many carried long walking staffs, and all bore some sort of pack on their back.

'They're dressed for travel,' Veil pointed out, peering forward.

'Missionaries,' Osh concluded with a grave face. 'The word's being spread beyond Byora.'

'Piss and daemons,' Doranei growled, pushing his wine aside and shoving a hunk of bread in his pocket. 'As soon as they pass we go to look at the ground around the Ruby Tower. If they're starting the next phase of their plan we need to stop it, and soon. I want Ilumene and the child dead by Prayerday.'

CHAPTER 13

Over the darkest hours Doranei's élite company gathered by fits and bursts. Men and women in small, subdued groups appeared out of the mist at the door of a warehouse adjoining the minor gate between Coin, Byora's financial district, and Breakale. At night Breakale was the quieter of the two – all Byora's upscale gambling dens were located in Coin, well away from the disapproving clerics of Hale and the gangsters of Burn.

When he arrived Doranei found most of the company already assembled, but unlike the rest of the King's Men he was unable to sit quietly. He prowled the warehouse, running the plan and escape route through his mind again and again, looking for flaws. The warehouse was crucial to their escape, providing a useful bridge between streets that were not quickly accessed otherwise – certainly not now a cart stood in the alley alongside the warehouse, waiting to block the remaining space.

He ascended the narrow staircase that led to a room above the rear entrance, from where Doranei could see the street and the gate into Coin. The gate was shut at this hour, of course, but since the warehouse was close enough to the wall for a nimble man to jump, that wouldn't be the case for long. Once in Coin a second gate – guarded by Menin troops most likely – would let them into Eight Towers, and to the gate of the Ruby Tower itself.

'More obstacles than I'd like,' Doranei commented softly when Veil joined him. 'This could go badly wrong, my friend.'

'Aye, that it could,' Veil said, looking unconcerned, 'but that's the way of it. On the other side of the coin we've got Cerdin-blessed thieves, mages and a fair amount of brawn, if it comes to that.'

The slim man was dressed in black from head to foot, unlike most of his comrades. They were going to make their way to the

Ruby Tower as quietly as possible, with Veil leading the way until the alarm was raised, at which point Coran and Daken would take over.

'What's taking that mad bastard so long?' Doranei muttered, still staring out of the window.

'Peace, Brother,' Veil urged, 'he's not late yet.' He paused. 'You're as jumpy as a raw recruit, Doranei. What's got you wound up?'

'A woman,' Doranei said darkly.

Veil frowned at that. 'You heard from her?'

'No, I kept her well out of this. Last time I saw her we, ah—' He faltered. 'Well, I don't know how I left it, really, but it felt sort of final. Can't tell whether she's been keeping an eye on me, but there's this itch at the back of my mind.'

'Reckon you'd be able to tell if she was tracking you?'

'I guess not, but I got a burr of something nonetheless.'

'You decided she's our enemy now?' Veil asked in surprise. Last time the subject had come up, Doranei had been emphatic that Zhia wasn't working with Azaer, and her actions had borne his assessment out. 'What's changed?'

Doranei rubbed a callused palm over his face. 'I don't know,' he admitted, 'just a feeling. I could be wrong o'course, she's had a hundred lifetimes to practise giving nothing away, but something's got me thinking all the same. She's a cold bitch when she wants to be – think she surprises herself when she's with me – but there was always a part of her that was closed off.'

'Aye, well that's her reputation,' Veil said. 'She might be a vampire, might be a heretic, but her heart's that of a blood-sucking politician.'

Doranei nodded. 'She's been doing it for too long, it's what she is. I'm just scared she might decide what Azaer did in Scree was a true demonstration of the shadow's power. Cursed with compassion she might be, but she'll still take sides with Azaer if she can break her curse.'

'And if that happens,' Veil finished, 'we're in a whole heap of trouble.'

As Veil spoke there came a quiet knock at the door downstairs. Both men were up and moving before it had even been opened, hands moving automatically to their weapons. When Daken slipped through the doorway, his face more animated than before, it was clear the operation was in motion.

'It's done?' Doranei asked.

'That it is,' Daken replied, lifting his mail shirt in evidence. The white-eye's broad chest was missing the large tattoo of Litania the Trickster; the skin where she'd been looked raw and painful. He grinned. 'She said she'd give me time to get here. I left her slipping into some servant girl near the Menin barracks.'

'Any idea what she's going to do?'

Daken's grin got wider. 'She's not one for plannin' but that girl's hungry for a bit o' fun. They'll be distracted all right!'

'Then we're off. Get moving, Veil.'

As Veil and the youngest of the four Tio He thieves headed for the roof, Doranei turned to the rest of his troops. 'Everyone remember their job? Any questions? All got your equipment?'

'Stop fussin' like an old woman,' Daken growled, 'we're good to go and you ain't in charge, remember?'

'The plan's mine,' Doranei reminded. 'If everything's in place, then I'm yours to command.'

'That's the sort o'talk I like.' Daken pointed past Doranei to the smaller of the warehouse's two doors, the one leading to the gate. 'Time to move.'

Upstairs, Veil pulled himself up onto the building's roof and hauled his companion up after him. The greater moon, Alterr, was hidden by cloud, and this deep into the night, the Poacher's Moon was hours off. Veil sensed as much as saw the swift dark clouds sweep east overhead. He made his way to the corner of the building closest to the wall and knelt to check the iron hook they had put there that afternoon.

'Ready, Dirr?' he asked softly.

'Hurry up old man,' Dirr replied, with an obscene gesture.

Veil secured a rope to the hook and slipped over the edge, lowering himself down until he felt his boots reach the jutting edge of a beam that ran down the side of the building, almost the height of the wall beyond. He retreated along the beam a little and let the rope play out, then signalled to Dirr before launching himself forward. He ran a few steps along the beam and jumped forward, pulling hard on the rope, using the hook as a pivot to swing himself up to the district wall.

Reaching it comfortably, Veil hooked his legs over and caught his balance. He found himself just above the guardhouse on the right of the gate. He eased himself down until his feet were touching the roof, then braced against the wall to take the strain on the rope as Dirr came hand over hand down it.

Once they were both safe on the guardhouse roof Veil crept to the edge and peered over. None of the guards were in sight, but the door was half-open, spilling light into the street and illuminating the barred gate where Doranei would be waiting. Veil dropped, using the door and lintel to swing himself into the guardroom and he was on the ground and drawing his shortswords before the guards realised what was happening. There were three, all seated, and only one had a weapon close enough to grab, so Veil lunged like a fencer towards him, catching the man in the throat.

'What—?' was all the next man managed before Veil turned and whipped both swords across him, slashing deeply into face and chest and sending him spinning over a table.

The third had more presence of mind. He grabbed a spear propped against the wall and had almost levelled it by the time Veil made up the ground, but it wasn't enough. One shortsword got him in the stomach, the other pierced his lung from behind, and he fell with an abrupt cough.

Not waiting to check whether there was need, Veil turned back to the second man face-down on the table and stabbed him in the back. The guard arched up, mouth open as though about to scream, but Veil slit his throat and the only sound was his dying breath.

'Gods, you really are fast!' came a gasp from the doorway.

Veil spun around, weapons raised and already moving towards the newcomer before he saw it was Dirr. He stopped dead, but Dirr had already retreated, a look of horror on his face.

'Get that gate open,' Veil hissed, indicating the gate behind him with a flick of a sword.

Dirr flinched as blood spattered across his face, but he obeyed without hesitation and trotted over to lift the bars.

Veil was about to follow him when he saw a key hanging from a nail by the doorway. 'That makes it easier,' he muttered, pocketing the key.

The gate had a postern that could be barred but was usually only locked. If the Brother who was staying at this gate could find a way to blockade all but the postern, they could lock up behind them on the way back and perhaps win one more precious minute. Once the whole company was through Veil pressed the key into the hand of a King's Man wearing the livery of the Byoran Guard.

'Keep the postern open,' he instructed. 'You won't get much traffic this time of night, but let 'em all through as wants to go; that should let you bar the rest and fix it that way.'

A growl from Coran indicated he was supposed to be off and he jumped to obey, trotting through the deserted night-time streets with Dirr and Telasin Daemon-Touch, who ran with his head covered and bowed as always. Instead of the rapier and dagger Veil had expected, Telasin carried a pair of brutal khopesh that looked custom-made, with basket-hilts and runes detailed in bronze on the forward-tilted chopping edge.

Coin was at its quietest, the cold wind and late hour ensuring the streets were deserted. Veil padded ahead of the rest so he could ignore the sound of their footsteps and scout the next section. The pace was slow and patient, his reward continued silence as he moved from one building to the next.

He reached a crossroad and crouched down to peer around the corner. The street was empty, and no lights shone from any of the houses as far as the near-invisible cliff of Blackfang that Coin backed onto. Veil couldn't help but look up at the broken mountain ahead. The steep, impassable slope started its climb up into the sky barely four hundred yards away. Something about it made Veil shiver; the presence of that brooding, broken mountain made him feel vulnerable.

Footsteps in the street brought him back to the mission with a jolt. He looked around the corner and saw five figures walking towards them. In the darkness it was impossible to tell who they were, but as he frantically waved behind him he heard their voices carry on the night air.

Piss and daemons, Veil thought, gesturing again. They weren't drunks on their way home from some bar but a Menin patrol.

'How many?' asked a strange voice beside him and Veil twitched in surprise, even as he realised it was Telasin who'd spoken. It was the first time he'd heard the secretive Raylin mercenary speak.

'Five,' he whispered.

'Keep clear.'

Veil bit down the question on his lips as Telasin met his gaze for the first time since they'd met. The former Devoted officer hadn't spoken the entire time he'd been among the Brotherhood. His head had remained bowed in shame and he'd allowed Daken to answer for him whenever words had been necessary.

In the darkness it was hard to make out much of Telasin's face beyond a broken nose and a strange difference between his eyes: either they were markedly different colours, or one was milky with blindness. He was older than Veil; a hard forty winters showed in that face.

Veil had an image blossom suddenly in his mind: yellowed ivory skin and long black tusks, rusting rings in the flesh of his cheek, and an eye that burned with orange flames. Veil fell backwards in horror, barely able to stop himself from crying out in shock.

Telasin didn't wait to see if he'd made enough noise to warn the Menin patrol; he had already leaped silently out into the street and gone on the attack. Veil scrabbled to follow the daemon-touched soldier, but as he rounded the corner and saw Telasin engaging all five Menin he faltered. A black cloud swirled around them all, shadows whipping up from the ground. Telasin's cloak lifted high in the sudden gust, revealing tarnished bronze scale-armour, as he hacked at one of the Menin and parried another in the same moment.

In a heartbeat the entire group was obscured by darkness. Veil could do nothing but wait, listening to the muted clash of steel. A hot, greasy wind swept across his face, bringing a sudden stink of sulphur and decay. Both Dirr and Veil gagged as the unnatural hot air enveloped them, and in the next breath it was gone. Veil dry-retched once more and opened his eyes to see Telasin standing over five brutally slain corpses, a red-tinged glow playing about his shoulders.

'Gods,' Veil and Dirr said in the same breath. As they spoke they felt a distant tremble underfoot and a crack of thunder split the sky.

'Don't just fuckin' stand there,' Daken snapped as he caught them up, giving both men a shove. He pointed to their right, where Veil saw a sudden red glow in the distance. 'That's Litania, that is; she's havin' her fun now.'

Veil blinked and realised the thunder hadn't come from the sky at all; it had been somewhere in Breakale and loud enough that it might have been an entire building collapsing. Daken gave a coarse laugh and went on ahead, clapping a comradely hand on Telasin's shoulder. The man jumped like he'd been stung and lowered his weapons, head bowed.

'Five for you, eh? I got me some catchin' up to do!'

Veil upped the pace of his scouting ahead. In the distance an orange glow grew steadily, he guessed somewhere close to the Breakale-Hale gates. When they reached the gate into Eight Towers he found it half-open, but guarded by both a squad of Menin soldiers and some Byoran troops.

Veil passed a signal back and hunkered down to wait for support, which came in the form of Cetarn, the oversized Narkang mage. As usual, he wore a cheery grin on his face, as though what they were about was nothing more than high jinks.

'What have you got for me?' Veil whispered.

'A little misdirection should do,' Cetarn replied.

The mage's attempt to keep his voice low sounded painfully loud to Veil, but he ignored it as Cetarn made him stand upright. Muttering under his breath, Cetarn ran a fleshy hand over Veil's head before repeating the process over himself. That done, the big mage grabbed Veil's arm and dragged him out into full view of the soldiers.

'We don't look any different,' Veil hissed, watching the soldiers notice them.

'Not up close, no,' Cetarn said cheerfully, 'but at a distance, trust me – we appear to be the most magnificently blessed young ladies those men have seen in a long while.'

Veil almost choked at the notion, and he would have tripped on the cobbles had Cetarn not had a firm grip on him.

'That's a good idea; don't we look so pretty and drunk?' Cetarn commented brightly.

Veil recovered himself in time to see four dark shapes ghosting through the shadows on the other side of the street, evading the soldiers' notice. When Veil and Cetarn were ten paces away the nearest soldier gave a cry of surprise and Veil realised the glamour had failed. The soldier reached for his weapon, but he was cut down by the first of the Brotherhood. As Veil ran to join the fight his Brothers were already cutting a path through the soldiers to the gate.

One tried to race through, only to be thrown back by the force of a spear catching him in the side. The next King's Man kicked out and snapped the shaft against the closed half of the gate, lunging with his sword at the holder and pushing on through.

Veil made for the nearest Menin, feinting right to get behind the tip. Keeping his swords close, he ran straight into the man and spun off his shoulder, stabbing him in the hip even as he darted away and trapped the next soldier's weapon. Out of the corner of his eye he saw someone's livery suddenly catch fire. The bright burst of light made the man he was facing hesitate and Veil used the chance to knee him in the groin and smash a pommel into his face. His opponent reeled and Veil chopped down into his arm, then his exposed neck.

As the last man fell and silence returned, Veil checked his surroundings. There were no other soldiers in sight aside from the remainder of their company, who were quickly making up the fifty yards between them.

'It's clear,' called the King's Man who'd gone through the gate as he dropped to kneel at his injured comrade's side.

'How is he?' Veil asked, watching the bulky shapes of Daken and Coran moving side by side as though in competition.

'Fucking hurting,' the injured man grunted, 'but I ain't dead yet.'

Veil turned. It was Cedei, one of the veterans of the Brotherhood. 'Good – but you're not coming with us like that. Cetarn, stop the bleeding and help him up. You'll have to make it back to the gate on your own.'

'Aye,' Cedei agreed in a strained voice. 'Luck to you. See you when the killing's done.'

'When it's done,' Veil confirmed and thumped his forearm against Cedei's as Coran reached him just ahead of Daken.

'The alarm will be raised soon,' Veil said, looking at the bodies on the ground. 'We've got a straight run to the Ruby Tower, so best we get Mage Firnin out in front now to clear the beggars out of our way.'

The white-eyes agreed and they set off jogging in two columns towards the Ruby Tower. The streets were still empty, but there were sounds in the city now, shouts coming from Breakale, and from the main gate between the two districts. Even Daken began to look serious: the real fight was close at hand. Whatever Litania had done, the panic had started.

Dawn was still more than an hour off by the time they reached the wide avenue that skirted the Ruby Tower compound. Behind it was a plateau of enclosed ground a hundred yards across, a series of peaked roofs, and pipes that channelled the floodwaters around the compound. A large statue of Kiyer of the Deluge was positioned at each corner, each with a wide, distended mouth from which the water was channelled into the avenue. The ground outside the gate was open cobbles for fifty yards before reaching the three main streets leading away from the tower.

Veil's company took a road parallel to one of these. It was blocked at the end, to protect the entrances to the houses on each side, but it gave them a concealed route for most of the way, with a narrow passage which took them to the north corner of the open ground. When they were all settled he moved forward with Doranei and Mage Firnin, the woman carrying a saddlebag with enough care that Veil was keen to see the back of it.

Firnin set the bag down and sat cross-legged on the ground, tugging at her breeches and shirt to put them perfectly in order. That done, she pulled a flask from her pocket, took a long slug of what smelled like brandy, and poured the rest down her front, ignoring the expressions on their faces.

'What're you doing?' Doranei snapped as he watched her. This wasn't what she'd outlined to him the previous day when he'd told her to take care of the beggars – that was what the saddlebag was for.

Firnin opened one eye and scowled at him, which twisted a scar down her face into an even more jagged line. 'Trying to avoid the death of innocents; the bag can help you get out instead. Have Cetarn signal me when you want the way cleared.'

'What are you doing now?'

The mage didn't reply, and Doranei realised he wasn't going to get an answer without interrupting her concentration. Camba Firnin's main skill might be as an illusionist, but she was still powerful, and now wasn't the time to anger her. Instead he made himself comfortable and stared out over the white-shrouded figures that even now knelt at the gates in prayer. There weren't as many as he'd feared, and he mouthed his thanks to Cerdin, God of Thieves, whom the Brotherhood had adopted as a patron God.

It was hard to gauge in the darkness but he guessed there were a little more than a score of them, perhaps thirty faithful, all in a circle with heads bowed. Along the wall fluttered scraps of paper and cloth, reminding him of prayers to Sheredal, the Aspect of the Goddess Asenn called the Spreader of the Frost. From the sheer number on show Doranei realised it wasn't just a handful of Byorans who were praying for intercession with the Gods. He couldn't begin to estimate how many prayers had been attached to the wall, but it looked like hundreds.

The scene of still reverence continued for a dozen heartbeats, until, without warning, a white misty figure stepped out from the compound gate. Doranei's heart gave a lurch. It was a child, robed in cloth-of-light, and resembling the ghostly Aspect of Vasle inhabiting Morghien, King Emin's long-time ally. Even before the praying figures had noticed it the figure set off down the main avenue, oblivious to the gasps it provoked as it passed the beggars. By ones and twos they struggled to their feet, looking around in bewilderment – one reached his hand out to the illusion, but when he tried to speak the words faltered in his throat.

'Karkarn's horn,' Doranei spat, 'you've just reaffirmed their faith, you stupid bitch!'

'Stop your whining,' Firnin said in a breathy whisper. 'Are they following?'

Doranei looked at the beggars, who were all staring after the child as it reached the top of the street and started off down it. When it became clear the child was leaving, they stumbled after it, a few crying out in wordless fervour.

'Yes, they are.'

'Good. Leave me here.' He could hear the strain in her voice now. 'I'll lead them as far as I can, then give them a nightmare that's hard to worship.'

Doranei opened his mouth to argue before realising it would waste precious time. 'Damn. Okay.' He signalled the rest of the company forward, carefully draping the saddlebag over one shoulder.

They came in a sprint, with Daken and the battle-mage Ebarn at the fore. There was no time to talk; everyone already knew their established positions, and they all knew how vulnerable they were out in the open. It was reasonable to think that news of the fire in Breakale had already reached the Ruby Tower – with luck the gate wasn't barred but they couldn't afford to make assumptions. Once she was standing in front of the gate Ebarn planted her feet firmly. Doranei gently placed the saddlebag on the ground to one side and took his place in the second rank.

'Close your eyes.' She stretched her arms out and braced herself while the soldiers immediately behind her, Telasin, Coran and Veil, were careful to give her room. The silver thread and crystal shards attached to her tunic began to glow, and sparks darted through the air around her. A moment later her skin glistened pale green and Doranei, knowing what was coming, ducked his head.

With a great gasp Ebarn threw her hands forwards and a flash cut the darkness, twin streams of magic leaping forward and exploding on the compound gates with an ear-shattering crash. The gates were ripped from their hinges and launched into the compound, while Ebarn staggered backwards into Veil's waiting arms.

As Doranei blinked and cursed at the effect on his night-sight, the white-eyes leaped eagerly forward, weapons raised. Telasin followed, into the stink of the Dark Place that filled the air and the chaos caused by the inrush of Brotherhood troops. A roar of wordless rage that could only be Coran cut through the clatter, shouting and screaming.

Once Doranei met the bewildered Ruby Tower Guards inside, his training kicked in. A spear jabbed out of the dust-filled gloom and he dodged to the side, feeling it catch the side of his brigandine. The fear flaring inside him came out as a shout and he launched himself forward before the Byoran had a chance to withdraw. His sword had pierced the man's throat and before he'd even fallen Doranei had turned and chopped with his axe into the arm of the next guardsman.

Past him there was only empty ground, and though Doranei looked around, there was no further threat. The wave of Brotherhood had crashed over the outnumbered defenders and slaughtered them with savage speed. It was only a matter of seconds before the attackers were the sole people standing, taking great gulps of air as Daken's laughter echoed around the compound walls.

'Let's go find more,' he roared, heading for the main entrance to the tower. Doranei followed him, as did Telasin, whose body now appeared to have fat strands of dancing black smoke attached. Osh, the Mystic of Karkarn, joined them, together with the four thieves and Mage Cetarn. The mage-killer, Shim the Bastard, hurried along in the rear, his axe as yet unblooded.

Coran led the rest to the barracks, in the other direction.

The cackling Daken was first to reach the entrance. He side-stepped a spear point with surprising agility and rammed the spiked tip of his axe into the guard's gut, driving him back through the tall double-doors. Doranei raced to follow and found himself staring at an empty throne in a dimly lit audience hall. There were no guards in the room so he followed Daken across the hall and headed for the smaller of the two doorways on the far wall.

Beyond it was a bare room with three more open doorways. It looked like this was the way to the rear buildings where the servants lived and worked, so he backtracked to the main hall. In the gantry above he saw a soldier with a crossbow looking down at him, and an unmistakable figure in mail and a steel skull-cap: Ilumene.

'Catch me if you can, puppy!' Ilumene yelled as the soldier levelled his crossbow.

Doranei ducked back through the doorway, shouting a warning to his companions caught in the open. The bolt went through the throat of the nearest, one of the thieves, who fell without a sound.

'Damned traitor!' Cetarn roared, his face scarlet with sudden and rare fury.

The mage looked around for a moment before his gaze alighted on Telasin Daemon-Touch. As Doranei ran for the other door to find a staircase he saw Cetarn run around the possessed soldier and place his hands on the man's back. Telasin, knowing what was going to happen, tensed, weapons at the ready.

With a burst of green-tinted light Cetarn punched forward and Telasin was propelled up to the landing. He hooked a leg and arm neatly over the balustrade as he reached it, in the same movement hacking at the archer's neck.

Instead of fleeing, Ilumene threw himself forward with a roar, his bastard sword swinging at Telasin's head with such ferocity that the daemon-touched soldier was almost driven back over the balustrade by the blow. Ilumene didn't give him a moment to recover, cutting again and again at Telasin with his longer sword and forcing the soldier back against a wall. In desperation Telasin smashed at Ilumene's sword with both weapons, knocking it to one side to avoid a killing blow, but he was head-butted by the bigger man.

Telasin grunted in pain and rode the blow, throwing himself to one side and half-falling back through the open doorway behind him. His khopesh crashed against the stone pillars on either side as he fought to remain upright.

'Where the fuck did he find you, freak?' Ilumene laughed, lunging with his long sword as he spoke.

Telasin batted the blade away, but succeeded only in deflecting it down and it nicked his thigh. He staggered and slashed wildly at Ilumene's head, forcing him to retreat a precious pace. They found themselves in a corridor where long, densely embroidered tapestries covered the inner wall. It was narrow, but still high enough for Ilumene to raise his sword without impediment. Telasin continued to retreat, a quick glimpse behind having shown him a short flight of stairs before the corridor widened.

He leaped down the half-dozen steps and raised his khopesh again. The stench of decay filled the corridor and a sudden hot wind blew past him towards Ilumene. The darkness wrapped around him was raised by the wind and grew to become thick tendrils that rapidly spread through the corridor.

'You think shadows can cow me?' Ilumene called contemptuously, and launched himself into the swirling black mass.

Holding his sword in both hands, Ilumene struck once, twice, matching Telasin's speed and continuing to drive the daemon-touched soldier back. Telasin tried to lure Ilumene on too far, but the big man caught one khopesh on his sword and leaned away in time to watch the other flash past his chest.

Telasin kicked out, but Ilumene rode the blow and smacked an elbow into his opponent's shoulder – then he surged forwards to slam Telasin into the stone wall, where he pinned one arm down. With his sword still locked with Telasin's other khopesh, Ilumene again lunged forward, skull-capped head leading, and caught him a glancing blow on the chest.

This time he followed up with a hefty punch in the stomach, thumping Telasin back into the wall, before grabbing a dagger from his belt. Quick as a snake Ilumene drove the knife up between the scales of his armour to pierce Telasin's stomach, then he made sure of his kill by slashing at Telasin's throat. He stepped away and Telasin staggered clumsily sideways, unable to bring up his free khopesh in time. The bastard sword hacked down and Telasin fell, a shriek of supernatural rage exploding through the corridor as the daemon was banished.

Ilumene wiped his sword, panting for breath as a sly smile spread across his scarred face. He looked around for threats and found none. The others had clearly taken the wrong stairway, or run into more guards. Then his face froze.

'They're not here to kill me,' he muttered, looking up and summoning a mental picture of the Ruby Tower's many staircases. On the east side was a servants' stair – though it was steep and narrow, it was the faster route up. 'They'll have to check each room; Ruhen's small enough to hide anywhere. We still have time,' he muttered.

CHAPTER 14

Doranei paused and stared at the stairway ahead, leading up and down. Daken had run off so fast he didn't have a clue which way the white-eye had gone – but before he could choose he heard footsteps and found Cetarn, Osh and the remaining thieves following him, with Shin the Bastard slinking up behind.

'You three, check every room on the ground floor, then head up the tower, in case I need your God's blessing with a door,' Doranei ordered the thieves. They turned back without question, far from unhappy at missing the bulk of the fighting.

'Cetarn, can you find Aracnan?' Doranei asked.

Before Cetarn had the chance to reply Osh suddenly launched himself forward at Doranei. The King's Man dodged to one side, turning and striking blindly. His sword caught nothing, but he caught a flash of movement before Osh swept past, his scimitars swinging in unison. The bulky Mystic of Karkarn moved with shocking speed, throwing his whole body into a full-extended lunge that felled the first attacker and left him crouching awkwardly as the second slashed above his head. With a roar of effort Osh lunged again and the scimitar point caught the guard in the throat and opened one side of his neck as Osh jerked it back.

'Fires of Ghenna!' The mystic hissed through gritting teeth, catching his balance on the wall and taking his weight off his left leg. 'Merciful Gods, that hurt!'

'Your knee gone?' Doranei asked, reaching out in case the older man needed a hand.

'Aye, right and proper,' Osh said, his face tight as he fought the shooting pain in his leg. 'Piss and daemons, an old man's wound. You'll have to go on without me – I'm not climbing any more stairs.' He waved Doranei away. 'Don't stand there gawping, get moving, boy!'

'That way,' Cetarn said, pointing as he knelt at Osh's side.

Doranei moved past, beckoning to Shim to follow, while the oversized mage clamped his meaty hands around the man's injured knee. Osh gave a strangled gasp and dropped one scimitar as he fought to keep his balance. Cetarn ignored him and began to mutter a mantra, clipped Elvish words, as strands of green light danced between his fingers.

'Better?' he asked, heaving himself upright.

Osh put his foot tentatively back on the ground and gave a wary nod.

'I've done nothing to heal it,' the mage warned as Osh tried his weight on the leg and winced. 'I've only dimmed the pain. It'll come back, and worse than before. Any weight you put on it will cause further damage.'

'Better crippled than dead,' Osh said with feeling, and gestured for Cetarn to follow Doranei. 'I'll be waiting for you downstairs.'

At Cetarn's direction they ascended the tower as fast as they could. He could sense Aracnan somewhere near the top of a building that had twelve floors in four distinct steps, connected by a confusing network of stairways. Doranei'd worked out from his hard-gathered intelligence that the duchess had private chambers near the top, just before the tower narrowed.

Following Cetarn's directions, he estimated Aracnan was a few floors below that. They could tell nothing more, but Cetarn warned him that the immortal was surrounded by a wild, unfocused corona of magic.

'It's a good sign,' Cetarn continued, seeing Shim's face pale. 'It means he cannot concentrate properly, that he will be sloppy, and will act without thinking.'

'Seadiamond venom'll do that to a man,' Doranei said, his face darkening as Sebe intruded on his thoughts. 'Also means he'll not use all his power if he can help it – the more he uses the more it'll burn.'

'Still hope we find the Mad Axe 'fore Aracnan,' Shim muttered in the gravely voice of a man who smoked a lot and spoke little.

Doranei didn't have to agree with that. They all knew Aracnan would outmatch any single member of their company, and the fact that Doranei couldn't smell rotting flesh any more made him fear for Telasin. They moved from floor to floor as fast as they could, the only opposition a pair of scared-looking guards running headlong towards them. Doranei killed one and knock the other off-balance for Shim to finish. The mage-killer was as quick as the rat the mercenaries called him.

'He's on the floor above us,' Cetarn said in a low voice after a while.

'Right, here's how we go,' Doranei said. He turned around to look both Shim and Cetarn in the face; the mage was careful to keep Doranei between them. 'Shim, you first, when you see him, you break left. I'll be going right, and Cetarn, you hit him with everything you've got. Your object is to keep him distracted. With luck he'll still be deciding between you two when I reach him.'

Not giving them time to argue, Doranei shoved Shim ahead and on up the last flight of stairs, bodily pushing him towards the door Cetarn indicated. The mage was silent now, and pale, and a silver-encased shard of crystal glowed white in his hands as he prepared to fight a vastly more powerful and experienced mage.

Doranei kicked the door open and charged through, the pommel of his sword in the small of Shim's back. The room was pitch-black and Shim yelped in fear as he stumbled blindly forward, then howled as two flashes of light illuminated the room. Doranei let him run and stepped right, dropping after a few steps into a forward roll across the rug-strewn floor. The lightning came again, deafening cracks of raw power lashing at Shim, who kept wailing even as he was thrown against the wall.

Cetarn replied and struck with a shimmering flood of light that hissed and crackled uselessly against a white shield Aracnan produced. Doranei caught his first glimpse of the immortal – he looked barrel-chested, until Doranei realised one arm was bound to his chest. Aracnan's face was so emaciated it looked desiccated, and zigzags of red blisters spread up his exposed throat. As he attacked Doranei found his blows parried with ease, Aracnan's sword spitting sparks each time metal caught it. With a contemptuous flick of the wrist Aracnan sheered through the haft of Doranei's axe and kicked him square in the gut.

Doranei hit the bookcase behind hard enough to drive the wind from his lungs. For a moment all he could do was watch, gasping for breath, as Cetarn threw a spiralling coil of green magic that wrapped around Aracnan before melting into nothingness. Aracnan howled in pain as he struck back, his sword tracing arcs of light that raced forward to hit both Cetarn and Shim.

The mage-killer was unaffected, but Cetarn, defending himself desperately, fell in a way that told Doranei he was badly hurt. Aracnan himself reeled against a long table in the centre of the room as a gout of blood burst from his shoulder, but when Doranei forced himself to attack, the mercenary continued to turn his strokes with ease. He would have died there and then, had a roar not suddenly come from behind the Demi-God.

Aracnan rolled back over the corner of the table as an axe crashed down on the last spot where he'd been. Daken barrelled on and batted an armoured forearm into Aracnan's throat, ripping his axe out of the table with his free hand and spinning into a second blow using all his Gods-granted speed. Aracnan caught the blow, but he couldn't move fast enough to stop the butt of the axe being smashed into his bound arm. He staggered back, checking a moment to let Daken follow then chopping savagely upwards. The glittering black sword would have torn Daken in two – but instinct made the white-eye dodge.

Doranei could see the white-eye's face contorted with rage as he attacked again, beating at the immortal with axe-head and butt as fast as he could – not looking for a killing blow, but striking faster than Aracnan could defend one-handed. Doranei ran to join in, but before he could reach Aracnan, Daken had pinned the immortal's sword and head-butted the Demi-God hard enough to make them both to stagger backwards, stunned.

From the shadows behind Aracnan jumped Shim, axe abandoned, and grabbed Aracnan by the throat with one hand, wrapping the other arm around it as though meaning to strangle him.

Doranei was about to shout a warning to Shim when Aracnan shrieked like a soul at the ivory gates of Ghenna. A pulse of raw power exploded all around the pair, knocking even Daken from his feet. Doranei was thrown onto his back, and though he caught only jerky, confused glimpses of what was happening, he realised the mage-killer was true to his name: Shim was holding on tight while Aracnan bucked and wheeled around the room like a maddened bull.

The mercenary continued to bellow in pain, but now it was all-consuming and he flailed like a man on fire, unable even to try to pull Shim off his back. The Crystal Skull on his sword-hilt blazed brightly, filling the room with white light, even after Aracnan dropped it.

Then, shockingly, his screams came to an abrupt end, and a second later the Demi-God crashed to his knees. Shim continued to hug the mercenary's head tight to his chest, his eyes screwed up tight, but when he found his feet on the ground again he risked a look up. His face was set in a rictus of terror.

Without warning Aracnan sagged and went limp and Shim toppled with the corpse. He fell with it as it flopped to the floor.

'Bastard,' Daken growled, his face still contorted with bloodlust, 'he was mine!'

The white-eye had raised his axe and taken a step towards Shim before Doranei shouted for him to stop. 'Daken, we don't have time for this!'

The white-eye turned towards Doranei, who retreated before him. Daken's teeth were bared, his breathing more like a rabid dog's snarl, and Doranei kept well back; he knew how Coran was when the rage was upon him.

'Ilumene's still in the tower,' Doranei shouted, trying to get through to the man behind the bloodlust. 'He must have killed Telasin – you take him, and you'll be a hero of Narkang!'

Daken peered forward, axe still raised. 'Not a fucking immortal, though, is he?' he roared. 'Not a fucking Demi-God! You think I'm in for the money?' The white-eye shuddered, the veins in his neck bulging as he fought to restrain the burning bloodlust coursing through him. With an effort of will Daken straightened up and lowered his weapon. Turning back the way he'd come he shot Shim a look of pure venom.

'We'll be havin' words later,' he snapped before disappearing through the open doorway on the far side of the room.

Shim didn't reply. He was still panting, and shuddering with exhaustion as he stared down at the corpse.

'You did good,' Doranei said, hesitantly taking Shim by the shoulder. The battered little man flinched and shied away, but he gave a grim smile when he was out of reach.

Doranei pointed down at the black broadsword on the ground. 'Spoils of war, if you want it.'

Shim gave a bitter, humourless laugh. 'No good to me,' he whispered hoarsely. 'Just a lump of metal in my hands.'

Remembering Cetarn, Doranei left the mage-killer to his thoughts. The big mage was still alive, curled around his left arm. There was blood all over his robes and his normally cheerful face was contorted with pain.

'Cetarn, how bad is it?' Doranei had to repeat his question before the mage noticed him.

'A fair scratch,' Cetarn croaked, his face white.

The mage lifted his right arm to expose the bloody stump of his left arm. The mage was trembling, but shock hadn't taken his senses yet. As Doranei watched Cetarn flexed his fingers and a red glow surrounded the wound, followed by a sizzling sound and a smell that made Doranei gag. The mage screamed, a sound that ended with a gasping sob. The King's Man rose and retrieved Aracnan's discarded sword.

'Will this help?' he asked, offering the weapon and pointing at the Crystal Skull fused to the hilt.

Cetarn gave Doranei a broken smile. He stroked his fingers over the Skull's glassy surface before slipping it off the black metal as smoothly as ice over stone. A brief pulse of light was enough to give Cetarn the strength to sit up.

'The pain is gone, we can continue,' he whispered.

Doranei stared at the mage then down at the massive sword in his own hands. 'No, you've gone far enough. Time for you to get out. We don't have much more time before the Menin garrison works out what's happening and our escape route's closed.'

Cetarn got unsteadily to his feet. 'I've still got some fight in me,' he said in a strained voice, sounding as weak as his long-time colleague Endine, who'd been left back at the warehouse to prepare their retreat.

'You're out,' Doranei said firmly. 'Shim, see he gets back down safely.'

'As long as he can walk,' Shim said sourly, 'no good in me helping him there.'

'I can walk,' Cetarn confirmed, taking a few wobbly steps before finding his balance. 'Doranei, go.'

The King's Man nodded and sheathed his usual sword, unwilling to abandon it. He hefted Aracnan's ugly black blade. It was as ancient as any he'd ever encountered, Eolis included – but where Eolis was a cool silver, this could have been made of obsidian, its matt surface dull, but for the faint pinpricks of light bursting on the surface. It took him only a moment to realise just how light and fast the sword was – it cut the air quicker than Doranei could have with a switch of willow, let alone a steel blade.

'Daken will find Ilumene first,' he muttered as Cetarn headed towards the door with Shim watching him warily, 'but if he doesn't, this will give the traitor a surprise.'

He headed for the door Daken had left through, pausing only to spit on Aracnan's corpse.

'Enjoy your time in the Dark Place,' he whispered. 'Your master will be following soon.'

Unseen by the men leaving, the shadows began to lengthen and deepen. One Land continued as normal while another, unseen, changed and grew heavy. The sharp lines of the stone walls faded behind a curtain of darkness, the texture of night becoming more tangible than stone or wood. A distant tremble ran through the floor and faded as silence reclaimed the room. All was still for a while, then the shadows grew thicker still. The one cast by the corpse became a pool of liquid black. It twitched like a maggot-ridden corpse. For a moment it seemed to strain against the dead-weight of the corpse, then it tore free and arose.

The lamps guttered before extinguishing as one. The air grew frosty and for a moment the darkness was absolute. Slowly a pale, sourceless silver light appeared, so weak it barely reached the walls on either side, but making the slow swirl of ice in the air sparkle. The shadow stood up straight and stared at the crystallising cold until a tall figure winked into being, hooded by absolute dark.

'You come to claim me now?' said the spirit with contempt. 'Never once acknowledged, never offered the place rightfully mine. Now you have the gall to summon me to the fold, when my life is over?'

'You were too weak,' Death replied, His voice heavy, emotionless. 'You were not strong enough to join the Pantheon.'

'Strong enough to kill one of your kind!' the spirit spat, its hatred undiminished.

The room grew instantly darker and more oppressive. 'What you did was a crime,' the cowled figure boomed, the very air shaking with His anger. 'To murder the divine is almost beyond forgiveness – and you did so with a weapon forged by the great heretic himself.'

'To the Dark Place with you and this feud with your creations; I want none of it – only what was due to me! I was the first of the Demi-Gods, and the greatest. You spurned me out of cowardice, not the infallible judgment your priests so cravenly claim as yours.'

Death stood silent for a while, regarding the soul of His unclaimed child as though the spirit had a face to see, an expression to scrutinise and fathom. All around them the darkness was suddenly filled with movement and life, as black shapes darted and fluttered just on the edge of sight.

'You were the first and greatest of your kind,' Death said without emotion. 'For that reason I offer you a boon. You may take your place in the land of no time. You will be conveyed there with all honour due to—'

'Spare me,' the spirit said furiously, 'I want none of your honour and none of empty charity! If you mean to grant me a boon let it be this; spare me your empty words and cast me down into the Dark Place. Let the creatures of Ghenna welcome me and reforge me in their fires as Aryn Bwr did the Crystal Skulls. Let the daemons make me one of their own if you think me so weak, so flawed. Let me choose the path and the consequences, as you chose for me all those millennia ago.'

'A boon I offered,' Death said slowly, 'a boon I shall give. If hatred is all you have left, so be it. There will be a place for you in Ghenna. The ivory gates will welcome you.'

The sparkle of cold vanished from the air. In its place came a deep red light and the stink of burning. The spirit turned its back on Death and spread its arms out wide as the floor trembled and shook. Distant voices came like shrieks on the wind, bloody light bursting from the cracks in the floor. The light intensified, flooding the room and shining like infernal rime on the edges of the shadows.

Death watched, unspeaking. The room around Him shook but His robes were unruffled, the mantle of night covering His head untouched by the red light. The shaking continued, but became no worse until He let go and vanished, leaving His son to his chosen fate.

As soon as Death was gone the red light filled the room and tore the floor open, a burning chasm appearing below. The distant voices became near and urgent, and screams of rage and pain echoed up to greet him. The roar of flames and howl of wind struck the spirit like a blow, but nothing could dissuade it. The spirit dived down towards the grasping hands within the chasm, reaching for their cruel embrace as the red light raced after him and the floor closed up. Behind him there was only darkness.

Doranei paused at a window and realised he could hear the clatter of combat from outside. It was too dark to see anything when he looked out other than indistinct grey movement in the darkness. He assumed that was a good sign. If the Menin garrison had worked out what was happening and arrived, the Brotherhood wouldn't wait; they'd fight their way out using the battle-mages to punch their exit hole.

Indistinctly he heard bellowing coming from elsewhere in the tower: Daken. It was random shouting, a white-eye's joy of battle rather than a man looking for him. He left the white-eye to it and headed further up to the duchess' private quarters. When he reached them there were two liveried guards on the door, but they were hesitant to leave their post to take the attack to him, which gave him time to grab a pouch from his belt and toss it, half-open, at the heavy door they guarded. As it hit a puff of dust was expelled, and weak though the lamplight was, it was enough to ignite the dust in a bright white flash.

As the men cringed and covered their eyes Doranei dispatched them quickly and recovered the pouch carefully, tugging the draw-strings tight before re-hanging from his belt. That done, he tried the door. He wasn't surprised to find it bolted, but he didn't bother seeking one of the Cerdin-blessed thieves. Instead Doranei placed the tip of Aracnan's sword where he guessed the door's hinge would be and stabbed forward with all his strength.

The weapon pierced the oak without difficulty and went straight through. He worked it up and down and quickly found the hinge, withdrawing the sword to get the tip against the metal. With a single pace as run-up Doranei slammed the sword in and felt the metal burst under the impact.

Doing the same with the lower hinge was a simple task and

soon the door was hanging drunkenly, half-open. Doranei slipped through the gap and blinked at the gloom inside, for a moment seeing nothing but indistinct shadows. When his eyes had adjusted Doranei found himself in a small ante-chamber with closed doors left and right, and a wide doorway ahead leading into an elegant study. He tried the closed doors first. The child's bedroom he tore apart until he was sure no hiding places remained, then the breakfast room got similar treatment.

The study straight ahead was empty too, and finally he headed for the duchess' bedroom, off the study. The room was very dark, even with a faint glimmer of moonlight creeping through the clouds. The lamps were barely warm to the touch. A lifetime of night exploits had given Doranei excellent vision in the dark, but he still managed to blunder into an unseen table as he headed for the window to look down. Still no light from below, but he was running out of time.

A sudden sense of being watched crept over him, causing the hairs of his neck to prickle as he whirled around, sword raised. The dark room remained still and empty, but the sense continued.

And well it might, Doranei thought, reaching for the pouch of sparkle-dust again. *That bloody door was barred from the inside.*

With a sweep of his sword Doranei smashed the nearest oil lamp and dropped the rest of the dust onto it, looking away with his eyes screwed up tight. The dust ignited and the lamp oil caught immediately, casting a weak light over the room. Doranei tugged a curtain from its rail and was about to set it alight when the shadows on the other side of the window suddenly billowed.

He dropped the curtain and struck out at the shadows, but a sword materialised from nowhere and caught the blow. Doranei hesitated; short blade and long handle – this wasn't who he'd feared.

'Zhia?' he said, startled.

The shadows opened like a black flower saluting the moon. Zhia Vukotic appeared, resplendent in a blood-red dress and white silk scarf, with her sword extended.

'My dear, you are one of the few people to ever look relieved when you find a vampire lurking in the shadows,' she said with a pained smile. 'I apologise for giving you a start.'

'What are you doing here?' Doranei demanded, lowering his sword and advancing on his immortal lover. 'Where are the duchess and Ruhen?'

'Escaped, I assume,' Zhia said, sheathing her sword on her back with a flourish. 'They had already gone when I arrived up here.'

'Why are you here? Why did you bolt the door?'

Zhia gave him a look that was almost too weary for irritation. Whatever she'd been doing, it had taken a toll on her.

'I was elsewhere in the tower on business; Lady Kinna has apartments on a lower level. When I heard the commotion it was not hard to guess who would be heading this way. I don't know how your Brothers would react to seeing me here, but I assumed King Emin's pet white-eye would be at the fore. His kind are hard to talk down once their blood is up and I have no desire to kill your friends. I thought the bolted door would slow them up; I hoped they couldn't waste the time it would require to break it.' She gave a wry smile – then suddenly screwed her eyes closed, as if in pain.

She gasped, shock blossoming on her face. 'By the Dark Place, I had forgotten how painful His presence was!'

'Whose?' Doranei asked, looking around.

Zhia straightened, as though a weight was lifted from her shoulders. 'That's better, He's gone now. Your Lord Death, that's who,' she added with a sour smile. 'What I crave the most I cannot bear the presence of. You must have killed Aracnan; He has come for His unclaimed son.'

Zhia stopped, noticing the sword for the first time. 'Even your mages would have found it hard to draw the bolts to this room. I had hoped to lurk here undisturbed until He had departed. I hadn't expected you to be carrying anything so powerful. Did you kill Aracnan yourself?' She sounded sceptical.

'I was there when he died,' Doranei replied, not wanting to waste time explaining any further. 'Can you find the child for me?'

'I have already tried, but there's too much of a swirl of magic around the tower for me to find anyone not a mage.'

Doranei faltered, his shoulders sagging. 'Then this was all for nothing?' he said distantly.

'Not necessarily.' Zhia pointed to the desk on which lay a few books, a writing box and a silver sand-shaker. 'I had a look around while I was waiting for your men to lose their ardour for slaughter.'

He moved to the desk, scanning the objects on it but seeing nothing out of the ordinary. 'And?' he prompted.

With a twitch of her fingers Zhia caused one of the books to rise up, green light playing around the edges and illuminating the monogram on the front. 'I noticed an enchantment on one of the books and found it bore my brother's initials.' She let the book fall into his hands. 'Is this the journal you were looking for?'

Doranei looked it over. It did indeed have entwined Vs on the cover, just as the novice Mayel had described to him. This had to be what Azaer had wanted from the abbot in Scree – what the shadow had sacrificed possession of the Skull of Ruling for.

When he tried to open it he found the pages stuck together, and when he ran his finger down the edge he saw a tiny spark of light and felt something as sharp as a knife slice his skin. He withdrew his hand hurriedly.

'It's a simple magical lock; it will not tax your king's mages for too long,' Zhia assured him, 'but right now, it is time for you to leave.'

The look on her face told him not to argue and he realised she was right. He had already stayed longer than he'd planned; it was time to make good their escape.

'Thank you,' he said awkwardly.

Without warning Zhia made up the ground between them and grabbed him by his brigandine. Pulling him close she kissed him hard and fierce. When she withdrew the taste of her lips and the heady scent of her perfume remained.

'Do not thank me,' she said, her face unreadable. 'Every step in your war against the shadow takes you further into pain. This may bring you a league of hurt.'

'It is necessary,' he croaked. 'I do what I must.'

She gave him a weak smile. 'As do we both.'

This time it was Doranei's turn to pull the vampire close, half-lifting her off the ground and kissing her before he fled through the door. When he had gone she stared after him, her lips pursed tight. With a wave of the hand she extinguished the flames and was left alone with the shadows.

'Do not disappoint me,' Zhia said softly. The shadows did not reply.

CHAPTER 15

It was not yet midday when Count Vesna reached the Tirah-Tebran border, and already he'd had enough. Advance warning of what was waiting there failed to lessen his disgust when he saw the banners in the distance – banners that had no place in this suzerainty. In contrast, the ruby shard upon his cheek tingled at the prospect of violence.

At his side General Lahk observed them impassively, his only sign of disapproval the ordering of his personal standard be carried by the advance scouts, alongside the red banners of mourning. The general was also a marshal of Tebran, and it was into his small domain they were riding. Lahk's obedience to tradition was absolute, but Vesna doubted Suzerain Temal or Scion Ranah would care about the small rebuke, if they even noticed it.

They had spent the previous night at the manor of Suzerain Tebran, once one of Lord Bahl's fiercest supporters; renowned for his strength, but now a broken man, drinking himself to death. His parchment-pale skin hung loose on his body, and when Vesna had broken the news of his scion's death in battle, he hadn't been sure if the suzerain had even heard him. Muttered apologies were all Tebran had given, and it had been left to his daughter, Anatay, to tell them why through her own grief.

'He was frightened for me, frightened for us all. There was only one of his hurscals here; the rest were with you, my Lord. He had to grant them leave to stay, to march under arms in the suzerainty.'

Vesna scowled and felt his armoured fist tighten around the reins. Threatening the weak to claim the protection of the law? It made the God in him bay for blood. Each suzerainty was a self-contained domain, subject only to the Lord of the Farlan – to ride battle-ready in another's suzerainty without permission was tantamount to a declaration of war, but with his troops not yet returned from the Circle City, Suzerain Tebran had nothing to back up his authority.

Technically they were within the law, but it was a gross flouting of custom, and at any other time Vesna would have sorted it out at the point of his sword. Now, however, he had to ignore the breach, the only way to avoid bloodshed on his return to Tirah. The heir to the Ranah suzerainty was a hot-headed thug who'd draw at the first provocation and whether a battle or a duel, it would only make a bad situation worse.

'Suzerain Torl?' he called, turning in the saddle to catch the attention of the grey-haired suzerain riding a little way behind him.

'My Lord,' Torl acknowledged, as formal in addressing Vesna as the rest of his fellow Brethren of the Sacred Teachings, despite their past years of close friendship.

Isak, Vesna thought sadly, *was this how your life was? Always set apart, even from friends? Never allowed to be just part of the crowd?* He shook the thought away. Time for that later.

'Do you know Suzerain Temal? I've met Ranah several times and he doesn't have the brains to get on his horse the right way round first try.'

'Yes, my Lord, well enough. Temal's got precious little affection for his subjects, but I'd never thought the man disloyal – or religious, for that matter.'

'So we have a whole new faction?' Vesna muttered. 'Gods, it's a wonder we ever got around to building a bloody nation here.'

Torl gave a noncommittal shrug. The ageing warrior had never been one for ceremony and was dressed like any cavalryman, only the badge with his Ice Cobra crest indicating he was a nobleman.

A red cape of mourning hung over Vesna's divine-touched left arm, hiding it from onlookers, but the rest of his clothes followed tradition. His oiled hair was tied down one side of his neck to cover the blue tattoos of knighthood there.

'General Lahk? How do you want to play this?'

Lahk looked back at the divisions of Palace Guard following them before replying, 'We cannot be sure of their intentions, and until proved otherwise we must assume they are allies. They have broken no law.'

'I suppose so,' Vesna said reluctantly. 'Riding on through would be insulting to their stations, however strongly Lord Fernal ordered us to return without delay.'

'They're not here to fight – no Farlan suzerain takes on the Ghosts, however mauled we might be.'

Vesna looked around. The Tirah Highway passed through mainly forested ground, but there were villages and towns around and clearings and fields dotted the landscape. Here there were sufficient trees to obscure his view, and space for a few legions of troops to wait for the order. The mountain-lines of the Spiderweb range stopped at Tebran's outer border, but ridges of high hilly ground remained and anyone advancing towards Tirah would continue to be at the disadvantage right up to the city walls.

'They might if they have reinforcements nearby – our scouts and scryers could have missed an ambush easily enough.'

'Of the nearby suzerains the only one whose loyalty was in question was Suzerain Selsetin, and he died in battle at the Byoran Fens. There is no man of Duke Certinse's ilk here,' Torl pointed out. 'What would be their reason for such a risky venture, my Lord?'

Vesna shook his head. 'I don't know – and that's what has me worried. The past six months has shown us that the usual rules of the great game need not apply. I'm inclined to see hostility in any move I do not understand.'

'Sir Cerse,' Lahk called, prompting the colonel of the Palace Guard to urge his horse up to Lahk's.

Vesna watched him approach with a sense of sadness. Sir Cerse had been an eager young soldier when they first met not long ago – a political appointment, but keen to earn the loyalty of his men. Now there was a grim set to his jaw and a bandage covering one ruined eye. The colonel of the Ghosts had earned the respect of his men, but Vesna recognised all too easily a soldier who'd lost something of himself on the way.

'Sir Cerse, call a halt and ensure the men are ready for whatever might happen. We'll take two squads as escort and proceed to greet our peers.'

'Are you sure?' Vesna asked once Sir Cerse had returned to issue the order. 'Won't that just encourage them to act rashly?'

'"If your enemy intends to act, encourage him to do so rashly",' Lahk quoted in response. 'My authority ends with the military side of matters. Suzerain Torl, Count Vesna; I suggest you discuss the politics with Ranah and Temal, it is not my domain. If they do indeed intend us harm, let that come about before they discover Count Vesna's new allegiance.'

'I take your point,' Vesna admitted. He sighed and touched his black-iron fingers to the sword on his hip. 'It will be easily done, but let's hope it won't come to that.'

Riding ahead with a battle-scarred squad of Ghosts on each side, the three veterans did not speak until they passed through the advance companies of troops. They found themselves at an inn where Suzerain Temal and Scion Ranah were waiting. It was a big place, a three-storey stone building overlooking the single bridge across a tributary of the River Farsen, which cut through the heart of Tirah.

Soldiers were all around, and Vesna could see the inn's serving girls were struggling to meet the demand just from the hurscals. The more he looked, the more troops he saw – mainly light cavalry, of course, but also what appeared to be a division's worth of archers and spearmen.

'Good morning Suzerain Torl, General Lahk,' called Suzerain Temal, rising from his seat at a round stone table on one side of the inn named after it. He spared Vesna a look, but nothing more, making it clear he did not expect the lower-ranked man to speak until invited to do so. Vesna might be a hero, and Isak's right-hand man, but he was still a count, and ranked below both suzerains and generals. 'Please, join us in a cup of wine.' Palms upturned, Temal had pointedly dispensed with the usual formalities, something Vesna hoped was a good sign. That he was excluding Vesna was no great surprise; a suzerain had the right to speak only to his peers if he so chose, and if Vesna didn't speak, it was less likely Ranah would either.

The suzerain was a man of nearly forty summers. He had a welcoming smile. He wore his sword on his right hip because a childhood injury had robbed him of most of the use in his right hand. He'd not joined the army when Lord Isak had called his nobles because of it, but Vesna had heard he was a fair left-handed swordsman all the same.

Torl and Lahk dismounted and returned the suzerain's greeting. Vesna followed them. He had no intention of speaking until

215

addressed, but the hatred on Scion Ranah's face made it obvious he'd be easy to provoke, whilst keeping within the bounds of protocol. Ranah disliked Vesna intensely – a matter of principle more than anything else. The fact that Vesna had seduced the scion's sister was less of concern than Ranah made out; in truth, he was jealous.

Ranah was a handsome man, and his unusually light hair made him striking among the dark Farlan. He was also a talented warrior, and he coveted Vesna's reputation more than he did his octogenarian father's seat. Count Vesna was the man Ventale Ranah was trying hard to be, but his exploits thus far had earned only his father's scorn, and he'd been completely ignored by the storytellers.

A man easily provoked into rashness, Vesna though as he reached for a cup and poured himself some wine.

'The invitation did not extend to you, Count Vesna. Your jewels are better-suited to a whorehouse than a table of peers,' Scion Ranah snapped.

'Suzerain Temal,' Vesna said, raising his cup in toast and ignoring Ranah, whose outburst had permitted him to join the conversation. Temal would have to keep control of Ranah or lose face. 'We would be glad for a chance to sit down and discuss the state of the Land with peers.' He drained the cup and smiled. 'But in the interests of harmony I suggest you send the boy away before his mouth gets him into mischief – unless it's mischief you intend?'

Before Ranah's coughs of fury could resolve into a challenge, Temal drained his own cup and raised a hand to stop the scion speaking.

'We do not intend mischief, I assure you; we are all nobles of the Farlan, after all. However, Count Vesna, perhaps a less antagonistic tone might be politic? I hardly think "boy" is the right description for a man only five summers younger than you.'

Vesna shrugged off the reprimand, deserved as it was. As a count he outranked Ranah, at least until the man inherited his father's suzerainty, and Vesna intended to make full use of that. 'The last time I met the scion he was less than gracious towards me. It was only admiration for his father that prevented me from calling the scion out.'

'That or cowardice,' Ranah interjected, which earned him an admonishing look from Temal.

Vesna ignored him. 'I choose not to acknowledge any man inviting a challenge, but my position within the Land has changed and I can no longer overlook an insult.'

With his iron-clad hand Vesna slipped his sword partway from his scabbard, just far enough to reveal the misty white lines of the Crystal Skull melded about the black-iron blade. 'Nor would I even break a sweat in a duel with any man present.'

Temal's eyes narrowed, and he gave a small nod of understanding. 'Be that as it may, I would ask you to show greater civility in future.'

He turned to Ranah. 'Any mention of a man's honour is similarly uncivil and goes against our purpose of being here. I would appreciate it, Scion Ranah, if you would retire and see to those messages we were discussing earlier.'

Ranah scowled, but as there was nothing he could do he turned without a word and stalked away, disappearing into the inn and slamming the door behind him. Once he was gone, Suzerain Temal broke into a relieved smile and gestured for his companions to sit.

'I apologise,' he began. 'I spoke to Ranah before you arrived and he assured me he would behave.'

'Easily forgiven,' Torl said, 'but the treatment of Suzerain Tebran is less so. Whether or not it was Ranah at fault, you choose the company you keep, Temal – you know what sort of man he is.'

Temal nodded, looking glum. Shrewd politician that he was, he knew the ramifications of implying a threat to gain the right to march under arms in Tebran. A suzerain ignored the customs surrounding their law at his peril; neighbours became far less friendly with a man they couldn't trust. 'Such are the times that a man must keep company he finds distasteful. I will make suitable apologies to Tebran; my intention is quite the opposite from setting noble houses against each other.'

'Then tell us plainly what your intention is,' Vesna said.

Temal scrutinised the Mortal-Aspect for a while. 'I will do so,' he said, 'but now I see you' – he gestured towards Vesna's face and left arm – 'well, I have questions of my own.'

'They will be answered,' Vesna promised him.

'Very well. First, let it be clear I am not acting alone today. I've been in correspondence with many like-minded peers and I represent them here.'

The statement prompted raised eyebrows, but nothing more;

Torl and Vesna were content to wait to hear something of substance before commenting, and Lahk had pointedly pushed his seat back from the table to indicate the other two were speaking on his behalf.

'I assume you know of Lord Isak's decree regarding his successor,' Temal began hesitantly. 'Perhaps you do not yet realise the extent of the outrage this has provoked.'

'If you are going to suggest insurrection,' Torl said sharply, 'I would suggest you stop all thoughts down that path. However much they might dislike it, the Ghosts wouldn't disobey an order to slaughter your troops to a man.'

'That's not what I mean,' Temal said, raising his hands placatingly. 'I mean only to set the ground for my words.'

Vesna stared at the man's expression and realised some spark of suspicion had flared inside him. Reading a man's face was important to any duellist, but the intent was not so clearly marked on Temal's face. There was something he wasn't saying, some agenda running behind the truth of his words.

'What you probably don't know is that High Cardinal Certinse was murdered by one of his own clerks. I'm told the man was a fanatic who couldn't accept Certinse's decision to ratify Lord Isak's decision regarding his successor.'

Interesting, he's been careful to avoid saying the name Fernal – either to avoid having to speak his title, or to avoid having to refuse to.

'Cardinal Veck has taken his place?' Torl asked, his face grim. Veck had been among the worst of the fanatics when they left the city, and this could lead only to more trouble.

'He has, and his first act was to rescind the Synod's approval. Now while—'

'Wait,' Vesna broke in, 'first tell me this: do you and whoever you claim to represent accept Lord Fernal's appointment?'

Temal sighed. 'We believe the decision has no basis in law, and on this point alone we are in agreement with the cults.'

'An edict by Lord Isak was not legal?'

'The law states the title Lord of the Farlan is for the Chosen only, and an appointed regent must come from the nobility. Lord Isak cannot simply nominate a successor; that invites the creation of dynasties.'

There was a moment of silence. The point was valid; the Synod approval had been vital to shore up an uncertain claim. It was an irony that the move intended to provide a rallying point to the tribe had instead sparked fresh divisions within it.

'And you think to make this point with an army at your back?' General Lahk asked suddenly. 'The politics are not my concern but I'm General of the Heartland, with orders enshrined in law that go beyond the current ruler of the tribe. If any army crosses this boundary into Tirah territory, I am bound to respond.'

'You did nothing while mercenaries ruled the streets of Tirah!' Temal said angrily, 'and the new High Cardinal has been consolidating his power since the entire Palace Guard left.'

'My duties are unclear regarding troops gathering on Tirah's streets,' Lahk said, unconcerned by Temal's tone, 'so Chief Steward Lesarl guided my actions and Lord Isak approved them. There is no issue of clarity regarding troop units exceeding a regiment crossing that border without permission.'

Temal stood. 'Unlike some suzerains I have heard of, military action is not our intention. We will only act if we hear reports of the cults breaking the law – but permit me to make this very clear: the power of the Farlan has always resided in the hands of the nobility, and that's always been kept apart from the cults. No court-ranked nobleman may take holy orders; no cleric may hold command rank – this is the law that has kept our tribe strong, and we will defend that position against all who threaten it.

'Inform the creature Fernal of our position. There are some who may intend insurrection – both for and against the cults, make no mistake about that – but I believe I represent a majority opinion among the nobility. We are willing to fight to stop the cults gaining any further control over the tribe, and we expect Fernal to withdraw his claim on the title of Lord of the Farlan.'

Interesting, Vesna thought, listening to the measured tone of Temal's voice. *I think this one's trying to be nice to all sides, and come out as the suzerain who helped avoid bloodshed. The more he smoothes things over now, the more useful he'll appear to any future leader desperate to keep peace.*

'Who would you have take his place?' Torl asked in a horrified voice, as though he was already expecting the answer.

'You, my Lord Suzerain,' Temal said stiffly, 'to be regent of the Farlan until our Patron God chooses one to take Lord Isak's place.

You can unify our tribe, Suzerain Torl – perhaps you alone can prevent civil war.'

Desultory drizzle welcomed the remaining regiments to Tirah; the faint patter wiped out by the sound of hooves on cobbles. Vesna rode at the head of the cavalry, watching the faces of those they passed and trying to gauge the mood of the city. There was no hostility in the faces he saw, but no celebration either. The citizens of Tirah looked tired to him, worn down by the struggles of the different factions, and the fear that accompanied those struggles. They waited impassively for the soldiers to pass, but as worried as that made him, the Mortal-Aspect of Karkarn saw other things to concern him more.

The presence of priests on the streets was no great surprise – their bile and fury would have dissuaded many from attending temple, so it had always been likely the priests would eventually follow – or chase – their flocks into the street. That every major street corner had a priest preaching was troubling, as was the venom with which they harangued passers-by – and even the cavalry, until their attendants hushed them.

Every preacher had at least a handful of penitents guarding them, a necessary precaution considering the raised hackles their words were causing among the people. Vesna knew that folk wouldn't go against armed troops, but angry words were being exchanged all over the city. He couldn't help but be put in mind of Scree in the days before the population lost its sanity completely. He shuddered.

When the procession reached the lower end of the Palace Walk, Vesna saw a crowd up ahead and called a halt. The people were blocking the street and he didn't want to lead the cavalry close enough to spark either a panic or a riot. As he edged nearer however, he realised this was no mob, but a crowd listening intently. Vesna looked over the heads to see what was happening and blinked in surprise.

There was what had to be a Harlequin standing on a makeshift gantry on the left. The diamond-pattern clothes and white porcelain mask were unmistakable, as was the entranced hush over the crowd.

'Now that's something I've never seen before,' he commented to Suzerain Torl beside him. 'A Harlequin preaching?'

He'd spoken too quietly to be heard by anyone else, but all the same the Harlequin broke off from what it was saying and stared straight at him. Vesna felt the air grow cold as faces turned to follow the Harlequin's line of sight. Their expressions were more annoyance at the interruption than anything else, but Vesna also smelled resentment in the air.

He started to turn his horse away from the crowd when the Harlequin called out over the tense quiet, 'Brothers, there you have the embodiment of war – sitting so proud with blood on his cheek, stained and burdened by the life he has led. Pity him, fellow children of the Gods, for men of war have lost the path of peace and pain fills their soul.'

Vesna checked behind him to ensure his soldiers hadn't instinctively drawn their weapons.

'I fight in the name of the Gods,' he called back, aware that he needed to respond in some way. 'I fight with the blessing of the Gods.' *Death's cold rattle, why is a* Harlequin *starting an argument with me?*

'You are as lost as the cults. It only remains to be seen if you wish to seek peace, or continue to add to the pain sickening this Land,' the Harlequin retorted.

'You claim greater wisdom than the Gods?' Vesna demanded.

The Harlequin gave a slow, pitying shake of the head. 'Not I – all I claim is a desire to fill my heart with peace, to be as a child and free myself of the burden of years that cloud a mind.'

I don't think I'm likely to win an argument about the merits of peace, Vesna thought, tugging his red cloak a little to ensure it completely covered his armoured arm. *But I'll find out nothing by backing off.*

'What of the wisdom that comes with age?' he ventured.

'That too is clouded by the fear driving the actions of men. It is only by letting the baggage of life fall away that men ensure their decisions are not tainted or swayed.'

'Let me guess: you have a suggestion for how to do that?'

'Not I,' the Harlequin intoned; 'I do not appoint myself arbitrator for the deeds of others. Every man and woman must choose their own path in this life. I offer no ritual for absolution, no mantra to cleanse the soul of its stains. We must all find innocence in our own way – we must all serve innocence in our own way.'

Before Vesna could think of a reply the Harlequin raised its hand, pointing at the part of the crowd that was blocking the centre of the street. 'My siblings, we cannot hope to find the path to peace just by blocking the path of war,' it called in a laughing voice, diffusing the tension in the air. 'Please, allow the men of war to pass; a child would not be so prideful as to mind standing in the gutter and nor shall we!'

A smattering of laughter accompanied the shuffling of feet and in moments the street was clear enough for the troops to pass. Gesturing for the column to advance, Vesna rode on slowly, giving the Harlequin a respectful nod as he passed. It did nothing in response, but he felt its eyes on his back until he crossed Hunter's Ride and started on the last stretch leading to the Palace. As he neared that Vesna realised there was another unpleasant surprise waiting before he made it inside the walls.

'Gods, I've got enough to worry about, haven't I?' he muttered under his breath.

'Soldiers?' Suzerain Torl said, casting Vesna a questioning look. Torl was older than the men under his command, and he had to rely on their eyesight for anything in the distance.

'Aye, they're penitents,' Vesna said grimly, 'but maybe this is one argument today I can win.'

'Are you going to reveal your full authority, my Lord?'

'How long would I be able to keep it a secret in any case? It's a surprise the city didn't all know before we arrived.'

Vesna spurred his horse into a canter and broke away from the column, covering the ground quickly. A regiment of penitents had formed up around the fountain-statue of Evaole at the centre of the Barbican Square. Vesna took in the whole scene with a single glance: the Palace gates were shut and archers stood ready on the battlements above. The rest of the square was deserted.

The penitents looked nervous, shifting restlessly while the priests in charge of them bristled at his arrival – or one of them did at least; the other was a priest of Karkarn, of middling rank by the hems of his scarlet robes. His reaction had been one of opposites; stepping boldly forward, then faltering, most likely when he saw the teardrop on Vesna's face.

'Count Vesna, the city rejoices in your return,' announced the other priest, somehow contriving to sound disapproving of what he'd just said. He was a man of Nartis, and as tall as Vesna, though he lacked a warrior's muscle. His features were small and rounded with cheeks like a baby's, but his expression was rapacious.

'Really?' Vesna said in a dead tone and looked around. 'I didn't notice anyone celebrating. Is that what you're doing here?'

'No, my Lord, we are here on the orders of the High Cardinal himself—'

'To besiege the Palace?' Vesna broke in, recognising the pious tones of a fanatic; it was easy enough these days.

'To ensure the rule of law and the will of the Gods are done,' the priest snapped back. 'The abomination Chief Steward Lesarl has installed in the Palace must be driven out, along with the Chief Steward himself. The impious ways of that wicked man have forced our hand, and we stand here in defence of the entire Farlan tribe, against the machinations of inhumans and all outsiders.'

'Last stand of the faithful, eh?' Vesna growled. 'I was present at one of those in Scree. I can tell you: it brought us only hurt.'

'Unmen Dors!' hissed the priest of Karkarn, 'perhaps it is time we left?'

'Leave?' Dors shrieked at his fellow unmen, 'and disobey the orders of the High Cardinal, the voice of our Gods himself?'

'Enough,' Vesna shouted, loud enough to make even the fanatic hesitate. The penitents were staring at Vesna with increasing apprehension. He knew his reputation as a warrior wasn't the cause; it was the effect of Karkarn's blood flowing through his veins. *Time to use that divine authority.*

'Unmen Dors,' Vesna continued in a quieter voice, 'you will lead your troops away from this place and instruct the High Cardinal they are not to return. You will do this now.'

'You do not issue the cults with orders,' Dors squeaked with outrage, 'you have no authority over us! It is our duty to see the abomination is removed from the seat of power and prevented from issuing his monstrous orders!'

Vesna didn't bother to respond; there was no reasoning with a fanatic. He felt something flicker inside him, something stir and grow. A coppery taste bloomed on his tongue and the Land grew suddenly sharper, each line and shadow more defined. He felt shadows spill from his shoulders like a mantle of boiling darkness and a sudden surge of rushing power flowed through his limbs.

The shadows cascaded all around and flooded the cobbled square around his horse. Vesna took a slow, deep breath and twitched back his red cloak to reveal the iron-clad arm. Tight, twisting energies snaked around the black-iron plates and Vesna saw Unmen Dors' eyes widen.

'Get out of my way and take your mercenaries with you,' Vesna snarled, feeling his face flicker as he spoke – the spirit of the God of War was coming closer to the surface. The ruby teardrop blazed with crimson light and cast a bloody corona around Vesna's head.

He felt the reverberations of his voice in his mortal bones; the whole of Barbican Square appeared to shudder with every syllable. The unmen's resolve collapsed and he staggered backwards, his hands raised as though to protect himself from a physical blow. The priest of Karkarn sank to his knees, white-faced and terrified.

The penitents, all mercenaries, no doubt, shrank back. Those among them who prayed would pray to Karkarn, and none would doubt the God's presence now. They began to shuffle away while Dors still cringed under Vesna's stare, but the tall priest was stirred to action when he heard the scrabbling footsteps of the penitents racing away.

'You may tell the High Cardinal he is not to send troops to the Palace again,' Vesna called after them. 'If he wants to debate religious authority with me he can come alone.'

He looked up; the archers were staring out over the battlements, the same look of horror on their faces as the fleeing penitents.

'What do you lot think you're waiting for?' he called. 'Get that damn gate open before your commander arrives or you'll wish it was a bloody prince of daemons waiting down here!'

CHAPTER 16

Count Vesna rode out from the tunnel beneath the Palace Barbican and hesitated. Nothing had changed except for the thinned lines of recruits assembled to welcome the Ghosts home, but, quite unbidden, his mind cast back to the day he first arrived here. The sights and smells had changed little in the intervening decades. While this return was a somewhat muted affair, Vesna felt his heart ache as the clatter and clamour of that day filled his ears, swamping his senses as completely as they had a young provincial noble on his first trip to Tirah Palace.

Not long past his seventeenth birthday and newly raised to his title, it had been a wary and angry youth who'd ridden into that massive hemmed space and looked around in wonder. Sotonay Shaberale had been at his side: a whiskered veteran of sixty summers who'd spent much of the previous two years teaching Vesna sword-craft. To Vesna's surprise, they had barely arrived when a bellow echoed out over the training ground.

All eyes had turned, first to the hulking figure of Swordmaster Herotay as he roared '*Shab!*' followed by a stream of inventive, anatomically impossible obscenities.

The Swordmaster had run from the crowd of nervous youths he'd been inspecting – hopeful farm-boys and proud young nobles alike – who watched with alarm as Herotay dragged Vesna's mentor one-handed from his saddle and enveloped him in a bearhug that made the older man gasp.

'*What have you brought me then, you whoring old bastard? How long are you staying?*' Herotay had demanded, casting his appraising eye over Vesna. Vesna had slid from his saddle and offered the Swordmaster an awkward bow while Shab battered the man away.

'*Just long enough to get you drunk and yer wife in bed,*' Shab said with a levity Vesna had never heard before. '*I made the journey to show the faith I got in this boy, but he don't need me here to hold his hand.*'

'*All the way from Anvee? Death's bony cock, boy, you must be good!*'

Vesna hadn't known how to respond to that; Shab had made it clear this wasn't the place for pride. The veteran had told only part of the truth in any case: the death of Vesna's father had hit him harder than he then realised, and Shab had come along as much to keep him out of trouble as to recommend his pupil.

'*I realise the honour Master Shab does me,*' he had stuttered, '*and I will endeavour to live up to it.*'

Herotay had laughed. '*Don't you worry yourself about his honour, boy. The man's been sniffing around my wife like a horny ferret for thirty years now; there ain't much honour for him in my eyes. Mind you, you're prettier than Shab ever was, so maybe you'll do him proud there too.*'

'How proud would you be now, Shab?' Vesna wondered aloud as he watched the Ghosts stream in, some to be reunited; all to share the grief of others. 'I doubt you expected this when you told Herotay I was destined for great things.'

For the hundredth time that week he rubbed the fingers of his left hand together, wincing at the numbed sensation – it was neither skin nor armour but something other. He could not inspect the join between the two; that was one thing he would have to trust Tila to do for him. The only visible join was at his shoulder where the pauldron sat; his cuirass had been no problem to remove, but everything from the pauldron to his fingertips was fused to his skin: from the mail that covered his inner arm and armpit to the raised ridge of the pauldron that deflected blows from his neck, it was all a part of him. It was maybe not flesh, but the loss of any piece would hurt like a bastard to remove, even the lion-embossed plate that protected the elbow joint.

Lost in his thoughts, Vesna was an island the wary mortals skirted as they went about their lives. Only a handful looked in his direction, and none for long – unlike that day twenty years ago. Then, they had all noted his face, and the special attention Vesna had received – it had been his first taste of the burden a reputation could build.

In the public trials Vesna had been the only one to knock down the Swordmaster facing him, but it had been mostly thanks to a slip and it worked against him in the end. Shab had told him that every man entered the Ghosts on his arse, and Vesna was no exception; Swordmaster Herotay himself had seen to that. The bruises from his wooden swords took a week longer than anyone else's to fade, but he'd given a good account of himself, and laid a clear marker.

Vesna shook the thought from his mind. He'd spent enough time thinking during the last few weeks to last any soldier a lifetime. Slipping from his horse, he beckoned over a groom and headed towards the main wing where General Lahk was waiting for him.

Before he reached the building a still figure caught his eye: a young man in the white robes of a chaplain, who was growing increasingly pale as he watched the returning Ghosts ride in. The cobalt-blue hem of his robe had a band of white running through it and the legion crest sewn over his heart was that of the Ghosts itself.

'Legion Chaplain?' Vesna ventured as he approached the young man.

The chaplain jumped, startled. 'Ah, yes sir, Chaplain Cerrat,' he said when he recovered his composure.

Vesna extended his hand, feeling a pang of sympathy for the youth. 'I've heard your name mentioned. Lord Bahl himself ordered your appointment, no?'

Cerrat's face flushed with nervous relief as he gripped Vesna's forearm. 'He did, sir, yes.'

'Stop that,' Vesna said sharply. 'I don't care how young you might be – you must remember your position, Legion Chaplain Cerrat. You are on Colonel Carasay's command staff now; your military rank is equivalent to mine, even if a chaplain can't issue orders.' He turned his head so Cerrat could clearly see the two gold earrings in his left ear.

'Take it for granted and they'll make your life a misery,' Vesna continued, 'but put it aside to avoid throwing your weight around and they'll never respect you. Without respect a chaplain's just an angry priest, and the Gods know we've had enough of those.'

Cerrat swallowed and bobbed his head. 'You're right, sorry. I've only been here a few days; this is all a bit of a shock, both the position and the influence I'm told I have within the cult. I arrived here as a novice.' The new legion chaplain had a boy's face but a soldier's build; he was bigger than Vesna had been when he first arrived, and he was unlikely to have stopped growing yet.

Vesna forced a smile and clapped his black-iron-clad hand on Cerrat's shoulder. 'As did I, as did we all.'

At the contact Cerrat's eyes widened. He wasn't a battle-mage, but he was an ordained priest of Nartis now, and he would be able to feel something of Karkarn's spirit within Vesna, even if he could not yet put a name to it.

'Some of us arrive with greater expectation on our shoulders than the rest,' Vesna assured him with a smile, 'men we've revered saying we'll surpass them, but you look strong enough to bear that weight. Only those who ask great things of themselves achieve them; just don't be in any rush.'

Cerrat nodded in understanding. The chaplains were the heartbeat of the regiments; the fiercest and most uncompromising among them; he had much to learn from his flock to be able to fill the position he'd been given.

'Enough of that,' Verna said. 'Do you know where I can find Lord Fernal and the Chief Steward?'

'They're in the main wing – meeting an envoy from Merlat who arrived a few hours ago.'

'Thank you.' Vesna looked back at the crowd of soldiers behind them. 'This evening, when they're all settled, go and find Sergeant Kishen and get drunk with him. That'll be the first lesson in your education in dealing with the Ghosts.'

Having dropped the new legion chaplain squarely into the middle of the lake, Vesna collected General Lahk and together they made their way through the Great Hall to the quieter private areas beyond. Just before the wide, ornately decorated main staircase was the ducal audience chamber. A pair of guards suggested Lord Fernal's presence within.

Vesna didn't recognise the livery, but it wasn't much of a surprise: a dark-blue snake coiled around a sheaf of arrows, its head raised toward an occluded moon. They were admitted without a word and entered to find five people standing before the massive ducal throne, the seat of Farlan power.

The throne, hewn from a single piece of dark wood and inlaid with symbols of the Gods, was built for white-eyes. It lacked the intricate detailing found on its equivalent in Narkang. Too heavy for two normal men to lift together and able to resist an axe-blow: everything about it said solidity, strength and permanence – and the blue-skinned Demi-God Fernal suited it perfectly.

At the sight of the new Lord of the Farlan Vesna was reminded of Lord Bahl. Fernal wore plain, loose breeches and a white linen shirt over which spilled his mane of dark cerulean fur. The last time they had met Fernal had been wearing only a tattered cloak, replaced now by one of blood-red, to show he too mourned Isak. But it was the silver circlet on Fernal's crumpled brow that gave Vesna the biggest start.

He had to move quickly to catch up with General Lahk and kneel before the bastard son of Nartis, barely remembering in time to unclip his sword from his belt and offer it forward. As he did so, Vesna cursed his own stupidity. He'd had weeks to get used to the idea of Fernal being named the Lord of the Farlan, but still the sight of Fernal wearing a ducal circlet had tripped him.

'General Lahk, Count Vesna, welcome home. Please, rise.'

Fernal still had trouble with the rolling vowels of a dialect unsuited to one with the teeth and tongue of a wolf, but his deep, booming voice was that of a lord all the same.

He looks the part, he sounds the part, Vesna thought as he returned his sword to its usual place. *Now we just need to find out how much he's willing to fight for the part.*

'Lord Fernal,' the pair said in response, for the benefit of the envoy as much as tradition.

'General, I'm sure you have much work to do dealing with your troops,' Fernal said. 'If you wish to leave and see to them please do so.'

Lahk bowed and left as smartly as he had arrived. He had no interest in the dealings of politicians.

Vesna glanced at the others in the room. His eyes went first to Tila – it had been all he could do not to seek her out immediately, but he knew the envoy would have been watching and any deviation from tradition would have been noted. When at last their eyes met he felt a weight lift at pleasure which had blossomed on her face.

Tila wore a plain white dress, and her luxuriant dark hair had been swept to one side and wrapped in a red mourning scarf embroidered with a prayer for the dead, one of the few in the Palace to have done so. The period of mourning was technically over, but it was traditional for the army to mourn until it had returned; Vesna guessed Tila was doing the same.

The envoy himself was a knight Vesna didn't recognise, despite being of a similar age; he too had battlefield honours tattooed on his neck. He bowed respectfully to Vesna while Chief Steward Lesarl, looking older and more fatigued than Vesna had ever seen, gave him just the briefest of nods.

Behind Lesarl were two armed men who looked like neither noblemen nor soldiers; each was carrying a rapier and long dagger, the weapons of a trained duellist, and Vesna guessed them to be agents of the Chief Steward. Curiously enough, they flanked Lesarl rather than Fernal, suggesting they were there to protect him rather than their lord.

'Count Vesna, your own business will have to wait until we are finished here,' Fernal said as the door was shut behind Lahk, 'unless there is anything you wish to say first?'

Vesna shook his head. Fernal was asking whether he still considered himself a subject of the Lord of the Farlan. 'No, my Lord, I await your pleasure.'

'In that case, Sir Jachers here was just outlining the position of the Farlan's westerly dukes.'

'Both of them?' Vesna asked sharply, looking at the envoy.

The Dukes Lokan and Sempes rarely agreed on anything since Lokan had poisoned his uncle – Sempes' distant cousin – to take the dukedom, and their 'disagreements' had resulted in one sea engagement and three outright land battles, not to mention an entire dossier of clandestine actions.

'Both. I am a man of Perlir,' Sir Jachers clarified, 'but Duke Lokan contacted my lord when he heard of Lord Isak's death. Their concerns on the subjects in hand are close enough that they speak with one voice.'

'And that would be your voice. What are the subjects being discussed?'

'Principally: the legality of Lord Fernal's appointment, Lord Fernal's intentions regarding this position, the continuing problems with the cults, and Lord Isak's crusade.'

'Has Duke Lomin added his voice to this discussion yet?' Vesna asked, wondering how Lord Isak's appointment would be reacting to the news.

Lomin had shown the rest of the tribe he was as independent as his peers when he refused to send troops to join Isak's 'crusade', but how he would react now was anyone's guess. Their information on the man was not complete enough for sensible guesses to be made, he'd proved that much.

Sir Jachers shook his head. 'The mind of Duke Lomin is not known to my master, they have met but once. Anticipating the wishes of Duke Lokan is somewhat easier. Duke Sempes has sent me here with all possible speed so that swift decisions might be made, if any agreement can be reached. He believes acting before the suzerains do so en masse is the best way to guide their actions.'

'In that he is correct,' Lesarl broke in. 'With your permission, Lord Fernal, might I suggest we bring the discussion to a close for the time being? There is much that needs to be done now the Ghosts have returned and you might wish to consider Sempes and Lokan's positions before proposing a resolution.'

Fernal nodded. He knew how little of the nation's politics – Isak had asked him to take this position because he wanted a leader who could be a symbol for all, as well as a warrior. A nose for politics would have been the least of Isak's requirements.

'A good idea. I will sleep on it. Now, if you would give me the room? I must speak with Count Vesna before he goes about his duties.'

The others left smartly, Tila ushering Sir Jachers away and Lesarl only too keen to be about his work. Vesna watched her leave, feeling fresh pangs of guilt over leaving Isak on the battlefield. His death would have hurt her badly. Tila was still young, and she had been closer to Isak than to either of her brothers. However much they had infuriated each other, the bond between them had only strengthened with every squabble.

'Vesna,' Fernal said softly, 'what have we done?'

He looked up, startled. 'My Lord?'

'Look at us,' Fernal continued, spreading his arms wide, 'was this a goal for either of us? You, the Mortal-Aspect of Karkarn? I, Lord of the Farlan? How did we end up this way?'

'I couldn't say, my Lord.'

Fernal shook his head sadly. 'I do not know what to do. Lord Isak hoped my appointment would heal rifts, provide the Farlan with a figure to rally around.'

'Lord Isak never fully understood his nobility,' Vesna pointed out, hearing the bewilderment in Fernal's voice, 'but the very fact that you claim the title has delayed outright civil war, that I promise you, my Lord.'

'And now? What do I do now? I keep being asked questions I cannot answer! The dukes claim my appointment is illegal, they are threatening to break away from the nation if I remain.'

'What do you want?'

Vesna's question seemed to catch Fernal off-guard. The massive Demi-God peered at him for a while, his mouth open just enough for Vesna to catch a glimpse of pointed teeth.

'Not this,' was the eventual answer. 'Power has never interested me, and the politics of men even less so. If my father chooses a new white-eye for this position tomorrow I will give thanks at his temple for the first time in my life.'

'You wish to return to Llehden?'

'Of course, it is my home. But I do not wish for civil war among the Farlan either; I fear leaving now will spark that.'

Vesna didn't speak. There was nothing he could say. Lesarl would have already told Fernal all he needed to know about the Farlan nobility. Without a ruler, they would fight. It was as simple as that.

'If it helps,' he said eventually, 'I am as adrift as you, my Lord. Lord Karkarn has given me only one order, to ensure the Farlan Army is ready when it is required. At present I am unsure how that will even be possible without killing every argumentative noble in the tribe.' Vesna gave a tired laugh. 'And there are a lot of them!'

'Then for that reason and several others I call you brother,' Fernal announced with a smile to share the humour. He gave Vesna a dismissive wave. 'Go, I need to be alone – how you humans think with the noise of a city all around you I cannot understand. Go and greet your intended; life does not stop with the death of any man.'

Before he went to find Tila, Vesna knew he had one more person to see first. It would take a division of Ghosts to drag him from her side once he was there, but she would understand the delay – indeed, when Vesna went back out onto the training ground, he caught sight of her face, and the little wave she gave told him she had anticipated his next mission.

Amidst the chaos of the training ground it took him a while to work out where to go. He knew Carel was a typical soldier, however long ago he had retired from the Ghosts. In grief they tended to go silent or loud, and drunk in both cases. Even after he'd lost his arm in battle Carel had been a formidable presence in the palace, never more comfortable than when he had a drink and an audience. With his world turned upside down, Vesna guessed the veteran would go the opposite way and seek out silence the way Vesna wanted himself.

'But he'll want to work; a man like that can't sit still for long,' he said aloud, starting off across the training ground as servants and soldiers parted before him.

The palace forge was the closest of his choices and when Vesna ducked his head inside and peered through the smoke he realised he'd been correct. None of the few men within looked like a marshal, but he spotted Carel's swordstick propped against a wall.

As he closed the door behind him Vesna felt a tremor in his eyes as they adapted with unnatural speed to the gloom. By the time the door was shut he could see perfectly clearly.

This was the main weapons forge, and Vesna could see it was running at full capacity, in anticipation of the Guards' losses. Keeping three furnaces and six anvils running day and night was gruelling work, not allowing time for idle talk. Vesna saw Carel at the back, working in unison with another man. They weren't doing the finesse work, that was left to the skilled smiths, but even a one-armed man could lift a hammer and beat a lump of steel.

'Change it,' said Carel's partner when he noticed Vesna standing behind them.

With a reluctant exhale, Carel let the hammer slide through his fingers. As he took the tongs, he noticed Vesna for the first time. Carel looked ragged in body and soul: sweat- and grime-stained, his white hair was grey with dirt and tied back with a fraying strip of material. His blood-shot eyes looked empty.

'Thought your count was off,' he said to his companion in a hoarse voice.

To Vesna he said nothing, but there was no need when the pain and years were plain on his face. The count felt a sudden pang of fear in his belly. He realised he had no idea what to say to the man who had been a father to Isak.

Carel watched him hesitate and gestured to his partner to

233

continue, turning the steel shard to the correct position. When the man did so Vesna realised the fingers of his right hand were frozen in a twisted grip and he was using his left: another damaged veteran, he assumed.

'You were there?' Carel called after three blows with the hammer.

Vesna shook his head. 'He ordered me to lead the army away. He died to save us all.'

Carel's expression darkened. 'Rode a long way to do that.'

'What do you mean?'

'I mean we should've seen it'd end that way an' stopped the boy.'

Vesna took a cautious step forward. 'Carel, he was Lord of the Farlan; the choice was his. It wasn't one he took lightly, I know that much. It was a risk he thought worthwhile, and no one would have been able to persuade him otherwise.'

'Really?' Carel snapped, glaring up at Vesna. 'Used to joke the Gods set me on the Land to keep that boy out o' trouble. Don't seem like a joke now, just a failure.'

'You couldn't have stopped him,' Vesna said firmly. 'His mind was made up.'

'What if I helped him make it? What if he made those choices 'cos of advice I gave him?' There was a waver to Carel's voice that betrayed the guilt hanging over him like a leaden cloud.

'When did you ever know him to do anything but what he wanted?'

The old man looked down. 'I told him to face what he feared – an' if he feared anythin', it were those dreams of death. He knew they weren't just dreams.'

'Carel, he wanted to strike at his enemies before they were ready, he wanted to take his destiny in his own hands and not let others dictate to him. The only fault to bear is mine and Lahk's, for not seeing how the battle was going to unfold.'

'Then maybe I blame you too!' Carel roared suddenly, his voice loud enough in the enclosed space to stop the smiths mid-stroke. 'You left that field greater than you were, as blessed by the Gods as he once was! Isak was barely grown, for all his size, alive for fewer years than you been a professional soldier. Aye, he were a wilful shit at times, but he always wanted to be more than the colour o' his eyes. He trusted *us* to keep him so!'

He turned away, staring into the wincing heat of the furnace, and

Vesna could see Carel's whole body shaking. The only sound was the scrape of steel on the anvil's surface.

'We failed him,' the veteran continued in a much quieter voice. 'We din't stand in his way when he needed us. His blood's on our hands.'

Carel looked at his palm as though looking for blood, and seemed to notice for the first time how hard his hand was shaking.

'Leave me be, Vesna,' he muttered, 'I got work to do here an' I can't do it like this. Go find your bride. She needs you, not me.'

Karkarn's Iron General stared at the ageing Ghost and felt the words dry in his throat. It was nothing he'd not said to himself on the long journey home, but to hear it from the mouth of another was completely different. To hear it from someone who'd loved Isak so deeply cut through his armour like a burning shard of light, scorching the hardened soldier's heart with frightening ease.

He felt himself stumble as he retreated, the weight on his shoulders even heavier now, hot shame gripping him as he fled outside. Only then could he breathe again, but it did nothing to ease the guilt rekindled inside him.

Mihn stopped in the woods and looked around. The gentle clatter of rain on leaves surrounded him, drowning other sounds – but for a moment he thought he had heard something, a faint noise . . . something out of place that set his palms prickling. After a while he realised he was holding his breath and relaxed, a wry smile on his face.

'I'm getting jumpy in my old age,' he muttered, starting off down the rabbit-run again. Hanging from his belt was a young hen pheasant, the fruit of a good morning's hunting. It felt good to be fending for himself again, brushing the dust off skills he hadn't used in a while and becoming less dependent on the locals.

What little silver he had brought with him had been enough to buy fowl for egg-laying. The witch appropriated half of everything he trapped as payment for the food she brought – just as well, now rumours of the ragged man had spread throughout Llehden. Few would come near the lake now.

Mihn wound his slow way back to the lake, checking each of his snares as he went. As he came out from the trees he saw Isak standing at the shore, staring over the water, Eolis drawn and by his side. He wore a long patchwork fur cloak the witch had brought, old and ragged enough to frighten Chera if she ever returned, but still serviceable.

The white-eye stooped badly, his left shoulder dipping as though the lightning-scarred arm was a lead weight, and his head was permanently hunched forward. The damage done to him in Ghenna had turned him old before his time: as old as the hollow look in his eyes.

Mihn hurried over, but he saw nothing at Isak's feet, nor any blood on his blade. The sky had remained dull all day, though the rain had lessened to a desultory smattering. 'Isak? Is all well?' he asked anxiously.

The white-eye didn't move. His eyes were fixed on the distant shore, though he wasn't looking at anything in particular; his mind was further away. The fitful breeze did little to disturb the surface of the lake. A flock of black-necked gulls hovered over the northern edge where ducks and geese squabbled.

Everything looked peaceful enough to Mihn. Isak's pup was watching them sleepily from the small shelter outside the cottage Mihn had built for him. The hound, finally named Hulf by Isak, tired easily still, his exuberance outlasting his enthusiasm. Even if he had been chasing the geese grazing too close to the cottage, it shouldn't have been enough to drag Isak outside.

'I dreamed,' Isak said at last, his voice distant.

Mihn's heart sank. Despite Ehla's best efforts, Isak still had more memories than were good for him, and his dreams were rarely pleasurable. 'What of?'

'An empty house by a lake. A cold house.'

'That is all?'

'I woke in the cold house. I couldn't remember my name. It was all gone – who I was, where I came from. Only the lake was real. The lake and the smell of mud on the wind. I was a ghost, empty and . . .'

There was silence as the pair stood side by side on the shore – until an abrupt bark from Hulf brought Mihn back to the present and he turned to encourage the oversized puppy over to them. He crouched down and draped an arm over Hulf's back.

'I couldn't move. As cold as the lake,' Isak continued, oblivious to Hulf's snuffles of pleasure as Mihn rubbed his ears. 'I was dead, but still standing.'

'He is gone from you, Isak,' Mihn said, looking up. 'You need not think about Aryn Bwr any more. You are free of him and his influence.'

'Still I dream.' Isak scratched the stubble on his cheek, then looked at his fingers, as though shocked at the state of them. The end joint was missing from both middle and little fingers, and the rest bore ragged scars from struggling against his chains. Quickly he lowered his hand, slipping it protectively under his armpit and shuddering as his body remembered the pain.

When he composed himself once more, he crouched also, reversing Eolis to keep it well clear of Hulf's inquisitive nose. 'I dreamed daemons came. To the cold house with chains in their hands. They came for me and I killed them. Their blood stained my hands and feet. It reminded me who I was. In the blood I remembered my name.'

Mihn looked at Eolis again, but the sword was spotlessly clean. 'It was only a dream, Isak; it did not happen. There were no daemons, the cottage is warm and cosy, and you are not alone. You are safe now.'

Isak nodded, his face caught between a grimace and a smile. 'Safe,' he echoed with a hollow whisper, 'but is it me I remember? Aryn Bwr's name remains in one place – the prison in Ghenna made for his soul. They wanted him to feel that pain again and again. Is the pain I feel from my scars, or from forgetting a part of me?'

'That I cannot answer, my Lord,' Mihn said, bowing his head in grief. 'But here I remain, to remind you of the man you were and the life you lived. We knew this would be the hard choice, the terrible choice, but it had to be made.

'You have broken the prophecy; the threads of history that bound you are all parted. You are free of it now, free to choose a new path – free to stop those who would have used you to their own ends. And you will never be alone in this. I am with you to the end.'

'But how can I trust you?' Isak asked with a curious, twisted expression Mihn could not identify, 'when you've not even noticed Hulf eating your pheasant?'

Tila trotted down the stone steps of the main wing and looked around. Vesna was not in sight and a flutter of alarm began in her heart. It had been an hour since she'd seen him head out to the forge to speak to Carel. She was under no illusions about Carel's grief; she had broken the news herself, and held him while he sobbed. Still, he'd been a long time.

Just the memory of Carel's fury and pain made Tila want to weep. The veteran understood death better than she. Even now Tila could barely accept Isak was dead; it seemed impossible, unthinkable. That seven-foot lump of muscle and foolishness hadn't been like the rest of them. Ever since returning from the battle of Chir Plains Isak had possessed an unnatural quality, some spark of vast power at odds with mortal life.

She'd watched Vesna spar a dozen times and his skill was exceptional, she'd lain in his arms and felt the strength in his chest. The count from Anvee was a soldier well-deserving of his reputation as a hero, but even so, him she could fathom. Isak had been something more: a force of nature who suited his nickname of the Stormcaller. And now the storm was gone.

She bit her lip and hurried on, forcing herself to scan the faces in the distance, however unnecessary it was. Vesna would stand out from the crowd easily enough; that she couldn't see him with one glance meant he was not here.

'Lady Tila?' said a cautious voice to her right. Tila whirled around to face the nervous young legion chaplain she'd met a few days before. 'Ah, my lady, are you looking for Count Vesna?'

'I am, Legion Chaplain Cerrat, have you seen him?' Tila's reply was rather more brusque than she had intended and Cerrat backed away a little. She had to remind herself that there were no women in the chaplaincy monasteries.

'My lady, he is ... Ah, come with me, if you would be so kind.'

Cerrat led her almost the length of the training ground, weaving through the bustle to skirt the barracks and stables that backed onto the long perimeter wall. He walked quickly, looking back every few seconds to ensure she was keeping up. As they neared the furthest corner of the compound they came to the much-repaired black tower, once the keep of Tirah's first castle.

Tila felt her alarm intensify as she saw a crowd assembled outside at the foot of the stone staircase that ran up the side of the tower. The people looked wary, shifting nervously as they looked from her to the door at the top of the stairs. There were wives and servants there as well as soldiers.

'The shrine?' Tila asked, dreading the answer.

'He is there. The mourners, they fear to disturb him, my lady, but they wish to offer for their lost.'

Tila nodded, understanding the anxiety she could see in the faces ahead. There was a shrine to Karkarn there; it was custom within the Palace Guard to offer sacrifices to Karkarn as well as to Death for their losses in battle. The scriptures told of great heroes wearing a ruby around their necks at their Last Judgment, an indication that they had killed, but the act was honoured by the God of War. The relatives would want to pray, to leave a drop of blood in the offering cup for each hero lost.

The crowd parted before Tila, and she made her way straight up, not trusting herself to linger at the bottom in case she lost her nerve. As she entered the dark shrine room, the light from the doorway spilled across the floor and illuminated the hunched form of Vesna in the far corner.

The shrine was in the form of an ornate weapon-stand in the centre of the room that bore a crossed sword and axe, and, underneath, a brass prayer bowl stained by decades of blood offerings. All around the weapon-stand were symbols of Karkarn and his Aspects. A fireplace on the left, behind the weapon-stand, was occupied by a black-iron dragon, burning the incense that filled the air in its upturned claws. The walls were festooned with weapons, and links of copper armour, each one inscribed with the name of a fallen Ghost.

Tila left the door open a finger-width and went over to Vesna, who was sitting on the floor, his black-iron-clad hand pressed against his temple as though praying to Lord Death.

'Vesna?' she whispered, trying to ignore the changes and just see the man she loved underneath.

He flinched and gave a great sigh before looking up.

Tila felt her eyes widen at the sight of the ruby on his cheek, but it was the exhaustion in his eyes that chilled her more.

'He blames me,' Vesna whispered, 'as well he might.'

Tila sat down beside him, taking his armoured hand in hers. 'Carel grieves, nothing more. Grief makes liars of us all. He does not mean what he says.'

'I should have stopped him,' Vesna insisted, 'I should have died in his place.'

Tila felt her breath catch at the very thought, but she forced it away. 'Do you think that is what he would have wanted? You never understood how Isak could be so accepting of your feelings for me, but it's because he realised what it meant to be a white-eye after that first battle. Violence flowed through his veins, but he found a reason to channel it. As he watched our feelings for each other grow, Isak realised he could live with the violence. He knew he had to accept it as his lot in life, so that others might find something different, something better.'

'And what about Isak?' Vesna said bitterly. 'What does he get for his sacrifice? *He was just a boy!*'

She pulled his unresponsive hand closer and finally felt his fingers close about hers. 'I didn't say it was a fair exchange, just that Isak was happy to make it. And remember; he's one of the Chosen, Isak's place in the land of no time is assured.'

A discreet cough came from behind her. 'Curious that you bring that up,' said a quiet voice behind her.

Tila barely had time to turn before Vesna was upright and standing protectively in front of her. After a moment she felt him relax and step slightly away so she could see the speaker. It was a man, that much she could tell, and he appeared to be dressed in shifting robes of darkness. As her mouth fell open in astonishment, the figure gave a dismissive gesture with both arms and the black swirl melted into nothing, revealing a white silk tunic and both arms covered in ornate bronze armour.

'Lord Isak has not knelt before the Chief of the Gods, he has not passed to the land of no time,' said Karkarn, God of War, bowing to Tila with all ceremony.

In her astonishment and horror Tila found herself unable to move, let alone kneel before the God, but his imperious face showed no displeasure.

'What do you mean? Say it plainly,' Vesna growled.

'Remember your place, my Iron General – it is not to question me,' the God said coldly.

'How am I supposed to serve you if you withhold information from me?'

'Stop your petulance,' Karkarn said sharply, his face flickering slightly between the cool, emotionless expression and the wild face that Tila guessed was his Berserker Aspect. 'It is not for you to know the secrets of the Land, especially if they were kept from you by the one you grieve.'

'Isak?' Tila found herself blurting out, 'this is his doing?' She stopped, casting her mind back to the months he'd spent in Tirah before leaving with the army. 'Is that what he was up to – what he and Mihn were conspiring? He was planning for his own death?'

'What happens after death is not my domain,' Karkarn replied, 'and Lord Death is not one to be questioned idly on the subject. I do know that your white-eye has not passed through the halls of Death, and that is no simple feat.'

'What does it mean?' she asked, her voice breaking.

Karkarn gestured towards Vesna. 'I merely answer my servant's plea,' he said, and vanished in the blink of an eye.

'Vesna, what did he mean by that?' Tila asked, bewilderment clear in her voice.

The count took Tila's hand once again. 'I questioned the choices I had made, the service I had given Isak. I don't know where this path will lead, but what hope do I have if I've already failed those around me?'

'But now you know that isn't true – you know Isak was fixed upon this path, wherever it took him?'

'I wish it were as simple as that,' he sighed, looking down at his love. 'But yes, it's at least clear now that Isak had a plan – why he could not trust me with it, I don't know— Ah, damnation! I've as many questions now as I had before—' He stopped for a moment, then said, 'No, maybe not quite. At least I can believe he didn't die for nothing. It's scant comfort when my dear friend is dead, but it's something.'

Tila stood on her tiptoes and drew him close. Vesna wrapped his arms around the young woman and bent to her, and she kissed him. They stood together, embracing closely, for several minutes, until Vesna returned the kiss with surprising fervour.

When Tila did at last pull back slightly, she settled her cheek against his. 'It's been too long since you last did that,' she murmured, breathing in the scent of his body. She kissed Vesna lightly on the throat and looked up at him, relieved to see some of the strain on his face had eased.

'It has, and I have needed it badly.' Vesna patted the pauldron fused to his shoulder. 'Anything more might be a bit uncomfortable, I'm afraid.'

Tila ignored him and ran her fingers tenderly over the black-iron plate. 'It's certainly not enough to put me off,' she declared, her fingers moving to his cheek, 'even if you are wearing more jewellery these days too. Has anything else changed?'

Vesna laughed, for the first time in what felt like years. 'Not the man inside,' he said. 'Karkarn was insistent that he was not looking for a warrior to fight in his name. He wanted the man I am, and so a man I remain.'

'But you are still changed; I can feel it in your arms. You've been touched by a God; you carry a part of him within you. Do you still need sleep? Food? Will Karkarn visit us every day? Will you age like a man, or a God?'

Vesna raised his fingers to her lips to stop the questions. 'I can't answer, not yet, but I can assure you that I'm still a man, with all of a man's needs and frailties. The rest is unknown; we'll have to discover the answers together.' He gestured towards where Karkarn had been standing a few moments before. 'As you've seen, my God is reluctant to reveal everything.'

'And what of me?' Tila asked in a small voice.

'What do you mean?'

Her eyes lowered and her hands fell away. 'Where do your loyalties lie now? This cannot have failed to change you inside. Whatever you believed when the offer was first made, you now have a God's interests to serve.' She hesitated, then, her voice barely audible, she said, 'What room is there in your life for a foolish girl half your age?'

'Tila, my Tila,' Vesna said, tilting her head up to look her in the eye, 'it would take more than the tears of a God to change my heart.' He took her hands again, and pulled her close, and kissed her, gently. 'Tila, I know the duty I now bear, but you have to believe that it will *never* eclipse what I feel for you. Just as the rage of the Gods turned mild-mannered priests into fanatics, so I have been irrevocably changed by you, and I am equally devoted to *my* cause.'

She blushed, and squeezed his hands. She was turning her head up for another kiss when her eyes widened and she stopped back half a pace. 'Vesna, that reminds me: Lesarl's been investigating the fanatics further and he thinks it was those who were actively praying when the spell over Scree was broken were the ones most badly affected. You mustn't expect all of Karkarn's priests to accept you easily.'

Vesna looked at his beloved. He had been agonising for days over how he would explain his new condition and that really wasn't the response to his declaration he'd been expecting. 'Well, thank you for ruining the moment for me! Do you have to think like a politician all the time?' He smiled to take the sting out of his words, and Tila blushed again, this time in embarrassment.

'I'm sorry, I just remembered, and it's important.' Suddenly she poked him hard in the chest. 'Hang on, didn't you just compare me to the bloodlust that's been tearing the Land apart these last few months?'

'I . . . ah—' Vesna stammered, 'no, no – I didn't mean it that way at all!'

'And yet that's how it came out. You soldiers really are as brainless as mules, sometimes.' Tila's face lit up, and she hugged him. 'You're very, very lucky I'm still going to marry you, Count Vesna; I can't think how you'd ever manage around all these Gods without me.'

Vesna held her close, immeasurably cheered. Just the sight of this beautiful girl, the scent of her perfume, the touch of her soft skin, had done much to lift the bleakness surrounding him, though his heart remained heavy.

'I should thank you for that, then – and believe me, I do,' he said. 'So. Have you set a date for this salvation of mine?'

'A month from now,' Tila replied promptly. 'I would drag you before Lord Fernal right this very minute if it were up to me, but my mother would never forgive me, and that is too great a burden for us both to bear into our new life. Much of her family live in Ked, and need time to get here. But Mother believes it is possible to organise what she's describing as "a modest celebration" in a month. And the Gods themselves help anyone who gets in her way – she may be my mother, but that woman would terrorise the Reapers themselves if they stood between her and her only daughter's wedding.'

'A month?' Vesna croaked.

'A month,' she confirmed, a steely look in her eye. 'As short a time as possible – because you may well be sent off to fight at any moment.'

Despite the turmoil in his head, Vesna had the sense not to argue. Very carefully, very deliberately he closed his mouth, trying not to swallow visibly. He loved this woman with all his heart, but he had been a bachelor – and a highly popular one at that – for many years, and couldn't help but feel daunted at the new trick this old dog was going to learn. But he had made his decision. 'A month it is then. If there's fighting to be done, I suspect it'll be in Tirah anyway.'

'Really?' Within a blink of an eye the quick-witted politician was back. 'Can you tell me why?'

'Suzerain Temal and Scion Ranah were awaiting us at the border – with troops. I doubt they'll be the only ones. Now the tribe's leadership is in question, support and swords will be up for sale – and don't expect them to all side against the clerics, either.'

'All the more reason for us to be quick about it then,' she said with a mock-stern tone. 'There'll be no wriggling out of it this time, my love.'

Vesna smiled and allowed her to take his arm and lead him to the door.

'I remember once,' Tila added with a sly smile as she closed to door to the shrine, 'being told to treat my husband like a God on my wedding night.' She patted his black-iron vambrace. 'It is good I won't have to pretend now.'

Mihn woke with the sense that something was out of place. This was an exhausting existence, not just caring for the two of them and hunting enough to feed a white-eye's appetite, but being constantly on guard, alert for dangers both natural and unnatural. Most mornings he drifted into wakefulness slowly, but today he found his eyes wide open and staring at the crossbeam above his bed. He had hung a blanket over it to give one end of the bed an element of privacy, though still able to keep an eye on Isak during his nightmares. He found it oddly comforting.

Now he peered at Isak's bed, and immediately reached for his boots as he realised it was empty. It was early, still chill, and the pale dawn light was just seeping into the cottage. He set the boots aside and instead pulled on a thick woollen shirt and trousers. As he slipped silently outside the charms tattooed on the soles of his feet glowed warm on his skin. The rising sun was hidden behind a low bank of mist, while the eastern horizon, over the lake, was as dark as a thundercloud.

Isak was standing by a crooked willow fifty yards away. Though old, the tree jutting out over the water was no higher than the white-eye. The puppy Hulf nosed through the hanging fronds at Isak's feet, a broken stub of wood jammed in his mouth like a cigar. When he saw Mihn, Hulf gave a snort and scampered over, his tail wagging furiously. The bark had been stripped off his little branch by his increasingly powerful jaws. He dropped it at Mihn's feet.

'Isak, could you not sleep?'

Isak watched the insects skittering over the near-still lake surface for a while, making no sign that he had heard Mihn.

At last, 'I once loved sleep,' he said wearily, 'and now it stalks me.'

From the trees came the warbling song of dozens of birds, all saluting the dawn. Mihn looked around to see a robin sitting on the topmost branch of the willow, watching Isak, its head cocked as though trying to puzzle out what he was and where he came from. Like all the robins he'd seen in Llehden, this one had a green cap, as bright as its red breast – something he'd never seen elsewhere on his wanderings.

'Do you want me to leave?'

Isak shook his head. 'You're as much a part of it as they are,' he said, looking back at the insects briefly.

'A part of what? The Land?'

'The patterns I see all around me. The threads that bind you to the tapestry.'

Mihn frowned. Isak's maudlin thoughts were often followed by listlessness and a deep gloom and he'd hoped today to be able to get the damaged white-eye up and working; exercising those still-powerful muscles and helping him continue his journey back to the man he'd once been.

'Come back to the cottage,' he urged, 'I'll make some tea – you must be cold out here.'

Isak was wearing only a thin robe, tied at the waist with a braided belt Xeliath had once worn. The scars on his throat and chest were plain to see, duller now that the day they had returned from Ghenna but no less terrible.

'It's strange,' Isak said, looking Mihn properly in the eye for the first time that day. 'I don't feel part of that pattern. We cut the threads that bound me. We had to – there was no other way.'

'I know,' Mihn said soothingly, seeing Isak's face tightening with anxiety. The witch of Llehden had cut many memories from his mind, leaving great holes there. Some things Isak remembered perfectly, but he sensed the frayed edges of his memory. 'We freed you. It was hard, but we freed you.'

'We cut too many,' Isak said with an abrupt, strangled cough of laughter. 'Ham-fisted wagon-brat, that's what she used to call me.'

'Tila? Aye, and Carel too.'

'Carel?'

Mihn shook his head hurriedly. 'Just someone you once knew,' he said, a dagger of guilt driving deep into his heart. *Merciful Gods, he cannot remember Carel? How do I ever forgive myself for taking that memory from him?*

He had to cough and clear his throat before he could speak again. 'Tell me how you know we cut too many.'

'I'm not part of the tapestry, not any more. A few threads still hold me to life, but I died, didn't I?'

'You did.' For a moment Mihn felt the weight of the Land upon his shoulders, but he shook off the mood. He didn't know what price he would have to pay for the audacity of his actions, but whatever it was, it could not be worse than what Isak had endured. 'You died, and we brought you back. We had to.'

'To free me of the ties that bind,' Isak intoned, 'and that bastard Lesarl,' he added. 'Never liked him.'

Mihn forced a smile at the glimpse of the old Isak; he didn't see them often, but they were coming more frequently now. The witch had been right to give Hulf to Isak. They were inseparable now and the dog, growing stronger every day – and starting to show the fierce spirit yet to reawaken in Isak – was tirelessly playful. Hulf was forcing Isak to remember his own love of silliness, running along the lakeshore with happy abandon, leaping over whatever was in his way, or stealing Isak's shoes in the hope of being chased. It had taken Isak a while to keep up, but just as the growing dog was developing a wilful, exuberant personality, Isak was unearthing

246

his own, buried deep, but not entirely cut away by their drastic measures.

'Can you see the pattern?' Mihn asked cautiously. 'Do you understand it now?'

Isak's gaze returned to the lake. 'I see the wind. I see the sun – the threads that tie flowers to the sun and bees to the flowers. I see the spirits of the forest and the Gods that rule them. I see the threads that bind it all, the weaves and colours of all things.'

'And me?'

Isak's face went suddenly grave. 'Especially you. You keep me in the pattern. I am the millstone around your neck.'

'Isak, that is not true,' Mihn insisted sternly. 'We both made this choice, and I would make the same choice again.'

'Would I?' Isak wondered. 'Do I have the strength?'

'Your strength is something I will never doubt.'

Without warning tears spilled from Isak's eyes. He stood there, unashamed, looking mournfully at Mihn. 'We must remake the pattern; tear out the threads and bind them anew – and you will have to live with the consequences.'

CHAPTER 17

Legana felt the light of the fading sun break through the clouds and settle over her as she sat on a stone bench in the centre of Kamfer's Ford. She turned her head a little to protect her sensitive eyes and waited. Life in the market square continued around her. The locals were used to the sight of her now, and had quite got over their nervousness, if not their awe.

'Mistress?'

Legana looked up at the broad woman bathed in warm orange light. She recognised the voice of the innkeeper's wife, a woman as respectful towards her as if Legana were the greatest witch in the west.

'I thought you might like a cup of tannay,' she said timidly, offering a small brass goblet. Legana smiled, and sensed the woman's relief.

Quickly Legana wrote —*Thank you* on her slate and held it up before accepting the goblet. The local spirit was served warm to bring out the flavour.

'You've brought us enough trade in recent weeks,' the landlady said. 'Your guests all come to the inn, and never a word of trouble no matter how much they drink – and whatever Unmen Poller says at High Reverence, the wisewomen say you've frightened off every bad spirit for miles. It seemed only right to fetch you a cup in thanks. My ma always said tannay should be drunk with a spring sunset.'

Legana sipped the drink and felt its warmth spread down her throat. She'd tried other people's tannay since she'd arrived at Kamfer's Ford, enough to tell this was the finest yet. A smile spread over her face and she gestured to the other side of the bench, inviting the woman to join her.

'Oh I wouldn't want to disturb you . . .'

Legana gave a dismissive wave of the hand and the woman tailed off. The divine spark was strong enough inside Legana that when she gestured again the woman sat immediately.

—*I am Legana.*

'Nanter Kassai,' came the hurried response. 'Mistress Legana, may I . . . may I ask you a question?'

Legana inclined her head and shifted in her seat to look Nanter in the face, who faltered at the sight of her gleaming emerald eyes.

Nanter had short auburn hair and a button nose that seemed out of proportion with the rest of her face. She cleared her throat and looked down. 'I was just wondering, why d'you sit here every evening? I don't mean to pry, Mistress Legana, but the women who travel here, they come at all times, but we never see you save at sunset.'

Legana considered the question a while, chalk in her hand. Eventually she began to write.

—*Do you remember the girl you once were?*

Nanter smiled encouragingly.

—*This is how I do it.*

Nanter looked a little puzzled by the statement, but it was as simple as Legana could make it. At twilight the Gods withdrew from the Land and the part of her that was divine became a shade muted. The sounds of everyday life around her reminded Legana of what it was to be alive, while the sinking sun was a memorial to the Goddess she had lost.

Whether pious or merely conditioned to the routines and rituals, every devotee of the Lady had lost something of herself when the family that raised her had been broken. Some would not want another to take its place, but Legana was sure many would be glad of anything she had to offer. Most people craved belonging of one sort or another. While Legana had spoken her prayers through rote rather than joy, she had still been glad to work – even to bleed – in the service of her family.

'Mistress, do you know how many there are of you left?' Nanter asked quietly, terrified of prying, despite Legana's invitation for her to sit.

Legana shook her head. She had been unable to reach the minds of any devotee beyond those she had brought to Kamfer's Ford –

two dozen now. She could feel them out there, glowing in her mind like candles in the fog. Those that had come at her call said they felt something in the night and been curious enough to investigate, which told Legana her efforts might at least serve as a beacon to those touched by the Lady.

Less happily, the newcomers had also brought tales of fanatical clerics turning on Fate's priestesses. Some had already been burned, amidst rumours that Fate had been cut down by Death and her followers were now heretics.

'How did it happen?' Nanter whispered. 'Did you feel it?'

Legana's hand trembled as her body remembered the beating it had received the night Aracnan killed the Lady.

—*I felt it*, she wrote hesitantly. *I saw her murder.*

'Who would do such a thing?' Nanter's face was white.

—*A daemon with the face of a child.*

Nanter shivered. 'Will it be hunting you?'

Legana shook her head. – *I am no threat, and it has other enemies.*

'As do you.'

—*I know.*

'What will you do if the fanatics come looking for you?'

Legana gave her a small, inscrutable smile, and the emerald gleam in her eyes intensified momentarily. Nanter drew back in alarm, but managed to catch herself. With a great effort of will she kept her seat on the bench.

'A Goddess' blessing,' she whispered, as enthralled as she was frightened, 'a blessing on us all.'

—*Tell the unmen that.*

'We've tried,' Nanter said sadly, 'but he won't listen. We are Godsfearing folk in these parts, but he drives away the most pious among us with his fervour.'

—*Worship without him.*

The innkeeper's wife froze. 'You want us to . . . ? Are you saying . . . ?'

Legana realised what Nanter was failing to say and almost choked as she tried not to laugh. Her ruined voice and damaged throat meant that laughter was dreadfully painful, and barely recognisable.

—*I am no God, nor priestess*, she wrote when the coughing had subsided.

The relief on Nanter's face showed she had been right, the woman had been asking whether Legana intended to take Unmen Poller's place as the heart of the town's worship.

—But I can get him away from the temple each evening.

Nanter bobbed her head in thanks. 'Thank you, Mistress.' She was about to say more when she caught sight of something past Legana's shoulder. 'Mistress, I think more guests have arrived.'

Legana turned and squinted in the direction Nanter indicated. There were four figures standing on the edge of the square, facing her. With the sky bright behind them she could make out little detail, but none wore hoods, and even her weak eyesight could make out the copper tint to their hair.

'It's time I left you alone,' Nanter announced, accepting the empty goblet from Legana as she stood. 'I thank you for your offer. Many folk hereabouts will be most glad of your help.'

Legana retrieved her silver-headed cane from the ground and used it to push herself upright, giving Nanter a smile of thanks. The woman half-curtseyed and fled, leaving Legana to walk, a little unsteadily, towards the newcomers.

'You are the one they call the Hand of Fate?' croaked the one at the head of the group, clearly an old woman.

'*Not to my face,*' Legana said directly into the woman's mind. '*What they refer to was not made by Fate.*'

She lifted the white silk scarf tied around her neck so the former priestess could see the shadowy handprint made by Aracnan.

'I have never known a sister to be a mage before,' said another of the women, sounding as old as the first.

As Legana moved a few steps closer, to see their faces more clearly, one of the remaining two stepped around the priestess, her hand on the hilt of her shortsword. She was the tallest of the four, as tall as Legana, and built for fighting, though she was young enough still to be a novice.

'*I was not, until the Lady made me her Mortal-Aspect,*' Legana replied. '*She called me nothing more than Legana. I would keep that sword in its sheath,*' she added, nodding towards the youngest, '*the Lady chose me because I was the best of her devotees – however damaged my body looks, I am faster than any mortal.*'

'Step aside, Dainiss,' the first woman said, placing a hand on her protector's arm.

As Legana's eyes adjusted to the light she saw the old woman's face was a mass of wrinkles, her skin a leathery-brown that spoke of a lifetime in the sun, but she could make out little more, and she couldn't place the woman's origin.

'I can sense our Goddess' flame within her; she is not the fraud we expected,' the woman said, musingly.

Legana watched the old woman, wondering how she was going to react to that statement, but the priestess did nothing but stare. After a while it became apparent that both sides were waiting for the other to explain themselves. Legana felt the impatience well up inside her. No doubt the old priestess had been a temple-mistress in her time, and had outwaited many a stubborn novice, though Legana was sure she would win that game, even against one so practiced.

'*Have you come to join us?*' she asked.

'What is it you are doing here?'

'*Looking for new purpose. The Lady is dead but her followers are not, and all we've ever had is each other. Some may wish to forget about their family and start afresh, but not I.*'

'You would appoint yourself our queen? Our Goddess?'

'*I appoint myself nothing, but like it or not, I carry the spark that binds us. There are only a few of our sisters here yet, but several have been permanently affected by the death of Fate. Those who were praying at the time of her murder were harmed in the mind and they need the protection of their sisters. I intend to gather as many as I can and take stock. Only then will we be able to find our way forward. Only then will we have a chance to find a new purpose.*'

The old priestess pursed her lips as she thought. No doubt she was wary of everything since the death of their Goddess.

'*You don't need to decide now,*' Legana continued, '*come with me to the castle and meet the others. They would be glad of a priestess here.*'

She gestured for them to follow and turned towards Camatayl Castle. After a moment she heard footsteps. Though she set a slow pace, Legana walked alone, feeling their eyes bore into her back with every step.

When she reached the castle Shanas, one of the devotees she had first arrived with, ran up and informed her that King Emin had been looking for her.

'*I thought as much,*' Legana said, gesturing at the activity within the normally sleepy courtyard. '*He will soon have need of us.*'

There were hundreds of men in the castle now, soldiers and workmen alike, the latter labouring to erect new buildings within the embrace of the castle walls: temporary barracks for the troops that would soon be passing through the area. A few regiments were already camped up against the outer walls, along with a large number of messengers. Flying from the main tower were half a dozen flags now – another two had been added during the day.

'My sisters,' she said, rounding on the devotees following her, 'I'm needed elsewhere. Shanas here will take you to the others. King Emin had granted us rooms in the gate-tower – it's not much, but as you can see, space is limited. His hospitality isn't charity, and if you wish to stay it will be on my terms.'

'And what are those?' demanded the priestess.

'Use of what skills we possess,' Legana said, 'and a guarantee from me that his secrets will be kept. I advise you not to test that; the devotees here have already made their choice.'

Before any of the four had the chance to argue Legana turned her back on them and headed for the main tower. There were now green-and-gold liveried members of the Kingsguard posted throughout the castle, but she was admitted without challenge and made her way up to the room where she'd first discussed a bargain with the king. This time he barely even looked up as she entered.

King Emin had chosen Camatayl Castle as his base of operations for the coming year, leaving his queen and newborn son in the relative safety of Narkang. He wore a ceremonial version of the Kingsguard uniform and a hat to match it that looked gaudy even to Legana's weak, greying vision.

'What about there?' he asked the man beside him, a decrepit old relic in a faded uniform.

The man's cheeks were scarred by drink and his uniform hung loose on his body. The dull gold braiding from shoulder to cuff on one sleeve indicated he was a general in the Narkang Army, the creasing suggested he had been retired for a while now. There were two other men looking over the map, both much younger, who sported the same braiding, and Legana guessed them to be newly promoted.

'Good ground, yes,' said the old general, with a cautious glance at the newcomer, 'but the river all along that stretch is impassable. There are only two bridges of use to us for more than a hundred miles. You'd need a local in command or they could get trapped.'

'It's worth the risk, within striking distance of the city. Three divisions, under your personal command. If the city falls you pull back past the river and the south bank is your boundary. Remember, hit-and-run is our mantra: constant movement, and no engagement where it is expected.'

King Emin at last tore himself away from the map and directed Legana towards an elderly, rather shambolic-looking nobleman escorted by a bored-looking Kingsguard. The pale, rather portly man sat at a small desk peering at another map that had been stretched out and held at the corners with brass weights. Alongside was a jumble of papers on which he was writing notes. The king had been expecting his arrival for a few days now; this was his uncle, Anversis Halis, an academic who had been recording and modelling the movements of the Harlequins for years.

Only recently had the king become interested in the work, though he was aware of most of the research being conducted within his borders, interesting or otherwise. It wasn't the first time the king had been able to harness knowledge of this kind for military use. Legana didn't know if they all got guards, but the king had been less than complimentary about his uncle's discretion, so she guessed it was as much to keep him out of trouble as anything else.

Legana made her way over and stood in silence at the table until Halis noticed her.

He gave a gasp of shock. 'Blessed song of seasons!' he exclaimed, half-falling off his chair. But he soon recovered himself and it wasn't long before Halis was peering up at her face with utter fascination. 'You, ah, you are . . .' he stuttered.

Legana inclined her head and the words died unsaid in his throat, but the acknowledgement didn't appear to diminish his curiosity. He even went so far as to edge around the table to get a little closer, but that just prompted Legana to back away.

—*Stop staring or I'll blind you*, she wrote on her slate eventually.

The man gave a squawk and retreated to his seat. 'Ah, my apologies, Mistress Legana. There are so many questions running through my head that I hardly know where to begin.'

Legana scowled, her fingers flexing around the silver head of her cane. It took a while, but the man eventually got the message that she was not going to answer questions and turned his attention back to the map.

'Ah, here is the working plan. The, um, subjects follow a reasonably simple path through the Land, as one might expect. They are only human, after all, and they are subject to the same habits as the rest of us.'

—How many?

'In total?' Halis frowned at her. 'It is impossible to tell for sure. King Emin assures me they have home clans and will return there periodically, but for how long is impossible to calculate, as is the incidence of their passing being reported to me.'

—How is that done?

He glanced away uneasily at the king, but at that moment Legana's balance failed her again and she swayed forward, grabbing the table with both hands to steady herself. Halis went even whiter and raised his hands protectively, as though she was going to strike him.

'A network of academics throughout the Land,' Halis blurted out, misreading her actions entirely. 'They study the writings of Verliq and aid the research of their fellows wherever possible.'

'And what kind fellows they are too,' added King Emin, joining them. He looked at her, concerned, but she waved it away and he didn't comment further.

'You will have heard of Verliq's Children, I assume? As I have reminded my uncle here, my patronage and assistance over the years has been invaluable to them, and I fully expect them to be delighted to assist our midsummer operation.'

'Delighted?' spluttered Halis.

King Emin raised a hand to stop him saying any more. 'I choose to believe they are delighted. They are, of course, not men of action, but I want this to be kept separate from my principal spy network, which has quite enough to keep it busy at present. To bolster numbers Legana has agreed to recruit for me among her sisters, both for the operation itself and the logistics of putting it into practice.'

—How many?

'To kill? Our aim is a hundred; we know we will not get them all, but that should still disrupt this current phase of the shadow's plan.' Emin pursed his lips in thought and stared down at the map. 'I have had news from Byora; we were not successful in our goal.

255

At the same time it was not a complete disaster, and our casualties were acceptable.' He hesitated. 'You can tell your sisters that the killer of their Goddess is dead.'

Legana felt her knees tremble and another wave of dizziness washed over her, but she fought it, and managed to keep herself upright. *Aracnan was dead.* She had been expecting this news at some point, ever since Doranei's comrade, Sebe, had managed to wound the mercenary, but still the news caught her off-guard.

Anger and satisfaction clashed inside her. There was some frustration that it had been done by another, despite King Emin's assurances that his end would have been painful. What more did she want? What more could she ask for?

Nothing. There is nothing more, she realised. *All I can do now is ensure his deeds do not define me any more than they must.*

—*Thank you. How many sisters?* she forced herself to write, ignoring the unsteadiness of the script.

To Emin's credit he continued with only a questioning look at her expression. 'As many as possible, more than we can manage,' he said. 'Some will have to leave today – we are limited by the distances involved – but some of Uncle Anversis' colleagues have faster methods of communication so we may be able to hire mercenaries, if nothing else. There is an additional matter, however. Doranei has reported preachers being sent out by the child, Ruhen. They are now secondary targets.'

—*Does it suspect?*

'There is no indication of that,' Emin said, his worry-lines deepening at the suggestion. 'The reports we're getting suggest Harlequins are laying the foundations for these preachers, adding legitimacy to what will follow. The agents I have here and those easily contacted will be sent furthest afield.' Emin picked up a sheet from the pile of paper his uncle had been making notes on. 'This designates the place and the local contact. The particular agents will be assigned here, and the page will be encoded and copied before it leaves this room.'

—*When do you need my sisters?*

'We will send them in groups; I need the first ready in two days.' The king took another piece of paper proffered by his uncle and scanned it before showing it to Legana. 'This is the first; do you have enough to fill these?'

Legana squinted at the page. The scribbled characters were hard to read, but she was able at least to make out the number of lines involved. She nodded.

'Send them to Dashain tomorrow morning. She will assign positions and give the contact names. Hopefully you will not have to remind them how skilled the targets are; they are not to be given any sort of chance, or drawn into a fair fight.'

King Emin paused and gave her a long, hard look. 'I'm taking a great risk in trusting so much to your sisters. Are you certain of their loyalty? I don't have a contingency plan here; my forces are stretched too thin.'

—*It will be done.*

The look in her eyes was chilling. It reminded Emin of Larat wearing his sister's face. There was no place for uncertainty in a God's mind, and Doranei had described Legana as uncompromising when she was just mortal. The current combination was not a comforting one. As he ordered murder to be done, Emin found himself hoping he wouldn't be the one to find out how far Legana was prepared to go.

CHAPTER 18

'Count Vesna,' Lesarl called from the massive stone stair that led to the Great Hall, 'where exactly do you think you are going?'

Vesna wheeled his horse around and stared with some incomprehension at the Chief Steward. All around him the soldiers hesitated, sensing something cutting through the tension in the air. Vesna was surrounded by a hundred men of the Palace Guard, now in the process of forming up around a small party of officers.

'What are you talking about? You heard the message too!' he shouted back.

Half the palace had heard the man shouting as he raced into the Great Hall to deliver his message to Sir Cerse, and they had all exploded into action at the news.

'Yes, Vesna, I heard it only too well – which is exactly why you should not be going anywhere.'

Vesna gaped. 'What in the Dark Place are you talking about? We've got soldiers under siege at the Brewer's Gate, man – men of the Ghosts!'

Lesarl sighed theatrically and folded his arms, looking down at Vesna as though he was just a foolish child. 'I know you men of action get excited easily, but think it through a moment. Go back to the source of the problem.'

Vesna turned to his companions on horseback, Sir Cerse, Swordmasters Pettir and Cosep, and a bearded captain of the Ghosts called Kurrest. From the bemused expressions on their faces, he guessed none of them had a clue what the Chief Steward was talking about. Vesna's horse, a black hunter with padded barding covering its flanks and a steel chest-guard, tossed its head impatiently, refusing to stay still even when Vesna jerked on the reins to quieten it.

Letting his new-found divine senses filter out the movement all around so he could concentrate, Vesna replayed in his mind the report that had prompted immediate action. Surely it wasn't just a ruse? A soldier had run all the way to the palace, bringing news of a unit of Ghosts who'd arrested a nobleman under holy orders, one Count Feers, only to find themselves attacked by a party of penitents and priests of Karkarn. The Ghosts had driven off their attackers and retreated to the nearest safe place, the nearby Brewer's Gate barbican, where a permanent guard was stationed.

Now they were under siege, by increasing numbers of troops, and they had rung the attack-alarm to summon help. While it was possible this was a set-up, to lure a few companies of Ghosts out of the Palace, Vesna didn't believe it, not when individual squads out on routine patrol could have been ambushed on a daily basis if they wanted to.

Go back to the source of the problem. The arrest? Vesna tried to remember what he could of Count Lerail Feers – they hadn't ever exactly been friends. Feers was a deeply religious man, one of those who'd regularly denounced Vesna's lifestyle when he'd been a member of the Ghosts. He had been arrested for siding with the clerics against Lord Fernal – not a crime in itself, but for a nobleman to take holy orders without relinquishing his title was.

It had been prohibited for a millennium or more: all noblemen automatically had military rank, so taking holy orders was strictly prohibited lest it place wealth and weapons in the hands of priests. Only the Lord of the Farlan had a place in the three spheres of Farlan power, spiritual, temporal and military. Normally Feers wouldn't have been arrested, but as a count he had a number of marshals and knights under his authority, and by ordering them to also take holy orders he had committed treason.

'Piss and daemons,' Vesna said suddenly, 'you're worried about *hypocrisy*? You think they'll accuse me of the same crime . . .' Vesna didn't have any position within the cult of Karkarn, but he was the War God's Mortal-Aspect, and rank didn't really apply when the divine spirit surged through his body and he wielded the wrath of the heavens.

'Dawn and dusk,' Lesarl replied with a shrug. It was a mark of the strain he was under that Vesna's late realisation wasn't enough to amuse the Chief Steward – in quieter times much of Lesarl's entertainment had been at the expense of the soldiers around him.

'Don't matter which way it's going,' Swordmaster Pettir said, absently completing the saying, 'it's all fucking grey to me.'

Pettir was Kerin's replacement, a former major of the Ghosts who'd joined the legion in the same trials as Vesna. While there had been Swordmasters more senior, General Lahk had chosen to promote the low-born Pettir to the position of Knight-Defender of Tirah and commander of the Swordmasters because of the respect the troops had for him. Vesna had been glad of it; he and Pettir had been friendly rivals from the outset and the last thing the count needed now was any sort of pious deference.

'The wisdom of soldiers,' Lesarl agreed. 'It might be foolish for the Mortal-Aspect of Karkarn to arrive bedecked in the livery of a famous nobleman and hero of the army. Sir Cerse can deal with the situation himself.'

'You think they're going to listen to a soldier?' Vesna retorted angrily. 'All that politics has addled your brains, Lesarl. Fate's eyes, they aren't going to negotiate with the colonel of the Ghosts!'

'Right now it's debatable whether they will negotiate with anyone,' Lesarl said, making his way down the steps so they could continue the discussion without shouting. 'Your presence is as likely to be inflammatory as it is useful. Either they speak to Sir Cerse and follow the law, or they draw weapons on a regiment of the Palace Guard. That is a line they haven't crossed before; it isn't like the skirmishes individual squads have been getting into.'

'You want this to happen? You want a pitched battle on Tirah's streets?'

'Don't be facetious,' Lesarl snapped, 'you know me better than that. You change any situation, just as Lord Isak would have. You are a being of power who affects events by your very presence. With just Sir Cerse and his Ghosts there, they will either submit to the rule of law and be arrested, or they will make a move that will have to be condemned as treasonous by every other party involved. With you there, *anything* could happen, and likely as not it will involve more blood spilled.'

'Their blood, not that of the Ghosts,' Vesna promised with a scowl. 'Without me they may not have the decisive force to end any skirmish before it heats up. Fighting on the streets doesn't just happen; it takes time to fester, like a dog working itself up to violence.'

'Now who's the one to go looking for bloodshed?' Lesarl demanded. 'If—'

Vesna cut the man off mid-sentence by wrenching his horse away, towards the barbican. 'Unless the order is Lord Fernal's, I go with the Ghosts. You do not know his mind as well as Lord Bahl; you do not yet give orders in his name.'

Lesarl hesitated. 'That is easily rectified,' he called, turning back towards the Great Hall.

'Then do so. You'll find me at the Brewer's Gate!'

At Sir Cerse's order, the columns of Palace Guard clattered to a halt. The officers on horseback looked over the heads and Swordmaster Pettir swore quietly, voicing the thoughts that were running through Vesna's head too. There was a makeshift blockade across the street ahead, manned by a handful of penitents with bows. Their robes were grey with red hoods – Penitents of Karkarn – and they were led by a priest of the War God. More worrying still, they were accompanied by two liveried soldiers, sworn swords of Count Feers, most likely, both wearing scarlet sashes. It was not much of a guess to assume those sashes bore the Runesword of the Knights of the Temples, whether or not the Order was banned in Farlan territory.

'Come no further,' shouted one of the soldiers, walking a dozen yards from the barricade towards them. 'If you attempt to interfere with the work of the Gods you will answer to Keness of the Spear!'

Vesna, his lion's head faceplate raised, shared a grin with his comrades. 'I'd like to see how that works out for you!' he yelled back. He quietly told Sir Cerse to hold their position, then nudged his mount into motion and slowly began to make his way towards the barricade. A single knight was hard to interpret as great provocation by the archers, and whatever their masters said, the rank and file would be painfully aware of the law: killing a nobleman in cold blood was something the nobility frowned upon, and the punishment made the eventual hanging something of a mercy.

The priest of Karkarn advanced also, reaching the man who'd called out before bowing his head in prayer. Vesna felt the air swirl around above their heads as the priest, clearly a mage as well, called his Aspect-Guide forth. The bitter coppery taste of magic filled the air and Vesna felt a responding pulse of energy from the Crystal

Skull moulded around the blade of his sword. The wind seemed to echo with the distant clash of steel and his horse slowed. Vesna urged it onwards.

The street, a wide avenue lined with shops, had been deserted when they arrived, and only a handful of nervous faces looked down from high windows out of the way of whatever was going to happen. The tensions of recent months had taught the locals to fear any potential confrontation; even the side-streets were empty.

Without warning a tall figure winked into existence beside the priest, as tall as Vesna atop his hunter, and carrying a cross-blade spear more than ten feet long. Keness of the Spear wore a shirt of chainmail, shining brass greaves and vambraces inscribed with prayers for safety in battle. The Aspect of Karkarn wore nothing on its head bar a knotted cord of red cloth like a circlet. It blinked and looked around, first at Vesna and then at the priest beside it.

'This is a city,' the Aspect rumbled, its words echoing around the street. It looked down at the priest beside it. 'My place is the battlefield. Why do you call me here?'

The priest gaped at the minor God beside him, astonished by its reaction. Unfortunately the sworn sword beside him was not so tongue-tied.

'They are heretics,' he shouted, jabbing his finger in Vesna's direction, 'here to arrest priests and commit crimes against the Gods.'

The Aspect gave Vesna another look and nodded slightly in acknowledgement. It gave a flick of the wrist and levelled its spear so the tip was an inch from the soldier's throat.

'You are aligned to Lady Amavoq. It is deference to her that stays my blade,' the Aspect said after a pause, slowly turning its head to look the soldier in the eye. 'Speak again and I will risk your mistress' wrath.'

The soldier backed away, his mouth open in terror, and the Aspect lowered its weapon. Vesna continued riding slowly towards the barricade. When he was fifteen yards away Keness bowed to him and lowered the tip of its spear to the ground in salute before stepping out of his way.

Vesna continued until he was level with the Aspect and the priest was within sword-reach. There he stopped and gave the soldier a cold look. The man was visibly trembling, despite being very obviously a veteran. It was one thing to see a few battles and take holy orders; quite another to see more than one embodiment of War standing before you.

'Keness of the Spear,' Vesna said to the Aspect, 'I apologise that you were disturbed.'

The Aspect inclined its head and calmly allowed Vesna to cut the flow of magic between priest and God. He vanished, and that done, Vesna turned his attention to the priest. From the markings on the man's robes he was a senior unmen, no doubt recently elevated because of his abilities as a mage.

'Unmen,' Vesna commanded, causing the priest to flinch, 'dismiss your men and go home to think about what you almost did.'

Without waiting for a response he waved forward the regiment of Palace Guard waiting behind. There was no word of argument from any of the penitents; they raced to clear the barricade and by the time the Ghosts trotted up there was a gap large enough for the troops to pass through two-abreast.

Swordmaster Cosep picked two troopers to disarm the penitents while Vesna led the Ghosts down the street and around the corner to where the rest of the action was happening. A dozen soldiers rounded it at the same time, and skidded to a halt when they saw Vesna and the column. The soldiers immediately turned and fled back the way they'd come, but as Vesna continued he realised that wasn't the good news he'd been hoping for.

The Brewer's Gate was a solid fortification in the northeastern part of the city. With produce normally flowing through it every hour of the day, it was no surprise that a small market had been established in the lee of the gate itself. Vesna saw the stalls had been abandoned, and the only people in the space now were armed – and well in excess of the numbers Vesna had brought with him.

The bulk of troops, on the right, were hurriedly turning to form line – they had not been expecting anyone to approach from the south, rather than direct from the palace – but Vesna ignored them, more interested in the squads at the gate itself. Men were huddling under raised shields, as though the occupants of the guardhouse were firing arrows down at them, while a second squad was keeping the gate itself firmly shut and barred.

There was no sign of blood having been spilled, and the only

indication of confrontation was at the guardhouse, a square building on the left of the gate, where the attack alarm on the roof was
sounding again.

'Who's outside the gate?' Swordmaster Pettir wondered aloud,
but he didn't get a chance to speculate as a group of soldiers and
noblemen marched up to address Vesna.

'Leave this place!' roared a middle-aged man wearing a single
gold earring of rank. He wore chainmail and a heron crest on his
brown and white livery. Vesna didn't recognise the man, but he
had half a dozen hurscals at his side, and they had their hands on
their hilts. 'You have no authority over the cults!'

'And what, pray, has that got to do with you?' Vesna replied in
a calm voice, ignoring, for the moment at least, the lower-ranked
nobleman's deliberate flouting of the traditions of respect. 'You are
a titled man. You can have no affiliation with the cults.'

The man shouted, 'My allegiance to Nartis is my own business,
not yours.'

'If you have taken holy orders, then it is my business,' Swordmaster Pettir interrupted. 'As Knight-Defender of Tirah, I am
charged with enforcing the rule of law in the city. What say you?'

'I say I am a man of piety, you damned jumped-up peasant, and
the Gods shall strike you down as a heretic if you claim otherwise –
just as the charges upon which Count Feers was arrested are
tyrannical, and against the will of the Gods.'

'But they are still the law,' Vesna answered, 'so you'll step aside
and allow the Palace Guard to do their duty.'

'Under whose authority?'

'That of Lord Fernal.'

The man spat. 'The creature Fernal bears no authority. It has no
right to claim rule over the noblest tribe of man.'

'That is a matter for your betters to decide,' Vesna said, nudging
his horse forward while signalling for his troops to remain. 'The
law on holy orders remains, however, and Count Feers has broken
it; he must answer for his crimes at the Temple of Law.'

'Count Feers is guilty of nothing but proclaiming the majesty of
the Gods and their authority over all,' the soldier roared.

'Then the Gods will see to it he is acquitted,' Vesna said. 'Until
then he is under arrest.'

'You may not have him, nor may your lackeys!' the nobleman

screamed, pointing towards the gate. 'We serve the Gods. We will die to protect their majesty.'

Vesna stopped. Clearly there was something he did not yet know about the situation. 'Who is outside the gate?' he asked.

'The heretics you sent to murder priests, the criminals who wish to plunder the temples and steal rule of the tribe from those the Gods intended,' he snarled.

Vesna scratched his cheek, where the ruby in his skin was suddenly itching fiercely.

'*Kill them all,*' whispered Karkarn in his ear. '*There is no place for madmen and fools in this Land.*'

Vesna instinctively shook his head at the sudden intrusion, as though he could dislodge the God from it, and his hand twitched towards his sword before he could catch himself.

The nobleman saw the movement and took a step back to plant his feet more firmly. He gripped his sword.

Enough of your help, Vesna thought as he drove the War God from his thoughts. *This must end without bloodshed, otherwise it will lead to civil war.*

Carefully, deliberately he withdrew his hand, and when the nobleman had relaxed a touch Vesna dismounted. A man on horseback had a clear advantage in battle – whether they would admit it or not, Vesna knew the veterans would see it as a pacifying action. He removed his helm so they would be able to see the ruby on his cheek more clearly and walked towards them, not deviating when they turned aside and opened up the path towards the guardhouse.

The penitents standing ready at the door retreated when he reached them. Vesna could feel the eyes of everyone in the market on him, watching every small movement, waiting for the action that would spark the violence.

He thumped on the guardhouse door and called out, 'Sergeant? Is all well in there?'

He could hear the scuffle of feet inside, then the sound of boots on a ladder before the reply eventually came. 'Aye, sir, we're not harmed.'

'Then open the door please, and bring your prisoner out.'

'Ah, beggin' yer pardon, sir, but who's givin' the order?'

'Count Vesna, acting under the authority of Lord Fernal.'

Using Fernal's disputed title seemed to do the trick. He heard

265

the screech of heavy iron bolts being drawn back, and something heavy being dragged from the reinforced oak door. It opened cautiously, just enough to catch sight of the man outside, but Vesna's armour alone was unmistakable to any man of the Ghosts. Quickly the door opened all the way to reveal the grim faces of a dozen Palace Guards, dressed in full battle armour. Behind them was the whiskered face of Count Feers, purple with outrage as he barged towards Vesna.

'You of all men come to accuse me? Murderer, adulterer, *hypocrite*—'

Vesna raised a cautioning hand. 'Think very carefully about your next words, Count Feers. Tensions are running high and there are already serious charges against you. If you incite others to violence against the Ghosts ... well, I doubt you need much convincing as to the Chief Steward's vindictive nature. He would extend any punishment laid down upon you to every member of your family.'

The threat had the desired effect; Lesarl's reputation among the nobility was well deserved. However deep his fanaticism, Feers had a large family and it was a fair bet at least one of them meant something to him. It took a few heartbeats, but then the count's shoulders sagged and he capitulated, allowing the Ghosts to lead him out without further resistance.

'Ah, my lord?' one of the soldiers still in the guardroom piped up.

Vesna turned to see four anxious faces. 'What is it?'

'Outside the gate, my lord, there's a couple of regiments out there, under the command of Suzerain Yetah.'

'Tsatach's fiery balls,' Vesna groaned, 'that's the last thing I need right now.'

Now he realised why the Palace Guardsmen were looking so concerned. Kollen Yetah being here right now meant trouble in some form or another, though this was a curious twist, considering the nobleman's words of a minute ago. Yetah's family had been as entrenched in the Knights of the Temples as much as any man's, for a century or more – although they had always complied with Lord Bahl's edicts about the Devoted. Suzerain Yetah was an unlikely person to be bent on defiling temples.

'He's demanding the gate be opened immediately.'

'I'm sure he is.' To himself Vesna muttered, 'Damn, what part is he intending to play?' He didn't wait for the men to respond; there was only one way he'd get an answer and that was by speaking to the man himself.

'Open the gate,' he ordered.

The sergeant saluted and directed his men to start the process of removing the great bolts locking the gate closed. 'Lot of angry soldiers out there, sir,' he commented in a neutral voice, not wanting to sound like he was questioning orders.

'I know, but neither of us has the authority to deny a suzerain, and General Lahk is not here at present.'

Vesna confirmed the Ghosts with Count Feers were not being prevented from joining their comrades. The various troops under command of the cults hadn't moved. They didn't look happy about the situation, but as long as no one was raising weapons, Vesna was happy.

As soon as the gate opened a tall man with a mop of curly hair stormed through, four knighted hurscals at his heel. He looked good for a man ten summers older than Vesna, though he walked was a noticeable limp, favouring the right leg that had been recently broken when Lord Isak had called for soldiers to join his crusade.

Yetah wasn't the only suzerain to have moved troops into Tebran, just the boldest. He was an experienced soldier, having spent almost ten years in Lomin commanding a cavalry division, but he appeared to have lost none of his youthful belligerence in that time.

He walked straight up to the count, making a dismissive gesture when Vesna made to kneel and offer his sword, and cried, 'Good to see you again, Vesna – I hear congratulations are in order. Some filly broken you at last, or are you just getting old?'

A cuirass was plainly visible under the suzerain's livery, and he carried a red broadsword with a lightning flash down the blade that reflected his family's long-standing allegiance to the Devoted.

'A bit of both, my Lord Suzerain,' Vesna replied coolly. 'I am glad to see you are recovering.'

Yetah pointed to his leg. 'This? Pah, teach me to jump fallen trees on an old horse. Have you arrested Count Feers?'

Vesna blinked. Yetah's information was better than he'd have expected; the arrest warrant had only just been issued and had barely been announced to the city. 'He is in custody, my lord; the stand-off is over.'

'But the bastards are still here?' Yetah exclaimed, looking past Vesna. 'They're still armed? What's stopping you? They should all be in irons and on the way to the gibbet by now!'

'Gibbet? Sir, why are you here, and leading troops into the city no less?'

'Doing what must be done,' Yetah snapped. 'If you will do nothing about this gradual coup by the cults, then it falls to the armies of the Farlan to protect our nation.'

'Coup?' Vesna said in a daze. 'Yetah, you're a member of the Knights of the Temples—'

'You will address me as "my Lord Suzerain" – need I remind you that we are not peers?' Yetah replied sharply. 'As for my allegiances, they are none of your concern. I am a nobleman of the Farlan and a loyal soldier of the tribe. Whether or not a usurper currently holds the ducal throne, my duty to the tribe remains. I will not stand idly by while bloody mutinous priests exploit the majesty of their Gods to take power.'

Vesna looked back and saw the penitents drawing back, but rather than fleeing they were taking a defensive position at the mouth of a side-street. 'My Lord Suzerain, what you propose would result in a pitched battle in the streets of Tirah – we would have civil war—'

'If there are traitors within the tribe, let them declare themselves so,' Yetah shouted towards the penitents. 'This creeping theft of authority must stop. The politicking and deal-making to sell the nation is over. They will learn our resolve and discover the consequences of their actions.'

Vesna raised his hands, a pacifying gesture that kept them away from the hilt of his weapon as much as anything. Yetah's hurscals looked as fiercely resolute as their master, and itching for a fight.

Vesna had been hearing reports of suzerains reacting against the cults since returning to Tirah, but thus far it had been small-scale actions in distant parts. Suzerain Saroc had routed a party of a hundred soldiers at a monastery on his land, where they had been conducting Morality Tribunals and Tests of Faith that amounted to torture, but that had been the biggest engagement so far. Every morning brought news of deaths from one part of the nation or another, but they were all skirmishes involving a few dozen combatants at most. This was on another level entirely.

No one could ignore a battle involving hundreds on the streets of Tirah, nor fail to react to it. From where he was standing Vesna's view was restricted, but he could see at least two regimental banners behind Yetah.

'Suzerain Yetah,' he said carefully, 'contrary to what you have heard, the rule of law still governs the streets of Tirah. If you bring troops onto the streets of Tirah, you would be breaking the law, and force us to respond.'

'Don't bother to threaten me, Vesna, your position in all this is as much in question as that of the monster you serve now,' Yetah growled.

'Lord Fernal was named legitimate heir and Lord of the Farlan by Lord Isak, and I act in his name.' Vesna paused, trying to slow things down as much as he could. 'Suzerain Yetah, you must see that Lord Isak realised we need a strong ruler this coming year; we cannot wait for Lord Nartis to appoint a new Chosen! Without a figure to unite the tribe we will be invaded and conquered by the Menin.'

'Whatever the consequences of Lord Isak's warmongering, we will not accept a non-Farlan to rule the tribe – otherwise we might as well submit to Kastan Styrax and see his flag fly from the Tower of Semar!'

Vesna took a step back and lowered his hand to his hilt. There was obviously going to be no reasoning with the man. The ruby on his cheek glowed bloody red. 'Sir, with the greatest respect, I cannot allow you to lead troops into Tirah; I will not let you pass.'

'You do not have the authority to stop me, damn you!' Yetah roared, drawing his sword. 'You should have already given up the rights and rank of title – whoever your master, you have no right to command the Ghosts now, so get out of my way. I am acting to protect the tribe, and to stop me you will have to cut me down!'

Yetah started forward, certain in the knowledge that Vesna wouldn't kill a man of higher rank, but when a sword-tip appeared at his throat Yetah nearly tripped in his surprise and outrage. He looked at the count and blinked. 'Vesna, I mean you no harm. Step aside and let me pass. If you kill me, you will be cut down, or the law will see you hang, you know that.'

Vesna nodded. He did know it, and he knew too there would be no defence he could bring that would avoid it. Suzerain Yetah was his superior, both in title and military rank, and if he killed the man and avoided a hanging, that would invalidate any claims Lord Fernal might make about protecting the tribe's laws. He just had to gamble that he wouldn't kill the man.

'Then lower your sword, sir.'

'I will not.'

Yetah lurched to the left, trying to step around Vesna, but the count was a renowned duellist and swordsman, and he was there before him, his sword still raised. Yetah swatted the tip away from his face with his own blade, but as he advanced Vesna stepped forward and dropped his shoulder into the suzerain, shoving him backwards.

'Damn you, Vesna,' Yetah snapped. He struck without warning but Vesna was faster and caught the blade, again stepping into Yetah and this time hammering the pommel of his sword against the suzerain's cuirass.

The move drove him back another pace, but the space was quickly made up by the youngest of the hurscals, who swung a wild blow at Vesna's head. The count retreated, fending off blows for a few paces before flicking his opponent's sword away and punching the man's arm with his black-iron fist, snapping the bone and sending the man reeling into the hinge of the now-open gate.

A second man attacked with more purpose, his shield raised high. Vesna, moving with blurring speed, stepped around the hurscal's lunge, and the man fell screaming. A diagonal cut had sheared his shield in two, and the arm behind it.

The others hesitated, stunned by the count's unnatural speed.

Vesna took a step back. He could feel the power of the Crystal Skull begging to be used. As soon as he focused on it the Skull emitted a bright white pulse, and the remaining hurscals stopped dead in their tracks.

'Enough – stay your swords,' Vesna called. 'Suzerain Yetah, order your men back. I will not kill you, my lord, but I will kill any other man who tries to pass.'

No one else stepped forward. Vesna met the eye of each one. None had the strength of will to keep their weapon raised. He pointed to the injured men.

'See to your comrades, then leave this place and return to your own lands. Tell any others you meet: the law is not yours to protect, unless so ordered by the Lord of the Farlan. If any man intends to kill his fellow Farlan, he must face me first.'

He turned away and stopped dead when he saw the companies of the Palace Guard were lined up in defensive formation. Sir Cerse, the legion's colonel, offered him a crisp salute, and after a moment he returned it. They had been ready to defend him, even to fight their own alongside him if necessary.

And that's a gift even Gods cannot give, Vesna thought as the ranks parted to allow him through. Swordmaster Pettir handed him the reins of his horse.

'Lesarl will be pleased with you,' Pettir said with mocking cheer.

Vesna scowled. 'This cannot continue.'

CHAPTER 19

Ruhen smiled, his face turned to the afternoon sun. Its diffused light cast a pale yellow tint over the valley, while long shadows enveloped the waiting soldiers. He felt its warmth on his face as he breathed in the fresh clear air. Winter's grip was lessening day by day and he could smell the change in the air, even if the arguing delegates nearby couldn't.

In the wake of the dragon, the valley housing the Library of Seasons had taken on a dismal air. All of the white stone buildings had been damaged and the beast's gigantic corpse still rotted below the southern cliff, but today Ruhen could taste something other than decay on the breeze. A hundred yards away there were tables set out on the grass, as close to the centre of the valley as they could judge. Without Ruhen close at hand Duchess Escral's wits had returned enough for her to lead the debate, but as yet there had been no progress.

Lord Styrax sat beneath a huge army standard emblazoned with his Fanged Skull, looking bored, while the white-eye Duke Vrill, his pet politician, stood at his side shouting something at the men in scarlet sashes opposite.

The Knights of the Temples were divided into three distinct camps, each desperate to assert authority over the others while the negotiations stagnated. The Knight-Cardinal led one, a pair of generals, envoys for Raland and Embere, comprised the second, while the scarlet-faced priests of several cults made up the third faction.

Two squads of Devoted heavy infantry were assembled behind them, watching the proceedings with as much bemusement as the Ruby Tower Guards behind Duchess Escral; Ruhen could see only contempt on the faces of the élite Menin soldiers around the valley.

'I've beginning to wonder,' said Ilumene from behind Ruhen, 'whether our presence has somehow only made things worse.' The big mercenary smirked as he spoke. He pretended to straighten the white patchwork robe he'd worn specifically to annoy the priests. The missionaries preaching Ruhen's message of peace had been first admitted to Akell, the Devoted quarter of the Circle City. Knight-Cardinal Certinse had given their presence his tacit blessing, but as soon as the cults heard their preaching, every priest in the quarter started screaming for blood. That Ilumene was attending the official negotiations dressed as one of Ruhen's ensured the priests were filled with bile and fury when they started proceedings.

'Let them dig their own graves,' Ruhen replied and closed his eyes to savour the warmth of the sun.

'Aye, every soldier there was disgusted by the reaction, I marked that well. It's even taught me to be civil. The more polite I am to the bastards, the more crazed they look!'

'Progress through discord.'

The boy contrived to look eight or nine summers now, though small and slender for that age he was in truth far younger. Ilumene realised he had shaken off the gangly awkwardness of early childhood, instead moving with the precision and elegance that normally only follows puberty.

'So when do you step in?'

'Not quite yet; let them tire a little more.' Ruhen opened his eyes again and focused on the Knight-Cardinal. The man looked beleaguered, as well he might, but he had not yet looked in Ruhen's direction. Certinse had accepted Luerce's offer of assistance readily enough, and he knew the part he had to play. The more Ruhen could be seen as the answer to the Devoted's problems – and in time the fulfilment of their prophecies – the more Certinse could wrest control of his Order from the clerics paralysing it ... yet he had not yet committed himself.

Ilumene fell silent, sensing Ruhen didn't want to speak any more. He could see soldiers watching the boy, trying to be surreptitious, but unable to stop staring at the child they were hearing so many stories about. The priesthood was at the very heart of the Knights of the Temples, with every officer an ordained priest, albeit usually in one of the less-demanding cults. Every cuirass was inscribed with a prayer, and every day was heralded with the devotionals spoken *en masse.*

Originally the religious aspect had been a veneer for the majority, a small matter, accepted in return for the Order's weekly stipend, but it was no longer such; the common soldiers were beginning to feel their holy charge more as a yoke around their necks. They were informed on by their own, even flogged for impious behaviour, and resentment had been building for months. Some had been mooting retaliation of some sort, but it was hard to fight back against the appointed of the Gods . . . unless the priests themselves were at fault, and then it would not be impious at all.

This was fertile ground for Ruhen's message of peace, his dismissal of the priests' role. They were far from ready, but even so, most of the Circle City had heard of the remarkable child Duchess Escral had adopted, the miracles he had performed.

And what better way to persuade a man, thought Ilumene, looking down at the slight figure beside him whose eyes were swirling with shadows, *than to give him what he hopes for in his heart.*

His gaze moved to Knight-Cardinal Certinse, presently exchanging angry words with his own spiritual advisor.

You're not a man to care why you have been given everything you asked for, are you, Certinse? You assume you'll be able to kill us when Ruhen has served his purpose. Ilumene smiled and ran his fingertips over the hilt of his own dagger. *Good luck with that. When you do, that's when you'll start to notice the shadows moving out of the corner of your eye.*

A few minutes later, Ruhen started off towards the bickering men and women. Ilumene kept back a while before following. He was there as a devoted servant of the child, nothing more. Ruhen had to look vulnerable, without guidance; his hypnotic eyes would do the rest.

'Tribute?' roared the general from Raland, 'what new insult is this? There was no mention of such a thing an hour ago!'

'An hour ago you were declaring yourselves ready to fight to the last man,' Duke Vrill retorted with a pinched expression, 'with the great dragon of your Order threatening to reach out with its claws and strike us all down.'

More than a few couldn't help but glance at the rotting corpse of the dragon Lord Styrax had killed. The body had been butchered, its claws and teeth taken by Menin soldiers as trophies, but a large enough chunk remained rotting in the sun.

'So much anger,' Ruhen said in a quiet voice. 'Where does it end?'

The general paused in his response as he noticed his presence for the first time.

'What is this child doing here?' demanded High Priest Garash, a tall man in the brown robes of Belarannar. 'Damned heretic – false idol of heretics!'

'High Priest,' Lord Styrax said in a cold tone, 'there is no call for incivility.'

Garash bristled visibly. 'That child's followers preach heresy in Akell and beyond, and I will not listen to the filth it has to say.'

Styrax looked from the priest to the small figure of Ruhen. 'Then get out of my sight,' he said. 'If you think a child of eight winters capable of preaching grave heresy, then you're a fool, and I do not treat with fools.'

The high priest opened his mouth to respond, but before he could Knight-Cardinal Certinse touched him on the arm. The pair conferred quietly, Garash's eyes widening with anger, but Certinse's expression was hard.

'Go,' he said softly, 'the piety of a small boy is not the concern here.' He looked past the priest to where his adjutant stood. 'Captain Perforren, please escort the high priest back to Akell.'

Garash scowled, realising he would have to physically resist if he wanted to remain at the discussion. He gave Ruhen one last hate-filled look before he rose and turned his back on them.

'Thank you, Knight-Cardinal,' Styrax acknowledged. 'Duchess Escral, perhaps your man would take the child away, and leave negotiations to the adults.'

Before the duchess could reply Ruhen turned towards her and fixed his shadow-filled gaze upon her. She froze, lost at once in the hypnotic swirl.

'Do you not want peace?' he asked, looking around at them all. 'Do you not think the bloodshed should end?'

'This is ridiculous,' Certinse muttered. 'What does a child know of diplomacy? Duchess, would you—' He stopped dead as Ruhen stared straight at him, the words dying in his throat.

Ilumene had to suppress a smile. So Certinse intended to use

Ruhen for his own ends? Ruhen could have that effect on many when he wished ...

It was a strange sight; the small boy standing like a presiding magistrate between the opposing parties. Ruhen was dressed in a simple fawn tunic and calfskin trousers. There was a small pearl at his throat, but apart from that the boy could have been a shop-keeper's son.

'Very well, what do you suggest, little prince?' Certinse asked.

Ruhen gave Certinse a small smile before turning to the envoys from Raland and Embere. 'Do you want to make war?'

The generals exchanged a look. 'Ah, of course not, if it can be helped,' one said hesitantly.

'Then do not fight.' Ruhen's high childish voice had them all transfixed now. His words were spoken without guile or inflexion, so plain that they sounded completely out of place around these men of politics – and that gave him his power.

'It is not quite so simple,' began the general, tailing off when he realised he was about to justify himself to a little boy.

'He does not want to fight,' Ruhen insisted, pointing at Lord Styrax. 'Murderers came to Byora to kill my mother, and he must fight them. But he only wants peace with you.'

All eyes went to Styrax. 'My offer remains, now that tempers are less heated. Sovereignty over your own lands, if you acknowledge my empire and rule. No occupying forces and only modest tribute, in return for protection against any and all enemies who may threaten your borders.'

'What of those of our Order in Akell?'

'They must remain,' Styrax said apologetically, 'for no less than a year. Their safety relies on your adherence to this non-aggression treaty.'

'We cannot treat with a heretic,' growled another priest, a bearded man who'd barely spoken throughout the negotiations.

'Why not?' asked Ruhen.

The priest looked startled at the question. 'He has turned away from the Gods, and such behaviour cannot be condoned!'

'How do you know that?'

'Our reports were quite specific.'

Ruhen blinked, and summoned an expression of innocent puzzlement. 'You want to fight because of a rumour?'

'One I deny,' Styrax broke in, 'if that's any help?' His face was inscrutable. The white-eye was careful not to let his lively enjoyment of the situation show in any way that might give offence.

'Can you not forgive?' Ruhen said. 'Does your God not allow forgiveness?'

The priest purpled. He wore the black robes of Death. 'Forgiveness is my God's prerogative, not mine.'

'What about judgment?'

There was a pause. 'Judgment is His alone,' the priest muttered, aware that the dogma of his cult was too plain on the subject to argue, 'but that does not mean we should comply with the threats of tyrants.'

'Is it a threat to ask for peace?'

Knight-Cardinal Certinse laughed. 'No, little prince, I don't believe so.'

'Then do not judge, unless you want men to kill each other.'

The little boy turned and headed back towards Ilumene, leaving a stunned silence in his wake. When he reached Ilumene and raised his hands, asking to be carried, the big soldier lifted him with the greatest of care and started back towards the ruined Fearen House, the library where Ruhen had been playing earlier.

Before he was out of earshot he heard someone break the silence.

'So, Lord Styrax; now that we are suitably chastised, what assurances can you offer us?' Certinse asked.

Ruhen smiled.

Venn stopped and looked up at the thin shafts of light pushing through the leaves. All around him the Harlequins stopped, their attention solely on the black-clad figure leading them. He ignored them. Breathless anticipation ran through his people whenever he paused or began to speak. Flies danced and swirled and winked in and out of sight as they passed through the dappled light.

'Oracle?' came a low voice on his left: Paen, the priestess with eyes of deepest amber, his first follower. 'Do you sense something?' Like many of the priests among them she had bleached her robe to a dull white – black remained a colour they would not wear, though now it was out of deference to Venn rather than Lord Death.

Venn turned to her. 'Only that evening is near,' he replied at last. 'We should camp for the night.'

'I will have Kobel post sentries.'

Venn looked over at the ageing Harlequin, who stood waiting for his command. The old man had been one of the last to come around. His resolve was stronger than most, but in the end Jackdaw's magic had found some spark of ambition within him and now he was Venn's general, commander of his followers, the eighty Harlequin warriors and trained youths.

'Do so,' Venn ordered, 'then see if we have any of that ice-wine left. We've covered a good distance today.'

Aside from the blades there were only two dozen others in the party, the priests and clan members who had begged to accompany their oracle on his search to find the child. They were making good time through the Great Forest east of Farlan territory, particularly since they had not yet had to take any diversions to avoid Elven encampments. They had few luxuries with them, but ice-wine was drunk in thimble-sized cups, so it was no great burden to carry.

'Oracle,' called a returning scout, and Venn went forward to meet the young man, resisting the urge to break into a run for the sheer pleasure of having his strength restored to him.

The youth was no more than sixteen summers of age, too young to have passed the tests yet, but he carried the blades like the others and even now he would be the match of any Elf or soldier he might encounter.

'You have found a camp?' Venn asked.

The young man skidded to a stop 'A camp, of sorts,' he said, and took a deep breath.

'Only sorts?'

'I—Capan thought you would want to see for yourself, Oracle.'

Venn ignored the youth's discomfort in suggesting what he should do and gestured for him to lead the way. The camp proved only to be a few hundred yards away, but even before he reached it Venn knew what was waiting for him.

'A perfume on the wind,' Rojak sighed at the back of Venn's mind, 'the scent of change.'

Venn knew what scents delighted the dead minstrel, he'd smelled enough of them in Scree. What he could detect on the wind here certainly fitted, and the sour smell of decay grew stronger as he approached. By the time he reached Capan he was guessing at dozens of bodies, rotting fast in the warmth of a spring day.

He looked up, taking a moment to pick out the high platforms that were usually built in the huge trees of the forest as both refuge and sentinel-post, then turned to the scouts.

The stoic Capan was the only one of the four not to have covered his mouth; he seemed barely to have noticed the stink. He moved only when Venn was close enough to bow to. The Harlequins used their bodies expressively, since they spent most of their time wearing white masks, but Capan gave nothing away through gesture, or through intonation.

'Oracle, it is like nothing I have seen before.' He turned and led Venn to the entrance to the camp, where a half-fallen tree was resting on a hump in the ground. Venn almost gagged on the smell as soon as he ducked his head under the thick tree-trunk, but he recovered himself to follow Capan in. A natural hollow in the ground had been dug out to extend it, though it was still small and cramped. It centred on a crudely built circle of stones that resembled a cairn. There was a hump-backed chimney arrangement that diverted the smoke away and over the earthen walls to disperse less obtrusively, which made Venn guess it was a communal fire.

The ground was littered with bodies, not long dead and as yet unmolested by scavengers, but that did not surprise him. The Elves hadn't been attacked and slaughtered, though some had weapons in their hands, and there were no signs of violence – other than the brutal effects of disease, including protruding black nodules on their necks, wide white blisters on any exposed flesh and strange orange-tinted scabs on the flesh of their fingernails.

Venn had no idea what diseases caused such outbreaks, but whatever they were, they had obviously come on too fast for the Elves to bury – or even move – the first afflicted. There were fifty or more bodies on the floor of the camp, adults and children alike, and whatever had killed them, it had been swift and terrible.

'*This cannot be natural,*' moaned Jackdaw. Venn could feel the man's revulsion, increased by the fact he had no body of his own with which to retch and shudder.

'I *doubt it is,*' Rojak said, his voice betraying his fascination. '*I smell magic on the air.*'

Venn looked around. Bodies, roughly made tables, discarded and rotten food – nothing he wouldn't expect to see here. All the Elves were dressed the same. If any of them had been mages, they lacked the human inclination to marry power with grandeur, which he found unlikely.

'*Jackdaw,*' Venn said in the privacy of his mind, '*what can you sense?*'

There was a long pause before the Crystal Skull he'd retrieved from the cavern's entrance-shrine one night gave out a pulse of warmth.

'*There is something here,*' Jackdaw said with a horrified whisper, '*like nothing I have ever seen – and it is not alone, it's like there are fireflies dancing all around the camp, all watching us.*'

'Capan, leave me.'

The scout had advanced further into the camp than Venn, picking his way through the piled bodies with balletic grace, but at Venn's words he at last showed some emotion, tilting his head in surprise to look at Venn, but when he said no more Capan ducked his head in acknowledgement and left, careful not to touch any of the bodies as he went.

Venn looked around at the scene of horror, frozen in time and undisturbed by wind, predator, scavenger or insect. As he wondered who or what had the power to do this, and who would bother with just a tiny camp, Rojak's mocking little laugh echoed through his head.

The minstrel had been quiet since first revealing himself, speaking to Venn only a handful of times, and refusing to answer the hows or whys of what had happened since his body had been consumed by a firestorm in Scree. Venn could guess, however: Rojak's soul had been bound so tightly to Azaer that it had not been his own for many years before his death. No doubt the day the minstrel had lost his shadow he'd suspected that instead of receiving his Last Judgment, he would continue as some subordinate shadow-Aspect of Azaer.

But Azaer had taken mortal form, and when Jackdaw started playing with magic to hide himself in Venn's own shadow, there had been a transference, whether intentional or not.

'*Well my pretty, won't you come out to play?*'

Venn blinked, and felt Jackdaw recoil in his mind. Nothing changed at first, then he noticed a pale wisp of light hanging in the air. He looked up and saw more, a spray of dozens in the late-afternoon air, some almost hidden by the pale sky behind, others clearly visible against the trees.

'Created in the image of your Gods,' came a whisper from nowhere, a woman's voice, soft and ancient, 'and like your Gods, you enslave those around you.'

From the mud-bank opposite him suddenly appeared a woman as terrible to behold as the ruined bodies all around him. Cold eyes shone out from a pale, emaciated face half-obscured by a curtain of tangled greying hair.

She wore a small crown of grey metal, as ragged and dull as her clothes. After the first moment of shock, Venn realised who she was, and a cold sweat broke out down his back. The Wither Queen was not known for her welcoming nature.

Venn pointed up. 'They are your slaves?'

'Bound as I am bound by another,' she hissed, her dead blue tongue flicking like a snake's, tasting the air, 'but not for much longer. My power grows, and a dead man's bargain is soon broken.'

'Bargain? Is that why you killed them?' Venn asked, indicating the dead Elves all around.

The Wither Queen reached up with long broken fingernails and caressed the nearest of the wisps of light. 'Such is the nature of my bondage, to scour the forest of Elves and leave the humans unharmed.' She stopped and peered at him with rapacious intent. 'But what human has three souls?'

'*One who would honour your work, my queen,*' Rojak replied before Venn could speak.

The Reaper Aspect cocked her head in curiosity – not in a human way; it reminded Venn more of a cat's unfeeling interest. There was no doubt she had heard the words, and she was surprised at the way Rojak had addressed her. Her eye narrowed. 'To do that you must free me of my bargains.'

'And if we did?'

Her expression went even colder. 'Do not think I would substitute one set of chains for another.'

'*Never shall you be chained,*' Rojak crooned, '*never caged like a God's pet.*'

She took a breath and her tongue tasted the air once more, flicking out towards Venn, as though lapping the sweat from his cheek.

'Tear down the temple to me in Lomin, defile the ground and break my chains – then you may ask one thing of me, so long as it does not leave me bound to another.'

'*A Goddess asks for her own temple to be defiled?*' laughed Rojak, his delight unrestrained at the perversity of the request. '*Such a thing would be a joy in itself.*'

Venn bowed to her. 'It will be done.'

CHAPTER 20

Major Jachen squinted up at the sun and wiped his forehead with his sleeve. It was mid-morning and they'd been travelling since dawn, making a final push to reach Llehden before the end of the day. The sun had been in their eyes all the way and Jachen's head was hurting because of it – that, and the questions running nonstop through his head.

Lord Isak's final orders for his Personal Guard had been to travel to Narkang and enter the service of King Emin. That in itself had been enough to provoke near-rebellion in the ranks. Count Vesna had limited the impact by returning the married men to their previous positions before giving the order, but still it rankled. Some of the men still refused to believe Jachen was as much in the dark as they, especially once they had found their new master at his castle outside Kamfer's Ford.

'You will go to Llehden,' the king had said, his face inscrutable. 'You will find the Witch of Llehden. She has a use for you.'

Jachen shook his head. He had been a mercenary for years, and had served many masters, but this was the first time he'd been passed around like a piece of currency.

'Can you not tell me any more, your Majesty?' he'd pleaded. 'What do I say to my men? They're the best of the Farlan Army, and they're ready to die for their lord without hesitation – but to be handed off like mercenaries or slaves . . . they're men of honour, your Majesty—'

'They are men of war,' King Emin had replied, with enough snap in his voice that the black-clad bodyguard at his side put a hand on his sword hilt.

Jachen had been given an audience by himself, while the rest of Lord Isak's Personal Guard were left in the courtyard below and told in no uncertain terms to stay put until Jachen returned.

The king's reaction had left Jachen even more confused; the Farlan and the people of Narkang were allies, were they not? Yet everyone at Camatayl Castle had treated them with suspicion and hostility, as if they were enemies in their midst rather than proven friends and comrades.

'What is more,' King Emin had continued after a tense moment, 'you will go to Llehden with only two of your men – am I right in thinking not all are Palace Guard?'

Jachen had been slow to work out what the king was talking about, and his silence prompted the bodyguard to take a warning step forwards. 'The Ascetites? Yes, your Majesty, three aren't Ghosts but agents of the Chief Steward.'

'They will stay here then, I have need of such men. Their names?'

'Ah, Tiniq, Leshi and Shinir – they are as thick as thieves and about as honest, but Tiniq at least can be trusted to follow order. He's General Lahk's twin brother.'

'Ah yes, now I remember. I have some knife work to be done. You may tell those three – and any of the rest with the necessary skills – to report to Dashain.'

'Your Majesty—' Jachen had begun, only to have his protests cut off once more.

'Major! Is there any part of that instruction you do not understand?'

Jachen hung his head, well-aware of his place and how far any objections could be taken. 'No, your Majesty.'

'Then carry out your orders, and without further question, if you please. Narkang shares your grief for Lord Isak, but it does not excuse forgetting your place – indeed, it shows just how serious events have become.' King Emin's face had hardened as he leaned forward over his desk. 'You may not fully understand your orders; you may not have all of the information you think you need, but that should be nothing new. This is a war, and you must do your part. The more you do not understand the reasons for your mission, the more you should realise the deadly importance of the task. Do you understand me?'

Jachen, chastised, saluted, not trusting himself to speak. He had talked his way into trouble his entire career, but he knew enough about the Narkang king to realise talking back now wouldn't just result in demotion.

'You all right, sir?' came a voice from behind him.

Jachen flinched, and Private Marad chuckled in a half-hearted way. The other member of their party, a grizzled sergeant called Ralen, just squinted at him, but as he looked back, the major couldn't tell whether Ralen's expression was one of concern or just discomfort at the sun.

'I'm fine, Sergeant, just wondering what's waiting for us.'

'Bunch o' jabbering monsters, sir,' Ralen drawled, 'if it's anything like the last time we was 'ere.'

'Nah,' Marad said, 'gentry only comes out a night.' He pointed past Jachen to a long line of huge pine trees that dominated the view. 'See them big stones at the base o' them trees? They're called twilight stones; gentry stand on 'em and watch the sun set. That's the first you'll see of 'em all day, so we were told.'

Jachen followed the line of Marad's finger. He thought he could make out shapes in the shadows under the trees, but with the sun so high it was hard to make out much more. 'We'll soon find out enough,' he said, urging his horse into a trot again. 'Let's hope we get more answers here than we did from the king.'

'From a witch?' Marad scoffed. 'Not bloody likely – 'bout as much chance as 'er lettin' the sarge shag 'er.'

Ralen gave a wistful sigh and started on after Jachen. 'Man's gotta have goals in life,' he said, prompting another laugh from Marad. 'Considerin' the closest thing she's got to a friend has blue fur and fangs, I ain't givin' up yet.'

The three soldiers found themselves riding through the belt of ancient pine that denoted the Llehden border in silence. There was an occasional marker stone, but it was clear few travelled this way. The woods were strangely hushed for a spring afternoon, the birdsong sounding distant, coming in clipped bursts, as though even the birds were wary to break the silence.

The pines extended a mile past the twilight stones, dwindling in number as the land rose, then dipped away. Only when the last of the huge trees were behind them did they start to see signs of civilisation, and when they reached the first hamlet it was the soldiers who were more surprised. At a fork in the path they came across eight cottages huddled along the bank of a stream, penned in by a wicker fence and cultivated hawthorn thickets. To the right the oak and birch trees thinned out and they could make out the long grass of pastureland.

Jachen assumed the thorny fencing was to keep the animals from wandering at night, but as they drew closer he began to pick out rabbit-bone charms and polished metal discs hanging amongst the branches. It was unusual to see so many charms on display like that – they didn't look religious, and it was the sort of thing priests objected to.

For a small settlement frightened enough to put so much effort into protective charms, they betrayed very little fear – or even interest – at the sight of strange horsemen. The few locals in sight – five women of varying ages and three scrawny children – watched them approach without abandoning their daily activities. A few long-legged dogs ran out and began to bark, but a word of command from one of the women was enough to bring them back to the open gate.

'We're looking for the witch,' Jachen called, but he received only blank looks for his troubles. 'No? Don't speak Farlan eh?'

He reined in his horse and tried to recall what little of the language he'd learned. King Emin's peace had limited the amount of work a mercenary could find within Narkang lands, but Jachen hadn't always been exacting about the jobs he took and a man who could read and write rarely starved. He said, 'The woman not like you?' – the best he could manage in the Narkang tongue – but it did at least get a reaction.

One of the younger women pointed southwest, saying something he couldn't understand and shaking her head as she spoke.

Before he could thank her, a man called out from the woods behind them, 'She's warning you, says you don't want to go past the village.'

Jachen turned, his hand instinctively going to his sword, but he froze, his mouth dropping open in surprise. It took him a moment to get the name, then he had it: Morghien, the man of many spirits. His weatherbeaten face was dirtier than the last time they'd met, in Tirah Palace, but he was certainly looking at the ageing wanderer who, with Mihn, had brought Lady Xeliath to the Farlan capital.

'You'll catch flies if you keep that up, Major,' Morghien added, bowing mockingly before starting towards them. 'I see you're still whole, Ralen; there really is no justice in this life.'

Ralen chuckled and gave the man a careless salute. 'Morghien, you ole cheat, still sneakin' up on folk then? I thought Marshal Carelfolden 'ad warned you about that.'

Morghien smiled, but his response was drowned out by an explosion of noise as the dogs caught sight of him and raced out again, barking with a far greater ferocity than they had at the riders. Morghien stopped dead while the woman Jachen had spoken to yelled at the animals. The three long-haired guard-dogs ignored the horses and stopped only when they were just past the Farlan, as though ready to protect them from the eccentric wanderer.

Jachen had met Morghien often enough for him to be wary at the wanderer's unexpected appearance. What he hadn't expected was Morghien's reaction to the dogs – only the woman's repeated shouts were holding them in check at all, and none were showing any sign of backing down, but Morghien had sunk to his knees, as if to make himself an easier target.

Without taking his eyes off the dogs Morghien untied a dead rabbit from his pack and tossed it to the dogs, closing his eyes and mouthing something, looking to Jachen for all the world as if he was praying.

To Jachen's complete astonishment, the dogs shut up. The largest of the three picked up the rabbit and fixed Morghien with a baleful look before carrying his prize back inside the hamlet fence.

'What in the name o' Larat's twisty cock did yer do there?' Ralen asked, clearly mirroring Jachen's own surprise.

'Just said hello,' Morghien replied, getting to his feet with the groan of a man far older than he looked. Morghien, a man who counted King Emin among his friends, had looked exactly the same when he met the king almost twenty years previously, and twenty years before that too.

'The hamlet's got a guardian spirit, one they've linked to the dogs somehow – that'd be your witch, I'd expect.'

'And it took exception to you?'

Morghien laughed. 'Took fright, just as likely, but it acts like a dog and they don't need much excuse to bark.'

'Were you waiting for us here?' Jachen interrupted. 'Did the king tell you to meet us?'

'Pah, he's got a war to think about now, and he don't know any more than you do anyway.'

'What do you mean?'

Morghien cocked his head at Jachen. 'Curious, he didn't tell you any more than he had to. You ain't here at his order; you're here at the witch's.'

'Lord Isak's last orders said we were to follow King Emin's orders, not those of some village witch,' said Jachen, looking puzzled.

Morghien nodded. 'Maybe so, but the witch sent Emin a message a few weeks back. She asked for you by name.'

'Me?' Jachen said in surprise. 'I barely met the woman.'

'But you have kind eyes, and women like that,' Morghien laughed with a wink at Ralen. 'Might be something else, of course, but we won't know until we find her.'

He called his thanks to the woman by the cottages and disappeared into the trees, coming back almost immediately. 'Come on, Major, let's see if love awaits you,' he said as he started off down the path she had indicated.

Morghien was silent as they continued on their journey, passing though a second charm-enclosed hamlet before the trees opened out and they found a village straddling what was now a small river. Compared to the rest of Llehden it looked bustling, and was apparently large enough to have no more of a protective fence than a boundary ring of charm-inscribed stones. They could see smoke from more than a dozen homes rising into the air, and hear the clash of a blacksmith at work, and there were figures visible working on half a dozen smallholdings in between the cottages.

'No lord of the manor here,' Morghien commented as they crossed the boundary stones, 'and they eat all they grow; you Farlan wouldn't approve.'

'Ain't they lucky,' Marad drawled, 'the king's law rules all round their border, so's they gets the best o' both.'

'Don't fool yourself; it's not so simple – or safe – in these parts. Start thinking that way, you might not last the night.'

'Bloody peasants an' their bloody superstitions,' Marad replied, spitting on the ground, 'if it can hurt you, you can hurt it. I'll put my glaive against anythin' Llehden's got.'

'I'd be interested to see that,' Morghien said with grin, 'from a safe distance.' He broke off to speak to a man with greying whiskers and a hoe resting across his broad shoulders, who had come over from the nearest smallholding. They talked briefly, and Jachen noticed a look of relief crossing the man's face when Morghien shook his head in answer to a question. After a while he pointed to a house on the far side of the village.

'The witch is here in the village today; one of the women is in labour,' Morghien reported back to them, and led them across the small bridge and into the centre of the village, scattering the hissing black-winged geese grazing on a patch of common ground.

As they headed to the house, Jachen asked, 'What about the first bit?'

'First?'

'What the man said.' Jachen said, jabbing a thumb behind them.

'Ah, nothing. He asked if we were hunting the Ragged Man.'

'Who?'

Morghien shrugged. 'Some local spirit, by the sound of it; he said it'd eat our souls if we went after it.'

'Let's not, then,' Jachen said with a shiver. War he could handle, but the supernatural terrified him. The sight of the Reapers slaughtering Scree's population still haunted his dreams . . . he had none of Marad's optimism.

At the house Morghien spoke to a stern-looking woman with greying hair and returned to the Farlan soldiers looking grave. 'She sounds worried; it's her sister givin' birth. If you're brave enough, go fetch the witch out – me, I'll wait.'

Ralen and Marad shook their heads violently and followed Morghien over to what proved to be a tavern. Finding himself alone and the sole object of the woman's scrutiny, Jachen beat a hasty retreat. The three soldiers busied themselves attending to their horses before they stretched out beside Morghien on the grass with pots of the potent local brew.

It was two hours before the witch appeared, arms bloody and a small bundle carried reverentially in her hands. She handed the dead infant to the sister, who bowed her head as she accepted her tiny charge. That done she crossed the green, not paying the new arrivals a moment's notice, but before Jachen could call out to her to attract her attention, Morghien stopped him.

'She'll not speak to you, not yet,' he said, gesturing for Jachen to rise and follow him.

The two men trailed the witch at a respectful distance and watched her wash her arms and apron in the river. Only when she rose from her knees and began to wring the sodden cloth out did Morghien allow Jachen to approach.

'You come on a bad day,' Ehla, the witch of Llehden, said in stilted Farlan.

'At your order,' Jachen pointed out brusquely.

She turned to face them and he found himself taking a step back at the look she gave him.

'Not my order. Isak's.'

Jachen stiffened. 'Lord Isak is dead.'

'He died,' Ehla agreed. 'Your loyalty died too?'

'Of course not!' Jachen growled. 'What in the name of the Dark Place are you suggesting?'

'That your service is not finished.' She didn't explain further but shook out her apron, draped it over her arm and headed back to the house. Jachen looked to Morghien for answers, but saw only amusement in his face.

'Don't give me that kicked puppy look,' Morghien said dismissively as they turned to follow the witch. 'I'm as much in the dark as you – just I'm more used to it.'

'And not even the king knows why we're here?'

'There's much Emin keeps from me, that's what kings do.'

Jachen bit back his reply, knowing he'd get nothing useful from the strange man. He followed in silence, determined not to speak any more than necessary until someone gave him a few answers.

The witch didn't stay long at the house; she checked first on her patient, then gave the sister a few stern instructions, rejoining the men a quarter of an hour later. She led them south at a brisk pace, ignoring the looks of alarm on the faces of those townsfolk they passed.

The path was little more than a rabbit run. After an hour the trees had become denser and the Farlan were forced to dismount and lead their horses. From time to time Morghien spoke to the witch in the local dialect, but her responses were curt. Morghien didn't appear to be put off, but the witch began to ignore him and the wanderer was forced to get Sergeant Ralen to bring him up to date instead.

With every mention of fanaticism within the cults, Morghien's voice betrayed a growing anger, one that Jachen had never heard before. Similarly, the news that Count Vesna had become the Mortal-Aspect of Karkarn was met with a snort of disgust, but it was news that a huge dragon had been awakened under the Library of Seasons that finally made Morghien fall silent.

As the afternoon progressed, a breeze picked up and Jachen realised he could smell smoke on the wind. He saw Ralen had noticed it too, and was similarly confused. The witch wouldn't have left the fire burning at her home, so clearly she was leading them to someone – but who would she want them to meet in this backwater part of Narkang? But he was determined not to say another word until he got some answers.

At last the trees petered out and Jachen saw a lake stretching out in front of him, beside which was a cottage. To his complete astonishment there was a man sitting on a small jetty, fishing, with a grey-furred dog at his side. At the sound of visitors the dog turned and began to bark; the man twisted and hooked an arm around the dog's chest. They walked cautiously, waiting for the man to quieten the frantic dog before risking getting too near, but at last the man released the struggling bundle of fur and jumped up to greet them, a welcoming smile on his face and a firm grip on the scruff of the dog's neck.

'Mihn?' Jachen exclaimed.

The failed Harlequin gave a small bow before gripping the major firmly by the wrist. He wore a shapeless woollen shirt with the sleeves half-rolled up, exposing the curling trails of the leaf tattoos on each arm that ended at his wrist. For the hundredth time Jachen wondered what the tattoos and the runes on each leaf did. The dog danced around them, watching all three warily as it crept forward to sniff at their boots.

'Good to see you again, Major,' Mihn said, greeting Ralen and Marad before Morghien embraced him. 'May I introduce you to Hulf? Toss him a strip of smoked meat and he will be your friend for life.'

'When did you leave Tirah?'

'Not long after the army, I had instructions to carry out.'

Jachen faltered. 'Ah, have you . . .'

'Heard the news?' Mihn replied gravely. 'I knew when you did.'

'Fucking spawn of Ghenna!' Marad yelled, dropping the reins of his horse and yanking his glaive from its sheath, and Jachen whirled around in time to see a shape retreat into the shadows of the cottage.

'What was it?' Jachen snapped, drawing his own sword as Ralen fell in beside Marad.

'Some bastard daemon,' Marad growled, his face white with shock, and advanced on the cottage, his glaive raised and ready to strike.

'Lower your weapons!' Mihn yelled, racing in front of Marad. 'It is not what you think!'

Beside Mihn the dog crouched, muscles bunching as it snarled at the angry voices. The guardsman blinked at Mihn and stopped, but he kept his glaive high.

'Not what I think? What I saw ain't possible, and it's damn sunny for that to be a ghost!'

'Mihn,' Jachen called warily, 'what's going on?'

'Lower your weapons and back off,' Mihn said firmly. He was unarmed but a steel-capped staff rested against the door just a few yards away. 'Marad, I mean it – back away now, or I will put you down.'

'The fuck're you t'give me orders?'

Jachen looked at Mihn's expression and grabbed the soldier by his collar. Without a word he dragged Marad back and Ralen followed.

Only then did Mihn relax and push the reluctant dog away towards the cottage.

While Marad still spluttered with anger, Jachen dropped his own sword and yanked the glaives from his soldiers' hands.

'Astonishing,' Morghien murmured, as if oblivious to the confrontation, staring open-mouthed at the cottage.

'His mind remains fragile,' Mihn said in a quiet voice. 'You cannot begin to comprehend the horrors he has endured. You will all compose yourselves, and you will not speak until I permit it, do you understand me?'

The three Farlan exchanged looks. Jachen agreed at once, but Marad, still stunned, remained silent until Jachen glared at him. Eventually both soldiers nodded while the witch, standing beside of the water, watched them impassively.

'Better,' Mihn said after a while. He collected his staff and gave Marad a warning look before stepping inside the cottage. The Farlan could hear soft murmuring, as if Mihn were coaxing the occupant out as he would a deer.

At first all Jachen saw was a huge stooped figure wearing a cloak made of rags, arms wrapped protectively about its body and head held low. Hulf ran straight to him, dancing around him with obvious delight before taking up a protective position between him and the soldiers.

Jachen could scarcely believe he was looking at a man. He was massive; even stooped he towered over Mihn, and he was far wider. One shoulder was dropped low, which reminded Jachen of men he'd known with broken ribs. Even when the man pushed back the hood of his cloak, the scars and the anguish on his face made Jachen the last to recognise him.

'Gods of the dawn,' Ralen breathed, sinking to his knees as though all strength had fled his body.

And in the next moment Jachen felt his heart lurch as the cold hand of terror closed about it.

The man recoiled – his timid movements so different to how he once was, but unmistakable all the same.

'My Lord,' Jachen said hoarsely, almost choking on the words as he dropped to one knee.

Isak looked at him and frowned, incomprehension cutting through his distress. 'I don't know you,' he mumbled before wincing and putting his hand to his temple. 'I can't remember you.'

'There are holes in his mind,' Mihn explained, putting a hand on Isak's arm to reassure him and draw him forward. 'We had to tear out some of his memories.'

'Why?' Jachen found himself asking, fearing the answer he might receive.

'Because there are some things no man should remember,' Morghien said, as though in a trance, 'some things no man could remember and remain a man. Merciful Gods, are you brave or utterly mad?'

He shivered and in unison Isak cringed slightly, screwing his eyes up tight before the moment passed.

Jachen didn't even hear the question. He continued to gape, lost in the astonishing sight of a man he knew without question to be dead. Mihn brought Isak a little closer and now Jachen could see the scars on his face and neck, the broken nose and ragged, curled lip, the jagged line of his jaw and a fat band of twisted scarring across his throat.

His lord had once been handsome, for all the white-eye harshness, but no longer. If the signs of torture continued all over his body, Jachen couldn't see how any man could have survived—

He felt his breath catch. No man could have survived it; *Isak* had not survived it. He had died on the field outside Byora, without these scars, or the broken look in his white eyes.

'How?' he breathed at last.

'The hard way,' Mihn said grimly, 'and not one taken lightly. The rest can wait for later. Go see to your horses.'

Jachen didn't move. He was still lost in the pattern of pain etched onto a face he once knew. Isak returned the look with difficulty.

'I see you in the hole in my mind,' he whispered, his scarred forehead crumpled with the effort. 'I'm falling, but the war goes on.'

'The war goes on?' Jachen echoed.

Isak seemed to straighten at that, and Jachen thought he caught a glimpse of his former strength showing beneath the lost look on his face.

'The war goes on,' Isak said, 'shadows and lords, the war goes on.'

'Isak, perhaps you should rest?' Mihn urged. He reached out and took Isak by the arm, but the broken white-eye ignored him.

With crooked fingers and awkward movements he pushed Mihn's hand away. 'No rest, not yet,' he said, his face contorted as though every thought caused him pain. 'Lost names and lost faces.'

'You want me to remind you of people?' Mihn asked, looking hopeful.

Isak shook his head and prodded Mihn. 'I want you to tell me what it means,' he said. 'Tell me what it means to lose your memories, to lose *who* you are.'

'Why?'

Isak prodded Mihn again, pushing him a few steps backwards, and this time Mihn glanced behind him to check how close he was to the water.

'The war must go on. Someone told me once to use what I have inside me,' Isak said.

'I don't understand, Isak.'

Isak's face became a ghastly smile. 'What I have inside are holes – and they'll be my weapons now.'

King Emin walked stiffly up the stairs, a jug of wine in one hand and a pair of goblets in the other, a slender cigar jammed in the corner of his mouth.

'Another long day,' he commented to Legana who was ascending silently behind him, her progress slow and careful. She steadied herself with a hand on the tower wall and her silver-headed cane in the other.

'It appears even a king must feel his age one of these days.'

Legana inclined her head and walked past as Emin respectfully held open the door to his breakfast room. It was a small room, and as sparsely furnished as the rest of Camatayl Castle, but it served the king's needs. This was not a place for luxuries: almost every room now contained food stores or cramped bunks for soldiers.

There was a fire alight and chairs set for them on either side of it. Emin poured drinks once Legana was settled. Over the past few weeks the pair, both strong-willed and impatient with others, had found an accommodation that suited them both. Their common understanding of their extraordinary positions had turned into a cautious friendship.

'Have the priestesses accepted your authority?' Emin asked, tossing his hat aside and easing down in his chair. He idly brushed dirt from his boot while Legana wrote on her slate.

—*They ask many questions.*

'Questions you cannot yet answer?' Emin nodded sadly. 'As do my generals. They believe absolutely in the might of Narkang's armies; defeat in battle has been a rare thing in my life, so they cannot understand my tactics now.'

—*The priestesses ask what the rest do not dare.*

'What the substance of your promises might be? It's the nature of people. Offer them a brighter future and they will cheer and shout your name, but sooner or later they want to know the details. How did you think I ended up in this mess?' Emin said wryly.

—*I promised only that a better future was possible.*

'But you don't have a form in mind? I hadn't taken you for a woman of faith.'

—*Of instinct,* she corrected, *even before I was joined to the Lady.*

I sense a future will come. I hope it will come before a God tries to subsume me.

Emin looked startled. 'Is that even a possibility, Gods fighting each other for supremacy? I know it used to happen in the Age of Myths, but now? Piss and daemons; could a God like Larat decide there is enough of the divine within you to take you as an Aspect?'

—*I don't wish to find out.*

Emin gave a snort. 'I can imagine. So we both may be running out of time.'

—*You don't believe in your armies too?*

'Hah! I know my strength well enough, and I also know my enemy. I've studied his campaign thus far; Lord Styrax is inventive and bold, but he's lacking the arrogance one might hope for. His armies are battle-hardened and replenished by the states he's conquered; mine are untested in ten years. He has made no significant mistakes, and only committed himself to vulnerability when he is certain of victory. This is not what one hopes for in an enemy. '

He grimaced and took a swig of wine, staring into the distance a moment before continuing, 'No – that's not correct; he has made one mistake. His allegiance is no longer to Lord Karkarn, it appears, or any of the Gods, it's to himself. However much they fear to walk the Land and risk death, the Gods do not favour the greatest of their creations.'

—*Can you exploit it?*

'Would that I could,' he said. 'It's a mistake I've also made. Even it were possible, I don't know how ...' He tailed off, then asked, 'Is that what Larat meant?' There was a pause and the king straightened in his chair a moment, then relaxed back down. 'No, it doesn't fit.'

—*What?*

Emin looked at her, unable to discern anything from the expression on her face. Curiously, it was one of the reasons why he liked the fierce Mortal-Aspect; she was beyond his abilities, both as a man and a king. Not even the intellectuals he welcomed to the Brotherhood-protected private club in Narkang could hide their thoughts from his scrutiny. He enjoyed feeling in the presence of an equal.

'Did you not sense it, a week or so after you first arrived?'

She hesitated, then scribbled quickly on the slate. – *Once*

I dreamed of laughter, and a face that shifted, yours to a young woman's.

Emin nodded. 'Larat came to speak to me that morning, he warned me to heed the lessons of the Great War.'

—*One favours you then.*

'True, but direct action is not his way – and having lost Death's favour, none of the rest will intervene. What do you know of the Crystal Skulls?'

Legana gestured to the blackened handprint on her throat and the cane she now walked with. – *I know one did this.*

'But the nature of them? I've read a number of Verliq's works – the great man mentions the Skulls several times, but he never studied them directly. Larat mentioned something, and I wonder about the significance.'

He fell silent again, and Legana waited patiently. Allies they had become, but neither expected undying loyalty of the other, and asking too much would invite questions in return.

At last he went on, 'He told me that the twelve Skulls corresponded to the Gods of the Upper Circle, and the bearer of a Skull had the right to ask a question of that God.'

Legana didn't move for a long while, her porcelain features crinkled in thought until her emerald eyes flashed and she opened her mouth to speak before remembering herself and writing on the slate.

—*Why ask?*

'Why ask?' Emin echoed, realising she was prompting him just as he had done so often with his pet intellectuals in Narkang, nudging their thoughts down new paths, harnessing their knowledge to a particular need.

'Why ask? You ask to secure an answer – expecting an answer. Larat said that some knowledge should not be shared, that there were some questions that might upset the balance of the Land.'

—*He is a God.*

'And a tricky one at that,' Emin added, feeling a spark of insight; he was getting close. 'What he told me was no doubt correct, but not the entire story. One asks a question to get an answer, to be so foolish as to do that with a God of the Upper Circle – well, you would have to be certain that an answer would be forthcoming. To have a God smite you for impertinence is the outcome one would expect for idle pestering, or seeking knowledge the Gods would not wish to share.

'So perhaps it isn't just a right, but a compulsion; something binding the God to answer truthfully – perhaps even something stopping them from simply reaching out and crushing the head of whoever has presumed to question them.'

He took a long draw on his cigar and cocked his head at Legana. 'Covenant theory: the idea that a contract of sorts must exist in magical actions – no spell so powerful it does not have a flaw; no great incantation that cannot be undone by something innocuous – and no dealing with Gods or daemons that does not have rules to frame it.'

Legana nodded encouragingly, and Emin, looking calmer, continued his exploration. 'This right to ask a question of a God, it confers a right to get an answer too. Perhaps that means there is a contract of sorts, and they're creatures of magic so they must be bound by the rules – and if they're bound in whatever way, that implies there's some power of compulsion over the God.'

Emin took a slow breath, ordering his thoughts as he extended the principle further. 'If Larat is willing to admit that much, no doubt the truth is something deeper, something more fundamental to their relationship with the Skulls – perhaps even the existence of the Gods themselves. The Skulls are stores of power; the Gods are power incarnate. Could they be the flip-side of the same coin?'

—*How does this help?*

Emin topped up her goblet with a smile. 'Lord Styrax is not collecting them to secure his rule or aid his conquest, those are just by-products. He wants that power over each of the Gods of the Upper Circle, not to ask questions but make demands.' He shook his head. 'As great and long-lived as he is, the man is only mortal. One day he will die, unless . . .'

King Emin puffed on his cigar and looked at the icons hanging on the wall. The empty cowl of Death occupied the centre; on His left was Kitar, Goddess of Fertility, on His right, Karkarn, God of War.

He said slowly, 'He will die unless he becomes a God. Unless this peerless warrior asks something of the Gods they cannot refuse.'

CHAPTER 21

Captain Hain looked around at the army and felt a strange surge of exhilaration. 'Damn but it's a sight,' he said, nudging Sergeant Deebek with his elbow. 'Shame the major's missing it.'

Behind his helm Deebek grinned as best he could, his mangled top lip lifting on one side to reveal the ruined gums underneath.

'Reckon 'e'd agree, sir. I 'eard 'e were sent to play spies in Byora 'til 'e's fit for duty. Can't see 'im takin' that over an honest fight.'

The entire Cheme Third Legion was lined up in tight ranks, as though on the parade ground. Ahead was the Second, and the other side of a copse, the lighter-armed troops of the First. Lord Styrax's favoured shock troops, his minotaur clans, were a few hundred yards north, alongside a division of light cavalry. On their other flank was a legion of Chetse, what was left of the Crocodile Guard bolstered by fresh recruits from the now-quiescent Chetse cities.

Hain had lingered on the sight more than once; he'd never believed he would see the day a legion of the Ten Thousand marched under Menin banners. Once each of the commanding tachrenn had kneeled to Lord Styrax, the enlisted had started to see him as something other than a conqueror: they saw a peerless warrior, a Chosen of the Gods who truly deserved the title.

'Don't hope for much of a fight today, Sergeant,' Hain warned. 'I doubt they'll dare.'

They had skirted the Byoran marshes and gone up through the Evemist Hills and just crossed the Narkang border. Now they stood less than a mile from the fortress town of Merritays, Narkang's first line of defence against aggression from the Circle City that had never materialised until now. Four square stone towers were connected by defensive earthworks and enclosed a small garrison town, accessible only by drawbridges attached to each tower. Some two miles behind Merritays stood a market town that had grown up in its protective lee.

Hain watched the First Legion advance to within bowshot of the defensive lines. The earthworks were built in two enormous steps and looked down over a water-filled ditch. There was a neat stone wall on each level. There weren't many soldiers on view at the moment; Hain knew they wouldn't commit their strength until the Menin attacked.

'What's the plan then, Captain?' Deebek asked conversationally.

'You think General Gaur tells the likes of me?'

'But you might 'ave seen summat, I reckon we ain't 'angin' around for a siege.'

'You're right there,' Hain admitted, 'but I still don't know what's planned. Shut up and we'll both find out.'

'Right you are, sir,' Deebek said. He reached out and gave the axe resting on Hain's shoulder a tap with his fingers, then balled his fist and thumped it against his chest.

'Fer luck, sir,' he explained without embarrassment. The medal he pulled out next was one he'd won ten years previously and he kissed it, as he had before every fight since.

Hain didn't comment. The axe was the one Amber had used to kill the Chosen of Tsatach; if the men now considered it a talisman, all the better. Ten minutes later, they heard the drums beat out the command over the whisking wind: *Advance to enemy.* Whatever General Guar planned, they were certainly going to get some sort of a fight today.

The Second Legion headed for the nearest of the towers. There was a scramble of movement on the earthworks in response as archers moved out to face the Menin troops. The Third Legion went up to the Second's right flank, five regiments in the lead with the rearguard division mirroring them at a short distance.

Hain's regiment was in the vanguard, nearest to the Second Legion. They were all expecting the next order and as soon as it was given they began to move forward, heavy shields raised against the expected volley of arrows. As the first began to fall a prayer to Karkarn whispered through the ranks, causing Hain to grimace. The pace was swift and steady, with Hain chancing quick looks through the spear-rest of his shield to check when he would have to give the order.

An arrow smashed into his shield and exploded into splinters, causing him to miss his step for a moment, but the soldier behind him half-caught him on the shaft of his spear and shoved him forward, back into place.

'Bastard,' Deebek growled beside him. Hain looked over and saw blood on the exposed side of the sergeant's scarred nose. A splinter of the arrow's shaft protruded from the small cut.

'There go yer looks,' Hain laughed with the men around him.

'Aye, sir.' Deebek glanced back at the man who'd steadied the captain. 'Soldier, you trample 'im next time, 'ear me?'

Still smiling, Hain chanced another look. Arrows were still dropping, but far fewer than he'd expected. Either the garrison was under-strength, or they were keeping the bulk of their men back. As the front rank neared the ditch Hain could see it wasn't going to be easy to negotiate. The slope was almost sheer on each side and the dozen ladders they carried weren't going to be long enough, unless the water was only a foot deep.

'Regiments to halt, defensive position,' came the shouted order, and Deebek instantly relayed it at the top of his voice. The troops slowed to a stop and the front rank kneeled behind their shields, allowing the second rank to rest their own shields on those in front.

'Come on, General,' Hain muttered as he peered left and right, 'don't let us be the decoys.' He saw movement to the right and called forward to the front rank for information.

'A company's left the line, sir,' called a trooper. 'Handful o' men – what in the name of the Dark Place are they doing? They're just standing with shields raised – and some're just sittin' down on the grass behind. Ah no, someone's lying on the ground too, reaching forward with summat.'

'Mages,' Hain and Deebek said together.

'Aye, sir, can't see what he's doin' but there's summat up down there. Some sort o' white mist fillin' the ditch.'

'Any mages on the rampart?'

'No, sir, but the archers are after 'em now.'

'In that case: ready to advance,' Hain said, raising his voice. He didn't know what was about to happen, but you didn't need an entire division to shield a few mages.

'Piss and daemons,' exclaimed one of the men in the front rank, 'that wind just got fuckin' cold.'

301

'Ice then,' Hain muttered to Deebek. 'They're freezing the ditch; Lord Styrax did just that in the Numarik campaign once.'

'It work?'

Hain shook his head and Deebek chuckled nastily.

'It didn't then, but it was Verliq himself who broke the ice. A mage has got to be fucking strong to shatter half a yard of ice; I reckon King Emin won't have any of those spare, not for a pissy border town.'

Hain lifted his shield a fraction, realising the archers were directing all their efforts at the mages. The mages were taking their time completing the spell, but Hain wasn't surprised. They would be weaker than the Chosen, and it was a long stretch of water. Fortunately for them, the ballista-stations couldn't reduce their elevation enough to hit them, and the shields were proving more than a match for the archers, given the groan of ice Hain could hear. The Menin archers were peppering the rampart to give them as much cover as possible and before long the trooper reported the mages were retreating again.

'Looks like we'll get that fight after all,' Hain muttered as the order to advance was yelled and repeated by every squad sergeant. He saw the first rank drop gingerly down on the ice. One soldier lowered his shield as he tested the ice underfoot – only for a second, but a sharp-eyed archer noticed it all the same and put an arrow through his neck.

'First blood!' came the cry from those around him, 'Heten Sapex!'

'Shift yourselves!' Hain roared as the name was repeated around the regiment in Cheme tradition.

His troops obeyed without a moment's hesitation and raced forward, several losing their balance on the ice but propelling themselves forward as best they could until they reached the other side. More men piled into the shallow impression, the first six ranks of each division, and the ladders were passed forward.

The front rank, pressed against what small cover was afforded by the earth wall, took the ladders and hoisted them, pulling them flat against the slope and locking their arms to hold them fast. The second rank began the terrible scramble up; Hain watched them with the familiar jangle of fear and excitement flooding through his body as he waited for his turn.

A loud roar came from their left and the Chetse warriors barrelled towards the remaining space in the ditch. As in all the Ten
Thousand, the bulk of the Crocodile Legion didn't carry shields,
only the first few ranks. The rest wore oversized bronze pauldrons,
vambraces and one-piece helms to deflect axe blows, and many
even eschewed mail shirts, going shirtless to display their painted
barrel-chests. Each man bore the legion emblem and Styrax's
Fanged Skull in ochre and woad, along with ritual scars and invo-
cations to Kao, Karkarn's berserker Aspect.

They had waited for the Cheme troops to draw the worst of
the artillery before making their move, but as soon as they
arrived Hain saw the focus turned towards them and a ballista
bolt smashed bloodily through the leading knot of four. The
next dozen were cut down by arrows before they even reached
the far side of the trench.

Hain gasped as he watched the first few reach the lower edge of
the rampart. The bare-chested warriors threw themselves at the
earth wall, using their enormous axes to climb up it, oblivious to
the damage being done from above.

'Mad li'l buggers!' Deebek cackled, seeing Hain's surprise, 'let's
move afore they kill 'em all!'

They started up the ladder, Hain in the lead with his shield
shipped over one shoulder. An arrow glanced off his exposed
pauldron, but he ignored the impact, intent only on getting to the
top. The first few up there were fighting for their lives, defending
the breach furiously until help could arrive.

As Hain scrambled onto the stone-topped rampart and swung
his legs over, he had to throw himself flat on his back as a spear
swung wildly forwards. He grabbed the shaft and yanked it back,
kicking at the man's knee while he got a better grip on his own
weapon. Recovering his balance Hain hopped up and hacked at the
man's head, felling him with one blow.

He looked down the trench, a walkway no more than an arm-
span in width. His troops were barely able to fight at the moment
as they stood two men abreast on each side of the breach and kept
behind their shields as the defenders battered at them frantically.
Hain made his choice, roared a curse in Menin and charged, swinging his axe down over a soldier's shoulder to catch the man pressing
him back. There was a yell and a spear flashed forward but Hain

dodged it and reversed his grip on the axe, stabbing forward with the spike that killed Lord Chalat.

They moved forward by inches, driving with shields and lowered spears into the terrified defenders while more troops swarmed up the ladders. Renewed roars of bloodlust came from the Chetse end, telling Hain that the crazed warriors had a breach of their own and were bloodily expanding it. After five minutes of fighting Hain found himself at the corner, looking up at a narrow cleft in the earth that led up to the next tier.

'Keep moving,' he roared, pounding the backs of the soldiers in front. 'Heten Sapex!'

'Heten Sapex!' came the reply as the first two charged up the cut steps, shields held high.

One was taken down by an arrow from the darkness, but the other found an enemy in front of him and barrelled straight on, smashing into the smaller westerner and knocking him to the ground. Hain followed up quickly, hammering the butt of his axe against the man's chest. There was a crack and a scream of pain, and Hain heard nothing more as he continued on, swinging his shield back around just in time to feel the thud of three arrows slam into it.

One passed almost straight through before catching on the steel rim, another glanced off the boss at the centre of the shield. The third went through shield and chain-mail to embed itself in his bicep. He gasped in pain, but he kept moving, unable to stop, even to break off the shaft.

The first blow on his shield ripped the arrow free, and Hain howled as he thrust forward, off-balanced by the wound. The spike of his axe missed its target and he slipped sideways onto one knee, but the welcome sight of Sergeant Deebek charged into view in the next moment. The westerner dropped screaming, Deebek's spear lodged in his armpit, and Hain struggled back to his feet.

On they fought, through the shadowed cleft and back out into the pale morning sun as they reached the larger upper level. There were more soldiers there, but the Menin went through them like butter, cutting a bloody path until the overwhelmed defenders threw down their weapons and the Menin were able to stream down the other side of the rampart into the town beyond.

Hain paused on the rampart, ordering a pair of soldiers to corral the prisoners. He dropped his shield and checked his arm, which was bleeding freely. Cursing, he unhitched the chain-mail and shoved his fingers underneath. The wound was shallow but wide.

'Private, wrap this tight,' he ordered, pulling a piece of cloth from around his neck. As the man was doing as ordered Hain paused for breath and looked at the prisoners they had taken.

'Piss and daemons,' he muttered, 'I know they're smaller here than back home, but this lot're the fucking dregs.'

The soldier looked up as he pulled the rag tight. 'Aye, sir, and not much fight in 'em either.'

The flow of blood stemmed, Hain set off after his regiment. There was a wide killing-ground where the steps opened out at the base of the earthworks, but not enough defenders to plug it. They had retreated to defend the towers and the gates attached to them, the thin lines of soldiers already looked outnumbered. He searched around and found his regimental banner in the thick of the fighting at the northern tower. By the time he got there, there were barely a dozen shields defending the fortified door to the tower.

Hain inspected the gate while his men killed the last of the enemy. He was trying to work out how to drop the drawbridge and admit the rest of the army, but as far as he could see it was controlled by a mechanism on the top, bound by steel clamps and far out of reach.

'That ain't openin',' Deebek opined, appearing as if by magic at the captain's side. 'Cables're cut.'

He pointed to the right of the steel clamps and Hain realised he was right; the drawbridges were never going to be dropped without significant work.

Hain turned and looked at the neat garrison town enclosed within the four ramparts. The only movement he could see was that of the Chetse warriors charging down the streets and kicking in doors to root out the remaining defenders. What he didn't see was civilians, fleeing, screaming, fighting, or any of the above. There was a strong smell of tar in the air, but a noticeable absence of panic.

'Town's been bloody emptied,' he muttered.

'No surprise; they know they're on the front line.'

'But where's the rest of the garrison? This was too easy.'

There was a splintering sound as the door to the tower began to give way.

'Get that door open,' Hain bellowed, suddenly desperate to see what was going on outside the ramparts.

The soldiers redoubled their efforts and hacked furiously at the door, and in half a minute it was sufficiently weakened that they could break it down. The men inside didn't put up much of a fight – most threw down their weapons, and any who didn't were easily dispatched.

As soon as he could Hain was up the spiral stair and onto the upper level, looking down at the earthworks and the troops beyond.

'Karkarn's horn; never trust fucking scryers when they're sure they're right,' he growled, thumping his fist against the stone wall. 'There's the rest!'

Out of the tower window he could see a mass of enemy troops, the best part of a division, he guessed, surrounding the minotaurs, while a second division advanced towards the hastily retreating Menin cavalry. Their speed of attack had been turned against them.

Most of the rest of the army were already at the ramparts, following the order to get as many men inside as fast as possible. A few officers were starting to shout orders to reform their units, but it was a disordered mess. For the next few minutes the minotaurs would be on their own.

'Get back out there,' he yelled, 'get that fucking drawbridge open!'

'It's bust, sir,' a soldier shouted back from the walkway above the gate. 'Ain't movin' no time soon.'

Hain fought his way back down the stair, furious at his powerlessness. He battered aside the soldiers in his way and made his way to the broken door, but before he reached it he heard shouts of panic that sent a chill down his spine. He ran into the sunshine, axe at the ready, and stopped dead.

'Oh Gods,' said someone nearby.

Hain could only gape.

A burning figure stood at the head of the central street, reaching out to the nearest building. A dirty plume of smoke was filling the air above it. The timbers of the building burst into flame with terrifying eagerness, but it was the figure Hain gaped at. This wasn't the Aspect of Death, the Burning Man, nothing like: this was a wild thing of whipping flames and jagged, brutal movements; this was a Chalebrat – a fire elemental, savage and mad.

'Gods preserve us – this king's too like Lord Styrax for comfort,' he whispered before remembering himself. 'Fifth regiment, form ranks!' he shouted at the top of his voice.

Startled faces turned and stared incredulously at him.

'Did I fucking stutter?' he bellowed. 'Shift, you bastards! No man of the Third's going to run away from a bloody elemental, and I don't fancy burning!' He gave the nearest man a shove forward and it stirred the rest into action. 'We ain't getting out o' here in a rush, so it's time to fight!'

He didn't need to point to the ramparts to make his point. There were troops swarming down, others starting back up, and a massed crush at the bottom of the stairs where men had left the high-walled walkways and caught their first sight of the Chalebrat advancing towards them. Some were staring in shock, others fighting to get back up the way they came, but meeting a solid wall of men coming the other way.

The sergeants of the regiment took up the call and Hain left them to it as he ran forward to yell at the confused mass piling over the ramparts. The Chalebrat gave an unearthly screech and drowned out what he was trying to say, but that had the same effect as the message to retreat was at last shouted back at those behind.

The elemental was taller than Lord Styrax, and had elongated arms of fire. A handful of Chetse mercenaries charged it as he watched, but two were smashed aside before they even brought their axes to bear. The others struck, but did no obvious damage and their frantic blows were soon halted as the elemental engulfed them. Once they were dead the elemental stopped and looked all around it, hunting for more to kill.

The Chetse had unwittingly bought him the time he needed. Hain gestured for his men to advance, while muttering, 'Now if I could only remember about Chalebrat, – come on, Gess, think!'

For a moment the wind turned and engulfed him in a cloud of dirty black smoke. He coughed and flapped ineffectually, trying to clear the air around him.

'Sir!' Deebek called as the regiment trotted up in formation, 'you sure 'bout this?'

Hain forced himself to straighten. 'Nope, but we're doing it anyway! Fore company, go left and flank it. Rear company, we're going straight.' He took a breath to clear the last of the smoke from his lungs and raised his voice. 'Work in squads, strafe it and go clear – every time you hit an elemental it weakens, so we need to hit it enough to send it running. Keep it turning and go for it when it turns after another squad.'

Hain caught the eye of a company lieutenant and pointed to the streets on the left. The man saluted and trotted off, half the regiment following him. The rest were already formed into ten-man blocks, ready to move at his order. The first two squads pushed forward. The small town was built on a simple grid: an outer ring of barracks, within which were warehouses and official buildings, each surrounded by a square of small, single-storey homes. Hain guessed the intention was to have easily demolished houses around each to prevent fire from spreading, but that relied on the fire not moving of its own volition.

The first squads peeled away and headed down the right-hand avenue, while the remaining three squads advanced slowly. The Chalebrat had moved out of sight, but the fresh flames leaping from a rooftop pinpointed its position pretty well. Hain, leading one squad himself, paused and waited for the other company to come around and catch them up. His men were hugging one side of the street they were on, the other side was aflame and the heat growing increasingly oppressive.

As soon as he saw a group of men appear from behind a house up ahead, Hain gestured to the warehouse and told them to circle around it before leading his own men around the corner. There they saw the Chalebrat hammering its fists against the closed door of a warehouse. The wood blackened under its touch, gobbets of flame remaining like fire-arrows wherever it touched. With a yell, one of the squads he'd sent around charged forward, shields raised and spears levelled. The Chalebrat retreated a step in surprise, then screeched its defiance as the squad barrelled towards it.

'Move!' Hain shouted as he watched the attack.

The first few spears just passed through the elemental's body, but at last one caught its arm and it looked like it ripped a piece of flame away. The Chalebrat roared and grabbed at the spear, jerking the man from the end of the rank and dragging him towards it. Another man threw his own spear over-arm at the creature; it missed, but distracted the Chalebrat for long enough for the captured soldier to scramble away.

'So becoming solid enough to grab a spear must take more effort,' Hain muttered, 'and when it is we can hurt it more.'

Seeing Hain's unit advancing, the Chalebrat hopped forward to meet them. Hain led the squad at a run, his men behind him, spears levelled. As the Chalebrat slapped a burning palm down onto one shield, three soldiers managed to score hits. The spears passed through its body with ease, but now they just had to keep on doing the same thing.

A third squad came forward hard on Hain's heels, but the creature was ready for them this time.

As Hain turned his men around he heard screams; the Chalebrat had leaped right into the centre of the squad and engulfed them all in licking flames. The fourth and fifth fared better, passing and striking almost as one before peeling off on either side of it.

Now the Chalebrat saw soldiers all around it and hesitated, confused by the choice. At last it picked a direction, but as soon as it began to move the squad retreated and another closed in from another angle.

Hain bellowed above the din of cracking flames from the warehouse and two more squads advanced from between buildings, moving at a fast trot with their shields and spears held high.

As the remnants of the decimated squad screamed in agony nearby, their skin blackened, their weapons abandoned, the creature appeared confused.

It barely moved as the two new squads approached – until they were close, when the elemental jumped forward and tried to smash through the interlocked shields with its fists. As soon as it had chosen a target, the free squad lurched towards it, their spears lowered, and passed it at a trot.

Three or four spear-heads passed through the Chalebrat's body without apparent effect, but as it struck down at the squad, the company lieutenant slashed up with his scimitar and as elemental arm met sword there was an explosion of fire.

Hain heard his lieutenant cry out as he fell to the floor, but the clash drove the elemental back too.

'Come on,' Hain roared, axe held high, and the circling squads obeyed, charging forward as one. Hain was the first to reach it and once again he led them past, strafing to get its attention off the beleaguered squad that had faltered. The elemental turned to follow them before it saw the remaining units.

Slashing wildly at the air, the Chalebrat tried to back away, then realised there was nowhere to go and turned towards Hain's squad. He yelled at them to stop, and his élite troops obeyed, hunkered down behind their shields and set their spears forward.

The elemental thrashed at them with a long whip of fire, but it burst harmlessly on their shields and within seconds the remaining squads were behind it, impaling it on their spears. The Chalebrat reeled and turned, snapping spear-shafts with savage slaps.

Now's our chance, Hain realised, and he pushed his way through the shields. Ignoring the scorching heat he ran forward as the elemental battered away the never-ending wall of spears. His eyes watering, his skin tightening, he could feel the Chalebrat like a brand pressed against his exposed lips and chin. Hain hacked upwards at its arm, and was rewarded by an impact. The contact drove him back a step, but he forced himself on, eyes half-closed and swinging blindly at the yellow glare.

The elemental screamed again and again, the light intensified and Hain felt a blow to his shoulder that knocked him over, but in the next moment the fires winked out.

Hain felt himself hit the ground and kept on rolling, abandoning his axe in a desperate attempt to put out any flames. When his mind registered cheers coming from all around him he stopped and blinked up. After the glare of the Chalebrat the smoke-tinted sky looked blessedly dark and cool. He fought his way to his feet and took a breath, gasping with pain as the skin on his lips split and blood spilled down his mouth.

'Sir!' he heard an urgent voice call as hands went under his armpits and helped him up. 'Sir, you 'urt?'

Hain blinked again and at last the blurs resolved themselves into shapes. 'Gods,' he croaked, realising it was Deebek's mangled features right in front of him, 'can't be in paradise yet.'

He heard the words slur and felt blood spill from his mouth, but the twisted grin on Deebek's face told him the injury wasn't as serious as the pain in his face suggested.

'Don't worry, sir, there's a special'un fer the likes o'us.'

'The ugly?' Hain asked drunkenly, prompting a roar of laughter that showed him far more of Deebek's remaining teeth than Hain needed.

'Bloody heroes, sir!'

Hain looked around at the cheering soldiers, then down at the scorched earth underfoot. There was a shapeless, blackened patch at his feet about a yard across, but no other trace of the Chalebrat.

'Bloody heroes,' he repeated before half-spitting and half-dribbling more blood from his mouth. Someone pressed his axe into his hand and Hain held it up to roars of approval from the survivors.

'Well, boys,' he said as loud as he could, wincing at the effort of a smile to make the old sergeant proud, 'you wanted a real war and an enemy worth fighting. Looks like we got one.'

CHAPTER 22

Witchfinder Shanatin sucked his teeth and thought, his round face screwed up with the effort. He was a large man, and his thinning hair and air of harmlessness led people into thinking him a fool. Shanatin had often wondered, in the quiet of night, why he'd ended up the butt of every joke in the Knights of the Temples, and the target for every bully. There must be something about his open, honest face that caught the eye and inspired malice, while a lack of coordination in his unwieldy frame meant he tended to come off worse every time he stood up for himself. The bruises on his face were now yellow and grey, still visible in what daylight crept through the shattered roof of the ruin they were standing in.

Luerce cocked his head and watched the man think. Significantly smaller than Shanatin and never much of a fighter, Luerce nevertheless found himself wondering what it would be like to punch the fool in his fat face. To see the dismay and fear blossom; to see blood smeared across his plump, greasy cheeks . . . he tried to clear the image from his head: today he was Shanatin's friend.

'Do you want me to explain it again?'

Shanatin shook his blotchy, melon-like head. 'Just don't get why.'

Luerce raised an eyebrow and the witchfinder raised his hands submissively, ever the coward.

''Course I'll do it, no fear – but why not Garash? He's the bastard giving orders to harass the preachers.'

'High Priest Garash is a useful man; I wish him nothing but the finest of health.'

'Eh? But—'

Luerce sighed. *You really are a fucking idiot, Shanatin. Lucky for you the master keeps his promises.*

'Garash is a fanatic; a sadistic and violent man. The more he abuses his position, and the soldiers of the Devoted, the faster he pushes them to the master's service. Remember, small steps in the shadows will lead us to greatness. We leave the grand statements of power to others; far safer to prepare the path and allow others to bring about their own downfall.' He smiled like a snake. 'If a few of Ruhen's Children fall along the wayside because of Garash's excesses, such is the sacrifice we must all make.'

Shanatin's piggy eyes widened. 'All? You mean they're going to find out it's not true?'

'Some more than others,' Luerce reassured him. 'As for your share, we'll apportion it to a certain sergeant who tore up your books.'

At last Shanatin smiled. His only true friends were the three books he owned – at least, he had owned them, until a drunken sergeant had ripped them to pieces and pissed on the remnants.

Not one of the master's greatest acquisitions, Luerce reflected, *but sometimes we must make do with what is available. If a few soldiers are the price of his service, I'd gladly pay it ten times over.*

'Now,' Luerce continued, not wanting the fat lump to get distracted by what might await his tormentor. The first time a snivelling Shanatin had been nursing his bruises alone and the shadows whispered his name, the result had been his abuser clawing his own eyes. This time might not be so dramatic, but it would suffice. 'Do you remember what to do?'

Shanatin affected to look hurt, but only managed constipated. ''Course I remember. I'll go now.'

'Thank you, my friend.' Luerce put something in Shanatin's pocket and patted it meaningfully. Then he tugged the hood of his white cloak up over his head and smiled at the witchfinder from the shadows within it. 'Stay strong, the twilight reign is coming. Our time is coming.'

The thin Litse turned and disappeared into the broken rear room of the building, secreting himself out of sight until Shanatin had gone. They were in the poor inner district of Akell, the Circle City's northern quarter, where few Devoted would venture.

Unlike Byora where the rich lived in the lee of Blackfang's cliffs, here the long, shallower slope led up to the highest side of the mountain. Parss, that malevolent – some said simpleton – child of the mountain Goddess, Ushull, tossed his boulders down this slope too frequently for the rich, for they hit the buildings as if flung from siege engines. Shanatin left and checked his surroundings before leaving, careful to wait until the street was empty.

The witchfinder headed east, following the tall spur of wall that was all that remained of a gaol once built here. A landslide had demolished the rest during a storm when Shanatin was a child. As he walked through a haphazard network of makeshift shacks, the sound of the landslide boomed again in his ears. That demonstration of divine power had been his reason for joining the Knights of the Temples, just as the petty cruelty of men had been spark for him to accept what Azaer promised him, years later.

When he reached the more respectable areas he started seeing Devoted uniforms and hunkered down low as he walked. He had been careful to not wear his uniform – the white and black of the witchfinders was as easily noticed as Shanatin himself – but it meant he had to return to the Brew House, where they were quartered. It was an island within the main garrison complex, so he'd be forced to pass the barracks. He gritted his teeth and walked with head down and hands in pockets, silently asking Azaer to watch over him as he went about his task. He'd never heard the shadow's voice or felt its presence except after sundown, so it didn't worry him when he didn't receive a response.

And Shanatin muttered words of thanks when, almost an hour later as the sun met the eastern horizon, he reached Cardinal Eleil's offices unmolested. He'd done his best to ignore the sights as he walked; the entire main thoroughfare was lined with punishments of various sorts, from stocks at the mouth of the street, at the junction of the main road, to the gibbets closest to the Cardinal's office. He didn't count the soldiers and citizens being disciplined that day; undue interest itself was a crime now. The priests had made cowards of them all, though it was a familiar sensation for Shanatin.

He was admitted to the courtyard with only a cursory inspection, the guards making it clear they thought him incapable of causing trouble as they opened the gate. Inside he discovered the offices were in fact two tall buildings connected by a central hall.

The cardinal himself was said to have a desk situated on a mezzanine in the hall – from which, if rumour was to be believed, he could see and hear everything that happened at the desks below, the administrative heart of the Devout Congress.

Outside the hall's wide barred windows, and blocking Shanatin's path, was a company of soldiers, dressed like regular Knights of the Temples infantry, except they were armed where most of the other soldiers in the city had turned their weapons in to the Menin. A few eyed him suspiciously, the rest didn't bother.

'You lost?' a soldier called out. Shanatin shook his head and approached the man, a sergeant with pox scars on his face.

'I need to speak to Cardinal Eleil,' Shanatin said in a quiet voice.

'The cardinal?' The sergeant snorted. 'Gen'rally speakin', he don't bother with any damn stray that wanders in.'

Cardinal Eleil, once head of the Serian in the Circle City, the Devoted's intelligence-gathering arm, was now High Priest Garash's deputy on the Devout Congress. While Garash was the driving force behind this moral vigilance within the Knights of the Temples, it was Eleil who administrated and instituted Garash's reforms.

'It's important,' Shanatin insisted, dropping his eyes to look at the sergeant's scuffed boots. The man looked like a bully to Shanatin; he just had to hope he looked cowed already.

The sergeant was silent a moment. 'Better be,' he muttered before walking past Shanatin and jerking open the main door. 'Hey, you – where's Chaplain Fynner?' he asked someone inside.

Shanatin didn't hear a reply, but the sergeant stepped back and a few seconds later a tall, white-haired man in the dark red robes of a chaplain came out.

'What is it?' Fynner asked in a deep, rich voice.

'Witchfinder's askin' for the cardinal, Father,' the sergeant explained, pointing at Shanatin. 'Says it's important.'

The chaplain frowned at Shanatin, who wilted under the look.

'Very well,' said Fynner with resignation, 'come with me.'

Shanatin followed him into the large, chilly hall. It was still bright inside; orange-tinted sunlight streamed in through the windows lining the wall above the door and lamps were lit below. There appeared to be no one looking down over the room, but a dozen or so priests of various ranks were busy at the lower desks.

Once the door had shut behind Shanatin, Fynner rounded on him. 'So, Witchfinder, you'll have to convince me before you see anyone,' Fynner said sternly.

315

'Yes, Father,' Shanatin mutter respectfully. 'I ... I overheard somethin' I shouldn't of a few days back. I been keepin' my eyes open since then and I don't think he's the only one.'

'The only what?'

Shanatin hesitated. 'Mage; a mage off the books.'

'You are talking about an officer of the Order? That is a serious charge, young man; a very serious charge for an enlisted to make.'

'I know, sir, important officer too.'

Fynner looked around the room. The other priests seemed to be busy with their work and oblivious to what was going on, but still he beckoned for Shanatin to follow him to one end of the hall, where they went through a door. Without a further word Fynner took him up a short flight of stairs, past a sentry and into the private quarters of the cardinal.

'Cardinal Eleil is eating,' he explained at last when they reached one doorway, 'which may be for the best; this is sensitive information after all.'

Shanatin nodded, looking relieved. Fynner knocked and entered without waiting for a response, ushering Shanatin inside and shutting the door behind him.

'Fynner?' inquired the cardinal, seated alone at the head of a polished mahogany table and with a laden fork raised.

Shanatin felt his mouth start to water as the aroma of roast pork filled his nostrils. He could see roasted apples and potatoes on the plate, all liberally doused in thick nut-brown gravy. For a moment all thoughts of his mission were forgotten – until Chaplain Fynner cleared his throat pointedly and Shanatin realised he was staring open-mouthed at the food.

'My apologies, Cardinal Eleil, but this man has just brought a matter to my attention that I felt sure you would want to hear.'

'Well?'

Cardinal Eleil was older than Shanatin had assumed; his face wrinkled and weathered, his hair perfectly white, which indicated he was probably pure Litse blood.

'Ah, your Grace,' Shanatin stuttered, giving an awkward bow.

The error put a slight smile on the cardinal's face, as Shanatin had hoped. He inclined his head to acknowledge Shanatin's respect and took a swig of wine while the witchfinder started to speak.

'I was comin' back from ... ah, meetin' a friend, four nights

316

back – past midnight. I was out past curfew so I was sneakin' back into the Brew House, but before I got in I saw two men speakin' in the shadows. I hung back 'til they left. One o' them was Sergeant Timonas, see, from the witchfinders.'

He hesitated and glanced at Fynner, who gestured for him to keep going. 'Right, well, the other were an officer, and he bought some dose off of Timonas, gave him money, right in front of me. For more than one person too – brew don't last too long after it's cooked, and I reckon Timonas gave him enough for two, maybe three. Before the officer left he told Timonas to make damn sure he was doin' the next inspection too. The sarge said the schedules had bin worked out right an' it was all sorted.'

The cardinal leaned forward, his meal forgotten. 'Did you recognise the officer?'

'Yes, sir. It were Captain Performen, the Knight-Cardinal's adjutant.'

The two priests exchanged a look, then Fynner spoke. 'You are certain that was what was being discussed? There is no room for confusion or explanation?'

'No, sir, they was clear enough, an' I recognised the bottles Timonas gave Performen – they're the ones we use for the dose.'

Shanatin fell silent, letting the news sink in. The Order's laws were specific: all mages within their ranks had to be registered and monitored. A man with ambitions, however, would know any ability as a mage would count against him when it came to promotion – certainly no mage would ever be elected to the Council, and Captain Performen was aide to the man who had led that Council for years. Corruption, bribery, wilful flouting of the Codex ... these were all breaches of the law, and they added up to a capital offence.

'They did not mention who the others were?' Cardinal Eleil asked at last.

Shanatin shook his head.

'Then we must move cautiously. What is your name, Witchfinder?'

'Shanatin, your Grace.'

'Then, Witchfinder Shanatin, under the Second Investigation Act you are hereby co-opted into the Devout Congress. Add his name to the register of devout, Fynner.'

The chaplain bowed as Cardinal Eleil continued, 'Shanatin, you will return to your duties and investigate further. Monitor this sergeant and secure a copy of the schedule for the next ... how long does the dose last?'

'Up to a fortnight, sir.'

'Very well, the next three weeks. You will be contacted in the next few days by someone who will act as your liaison from now on. Do nothing that will alert them. This conspiracy may be bigger than we have seen thus far.'

The cardinal's tone made it clear the meeting was over. Shanatin didn't seem to notice, but Fynner did and took the witchfinder's arm, directing him outside again. The chaplain lingered a moment longer in case the cardinal wanted to speak to him further, but he had already returned to his pork. Fynner shrugged and accompanied Shanatin outside.

Once the door was closed Cardinal Eleil sat staring at it a while, slowly chewing the meat while he thought. He was naturally suspicious – a lifetime of the Serian did that to a man, and Witchfinder Shanatin had prickled his paranoia.

'He's just the sort I'd use myself,' he mused, spearing a piece of apple and holding it up to inspect. 'Simple and stupid, too obviously a fool to be a good ruse, and therein lies his value.'

He ate the apple, enjoying the sensation of the cooked fruit melting inside his mouth.

'An attempt to discredit the Congress?' he said eventually before shaking his head. 'No, surely anyone trying to make us act rashly would take such information to Garash instead. Misdirection perhaps? Have us waste our efforts on the Knight-Cardinal's men so others find a little more freedom to move?'

He finished the pork, saving the crackling until last. The first piece he tried was overcooked, too solid for his ageing teeth so he sucked the juices off it and discarded it in favour of other bits.

'There is of course the possibility that the fat cretin is telling the truth,' he had to admit finally, 'that he's stumbled across something and seen a way to profit from it.'

He pushed the plate aside and stood. Immediately something caught his eye, a small glint half-obscured by a chair near the door. Curious, the cardinal tilted his head sideways. It appeared to be a coin, a gold coin, lying on the floor.

'Where have you come from?' Eleil asked the coin, rounding the table. 'Did I not notice you when I came in? I can't believe Witchfinder Shanatin would have any call to be carrying gold with him, nor Fynner.'

He stood over the coin, looking down at it, but making no effort to pick it up. The coin was large, but not one he recognised, certainly not Circle City currency. While each quarter had its own, none of the gold coins used there were even similar. After a moment he crouched to pick the coin up, hissing at the clicks in his knees as he did so.

The coin was a thin disc, half the width of his palm, flattened at the rim to produce a very dull edge. There was nothing on it to indicate its origin; it wasn't really a coin at all since there was no sign of currency stamped on it. He carried it back around to the table and set it down, peering closely at it.

'So what are you then?' he asked.

Now he could see that symbols had been badly engraved onto the surface, around a crude cross. Something about that made him think of Elven core runes, but his education on such matters was limited. The cross was not composed of single lines, but half a dozen or so roughly parallel grooves.

He picked up the coin and was about to turn it over when he felt a tingle in his fingertips. On a whim he placed it upright on its edge and turned it around instead of flipping it over. The other side also had a strange script engraved on the surface, so lightly it looked almost like scratches, but the main symbol was a circle of several grooves around the flattened edge. The coin – disc – was old, and the gold had more than a few minor dents and scratches, but still Cardinal Eleil could see a distorted reflection within the polished circle. He turned it again, then flicked it with his fingernail to set it spinning on its edge.

As he watched the runes and faint reflection merge, he thought he heard a tiny sound from somewhere behind, the softest of whispers. He jerked around, but there was no one there. Doors set with two panes of glass led out onto a balcony, but he could see no one though the panes and the bolts top and bottom, out of reach of anyone breaking the small windows, remained firmly closed.

'Foolishness,' he muttered, and returned to the coin, which was lying flat on the tabletop, cross side up. Again he put it on its edge and set it spinning to watch the two sides merge. It reminded him of a toy he'd once had as a child, a piece of painted wood on strings which, when turned quickly, merged the image of a bird on one side with the cage on the other.

A susurrus sigh came from his right and the cardinal half-jumped out of his seat. He slapped a palm down onto the coin as he turned to where he'd heard the sound. There was no one there; nothing was disturbed, and the only piece of furniture that could possible have hidden someone, a padded recliner he often took an afternoon nap on, was at such an angle that it would have been impossible.

He resisted the urge to ask, 'Who's there?' and rose instead. He went to the bureau against the wall behind him. With one eye on the far side of the room he pressed a catch just inside the footwell and opened one of the drawers, reaching inside to pull a thin dagger from its hiding place.

With that in his hand he advanced to the other end of the room. The light was starting to fade and Cardinal Eleil realised the room was gloomier than he'd realised while eating. This end of his study had only one small window, above head-height. Set into the wall was an elegant fireplace with a tallboy on either side and a gilt-framed mirror above.

He glanced back at the coin, on the table where he'd left it. Its warm yellow colour looked markedly out of place in the dimly lit room. A slight scratching sound came from the wall by the door and he whipped around – to see nothing there at all . . . but his heart gave a lurch when, out of the corner of his eye, he saw something reflected in the mirror. He faced the wood-panelled wall, but still he saw nothing unusual there at all, and when he looked back at the mirror it was empty.

'Gods, am I going mad?' he whispered, his fingers tightening around the grip of his knife.

He looked back at the other end of the room, almost certain that for a moment he'd seen someone stood in the corner there – a grey figure – but it remained steadfastly empty. When he inspected the mirror that too looked fine, free of dust or dirt that might blur the image.

Again he heard a tiny whisper somewhere behind him, this time more like the rustle of pages, and so faint it was nearly drowned out by the frantic drumming of his heart. Each of the tallboys had glass-fronted shelving at the top, filled with leather-bound books. Nothing within them moved.

He waited a while, standing still and listening until he was forced to breathe deeply. Immediately there came a different sound, like fingertips being brushed gently against the wallpaper of the far wall. When he looked the sound faded to nothing, leaving him uncertain whether he'd heard anything at all.

'Ah, my imagination's playing tricks on me now,' Cardinal Eleil declared rather more boldly than he felt. 'You're a foolish old man whose hearing isn't as good as it once was, nothing more.'

He opened one of the glass cases and ran his fingers down the spines of the books. 'I refuse to pander to my imagination,' he said aloud, finding the book he was looking for, 'so I'll look up that rune instead.'

He flicked through the pages of the book with forced briskness, finding the section he was after easily enough. His familiarity with Elven runes was only very basic, limited to what he'd learned over the years within the Serian. The knife he kept in hand, underneath the book. It was an ornate weapon with a slim guard, gaudy but wickedly sharp.

Heretical academics frequently used the runes in their correspondence to each other, often using them for code, though sometimes the cardinal suspected it was mere pretension on their part. The closeted idiots had no conception of the dangers their research could result in. The Serian had saves thousands of lives over the course of his service, stopping reckless and foolish academics playing with forces far beyond their control.

'Aha,' he announced to the empty room, 'here we are. Azhi? Azhai?' he read, fumbling slightly over the pronunciation since the book was written in Farlan, 'and it means ... oh. Well, not a lot.' He sighed and glanced up at the room to check. It was still empty.

'Azai; a concept requiring context, potentially implying weakness or absence,' he read aloud. 'Other possibilities are substitution, usurpation, manipulation or corruption. At its most basic it can mean the shadow of something.'

His eyes flicked up to the mirror and he gave a gasp. At the corner of his vision he saw a faint movement on one side – too quick to catch, indeed, could have been the flash of an eyelash or trick of an ageing eye – but it had looked as though someone peeking through a window had ducked to the side of it.

He checked the room again, knife held ready, but there was absolutely no one there ... but still he imagined soft whispers on the edge of hearing from the far corners of the room. Heart hammering, feeling both foolish and terrified at the same time, he moved back to the mirror and edged carefully around it, as though wary of something reaching out from the reflection. There was nothing there; the reflection showed an empty room and nothing more—

He turned away, but as he did so he glimpsed a face, grey and formless in the glass, as though staring straight over his shoulder. Cardinal Eleil yelped with terror, dropping the book as he tripped over his own feet in his haste to turn. Behind him there was nothing, no man or shadow beyond those cast naturally.

The room was grey now, a layer of gloom covering everything as twilight began its reign over the Land. With shaking hands Cardinal Eleil looked down at the book, but he couldn't bring himself to retrieve it. It could stay there for the night happily enough. Only his trembling knees that threatened to give way underneath him prevented him from fleeing the room entirely.

The ageing cardinal gripped the mantelpiece in an effort to steady himself, but as he did so the whispers from the far corners of the room increased. A fresh lurch of panic surged through his body. He looked into the mirror and for a moment thought he could see a faint shadowy face in the gloom, smiling malevolently over his shoulder. Then the image faded and he realised he'd been holding his breath out of fear. He put both hands on the reassuringly solid mantelpiece and bowed his head, his eyes closed as he drew in heaving breaths of air.

'It's pronounced "Az-ae-ir",' came a murmur in his ear.

A moan of terror escaped his lips as pain flared in his chest. His eyes flashed open again, but this time the mirror was empty. A chill whisper of breath brushed his ear and Cardinal Eleil fell, his chest wrapped in burning agony.

Ilumene leaned forward over the bed, a cruel smile on his face and a dagger in his fingers. The tower bedroom was dark, lamps still unlit though Blackfang's shadow made the twilight even darker. Ruhen lay on the bed, fully dressed and laid out like a corpse, but as Ilumene watched his eyelids flickered and his lips twitched. There was a slight movement in the small boy's cheek, then another. His eyebrows trembled . . . At last his lips parted and Ruhen gasped for breath, as though returning to life.

'Old ones still the best, eh?' Ilumene said with a grin.

Ruhen turned his head to look at the big soldier from Narkang, the ghost of a smile on his face. He nodded solemnly as shadows danced in his eyes.

Venn turned to the yellow eye of Alterr and listened to the silence around him. He stood at a tall arched window, opened wide to admit the cool night breeze. Capan stood at his side, and behind them were two of his best fighters. Each of the Harlequins was silent and motionless, waiting for the signal that their Oracle was satisfied.

His three companions still wore their brightly patterned clothes. Their white masks shone in the greater moon's weak light, while the bloody teardrops on their faces looked perfectly black.

'Lomin sleeps,' he said after a long moment. 'It is time.'

They had entered the city during the day, walking straight through Lomin's formidable defences, and shown every courtesy by the guards on the gate. Venn had enjoyed the curious looks he'd received: a man in black with tattooed teardrops on his face travelling with a group of Harlequins. They'd erred on the side of caution and assumed he was to be treated with all possible respect, an intoxicating sensation for Venn after years of living in the shadows, of acting with all humility and resisting the urge to ever walk tall. Such respect from every person they met was more than welcome.

Venn slipped out of the window and balanced on the sill before pulling himself up onto the roof with barely a sound. They were in the house of a local merchant and they needed to avoid alarming the man's guards. Within a minute he was joined by Capan and Marn, one of the few female Harlequins under his command – though there was little to distinguish between the sexes within the clans. Marn stood a few inches above both Venn and Capan, and from her lithe movement Venn guessed she would push even him in combat.

'Kail, follow us at a distance,' Venn called down quietly to the last Harlequin, who had just come out onto the window sill. 'We can spare your blades easily enough. Watch our backs in case I am more flawed than I realise.'

Kail pursed his lips, but acquiesced, going back under cover. Venn didn't believe the Wither Queen's request had any hidden agenda, but caution was rarely punished. Like all Harlequins Kail was careful, and Venn knew nothing would escape his attention if there was anything to see.

With Capan and Marn trailing him, Venn ghosted along the peak of the roof, spending as little time as possible in the moonlight. He hooked an arm around the neck of a stone gargoyle looking over the street and dropped beneath it. Its reaching claws provided an easy handhold and Venn hung by one arm as momentum carried him past. He kicked out and felt his toes touch the jutting capstone of the house's double-height rear door. He let go, and for a moment he stood flat against the wall, on the balls of his feet, his arms pressed out wide as he caught his balance.

Then he dropped, pushing off the wall so he fell freely, grabbing the capstone as he reached it and spreading his legs to catch his feet on the stone door jambs to silently absorb the force.

A second kick to the side allowed him to reach the sill of a window beside the door and from there he dropped the remaining few feet to the ground. He stepped back and checked the street for watching faces, but it was deep into the night and there were none. His descent from the roof had been virtually silent, with nothing more than a shoe scuffing on the stone.

The others followed, perfectly mirroring his actions.

Lomin was a compact city of tight, weaving streets and alleys, so close to the Great Forest that the inhabitants didn't have the luxury of expanding beyond the city's current boundary. The local laws were enshrined on the assumption of periodic siege, so nothing was permitted outside the thick stone walls, and the city elders had gone so far as to connect many of the largest buildings within the city to provide a second line of defence, should it ever be needed.

Venn was already within the inner city, where most of the temples could be found, and from there it was a simple thing for the Harlequins to make their way to the Grand Square in the north-western corner, avoiding Lomin's Keep, the ducal residence.

The Grand Square itself was a misnamed, misshapen amalgamation. Centred on a monument to a past duke, it presently consisted of three expanses of open ground: the market to the north, the Temple District, that straddled the western piece, and a chaotic mass of open-air taverns and eateries in the southeast. There were some buildings in the Temple District, but they were all small and well spaced, so it looked more a part of the square than the rest of the cramped city.

Apart from the multi-level many-roofed Temple of Nartis that marked the boundary between the secular and spiritual parts of the square, the temples were all single-storey constructions. Several were strung together and enclosed garden-shrines that the locals flocked to, but this night even the Temple of Etesia, Goddess of Lust, was quiet. The red and purple lanterns hanging from the temple's eaves swayed gently in the breeze, and Venn heard only soft snores from within as he passed.

He slipped into the jagged shadows of Vasle's temple, any sound masked by the burble of water. The newest addition to the district was directly ahead of him, facing the cross-shaped Temple of Death on the edge of the square. The Wither Queen's wooden temple looked poor by comparison; but for the sharp grey-blue painted spire rising from the centre of the peaked roof it could have been a sombre-looking barn.

The roof and walls were black and the shutters covering the windows grey-blue. It looked far from welcoming, not least because of the dead garlands hanging from each corner of the temple.

'Spread out, keep a watch for soldiers while I deal with the temple,' Venn commanded Capan and Marn.

Neither Harlequin argued as he set off, skirting the building to ensure there was no one awake nearby. The temple had been guarded earlier, but only by two soldiers stationed on the nearer side, either side of the door. He slipped on a black hood and crept forward, using the spire as a guide.

When he reached the last piece of cover Venn paused. He had no doubt that he could kill both soldiers with ease, but he didn't want to risk them shouting as he did so. He climbed the low building he was hiding behind and crouched on the thatch roof, keeping the peak between him and the guards as he drew his swords. Then he walked along the roof's supporting beam until he was at the peak and peered over the top: the two guards were lazing almost exactly where he'd pictured them.

Venn took a deep breath and launched himself forward, cresting the roof and sprinting down the other side, leaping from the edge with one sword raised. He landed a little from the nearer guard and slashed his sword into the man's neck as he passed. The man had barely begun to turn when Venn opened his throat; he released his sword, dipped his left shoulder and rolled, bringing his legs under him and pushing hard to drive him onwards. He was back on his feet and lunging forward at the second guard in the same moment, but the man had not moved more than an inch when Venn's slender sword pierced his heart like a stiletto.

The former Harlequin made up the ground in a flash and grabbed the soldier by the arm just as the man's knees realised what had happened and gave way. Venn punched him in the throat to crush his windpipe and ensure quiet and he sank to the ground without a sound.

Venn looked around. There were no startled faces or vengeful comrades watching, just Rojak chuckling away at the back of his mind.

He pulled the bodies into the shadows of the recessed doorway and retrieved his swords, sheathing one as he went around to the rear of the temple. He was keen to get out of sight of Death's temple as soon as possible – though it was unlikely any priests were awake at this hour, all of Death's temples lacked doors and the torches were kept burning outside and would need replenishing from time to time.

At the back of the Wither Queen's temple he found an annex, half the height of the temple. The door was locked, but Venn placed one finger into the lock and put his other hand on the Skull of Song hanging from his waist. In half a dozen heartbeats he felt the slight click of the lock opening as Jackdaw did his work.

He slipped through the door and closed it behind him, finding himself in a small kitchen. On his left was a pallet where a young girl sprawled, still asleep. He put a hand over her mouth and stabbed down into her heart and her eyes flashed open, the whites shining bright as she struggled for one moment of utter panic before falling limp.

The priestess through the next door was lying face-down on her bed, a naked youth beside her. He stabbed the boy, then dropped down to kneel on her back and yanked her head back hard enough to snap her neck. The lovers died within an instant of each other.

Venn checked the main body of the temple quickly. There were only supposed to be three people inside and he'd taken care of three people . . . He spent a minute standing at the entrance listening, trying to ignore the beat of his heart. It was pitch-black inside and he could see nothing at all. Once he was certain he was alone he ordered Jackdaw to cast a faint illumination around the room and saw eight rows of pews running down the centre of the room, icons of the other four Reapers on the side walls, a bedroll in a corner, still done-up, and little else. Long hanging drapes covered the walls, except where an icon or lamp had been fixed to the wall, leaving the bare wood visible.

The altar was a table covered in cloth, too dull in this light to be plain white, below a larger icon of the Wither Queen. Venn examined the image of the Reaper Aspect, which depicted her as tall and imperious. Her bearing was a little more regal and a little less cruel than the God he had met.

He sniffed; there was decay in the air. It took him a while to trace it, until he spotted a cage of some sort. As he got nearer he realised there was a dead dog in it – no doubt it had been diseased when they brought it here as some sort of tribute, but even in the dim light Venn was able to see it had been dead for a while.

'When you are a God, minstrel,' Venn said softly, 'your temple will look like this.'

He didn't wait for a response from Rojak as he dragged the bodies of the soldiers inside, dumping one with the novice and the other with the priestess. It was unlikely he would be fooling anyone, but there was no point advertising what he'd done. Once he'd finished Venn went around the drapes in the main room and Jackdaw set them all alight before doing the same in the two smaller rooms.

Confident the blaze would soon take the whole building Venn headed for the refuge of the dark narrow streets beyond the Temple District. At the Temple of Tsatach he hesitated, but the cordon of bronze fire-bowls around it were all burning low, the light they cast fitful. He weaved his way between the stone pillars that supported the shallow bowls, but stopped when he reached the other side when he spotted a unit of armed men dressed as Penitents of Death.

They hadn't seen him yet, but Venn had no illusions; it would take them only moments.

A shame for you I didn't come alone, Venn thought, advancing towards the penitents.

The first man to notice him took a step back in surprise, his mouth opening to cry out, but no sound came. Marn darted out from behind him, leaving her leading sword in his throat. She pivoted around the man and slashed across the face of the next penitent to turn her way. The group had barely registered her presence when Capan danced forward from the other side, his blades swinging in unison. One fell, then another in the next swift stroke. Venn himself was already moving, slicing across a wrist, dodging sideways around a spear, cutting across a man's mouth . . .

He didn't wait to watch the penitent fall but kicked the one he'd winged and drove him back into the last man standing. Before either could recover their balance Marn had finished them both off with an elegant double swipe.

Venn didn't see any point in hanging around waiting for more temple troops to arrive. He led the Harlequins into the tight, twisting streets and on to find Kail. As they arrived, Kail stepped out from a covered walkway, dragging with him a woman with dyed coppery hair and a split lip, cradling a broken arm.

'Your instincts were correct,' Kail informed Venn with a bow.

'A devotee of the Lady?' Venn wondered aloud. 'What is your argument with us?'

The woman spat on the ground at his feet.

Venn could see she was trying to fight pain and shock. 'I do not have time for this,' he declared. 'Bring her.'

Kail grabbed the woman by the arm, but without warning her legs went from under her and with a gasp of pain the devotee collapsed onto the ground, protecting the arm Kail had broken to subdue her.

Venn frowned. She hadn't passed out, so the fall was intentional.

'Going nowhere,' the woman hissed through the pain. 'You want to kill me, do it here.'

Venn had to laugh at her defiance, however short his humour was. 'All I want is to know why you were following us.'

'Piss on you,' she snapped, 'whoever you are. I was sent watchin' the merchant.'

'I can hardly let you go now,' Venn said, drawing his sword once more.

'That blood on your sword?' she asked derisively. 'Oh sure, an injured devotee of the Lady'll run to the guards as quickly as she can when murder's been done. Bloody love gaols, me.'

Venn thought a moment, then sheathed his sword and gestured to the others to move on. The woman looked up in surprise, but it was short-lived. He slapped away her raised hand, gripped her head and twisted it violently. There was a sharp snap as her neck broke and she fell limp.

'Nice try,' Venn muttered as he smashed her head against the ground, then arranged her broken arm underneath her body, 'but I prefer not to gamble.'

He looked up at the buildings above them; the fall was easily high enough to be fatal. Quickly he climbed up on top of the walkway and stamped hard onto the overhanging tar-covered boards covering it, enough to snap a pair of them and send the pieces down to lie on the ground beside the body.

'Plausible enough,' he announced quietly as he lowered himself to the ground. 'And now we must lose ourselves in night's embrace.'

Capan gave a curt nod. 'These deeds are done,' he said, recognising the play Venn had quoted, 'let the veil of darkness be our only witness.'

'And so the game changes once again,' Ruhen said softly. The unnatural boy was standing next to Ilumene at a high window, looking down at Byora. The room was pitch-black, lit only by the pale light of Alterr shining through the windows. This was how they both liked it, caught in the embrace of the concealing night.

'A change too far, maybe,' Ilumene added, idly balancing a stiletto on the back of his scarred hand.

'How so?'

The big soldier squatted down at Ruhen's side so he could look into the child's shadow-laden eyes. 'This is all happening too fast, you can't deny that.'

'Change is inevitable.'

'Don't give me that,' Ilumene said firmly, trying to restrain his growing impatience. 'I'm not Luerce or even Venn – I won't swallow that without question.'

'Good.'

Ilumene waited but Ruhen's gaze was unblinking and eventually he realised the child was expecting him to provide the reasons himself. He sighed and sat down on the floor. With the stiletto he pointed out over the city. 'Since he was Chosen, the Farlan boy accelerated this war with every breath he took – it's burning hot, fast and out of our control.'

'Fortunate he died before he achieved further mischief.'

Ilumene shook his head. 'The damage is done. If the Menin conquer Narkang this season we may not have enough time.'

'Kastan Styrax has many Skulls yet to track down.'

'At the pace he's going? He'll regain Knowledge and Ruling when he cuts out Emin's heart, and he'll most likely find the journal sitting on the man's desk. Smart money is on the vampires offering theirs, believing it worthwhile to believe what he would promise in return. That brings his total to nine.

'When Venn arrives it could become ten without much strife. All we're missing are Hunting and Dreams, both in Farlan hands and both on the list for next summer, if not earlier.' His voice came more urgent, 'Master, we planned for five years of long, drawn-out war, to give us time to prepare the way.'

Ruhen was silent for a time, staring out over the great buildings of Eight Towers and the districts beyond.

'Your tune has changed since we last discussed this.'

'I've had time to think since.'

'And the new melody?'

'What would it take to be ready by the end of next year?' Ilumene sheathed the knife and leaned closer to Ruhen. 'I know the goal, but not the exact method – if we were to gather the objects we need by the end of next summer, what would be lacking?'

'A power-base,' Ruhen replied, turning to face his scarred protector, 'the foundation of worship.'

'Exactly. Your preachers were to spend those five years of war drawing followers away from the Gods and to your own worship, thus weakening the Gods and building your own foundation. Gods and daemons and everything in between: the worship does Styrax no good while he is mortal, but you are not mortal, no matter what form you appear in.'

'I thought you more intelligent than this,' Ruhen said, his expression turning cold. 'If I drew my strength from the worship of mortals, I would already have done so.'

Ilumene grinned. 'Appearances can be deceiving,' he said, before hurriedly continuing, 'A God receives worship, a daemon thrives off fear and pain – but both are strengthened by the followers they possess, and I'd guess the same goes for everything in between. King's Men aren't just soldiers or spies; Emin insisted we knew more of the Land than the folklore of childhood. We spent too much time in the wilds to be ignorant of such things; I might've forgotten much, but I remember one thing the old witch who taught us used to say: "the only hierarchy more rigid that the Pantheon of the Gods is found in the chaos of the Dark Place". No matter where they're from, beings of magic can be subsumed by others, just as they can *offer* their power, no? A power base is the only way they can maintain their position.'

'Our new friend?'

'She ain't strong enough yet, not for her needs. She was once an Aspect of Death, so how long 'til He rectifies that situation? She can't hide forever, but maybe we can help her prepare.'

'Offered the right covenant,' Ruhen said, 'perhaps, yes. She will be resistant to the very idea of a new master.'

Ilumene snorted. 'Whatever her bluster, she'll know it's a straight choice.'

'Dare we expect logic from a God?'

'Fair point,' Ilumene admitted, 'but you're known to be persuasive.'

Ruhen smiled at last, his small, neat teeth bright in the moonlight. 'It will take Venn a few days to return. I have until then to decide,' he said, but the expression on his face was enough for Ilumene. It would be done.

With that, the twilight reign crept closer.

Through a break in the canopy Venn looked up at the early evening sky. Long trails of cloud reached over the paling sky to where the sun was just about to set. As his custom since leaving the snow-bound home of the Harlequin clans, Venn crossed his hands over his heart and inclined his head towards the orange ball at the horizon.

He'd seen this done in Mantil, throughout the pirate havens and fishing ports of that island. It was a gesture of deference, echoing Azaer's small contribution to the Elven language, and he had adopted it himself to greet twilight.

I have seen how flawed my people are, Venn thought with a smile, *how enslaved they have been to telling one particular notion of history and refuting Aryn Bwr's heretical truths . . . And yet still I am drawn to tradition with all the rest of them; still I feel the need for solemnity and reverence. 'Flawed and frail is man and so we raise Gods in our better image' – Verliq had a point there.*

The black-clad Harlequin pointed to a fallen oak ahead. 'We'll make camp there,' he said, slipping his pack from his shoulders and holding it out for Marn to take from him. 'There is something I must do first.'

Capan shot him a questioning look, but led the others on.

Venn watched them go, walking with the lithe grace of all Harlequins. 'And what a sight they will look when they are all gathered,' he whispered to the twilight. 'Not even the Reavers could stand against two regiments of Harlequins. Never will death have looked so beautiful.'

He turned away and headed to a spot he'd noted earlier: a long dip in the ground that curved slowly off to the right, a natural ditch covered in lush bracken. The ground fell away after that so Venn had to walk only a short distance before he was out of sight of the others. Somewhere above his head he could hear the chatter of sparrows and, closer, the high abrupt chirp of bluecrests as they chased the evening midges.

'Jackdaw,' he said, 'do your work.'

Unbidden, Venn felt his lips move and as the Crystal Skull at his waist drew in the air around him the smell of earthy undergrowth filled his nose. It was overlaid by another, sharper tang, and Venn wrinkled his nose as that developed into a stench of decay he could taste at the back of his throat like bile. He looked around, but saw no one.

Rojak spoke in his mind. *'Cautious in your freedom, my queen?'*

Venn saw movement off to his left and turned as the Wither Queen rose from the tall bracken and closed on him. She was eying the former Harlequin with naked suspicion. She came close enough to reach out and touch him, but there she stopped, looking all around while her tongue, serpent-like, flicked her lips. Her skin had the pallor of the dead. It was stretched tight over her bones, and looked fragile, as if it might tear at the slighted touch. Matted hair partly obscured her face and strands stuck to a weeping scab on her jaw.

'There is no charity in your heart, spirit,' she replied, peering at him as though she could see Rojak's soul through Venn's eyes, 'so cautious I remain.'

From the undergrowth wisps of black fog pulsed and shifted with restless energy, and he could see shapes resembling rats moving along the ground. They surrounded the former Aspect of Death, forming a cordon that Venn believed to be more substantial than it looked.

He looked at the nearest of the rats and saw it watching him, its spectral jaw hanging slack. Venn suppressed the urge to draw one of his swords and looked away, putting the spirit's hungry eyes from his mind.

'As you wish,' Rojak replied, unperturbed. 'I come to claim that which you promised.'

'Then ask your boon and be gone.'

Rojak laughed his strange, girlish laugh, but the Wither Queen made no sign of whether she'd heard it. 'It is only this – that you listen to me a while longer.'

'The Harlequins prove a dull audience for your prattling?'

'They have heard all my stories,' Rojak agreed, 'but what I ask of you is something different. I have a proposal – I wish you to listen and make no decision until I have finished.'

'What trickery is this?' she asked angrily, and half a dozen more insubstantial spirits appeared in the air between the Wither Queen and Venn.

'No trickery,' Rojak assured her, 'but you will need persuading before you agree to my suggestion.'

Two of the pulsing black spirits raced away suddenly, darting through the trees like startled sparrows to scout the nearby forest more properly. Venn saw the Wither Queen mouth silent words as she turned to watch them go.

'Speak your piece,' she commanded once they had gone. The

333

Goddess tasted the air again, but this time it was a predatory action. The stink of her presence became a cloying force in Venn's nose and throat. It was all he could do not to gag as Rojak cheerfully continued, apparently enjoying the sense of corruption all around him.

'These forests are not only your hunting ground; they are also your refuge.'

Venn saw the Wither Queen's eyes narrow, but she kept to the bargain they had made and did not speak.

'*You have grown stronger away from Death's presence, but not so strong that you can prevent Him from leashing you once more. To do that you need more than brute strength, you need stature – in the divine sense.*'

There was a note of enjoyment in Rojak's voice that Venn recognised all too well. The minstrel had always loved to lecture, to present truths to others and let them walk the dark paths he revealed. To do so with a God would be a pleasure worth savouring.

'*We have the means to bring this about, to secure for you a place in the Pantheon that Death himself will not wish to disrupt.*'

'How?' The Wither Queen asked, her expression turning from suspicious to one of burning hunger.

'*A king is measured by his subjects, a God by its followers. Death must respect a position within the Pantheon because He is the epitome of rank, of authority – but spirits of the forest do not convey the worship a God needs to be called a God.*'

'My mortal followers are few and reluctant; their prayers full of bitter tears.'

'*And there you are a God most rare,*' Rojak said, as softly as if he were whispering to a lover.

The Wither Queen stared, waiting for him to continue.

Rojak chuckled, enjoying the moment. '*Others of the Pantheon, however, are more fortunate and it pains me to see such beauty lack the majesty it deserves. My suggestion is this – permit us to help you achieve this position and ally with us in our endeavours. In return, when the time is right and our need is pressing, lend my master your power when it is requested.*'

'Your master wishes to bind me as Death would? What good is it to exchange one lord for another?'

'*It would be a loan, to last no longer than a moon – it is not domination*

334

over you my master seeks, merely assistance to ensure a similar freedom as that we offer you.'

The Wither Queen was silent for a time; even the spirits surrounding her stilled and the darkening forest itself became hushed.

Venn realised every muscle in his body had gone taut with anticipation.

'A term of service, when asked for, to last until the moon is new,' she said at last. Venn felt the tension drain from his body. 'In return for providing me with the power to resist Death's call. Prove you have the power to do such a thing and there shall be a covenant.'

'It would be a pleasure,' Rojak purred. *'If you are ready to take what is deservedly yours?'*

Venn heard a second voice in his head as Jackdaw started murmuring; he could not make it out at first – then he froze, recognising the form easily enough that the words did not matter. Jackdaw was praying. Once he had been a prior at a monastery to Vellern, until Jackdaw had renounced his vows and become sundered from his God. Needless to say, the Gods disapproved of such behaviour – using prayer to summon one was like poking an already-angry bear. The God of Birds might well be diminished after Zhia Vukotic killed an Aspect and high priest of his in Scree, but feeble he was not.

Venn smiled; Vellern wouldn't even think twice before incarnating. A greasy sensation slithered down the former Harlequin's spine as Jackdaw drew on the Crystal Skull he carried. The forest went completely silent and even the breeze drifting through the leaves vanished as the dusk birdsong faded to nothing. Venn felt a prickle of excitement and his heart began to beat faster as the Jackdaw's incantation grew louder.

The Wither Queen was busy herself, her eyes firmly closed, her arms held outstretched as she performed her own summoning. Pinpricks of pale light began to appear all around her – five, ten, twenty – forming sickly constellations above her head. A handful sank to the ground and wriggled like diseased mice before abruptly spasming and splitting open for new rat-like wisps to emerge. More rats scampered from the undergrowth with unnatural speed to gather and fawn at the tattered hem of her skirt.

Jackdaw's intonation broke off suddenly and Venn looked around. The forest was empty, but there was a sudden sense of weight in the air like the heaviness before a storm.

'*He comes,*' Jackdaw whispered from the recesses of Venn's mind. He sounded terrified. The taste of magic appeared thick in his mouth, eclipsing the Wither Queen's putrefaction. Venn gripped the Crystal Skull firmly with one hand and reached for a sword with the other. He didn't know whether it would do any good, but if this all went wrong he didn't want to die empty-handed.

A dark shadow descended over them all. For a moment Venn thought it was Vellern, swooping from on high, but then he felt the familiar touch of Azaer on his mind and relaxed.

The moment didn't last long; in the next instant there was a swirl of air a few yards away that seemed to fold in upon itself and Venn blinked and found himself staring at the stern, hairless face of Vellern. Standing eight feet tall, with a mantle of peacock feathers that reached all the way to the ground, the God of Birds glared around, searching for Jackdaw.

The God carried a long jet-black javelin in his taloned hands. He levelled the weapon at Venn, who took a step back, his hand tightening on his sword. Vellern advanced a step, half-turning his back on the Wither Queen in his fury.

'You elude me no longer, traitor,' Vellern said, his voice sharp and quick like an eagle's cry.

Jackdaw was busy and Venn didn't reply, but he drew his sword, which enraged the God further. Venn took another step back and Vellern followed, raising the javelin high, ready to stab down at him.

The blow never came. As one the spectral rats leaped, and the swirling spirits darted at Vellern's face. He ignored the rats entirely and slapped away the first spirit to reach him. Its smoky form dissipated entirely as Vellern's hand passed through it without resistance. The second fared no better, casually destroyed without regard, and though the rats tore and raged at Vellern's legs their efforts were too insignificant to warrant attention.

But they were just distraction, and a fat arc of raw, spitting energy raced from Venn's sword tip and struck Vellern hard enough to make the God reel. It was followed by another, then another, each one driving Vellern a pace back as it hit home. The Wither Queen stepped forward now, a long stiletto in each hand.

Jackdaw changed his attack and threw a writhing coil of white energy that blew apart Vellern's javelin, while the Wither Queen stabbed her knives into the God. Vellern parried the blows with his hands and kicked out at her, raking talons down her chest and causing her to screech in pain.

Jackdaw renewed his efforts, lashing out and tearing great rents in his peacock mantle. Venn felt a shudder run from deep inside him and he howled with pain as Jackdaw punched forward, knocking Vellern from his feet.

The Wither Queen and her rats pounced, a swirling mass that swarmed over the supine figure.

Venn's every sense was spinning and he was struggling to move as he saw the rats tearing at Vellern's white speckled tunic, trying to rend the flesh beneath. The Wither Queen had greater success, stabbing one stiletto into Vellern's shoulder and pinning him to the ground.

Venn felt a burning sensation on his fingers as though they were aflame. When he looked down he saw his fingers were blackened trying to control a crackling ball of energy. In his mind Jackdaw gibbered with drunken delight.

'Yield to me,' the Wither Queen screeched triumphantly, 'yield and submit – accept me as your God, or you die now.'

Venn saw the horror in Vellern's eyes. The God looked past the Wither Queen and directly at him, fearing the surging ball of magic in his hand. Venn raised his hand and his intent was obvious. The rats continued to attack and now the God could feel them, writhing under their assault as he lay there with one shoulder pinned to the ground. With a gesture the Wither Queen halted the rats and underlined her demand by putting the other stiletto to Vellern's throat.

'I yield,' the God cried at last. 'In your service I will live.'

The last words were said in a resigned pant, but the Wither Queen was not yet satisfied. The glee plain on her face, she slammed her free hand into Vellern's chest and drove her broken fingernails through the flesh. Vellern howled, but the Wither Queen ignored him and pushed down to where a mortal's heart would be.

The Goddess found what she was looking for and wrenched her hand out again, this time closed around something. She held her prize up and laughed, the noise like a person choking their last few breaths. She raised her hand to her mouth and opened it, and Venn caught a glimpse of a golden wisp of light before it was devoured.

The Wither Queen licked the dripping ichor from her palm and crouched to allow the rats their share. At last she was satisfied. and looked down at Vellern. She placed her hand on the injured God's chest and he vanished, leaving only an indentation in the earth and a few last spots of divine blood that the rats fought to lap up.

'Tell your master,' she croaked, looking up at Venn with the smile of a sated glutton, 'I agree to his bargain.'

CHAPTER 23

The sweet scent of azaleas drifted in the breeze as Major Amber eased his leg up onto a stool and hooked an arm over the rail of the balcony so he could better look down at the tables below. It was early evening, but the terrace was full, every chair in use. He took another sip of wine before catching the eye of a woman with a yellow sash tied across her solid body. Amber raised his goblet and she nodded, moving swiftly to fetch him more wine.

This tavern dominated the northern edge of the Stepped Gardens, the three-tiered heart of Byora's Breakale district. The tables below, which had long since spilled over onto the hedge-bordered grass of the middle tier, catered for a general clientele, but the upper room was for more exclusive guests.

This early in the evening his only companions in the room were a trio of Litse, two merchants, and the wife of the elder. All three were typical of their tribe: fine-boned and very pale-skinned, and Amber guessed them to be as wealthy as anyone in Breakale; no doubt voluminous sleeves and oversized collars were the height of fashion among the people of Byora, no matter how ridiculous they looked.

The younger, a man of some twenty summers, couldn't hide his distaste at sharing a room with a Menin soldier, but Amber was determined to enjoy himself. Though his injuries had healed, he still felt fragile, and the last thing he wanted was start a barroom brawl, no matter he'd easily win.

Relief came in the form of Nai, former manservant of the necro-mancer Isherin Purn – and staunch opponent of footwear, however fashionable. The mage padded up to Amber's table and sat without invitation. He had a preoccupied expression on his face, and if he even noticed the outrage from the Litse, he didn't show it.

'At least you've visited a tailor,' Amber commented, looking Nai up and down. He lingered on the mage's bare, odd-sized feet. 'Did the cobbler laugh at you though?'

Nai's expression soured further. 'If you called me here to mock me, I'll be leaving.'

'It wasn't the only reason,' Amber protested, 'just my preferred one.'

The woman in the yellow sash arrived before he could say anything more, and deposited a fresh carafe of wine and a second goblet before sweeping up the silver level Amber had left for her. Once she'd gone Amber poured Nai some wine and gestured at the bowls on the table. The mage selected a small stuffed pepper and sat back, his eyes fixed on Amber while he sucked out the filling. Amber grinned, his slightly malicious smile faltering slightly as the fiery spices appeared to have no effect on the mage.

'I hear you've been busy,' he said at last. 'Running all over the city.'

Nai reached for another pepper. 'I'm only doing what you ordered me to.'

'And do you have anything to report?'

'Nothing you couldn't have found out yourself.'

Amber shifted forward in his seat. 'Don't get petulant. You're in the Menin Army now, and there's no place for it here.'

'Funny sort of army,' Nai retorted. He knocked back his wine in one gulp and eyed Amber suspiciously as he poured himself another. 'For one thing, loads of soldiers marched away a while back and left us here.'

'The term "army" encompasses many meanings,' Amber said, a warning tone to his voice. 'Perhaps you'd be good enough to tell me what you've learned?'

Nai grunted and began, 'Not all that much, except Sergeant Kayel has good taste in whores and is paying a lot of attention to the various Walls of Intercession cropping up all over the city.'

'Is that what they're calling those walls covered in prayers to the child?'

'Not just walls either, but that's what they're calling them, so the difference probably doesn't mean much. The wall at the Ruby Tower compound's as much a cenotaph to those who died in the assault, for example. Your friend the sergeant is showing his face at each one, turning up as soon as he hears of it … Doesn't do anything once he gets there, mind, unless those sitting in vigil speak to him, and few enough dare. Otherwise, he just stands for half an hour, looks at the faces and leaves.'

'Hmm. Just telling the people of the city he's watching over them,' Amber concluded. 'He does nothing else all day?'

The mage shrugged carelessly. 'Not much. He's often in Hale overseeing the resettlement, of course, but you know that already. It's hard to follow him there, but even so, I'm certain he's doing nothing more than watching and giving orders. There haven't been any clerics openly resisting the reallocation of temple land, so he's had no excuse to arrest any, and he shows no great zeal for that to change. The leader of the beggars spends much of the day meeting with agents, but he's always surrounded by his faithful flock so I can't get close enough to hear what's going on. All I know is his name, Luerce; he's a local, but he looks to be in charge of sending the missionaries out. Kayel may give him his orders, of course, but not when I've been watching.'

'So it's really just these Walls of Intercession, drawing worship away from the Gods?'

Nai scoffed at the suggestion. 'Before you start throwing charges of impiety around, take a look at yourselves first!'

'What do you mean?'

'That damned Victory Memorial right inside the Carter's Gate!' Nai exclaimed. 'Skulls and icons glorifying our lord – right where everyone can hardly fail to see it! It's looking more like a shrine than any rag-strewn wall.'

'I don't remember your orders including the instruction to think about anything,' Amber said quietly.

Nai slammed a palm on the table. 'If that's the case, get yourself some pet adept of Larat to spy for you instead!'

Amber sighed. On the other side of the room the three Litse sat bolt upright with alarm, like deer ready to flee. 'I can't trust any of them,' he said in a low voice, 'you know I can't.'

'Then don't forget I'm no damn soldier,' Nai hissed. 'I'm not even Menin, and my loyalty isn't blind. Your coin might look like army wages, but don't think for a moment I can't manage without you.'

Amber paused. 'I'd never thought of it like that. How did you earn your keep, back in Scree?'

Nai gave him a cold smile. 'Do you really want an answer? You really want to ask how my master came on his wealth? There are more than enough ways for a mage to easily earn an honest living, but as you can probably imagine Isherin Purn didn't believe in any of them.'

'You're right,' Amber agreed, 'I really don't want to know. As for impiety, no, I don't care about that. I'm trying to work out what Sergeant Kayel and his friends are up to in Byora – whether all these prayers for intercession and missionaries to other cities are the scheme or the smokescreen.'

'It would be a complicated smokescreen,' Nai pointed out. 'Their resources are limited, their numbers few. The missionaries are all, from what I can see, locals being recruited to the cause – the mad and the sick, beggars who've lost all hope and are desperate for salvation. What's telling is that the Harlequins are in on it now.'

'What do you mean?'

Nai grabbed a heel of bread and jammed it in the side of his mouth, talking as he chewed. 'Aha, some real news to justify this sinner's wages. There's a Harlequin in the city. It was speaking in Burn the other day.'

'What's new about that?'

The necromancer grinned. 'It wasn't the usual stories the Harlequin was telling – some, but not all. It was mostly speaking of a child, one that would set us back on the path of the righteous. Damn storyteller did all but denounce every cult in the Land as self-serving criminals, leading us away from the embrace of the Gods.'

Amber gaped. 'A child? They're in league with the Harlequins? But, that's . . .' His voice tailed off and he sat back in his chair.

'Surprising, aye,' Nai said. 'Means you've got to take them more seriously now. The Harlequins have never sided with anyone before, but all this fits together so neatly there's got to be a plan there somewhere.'

'But what's the plan?' Amber asked helplessly. 'What am I missing?'

'That I don't know,' Nai said as he tipped his chair back to balance it on its rear legs. It creaked and wobbled alarmingly. 'But this plan's not secret now, parts of it at least. Getting the Harlequins on your side will make every power-broker in the Land sit up and take notice, them and the preaching missionaries. That means they're confident, either because they're strong enough to survive on their own, or because what they're up to doesn't threaten anyone nearby.'

'They're not strong, even with the Jesters. The tribes that worship them aren't an army and they aren't here. They're just a few Raylin, plus a bodyguard.'

'But we're the only ones who can hurt them,' Nai said with a pointed look. 'What if they don't fear us – their Walls of Intercession are more than a shade akin to the memorials Lord Styrax has raised after every battle he's won. If there is a purpose behind them, maybe it's the same purpose.'

Amber leaned forward over the table and said in a hushed voice, 'You think Lord Styrax is in league with the shadow?'

'I'm not someone he confides in,' Nai replied. 'I don't know if you are or not – I doubt even you really know – but the Lady of Luck's dead and I don't believe in coincidences.'

Amber looked bleak. 'I don't know all his secrets, but if you think Lord Styrax follows the order of any man, let alone some shadow, you're the fool.'

'So go and ask.'

'Eh?'

'That scarred bastard, Sergeant Kayel,' Nai said brightly. 'You think he's one of Azaer's disciples, and my money's on you being right. Now I don't know much about Azaer, but what I do know leads me to believe it isn't one to advertise. To those in the know, all this preaching's a lot of noise coming from a corner that's normally quiet. They won't believe all this has gone unnoticed by the man who's just conquered this city, and still they don't hide – so go and ask Kayel. No one draws attention to themselves while under Kastan Styrax's thumb unless they've got nothing to hide.'

Amber nodded slowly. 'Or they've got something to offer. You could be right there.' He paused. 'What's your part in all this?'

Nai looked startled at the change of focus, immediately wary. 'What do you mean?'

Amber was about to leap on the shift in the mage's demeanour when he caught himself. *He's not just a mage*, he told himself, *he's a necromancer; as a breed they don't like scrutiny, and they don't like questions, so this doesn't tell me anything.*

He changed tack slightly. 'You heard me. What part are you playing in all this? You've sat in more than one camp, but exactly how many? One whole lot o' things bugged me about Scree, and one of them was Zhia Vukotic not once showing any sign of sensing that abbot using the Crystal Skull they were all chasing.'

Nai's brow crinkled in confusion. 'I don't understand.'

'Remember when we walked out into the Library of the Seasons, when it was a dead area for magic?' Amber reminded him. 'The change was clear as day on your face. There was no reason for Zhia to hide it if, during the course of a day, she'd sensed someone using a Crystal Skull, yet long before that Purn had detected it and contacted us. Purn's house might have been closer than Zhia's but she's by far the stronger mage and she never seemed to notice.'

'Zhia Vukotic is a politician,' Nai argued, 'and as gifted at it as her brother is with a sword. If she doesn't want to give something away, she doesn't.'

'That's crap – if she wants to hide something, she does, but that's not the same as never giving nothing away – so why should she bother? She knew why I was in the city because Mikiss told her. And how she was around that lovesick boy from Narkang, that wasn't an act either. So if she wasn't hiding everything all the time, why would she have chosen something that didn't matter? You better believe I was paying attention, and thinking of the debriefing I'd have to give if I survived.'

Amber took a deep breath. The flicker of suspicion at the back of his mind was growing with every moment. 'If Zhia went looking for it, then sure, she'd find it – but why bother?'

Nai inclined his head to agree, but he didn't speak, which only added to Amber's certainty.

He continued, 'And on the paranoia stakes, what sort of man could compete with one of the greatest heretics in history? A necromancer, maybe – but if Zhia Vukotic didn't bother searching for such a thing, why would Isherin Purn?'

He rose suddenly from his seat, startling Nai and causing the mage to nearly fall backwards. 'You fucking rat-bastard necromancer!' Amber shouted, grabbing at Nai's arm.

The mage tipped himself back out of his chair and rolled onto his feet out of the major's reach.

'What are you doing?' Nai yelled, almost colliding with one of the Litse merchants as he scrambled back. The three stared in horror as the big Menin lurched forward, still unsteady after his injuries but no less brutal-looking for all that. The conversation had been conducted in the Menin dialect and they had no idea what was going on.

'I'll fucking gut you in a moment,' Amber roared, drawing a scimitar. 'Bloody Purn didn't sense that Skull; he was taking orders from Azaer!'

'How would that be my fault?' Nai shouted back, retreating as far as he could with hands outstretched towards Amber. 'If it's even true, I did nothing!'

Amber kept on moving. 'Don't pretend you didn't know, there's no way he'd be able to hide something like that from his acolyte!'

'You expect me to be privy to every conversation?' Nai yelled back. 'Purn was far more powerful than I! How would I know his orders?'

'Maybe not, but you damned well must have known his links to Azaer, and you kept it from me.'

Nai gaped, his alarm suddenly eclipsed by outrage. 'And you blame me for that? He was a necromancer, most likely one of the most skilled in the entire Land – of course Azaer had noticed him – but whatever dealings went on *if* there were dealings, I didn't know the details!'

Amber stopped and lowered his scimitar. He started to think about what Nai had just said – then a greenish light flared in the mage's open palm and the major felt a blow to his gut like a mule's kick, throwing him backwards. He hit the ground hard, black stars bursting before his eyes.

His vision still blurred, Amber felt a foot press against his shoulder and instinctively curled, anticipating a second blow, but instead he was rolled roughly onto his back. He could just make out Nai's furious face looking down at him.

The mage no longer looked in the least bit comical. Twin trails of green fire swirled around his right hand, which he'd drawn back, like a boxer ready to throw the final punch. 'All you damn Menin,' Nai spat, 'you think you're the chosen people; that someone like me doesn't count, and you can treat us like dogs. That's why the Litse hate you: they can see that arrogance in your eyes – that calculation that anyone not on your side must be an enemy, someone to be dominated. I didn't tell you about Purn's link with Azaer because by association it'd mean one more reason not to trust me.'

With an effort of will the necromancer took a step back and let the trails of magic dissolve harmlessly into the air. 'Politics interested Isherin Purn just as little as they do me – who sits in which palace hardly matters when you're unravelling secrets of the Land itself.'

He made to walk away, then stopped and looked back. 'Despite the limitations of your tribe and profession, Major Amber, I respect you. But in my world we can't afford uncertainty. My choices are to kill you now, or disappear well beyond your reach.' His voice took on a cold tone. 'Ready for me to decide?'

CHAPTER 24

'Lord Fernal, this is madness!' Count Vesna shouted, bursting through the door. 'You cannot sign this treaty!'

Fernal looked up from his desk, then turned to the Chief Steward standing on his left. 'Is this the sort of obedience I can expect from all nobles now?'

Vesna ignored the comment as he marched up to the desk. The braiding of his formal uniform was swinging wildly. 'You're signing the treaty?' he demanded.

Fernal growled and stood. The Demi-God was large as a white-eye, and he towered over Count Vesna. The new Lord of the Farlan wore a strange amalgamation of robes and tunic, made of some silky grey cloth seamed with gold thread, with his snake-and-arrows crest embroidered on the front. The ducal circlet sat on his head, and the clasps holding his cloak were solid discs of gold. It was as formal as Vesna had ever seen Fernal, but as with Isak, it did nothing to hide the dangerous potential rumbling underneath.

'I am signing the treaty,' he said deliberately slowly, pronouncing each syllable with care, even as he ensured his massive canine teeth were on full display. 'It must be done.'

Vesna remembered his place and backed off, turning to Lesarl instead. 'Did you counsel this?'

'Despite my appearance,' Fernal continued, 'I am not some unthinking monster. Lesarl advised me of the alternatives. The decision is mine.'

Vesna looked around the rest of the room, as though expecting to see a Menin envoy hiding in one of the corners, but seeing no one seemed to deflate the Aspect of Karkarn and he lowered his voice. 'You cannot believe their assurances?' he pleaded.

'Lord Fernal is well-aware of the Menin's trustworthiness,' Lesarl answered for his master, 'or lack thereof, but signing the treaty was the price of the dukes' official recognition.'

The Menin had arrived only three days before, offering a non-aggression treaty that effectively drew a line under the whole matter of Isak's crusade. Unlikely as the offer was, the three other Farlan dukes had all demanded it be signed.

'So we abandon everything?'

Lesarl's eye narrowed. 'So we deal with one problem at a time. We need the nobles to fall in line; this is the only way it can be done.' He raised a hand as Vesna started to object. 'We're in no position to go to war until the nobles are happy with their lord. That we are abandoning our treaties with Narkang I know all too well, but treaties are of little use when we cannot follow through on them.'

'So you would allow the Menin to pick us off one by one?' Vesna said with contempt. 'The dukes and suzerains may force you to honour this treaty even when we're ready, but it won't stop the Menin.'

'What happens next year is uncertain,' Lesarl assured him, 'and the nobility may yet be brought around with careful management. If the Menin have moved against Narkang by then the picture will look very different; they will start to feel vulnerable, more open to persuasion. Until that time we need them to recognise Lord Fernal's title and authority for without that we have civil war. Only with the unified support of the nobility will we be able to regain control of the cults.'

'There is a greater war to be fought,' Vesna argued, feeling increasingly desperate. 'Are we going to sit here and do nothing? Isak lost his life trying to stop Azaer before his power-base developed further. Are we to do nothing?'

'We can do nothing,' Lesarl said very deliberately. 'There can be no officially sanctioned action against either the Menin or those within their sphere of influence.'

'What in Ghenna's name is that supposed to mean?'

Lesarl gave him a cold, reptilian smile. 'It means, *Count* Vesna, that no soldier or nobleman of the Farlan nation can act in any way that might contravene the treaty Lord Fernal will be signing this afternoon – while you are off marrying the delightful Lady Tila.'

Fernal pushed forward a piece of parchment that had been sitting in front of him, one bearing three official seals and the angular marks Vesna recognised as the Demi-God's signature.

'What's this?'

'The deed of trust to your estate,' Lesarl said. 'As a man of religious status, you are ineligible to hold military rank or title. This deed, back-dated to your return, entrusts all such affairs to the Lord of the Farlan until such a time as there is an individual to legally take possession of such things.'

'Such as a wife?'

'I believe a wife would suffice, yes.'

Vesna looked from the slender politician to his massive lord. 'What's the point of all this? The wedding's this afternoon; surely this is a technicality hardly worth the time of the Lord of the Farlan.'

'Nevertheless, such matters are best attended to in the correct legal manner,' Lesarl replied smoothly, 'so please sign and renounce your title in favour of any offspring the future Countess Vesna may bear you. You should also resign your army commission – unless you intend to join the chaplaincy branch of the cult.'

'Are . . . are you telling me I should continue a fight alone?' Vesna asked hesitantly.

'Not at all. Lord Fernal could never condone such a decision. However, without the constraints of title, you would be free to act as you see fit, and as your God commands – this you should have realised by now, but since you failed to I thought it best the matter was brought up *before* your marriage. What opinions the God of War might have regarding the subject of continuing the fight I leave to theologians.

'Furthermore, whether or not others choose to join you in this matter is entirely up to them. Special Order Seven has been rescinded and all constraints upon military personnel are removed.'

Vesna was silent a while as he signed the document. 'Men under arms are no longer landlocked, and title regains precedence over military rank,' he said slowly. 'They may cross borders without written orders and release those in their service if they so wish.'

'That was but one of the constraints of the Special Order, Count—ah, I believe *Iron General* is the correct term to use now?'

'What in the name of the Dark Place am I supposed to do, then?' Vesna whispered, ignoring the question.

349

'To pursue a war against Azaer? I believe King Emin is the expert there; perhaps you should ask him. But first, there is something else you must do.'

'What's that?' Vesna asked sharply.

Lesarl gave him a broad smile and indicated Vesna's dress uniform. 'Marry that poor girl, Vesna, if she'll still have you. I believe your bride is waiting for you.'

Outside Tirah Palace the air was heavy and a cold wind blew. Vesna stopped on the stairs leading down to the training ground and squinted up at the sky. He couldn't see the sun and a dark grey bank of cloud had appeared on the northern horizon and was being driven by the wind towards them. There was a promise of rain in the air. The Farlan considered that a good omen – he was, after all, to be married at a shrine to Nartis, so peals of thunder and pouring rain could hardly be anything but a blessing from the God of Storms.

'Vesna,' called a slim man in armour hurrying over from the forges. He carried a teardrop shield and an eight-foot spear, both new, beautifully forged by the palace armourer. 'You're early; we don't need to leave yet.'

'I have to speak with Tila before the wedding,' Vesna said once he'd gripped the man's arm in greeting. 'I know, Dace,' he continued as the man opened his mouth to argue, 'but this is more important than tradition.'

Sir Dace laughed and took a pace back, standing to attention, presenting spear and shield formally. His sleeves and trousers were fitting to the occasion but the rest, as was traditional, were what he would wear into battle. 'You're telling that to the wrong man, my friend,' he said with a smile. 'You might have always been my better with a sword, but there's no damned way I'm crossing Lady Tila!'

The two men were the same age; they'd known each other for decades. Dace sported the single gold earring of a knight under his wild black curls, and the same blue tattoos on his neck as Vesna. Born to a cobbler, he had won a place in the Palace Guard the year after Vesna and the two had soon become friends. The day Vesna won his martial honours on the battlefield, Dace had been close behind his friend; he was one of three men knighted that day. Family life had taken Dace away from the army, but for ten years he had stood at Vesna's side, both on the battlefield and on the duelling ground, just as he was about to as the famous rogue at last followed his friend's example and married.

'My circumstances have changed,' Vesna explained in a lower voice, 'and Tila needs to know before we marry.'

Sir Dace's smile widened. He handed his friend the spear and reached into a pocket to out pull a letter. 'Something you need to learn about married life,' he explained. 'They'll outflank you more often than not, especially when they're as smart as your intended. Best thing is to accept it without a fight.' His grin widened. 'Let that be my first act as sentinel for your marriage!'

'What are you talking about?' Vesna swapped the spear for the letter and saw it bore his name in Tila's handwriting.

'Read the letter,' Dace advised. 'A God I might not be, but Karkarn himself could give you no better advice.'

Sir Dace had travelled south from Anvee after news of the crusade had reached there and all able nobles had been called up. Despite having four children waiting at home, Dace had stayed at Tila's request. A Farlan wedding called for a man to assume the position of sentinel to the marriage, to watch over the happiness of both parties – and, occasionally, to defend the honour of one or the other, which explained why Vesna, hardly the guardian of marital fidelity, was sentinel to several marriages.

Vesna tore the letter open and scanned the half-dozen lines. As he read it his frown slowly softened.

> My dearest,
>
> By now I am sure Lesarl has given you the deed of trust and intimated that you are no longer bound by your military obligations. Let me remind you that Isak was my friend also, and I grieve for him as much as you. You must do what you can to further the cause he died for, but that has no bearing on our marriage. Today we will be married, no matter what tomorrow may bring – and this I do with full understanding, so let Lord Karkarn himself defend you if you try to make my choice otherwise.
>
> With all my love on our wedding day,
> Tila

'See what I mean?' Dace said cheerfully, 'anticipated and out-flanked. You never stood a chance, my friend.'

He thumped Vesna on his plate-armour shoulder, wincing slightly as he caught his palm on the black-iron.

'I can still ask Karkarn to be my sentinel,' Vesna growled, trying to be stern, but feeling his irritation melt away as he reread the letter.

'And he too will have better sense than to cross a young lady on her wedding day,' Dace declared. He thoroughly enjoyed being a family man, and he intended to savour every moment as his renowned friend followed in his wake. 'And anyway, I didn't see Lord Karkarn taking a paddling in the barracks last night – if I have to share the pain from your wedding rites I'm damned-well going to get some of the pleasure too!'

Vesna grinned at last. 'Aye, and cruel on you that I don't feel pain like a normal man these days.' He took a last look at the letter and pictured Tila writing it. 'Who am I to argue then?' he said, unable to restrain his smile.

'That's better; at last the face of a man getting married!' He grabbed Vesna by the sword-arm and started to drag him towards the barracks. 'Now come and have a last meal with us; there are still a few filthy stories about you that need to be aired before you mend your ways.'

Vesna complied willingly and they repaired to the officers' quarters, where, surrounded by men he'd fought alongside for years, he found himself the butt of altogether too many jokes. Vesna's grin was even wider by the time they filed out and mounted up to proceed north to the New District, where Tila's family lived.

While Vesna had the right to be married in the grandest temples in Tirah, too many were under the direct control of clerics hostile to the nobility. The cults had withdrawn their military threat as soon as it was clear the nobles would unite behind Lord Fernal, but tensions remained.

High Chaplain Mochyd was willing to conduct the service, so Tila had instead chosen an old shrine in the New District and scaled down the ceremony so Lord Fernal, along with half the guard, would not have to attend. As Vesna led a column of fifty Ghosts in dress uniform through the streets he felt a rare jangle of nerves in his stomach.

'Okay?' Dace asked, leaning in his saddle towards Vesna.

The Mortal-Aspect of Karkarn nodded, his face pale. 'Just wondering what comes tomorrow.'

'Tomorrow? You wake up with a sore head and a better girl than you deserve!' He laughed. 'What comes after that is in the hands of the Gods, so you just need to get the first bit right before you start worrying about the rest. And for pity's sake get that damn look off your face or she'll want me for her wedding night instead!'

Vesna laughed at the suggestion, but it shook him from his gloom. They continued in cheerful spirits the rest of the way, the Ghosts singing lewd marching songs until they were within sight of the shrine. A few yards out they dismounted and left their horses in the charge of a young lieutenant and formed up in two columns, flanking Vesna and Sir Dace.

The shrine was on a fork in the road, with a door at the top of a dozen stone steps on either street. It was an ancient building, even by the standards of Tirah, and comprised three concentric circles of pillars below a curved roof that rose to a sharp peak in the centre. Directly below that was the carved heart of the shrine: a strung bow resting in crooked stone branches, surrounded by images of Nartis' face and stylised lightning bolts.

Behind the shrine was a raised garden, enclosed by a stone balustrade, that stretched twenty yards to the stone side wall of the building behind it. Over the slanted roof of the shrine itself he could see a pair of trees that shaded the garden.

There was quite a gathering there, despite this being a restrained affair. A group of nobles clad in all their formal finery were gathered around the steps, while Tila's immediate family, the High Chaplain and a handful of her closest friends stood around the heart of the shrine.

As he approached, Tila stepped into view from behind the High Chaplain. His beaming bride was wearing a formal dress of blue and white, its simplicity serving to highlight her beauty. Her head was partially covered by a matching blue shawl embroidered with white and gold, and she wore charms to various Gods and Goddesses woven into her hair – a wedding was the only time all Gods were welcome at any temple, so Tila wore her favourite charms safely.

Vesna felt a pang of guilt. The only God accompanying him to his wedding was Karkarn, the God of War. All Gods might be welcome to bless a wedding, but some more so than others, he suspected.

'*Now, my Iron General,*' said a cold voice in his mind, '*do you ask my blessing on this happy day?*'

'*I do, Lord Karkarn,*' Vesna replied silently. '*Above all other Gods I ask your blessing.*'

'*And it is so granted,*' Karkarn replied. '*Just remember the saying; "War is a jealous mistress" – never has it been so true.*' Without waiting for a response Karkarn receded into the depths of Vesna's mind, returning to the distant echo that was a constant presence. Vesna understood his God's meaning.

He fell in behind his sentinel and Sir Dace led him up the steps, calling his greetings to those assembled. Tila's father stepped forward and Vesna bowed low to the man. Introl was a slim man with weak eyes; he looked fragile compared with his son-in-law-to-be. Vesna knelt and unbuckled his sword and Introl took it. Next Vesna pulled off his tunic, fumbling a moment with the toggles that had been added to his left side so it could be pulled over his black-iron-encased arm. His stomach tensed instinctively as the cool air rushed in and enveloped him, but then the sensation faded.

Vesna chanced a look up at Tila; she was watching him with a half-smile on her lips. The other women in the party didn't look so impressed – Vesna's broad chest was as heavily muscled as any man there, but the scars on his torso from past injuries were now deep red, and starkly obvious. He might be in good condition for a man approaching forty summers, but there was no doubt his body was a monument to the abuse it had received during years of military service. The sight was clearly shocking to Lady Introl and her sisters, but Tila blew him a kiss.

He grinned, then quickly lowered his eyes as Master Introl threw a white sheet over Vesna's shoulders, unsnagging it as it caught on his jutting pauldron, symbolically clothing him. He rose and continued up the steps to Tila's side.

As he looked at the faces assembled around the shrine he caught sight of Carel at the rear and felt a knot in his stomach. The marshal was dressed formally, but there was little joy on the old soldier's face. He stood just outside the consecrated area of the shrine, under the garden's trees, where the ashes of the dead were scattered. Vesna offered him a half-bow, trying not to dislodge the sheet, and received a cool nod in return. In that moment he knew their friendship was dead. Carel was attending the wedding out of love for Tila and as a memorial to Isak, nothing more.

In the next moment he saw Carel's eyes narrow, and the veteran was already starting down the steps, thumb on the catch on his sword-stick, by the time Vesna turned. A mutter ran around the crowd of witnesses and faces turned to the door Vesna had entered by.

The street was a hundred yards long, and it sloped up away from the shrine, leaving the Tower of Semar visible behind the buildings. There seemed to be some sort of commotion at the head of the street as two Ghosts advanced towards a third, who drew a massive sword.

Vesna's breath caught as he tasted magic on the air and he saw two lightning-quick blows take out both Ghosts. As they fell Vesna saw Sir Dace and Swordmaster Pettir were already heading towards him, their weapons drawn – but before they'd gone more than a few steps Vesna saw the Ghost level a black longbow.

Without thinking Vesna called on the magic inside him, reaching out with his empty armoured hand at the archer. The Land fell away from his senses as blistering magic flowed over his body. As the archer fired, Vesna created a smoke-grey shield which appeared in the air to block the arrow before it reached the shrine – then, without warning, he felt the God of War invade his mind.

Before Vesna even had a chance to cry out Karkarn had wrestled control of the magic from his Mortal-Aspect and roughly ripped away the threads binding the shield together. It exploded in white-green light, the energies screaming as they were cast asunder.

Vesna froze in incomprehension as his divine-sharpened eyes watched the arrow race towards him. Then ingrained instinct kicked in and he turned himself left-side-on, bringing his armoured arm across his face to protect himself.

The arrow hit his forearm, driving the black-iron into his face as a searing flash of light exploded all around him. A thunderclap of shattering glass and the copper taste of magic filled the air as a spell blossomed into life upon impact. Vesna felt tiny teeth tearing at his back and shoulders as the force of the blow sent him reeling. He was forced back, barely keeping his feet, as he was buffeted by streams of magic flowing past him. Noise crashed against his ears, and dark stars burst in his eyes as a sudden weight of raw power enveloped him.

He staggered again as he heard the crash of glass on the shrine. The pain fled as a cold, black dread struck him in the gut. He tried to see, but he could make no sense of the blur before him. Shards of glass, droplets of blood and tiny pieces of linen and silk were whirling in the air like snowflakes, covering the shrine. His breath caught as a fragment of blue cloth caught by the storm whipped past his eyes and then, as suddenly as it had struck, the magic winked out of existence.

Vesna lurched forward, pieces of glass crunching under his boot. He alone was standing; the shrine had been scoured of everyone behind him. As he skidded on the blood he grabbed a pillar to steady himself. He felt empty as he saw the bodies at his feet. They were covered in blood from head to foot, their finery shredded by the lethal shards, and at first he could not recognise any of them. He made a grab for the nearest – a man ... He shoved the corpse aside and scrambled for the next.

From the back of his mind Karkarn's spirit cut through the panicked cloud of his thoughts and he focused on one body: Anad Introl, Tila's father.

He ran forward and pulled the man up. Introl was wrapped around a figure trapped underneath him, as if he had thrown himself on top as protection. His arms were slippery, and far too thin – distantly Vesna realised with horror they'd had been flensed to bone, and the wetness was his blood. A terrible pain was blossoming in his chest. The person he had been trying to protect was his beloved daughter.

Vesna felt a great scream building up inside him. Tila's face had been barely touched by the glass – Vesna could see only one small scratch on her forehead – but it was contorted in pain. He made to lift her body, but stopped, his heart pounding ... did she just *move*? He knelt, ignoring the lethal debris, and slipped one hand gently underneath her. Tila began to tremble, then took a shallow, shuddering gasp. Vesna's most ardent prayer and worst fears were realised: Tila was alive, but he could see she was grievously injured, her back sliced in ribbons ...

'No,' Vesna whispered, cradling his bride as gently as he could, 'lie still, stay with me.'

Tila's lips parted, as though she was about to speak, but even that slight movement sent a spasm of agony across her face.

'Hush now,' Vesna whispered, half-sobbing with terror, 'dearest love, Tila, stay with me . . .'

He saw her eyes focus on him suddenly as his voice momentarily cut through her pain. She looked into his eyes so intensely that he felt her touch his soul . . . then, with a tiny gasp, she was gone. Her bloodied body went limp in his arms, and Vesna screwed his eyes closed and set loose the scream that had been building, howling like the very damned. His entire body shook, and his cry filled his ears, but nothing could blank out the pain that was all-encompassing . . .

When his breath finally gave way and he stopped, he gasped, 'Karkarn, do something!'

'I am no healer,' came the growling reply, 'and Death's die is cast.' A wisp of light stroked her cheek, a last goodbye. 'But she will be honoured in death. The Bringers of the Slain shall escort her on Ghain's slopes and see her untroubled to the land of no time.'

Vesna looked around in desperation, but there was no one: the icons had been destroyed, the people brutalised beyond recognition. 'You can do nothing?'

'No more for her.'

Something in Karkarn's voice made Vesna look up. He saw his sword lying discarded on the ground, the scabbard reduced to slivers of leather.

'What was that?'

'A weapon designed to bypass whatever first defence you offered. Had the shield remained, you would be dead.'

Vesna turned back to his bride. The pain was gone from Tila's pale face; she looked peaceful, as if she were sleeping beside him. He bent and kissed her on her lips.

Then he reached for the sword.

'Get me there,' Vesna rasped, pointing to the other end of the street as he rose, 'and keep out of my way.'

Karkarn did not reply, but Vesna felt a force close about his shoulders and wrench him from the ground. His vision blurred as he was moved through the magic-heavy air. Dark shapes flashed past, then he was tumbling forward. He landed heavily, driven to his knees by the impact, but he didn't wait for his senses to return; his sword was up and ready to ward off a blow—

—that never came.

Vesna blinked, but the archer hadn't moved. The man wore the uniform of a Ghost cavalryman, but there was something blank about his face that made Vesna realise it was unnatural. He narrowed his eyes, trying to focus, and his divine-touched senses cut through the illusion – but as he felt a terrible pressure built around his eyes, he barely registered the long, narrow features of a true Elf, let alone felt surprise. His legs threatened to give way for a moment before Karkarn's divine touch dissipated the clouding grief.

It was pierced by the fierce white light of hate, as palpable and strong as a daemon rising from the Dark Place.

The Elf laughed and unhooked something from its throat. The illusion fell away, leaving a slender figure in dark, functional clothes, over which was draped one of the Ghosts' black-and-white tabards. It had an unearthly beauty, as much female as male, but its body shape was clearly male, even if it lacked Vesna's muscular bulk.

As Vesna watched it nonchalantly tore off the tabard, revealing dragons on its tunic and belt-buckle. The Elf's cold regard reminded Vesna of Genedel's unblinking stare after the dragon had won the battle of Chir Plains for the Farlan.

'So this is what the Gods turn to?' the Elf commented in its own tongue, sneering. 'A magic-twisted ape?'

Vesna realised he was half-naked, and bleeding from a dozen small cuts, and his body was slick with sweat and blood – *Tila's* blood. He advanced on the Elf without speaking. There was nothing he wished to say. It retreated casually, dropping its longbow and tugging a large sword from a loop at its hip. Something at the back of Vesna's mind screamed danger at the sight of that copper blade, and he realised he'd seen the sword before – in the hands of the white-eye Chalat, former Lord of the Chetse.

The weapon was like Eolis, far more powerful than his own minor blade. Vesna had seen Isak use Eolis to shear right through other magic-hardened weapons. How well his armoured arm would fare against such a powerful artefact, Vesna had no way of knowing. Unbidden, Tila's face swam before his eyes and Vesna felt his gut tighten. She had been murdered by someone – some *thing* – that neither knew her name nor cared ... But he would whisper her name as he killed the creature; he would scream her name in his face as it choked on its own blood.

The Elf lazily swept the ancient weapon left and right, loosening its shoulder, observing the Mortal-Aspect's reaction. It made the blade look almost weightless in its grasp.

Vesna did nothing. He ignored the movement, just stared straight into his enemy's eyes. He let his rage warm his muscles.

Without warning the Elf exploded forward, swinging his great sword at Vesna's unprotected head, but the count stepped back out of range and flowed right, parrying the follow-up blow aimed at his ribs. He used his armoured knuckles to try to beat the sword wide and create an opening for himself, but the Elf avoided his lunge with ease.

So you do know how to fight, Vesna thought, forcing himself to block out every thought beyond the enemy in front of him. *Time to change the game.*

With a thought he flooded his body with magic, raw coursing power that thrummed through his bones and crackled over his armour, the same way he'd seen Isak do it, many times before. White-hot sparks hissed and danced as they wrapped his gauntlet with spitting power. When he saw the Elf's eyes shift towards it, he felt cold satisfaction: he knew he had made it uncertain. He increased the flow of magic and let it bleed out over the ground around him, sending jagged lines of light snaking over the cobbles in all directions.

When the Elf glanced down, Vesna attacked.

Holding his sword in both hand he cut across the Elf's body, then down, then up. It gave ground as it parried each blow without much finesse, until it was able to plant its feet and start trading blows. The swords flashed through the air with unnatural speed, as the smallest nick might be enough to make the other hesitate.

Vesna's arm screamed under the jarring impact of the greater blade on his own, but he refused to slow down. He caught a high cut and blocked it, then stepped in towards the Elf and swung his armoured fist at its face. Magic crackled in the air and the Elf howled as it stepped through the web of seething power and pushed its shoulder into Vesna's midriff.

Despite his greater bulk, Vesna felt the body-blow hit his chest like a hammer and found himself being driven back. He tried to punch the Elf in the shoulder in return, but he swung short and had to throw himself to one side, the copper sword just missing his stomach.

Vesna found himself with a moment to regain his balance while the Elf was shaking its head from side to side and cursing – its cheeks and narrow chin were scorched black by the magic, and only its height had saved it from being blinded.

Suddenly, each realising at the same instant that the other was catching their breath, they both ran forward—

They barely avoided impaling themselves on each other's swords, but Vesna had the faster reactions; he had twisted left, and used his own sword to force the Elf's weapon aside, at the same time stepping close and smashing his armoured elbow into its arm. For a moment he thought he had it – then he felt the resistance vanish as it spun away.

Vesna lurched to the right as the Elf turned right around and lunged for his face. He twisted violently, avoiding being impaled, but he felt the weapon bite into his pauldron, slicing away a chunk of metal. He batted the blade away with his left arm, ducked and thrust his own sword underneath it, hearing metal clash with metal, before he was facing his enemy again.

He cut high, then low, and the Elf blocked, then as his third strike whistled through the air the Elf stabbed at his left shoulder, trying to bring the copper sword's power to bear, but Vesna twisted out of reach and attacked again, relentlessly. He pressed forward, parrying blows, trying to get inside its guard, but when he got close, it kicked out at his leg with frightening speed.

He moved just in time, turning his half-bent knee into the blow, and though pain exploded in his kneecap, he was ready and it didn't knock him over. Vesna saw the impact of its kick had hurt the Elf too; it had retreated a step. Scowling, it charged straight back into the fray, hoping to take advantage of Vesna's disorientation, but it moved too slowly and he dodged, deflecting the copper sword as it swung past him.

Vesna struck at the Elf's back, but he missed, his reach too short. Now the monstrous copper sword arced down towards his head and this time when Vesna tried to move, his feet failed him and he froze, his arm still extended in the lunge as he watched his own death coming towards him.

At the last moment he threw his left arm up, as he had at the shrine, and the broadsword smashed down onto his armoured limb in a coruscating explosion of light and pain. The force drove him to one knee and he swung blindly at the Elf's ankle, but its knee hit his face before his blow could connect.

The impact snapped his head back, but his greater bulk let him ride the blow and he brought his sword up to catch the lower edge of the Elf's gleaming weapon. He forced it up and hooked his armoured arm over the flat of the blade. The Elf tried to lift it away, but that only succeeded in helping Vesna to his feet again.

Releasing his grip on his own sword, he tugged down with his left hand to pivot his weapon around the other blade. The momentum of the movement brought the hilt up and Vesna, turning away from the Elf, ignored a vicious punch to his kidneys, grabbed his sword in a reverse grip and jerked it back as hard as he could.

His aim was true and the sword bit deep into the Elf's guts. The Elf staggered under the force of Vesna's blow, and its own blade clattered to the ground as its hands moved to its belly.

A gout of blood gushed onto the cobbles as the Elf managed to pull itself off the weapon on which it was impaled.

Vesna turned and chopped down into the back of its right knee, nearly severing the joint. The Elf dropped, but before it could hit the ground Vesna had grabbed it by the throat with his left hand.

'Her name was *Tila*,' he shouted, and raised his reversed sword. He punched the pommel into the Elf's beautifully shaped nose.

The Elf gurgled something, but Vesna couldn't make out the words, nor did he care. He held it upright, ignoring the blood that spilled out over his polished boots. He punched its face again and again until the right-hand side was reduced to a pulp.

'Her name was Tila,' he repeated in a whisper, and the boiling sea of rage inside him suddenly drained away. He released the Elf and it crashed onto the cobbled street, where it squirmed weakly, pawing at the wound to its stomach. Dark blood had drenched its clothes, but it had some time left yet. Normally a soldier would pray to Karkarn for such a wound to be quick, but as Vesna stared down at the mewling figure at his feet, no words would come. He realised tears were falling down his cheeks and he sank to his knees, his strength sapped. His hands shook and the aching blackness in his stomach returned, but as the Elf died he did not move, only trembled, sobbing silently as Tila's face filled his mind. Above him, thunder split the clouds.

CHAPTER 25

'Major, we've found the trail!'

Captain Hain and Major Darn turned to see a sergeant of the scouts running up to them. Though it was midday, the sun had crept behind a cloud as they stopped to rest and sketch their route. The Menin maps of Narkang lands were poor and untrustworthy; more than once that week they'd been forced to stop and retrace their steps as rivers appeared to block their way, or some other obstacle appeared, making them wonder whether they'd misread the things entirely, or if the original cartographers had been blind drunk when they drew these particular maps.

'How far?' Major Darn asked once the scout had reached them. He grinned at the prospect of catching up with the enemy at last, some four hundred men, the remains of a small town's garrison that had fled when the Menin approached.

'An hour's march, no more.'

Major Darn looked past the scout. An elongated hump of ground stood between his men and the enemy; what was marked as just a blob on the map was in fact a steep rise, and now he was within sight of it Darn knew he'd have to take his troops around.

'The map says woods all beyond that,' he said, pointing at the hill.

'Some, aye, sir, but it's grassland for the main – the forest's north o' it, dense ground – it'd be a bastard t'march through, no space t'move. The road leads to a village, two miles past, and there's probably another a few beyond that, too. The way they're going they'll be just past t'village – sorry bunch o' stragglers they look now too. There's open ground all the way left o' the hill; we'll catch 'em before t'day's out.'

'I've heard this before,' Darn growled, unconsciously fingering a roughly stitched cut on his cheek, 'and I've lost my taste for taking the inviting option.'

The last fleeing garrison they'd tried to catch had been a decoy. In his eagerness to chase them down, Colonel Uresh, Major Darn's legion commander, had sent him on ahead without waiting for scouts to find out how many men were left in the town. The first division had been badly mauled that day, despite Darn's efforts to pull them out, and Uresh, realising his mistake, had walked straight into another when he charged straight in with the second division.

They lost the colonel and two hundred men that day, a quarter of their remaining troops, with as many again injured. The previous day Major Darn had been a middle-aged man with prematurely grey hair; this morning the years looked to have caught him up.

'You don't want to follow 'em?' Hain said, surprised. For days now Major Darn had looked like a man champing at the bit to exact some revenge.

'Of course I do, but how many straight engagements have we had since crossing the border?' There was no doubt the Narkang forces were engaged in a fighting retreat. They might be steadily giving ground, but they were avoiding direct confrontation in favour of guerrilla tactics, ambushing the Menin wherever they could hurt the invaders. They were only a few days' ride from Aroth, the most easterly of King Emin's cities, and had yet to see a real battle.

He looked at his captains and the Dharai assembled around him. He wasn't surprised when the two warrior-monks remained silent – they were impassive at the best of times – but none of the captains spoke either.

'There's scrub all round that hill, easy enough to hide troops in if you're looking to ambush,' Darn continued, 'unless you got close?' He looked at the scout.

'No, sir, but ain't many going t'hide there, doubt enough t'worry us – the garrison's too far away, couldn't double-back fast enough t'catch us on both sides without bein' too blown t'be any use.'

'There could be more in the trees on the right flank,' Darn said dismissively, 'enough men to strafe us.'

'Nothing at our backs still,' the scout said, looking anxious about contradicting the major, however certain he was. 'We'd've seen anyone strong enough t'threaten more'n a division o' heavy infantry. My men din't go inta the woods, but they were close enough t'see signs o' a legion easy enough.'

Darn gave a curt nod. 'I understand, sergeant, but the fact remains this is a fine place for an ambush and I don't want to be surprised again.'

'Send the cavalry through the trees? Maybe ahead of a regiment or two? We meet on the other side and if anyone's in between they're going to get it from both sides,' Hain wondered aloud.

Darn shook his head. 'It leaves us fractured. Neither flank can move fast, and if there is an ambush waiting, it gives them what they're looking for. We've barely more than a company of cavalry, including the scouts, and that's not enough to be of use if they're hit. However, even a regiment or two on the hill or in the trees can wait for us to pass, then follow us – and if we do that, we're the ones getting it from both sides. While they're sticking us full of arrows and running away if we react, that garrison'll make up the ground in double-quick time – and I'll bet they'll miraculously stop looking like a sorry rabble. Either way we're left chasing our arses like half-witted dogs.'

'Where's a bloody scryer when you want one?' Hain growled. 'Even that piss-poor fool was better'n nothing.'

An infiltrator had somehow managed to stay concealed in the high branches of an oak while the Menin made camp around it, and he'd managed to assassinate their only mage before he'd gone down fighting. What had shocked Hain the most was the assassin's youth – he was fearless and beardless, and well short of his twentieth summer. A fanatical loyalty to one's lord was hardly surprising to a Menin, but Hain had never before seen it shine so fiercely in the eyes of an enemy.

'Our God will provide,' rumbled the smaller of the Dharai unexpectedly. The shaven-headed monk had as many scars as wrinkles on his face, and the diagonal band of swirling tattoo crossing one eye showed him to be a Dharach, the highest rank. But even those with years of military experience rarely interfered with decisions, choosing instead stoic acceptance of orders.

The soldiers all turned in surprise as he continued, 'The hill is too steep for troops, but not for my Dharai. If there are men there, we will find them.'

'If there are men there, you'll be cut to bloody pieces,' Major Darn retorted bluntly.

'If that is Lord Karkarn's will,' the Dharach said solemnly.

'Karkarn's will be—' Darn snapped his mouth shut before he finished the sentence and swallowed his irritation. 'That is to say, Dharach,' he continued rather more respectfully, 'I do not intend to sacrifice any troops today, certainly not those of your calibre. No, the cavalry scouts will lead the way, and we will move in two blocks, one wide, one tight behind the hill. The cavalry will sweep the way before we advance. We'll deal with the garrison troops tomorrow.'

'No, Major. If we die in battle, then that is Lord Karkarn's will, but one more day may see them to safety,' the monk said firmly. He hefted his halberd, damascened to echo the tattoos on his face, and pointed northwest. 'We are too close to Aroth to delay. It is our calling to embrace such risks, to perform the twelve noble actions when such deeds are required. It is how we honour our God.'

Darn had no actual authority over the Dharai, and it was obvious he had no say in the matter now. The Dharach had made his decision, and they were separate from the army structure precisely for such eventualities.

Darn scowled, his lip twitching as he stroked the stitches in his cheek. 'So be it. Drummer, signal the advance. Dharach, get your men up that hill, double-time.'

'Oh fuck me,' moaned the lookout, turning round in search of his officer, 'Sir, the bastards are sendin' a company o'men right over us.'

Doranei scrambled after Count Reshar as the burly nobleman went forward to join the lookout. Crawling on his belly, the King's Man wormed his way through the thick tufts of grass until he had a view of the other side. He winced as the pommel of his new sword caught him on a long cut down the side of his head. The cut had been fire-sealed by Ebarn, the Brotherhood's female battle-mage – not a fun way of dealing with injuries, but it was the best patch-up she could offer in the circumstances, and it was a fair defence against infection.

'We'll have to pull back,' Count Reshar muttered to Doranei, keeping his eyes on the red-robed figures at the bottom of the hill. 'Back into the woods, where they can't see us.'

'Where you think they're going next?' Doranei said firmly. 'We hold here.'

The count turned as best he could, anger on his face. '*Master* Doranei, you are not a man of rank nor a man of title and you are not the one giving the orders here: you will do whatever in the Dark Place I tell you to do!' he snarled.

Doranei matched the look. Count Reshar was a good soldier, and he was a count, but Doranei was a King's Man and he knew the full story. 'Make no mistake, my Lord, my orders come from the king,' he said softly.' You agree with me when I tell you what we doing, or I will take command. Do you understand me?'

'You've lost your mind, man,' the count hissed, his face darkening as he tried to stop himself from bellowing. He was an experienced officer and utterly loyal, and he had raised no objection to the presence of a King's Man in his regiment, however obviously he disliked it. 'We've a few minutes before they discover us, and after that we're as good as dead.'

Doranei's expression was one of a man resigned to his fate. 'We hold here,' he said firmly.

'I will not condemn these men to death!'

'The decision ain't yours to make. If you prefer I can kill you now, waste of a good soldier or no.'

Doranei's tone didn't leave any room for uncertainty and Count Reshar hesitated. He was dressed like the rest of them, not too proud to wear dull, dirty leathers and mail instead of noble battle-colours. Only the small bronze device on his collar and the quality of his weapons indicated his rank.

'Why?' he asked at last.

Doranei scowled. The last thing he wanted to do was admit their fate had been decided days ago. He settled on part of the truth. 'This legion needs to be held up, and we're on the best defensive ground.'

'How long do you think we can hold?' he asked in disbelief.

'We hold as long as we can.'

'Alone?'

Doranei shrugged and looked to the west, towards the village and the remaining garrison regiments. 'You gave the others their orders; you know how they'll react.'

'We're outnumbered and facing heavy infantry!'

Doranei craned around the count to check on the progress of the men ascending the hill. A band of sunshine drifted over them, sweeping the slope with momentary brightness before moving on towards the hump of road that went around the hill. It wasn't an easy climb and they were taking their time, picking their way along a winding path to avoid the steepest parts. They were obviously not normal troops: they weren't in livery but red-robes, longer than anything a soldier would wear.

Great, some sort of élite, Doranei thought sourly. He looked back at his own men: a score of archers of varying ability, the same again of green recruits, two score regular infantry, Mage Ebarn and Veil of the Brotherhood. There had been one more of the king's élite agents, but Horle had died in their first raid on Menin lines.

'Outnumbered on high ground,' Doranei said at last, 'it's as good a place as any to be outnumbered. They'll think twice about trying to take us, and they can't leave us here.'

'They can detach two regiments to guard their backs and still roll right over the garrison troops!' Count Reshar's voice was anxious now as he also looked down the slope. 'Ah damn, we'll never get out of sight in time now!'

'Then we fight,' Doranei said plainly. 'Get the archers here and start picking off some of those red robes. If the main troop moves past we'll snipe at their rear, and if they assault the hill we'll hold our ground.'

'We don't stand a chance,' snapped the count, even as he gestured for the archers to move up.

'If you can't take a joke . . .' Doranei muttered under his breath.

Count Reshar spat on the dusty ground. 'You've killed us all,' he said, not meeting Doranei's eyes.

The King's Man reached out and grabbed him by the throat, and the count gave a croak of shock. Doranei hauled the man bodily towards him, swatting away his hands as he attempted to free himself of Doranei's grip. 'Now you listen to me,' he growled, dragging Count Reshar's face to within inches of his own, 'this ain't some border skirmish! Thousands are dead already, and if we're to win, it'll be off the back o' sacrifice. Get that into your thick skull and deal with it. There's no room for anything else.'

'Doranei,' Veil called from behind him, 'archers ready.'

The King's Man released the nobleman and looked back at his friend. Veil matched the look. His blank expression would be enough of a reminder to his Brother to curb his temper.

Veil's dark hair poked out from under a small helm and spilled onto his curved pauldrons. In fire-blackened greaves and vambraces he was as heavily armoured as Doranei had ever seen him. Veil looked as unperturbed as ever, but Doranei didn't like it: the slim King's Man looked out of place on a battlefield, however good a street fighter he was. This was even less Veil's domain than it was Doranei's.

'Archers, aye,' Doranei said, ducking his head in acknowledgement. 'Time to make our presence felt.'

At Veil's order the twenty-odd archers edged over the crest of the hill and took up position. Doranei, crouched just behind them, watched the first of the attackers fall – they were barely forty yards downslope, and sitting targets whether they advanced or retreated. Two men fell in the first volley, and three more as the attackers struggled on up the slope. Doranei guessed they were warrior-monks of Karkarn, in which case it was a safe bet they could put those halberds to good use, but their ascent would be slow.

'Ebarn,' Doranei called, beckoning the stocky woman over. 'Give them something to make the rest of 'em think twice, Veil, signal the troops.'

As Veil went to signal the garrison soldiers Ebarn joined Doranei. She let her dirty green cape fall from her shoulders, revealing a rust-coloured tunic adorned with thin silver chains and crystal shards. As she knelt, trails of light began to drift over her body, slipping from one silver chain to the next, then swirling around the shards. as though driven by a breeze Doranei couldn't feel.

The dancing strands of light became a flurry, changing from white to yellow and orange and as Ebarn raised her arms as though in supplication, fat coils of flame raced up them. With a shout, she threw her arms forward and twin lances of flame streaked away towards the monks. One was caught full on and consumed, and as he fell back into a comrade, he too was set alight. The other streak of flame hit the ground and a fiery barrier sprang up across the enemy's path. As the monks stopped for a moment the Narkang archers took advantage, catching one more in the throat.

The monks turned and began to make their way around the flames.

'First squad to the left flank,' Count Reshar called in a hoarse voice, 'second squad up on the peak.'

Doranei looked at the ground where they would meet as Ebarn unleashed more scorching magic to thin the enemy ranks further. The archers were on an outcrop that dipped away steeply in front, but a curved slope arced round that up to their left, the natural path up the slope and the one the monks were making for. They had their heads down and their legs were pumping as they struggled up the hill. It was madness for them to keep coming – but they were doing it all the same.

'Better you than us,' he said aloud, ignoring the look he received from Count Reshar as he unshipped the large weapon slung on his back. Aracnan's sword still felt oversized and awkward in his hands, and its speckled black surface looked unreal in the afternoon sun. Behind the monks the Menin legion had been spurred into activity, breaking into defensive regimental blocks, the first of which had already disappeared out of sight around the hill. The rearmost block dissolved and began to follow the monks, but laden with armour and shields they'd be even slower to get to the battle ground.

'They're sending the cavalry around,' a sergeant called from the right flank.

Doranei looked behind him. There were two score cavalrymen left, and he doubted they'd try and ascend the hill – that would leave them no room to manoeuvre, and even the shallow part of the slope would prove treacherous on horseback.

They're going to try to slow up the garrison, he realised. *We're both trying to make the other side hesitate.*

Veil appeared on Doranei's left, weapon in hand, as the count waved forward the two squads of recruits. They assembled behind the archers, waiting until the monks were no more than ten yards away, then Doranei yelled for them to charge. With spears levelled they ran into the group, screaming wildly, with Doranei at the fore. He smashed aside the halberd of the first monk, cutting through the shaft with blinding speed, but the monk didn't hesitate, dropping to the ground and hammering the shaft into Doranei's shin as the

King's Man slashed down at his face. Doranei took the blow on his greave and beheaded the man with his next blow. He almost overbalanced as the magic-imbued sword parted flesh with frightening ease, just avoiding being spitted by one of his own men.

Veil appeared in his lee and deflected a halberd down into the ground with his shield, only to be kicked in the ribs by the Menin monk. He staggered, his full weight keeping the halberd down, while the enemy tugged at it, desperate to free it. Doranei never gave him the chance, and hammered the pommel of his sword into the man's face. The monk fell without a sound, but Doranei was already throwing himself at the next man.

Yells from either side told him the flanking squads had engaged, but he was too busy with the remaining two monks ahead of him. He dispatched them both with savage ease, looked around and saw one remaining monk behind him, desperately fending off Veil – only to be spitted by a recruit. Half a dozen more were reeling under the assault from the right and as they faltered, the recruits couldn't resist what looked like an easy target and charged forward wildly.

One monk died in the initial rush, but the others exploited the gap in the line and began to lay about them with their halberds, felling four of the young men in a matter of seconds – but the second squad, finding themselves presented with unarmoured backs, cut the monks down where they stood.

A cheer died in the throat of the nearest man as Doranei turned and glowered at him.

'That's as good as it'll get,' he bellowed at the youth, 'so shut up. You only cheer if you last the day.'

The soldier averted his eyes quickly and muttered an apology. Doranei continued to glare until Veil moved between the two, then it was Doranei's turn to look abashed.

Veil put his hand on Doranei's shoulder. 'Peace, my friend,' he said softly, 'you've enough enemies already down there, too many even for your grief.'

My grief only needs one, Doranei thought with a heavy heart. 'Grief is a shadow,' he said, quoting King Emin's words whenever one of the Brotherhood was killed.

Veil nodded. 'And we don't submit to shadows,' he said fiercely. 'We can mourn when the war is won.' He thumped Doranei on the chest with his fist and turned. 'Let's see what they're up to back here.'

Doranei followed him back to their previous position and the two men looked down at the grassy plain leading to the village. The first of the Menin infantry regiments had rounded the hill: five untidy ranks of twenty. In the distance he could see the garrison troops advancing about half a mile off. Their orders were to approach close enough to threaten, but to retreat when threatened themselves, unless Doranei's band had attacked. A red flag fluttered nearby, the signal they were in need of support.

'We've made them think at least,' Ebarn commented, joining the pair, 'but we haven't got enough arrows to deal with a full assault.'

Veil nodded. 'Let's hope you've given 'em cause not to.'

'They'll have to,' Doranei said. 'They can't leave us sitting behind them while they chase those garrison troops – and they won't turn tail and run.'

'More's the pity,' Ebarn agreed. 'Reckon we've got some time; they don't look like men in a hurry.'

'Waiting for nightfall?' Veil wondered. 'If we can't see to shoot the ascent's a damned sight easier.' He pointed. 'The slope there'd be easy enough.'

'Means they can't see what we're up to, though. Once night falls we creep down the poorly defended side and cut throats on our way.'

'It won't get to that,' Doranei pronounced. 'They know we'll fuck off soon as it gets dark, so they won't wait.'

'Aye,' Veil agreed in a resigned voice, 'they're élite infantry; they know what they're about. They've got all afternoon to advance behind shields up that slope. We either attack a greater number behind a shield wall or head down and find enough waiting to slow us up 'til we get it both ways. The garrison troops won't get too close, in case they get pinned down by cavalry.'

'So we let them come at us.'

'You sure?' Veil asked quietly.

'Aye, no other choice. Archers and one squad stay here, deal with those coming up on our backs. The rest we string in a defensive line, hold 'em off as long as we can. The garrison can snipe at their backs. Maybe we can string it out 'til nightfall.'

'That gives Daken a chance,' Veil agreed, 'but the king won't want to pay the price of Ebarn for it.'

Only Veil and Ebarn knew Doranei's full orders: to delay this legion long enough to give a mobile strike force time to slip in behind them. The five-thousand strong force commanded by Daken, the white-eye mercenary, comprised the finest troops King Emin could put together. Thus far his tactic had been one of steady retreat and ambush, using local knowledge to stay ahead of the Menin.

The invaders had had to break up their larger armies as they were forced to chase many smaller units. Now the pattern had been established, they were relying on the Menin not expecting a full-scale assault – and certainly not one with the ferocity the Mad Axe was likely to bring.

'If that's what it'll cost, that's what we pay,' Doranei said after a while. He knew Ebarn was a superb military asset, and one the king would be loath to lose, but Emin Thonal would not shy from the deed if it dealt the enemy a grievous hurt.

'The pair of you are too important,' Veil insisted. 'If we last 'til dusk, you must slip away.'

Doranei met his friend's determined gaze. 'And leave a Brother to die? Fuck you, not again.'

From the shade of the trees two figures in all-black armour watched the Menin regiments. They were alone in the forest except for their horses, tethered nearby.

'These tactics are somewhat familiar,' Koezh commented. 'Perhaps someone should tell King Emin what happened last time.'

'I suspect he is fully aware,' his sister said. 'No doubt it was part of the attraction.'

'Ever contemptuous of men of war, dear sister – I thought you had a higher opinion of him than that.'

Zhia turned to look at her brother, but Koezh's helm was down and she could discern little from the whorled black metal. 'Genius has its own concerns. Would you wager King Emin has never refought Aryn Bwr's wars in theory and wondered where he could surpass him?'

'Perhaps not,' Koezh admitted. Without taking his eyes off the soldiers ahead, he sat down on the raised root of the oak tree shading them from the afternoon sun. With fingers made clumsy by gauntlets Koezh unfastened the baldric holding his sword on his back and placed the weapon on his lap.

'The birds are silent,' he said after a long pause. He looked around at the trees. The forest was unnaturally quiet. 'Do you think that's our fault, or the soldiers?'

'You know the answer,' Zhia said sharply, 'so save the banalities for your servants back home.'

'Really, sister, it's not like you to get so emotional over a pretty face.' Koezh leaned forward to look at her face. 'Do you intend to intervene?'

'You would prefer me to leave him to his fate?'

Koezh made a noncommittal sound. 'He was present at Aracnan's death, a man I have known for a long time.'

'A man who deceived you over his allegiances,' Zhia pointed out, 'and one I doubt you owed a debt of any significance.'

'It sounds like you do intend to.' When Zhia didn't respond Koezh leaned back against the trunk of the oak. 'I take it back; I have seen this sentimentality of yours before – once, at any rate.'

'Careful, Koezh,' Zhia warned, 'let's not discuss the past too deeply. Of those left to blame for my curse, you are principal among them.'

'I do not deny it. I merely sought to remind you that sentimentality in war can only ever lead to hurt. I joined Aryn Bwr out of belief; you followed him out of love.'

Zhia touched her fingers to the Crystal Skull fused to her cuirass. The Skull was flattened to a disc on the metal's surface, the round plate underneath it etched to show a death's head when covered by a Crystal Skull. She had never been able to decide whether that was a joke of Aryn Bwr's, or not. The last king had forged both, and each of the Vukotic suits of armour had a similar plate, but his humour had sometimes been alien and unknowable, even to the young woman who shared his bed for so many years.

'Saving him does not mean I join a cause,' she said, and Koezh tasted magic blossom on the air, 'but nor will I stand by and watch him die.'

Koezh didn't reply as he watched his sister deftly sculpt a spell. It was far beyond the skill of most mages: a complex, intricate blend of arcane words and shapes that he sensed hovering in the air like a cloud of moths drawn to her flame.

Indeed it does not, he thought as Zhia drew the spell into the body of the Skull, placing one hand over it and crouching to place the other flat on the ground. *What will force you to choose, I wonder? Love brought you to ruin during the Great War; is that why you avoided Doranei before the Farlan arrived outside Byora? Do you fear making the same mistakes again, or are we beyond mistakes, just as we are beyond redemption?*

CHAPTER 26

Corl went to the window again and peered down at the street below. Sundown had come and gone without remark by those outside, only Corl and his two companions seemed to have noticed. Within their room all was calm, outside reigned chaos more frenzied and desperate than usual. Tirah was draped in the colours of high summer; a haphazard network of ropes linked the rooftops, from which trailed twists of ribbon and cloth – in bright greens and yellows, for the main. In the sky, long furrows of cloud whipped by overhead, swallowing starlight like ravening dragons.

From his narrow window Corl could see effigies of half a dozen Gods, hanging from the ropes and painted on walls. Nartis was present, of course, but this was one of the few days when he was outnumbered in the Farlan cities. Tsatach, Belarannar and Kitar were just as dominant, while the Goddesses of Love were cheered and toasted as a trio, even at this late hour when the thoughts of many had turned to worship Etesia, Goddess of Lust.

A statue of Vrest made of sticks and animal skins stood tall over long spits of pork that dripped into a makeshift fire-pit just off the main street. As Corl watched, the woman tending it cut the first choice slice and tossed to her drooling dog, an offering to the God of Beasts. Corl smiled, remembering the festivals of his childhood, how the wonder had filled his whole body. Fate had taken him on difficult paths since then, but the memories endured, and despite his chosen profession, Corl remembered the boy he had been with a light heart.

It was the Midsummer's Day Festival, and throughout Tirah the drink had been flowing freely for hours. Corl leaned out of the window again to check on the old woman passed out below – she'd found herself a snug little nook in a stack of wooden pallets just as the sun had been falling; either she was so drunk she couldn't remember the way home, or she had no home to return to and was taking advantage of the cheap festival beer to solve her problems for a night.

Corl hadn't been the only one to spot her settling down to sleep it off; if he'd not whistled and wagged a warning finger at the pair of youths sidling up to her hiding spot, she'd probably have had those problems solved forever. As it was, they'd left her alone. He could make out the outline of her bundled shape well enough to see it hadn't been disturbed since last he checked.

There would be rich pickings elsewhere for the youths, Corl had no illusions about that, but it wasn't just the risk of their actions attracting the Palace Guard that prompted his intervention. It was Midsummer's Day, and whatever he had planned for the dark hours of night, Corl was not a man angry at the Land, a detail that had served him well over the years. His childhood had been poor but loving, and Midsummer's Day remained a fond memory for him. No one deserved to be robbed and murdered on this day if he could prevent it with a look.

Unless I'm being paid for it, o' course, Corl reminded himself. His scarred cheeks crinkled, distorting the tattoos and scars that had scared the boys off. Whether or not they understood the markings on his right cheek, few cutpurses would fail to recognise the mark of Kassalain on the other.

Those that don't, don't last too long.

The Goddess of Murder's shrine might be hidden away in the cellar of a long-abandoned house well away from the Temple District, but her mark was well known, and always afforded respect. Corl was a short man who didn't look that strong; without Kassalain's sign on his face, he'd have provided his mistress with many more offerings over the years as men mistook him for an easy target. The irony was not lost on the Priestess of Kassalain, but she was as fickle as her Goddess, she found the irony amusing.

'Not long now. Light the burner,' Corl called softly over his shoulder.

He received no reply; neither of them liked following his orders much, but Corl was well aware anyone who ended up a blade for hire was bound to have a few flaws. He'd worked with this pair on and off for several years now, and they respected his skills, enough to do what he told them, at least. The younger of the two, who called himself Orolay, was keen to join Corl as a devotee of Kassalain, but the older – Isen, a sour-faced ex-soldier like Corl, didn't care about anything beyond earning enough coin to survive.

In a city where the Hands of Fate, those devotees of the Lady trained as spies and assassins, had been numerous, there had been little work for the followers of the weaker Goddess of Murder. Corl was the best of those aligned to the hidden temple, but following the Lady's death, the priestess had started receiving overtures, a few making attempts to court the Goddess' favour. The most recent had provided them with a commission – some rat-faced foreigner needing a most unusual job done, and without the ability to do it himself. Whatever quarrel there might be was beyond Corl's fathoming, but the coin offered was good.

Corl caught a sniff of the pungent, earthy smoke coming from the burner on the table behind him and he turned. As he approached the table he wafted some of the smoke towards him, filling his lungs with it. He muttered a mantra to Kassalain and drew his longknife, holding it edge-on to the burner so the smoke caressed it, then repeating the gesture and saying a second mantra. He did the same with each of his weapons – two longknives, two shorter blades, a stiletto and a blowpipe – and with each there was a growing awareness of the textures under his fingers, the hang of his clothes on his body, the clamour of merriment surrounding their room like a cocoon. He gave a slight shiver of pleasure as the drug raced through his body; he felt a heady jolt in his muscles.

Corl ignored Orolay as the young man copied him, doing his best to smother his coughs on the drug-smoke. Isen drew his own fat knife with a studded finger-guard and tapped it on the table, then, that small gesture of respect done, fetched his costume and pulled it on over his regular clothes. Orolay and Corl followed suit a short while later. Corl's was the most dramatic – he'd found something approximating a Chetse's desert robe, albeit one he suspected would make a Chetse burst out laughing, but it came with a headdress that would hide his tattoos as effectively as it would protect against a desert wind.

Corl felt the drug-smoke increase its grip on him. It started with a tingle in his head: a bright, sparkling warmth that flowed down his spine and into his limbs. Orolay now had a broad grin, exhilarated by the sharpening effect of the drug on his senses. Isen refused to allow himself to enjoy it, but still the man shook out his arms and shoulders, flexing muscles now brimming with renewed energy. Corl smiled himself and tasted the air, breathing in the musky odour of the room and the dusty pine scent of its walls. He remembered the clouds racing outside and for a moment felt his spirit move with them, surging on with swift, joyful purpose.

Kassalain's Milk affected people differently. For Corl it heightened his senses – hyper-awareness of everything around him was her gift. As an assassin he valued that more than the sense of strength and invulnerability Isen got from the smoke.

Fast way to be killed, that, he thought, watching the taciturn man suddenly become animated, like a restless wolf. *Orolay's got it like me; maybe he'll make a decent devotee after all.*

'Come,' Corl breathed, savouring the delicious sensation of the word slipping out through his lips.

Isen moved forward so quickly only his sharpened reactions stopped him being hit with the door as Corl opened it and went through. Isen, desperate to be moving, was almost hopping behind Corl as the smaller man walked down the dark, narrow staircase to the open doorway of the tenement block. Laughter rang out from rooms on both sides: families celebrating together, having exhausted themselves dancing and cheering on the many entertainments.

The Chief Steward had supposedly distributed thousands of gold crowns so the population might drink to the memory of Lord Isak. Corl hadn't been able to tell if there had been genuine affection for the young white-eye, but his name was certainly being shouted in toast, so he guessed Chief Steward Lesarl would be satisfied. The cults were keeping a low profile this year – that was understandable given the place was teeming with soldiers ready to forcibly disarm any penitent forces stupid enough to get caught.

Corl chuckled to himself. Things certainly weren't dull around Tirah, not now at any rate, with the so-called peace treaty with the Menin overshadowed by the assassination attempt on Count Vesna. Some said it had been a beast from the Waste, but Corl took that with a pinch of salt; a friend heard it was Corl himself dead at the sword of Count Vesna – the man damn nearly shat himself with fright when he walked into a tavern to find Corl drinking at the bar.

It had been a hard few months, blood being spilled on all sides, but today was Midsummer's day and the people were damn well going to celebrate. The flutter of cloth above their heads was like a riot of swooping birds. That suited Corl, he thought, as he led them into the street to the tavern on the other side. *Lots of crowds to get lost in, none of 'em sober enough to notice much.* The door was wide open and some drunk was leading a song within, but there was also a tapped barrel outside manned by a man with thick arms and a thicker waist. He was taller than any of the three assassins, and his hair hung about his shoulders in many braids, each of which was tied with a red ribbon. Corl noticed the man had one finger missing, and a mass of scars down his wrist.

A veteran, he thought, *one who cashed in better than I did when he retired.* He inclined his head respectfully to a fellow ex-soldier and ordered two beers for his comrades and a jug of wine for himself. The desert-robe trembled in the breeze, flattening against his front and leaping madly behind him. Corl could feel the air rush past his body, given form by the long, smooth cloth.

'You seen battle?' the barman said cheerily, clearly having sampled his own wares during the day. 'Got soldier's eyes, y'have.'

'Aye, more'n enough,' Corl confirmed. While the other two drank thirstily, he contented himself with running his fingers down the side of the fired clay jug. 'But since it's Midsummer we're for Stock's Circle, find a more friendly tussle.'

That earned Corl a wide grin. 'Was a time I'd join yer; been seven year since I woke up after Midsummer happy an' no damn clue where I was!' The man laughed, lost for a moment in the memory. Stock's Circle was where many folk gravitated to on Midsummer if they were looking for someone to celebrate with.

Corl gestured to the tavern. 'Well, marriage happens to us all, so my da used to say.'

Laughter boomed around the street as the barman roared his agreement and tossed his knotted hair back from his face. 'Damn right,' he agreed and thumped Corl on the shoulder. 'That obvious?'

'Nah, I saw your offerings earlier.' Corl pointed up at the garlands hanging above the doorway and from the stone faces peering down from the corners of the roof. 'They're a woman's work, not a soldier's.'

The barman looked up, puzzled for a moment. It was traditional on Midsummer to put out offerings to appease the city's gargoyles and spirits, and whatever else might be roaming the rooftops and night-time streets. The garlands were bound hoops of hazel and elder twigs with beef bones or pigskin in the centre, each one threaded with thin strips of dyed cloth like to those hanging down over the cobbled street.

'Hazel leaves, friend? Your wife knows a witch, I'd guess, to use that. And anyways, you'd have just soaked rags in blood and hung them, not gone to all the trouble of colouring 'em yoursel'.'

The barman slowly nodded. 'You ain't been drinking enough this night,' he said reproachfully before the smile returned to his face. 'That's better attention than a man'll wanna pay at Stock's Circle.'

Corl agreed and held out payment. 'Slept off the first round – time to top misself up!'

The clatter and stomp of boots ended the conversation, as a horde of shouting, laughing people spilled around the corner. Corl thanked the barman and turned away, twitching aside his shawl to take a long gulp of the wine before the parade arrived. The parade always passed this way before winding up at Stock's Circle, and Stock's Circle was where one of the several Harlequins currently performing in Tirah would be until well into the morning.

Isen cheered and walked out into the centre of the street, arms stretched wide, to the jeers and yells of the folk in the parade.

The Wanton Woman and her Beasts: this same parade was happening in every Farlan town and village, in some form or another. There'd be half a dozen at least in Tirah, but in the poorer districts like this they were invariably more fun.

The parade was led by a wagon made up to look like a chariot and dragged along by more than a dozen men, some of whom were so drunk they couldn't even walk in a straight line. The Wanton Woman herself was standing in the driver's seat, and behind Corl could see a tangle of limbs poking out – someone getting a head-start on the fun, obviously.

Corl looked at the driver again – and gave a start. He couldn't recognise anyone under the black feathered mask – a woman's face outlined in white with full lips and pronounced cheeks, an echo of the ceremonial headdresses the eunuch-priests of Etesia wore for ceremonies – but when the wind caught the cloak, he recognised the diamond-pattern patchwork: it was remarkably similar to that of a Harlequin.

That's a bad omen, Corl thought as he approached the wagon.

'Beasts!' the Wanton Woman bellowed, to roars of approval from the screaming rabble. 'More beasts for my wagon!'

Laughing, Orolay and Isen grabbed at the traces of the wagon, shoving aside a couple of the more hopelessly drunk, who left without complaint, having spied the barrel of beer nearby.

'Drink, you harlot!' Corl shouted back at the Wanton Woman, 'you need a man riding up here!' Without waiting for a reply Corl hauled himself up to stand beside her and offered her the jar of wine. As the crowd behind booed at his impertinence, the Wanton Woman regarded him a moment, then reached forward and grabbed him by the crotch. Corl yelped as she squeezed a shade harder than necessary, but the gesture won the crowd's approval and their booing turned to a swell of cheering and vulgar suggestions.

'You'll do!' the Wanton Woman announced, releasing Corl and taking a swig of the wine he'd offered. She leaned closer and Corl realised the mask had a dark hood attached to it, hiding the fact her hair was cut so short underneath it – he had more on his chin. Her breath swept sweet and hot across his face. 'You'll get your lift, but no ride less it's from one o' those in the back, hear me?'

Corl nodded and she gave him a friendly slap on the shoulder. Her strength took him by surprise and the gesture nearly knocked him off the driver's seat, but she only laughed and yelled for her beasts to march on.

'And keep an eye on the fat one,' she muttered as she continued to wave and blow kisses at onlookers, 'he likes ta get rough – he does it again, I'll cut his bloody nuts off.'

Corl looked behind him at the half-dozen men and woman in the back of the wagon. They all appeared to be enjoying themselves; one entirely naked woman was riding a gasping bean-pole of a youth, her elbows on his shoulders and his head pressed against her breasts. At the back was one far fatter than the rest. He was shirtless, with his belly hanging out; he and another man were fondling a beautiful woman dressed like a dancing girl.

He faced the front again, took the wine back from the driver and drank, long and slow, enjoying the sensation of the liquid slipping down his throat – until the driver grabbed it back. He looked around. Behind him, the fat man had unbuttoned the dancing girl's blouse to expose her beautifully rounded breasts. In front of him Isen and Orolay looked perfectly happy straining away at the traces.

He hopped into the back, shoved the fat man off the back of the wagon with his boot and bent over the dancing girl. He let the shawl drop from his face, trusting to darkness and drink that she'd not recognise the marks on his face, and kissed her, long and hard. She wrapped her arms around his head and the other man got the message and shifted to the side, joining the naked woman and her youth. The journey to Stock's Circle was short, but deliciously sweet.

When they arrived Corl took his time saying his goodbyes. Stock's Circle was still full of people, doubtless waiting for the Wanton Woman to arrive and signal the culmination of the night's fun. He felt the press of voices and movement all around, mingling with the salty taste of the dancing girl's sweat and the heat of her body.

Their destination had once been a place of punishment, but the pit at the centre of the crossroads had been converted for entertainment decades ago. Now steps led down into the pit, and when fruit was thrown it was only a commentary on the performance. On the eastern edge was a half-moon gallery a hundred yards long, occupied by taverns and eateries, and a renowned glass-blower's workshop. With food, drink and entertainment all close at hand, the Circle had become the natural heart of entertainment in this part of the city.

Midsummer's Day was a festival for the common folk, one of the few sanctioned by every cult that mattered, and a Harlequin was guaranteed to be here, performing for the masses. As an impatient Isen dragged Corl away from the delicious dancing-girl, who was still pouting prettily at him, a chill went down his spine. Their prey was singing bawdy songs, accompanied by a choir of hundreds. Corl's ardour was immediately dampened; the dancing-girl vanished from his mind, replaced by the images of Kassalain in her temple.

Once again he wondered about the strange nature of his commission: to kill a person who had no identity, who bore no allegiance and took no sides. Isen and Orolay had both been incredulous when he'd told them. The younger man had been outraged, while Isen had been mostly mystified. The three of them had debated the matter for hours, but when they reached no conclusion, Corl had decided to do what he always did: take the money and try not to think too hard about the victim. After all, there was *always* a reason, good or otherwise, even if Corl himself did not understand it and that was not much different to serving in the army.

All the same, Corl could not help wondering: why a *Harlequin*? Who could possibly have a grudge against the blessed tellers of stories? What madman could imagine a Harlequin harming him, or posing a threat? It was foolish . . . but as he stood there, the swell of bodies pressing from all sides, Corl still found himself checking the weapons secreted around his body.

'Coin all spends the same,' he muttered, too quietly for Isen to hear properly. He waved Isen to silence as the song ended and the Harlequin started its last tale: one Corl had heard years back: the Goat and the God. They laughed as hard as anyone as the Harlequin acted out Vrest's amorous mishaps as he took the form of a Billy-goat, booed with gusto at the theft of the prized doe and cheered at the hoofprints adorning the God's buttocks afterwards . . . although Corl felt a vague sense of puzzlement as the story unfolded, the course of events differing to how he remembered them – but it was all too long ago to recall accurately, and Harlequins never forgot a single word, everyone knew that.

The swell of laughter and cheering swept him up and Corl tried to ignore his qualms. The Harlequin took its bows and as the drummers started striking the first bars of the salute to the night, the brisk, heavy thump of the drums reminded Corl of a heartbeat and his thoughts returned to the night's task. At his gesture, Isen and Orolay began to make their way around the pit to where the Harlequin was gathering its meagre possessions.

As they crossed the open ground, a pair of fiddlers took up the mournful salute and the Harlequin was slipping away with only a few words of thanks and blessing from the grateful crowd, who were mostly listening, rapt, to the final song, an ancient tradition.

It was Farlan custom for all who could afford it to offer a Harlequin food and lodging whenever it arrived in a town or city. Neighbours would bring gifts, to honour their presence; on Midsummer that was doubly important. Corl reckoned the Harlequin would have accepted an offer of bed and breakfast closer to the city gate, and as asking would be a bit obvious, he'd decided following the Harlequin was their best option. With luck the revelry would have died down before he reached his destination and they wouldn't have to slaughter the whole household.

Corl slung his arm around Isen's neck, raised the jug of wine to the man's lips and poured some down his front, roaring with laughter. He lurched into the middle of the street, keeping one eye on the Harlequin's back even as he hugged Isen to him.

'Easy now,' he said in Isen's ear, 'you're wound tight as a ratter – chase this one too hard and he'll turn on us.'

With that he lunged towards Orolay, shoving the jar into the young man's hands, then falling to the ground and dragging Isen down on top of him. As the bigger man's weight thumped down on him, Corl roared with drunken laughter and Orolay, catching on, quickly joined in.

'You ain't payin' me ta play fool,' Isen hissed, 'use the boy fer that.'

'Piss you on,' Corl replied under his breath, theatrically struggling to his feet. 'Pride's easiest to lose, it's everythin' else as hurts.'

Isen scowled and grabbed the wine off Orolay. 'Lose yer own then,' he said, and headed off down the street.

Corl watched him go. Isen wasn't giving up on the mission, he knew that, but the last thing he needed was the man trying to earn the fee alone. Whatever the reasons behind their commission, it wasn't going to be easy – the biggest question was how they were going to get it done and remain alive. Corl was good with a knife, *really* good, but he wasn't planning to tangle with a Harlequin unless he had a company of Ghosts at his side.

Shame you're not this good an actor, Corl thought as he watched Isen stamp away after the Harlequin, who was heading down a fork in the road, *this is better than the happy drunks routine.*

'I'm sorry!' he bawled after the other man with mock anguish. 'Forgive me!'

Corl ran a few steps forward, enough to make Isen flinch, before turning away and beckoning Orolay closer. Out of the corner of his eye he could see the Harlequin looking around, and seeing nothing but a drunken argument between friends. Corl splashed the remains of the jar of wine over the two of them so they were as stained and stinking as Isen.

'Know any songs?' he asked Orolay with a chuckle, but when the young man looked blank, Corl thumped him on the shoulder and said, 'Hah, never mind, we'll keep to the "drunken friends making up" routine.' He cupped his mouth and shouted, 'Balar, wait up! Don't walk away!' his voice echoing down the near-empty street. When they caught up with Isen, he pointed wordlessly after the Harlequin as it disappeared through a crumbling memorial arch heading towards the Golden Tower district. The street was empty other than them, and Corl felt the essence of Kassalain stir in his blood.

'Perfect,' Corl said, struggling to cast off the desert robes. 'I'll cut through the alleys and catch it on t'other side. You two keep following, 'case it turns away.'

He didn't wait for them to reply but set off at a sprint, slipping a longknife from its sheath as he moved alongside a building. There was an alley there that he knew well, kept in near-total darkness by the tall buildings, which was a good cut-through to the Wood Gate crossroads – as long as you were willing to risk the chance of a footpad lurking in wait. This was his chance.

He kept his knife low and ran as fast as he dared, keeping to the centre of the alley. Twenty yards in he heard a woman's voice whisper in his ear – Kassalain, smelling murder in the air – and he dropped, tucking his head down into a roll, and slashed at the shadow moving to his right. The footpad yelped and fell back as Corl, already back on his feet, made up the ground in one step and lashed out, this time slicing open his ambusher's hand. The blow drove the man back the way Corl had come and he saw him clearly for the first time, silhouetted against the mouth of the alley.

No second blade, flashed through Corl's mind as he grabbed the footpad's injured arm, yanked him sideways and kicked the man's legs out from under him.

'Wait!' the man gasped as he thumped to the ground, *'please—!'* He broke off as he felt the edge of a blade at his throat.

'Sorry, friend,' Corl whispered, 'but you tryin' to kill me's a promise to Kassalain, and I do her collecting.' He drew the knife across the man's throat, cutting as deep as he could in one movement. The man spasmed as the lifeblood flowed out of him, but in a matter of moments his heart stopped and he went limp.

Just another sacrifice to my mistress, Corl though grimly. *Better him than me.*

The body wouldn't be discovered tonight, so he didn't need to waste any more time. When he reached the other end of the alley he dropped to one knee and caught his breath. In a few moments he felt the veil of silence descend over the alley again. He chanced a look round the corner – and froze.

There it was, apparently still unaware of its pursuer, its patchwork clothes and white porcelain mask stark and ghostly in the pale moonlight.

Corl drew slowly back and reached for the blowpipe sheathed on his thigh. He allowed himself a quick flush of relief as he ran his fingers down its length and discovered no damage, then removed his darts pouch and selected one. The range wasn't great compared to a bow, but he preferred a lack of moving parts in his weapons. He loaded and raised the pipe, and set himself to wait patiently for his target to appear at the alley entrance.

Half a dozen heartbeats later he felt a prickle of fear – he couldn't hear the Harlequin's footsteps on the cobbles – then it appeared straight ahead of him, its head turned slightly away. There was no wind; it was as easy a shot as it could be. Corl filled his lungs, aimed the blowpipe and blew—

—and the Harlequin flinched. One sword was halfway out of its scabbard before the Harlequin even saw what had happened. Corl slowly lowered the blowpipe, feeling secure in the shadows, and watched the Harlequin twist around to look at the finger-long dart in its buttock. With a flick of the wrist it slapped the dart away, then whipped a dagger from its belt and slashed down at the cut.

Corl's eyes widened, he'd never seen that before. The toxin on the dart was insect venom, fast-acting, but not instant. As he watched blood run down the Harlequin's leg Corl found himself wondering how much had entered its bloodstream. *Not much, I guess . . .*

He shook his head. *Really not the time,* he chided himself, stowing the pipe and drawing his longknives. The Harlequin detected his

387

movement, even in the darkness, and peered forward, fully drawing one of its slim swords. It took a few steps forward and Corl felt a chill breath of wind on his neck, as though Lord Death had arrived to claim him.

Larat's Teeth, it knows it can't wait for the venom to kick in.

Corl took a step back. The Harlequin continued forward, still straining to make out any shapes in the black alley. Corl sheathed one of his longknives and drew a shorter blade, moving slowly and bringing it back behind his head, so the Harlequin wouldn't see. As he readied himself, footsteps came from the street beyond – footsteps *and* voices.

He hesitated, and so did his prey. Then a forced laugh rang out, echoing off the stone walls of the street and Corl realised it was Orolay, obviously as poor an actor as Isen.

The Harlequin, a trained performer, recognised the same and it turned to face the new threat just as Alterr, the Greater Moon, broke from behind a cloud. Her light spilled over the street, illuminating the scene as though they had fallen into some myth and it was Kasi Farlan himself they hunted.

Oh, another poor omen, Corl thought, his stomach clenched.

The Harlequin drew its other longsword, the slender blades as luminous as its mask, and, thanking Kassalain for that moment's distraction, Corl threw the dagger, straight and true—

—and the Harlequin moved with blinding speed, arching backwards even as it swung up a sword up to deflect the missile. Corl's mouth dropped open. What mortal could do that?

He didn't get a chance to find out. He heard Isen snarl and break into a run, and, inexplicably, the Harlequin broke and sprinted as gracefully as a gazelle for the side-street it had originally been headed for.

Corl blinked in surprise as the Harlequin disappeared from view. It didn't look as if the venom or the cut on its buttock had hampered it in the least.

A few moments later Isen and Orolay barrelled past, chasing after it, and the sight of them started him into action again.

'Wait,' he croaked, and stumbled after them, rounding the corner into the street in time to see them clatter to a halt. They stood looking around the empty street in bewilderment.

'Where the fuck's it gone?' Isen growled.

The answer appeared like the wrath of Nartis from the heavens as a blur of bone-white and glittering steel dropped between the pair of them. One sword plunged deep into Isen's chest, throwing him off his feet while Orolay reacted with the speed of youth and Kassalain's milk, slashing wildly and – through sheer luck – managing to deflect the blow.

The Harlequin spun around, raising its sword and slashing at his ribs, and Orolay tried to deflect the blow, only to find it was a ruse: the Harlequin pulled back and withdrew, then gently rocked forward and stabbed at Orolay's shoulder while the young man was still moving to parry the first blow to his ribs. The thrust sent him reeling, and the Harlequin pressed forward its advantage, twisting one sword to disarm Orolay, then lifting the other and slicing deep into his neck, the gleaming steel cutting through flesh as easily as butter.

Corl faltered. He'd barely had a chance to move while his comrades died. As he raised his longknives, he felt his hands waver under the sudden weight. He had no hope at all of matching a Harlequin's skill; his attack had relied entirely on stealth.

Do I have time to run? he wondered, knowing the answer.

'What venom?' the Harlequin demanded in a voice so calm and controlled it could have been reclining in a chair rather than engaged in combat. 'Tell me, and you can live.'

'Ah, venom?' Corl's mind went blank for a moment, then as the Harlequin advanced his survival instinct kicked in again. 'Wait! It's ghost centipede—'

From nowhere an arrow struck the Harlequin in the side, the force of the blow driving it backwards a few steps, and Corl heard it gasp as it grasped the shaft and realised it was a crossbow bolt. The Harlequin sank to one knee, dropping one sword to press a hand to its side.

Corl didn't get any closer; he had just had ample demonstration of the Harlequin's ambidextrous skill.

'Never send a man to do a woman's job,' announced a dismissive voice on Corl's left.

He turned, and nearly dropped his knives in shock as he recognised the diamond patchwork cloak and black mask pushed up on top of a shorn head: his Wanton Woman. Of course, the last time he'd seen her she hadn't had a large black crossbow held carelessly in her hands, or a cigar jammed into the corner of her mouth.

The woman dropped the crossbow, reached behind her back and produced a cocked pistol-bow and dropped a quarrel into it. The end of the cigar glowed orange for a moment, then she pulled it from her mouth.

'Why?' wheezed the Harlequin, looking up at her while blood, pitch-black in the moonlight, seeped between its fingers.

'For what you might do,' the woman replied simply.

Corl looked at her. She barely looked Farlan, with her cold eyes, cropped hair and scarred cheeks, but he'd seen this before. This one was a Hand of Fate – or had been, until the Goddess had died. It looked like Kassalain still had competition in Tirah; the woman's profession hadn't been removed with her copper-dyed hair, just her allegiance.

Without warning the Harlequin launched forward, lunging for the woman, who calmly hopped backwards, away from its sword's tip, even as she fired the pistol-bow. The quarrel hit it just below the shoulder, its sword clattered onto the cobbles and it dropped to its knees again. It bowed its head, as though in prayer, but all Corl could hear was shallow breathing as the Harlequin panted its last.

The woman used her foot to nudge the sword out of the Harlequin's reach before bending to pick it up. She hefted the weapon with an admiring look. 'A thing of beauty,' she whispered. 'Perhaps I'll keep it.'

She swept the sword down and the Harlequin's head tumbled away. Its torso flopped flat at her feet as the Wanton Woman stepped delicately out of the way.

'Double pay for me, it appears,' she said – not callously, to Corl's surprise, more wearily.

He bobbed his head and looked back at the corpses of his comrades. *Double pay? She's already killed one tonight? Gods, are they being wiped out?*

'Leave them,' she ordered, 'I'll dispose of this one. The guard can find them and think what they like.'

'I wasn't told to hide the body,' he said, returning to his senses.

She gave him a fierce grin and raised the sword. 'If I'm taking a memento, best they don't find the body straight away.'

With that she unclasped her cloak and wrapped the sword before fetching her crossbow. When she'd picked that up she carried on walking away, looking for a suitable hiding place, and Corl realised she was right. There wasn't anything more to say; it was time to leave.

Anyways, the night's not over for me, he reminded himself as he paused over the bodies of his former colleagues. *Someone with a grudge against Harlequins; that makes my next job look obvious by comparison.*

He sighed and sheathed his weapons. It would be foolish to linger. He summoned a map of the city in his mind and set off at a brisk walk.

The Temple of Karkarn it is, then, and all by myself now ... think I'd better pick up a crossbow on my way.

CHAPTER 27

Kastan Styrax waited, the dying sun on his face. A faint breath of wind danced across his cheek like a ghost's lament, as unnoticed as the discordant song of cicadas all around. He watched the orange smears of cloud as though searching for meaning in their patterns, but they answered no questions. The beauty of the sunset was similarly lost on him. Styrax had always been a man of the dawn, as the mysteries of the darkness were slowly unveiled. Any fool could enjoy dusk, thinking it heralded the reward of another day survived. Great men preferred dawn.

'You found me at dawn, Fate,' he said to the sunset. 'You sought me out when I was barely a man and told me I had a future like no other.' He raised a wineskin and drank, but when he lowered the skin, he realised his thirst had not been assuaged, and tossed it carelessly behind him, prompting a snort from the wyvern crouched nearby. The beast sat low on its hind legs, dusty-blue wings half-outstretched as though ready to catch the dusk wind. A voice in the back of his mind told Styrax he too should shake out his muscles, loosen the knots in his body with a few repeated forms with his sword. He did nothing. He felt like the weariness of his soul was a well of ice deep inside him.

The hillside was almost bare; low, gorse-like bushes with pale green leaves providing the only cover for the birds that nested there. Their nervous calls punctuated the summer evening, frantic chirps coming from all directions as though they were attempting to confuse the massive predator that had landed in their midst.

'You told me it was a future you could not affect, that the choices were mine alone. All this has come about because I willed it.' Styrax gestured to the Land around him, the open fields and olive groves, the glinting stream and serried ranks of sheltered vines. 'So who could be blamed for Kohrad's death but I? The Farlan boy? He sought to wound me; to distract me from the fight ahead, or excise the motive for conquest. As much as he deserves the lonely tortures of Ghenna, he was only reacting to my own actions. Thus the blame is ours to share.'

He walked forward a few paces until he reached a big boulder and sat. The weight of years had never before pressed so hard upon his shoulders; it had increased tenfold since Major Amber had roused him from his murderous grief. Now Styrax slumped forward, resting his elbows on his knees as he stared down at the dirt. It was dry and dusty on the hillside, what little water in the soil used up by the bushes. He paused as six pairs of dark eyes peered up at him: some sort of game-bird, with grey mottled plumage. Her five brown chicks were looking anxiously up from underneath their mother's wing.

'Hello, supper,' Styrax whispered. The bird bobbed its head in response, a nervous, wary reaction to the sound, no doubt, but one that filled him with a sudden sense of kinship. 'Oh, see now I can't eat you,' he continued reproachfully, 'not when you've welcomed me so respectfully.'

From somewhere behind the bird was an urgent chirrup, and the call was taken up in all directions, producing a sudden riot of sound. The cacophony was interrupted by the voice of someone calling, 'My Lord?' from further down the hillside.

The wyvern gave a hungry hiss, followed a ragged flapping sound as it hurriedly folded its wings in readiness to leap. The white-eye whispered a few soft words and a drift of magic slithered off his tongue. The wyvern quietened immediately, needing little encouragement to settle back down. It had flown for several hours that day and it was tired – no matter how tasty a morsel General Gaur might be.

'Come, my friend,' Styrax replied, not bothering to get up from the boulder, 'how fares my war?'

'About as hard as we anticipated,' the beastman said, trudging up the slope towards Styrax. He had a plain breastplate strapped on and his axe was slung on his back, ready for battle. 'And you?'

Styrax's gaze hardened, but the look had no effect on his long-time friend. He opened his mouth to speak, then the sight of Kohrad's body appeared in his mind and momentarily paralysed him. He looked away, unable to meet Gaur's bronze-flecked eyes any longer. 'Bored by the Circle City,' he said at last.

'They like to talk, sure enough,' Gaur agreed, the contempt obvious in his thick, deep voice. 'I don't have much good news for you, though.'

'How far from Aroth?'

'At the gates. King Emin pulls back at every thrust like a girl with pious guilt.'

'That is not good news?'

Gaur shrugged with a chink of steel. 'Good enough, but no victories to speak of. I have strike forces ranging ahead of the main armies, chasing down the score or more warbands raiding our lines. The Cheme Third got close to wiped out, major sorcery of some sort finishing what, to hear the survivors tell, Colonel Uresh's rashness started. Was timed with the only real assault they've ventured, one that decimated the Third Army's supplies and stalled our centre entirely.'

'Something tells me Major Amber won't thank me for keeping him away from that.'

'You're not sending him forward?'

Styrax shook his head. 'Byora's his mission now, Byora and Azaer.'

'I understand – it's a shame though. Spirits are low in the camps. It would be good for them to see their newest hero.'

'*Low?*' Styrax exclaimed. 'The enemy fears to face us in open battle and it's *our* morale that's affected?'

Gaur shook his dark mane. 'The raids are sapping strength and will. They've lost friends, without being able to strike back properly. King Emin's tactic is working, to a degree.'

'His tactic is flawed,' Styrax corrected, one finger raised. 'King Emin knows it, and so do I, for it is Aryn Bwr's own battle-plan.'

'He casts you in the role of the Gods?' Gaur gave an abrupt laugh. 'How prophetic of him.'

Styrax did not share his friend's humour. 'How reckless of him. His nation is nothing like as large as the last king's. How long can he run before he meets the ocean – long enough to wear us down? He hopes to force us to turn, to slow our pace and buy himself time for the Farlan to recover and honour their agreements.'

'Has there been word from our envoy?'

'No, but the more I think on it, the more I believe he'll be successful. Every report I get from the Farlan confirms my assessment. They've no stomach for a protracted foreign war, and they remain too divided for any ruler to sustain it.'

Gaur was silent for a while, his attention focused completely on Styrax. The beastman had smothered his grief for his lord, taking up the slack when the white-eye had raged alone. When Styrax lifted his head he saw the pain in Gaur's eyes that was eating away inside him. Kohrad, the youth Gaur had loved as a son, was dead before his eyes, while he had been brushed aside, left uninjured by the Farlan white-eye.

I could send you back, Styrax thought, forcing himself to look at Gaur despite the horrific, gut-clenching images of Kohrad's corpse that burst in his mind. *I could send you away to Thotel and let you oversee the garrison there. The Chetse are mine, body and soul, so there you could grieve . . . and yet I will not. A general's compassion is smoke on the wind; you know this though it may leave you dead inside.*

'What will you do in response?' Gaur said, looking down as if he had heard his lord's thoughts.

Styrax gave him a grim, mirthless smile. 'I will obliterate all he holds dear. I will be as the Gods of past Ages and lay waste to all before me. I will make my enemy realise he has no choice but to face me in battle.'

He stared off to the east, where the sun had dropped below the horizon, and far beyond to their homeland, where a mother too grieved the loss of her son. Selar, Kohrad's mother, was capable of cruelty and viciousness surpassing most other white-eyes, but she had loved her son. Her heart would be breaking at the news of his death – it might even eclipse the simmering hatred she felt for Styrax for a while.

You sought to stop me, Lord Isak. You sought to take away my reason for conquest. It would have been better for you if the Lady had not died. She would have been able to dispel your illusions. His hand tightened into a fist. He was burning to unsheathe his weapons and scour the Land around him.

She saw . . . All those years ago, when I was about to leave home and join the army . . . She came to me at dawn, to tell me of the choices ahead, and she saw my heart and knew my choice even as I made it. Only a fool builds empires for his family. The Lady saw my will, as deadly as any blade, sharp enough to carve a path through history itself. The loss of my son will not stop me; Fate knew that: Nothing will stop me.

Styrax spat in the dirt as the last sliver of sun sank beneath the distant horizon. He bent down to the bird on its nest. Moving as quickly as a snake he grabbed the creature by the neck and had wrung the life from her before she had even sounded the alarm. Her chicks scattered, but Styrax ignored them and turned away, leaving them for whatever hungry animals hunted the hillside at night. He slipped a knife from his belt and started to gut the bird as he walked back towards the wyvern.

My compassion is at an end. It died alongside you, Lord Isak. Now your allies will see my wrath, and it will be a righteous fury worthy of the Gods.

King Emin glanced round at the sound of footsteps, then resumed his position on the wall of Camatayl Castle. A cigar burned unnoticed in his fingers as he stared down at the fields beyond, where, in the distance, fallow deer were grazing.

—*The reports have started to come*, Legana wrote as she joined him at the wide embrasure, leaning back against the crenellated wall so she could observe the king. She rested her silver-headed cane against the stone and wrote – *A success?*

Her words provoked a sudden exhalation from King Emin: the laughter he couldn't bring himself to voice?

'A success,' he murmured, 'so it is reported. Most eliminated with great efficiency, as far as reports go. I've only heard from the cities, where I can communication directly with my agents through the slates, but if we extrapolate ...' He didn't bother to finish the statement.

Legana looked at him for a while. His shoulders were hunched, as though weighed down by the burden of his decisions. The king, she realised, was starting to thin on top. Age was at last catching up with the man most still thought of as having the brilliance of youth.

What if that's behind him? What if the candle is now burned, the fuel spent? What then for this war? she wondered.

The Harlequins had a special place in the Land. Their mandate and skills had come direct from the Gods; to kill one was a crime beyond murder, it was treason, heresy – to slaughter them all, systematically, as Emin and Legana were doing was unthinkable, horrifying. The Harlequins had always represented the rebirth of civilisation, and something more intangible still: the heartbeat of the Land. The human side of Legana railed at the deed, but the divine fragment cared little. All mortals could be tools when necessary.

—*I have noticed something*, Legana wrote, *about my new self.*

'Oh?'

—*My poor balance, my trembling hands – they come most often when I rest. My body hates inaction.*

If he smiled, she didn't see it; it was hard for her to make out much detail in the twilight. 'I'm sure I could swing you a position in the kitchens to keep you busy.'

—*Still good with a knife.*

'As is your friend Ardela, according to my agent in Tirah. Two Harlequins in one night – impressive by any standards.' Emin sighed. 'And yet it might still be for naught. There were two pieces of news from Aroth. The Menin Army has been sighted from the walls.'

—*Siege?*

He stubbed out the remains of his cigar and tossed the butt off the battlements before turning to face Legana. 'I doubt for long. He has yet to lose a direct confrontation in his invasion of the West, and Aroth's defences are not so formidable I can afford to hope they'll slow him for long.'

—*And then?*

'Hah, and then he and I both know there's nothing of consequence between Aroth and here. The ground is open and level for the main, providing few suitable spots to set raids. We could demolish every bridge across the Goeder but that would barely slow them. This fortress is the only defence between Aroth and— ah Gods, Moorview, I suppose. It's too much to hope that he'd go west around the Blue Hills; that'd invite attacks from Canar Thritt.'

—*Moorview?*

'A castle overlooking Tairen Moor. It's built on a small hill that gives it command over the whole area. If I could make a stand against Lord Styrax it would be there.'

—*But you do not yet dare?*

'Until I can think of a way to defeat him in battle, some ruse that bypasses the entirely unsporting attributes he is blessed with, no. Aryn Bwr forced a confrontation in his war; he tried to meet the power of the Gods head-on and he failed.'

—*How far will you retreat?* Legana watched in shades of grey as Emin's face fell.

'As far as I must,' he said in a soft, almost apologetic voice. 'He tries to lure out my army, to force battle. It isn't cowardice that stays my hand. We must wait, we must delay for as long as we can – the longer we can hold out, the more problems he will have with his new "allies" and his conquered cities. Supplies will become scarce, even in our farming heartland, and who knows? Perhaps your fellow Farlan will honour our treaty? If the Farlan Army marched to my aid, the Menin would be massively outnumbered, and they would be forced to evade for a change.'

—*While Azaer grows stronger.*

Emin scowled. 'I know that, only too well. My one consolation is that the shadow's goal appears to be promoting chaos in the nations of the West.' He managed a bitter laugh now. 'It's in Azaer's interests for me to last as long as possible too. A quick war does not serve the shadow's purpose.'

—*Forget Styrax for a moment. How can you defeat Azaer?*

The question made him turn back to the evening sky. 'A question I have asked for years now,' he said eventually, 'and one I have posed to some of the finest minds in my kingdom. And still I am unsure.'

—*What do you know?*

'Of Azaer? Little enough.' He grimaced. 'All these years, and still I do not know my enemy. Azaer is a shadow, neither God nor daemon. It's an entity with a similar origin, most likely, but it draws no strength from worship as a God does, nor from fear and suffering, as might a daemon. It simply exists, neither expending power, nor requiring its harvesting. If anything, it glories in its weakness, it finds power in its flaws.'

—*And flaws in power.*

Legana's observation made Emin frown, but he could not deny it. He hunched down further, as though assailed, and continued, 'Perhaps the shadow was once a God, in the time before the Age of Myths, when the laws of magic and the Land were still malleable. Perhaps there was no death then, as we know it. Maybe the God was defeated to the point of death, reduced to the existence of a shadow.'

—*Never to gather followers again?*

'Never to risk it, you mean? To be reduced once and in glimpsing oblivion, seeing the choices of death, or service as an Aspect to some other God, so it forged its own path? The case for that is strong, certainly. Even now, the Lady isn't dead, not in the mortal sense, however reduced she is, lacking in everything that made her the Goddess you knew.'

—*But you do not believe.*

'It is the best theory I've come across, but no,' Emin admitted. 'It contains the beginnings of understanding, but I suspect there is more to it than that. There is no God Azaer particularly hates that I can tell, which would be strange if one had killed it, no? While all the accounts I have are secondhand at best it—' He hesitated a moment, as if trying to pluck the correct word from the aether.

He shook himself, and went on, 'In the years of fighting Azaer's disciples, I have seen many things – I have dreamed of the shadow half a dozen times, and I do not believe they were merely dreams. For certain it has a scheme in everything it does, its actions are carefully calculated, and yet I have never detected hatred in its actions, nor a need for revenge. Azaer delights in cruelty, but its evil is motiveless.

'When it sent Rojak to the village of Thistledell to wreak its horror, it was for a purpose – it was refining the magics it ultimately used in Scree. I have read the few survivors' accounts; it took pleasure in what it did to those innocent souls, but it was for pleasure's sake. It cannot compel; it must persuade – although it is very persuasive. It prefers to offer its victims exactly what they desire, and then twist that desire to wring out any value it might have had.

'To choose to believe all this comes from Azaer's fear of death or its cowardice . . . I feel that would be a fatal mistake.'

—*What does it want?*

'To tear down the Pantheon,' Emin said with sudden conviction. 'The shadow loves power over others – over its disciples, over those it tyrannises. Plans formed over millennia, a hand in the Last King's rebellion; an end-game with the foundations of empty temples and war tearing through the entire Land – where Crystal

Skulls are being collected by a peerless warrior and the weapons of Life and Death may soon come into play.'

King Emin took a weary breath and looked Legana straight in the eye. The cold glitter of his pale blue eyes seemed to shine in the burgeoning twilight, just as she knew her own, divine-touched eyes did.

'Azaer is playing for keeps,' he said almost in a whisper. 'There will be no limit to the stakes when the shadow plays its final hand.'

—*So we must work out how to kill a shadow*, Legana wrote, a smile creeping onto her ethereally beautiful face, *preferably by giving it everything it wants.*

Awkwardly she reached out and put her hand on his shoulder. She could feel the king tense under the contact, but after a moment Emin relaxed and covered her hand with his. They stood together until the last light of day had gone, silently sharing the burdens of their callings.

CHAPTER 28

Dawn intruded. His head felt heavy, unwieldy and as he forced his eyes open and the hot needles of sunlight drove in, he gasped and wrenched his head away. As he shifted from his awkward sleeping position the pain moved to his neck, a spiked collar that sent arrows of agony down his spine. He tried to move his unresponsive fingers, making a weak effort to massage away the pain, while a hot throb ran down his arm from the point of his elbow, which felt as stiff and hurt as much as his neck.

He blinked until the blur of light and dark slowly came into some semblance of focus. A broken table lay a few feet away amidst the pottery shards of several wine bottles and piles of abandoned clothes. For a while he stared at the mess, not understanding what had happened. A shaft of sunlight cut a thin white line across the rug-strewn floor and ran up his leg and chest like a sword-cut. It hit another bottle, clasped between his legs, still intact but empty. It looked as if the wine that had spilled into his lap was now mostly dried.

He lifted an arm to remove the bottle and froze. The arm wasn't his; it was bigger, and unnaturally black – like some creature of the Waste. He turned it over and tried to make out the markings on it—

—and grief hit him like a thunderbolt, slamming into his head and racing down into the pit of his stomach. Count Vesna doubled over as the void in his gut twisted violently, and he wrapped mismatched arms around his body as he started retching, spewing a thin stream of sharp, sour bile onto his battered boots. A coughing fit followed, deep, shuddering exhalations that ended in a choked howl of sorrow.

The ruby teardrop on his cheek flared warm as his armoured

fist tightened around the arm of his chair, snapping the polished wooden armrest like a twig. Memory flooded back as black stars burst before his eyes: the scratch on Tila's face as she tried to speak, her last words to him. It had been such a small thing, barely more than a graze. As the image appeared in his mind he recalled that sickening sense of hope he'd felt at, the cruel momentary waning of horror, the second before he felt the ruined mess of her back.

Trembling, he wiped the stinking spittle from his chin with a grimy sleeve. Away from the shaft of light, the room looked dark and still, wrapped in cold shadows. Nausea shivered through his body again, but Vesna did not care enough to fetch a bowl or move away from the puddle of puke. A black knot of pain was building behind his eyes, eating away at his mind.

'Why her?' Vesna whispered. The effort of speaking, even to an empty room, drained him of energy and his head sagged onto his chest. For a while he looked at the torn threads on his tunic where buttons had once been, and the wine-stains on the fabric. He didn't remember putting that tunic on; his memory was a jangled mess. Only Tila's face was clear.

What happened then, the glass arrow, was in the distant past, as was the duel he'd fought with the Elf. There were clouds in his mind, after that, voices talking over one another, faces overlaid with pain and blood, someone shouting in his ear, tentative hands leading him through the streets, faces filled with horror and terror . . . such a *long* time ago . . .

There was a sound behind him, a click and creaking. Once he had been able to recognise the noise of a door opening. Now, he didn't turn. The sound belonged to a different time, one where Tila lived. Nothing mattered now. As a voice began to speak he tuned it out, staring, unfocused, at the wine-stains. The words flowed over him unheard as the ache behind his eyes sharpened with every beat of his absent heart. The sound filled his ears and rattled his ribs long after the voice stopped and he realised he was alone with his pain again.

'She can't be gone,' he muttered, 'she can't be.' But no matter how often he repeated the words, the hollowness in his belly remained and he knew the words were a lie. His God-given strength was useless against such overwhelming power. Karkarn's *iron general* was surrounded and helpless; his forces were broken, his stratagem in tatters. He had been defeated. Nothing was left but pain—

The cloud of shadows was suddenly thrown back and Vesna felt an explosion of pain in his head as he was thrown sideways onto the floor. He crumpled, content to lie there, even as the years of training tried to cut in and force him to stand.

'Get up, you useless streak of piss!' yelled a voice. 'On your feet, soldier!'

Vesna found himself dragged upright as he stared blindly at blurs that lurched and swayed. Before he could focus on anything he felt a hand slap him across the face with enough force to snap his head back.

'You pathetic, fucking drunk! You shame her memory, boy!' the voice roared, choked with rage.

Tila. Energies caught life inside him, sparking like a lit fuse, and Vesna caught the next blow with one hand and struck out with the other, trying to shove his attacker away. From somewhere his sword slapped into his palm and then the blur disappeared from his eyes.

In front of him stood Marshal Carelfolden, his face red with rage, and Sir Dace, his cheek yellow with old bruising.

'Get out,' Vesna growled.

Sir Dace opened his mouth to reply, but Carel beat him to it. 'Fuck off, you whining little brat! You want to be alone? You get out.'

Vesna took a step forward, power flooding though his body as the lit match became a mighty flame. 'Get out or I'll kill you,' he growled.

Carel raised his head slightly, like a duellist en guarde. He held a long log in his hand, the one he'd smashed around Vesna's skull. 'Go on then, you damned coward. You can kill me, but don't think you frighten me.'

'I will kill you.' Vesna raised his sword.

Carel spat on the floor at Vesna's feet and tossed the log aside. 'What are you waiting for then? I spent years around Isak and his temper; your grief's nothing new. Want me to count the number of times he threatened me? From his thirteenth summer, that boy was strong enough to kill any man in the wagon train, and I've got the scars to prove his temper – and so does' – he faltered momentarily, but caught himself – 'and so did he.' The rage in his eyes lessened, to be replaced by something Vesna recognised.

When Carel continued it was in a much quieter voice, though he was no less defiant. 'You ain't the only one who's lost here, Vesna. You ain't the only one who grieves for Tila.'

'What do you want from me?' Vesna asked.

Carel shook his head and his shoulder sagged. Now more than ever he looked the old man he was. 'There's no one here can tell you what to do. You've got to figure that out yourself – but if you just sit there I'll keep swinging this log 'til your brains spill out or you gut me.'

'Is this some sort of joke?' Vesna said in bewilderment. 'Just get out and leave me alone.'

'Sorry, my friend,' Sir Dace said with an apologetic shake of the head. Vesna's oldest friend took a pace forward and pushed aside the Mortal-Aspect's raised sword. 'It's no joke. You've been sitting here for more'n a week, and we won't take it any more. Whether the words were spoken or not, you were married to Tila, and I swore to stand sentinel to that marriage.'

'There's no honour to defend now,' Vesna whispered, dropping his sword. Dace stepped forward and slipped a shoulder under his friend's arm.

'Yes, there is,' Dace said, his face tightening, 'yours and hers. You think she'd want this? You think this is the memorial she deserves? A hero crippled with grief? A man both blessed and useless in one?'

Vesna shook his head. 'What Tila would want?' he whispered. 'She's dead, Dace, she doesn't want anything now, and I— I can't go on, not this way.'

'No,' Carel declared. 'No, you can't go on this way. I don't agree with what you've done to yourself, but it's done, and if your wife could accept it, so can and must I. And she did accept it, wholeheartedly and without reservation. She knew she'd be sharing you with Lord Karkarn, and there was never one word of complaint, not even after you left with the crusade. It was the duty you felt, the duty you chose, and she would never have stood in the way o' that.'

'You made her proud,' Dace said, his voice soft, 'so damned proud I could hardly believe it. You're my best friend, and the finest soldier I ever met, and I'm proud to have served with you and fought alongside you – you know that. But for Lady Tila, it wasn't just that. You were far more to her than your skill with a blade, much more, and I'd rather die than see you disappoint her that way. I won't allow you to be less than the man she believed you to be.'

Tears were streaming down Vesna's face, every time Tila's name mentioned hitting him like a punch in the belly. In his mind he could see her, looking at him from the doorway, seeing the state of him now: hair matted and greasy, earrings of rank discarded, his body rank, his clothes filthy and stinking. 'I don't have the strength,' he mumbled, 'I don't know what to do.'

'You do your duty,' Carel said gravely, 'for better or worse, you do your duty. Karkarn's your lord now, and Isak showed you the path. You make your fear and your pain a part of you; you use them as weapons, if what's needed.'

Vesna sagged, leaning heavily on Dace. 'How?' he asked. 'I don't even know where to start.'

Carel and Sir Dace exchanged looks. 'You start with a bath,' they said together.

'Ah, Vesna,' the Chief Steward said, seeing the door to his office open, 'do come in.' He gestured to one of the chairs. 'Please, have a seat.'

'What do you want, Lesarl?'

The Chief Steward gave him an appraising look. The count still looked ragged around the edges, but it was a vast improvement on the wreck of a man Lesarl had tried to speak to a few days before.

'What have you done with my clothes?' Vesna continued, doing a poor job of hiding his mounting anger, but if Lesarl noticed it he gave no sign.

'I removed them,' Lesarl said eventually, sitting down behind his desk. There were leather-wrapped files scattered everywhere, but Lesarl didn't take his eyes off Vesna as he reached out and touched one of the files with two fingers. 'They are the accoutrements of a count of the Farlan, and legally you cannot possibly be that.'

'You stole my clothes?' Vesna gestured at the dark grey brigandine he wore, far plainer than anything he would normally wear in the palace. The only detail was a small bronze pin on the collar bearing Karkarn's device.

'And your earrings,' Lesarl replied brightly.

Vesna's black-iron-clad fingers flexed. 'You think now's the time for this conversation?'

'I am bound to enforce the law,' Lesarl said by way of reply. 'Naturally the cults are demanding all your worldly possessions and deeds now belong to them, but given the unusual circumstances, it will be easy to delay any ruling for as long as you need.'

'Need?'

Lesarl again pointed to the chair. 'Please, Vesna – sit.' When at last the Mortal-Aspect of Karkarn did, Lesarl continued, 'Your title and noble possessions will be held by the Lord of the Farlan until such a time as you express a wish as to what should be done with them.'

Vesna leaned forward. 'You can piss them away for all I care. They hardly matter now.'

'They matter quite a bit,' Lesarl corrected, 'symbolically, as much as anything. You have been a faithful servant of the tribe and you are a hero of the Farlan Army – I tend not to piss away, as you so delightfully put it, such powerful symbols.'

'As you wish. I've no use for them,' Vesna growled. 'Is that all you wanted from me?'

Lesarl pushed forward a second file, a slim one this time. 'Not quite. First you should read this.'

'Why?' There was no reply and after a moment Vesna gave in and grabbed the file, knocking some on the floor as he did so. He flipped it open and read the top page. 'It's a murder report.'

'Indeed it is. Look underneath.'

Vesna did so and frowned. 'Another murder report. Both priests; what's wrong, Lesarl, one of your agents go beyond their remit again?'

'Can you see the link between them?' Lesarl asked. 'It's rather easy to spot.'

'They're both priests of Karkarn – is that why you think I'll care?' Vesna stood. 'In case you hadn't noticed, Karkarn and I aren't exactly speaking right now.' The iron fist tightened again. 'If he hadn't interfered at the shrine there's a good chance . . .' He stopped, then whispered, 'There's a good chance Tila would still be alive.'

'And you would likely be dead,' Lesarl pointed out. 'Karkarn saved your life, and like it or not, it was the right thing to do.'

'Right?' Vesna yelled, slamming his fist onto Lesarl's ornate monstrosity of a desk, hard enough to make it shudder under the impact. 'You had better carefully consider the next words to come out your mouth.'

'Vesna,' Lesarl said in a quieter voice, 'I do not pretend to know your pain, I would not presume that.' He took a long, slow breath, and saw Vesna do the same after a moment. He had had years of practice with Lord Bahl's grief and temper over the murder of his lover, replayed in Bahl's dreams, thanks to the Menin. He could recognise the tipping points well enough. 'Vesna, you must believe me: it gives me no pleasure to remind you, but someone has to.'

'Remind me of what?'

'As much as it will make you laugh until you're sick – remind you of your duty.'

Vesna gaped. '*Duty?* You think I care about duty now?'

'Of course not.' Lesarl held up a hand to stop the angry retort he could see forming on Vesna's lips. 'Lord Bahl taught me about duty: it's a heartless mistress, but it binds as powerfully as love, or grief.'

He stood up and walked halfway around the desk. 'Vesna, we've known each other for many years, and in all that time your duty has guided your actions and shaped the man you have become – a man who realised he was being offered a difficult, unforgiving path, and who had the courage to take it all the same.'

'Whatever you're getting at,' Vesna said, rising and heading towards the door, 'I'm not interested.'

'Really?' Lesarl said in a sour tone. 'Then perhaps I was wrong all those years ago when I first asked you to work for me. I had thought you more than just a thug for hire. I didn't think you'd ever be one to run away from your duty, not ever.'

Before he could blink Vesna had moved back to the desk and grabbed Lesarl by the throat, driving him backwards into a bookcase of files.

'Enough of your shit! You've used me like a toy for years – in the service of your own sick sense of humour more than the tribe. Is this anything more than the petulance of a twisted child whose plaything has been stolen away? You sicken me, you and all those who play games with the lives of others! I've had enough of it; I've lost more in your games than anyone could be asked to give, and I'm not playing any more!'

'You've lost?' Lesarl gasped, 'you accuse *me* of petulance? You claim you've lost more than anyone should?' Vesna shook him like a dog, but Lesarl continued with sudden, rare anger, 'Damn you, Vesna, you're not the one who's lost here; you've come out ahead of the rest of us and now you think you can just walk off with your winnings? *Tila* lost, *Lord Isak* lost, *Lord Bahl* lost – the Gods alone know how many soldiers who looked to you for inspiration lost as they died in battle. It wasn't their fight, it wasn't their war – but they marched for the tribe, *and they died for the tribe!*'

Lesarl struggled out of Vesna's grip and wrenched at his tunic to right it. '*They* are the ones who've lost in this war,' he said contemptuously, 'and you honour their memories by running away. You're wrong, Iron General – this is a game you'll see to the end, and that's a choice you've made already. The only question is whether you realise your duty must come before your grief in time to ensure their sacrifices were not made in vain. You need to act – you need to find the courage your friends have shown and do your duty, *no matter the cost.*'

'You want me to chase after Lord Styrax and die at his hands too? Maybe run away like Mihn on some witch's errand—?'

Lesarl's face purpled. 'You think Mihn's run away? Nartis preserve us, you really are just a stone-headed soldier, aren't you? *Didn't you see the tattoos he put on himself?*'

Vesna frowned, confused. He realised he had never seen Lesarl so incandescent with rage. 'Of course I did – but I've no mage's schooling.'

'And you never even bothered to investigate.' Lesarl shook his head in disgust. 'I don't know whether it was something he cooked up with Lord Isak or if he just guessed his lord's mind, but Mihn has made as much of a sacrifice as you – probably even more; I imagine it will last a great deal longer. He's not let anything get in the way of his duty.'

'What in Ghenna's name are you talking about?'

'Hah, exactly! Charms of protection, charms of silence – even a rune that echoed the one on Lord Isak's chest! He linked his soul to a white-eye, one who had been dreaming of his own death for months, who believed it would be at the hands of Lord Styrax –

and who then marched south towards that death.'

Vesna found himself sinking back down into his chair. 'At the battle—He said—He was talking about being a gambler, and the quality of his friends . . . I thought he was just talking about the battle, about saving the army.'

'I don't think he wanted anyone to know,' Lesarl said, more gently now. 'I doubt he wanted anyone counting on something as crazy as that. After all, who knows how it might work out? All I have are my suspicions, and the certainty that Mihn wouldn't ever let fear interfere with his duty. If duty took him to the Dark Place then there he would go, without hesitation.'

Vesna realised the wetness on his cheeks was tears, and a hundred clamouring thoughts were filling his mind. 'Then maybe he's a stronger man than I,' he muttered, 'because I don't have the strength to carry on.' For the first time he felt embarrassed at his weakness, but he was done. He truly had nothing left to give . . .

'Yes, my friend, you do. You have the strength of a God running through your veins, and you have a task ahead of you. This war isn't over, and you must play your part to the end.' Lesarl's voice was breaking.

'Where . . . Where do I even begin?' Vesna could not hide the sob.

Lesarl gestured to the reports on his desk. 'You are now Lord Karkarn's man; as Chief Steward of the Farlan I can no longer give you orders.' He managed a sly smile. 'However, there are pieces of a puzzle here that you may draw your own conclusions from.'

'The dead priests,' Vesna said slowly, 'someone is murdering priests of Karkarn. An assassination attempt was made on me – by a true Elf assassin with a magical arrow . . . and that's something we've heard before. The Krann of the Chetse was possessed by a daemon after being shot with a magical arrow, at the orders of Lord Styrax.'

'The Chosen of Karkarn,' Lesarl repeated, 'apparently weakening the God he is, or was once, aligned to. What else?'

'My noble status? How does that fit in?'

'Do you remember our conversation the morning of your wedding?'

Vesna felt a black weight descend on his mind and it took him a moment to collect his wits again. 'About my religious status, and continuing the war alone.'

'Indeed – although you will not be alone. General Lahk has expressed a wish to take holy orders, to devote himself to the service of your God. Recent history aside, the structure of our military does not allow for religious status. I have consulted the law and the matter is unclear, but I believe any soldier or officer who takes holy orders must be relieved of their military positions.'

'You would allow the Farlan's most experienced general to leave?'

Lesarl shrugged. 'If he were a priest, I would have no option – my only choice would be whether or not to prosecute him. That aside, he – and any other soldier in that position – would be free to chart their own course, or that of their God, naturally.'

'I see,' Vesna said. 'And if those soldiers took some mementos of their former lives, such as horses, weapons and armour, that might be overlooked.'

'If their commanding officer were a sentimental type? Doubtless.' Lesarl gestured to the open door to his office. 'None of this could possibly be condoned by the Lord of the Farlan, of course, having signed a treaty with the Menin, but he can hardly be blamed for the actions of a few religious fanatics.' He paused. 'Not twice, anyway. At any rate, Vesna, I have much work to be getting on with and you look like a man with some hard thinking to do. Perhaps you should consult your God, as my father used to say.'

'My God? I'm not sure I can stomach that yet.'

'Duty, my friend, does worse than sicken us,' Lesarl said gravely as he ushered Vesna out, 'but either we endure it, or we fall. There will be no second chances in this game.'

The Chief Steward returned to his desk and brandished another leather file. 'We live in times where men kill even Harlequins – *Harlequins*, for pity's sake! Whether or not that has to do with Mihn's self-appointed mission, it's astonishing; it's madness. These are the times we live in now, Vesna, when nothing is sacred. Our efforts now may be all that determine what of the Land survives these events that have been set in motion – whether they be they men, tribes or Gods.'

Vesna's face was ashen as he left. Lesarl shut the door behind him and stood with one hand pressed against the wood for a while. It was cold to the touch, polished smooth, and stained by age.

He faced the seat where Tila had worked alongside him the past few months, and murmured, 'Thank the Gods I was not born a hero. I would not wish that on any man.'

CHAPTER 29

'Well, engineer, will it work?'

The engineer froze in his tracks, like a rabbit that had seen the eagle's shadow. Lips pressed firmly together, he turned to Lord Styrax, but it didn't do any good. As soon as he looked directly at the black-armoured warrior his nerve failed and he began to hiccough.

The wyvern behind him was constantly trying to eat any horse that came near, and, according to the sergeant escorting him, it had only recently learned not to try and eat General Gaur. Its savagery was blunted, rather than tamed, and he was scared of it, yet the statue-still Lord of the Menin somehow unnerved him more.

'Aye, I believe so, my Lord,' he replied cautiously, remembering to bow only after he'd spoken. 'It's a battering ram; there's not much to go wrong.' The engineer wasn't a real soldier, and the campaign had taken its toll. He felt exhausted, and as out of place as he looked, this fat little man of fifty summers, but every battle won took him a step closer to home, so even the task of fitting wheels to a huge tree-trunk had been carried out with exacting care.

Styrax turned and the man wilted under his scrutiny. 'I know that, engineer,' he said, no trace of emotion in his voice. 'You are not a man of nostalgia, it appears.'

For a moment the Menin lord's gaze drifted away into the distance. There were dark circles around his eyes, indications that Kastan Styrax was still just a man, and grieved as any would, but the white irises were colder than ever.

'Ah—' He tried to reply, but found his mind empty of words. Last time Styrax had spoken those words to him, Lord Kohrad had been at his side, ready to prove himself to his father. The very idea of bantering with a grieving white-eye made his limbs tremble.

As the tribe's foremost expert in artillery and siege weapons, he knew only too well what terrifying forces could be produced by wood, sinew and metal, to be unleashed as required. Such weapons had a resonance, a restrained stillness, like that he felt now in Lord Styrax's presence. Power hummed through the man and strained at the clamps keeping it in check. The engineer fought down the urge to run, his deepest instincts screaming to be away before such catastrophic force was unleashed.

When Styrax turned away sharply he nearly sagged with relief. His shoulders jerked as he tried to hold back another hiccough, and he flinched as the ugly old sergeant appeared beside him.

Sergeant Deebek clapped him on the shoulder and grinned toothily, about to lead him away, when Lord Styrax spoke again. 'Engineer, estimate the range of their fire-throwers.' He pointed to the nearest of Aroth's two high bastions.

Though no rival to Tor Salan's defences, the fire-throwers of Aroth were still formidable, if their intelligence was to be believed. From what they knew, when it was fired, it released a curious horizontal main beam that whipped around the entire tower, then disengaged from the powering mechanism and pivoted back to its starting point, leaving the hanging bowl ready to be refilled while the mechanism was swiftly reset.

'I —That is difficult, my Lord,' the engineer stammered, 'the mechanism has magically enhanced sections and we have yet to see it in action.'

'I understand that. My concern is whether it could be employed against anyone attacking the causeway.'

Aroth was built on the shores of two lakes – a larger one, three miles across, that comprised nearly a quarter of the city's perimeter, and a smaller body of water that had been artificially created; it was less than a mile wide. Between the two was a narrow belt of land no more than a hundred yards wide that served as the main entrance to the city. This was considered Aroth's strongest point, and it was heavily defended with artillery-barges, positioned on both lakes, to turn the causeway into a killing ground. Naturally, that was where Lord Styrax had chosen to attack.

'Would it have the range? Aye, I'd expect so,' he said after a long while. 'Whether it could be brought to bear, that's more the question. They must have a way to tilt and turn it, because it's covering that entire flank, but it's one thing to cover half the circle; another entirely to go beyond that.'

'Especially with that loading system,' Styrax added, staring at the city. Aroth was set on a slight rise, making the tops of those towers the highest point for fifty miles in either direction, the lakes the lowest. Cultivated fields stretched into the distance on all sides, fertile lands that begged the question of whether King Emin could afford to continue his fighting retreat. Taking Aroth would shore up the Menin Army's supply-lines and change the complexion of the war – but Styrax had a different plan in mind to change the game here.

'Most likely they'd need a second reloading station, on the other side,' the engineer said, swallowing a hiccough.

'The effort would be worthwhile though,' Styrax mused, almost to himself. 'The smaller lake will have far fewer artillery-barges; it's the weaker flank – unless the fire-thrower can hit its far bank.'

The engineer didn't argue. He thought it unlikely they would have bothered; the long city wall at the back of Aroth unguarded by water was still the weaker point, and these defences had been designed before King Emin conquered the city. Chances were the builders hadn't worked through every scenario as the King of Narkang might.

'Gaur,' Styrax said over his shoulder, 'are they all in position?'

'They are, my Lord. Shall I give the order?'

'Not yet.' Styrax set off towards his saddled wyvern. As he put on his whorled black helm the creature snarled and crouched down, hind legs tensing with anticipation as Styrax climbed into the saddle and clipped the silver rings of his dragon-belt to it.

General Gaur advanced towards Styrax, stopping short as the wyvern's head lifted and its mouth opened hungrily. 'My Lord, this is not necessary. The Litse white-eyes have already scouted from the air.'

'Their mages weren't unduly panicked by the scouts, so another demonstration is in order. It—' The white-eye paused and gathered up the wyvern's long reins. 'Trust me, my friend.'

With that he tugged hard on the reins and the wyvern unfurled its wings fully, with two half-beats to ready it, then, driving up with its powerful hind legs, it leapt into the air and caught the cool morning air. A longer stroke propelled it higher, and now it was turning in a lazy circle above their heads, climbing all the while.

Gaur watched the creature rise until it was hard to make out the figure on the wyvern's back, then he stalked over to the engineer, who took a half-pace back.

The engineer couldn't decipher the beastman's expression, but he recognised the sense of purpose in his stride.

'Get back to the baggage-train,' Gaur growled at the engineer. 'Your work here is done.'

Beyn peered forward, ignoring the bubble of chatter behind him. The King's Man was intent on movement several miles away, beyond the Hound Lake.

'Knew it,' he whispered to himself, 'I damned well knew it.' He turned and looked down the line of frightened soldiers until he found the general, half-hidden by an enormous nobleman and his white-eye bodyguard – one inferior in every way to the vicious ogre who'd inspired that latest Narkang fashion. General Aladorn had withered in his retirement; now he could barely see over the shoulder of a normal man, and whatever he was trying to say was being ignored as the nobleman, one Count Pellisorn of the Arothan Lords' Chamber, continued to fire demands at him.

'General, have the mages turn the weather, now!' Beyn called.

As he expected, Pellisorn just increased his volume, turned his back on Beyn and loomed over the elderly general.

'Soldier,' Beyn said quietly to the crossbowman next to him, holding his hand out.

The soldier handed over his weapon with a grin and watched Beyn quickly load it, raise the bow and put it to the bodyguard's ear. To his credit, the white-eye didn't flinch or move; he very sensibly stood stock-still.

'What the—?' the count started, but Beyn cut him off.

'Honour Council Pellisorn,' Beyn said in a calm voice, 'the enemy have made their first move. That means your authority is no longer recognised. The task appointed to me – *by the king himself* – is to ensure General Aladorn is unimpeded in his duties.'

Count Pellisorn leaned back with a look of distaste on his face, as though a favourite pet had just revealed yellow eyes and a forked tongue. Unlike most of the men assembled he was dressed in court-finery, his only armour a ceremonial gorget displaying his position on the Honour Council, the ruling body within the Lords' Chamber.

He was, however, a consummate politician, and he recovered as soon as he realised it was his bodyguard in danger, not he. 'I don't give a damn for the opinions of some low-born thug!' the count announced, his hand moving to his sword hilt. 'Unless you think threatening my man will earn you anything but a slow walk to the headsman, you will lower your weapon immediately.'

'Take your hand away from your sword, Honour Council,' Beyn advised. 'You're as fat as you are past your prime, so don't embarrass yourself further. I suggest you get out of my sight.'

'You a King's Man?' the white-eye rumbled. He was a block-faced specimen of indeterminate age with a bulbous brow and a nose broken many times – and old enough to have a shred of common sense, Beyn guessed from the look in his white eyes. He had to hope so, at any rate; they didn't have soldiers to spare in Aroth.

'I am.'

'Then ah'm takin' your orders,' the white-eye said ponderously, trying to watch the point of the bolt out of the corner of his eye. 'Is the law, I were told.'

Beyn heaved a sigh of relief that the king's decree had reached the white-eyes here. He lowered the crossbow and ordered, 'Step back, and remove your former employer from my sight, soldier. Use as much force as you think necessary.'

The white-eye's face split in into a grin, and Count Pellisorn's objections were cut short when his erstwhile bodyguard grabbed him by the scruff of his neck and hauled him towards the door by his jewel-inlaid gorget, leaving Beyn free to approach the general.

'What was that you said?' Aladorn demanded, squinting up at Beyn. 'Are they advancing?'

'I saw the wyvern; you have to get the mages to turn the weather, sir.'

'He's not going to attack all by himself,' Aladorn croaked, waving a liver-spotted claw dismissively. 'No need to waste their strength.'

'He can soften us up first,' Beyn said, 'we've nothing that can fire so high. You need to order the mages now, the only way to stop him is to threaten a storm.'

The general made a contemptuous sound. 'Afraid of thunder, is he?'

Beyn ground his teeth with frustration. He was used to folk believing him on matters of war. While General Aladorn might have been pretty good during the conquest of the kingdom, magic hadn't played a great part. Now he was just a stubborn old man, as far as Beyn could see.

'Lightning is attracted by magic,' he explained, as calmly as a man facing imminent death could, 'and he'll be up there raining the fury of Ghenna down upon us unless we do something to stop him!'

'And tire our mages in the process.'

'They can't stop him head-on, any road,' Beyn snapped, his patience gone. 'Magic ain't going to win this for us, only our bloody artillery.'

General Aladorn scowled at Beyn, his mouth becoming even more pinched and wrinkled as he thought. 'Very well, lieutenant, give the order,' he said at last to an aide standing by the door.

The man saluted and turned stiffly about.

'Run, you fuck!' roared Beyn after him, startling the man out of his formality and sending him scrabbling through the door.

Once the lieutenant had gone Beyn turned his back on the rest of the assembled command staff and remaining councillors, uncaring of their reproachful faces. He wasn't there for decorum, after all, and right now he had bigger concerns. Out of those assembled, all of Aroth's ruling circles, Beyn was the only one showing any genuine concern for the coming siege. The councillors and nobles alike were all claiming they had supplies enough to outlast the enemy, and the soldiers were confident in both their defences and their prowess. But Beyn had seen nothing to give him any confidence at all in either claim.

The king's order to refuse battle was pronounced cautious prudence, nothing more, conceding unimportant ground. That the kingdom's second city might actually fall to the Menin didn't appear to have occurred to any of them, and Beyn knew if he mentioned the possibility he'd be laughed out the room.

Damn fools, Beyn thought, as uncharacteristic doubts marched through his mind. *Not one person's noticed I'm the only King's Man here. None of the king's best warriors or mages have been sent to join this defence.* His hand clenched as a sense of helplessness unexpectedly washed over him. *When the king himself doesn't believe we can stand against them, what chance do we have?*

Styrax pulled back on the wyvern's reins and brought it around into a thermal to climb higher. The beast resisted his urging for a moment, eager to be at the prey ahead, before tilting its wings in response.

Patience, Styrax thought, as much to himself as the wyvern. *Let them see us and react. Let them have the small victory of driving me off.*

Every fibre of his body railed at the idea, but he battered it down. He knew the flaws of his kind well enough, and he possessed every one, but there had been one guiding rule to his life: that *he* would choose his own path – not the Gods, not daemons, not the will of other men. *And certainly not my own rage.*

Just the thought of Kohrad was enough to produce a spiked knot at the back of his mind, but he gritted his teeth and fought it, letting the wyvern climb and circle above the city.

Without control I am no better than Dervek Grast, Styrax reminded himself, *and that I refuse to be.*

The words were like a mantra, one oft-repeated of late. Grast, the reviled former Lord of the Menin, had been a monster, made worse by his intellect. The man hadn't been a savage, the unthinking and deranged killer most preferred to think him; there had been method, and strength of will to support his vicious delusions. For all of his forerunner's brutality, Styrax believed Grast's crimes would pale into insignificance next to the devastation he would wreak if he allowed grief to sway him.

If I allow myself to be ruled by grief, he thought firmly, *if. There will be crimes enough without that.*

He thumped a fist against the side of his helm to wake himself up. The wyvern began to strain beneath him as it continued to climb so he corrected it with a twitch of the reins and it settled immediately, wings outstretched. It could soar like this, many hundreds of feet above the city, for hours, travelling faster than any horse, and in theory a mage as powerful as Styrax could shatter a city's walls in that time.

It wouldn't happen, though, there must be more than a dozen mages living inside a city of that size, quite enough to call the clouds above closer. He would cause some damage certainly, but not enough to risk being plucked from the air and smashed on the rocks below. No, he would resist the temptation, just as he would the growling animal in his gut that wanted to attack, to dive scream-ing onto the enemy and cut them to pieces before the rest of the army even caught up.

From the city below he detected a vibration in the afternoon air: a subtle, gentle stroke of magic, soaring up like the first notes of a symphony. It was joined by others, though most lacking the finesse of the first, a few exceeding it for power, and each a variation on a common theme.

One of their mages knows what he's about, Styrax thought approv-ingly, pushing briefly on the wyvern's neck to send it into a long, shallow dive. *You could have taught the Farlan boy a thing or two; the elements are to be cajoled, not compelled. A mortal makes demands at their peril.*

He could almost taste the thin streams of magic rising above the city. The air whipped past his face until the wyvern banked of its own accord and the buffeting lessened. A sparkle of energy tingled over his skin, adding renewed vigour to the breeze and sending a familiar *frisson* down Styrax's neck.

Styrax peered down at the defences below as a few hopeful archers fired up at him, but their arrows fell hopelessly short. Now the wyvern had carried him down, closer to the city, he could pick out where the enemy mages were located.

I could pluck out your hearts right now, burst them like overripe fruit and leave you dead on the ground as a warning to the rest, he thought grimly. From the lower plain he surveyed the staggered defences of the causeway: earthworks flanking a long stone building that was built around a central archway straddling the road. A pair of guard-towers were set behind the earthworks, but they were small, barely big enough to hold more than two squads, and the Tollkeeper's Arch itself would prove little more of an inconvenience.

The causeway defences had been built for commerce, not war. Further back, strung between buildings, was a hastily built defen-sive wall – it was feeble enough to show they didn't really believe anyone would make it that far. On either side of the road the ground was broken up by angled ditches, and at one point between the wall and arch, a small canal allowed shallow-hulled scows to pass between the lakes. Though the two bridges across the canal had been dismantled, it was small, and anyway, the Menin Army had their own bridges to hand.

It would be a slaughter ground if the artillery barges were allowed free reign, but with a little help from Aroth's mages, those would be dealt with before the troops arrived.

Didn't you hear? Styrax asked the distant mages below, *I've already conquered Ilit's chosen people. The wind is mine to command now.*

He turned in a long circle, following the perimeter wall of the city and noting what he could of the defences. The bulk of their soldiers were mustered in ordered blocks in the southwest of the city, where the ground was most open. From the air Aroth looked kidney-shaped, with a mile-long jetty protruding into Lake Apatorn. From here it was impossible to make out the delineation between the part built on stilts hammered into the lakebed and where the foundations were dry ground. But soon enough that wouldn't matter.

Guiding the wyvern lower Styrax placed his unarmoured hand against the Crystal Skull in the centre of his cuirass, the one named Destruction. He'd found the differences between them were small, like the minuscule flaws that made each of a dozen gems unique.

Styrax could name each of his Crystal Skulls solely by the way it caught the light, but from his experiments he believed the only one markedly different was the last; Ruling. That one would be a handful to use in battle, he suspected, but the rest had only slight tendencies towards certain magics – tendencies that made Destruction less effort to use now.

He drew energy into a ball around the Skull and heard the thump of his heart echo through the magic. The bloody stains underneath his fingernails seemed to lighten and come alive as a smooth lattice of red-tinted light formed around the magic-scarred hand. Even as his heartbeat quickened, Styrax felt a calmness descend as the magic washed all emotion from his mind.

Up above the clouds rolled in, coiling like a threatened snake above his head. He felt his ears pop as the pressure started to fall and the wind streaming past turned cool. Styrax looked down to gauge the distance to the yellow mud-brick walls of Aroth below. Still out of bowshot, he reined the wyvern back a little and it arced neatly up, head stretched out and watching the scuttling food beneath.

At the end of the wall was the nearer tower, an enormous construction that, with its mate on the larger lake, dominated the entire city. The tower was round, and two hundred feet high, with wooden platforms attached to the outside and a mess of timber on top that at first glance looked like a collapsed roof.

Styrax leaned out from his saddle, twitching the reins to correct the wyvern's flight as it adjusted to the shift in weight. The energy around his fist was coalescing and growing hotter with every moment, tiny licks of flame beginning to drift from one strand of the skein to another. Styrax grimaced as the heat stung his more sensitive hand, the ragged swirls of scar becoming dark shadows against the white before it was obscured entirely by the magic.

They reached the tower and Styrax wrenched the wyvern over, tilting it to glide with one wing pointing at the wall below. At the same time he tore his hand away from the Skull and released the strands of magic engulfing it. He watched them leap away like a net cast behind a boat. Holding tight to his saddle with his right hand, Styrax guided the wyvern around in a tight spiral, swinging dangerously low over the city to avoid its slender tail catching on the trail of magic.

As they passed, the net of magic snagged on the tower's wall and latched on. The remaining energies unravelling from his hand were violently jerked clear and the unfolding net dropped down over the contraption on the tower roof. It caught two thirds of the entire roof surface, a close-knit blanket of fire that sagged off the weapon's protruding edges and ran like molten iron down its sides.

This close he saw the faces of the gunners manning the fire-thrower, staring up in horror at the descending threads of light. The quickest few ducked under the wooden arm of the thrower, but the threads burst into flame as soon as they touched wood or flesh. As the first started screaming, Styrax pulled the wyvern up into a climb. He had no need to hear the cries of pain as the threads cut through flesh and bone. He knew none would survive. The trailing threads had caught it squarely enough to set the entire tower alight.

The wyvern flapped heavily in the suddenly close, heavy air, struggling for a moment to climb before rising above the handful of artillery boats stationed on the Hound Lake and pushing on to the Menin Army beyond. Styrax turned and sensed the calls to the sky renewed with fearful vigour, the magic becoming ragged with haste. Before his eyes the clouds darkened and turned threatening.

'Most obliging of you,' he murmured. He looked towards his own army and saw the troops had begun to advance to the edge of the artillery barges' range. 'Now see how the winds come to your aid,' he shouted.

Beyn charged up the wooden stair, his boots drumming a hollow tattoo that warned those in his way to move. The Tollhouse was an odd-shaped building, the guard platforms at the top a mere afterthought of construction. He ducked his head through the doorway and blinked away the gloom of inside, heading straight towards General Aladorn, who stood at the thin horizontal window on the eastern wall.

'General, the fire-thrower's almost entirely destroyed,' Beyn blurted out, not bothering with formality now. 'It's inoperable, even if we could replace the gunners quickly.'

'But why,' asked the general, still squinting out of the window, though Beyn knew the old man's eyes were not good enough to see the enemy. 'Why destroy that one in particular?'

'Because he intends to attack that flank,' blurted out Suzerain Etharain, standing next to the general. He was the ruler of the region west of Aroth, and second chair of the Honour Council, but he was an inexperienced soldier.

'Bah, too obvious for this one. Beyn, any reports of the other legions moving?'

The King's Man shook his head. 'They're holding position beyond artillery range.'

The Menin Army had split into three groups to surround the city, each digging defensive encampments to ward off Narkang sorties. Worryingly, one of the armies was composed mainly of Chetse legions, which suggested the invasion force had increased in size since crossing the Waste.

'Daily runs?' Aladorn said, cocking his head at Beyn. 'He waits for the weather to clear and takes out the next – before long his troops have a free run at the walls, eh?'

'It gives us time to repair,' Beyn pointed out. 'The sky looks ugly now, might take days to clear, and the man's in a hurry – sooner he takes Aroth, the less time he gives the king to prepare.'

Aladorn shook his head. 'Only a fool would plan it so – to try and win the war at a stroke is to forget to win the battle. Let them try to take the city in a day; I would welcome it!' The old man had a defiant look in his eyes, as though daring Beyn to argue.

The King's Man looked away, realising he wasn't going to win any arguments here. Before the silence could stretch out further the first fat raindrops began to fall on the flat tarred roof of the guardroom. Etharain raised an eyebrow as the rain increased rapidly in the next few moments and a rumble of thunder echoed from the heavens. In less than a minute the rain had developed into a deluge.

'The mages know their work,' he commented. The suzerain was a fit-looking man of forty-odd winters. His father had been a trusted captain of General Aladorn's during the conquest of the Three Cities and he had made sure his son knew how to use the sword he carried, but like so many of Narkang's soldiers he'd never been tested in battle. 'Gods, look at it out there. The ground'll be hard going for anyone marching on our walls.'

'Don't rejoice yet,' Beyn said, looking out. The suzerain was right, the mages had done well and a furious rainstorm now battered the city. 'It cuts our visibility, makes life tough for our artillery – Karkarn's iron balls, I reckon they've overshot this time!'

Deafening peals of thunder crashed out across the plain. A great gust of wind flung a curtain of rain across their view, briefly obscuring everything apart from the dull yellow of the Tollkeeper's Arch ahead. The wind continued to strengthen, becoming a great fist of rain sweeping across the Land. Beyn could just make out the inelegant shapes of the artillery barges, lurching on the lakes.

'Hastars?' General Aladorn snapped, turning to glare at the mage behind him. 'Order them to desist!'

The mage blanched at Aladorn's wrinkled face, despite the fact he was more than a foot taller than the general, bigger even than Beyn. 'This is not the work of the coterie,' Hastars yelped in protest. 'They broke off before he returned!' he added, pointing at Beyn.

'This isn't natural,' Beyn said, advancing towards the mage. 'Look at it.'

Hastars closed his eyes, mouthing a few words then pausing, as though listening to a voice inside his head. The man was modestly gifted, but he was knowledgeable, and able at least to communicate from afar with the two dozen others sitting with linked hands in a nearby warehouse. There were only two battle-mages, but this coterie in unison would most likely serve a more useful purpose against the Menin's overwhelming strength anyway.

Hastars gasped and staggered back, hands clutching his head. A grizzled marshal grabbed him before he fell, but Hastars still looked dazed when he opened his eyes. 'Gods preserve us!' he moaned, 'the storm is being fuelled— The Menin, they are pouring energies into the sky!'

The mage sank to his knees, gulping down air. 'Such power, such power! I barely reached out and ...' he tailed off, shaking uncontrollably.

Beyn scowled as the rest of the room fluttered round the mage, returning to the view with a growing sense of trepidation. Outside the weather was worsening, grey trails dancing and whirling through the air with increasing fury. Two bursts of thunder boomed out in quick succession, then another as a lance of lightning flashed down to strike the Tollkeeper's Arch.

Oh Gods.

On the surface of the lake something rose up from the water. Though they were indistinct, the grey-blue shapes were far from human. Beyn felt his guts turn ice-cold as the figures reached up to the heavens and began to grow, drifting over the water to form a circle. All around them the storm slashed at the lake and ripped furrows through the surface, churning and spinning into ever-tightening spirals. The figures twisted and danced, writhing with frenetic energy as the lake became increasingly choppy.

'Oh Gods,' came a distant voice, muted against the howl of the wind through the gaps in the wooden walls. Beyn found Suzerain Etharain beside him, face white with horror as he too realised what was happening.

The artillery barges and their attendant boats were rocking violently; Beyn caught sight of one smaller craft just as it was smashed against a massive catapult platform. A great spinning column of water heaved up from the surface on the furthest part of Lake Apatorn, and a terrible, unnatural shriek pierced the air.

Around the tower's base danced half a dozen water elementals, the spirits of the lake, whipped into a frenzy of power, while the wind heaved and thrashed around them. Malviebrat were known for their savage, remorseless nature, and now they were being fed power by a grief-stricken white-eye.

The clouds reached down to embrace the huge waterspout,

enveloping it with dark, nebulous hands. Thunder continued to crash all around as the storm surged. A sheet of water washed across the narrow window and Beyn and Etharain both flinched back. The King's Man realised he was digging his fingernails into the wooden sill. With a great groan the waterspout lurched abruptly forward and Etharain moaned with dismay as it started for the barges.

The smaller craft started away from its terrible path, only to be hunted down by the tornado's savage outriders. Standing tall on the water, twice the height of any man, the water elementals smashed and pummelled at men and boats alike, battering both into broken pieces while the waterspout roared on. With one final lurch it caught the first of the artillery barges and ripped the arm from its catapult.

The great wooden beam was tossed high in the air, discarded like a broken match. The rest of the weapon soon followed, then the entire barge was flipped on its side with careless ease and hurled end-over-end to carve a path of destruction through the remaining scows.

The tornado charged inexorably for the next, driven by a vicious will, and ripped it apart, plank by plank. One, then two, then four, all of them torn apart like the toys of an enraged Godchild, while the Malviebrat danced and worshipped at its base, the shrieking wind a fitting prayer for their monstrous fervour. In seconds the artillery barges had been reduced to kindling, and now the waterspout lurched again, changing direction to rip a path over the stony shore of the causeway. The air filled with dirt and the tornado took on a darker hue as it gathered weapons to smash the remaining flotilla on the Hound Lake, already abandoned by its terrified crews.

'Summon the troops,' Beyn whispered hoarsely, his throat suddenly dry. 'They're coming up the causeway. Piss and daemons, they'll punch straight into the city unless we stop them at the wall!'

'Move you bastards!' the sergeant roared as wardrums sounded from the back of the legion.

The heavy beat rolled over the thousand soldiers who moved off, spear-points high. Behind them the scarred savages of the Chetse Lion Guard bellowed, axes raised high as they screamed

425

their berserk rage at the distant enemy. The rain continued to beat down, smearing the blue painted symbols adorning their segmented bronze breastplates.

The Chetse warriors wore bronze helms sporting Lord Styrax's Fanged Skull emblem, with gauntlets and greaves all built to be used as additional weapons. Every other man carried a heavy shield on his back, for when arrows were raining down or they were about to charge a wall of spear-points.

Lord Styrax nudged his wyvern forward and looked down the line of troops. The massive creature huffed and waddled forward, unused to walking with its wings furled but obeying. The flight had temporarily drained its eagerness for battle, he was glad to note, not intending to use the creature further. For the first time his Chetse allies and own heavy infantry would fight side by side. He wanted to be in the midst of them, leading from the front and reminding them all why they followed him.

A bolt of lightning arced down from the heavens with an ear-splitting crash, striking the smoking tower Styrax had already attacked, adding to the ruin. From his position atop the wyvern he could see the wreckage of boats and barges on the two lakes. His arm was outstretched toward the Hound Lake, fist half-closed, as he contained and controlled the power of the waterspout. It was smaller now, its energy bleeding up into the ever-darkening clouds above as the storm howled with increasing fury, driven on by Styrax's steady release of the magic until it was safe to let free.

The Menin troops were undaunted. With two regiments out in front they tramped with grim purpose towards the causeway, tight ranks of steel-clad infantry forcing their way through the deepening mud.

Styrax dismounted and beckoned over a messenger. 'Tell General Gaur he has the command,' Styrax roared over the shrieking wind. Once he was stuck in the thick of the fighting, Styrax knew he'd be in no position to issue tactical commands.

The messenger's reply was lost in the tumult, but his salute indicated he'd heard the white-eye's order. Gaur was stationed with the rearguard, waiting to give the order to the flanking divisions to march on the city, assuming there were no surprises waiting.

As the messenger hurried away Styrax waited for the legion to move ahead and his bodyguard to fall into position beside him. A regiment of Bloodsworn knights, much of their heavy black armour stripped down so they could march on foot, quickly took up their positions around him. The fanatical Menin élite numbered only five hundred in total: a mix of young nobles and experienced soldiers, the match of any troops in the Land. It was rare to see them on foot – they were normally the heart of a Menin cavalry charge – but their horses would be no use here.

The troops on the road made good progress, unassailed by defenders on land or water, and within minutes they were at the Tollkeeper's Arch. The long stone building had been abandoned by the city's defenders, and although regiments of archers were stationed behind the shallow canal, a hundred yards from the Tollkeeper's Arch, the wind and rain took their toll.

The leading regiments barely noticed the falling arrows as they swarmed over the yellowstone building, and when the remaining legions reached the arch and began to negotiate the ditches flanking it, the archers and crossbowmen gave up entirely and scampered back towards their lines, leaving the Menin free to reform their ranks at leisure on the causeway.

Styrax made his way to the long central hall of the Tollkeeper's Arch, past the abandoned stations where goods were checked and taxed before entering the city. At the other end he stared out at Aroth. On his right the rain, funnelled by some quirk of the roof, formed a sheet of falling water that almost entirely obscured his view of the larger lake. He took a long breath and tasted the air; the rain had washed away all other scents, leaving the morning air clean. Under the deluge Aroth seemed smaller, diminished somehow. Its sandstone towers took on an aged and decrepit mien, like long-abandoned watchtowers on an unused frontier.

'My Lord,' called a man behind him, and Styrax turned to see Army Messenger Karapin standing to attention, a rare fervour in the man's grey eyes. Karapin had volunteered to follow him into battle, his ceremonial brass vambraces and a broadsword his only protection as he waited to carry his lord's orders. He had been born less than fifty miles from Styrax's home village, and he considered the risk to be the greatest honour of his life.

'All ready?' Styrax asked.

'The legions are in position,' Karapin confirmed with a bow.

'Drummers, sound the attack.' Styrax heard the hunger in his own voice, the red rage straining to be released. If Karapin noticed, he made no sign as he stepped out into the rain and signalled the nearest regimental drummer. In moments the call was taken up and the Menin troops roared their approval.

Amidst the tumult he could still make out the thousands of Chetse voices bellowing lustily, ready to follow him to war. Styrax stepped out from the arch, surveying his men as he drew his fanged broadsword. The clamour increased a notch as the first ranks set off, within them units of engineers who carried the temporary bridges for the canal.

The Bloodsworn knights gathered around him and one unfurled Styrax's stark black and red banner. Styrax reached over and plucked the tall standard from the man's hands, raising it and turning to the troops behind him, both Menin and Chetse.

'Tell them!' he shouted over the tramp of feet and the pouring rain, 'raise your voices and tell them we're coming! Tell them even the Gods themselves should fear us!'

The thousands of soldiers howled in response and hammered weapons on their shields. The sound boomed out across the Land in rising waves, almost drowning out the thunder that crashed over the city. Legion after legion lifted their heads and roared a warning to the skies. In the distance the towers of Aroth reverberated, shuddering behind the curtain of rain.

Beyn ran forward, beating at the disordered mob and screaming himself hoarse in an effort to get them to move. Frightened faces turned his way, uncomprehending, until those in the lead finally set off again.

'You! Captain! Look at me, you fuck!' Beyn yelled, lurching to the left as he spotted another regiment of pikemen appearing around the corner of a building. It was only when Beyn fought his way over and grabbed the captain by the throat that he caught his attention. 'You, what's your name?'

The young man looked at him in blind panic for a moment, struggling in vain to free himself. The soldiers around him started forward, then shrank back as they saw the golden bees on Beyn's armour, the mark of the king.

Beyn shook him like a terrier, and screamed for the third time, 'Your name, soldier!'

'Dapplin,' the young captain croaked shakily, 'Captain Dapplin of the First City Legion.'

'Congratulations, Captain,' Beyn shouted, 'you've got a mission.' He gestured at the ground between them and the makeshift wall they'd constructed across a bottleneck of loading stations at the wharf. In the centre stood the Tollhouse, the semi-fortified building where the customs-tolls were kept before being moved to the city treasury. General Aladorn and his cohorts had been evacuated and replaced with archers. Behind the wall was a line of troops, three-deep at the moment, with officers frantically trying to drive more in behind. Thought they looked formidable, they were raw troops holding spears in trembling hands, and the Menin had more than just minotaurs to breach the line.

'Grab another regiment from your lot and form up in squad blocks behind the main line of archers.' He gave the captain another shake. 'Don't get sucked in until your job's done, and don't, for pity's sake, get in the way of the reinforcement troops!'

'You don't want us to fight?' Dapplin yelled back, recovering his senses. 'The order was to send every last man on the streets to the wall.'

'You get a shittier job,' Beyn said. 'They'll use the Reavers to breach the line; your job's to stick those bastards full of steel before they get that chance!'

'Reavers?' Dapplin gasped, the colour draining from his face.

'Aye, Reavers – now you just shut that fucking mouth before I shove my fist down it! They'll be coming a handful at a time, so each squad surrounds 'em and works together. Do it as soon as they land and you'll have a better day than the rest of us.' Beyn grabbed the captain by the arm and shoved him towards the mass of soldiers. 'Move it!'

Once Dapplin had started to lead his men away, Beyn surveyed the chaotic mass of soldiers. The line was forming as well as he could hope, and tight knots of archers were grouping behind, waiting for the order to fire. What state their weapons would be in was anyone's guess.

The ground either side of the road was sodden, so at least the Menin would have to struggle through a sucking swamp to reach them, it was a poor blessing when the storm was soaking bowstrings and blowing away range-finding arrows like dandelion seeds.

'Cober,' he shouted, looking around blindly until he found the white-eye most recently in the employ of Count Pellisorn. Since the count had been packed off to command the defence of the north wall, Cober had been following Beyn around like a puppy – albeit a puppy carrying a very large axe. Like Daken, King Emin's newest pet, the white-eye was actually an inch shorter than Beyn, but he was far more powerful – and unlike Daken, Cober seemed happy enough to follow Beyn's orders, trusting there would be a fight at the end of it.

'Come on,' Beyn beckoned, leading Cober towards the wall. 'We've work to do.' They gathered every man holding a weapon they could and handed them over to one of the officers commanding the wall, who squeezed them into the defensive line. It was untidy, but Beyn knew they weren't going to win this battle on the straightness of their columns. Their only – slim – chance was to hold on weight of numbers, and that meant pressing into service every man who could hold a spear, and keeping such a press of bodies there that the Menin couldn't break through.

Before he reached the wall warning cries began to come from the front rank. Beyn craned his head until he could just make out the line of spear-points advancing on the wall.

'Down on one knee,' he snapped at Cober.

The white-eye didn't question him, but dropped immediately, as ordered, and Beyn pulled himself onto Cober's substantial thigh, balancing himself with a hand on his shoulder, to raise himself above the defenders. The Menin were close, less than a hundred yards from the wall.

'Archers!' he bellowed, waving frantically, 'Fire, as low as you dare!'

The order was relayed quickly. Half of the raised troops were farmers and citizens, conscripted into service, and useful for little more than wielding a spear and swelling the ranks, but amongst the professionals, there were hundreds of fair archers, and Beyn had seeded the units with as many experienced soldiers as he could spare.

Now they took over, screaming themselves hoarse and leading by example. Though the first volley was ragged, the second was an improvement as the bowmen started to get a feel for the cross-wind.

Beyn left them to it and went to shout with the sergeants in the line bellowing for the troops to hold their ground. More men appeared, running to join the rear ranks, waiting for their time of need.

A deep roar rang out: the sound of a thousand voices, foreign voices and more, shouting as they charged. Beyn felt the impact through his feet as much as he heard it, and he was tugging his axes from his belt as the first screams came.

'Aroth and the king!' he roared, holding one axe up high, and the call was picked up by all those around him and rippled through the defenders.

From behind the archers a line of trumpeters and other musicians began to sound their instruments: they all played the same notes, a repeated refrain with no specific meaning other than to add to the noise of battle. He hoped the strange cacophony would remind the soldiers of their homes and their families, whose survival rested on their men holding the line. It wasn't much, but Beyn knew soldiers would cling to any small hope to give themselves cheer.

'Not today,' the King's Man growled. 'I'm not fucking dying today.'

Kastan Styrax watched his troops throwing themselves with abandon at the enemy. As they slammed into the wall, some succeeded in driving the spears aside with their shields before stabbing with their own, others were impaled, and in their haste some smashed straight into the wall itself, a hastily built mishmash of rubble and sodden wood that stopped them in their tracks and left them staring at the face of some astonished Arothan barely inches away.

The Menin infantry pounded at the varied array of weapons, driven on by bloodlust and the press of ranks behind. Styrax himself couldn't reach the defenders, such was the mass of his men attacking the wall. Another volley of arrows flew into the Menin and Chetse troops, and more came from the buildings, though most were blown about by the gale and dropped like exhausted sparrows, their energy spent.

Styrax threw a lance of flame at the nearest city building, and an orange-gold stream of fire illuminated the sodden combatants below. Before it struck, the flames were wrenched upwards and soared over the roofs of the city like a comet before dissipating into nothingness.

Styrax smiled grimly and drew on the Skulls fused to his armour. He threw a crackling burst of iron-grey energy at the building, and this too was diverted by Aroth's mages, although its tail clipped one corner of the roof, exploding some tiles. The pieces clattered down onto those below, and told Styrax all he needed to know about the mages defending the city.

He was quite safe from attack by them; that much he was certain. The vast majority were men and women with minor skills, sitting within a network of defensive wards and channelling their power to the strongest. That one knew what he or she was doing well enough, whether or not they were a battle-mage. How long they could defend against his efforts depended on how many they numbered, but Styrax didn't care – endless power was his to command . . . It would be easy, he thought, to get carried away as he punched through the mages' defences. For the first time in years, Styrax didn't trust himself not to get lost in the storm of magic. Even a white-eye of his skill could easily be overwhelmed by such colossal energies, and grief had made him ragged at the edges. It would be easy for him to become careless and unfocused.

Let this be a victory for the army, he thought with a quickening sense of anticipation; *let it belong to the soldiers alone.*

He turned and waved forward the minotaurs, who were straining to drag the battering ran along the road that was swiftly turning to mud. Behind them came the Reavers. He would commit the regiments of white-eyes soon enough – their value was in exploiting vulnerabilities once he threw them into play.

As Styrax advanced towards the wall and joined the press of soldiers, a burgeoning corona of light played around his shoulders. The troops made space for him quickly enough so he could attack the nearest Arothan troops with his spitting whipcords of bright white energy.

At such short range the coterie of defending mages could do little to defend the men and as their screams of agony rang out, so the Menin soldiers cheered and pressed harder against the line, ignoring the dead at their feet except to step over them.

On the right the minotaurs got the battering ram into position and started to drive it forward. A bronze head capped the pointed tip of the ram, inscribed by Lord Larim with runes of fire and strength. As it struck the heavy door to the Tollhouse with an almighty thump, so fire burst out from the bronze head and licked over the iron-bound wood of the door.

The fire quickly dissipated when the ram was dragged back, but the wood remained scorched, and every time the head hit it burned a little more. The minotaurs bellowed with frustration and rage as the door continued to resist, most likely blocked with rubble behind, but they kept at their task.

Above them a handful of archers braved the Menin arrows to lean out and shoot down at the minotaurs. One was successful, catching the largest of the beasts in the neck and causing it to reel away in mortal agony, then the Menin bowmen responded, peppering the upper levels of the Tollhouse.

Styrax added to their efforts as the archers reloaded, casting deep-red tendrils at the wooden upper levels. The tendrils grew rapidly, reaching out like blind snakes. When one reached the window it slid inside and Styrax heard screams a few moments later.

Shortly afterwards the city's mages came to their rescue, deftly unravelling the skein of magic and allowing the force to dissipate on the wind. Only a black stain, darker than flame-scars, was left, but it had done its work and Styrax returned his attentions to the ranks of defenders.

He could feel the presence of the defending mages all around him, waiting to unravel his next spell, so instead he fed the inexhaustible power of the Skulls into Kobra, his unnatural black sword – and there was nothing they could do to divert that as Styrax began to barge his way towards the enemy, his weapon raised and humming with barely restrained power. The air seemed to darken around him, turning mid-morning to dusk as Kobra's bloodthirsty magic shone out from the sword's blade. In response, Styrax's black whorled armour began to leak smoky trails of magic that swarmed and coiled like a mass of snakes. Before he reached the enemy he could see the fear etched clear on their faces.

Beyn wiped a palm across his face, clearing the rain from his eyes. Voices came from all directions; there was a clatter and crash of weapons from the wall and a deep, reverberating thump from the

Tollhouse. He and Cober entered the fortified treasury by a side door, to be met by anxious faces.

'The rubble's not going to hold!' one young lieutenant said, terror making his voice high and strained. He pointed through an open doorway to the mound of stone and debris that occupied half of the far room.

'Well, make sure it bloody does!' Beyn snapped. 'Shore the damn thing up – we're in a city, aren't we? How hard can it be to find rubble – or make some?'

The lieutenant blanched and gave Beyn a shaky salute before hurrying outside. Men sat or squatted in the empty interior of the Tollhouse, working the stiffness from their fingers. They were working in shifts, shooting from the slit windows, and the blood on several uniforms told Beyn it wasn't all one-way traffic.

He went through into the front room; the makeshift barricade was indeed shuddering and shifting with every impact on the door. While the main doorway was blocked right up to the lintel, once the wooden frame gave way, the doorway was wide enough that they'd be able to haul much of the debris away.

'Damn,' he muttered, stalking outside again.

There were soldiers everywhere: reinforcements, running up to the wall in groups of fifty or a hundred, and auxiliaries, humping fat bundles of arrows forward for the archers. The sky had lightened a little, but that only served to make clearer the true horror of their situation.

A line of men was strung across the causeway, thousands committed to the fight in one go, and hundreds were already dead. Those at the front were barely fighting; they just stood behind shield and spear and allowed those behind them to hold spears above their heads and thrust at the enemy, who were doing likewise. It was a battle of attrition. Beyn had several thousand men in reserve – but so did the Menin.

A piercing shriek of jubilation cut through the brutal clash of steel on steel, sending a chill down Beyn's spine. He looked up, and saw a pair of dark shapes in the sky hurtling towards him.

'Dapplin!' he roared at the nearest unit of pikemen, 'get ready!'

The squad moved forward as the captain yelled orders, but still they barely had time to get into position before the first of the Reavers arrived. Squatting low over a blade-edged shield, the Menin white-eye smashed into Dapplin's men. His long braided black hair flying, the Reaver tore a bloody path through them, the shield cutting through flesh wherever it touched, until it slowed enough for the white-eye to roll off, grab it and loop the leather hold over his shield-arm, and start towards the archers beyond.

Beyn caught sight of the weird tattoos and scars that adorned his face, which was contorted in berserk rage as the Reaver hacked at the archers with his great spiked axe. Two men fell almost at once, then another as the white-eye turned around and slashed a man's chest with his razor-edged shield.

As Beyn raced towards the frenzied white-eye, Cober hard on his heel, the Menin abruptly changed direction and launched himself at the pair like a whirlwind of steel. His speed almost caught them out, his axe whipping around to catch them mid-step. Beyn managed to abandon his charge in time, throwing himself to the ground and skidding under the warrior's outstretched arm, but Cober was not so lucky – Beyn heard a crunch of blade parting mail.

The King's Man twisted as he slid on the rain-slicked cobbles and hacked at the Menin white-eye's foot as his momentum took him through the Reaver's legs. Before he'd come to a halt Beyn was turning, one weapon above his head, while he jabbed the other at the unprotected back of the Reaver's knee. The Reaver arched in agony, but his howl of pain was cut short as one of the archers fired at almost point-blank range. The arrow punched a hole in the Reaver's cuirass and threw the white-eye backwards onto Beyn, who collapsed under the enormous white-eye. He desperately tried to free his weapons before realising it was dead weight on him, not a living enemy.

'Don't just stand there!' he cried, struggling to get the dead man off him, 'bloody shoot the rest of them!'

As he got to his feet he saw the other Reaver had been surrounded and impaled, but several soldiers had been lost in the fight. The victory was short-lived as four more Reavers landed, flying directly into the defending line like an artillery strike. Those at the back turned to the nearest reserve squad, while the other two charged into the undefended rear of the battle line and began to slaughter the spearmen.

'Get to them!' Beyn roared, then he faltered as he looked down and saw Cober, still on the ground. The white-eye's hands were clasped around his neck and blood flowed freely from between his fingers. His mouth was open, as if he was trying to speak. Beyn looked into Cober's eyes and saw the horror there: the pain, and the fear of his impending death.

A wave of anguish swept over Beyn and his knees wobbled for a moment, but there wasn't time, not even for a man's last moments of life. Cober's body spasmed, and his mouth moved again, but no words came out.

His face tight with rage, Beyn turned away and headed for the fighting.

Styrax heard the door finally shatter to triumphant bellows from the minotaurs. The huge horned beasts started on the barricade filling the door, eagerly grabbing the lumps of rock and tossing them carelessly behind, drool hanging from their gaping jaws as they worked. The Menin lord fought his way clear of his soldiers and went around to the shattered remains of the Tollhouse's main entrance. The bronze head of the ram was a mess, but it had done its job, and inside the pile of rubble had already started to slip away.

Realising others would fit through the breach more easily Styrax let a sliver of magic run over his tongue as he shouted to the minotaurs, 'Withdraw! Be ready to breach the wall.'

The great beasts turned and regarded him. Bloodlust clouded their senses for a moment, before they understood the order. Even the smallest were bigger than Styrax, with their limbs like tree boughs and great jutting horns that were as much weapons as the maces and clubs they carried. They wore no armour, but one lucky neck-shot aside, the several who had arrows protruding from their flesh were unconcerned, for their skin was tougher than leather.

Without waiting for a response Styrax gathered a fistful of flame and launched it into the building. The fire flowed over the chunks of rock and debris with serpentine speed, and Styrax was rewarded with the chilling screams of the defenders. He reached up and grasped the inside edge of the doorway, bracing himself against it while allowing more power to flood through his body. He swung himself up and kicked forcibly at the top of the rubble. For a moment nothing happened, then a great rumble heralded a landslide on the other side and Styrax clambered through the gap at the top. He heard whoops and warcries from the Chetse troops as they followed him, dragging more stones out of the way to clear a path for their comrades.

The moment he was inside, he swept Kobra forward to behead the one soldier still standing, then moved through to the next room and cut down the three archers who had left it too late to flee. Two more soldiers ran in, their spears levelled, and charged the Lord of the Menin, but with a wave of his hand a shield of misty grey appeared before him, the spearheads glanced sideways, and Styrax stepped around his magical defence and beheaded the pair.

Now his Chetse warriors were through too, and half a dozen moved past him, their axes ready for the next defenders foolish enough to try to plug the breach. Styrax let them go on ahead as he turned to the left-hand wall. He took a deep breath and flattened his pale left hand against the Crystal Skulls on his chest. The shadows inside the Tollhouse were banished by a bright light which wrapped around his black armour. Styrax felt a small pain at the back of his head as he drew deeper on the Skulls than he'd intended, but he didn't relent.

There was a bricked-up doorway in the wall; he'd seen it from the outside. It looked as if there had once been another part to this building, and this originally an internal wall, and so it was likely weaker than the rest. Styrax dipped his shoulder and ran straight into the wall beside of the doorway. The entire building shuddered as a blaze of light exploded from his magic-laden armour, moment-arily igniting the mortar between the stones.

Styrax backed up and charged again, and this time he felt the stones buckle under the pressure. A third blow, and a section of the wall toppled down onto the soldiers behind it. For good measure Styrax kicked the doorframe again, sending another cascade of stones onto the Arothans outside. For a moment all he could see was the dust of the fallen building, then the screaming began as the Menin soldiers surged forward.

Behind them charged the minotaurs, shoving aside the Menin infantry in their eagerness to get at the enemy. They leapt nimbly over rubble and bodies alike, and the line of defenders buckled, then collapsed, brutally ravaged by the minotaurs. Styrax left them to it and headed out the back of the Tollhouse, following the stream of Chetse troops still piling through the broken doorway.

He emerged into a sea of enemy soldiers, the bulk of whom were formed up behind a line of archers. The berserker Chetse charged straight for the bowmen, who managed to take out a few before breaking ranks and running for their lives.

A squad of soldiers charged Styrax, their pikes levelled, and he dodged to one side to avoid them, deflecting the last with his sword. They had no chance to reform as he pushed on past the long weapons and into the tight squad, cutting around him with superhuman speed. Only two men survived his blistering assault, but they backed into an advancing minotaur, who clubbed one and gored the other, tossing him high in the air before he fell, broken, upon the ground.

More Arothan soldiers ran for Styrax, who found himself parrying three, then four desperate men. One black-clad soldier armed with two axes came in on his left, turning into Styrax's sword as it came up to stop his axe, bringing his other axe around to catch Styrax's arm in the next movement – and the manoeuvre would have worked, had Kobra not pushed back the guarding axe and shorn through the shaft. The red-black blade carried on forward, chopping through arm and into his ribs.

Styrax saw the soldier's mouth fall open in wordless agony as he hung there for a moment, the fanged weapon snagged on his shoulder, his body torn open and his life's blood flooding out. Their eyes met, and the soldier's jaw worked for a moment, as though he was trying to give Styrax a message with his last breath.

No words came, and the soldier's eyes fluttered as death took him.

Styrax tugged his sword from the corpse.

Behind him the Chetse reserves surged on, widening the breach in the wall and reducing what was left of the defensive line to mangled bodies and shattered bone.

'No quarter!' Styrax roared as he threw himself forward with his Bloodsworn bodyguard, following in the wake of the crazed minotaurs. More troops joined them, both Chetse and Menin, breathlessly stampeding into the belly of the enemy.

'Raze the city to the ground – kill them all!' cried the Lord of the Menin, and the soldiers heard the savagery in their lord's voice and watched as Styrax threw himself into the fight with reckless abandon, memories of Kohrad's death filling his mind as he waded through the collapsed city defences. They hurtled further into the city, killing everyone, and setting light to the buildings before they'd even finished the slaughter.

Even before evening drew in, the sky was so dark with smoke that it seemed Tsatach himself, refusing to witness such horror, had turned his fiery eye away from the Land. The rain fell like tears, washing a river of blood from what had once been Aroth into the two lakes.

CHAPTER 30

Mihn ran his fingers up the back of Hulf's neck, digging into the grey-black fur to scratch the dog's skin underneath. The oversized puppy arched its neck appreciatively and licked at Mihn's wrists, and shuffled forward to press its chest against him. Hulf was already bigger than an average dog now, and his shoulders were developing real muscles, but he was still growing into his body, and Mihn reckoned he had a way to go before he had reached his full size.

He turned closer into Mihn, demanding the attention continue, and lifting one huge furry paw up onto Mihn's thigh. Before Mihn could move, Hulf caught sight of Isak leaving the cottage and bounded forward with a bark, shoving Mihn aside. He turned to watch the exuberant dog charge into Isak and slam both paws into the white-eye's midriff. It took Isak a moment longer to react than anyone else might have, but once his mind caught up with events a crooked, distant smile crossed his face.

'It's a good sign, that,' Morghien called from the lake shore, where he was fishing.

'Why do you say that?'

He pointed at Hulf. 'Dogs have a fine sense for the unnatural. However you brought him back, he's here now, and with no stink of the Dark Place about him.'

'Hulf doesn't smell it,' Isak said, looking up at him, 'but I do.'

'What, the Dark Place?'

The white-eye nodded sadly. 'On the air, in the fire: a song on the wind.'

'It is a memory,' Mihn said firmly. 'You are here, you are alive – and the Dark Place has no claim on you.'

'But there I walk,' Isak said, 'one foot within, one without, unbound and unchained, but yet the chains mark me still.'

440

Accompanied by the leaping, fawning dog, Isak joined Mihn and sat. Hulf wedged himself between them for a restless minute before he bounded up again and headed off to make a nuisance of himself with Morghien's feathered fishing lure.

'Do the scars still hurt?' Mihn asked as they watched Morghien playing with Hulf, sending him chasing after the lure with practised flicks of his rod.

'Without the pain, what would I be?' Isak replied, his eyes on the far shore.

'Still yourself, always yourself.'

He turned to look Mihn direct in the face. 'And what's that?'

'A man, blessed and cursed equally,' Mihn said eventually. Isak had taken to asking questions that Mihn had no real answer for – questions he doubted anyone but the Gods could manage.

'Blessed? No,' Isak whispered, pulling his robe tighter around his body as though to hide the scars on his chest and neck. 'No blessings in the grave, and no curses either, not any more.'

'So you are just you, then, free of everything that was heaped upon you – the conflicting destinies, the prophecies and expect-ations, exactly as you intended when you faced Lord Styrax. You are free of obligation now.'

'All that's left is me, all of me I have left,' Isak said, watching Hulf struggle through the water. The ripples raced towards them and although they were a yard or more short of the edge, Isak still drew back his legs protectively. 'Ripples through the Land, change and consequence unbound—'

Hulf paddled his way to shore and raced past them, barking furiously at the figures emerging from the forest path, leading a pair of horses. One moved ahead of the others, obviously unafraid of Hulf's bluster, and Mihn recognised Major Jachen, returning as ordered.

'Major,' Mihn called, hurrying over, 'did you—?'

But he didn't bother finishing the sentence as he recognised two of the people following Jachen: the King's Man, Doranei, looking distinctly puzzled, the other – while Mihn hadn't actually met her, he could hardly mistake Legana's piercing emerald eyes, even at that distance. They were as conspicuous as the shadowy handprint at her throat and the seams of copper in her hair. The Mortal-Aspect of a dead Goddess stood awkwardly, using a long oak staff for support. She and Doranei were dressed much alike, in green tunic and breeches, but still her presence screamed for attention.

She cocked her head at him. As they had left the shadow of the trees she had screwed up her eyes against the afternoon sun. As Hulf, finished with the major, edged forward to sniff at her, Legana recoiled at the unexpected movement, and she had a knife in her hand before she caught herself. She tucked it back into her sleeve and hesitantly held her hand out towards the dog, who sniffed again and retreated with his head low, obviously unnerved by her scent. A slight smile appeared on her lips.

'Welcome, both of you,' Mihn said.

Doranei looked wary, and older than when Mihn had last seen him. King Emin's agent look distinctly drained, ragged around the edges.

And for that we call you brother, Mihn thought as they grasped each other's forearm in greeting. Doranei's grip at least was a strong as ever, Mihn was glad to discover.

'Good to see you again,' Doranei said, unable to stop himself peering over Mihn's shoulder at Isak. Mihn turned briefly; the white-eye had not moved from his position, or given any sign that he knew someone had arrived.

'And you,' Mihn said warmly, 'as they say in Ter Nol, "Too much has come to pass since last we met".'

Doranei scowled. 'Too damn much, aye.' He released his grip as Morghien arrived and embraced him.

'Brother,' Morghien, 'how fares the king?'

'As well as can be expected, but the strain's taking a toll on us all and ... well.' He rolled up his sleeve and showed his arm to Morghien. 'Beyn was in Aroth. He used the wyvern claws to send me an' Coran this message two days ago.'

Mihn turned his head to read the three words in the Narkang dialect, now scabbed over: We are lost. 'So Aroth has fallen.'

The King's Man nodded and looked away. 'No more word after this. Beyn didn't respond to my reply. That's another Brother dead.'

A moment of silence descended before Hulf whimpered and pressed against Mihn's legs. When he looked, he saw Legana had advanced a few steps. Her face was unreadable, not unexpected, he thought, of one so profoundly touched by the Gods. Mihn realised she was looking past him, but he couldn't see anything himself.

Grimacing in the light, even with the sun covered by cloud, Legana walked clumsily for a few moments, leaning heavily on her staff, until she got into her stride. Her face set, she ignored the three men.

'So it's true then?' Doranei asked, his voice a half-whisper.

'The message?' Mihn replied, still watching the Mortal-Aspect, 'it is true.'

'How?' He sounded incredulous.

Morghien snorted. 'Which part? The resurrection, or the fact he reckons he'll get lucky second time around.'

Mihn shot the cantankerous old man a warning look. 'No more of those comments; they try my patience.'

'Hah! Well, meself? I'm fresh out o' blind faith,' Morghien growled. 'Alive he may be; sane? That I ain't so sure about. You want to trust the future of us all to a man driven at least half-mad by his own foolish schemes?'

'Isak was bound by prophecy and destiny,' Mihn said, turning to face Morghien. He was not quite squaring up to the man, but he'd moved close enough to make his point. 'Kastan Styrax was born to kill the Last King, and that fate also bound Isak. But you know perfectly well no obligation nor tie can follow a man beyond the grave. And that means that now there is no link between the two, no predetermination of the outcome of a second meeting. The slate is blank.'

Doranei sucked his teeth. 'Gotta say, there's nothing binding me to Lord Styrax's destiny either, and I ain't keen to cross swords with the man any time soon.'

'The message said nothing about *fighting* the man, only *defeating* him.'

'But he won't say how, and that's what bugs me,' Morghien continued stubbornly.

'That does not interest me.' Mihn turned away to watch as Legana at last caught sight of Isak. 'He is most certainly damaged, broken, both as a warrior and as a lord, but he has seen what lies behind the veil of this Land.'

'Death's halls? He's not alone in that, I'd bet the witch has too.'

'More than that,' Mihn said, 'the fabric of the Land, the subtle balance of all things – Gods, men, even daemons. He was blessed by the Gods, not to be the greatest of warriors, but in a way both more delicate and more profound. You've seen the results of what he can do unwittingly already.'

'You mean the Reapers? Can't argue there, I suppose,' Morghien said gruffly. 'Severing an Aspect's link to Death wasn't something I thought possible.'

Mihn dipped his head. 'My point exactly. The minstrel's magic opened the door, but it was Isak's hand that performed the impossible in Scree. Intentionally or not, he summoned Death's Herald and tore the Reapers from Lord Death's grasp. Even more telling, perhaps, is the fact it was unintentional – the Land is his to command in a way no mage of Narkang could claim. Even before Scree he had defeated Aryn Bwr and chained him in his own mind – a feat only Gods had previously managed, and all this achieved by an untutored youth barely a year after his Choosing.'

'Somethin' I had a hand in,' Morghien pointed out.

'Undoubtedly,' Mihn agreed, 'you gave him the tools – but he acted alone. The Gods made Styrax the great champion, the unbeatable warrior, and then he rejected them – though they have come to realised how disastrous their direct manipulation was, it is too late to undo that. Isak was never intended to be the equal of Styrax; he was not created to be a great general. If anything, they intended him to be a fulcrum, a point on which history could turn, so that Styrax's power alone would not determine the future.'

'Whatever was intended, it got twisted awry,' Doranei interjected. 'Azaer, the Last King, maybe others too – they all tried to get a hand in, and they sent the whole thing spinning off-course.'

'So Isak was left with nothing?'

'Well, no, not exactly nothing,' the King's Man admitted.

'Consider what he has already done, even bound by all these efforts to control and direct him. He *is* that fulcrum. He has become a catalyst of events, for good or for ill, intended or not.'

Morghien pursed his lips. 'You sayin' that scarred wreck of a man can remake the Land as he sees fit? He can determine the course of history because it's him making the decisions?'

Mihn looked at Isak, then said to them both, 'I am saying Isak has already done many remarkable things. I am saying his mind is a tool as much as his body, and it has been forged in the fires of

Ghenna. To unpick and reshape the works of Gods and emperors requires an understanding of the very fabric of the Land such as mortal minds could never grasp. We were never intended for that. What you see as madness might instead be Isak discovering a part of him more akin to the immortal mind.'

The three were silent as they watched Legana catch Isak's attention and eventually down sit beside him.

Then Doranei spoke, his voice a rasp. 'Or it could be he's just fucking mad and we're all screwed.'

Mihn nodded. 'True.'

—Do you remember me?

Isak looked up at Legana's face. There was no recognition in his eyes, but eventually he nodded. 'We are both broken,' he said, returning his attention to the surface of the lake. 'All twisted and broken.'

She looked at his face side-on. The lines of his head were unnatural, reminding her of a copper bowl battered by years of careless use. White-eyes could heal remarkably quickly, and often with barely a trace of the original injury, but Isak's head bore the record of the abuse inflicted upon him.

Scars ran up his cheek from jaw to hair-line. The curve of his earlobe was frayed, like the wing of a dead butterfly. A furrow ran down the ear that looked remarkably like a massive claw had raked it. The furrow petered out where it reached the clear indentations of a massive chain pulled tight around his throat, each link looking like it had been burned into the skin with acid.

The extent of the damage shocked her, and she was reminded of the battle between the Lady and Aracnan. Her last memory of her Goddess had been one of agony, both personal, and that radiating out from the Lady as the power of a Crystal Skull burned through her divine form.

—Not completely broken she wrote. She held the slate in front of Isak's face, but he said nothing.

—Mihn sent a message to King Emin. About Lord Styrax.

Isak shrank back from the name in front of him, drawing his hands protectively up to his chest until Legana pulled the slate away. Eventually he took a deep breath and turned to look at her again, and this time Legana saw a spark in his eyes, the return of something human that was hiding behind the damaged remnants of his mind.

'There are holes in my mind,' Isak said. 'I will never be remade – not even the Gods have such strength.'

—*What do you see in those holes?*

'Shadows,' Isak said, with a lopsided attempt at a smile that would have terrified children and unnerved the mortal Legana ... but it was pity that filled her heart now. 'I see shadows where once there were memories, the parts of me I've lost.'

Legana looked at him, and Isak reached out a hand to awkwardly pat hers; he had two fingernails missing and not one finger followed the natural line. A man's touch had always made her skin crawl, sparked a flutter of panic in her heart. It had taken her years to learn how to keep such reactions in check, even with her unyielding strength of mind ... but Isak was as a child.

She took his hand and held it between her own, feeling him tremble slightly as he spoke.

'These holes are the only weapons I have.' He raised his other hand and Legana flinched as she realised he held Eolis in it. 'This I have no use for, I'm just waiting for someone to need it.'

Legana let Isak go and wrote – *Will holes be enough?*

'Perhaps,' Isak replied, enigmatically, 'but no. There will still be sacrifices. How it may be done I don't know.'

—*I don't understand.*

Isak stood, and looking down at Legana, said, 'I know what will stop ... him ... but ...' He flexed his damaged fingers, as if reaching for a solution, then said sadly, 'The pieces are not yet complete.'

—*And Azaer?*

'How do you kill a shadow?'

—*There are ways. There has to be.*

Isak held up a bag that hung from his waist. 'These are the key, hidden somewhere inside them.' He opened the bag and showed Legana the object within, a Crystal Skull. It wasn't one of those given to Isak by the Knights of the Temples, but the Skull of Dreams, the one fused to Xeliath's skin until her death.

'Look inside and find the answers. That's what I was born to do: crack open skulls and expose what lies within. These were there at the beginning, when Aryn Bwr set out on the path of rebellion. They were old when he found them, they were old when the shadow led him to a barrow caught in twilight and twisted history. To understand this war I must understand them and their place in this Land. Until then, we are lost.'

Legana shivered, the small spark of Fate that remained within her vibrating as he spoke the words inscribed on Doranei's arm.

—*We must go*, she wrote, pushing herself upright again.

'Where?'

—*To find the king. His last chance may already be in his hands.*

CHAPTER 31

Major Amber stopped as an unexpected cool breath of wind drifted over him. He turned and looked at the city behind him, the dirty-white stone of Ismess nestled around the base of the slope he had been climbing. The wind tugged at his clothes with renewed force and Amber closed his eyes, imagining being carried up into the sky. When he'd started up towards the Library of Seasons there had been a Litse white-eye flying high above him, staring down at the grand, dilapidated temples and the sprawling Palace of the Three Winds.

The slope, a huge stepped incline two hundred yards long, was called Ilit's Stair. It was the only official entrance to the library, located inside Blackfang Mountain. The rulers of the Circle City's other quarters had tunnelled through miles of rock to provide private entrances, so they could meet on relatively neutral ground. The rigid white lines of the library looked even starker against the black rock of the mountain, especially when lit by the summer sun high in the sky.

Amber had ignored the hostile looks while travelling through the city of the Menin's ancient enemy; he was used to them now. Walking up Ilit's Stair however, he was reminded of the weapons stores in the guardhouse. Amber was from a military family, and his ancestors had doubtless taken part in the Menin slaughter of the Litse. The weapons – bundles of arrows and ballista-bolts, enough for every Menin who had participated – were stored even today, to prevent the quarter and the library being sacked again.

'Didn't help you though, did it?' Amber called up to the dark shape in the sky. 'You let us in this time.'

He resumed his ascent, part of him still anticipating the flash of an arrow from the shadows, but he reached the open gate without drama and stopped to inspect the changes that had happened since he was last there. The damage to the buildings took him by surprise; he hadn't been back since the guardian had been woken.

As he walked through the gate, Amber realised the library was busier than it had been in years, centuries more likely. Blond-haired labourers swarmed over every building, even those that looked damaged beyond repair. As well as the workmen, he could see teams of engineers, soldiers and scholars, servants wearing the livery of the Ruby Tower – there were even some courtiers lazing in the shade or eating at long stone tables.

'So it's true,' Amber murmured to himself, 'Duchess Escral has moved herself to the library – but at whose suggestion, I wonder? If there really was a Devil Stair created in the tower by the assassins I can see why she would, but this isn't the most obvious alternative.' Intelligence on the assault on the Ruby Tower was sketchy, to say the least, but one mage had suggested the assassins had killed Aracnan by somehow casting him down into Ghenna. Amber suspected that before long the Menin would be getting the blame for it all, their lord having created that terrifying precedent in the recent battle.

The duchess' scrawny steward caught sight of him and hurried over. He bowed low as he said, 'Major, welcome to the Library of Seasons.'

Amber grunted in response and continued to scan the faces. Just emerging from the remains of the Fearen House, where the dragon had made a lair for itself, he spotted the waddling form of Lord Celao. As nominal custodian of the library, the obese white-eye should be securing his valuable property, but from the few Litse guards in view it appeared that wasn't as great a concern as Amber had expected. Servants in a variety of liveries bustled around him, but he ignored them all – despite the fact some were carrying books from the Fearen House.

Interesting. Celao's not only tolerating the Byoran presence; he seems to be giving tacit agreement to it, else he'd be throwing his considerable weight around.

'I hope you're not going to ask me for my weapons, Steward Jato,' Amber said eventually.

'Aha, of course not, Major.' Jato's beaky face was a mass of wrinkles as he tittered obsequiously. 'Can I fetch you some refreshment on this warm day?'

'Just Kayel, please.'

Jato straightened and frowned. 'Sergeant Kayel? Certainly, Major. I believe he is attending the duchess in the Summerturn House.' He pointed towards the building just past the ruined Scholars' Palace. There were deep-scored claw-marks on the stone, but no apparent structural damage.

The steward started off in that direction, but before he'd gone a few yards Amber called him back. 'Wait, I want to talk to you first.'

Jato looked at him with an expression that Amber eventually realised was intended to be sombre concentration. 'Of course, Major, how may I help?'

'The child, Ruhen – what do you think of him?'

'The little prince, sir? Why, he is a blessing for us all!' Jato looked almost hurt at the question, and his pale cheeks coloured.

'Does he—? Well, does he seem like other children to you?'

'Certainly not!' Jato gasped. 'He is above us all; untouched by the cares and fears of this life. He will lead us to salvation – to peace.'

'And you're his devoted servant, eh?'

The hectic colour drained from Jato's face. 'Of course I am . . . why would you ask such a thing? What lies have you been told?'

The fear was plain to see on Jato's face, but Amber ignored his questions, saying, 'That will be all, steward, thank you. Please fetch Sergeant Kayel.'

Steward Jato squawked breathlessly for a few heartbeats, until the big soldier pointed towards the Summerturn House, whereupon he flinched away and bowed hurriedly.

Maybe the link between Kayel and me remains strong, Amber noted as he watched Jato scuttle away. A magical link had been created in Scree between Amber and Ruhen's big guardian, one that remained to this day. His best guess was it had been created by some follower of Azaer to add to the confusion and chaos that ended in the city's destruction. He'd still not worked out how to exploit its existence. *I shouldn't have that effect on a man used to Kayel's presence, not unless he had reason to fear.*

His thoughts were disturbed by a peal of high notes chiming out from behind him. Amber turned and saw a long bank of shutters had been opened on the top floor of one of the smaller buildings on the bank of the small stream that ran through the valley. It was called the Watersong House, if his memory was correct, and he could see a rail inside the now-open windows, hanging from which were long steel chimes and small polished bells. A team of servants were ringing out some strange tune Amber didn't recognise, as they did every Litse feast-day.

He looked back towards Ismess, suddenly remembering the drapes and flags he'd seen on the way here; at the time he'd been more interested in the Wall of Intercession set up at the arched entrance to the Garden of Lilies. The garden was one of the few elegant places in the city. It surrounded the foot of Ilit's Stair, one of the most prominent positions in the quarter, so clearly it wasn't just the Byorans who saw Ruhen as the answer to their desperate prayers – or, perhaps more accurately, the only one listening to their prayers in this time of violent fanaticism. One thing the citizens of Ismess had in abundance was desperation.

'Well, if it ain't the hero of the Byoran Fens?' said a rough voice behind him. Amber turned to see Hener Kayel, wearing his usual evil grin. 'Should I curtsey for the great man?'

'Whatever you're used to,' Amber replied, disinterested.

The sergeant wore his uniform breeches and high boots, but he had discarded the jacket for an open-necked white shirt – which looked incongruous paired with the long steel-backed gloves that covered both arms. Amber felt distinctly overdressed in the heat.

'I'm not really used to heroes,' Kayel replied, mockingly, 'so I'm a bit out of practice. Best I leave it out entirely – wouldn't want to get it wrong and cause offence.'

Amber snorted, but before he could reply he sensed a sudden shift in movement. He looked around, and saw a group of Devoted soldiers approaching from the direction of the Akell tunnel, their red sashes, bearing the Order's Runesword emblem, making them obvious, even at that distance.

Kayel, watching people's reactions, gave Amber a comradely tap and pointed to the Litse lord. The grossly obese white-eye, Ilit's Chosen, was looking like a man afraid as he sensed the shift around him. His hand reached for his scimitar-bladed spear, which was carried by a servant. Gesh, first among the library's white-eye guardians, stood near Lord Celao, watching heads turn impassively.

There was no sign that he'd noted Celao's fearful reaction, though he could hardly have failed to see it.

'Fat-boy's scared,' Kayel commented with a chuckle. 'A noble-man from Tor Salan arrived in the night and demanded to speak to him.'

Amber considered both Gesh and the statement a moment. The white-eye was still wearing his ceremonial armour, but he now carried an ornate bow rather than javelins.

'Gesh has been made Krann of the Litse?' he inquired.

'That's the one. Turns out the nobleman spent his entire fortune to commission a bow from the mage-smiths of Tor Salan, bank-rupted himself a few weeks before you lot arrived at the gate.'

'Our Gods are caring, then,' Amber muttered, looking at the contrast between white-eyes. Gesh already looked more of a lord than Celao ever had, so he guessed it wouldn't be long before a true ruler took charge of what Litse were left in the Land.

'One of 'em, maybe,' Kayel said with a wink. 'I heard the man had the Lady's luck – you lot killed all the mages in Tor Salan, so none of 'em lived to collect his final payment!'

Amber smiled distantly and looked at the approaching Devoted, led by Knight-Cardinal Certinse, without his attendant priests for the first time in months. More curiously, they were ignoring the unmistakable shape of Lord Celao and instead headed towards the Summerturn House.

'Quite some allies you've got here, Sergeant,' Amber com-mented. 'The frightened Lord Celao I can understand; the only way to keep the support of his people is to unite them against us, but the Devoted?'

'As Ruhen says, it's always good to have friends.'

Amber frowned. 'Are they Ruhen's friends, or Duchess Escral's?'

'The duchess is the ruler of Byora,' Kayel reminded him, 'Ruhen's a special little boy, but he's not telling the duchess what to do.'

'Leaves that part to you, does he? No, don't bother answering that. I know the Devoted are having problems with their priests, but is it bad as all that?'

'Depends whether you'd enjoy being strung up for impiety. As I hear, Akell's at boiling point.'

'But the Knight-Cardinal's authority is based on the cults; isn't every officer of the Order an ordained priest? It would be quite a step for them to seek outside help against their own.'

Kayel nodded. 'Their problem, not mine.'

'But to look to Ruhen for help? Half the Order must consider Ruhen and your band of preachers heretical.'

'Don't you think everyone needs to wallow in the glory o' the Gods?' Kayel said in a deadpan voice.

Amber glanced around, then gestured for Kayel to follow him back out onto Ilit's Stair, where they wouldn't be overheard. 'I don't think you do, no.'

'What makes you say that, soldier-boy?' Kayel asked, an edge of menace creeping into his voice. Amber felt his fingers ache for the feel of his scimitars.

'Because I might not be as slow as I look, and nor's Lord Styrax.'

Kayel gave him an appraising look. 'Jury's out on that one, soldier-boy. You got a problem with me, spit it out, or draw those pretty swords, but don't just stand there catchin' flies.'

'I don't think it'll be a problem,' Amber said, forcing himself not to square up to the man. There was something about the big sergeant that reminded him of a white-eye; that air of aggression and belligerence that could spark a fight from thin air. 'But you're not just a mercenary, and you're not serving the duchess. Pretending otherwise is a waste of time and an insult to Lord Styrax.'

'I think you better explain yourself better than that – so far I don't like what I'm hearing.' Kayel had his hand on his bastard sword now, and Amber could see by the set of his shoulders that the man wasn't joking any longer; he recognised the readiness of a warrior ready to kill.

'First of all, I don't think there's a problem between us, or our masters,' Amber said in a calm voice, 'so let's not get straight to the cutting. I was in Scree, and I heard a name or two being thrown around. One was Azaer, another was Ilumene. Now any fool who lived through that little corner of Ghenna saw things that probably didn't add up, pieces of the puzzle that were missing.'

'Get to the point.'

'I will. Your name is Ilumene; you're a renegade agent of King Emin's; you're a high ranking follower of Azaer and you're not in Byora just to kill time.'

Kayel paused, not for long but enough all the same that Amber knew he'd surprised him. 'And what would that be to you?'

'Maybe nothing, but from what I hear your master isn't one for small ambitions. There's a purpose in all you're doing, and it ain't a power-play for one minor city. However, my guess is we're not in competition here.'

Kayel's – *Ilumene's* – grip seemed to relax fractionally, although his hand stayed on his swordhilt. 'Could be that's the case – but why'm I the one being interrogated here? You show me yours first, major.'

Amber shook his head. 'Don't get ideas above your station, *sergeant*. You're operating within the Menin Empire; that you're doing it openly makes me think you've got nothing to fear from us, and vice versa.' He took a step forward and prodded Ilumene in the chest. 'But that's a far call from equal terms, and don't you fucking well forget it.'

Ilumene stared him down, not rising to the bait, but he was obviously a long way from being cowed. He paused before he spoke, long enough for Amber to realise he'd got under the man's skin. *Ah, the guard-dog's learned to count to ten when he's on official business, but Gods, how he wants to bite!*

'Your point's taken,' Ilumene said in a controlled voice, a tight and mirthless smile on his face. It was clear the renegade Narkang agent had been taught not to lose his cool easily. 'Just remember this,' he continued, 'you lead troops into the Ruby Tower, you'd win because you got the numbers on us. Don't let that fool you into thinking *you'd* be walking out alive, though, because I'll be making it my business to personally take you down before I fall.'

'We'll just have to wait for that little test,' Amber said, 'unless you want your temper to get the better of you? I doubt your master would be too happy about that. How do things work out for the disciples who disappoint Azaer?'

Ilumene laughed. 'Don't know much of the Brotherhood, do ya? The mission's everything. If you're invading Narkang you'll be finding that out soon enough. Dumb little children, most o' them might be, but there's no doubt they're damned well-trained.'

'I'll bear that in mind. Now, if you're intending to enjoy Menin hospitality any longer, you'll be telling me your master's goal.'

Ilumene shook his head. 'That's not my call, just as you ain't got permission to tell me what your lord's up to. Let's just say we've got a bit o' revenge planned.'

'Revenge?' Amber took a step back and turned to spit on the ground. 'You best spin me something better than that – 'less it's revenge against all the Gods, I don't buy it. It doesn't fit what you're up to, and if that's what I report to Lord Styrax, he'll laugh at me and take offence at you.' He smiled. 'I imagine you can guess how he expresses his displeasure.'

'Okay,' Ilumene said with a scowl, 'so our scores ain't the main goal, sure enough. I can't tell you much – *can't* – you get me? Just as you can't choose to tell me why priests of Karkarn are meeting nasty ends recently – aye, we've noticed that too. So far we're the only ones paying attention to the patterns amidst the chaos, but don't kid yourself that'll last through winter. All I can say is the master reckons there's space for a new player among the immortals of the Land.'

Interesting; he said immortals, not Gods. 'A new player? Azaer's been playing for a while, so I hear.'

'But on the lower Heartland board,' Ilumene argued, 'not the board of the heavens. The game'll continue, just with some pieces moving in different ways.'

Amber got the message. Heartland played on two boards: the main board, where the bulk of a player's pieces moved, but a second, smaller board, known as the heavens, where the most powerful pieces were. A player had to play both, with different ploys, or find themselves disastrously caught out.

'My lord may require more.'

Ilumene cocked his head to one side. 'A shakedown, is it? Well, let no man say my master ain't accommodating. How about a gift, to prove our enduring friendship?'

'What sort of "gift"?'

'One your lord will appreciate.'

Amber gave Ilumene another jab. 'We'll have less of the secretive crap.'

'Not a fan of surprises, eh? You the sort of kid who'd search the house for presents on his birthday? As you wish. It's a Crystal Skull.'

Amber blinked. 'Ah. Good.'

'Good? Bloody generous is what it is. I don't know, you try and do something nice . . .' Ilumene gave a theatrical sigh.

'Which one?'

Which one? You're a picky bugger, ain't you? Is sir a connoisseur of the apocalyptically powerful artefact? Does sir want to peruse the selection out the back instead? Skull of Time? Pah, waste of it, more like!'

'I'm waiting.'

Ilumene threw up his hands and called up to the sky above, 'You made this one impatient, didn't you?' He cleared his throat noisily. 'It's the Skull of Song, Major Amber – don't believe that's been ticked off Lord Styrax's list now, has it?'

Amber ignored the question. 'And what's the price of this gift?'

'It's a gift, there's no price,' Ilumene said with a grin. 'What sort o' birthdays did you have? Now it might so happen we know the location of another, one you don't, and for that, we might want your boss to make sure we get the leftovers once he's finished his sweaty exertions. I reckon he'll realise by that point we'll both need allies, and it'd be a damn sight better than the alternative, namely Lord Larim getting his sticky little paws on them.'

'And when will this gift be delivered?'

Ilumene smiled and turned away. 'All in good time, Major Amber,' he called over his shoulder, heading back to the shade of the valley. 'All in good time.'

CHAPTER 32

They arrived at Moorview early in the ghost hour, just after sundown. Tairen Moor was a place of vibrant colour in the summer months, with great swathes of purple heather and yellow gorse carpeting the distant hills. It was a far cry from where the forest reigned in Llehden, forty miles away on the north edge of the moor. The moor was a long, shallow slope that ran northeast from this point for sixty miles and southeast for longer, studded by small hills and outcrops of granite. Doranei had travelled this way many times, and he always saw Tairen Moor as a rampart, protecting a dozen small towns and villages clustered in the crook of the moor from distant Helrect. They avoided civilisation, all of them sensing the mounting tension in Isak as they headed towards battle. Though Mihn did his best, it would take more than songs and stories to ease the white-eye's fractured mind, where the memories of Lord Styrax's blows remained fresh.

At the first picket Doranei showed his golden bee device and warned the soldiers not to interfere with those following him. The lieutenant got the message and ordered his men to clear the path leading up to the castle. They watched with curiosity as the small group passed. Doranei could almost taste the sense of apprehension in the air above the camp, like a storm building as the Menin marched closer. While the soldiers didn't know who was being ushered through their lines to an audience with the king, Doranei was far from alone in feeling a prickle run down his neck as Isak Stormcaller once more walked amongst them.

And just like Scree, Doranei realised, *the brewing storm will be more ferocious as a result of his presence.* He shook his head sadly and looked around the troops assembled: as large an army as King Emin had led in decades. There were twenty thousand men already, and that was expected to double at least before the Menin arrived.

This is our last chance – our last stand. Perhaps ferocity is what we need, a storm so terrible no invader can overcome it.

The witch of Llehden and Major Jachen led the way up the path towards Moorview Castle, the witch's fierce stare enough to turn away curious eyes. Isak, Legana and Mihn followed, with the two soldiers, Marad and Ralen, bringing up the rear. Hulf walked beside Isak, padding along with heavy paws after an exhausting day chasing butterflies and other interlopers, and guarding his flock. Isak trudged on, unmindful of everything, his arms held tight around his body, as though cringing from the curious faces.

Morghien had left them in the night, pushing on to reach the king as soon as possible. Doranei thought the strange wanderer had been missing something for a long while now, some inner fire that Doranei had grown used to seeing. The Brotherhood knew Morghien to be irascible and complaining, but he shared the same dark humour. Coran had told him the man had been changed by the sundering he'd performed to free King Emin of Death's influence. But now, Doranei thought, something of Morghien's spark had been restored – though he had raged and sworn with a playwright's invention two days previously, the day Morghien had discovered Isak alive – or at least, not dead – some part of his former spirit and energy had returned. The man of many spirits might have his reservations, but before, he'd lacked the strength even to argue properly.

It gives me a little hope, that the people we once were aren't gone forever, Doranei thought. *Let's hope it works the same for the king. I doubt much of the news he's received recently has been good.*

They walked through the lines of tents, a thousand faces looking up from their supper and wondering at the cloaked and hooded strangers in their midst. In addition to his long, tattered cloak, Isak wore a faded shawl the witch had given him to shade his eyes from the afternoon sun. It hid his face, but even with his awkward stoop Isak was large, even for a white-eye. Doranei heard whispers of 'Raylin' more than once as they made their way across newly dug ditches and defensive lines of stakes.

Legana provoked as much interest as Isak, but while the white-eye shirked from the whispers, she rose to the occasion. Doranei had wondered how she would manage to keep up, with her inability to face the sun and her ungainly walk, but during the day she'd effectively blindfolded herself, and still matched the brisk pace he set without complaint.

With the sunset, Legana had uncovered her head and eyes and, walking with the aid of her gnarled oak staff, she looked like a figure of legend come to join the battle. The copper seams of her dark hair shone bright, caught by the waning light, and her emerald eyes were never brighter.

'Doranei,' called a voice from the small bridge that crossed a deepset stream and Morghien stepped forward, Veil beside him.

Doranei hurried over to embrace his Brother.

'How goes it?' he asked.

Veil's face darkened. 'Not good. From what we hear, Aroth was destroyed entirely. Lord Styrax put the whole fucking city to the sword, and since then the Menin have done the same to every town they've come upon. They're not interested in prisoners; they're even chasing down refugees fleeing the fighting. He's sent a message, as if he hadn't already made the point: he'll kill everyone who crosses his path unless the king surrenders – or faces him in battle.'

'Best our mages can tell, Styrax has sent one force roving west, laying waste to every town and village they can find,' Morghien added, his face reflecting Veil's anger. 'The other, larger, army is coming this way, looking for a fast run to Narkang. No doubt his scryers have found us by now; it's a matter of weeks before they reach us.'

'I take it you're still not happy about facing them?'

Morghien's voice dropped to an urgent whisper. 'I ain't the only one – turns out bloody Larat himself warned the king not to face him in battle. Suggested he follow Aryn Bwr's tactic, sapping the enemy's strength in his retreat, using ambushes, rearguard actions, the lot.'

'The last king lost that war,' Doranei pointed out, 'and I for one don't intend to follow him all the way to the Dark Place. Besides, his intent's clear enough even without the messenger. If we don't face him somewhere, he'll put the entire kingdom to the sword. It's as much a warning to the Farlan as showing the king the price of retreat.'

He watched as Legana approached, Isak behind her. The white-eye walked with his hand on Mihn's shoulder, as he had for much of the journey. Hulf trotted alongside, warily watching the soldiers.

'You think this is the answer?' Morghien said quietly. 'The mad mystic converted you while I was away?'

'Enough of that,' Doranei warned. 'You start that again and Mihn's going to make good his threats. It ain't for us to decide these things, not even you. We leave that for the king.'

Morghien made a disgusted sound as Legana had reached them. She stopped and looked at Veil for a moment. Her pale skin was almost luminous in the gloaming, and it made the shadowy hand-print on her throat even more obvious. Doranei noticed Veil staring at the mark, looking as if the sight of Legana in the twilight was making him feel Azaer's creeping presence.

It's not the first time he's seen her, though, Doranei reflected. *I guess some of us are more used to the unnatural.* He cleared his throat. 'You're to lead us to the king?'

Veil ducked his head. 'Aye, follow me.'

He led them up the stepped slope towards Moorview Castle. It didn't look much militarily – a smallish tower set against the southern side of a defensive perimeter wall – but inside there was a newer, highly fortified keep. It stood on a bald outcrop surrounded by thick forest, dominating the landscape. It was, in the eyes of the king and his Brotherhood, a fine place for a last stand. There was one proper road running through the forest to the castle, and a few animal paths used by those who could find them, but for the main it was impassable to large bodies of troops. They crossed a defensive ditch around what had been formal gardens until two legions of Kingsguard had camped on it, and laboured up the last hundred yards to the main gate.

With Veil leading, they were admitted without challenge. The high walls concealed ground that was teeming with uniformed officers, their weapons and finery gleaming despite the advancing gloom. Veil headed for the keep, but before they reached it a black-armoured King's Man came out, followed by the king's bodyguard, Coran, and Veil had already moved to Isak's side as he saw the last man stop in the open doorway.

A slight hush descended upon the scene as the officers and soldiers on the wall all turned to watch as King Emin advanced from the shadows of the doorway, a curious, almost pained smile on his face.

'So it is true,' he said softly.

The king was resplendent, although dressed for war – not in all-enclosing plate, but in something more akin to the heavy armour worn by the soldiers of the Kingsguard. His cuirass was green and gold, of such intricacy and artistry only a king would ever consider wearing it to battle. Doranei picked out the angular Elven runes woven into the design: there was magic imbued in the metal.

His greaves were magnificently detailed, with knee-guards of bees in flight; Doranei's sharp eyes noticed their gilded stings protruded slightly from the metal plate.

'It is true,' Mihn said, stepping forward when no one else spoke, 'but it was not done without consequences.'

The king nodded, looking haunted. 'Aye, that I cannot doubt,' he murmured. Abruptly he swept off his feathered hat and bowed low to them, but Doranei realised it was only when he looked at Legana that his welcoming smile reached his eyes.

'That it was done at all is a miracle,' the king continued, 'and one I scarcely know how to begin asking about.'

Mihn held up a hand to stop him. 'Your Majesty, there will be time for questions another day, and I will answer them – yours is, ah, an *inquiring* mind, and naturally you will wish to know every details.' He looked apologetic as he glanced briefly in Isak's direction. 'However, there are some memories best not unearthed.'

Isak hadn't looked up through the whole exchange, but when Mihn turned in his direction he seemed to sense it and he flinched. Hulf started at the unexpected movement and Isak knelt, running a hand down the dog's back to sooth him. The sight of his abused flesh made more than one man gasp and Isak quickly withdrew his arm.

King Emin gave Mihn a puzzled look, clearly not having expected Isak's self-effacing bodyguard to be so assertive, but he was right; now was not the time. He walked forward and went down on one knee in front of Isak.

Hulf immediately moved forward and placed himself between the two men. Though not yet fully grown, Hulf was no longer a puppy, and he was piling on muscle every day. His growl was threatening enough to make the King's Men on either side edge forward. But the king ignored them and reached slowly forward with one hand for Hulf to take his scent.

461

Isak remained very still while Hulf sniffed at the king's fingers and quietened.

Emin heard the white-eye's breathing, shallow and uneven, but still Isak would not look up at him.

'Do you remember me, my friend?' he said softly.

'We fought side by side,' Isak whispered.

At last he raised his head. Emin had to struggle to retain his composure as he finally saw the young white-eye's face, not just the many gruesome scars, but the pain in his eyes.

'We did,' Emin agreed calmly, offering his hand to Isak and slowly standing. The white-eye didn't take the hand, but he followed Emin's movement. 'It was an honour to do so,' the king continued, looking up at Isak.

Isak's cheek twitched at the word 'honour' but he looked Emin in the eye all the same. 'There is no honour in my shadow,' he said sadly, 'only daemons.'

'We may need daemons soon enough, my friend. There is terrible work ahead of us. I pray you bring us the answers we need.'

'Prayers,' Isak agreed mysteriously, 'I bring prayers – but it's the prayers you hold that we need.'

Emin frowned. 'I'm not sure my prayers will be welcome – in fact, I'm quite certain they're not.'

'It's the prayers you hold,' Isak repeated.

As he straightened a little, his unfastened cloak swung open to reveal the unmistakable hilt of Eolis, tucked through his belt, and a small leather bag, which Isak was holding.

The shape of the bag made Emin hesitate, and almost unconsciously he touched a similarly shaped item hanging from his own belt. He gestured to the open door.

'Come. We need to speak more, and in private.'

Isak, Mihn, Coran, the witch and Legana followed Emin inside, but Doranei held back. Veil gave him a questioning look, but he ignored it and after a moment his Brother indicated the door be shut behind them.

Doranei didn't speak, but reached into a pouch and pulled out his leather cigar case. Veil produced an alchemist's match and held it up. When the initial burst of black smoke had subsided, Doranei put the cigar to the flame and drew on it until it was alight.

'The presence of great men,' Doranei said at last, looking at the

462

top of the keep. He'd stayed here once, as part of the king's retinue.

It was an unlovely construction, built by a local tyrant three hundred years previously, more for practical reasons than for architectural elegance. Once it was open to the elements; now it was partly roofed-over, and there were long banks of shutters on two sides of the square to allow light in.

'Had enough of it at last?' Veil said. There was no condemnation in his voice.

Doranei still scowled, even as he agreed. 'Never meant to get into it in the first place.'

Veil chuckled. 'Aye, the master-thieves in the Brotherhood always laughed at you for never looking where you put your feet. Sure you can keep out of things so easily?'

Doranei watched the lamp-light in the highest room grow brighter. 'I got to try.'

The sight of Morghien recovering some of his old passion had sparked an ache in Doranei's heart. *I just want to do my job again, serve my king. All this 'grand scheme of things' is beyond me; I'm just a simple Brother. Can't I leave it to someone else again?*

He sighed and puffed away at his cigar, the distraction greatly welcome.

But how do I go back to a time before I called lords 'friend' and vampires something more? he wondered.

Above the keep the clouds raced, indistinct, looming shapes in a darkening sky. The breeze freshened, carrying a scent too faint to recognise, and yet it put him in mind of the peppery smell of a summer storm ... but left him uneasy, in the way the promise of rain didn't.

'What do you think he's going to say?' Veil asked after a long while.

'I don't even care,' Doranei said sulkily. 'They can tell me to kill, or to steal, for the good of the nation, and that's my duty. They can't make me *want* to get more involved.'

'Could be worse,' Veil said cheerily. 'Cedei had to spend the day keeping General Daken busy and out of the way. I tell you, that bugger can sniff trouble out better'n a dog after a bitch on heat. The king's kept this from him, as you might guess – last thing we need is two bloody white-eyes gettin' under each other's skin.' He plucked the cigar from Doranei's unresisting hands.

The pair stood together for a quarter-hour or more, sharing the cigar as Veil patiently stood guard and his friend, eyes half-closed, stared into the night sky. The sounds of the army camp had returned to normal: the clatter of cooking pots and bellowed orders overlaid by the clump of boots on dry, packed earth. They washed over Doranei without effect as he closed his mind to everything but the clouds overhead, losing himself in their swift, silent passage. He let the breeze sweep away the tangle of his thoughts, dissipating them like smoke.

Then the door to the tower opened again and the Brothers saw Mihn staring fixedly at Doranei.

Mihn had removed his cloak and pack. He wore his customary black linen trousers and tunic. The failed Harlequin was a short, slim man, especially compared with the men of Narkang, and that difference was highlighted by everyone around him wearing armour. It was somehow hard to believe how capable Mihn was – until you saw him moving with purpose, Doranei thought.

'You want something?' he said eventually.

'You,' Mihn said. 'We have some questions for you.'

Doranei felt his hand tighten. 'Of course you do.' He carefully handed the stub of his cigar to Veil and followed Mihn. 'Don't suppose I'd be lucky enough you'd be asking about swords and the like?' he said dryly.

Mihn hesitated and looked back at Doranei for a few moments. Then, his eyes twinkling in the darkness, he started up the stair again.

'I am sure King Emin could phrase the question in terms of your sword, if that would help,' he murmured.

Doranei sighed.

CHAPTER 33

Doranei slept poorly in the humid night air. Words and faces danced on the edges of his consciousness, questions and memories colliding uncomfortably. Some part of him sensed the bedroll underneath him, and the pack he was using as a pillow, but at the same time he could feel the cool, clean sheets of Zhia's bed in Byora.

The sensations mingled and added to the mess of confusion in his dreams, and everything was dominated by Zhia's darkly glittering sapphire eyes. The questions continued, voices speaking at once: Mihn's soft lilt, King Emin's crisp, aristocratic tone, and they were all asking about those sapphire eyes.

Can she be trusted? Where do her allegiances lie? Will she take sides?

He couldn't answer any of them. In his dreams his tongue swelled, making speech impossible, but even if he had been able to speak, there was nothing he could say, no assurances he could give.

An unexpected chill shivered down Doranei's spine and he jolted awake, heart hammering and dread slithering across his skin. The room was dark, and as he sat up his head cracked against the underside of the dining table under which he'd been sleeping. A deep thump reverberated around the room as Doranei fell back onto his bedroll, gasping.

'Told you,' whispered someone nearby.

It took Doranei a few moments to focus as he winced and rubbed his stinging head. When the stars cleared he saw Veil, watching him owlishly from the other side of the table.

'Told me what?'

Veil grinned. 'That you wake up sudden-like sometimes, so maybe under a table ain't the best place to sleep.'

Doranei looked around at the rest of the dining room: a long, ancient hall – older even than the keep – that had been incorporated into the newest wing of Moorview Castle. Apart from the huge, empty fireplace there was precious little space not occupied by dozing King's Men. He opened his mouth to reply, but hesitated, remembering the strange sensation that had woken him.

'Thought I heard something,' he said at last.

'No, you didn't,' Veil said. 'You'd have a sword in hand if you did. You dreamed you did, or some girl with sapphire eyes just reached out and touched you.'

Doranei frowned and tried to order his thoughts. He didn't remember dreaming of anything that would wake him so abruptly. Zhia's touch was accompanied by a memory of her perfume; this was neither, it was something unfamiliar.

'Think I'll go get some air,' he muttered.

Veil watched without comment as Doranei picked up his sword; unnatural happenings and strange sensations were familiar to the Brotherhood, as were overactive imaginations in the dark of night. However, the need for caution was ever-present, and confusion hadn't overridden Doranei's natural mistrust.

Doranei slipped out of the darkened hall and found himself in a moonlit corridor. He didn't know what bell it was, but the stillness indicated the depths of night. He looked around and as he shivered involuntarily, his hand closed around the sword grip . . . but nothing happened, so, feeling foolish, he released it again and buckled the scabbard properly to his waist.

He still felt better when he was holding the sword. King Emin's belief that Lord Styrax would not use subterfuge to win this battle was small comfort in the dark hours of the night.

Magic had always been feared by the common folk; its use in battle was accepted, but few generals made their name off it. Styrax might have the advantage there, with his awesome powers, but his plans extended further than mere victory. Intelligence reports were coming in all the time: four Menin armies of ten to fifteen thousand men were destroying great swathes of the Narkang nation as three of them made their way towards Moorview Castle. Each army comprised soldiers from all his conquered cities, most particularly the remnants of the Chetse élite known as the Ten Thousand.

Part of the reason for bringing them here was to keep the vanquished troops under control – if they were ravaging King Emin's lands, they would not be fomenting rebellion in their homeland.

But that was not the whole of it: Lord Styrax had amassed a larger host than ever before for a more fundamental reason. Forty thousand or more men were marching on Moorview to take part in the battle he wanted every bard to sing of for centuries to come.

Somewhere up ahead Doranei heard the scuff of a shoe on the flagstone floor. He started to draw his sword – and stopped, struck by the sight of the black blade in the darkness. The provenance of the sword he'd taken from Aracnan's corpse was unknown, but it was certainly old and powerful. In daylight it prickled faintly with tiny sparks of light. Now it was more like the night sky on a clear night, casting a very faint light of its own. He sheathed it again, suppressing his fascination for the time being. When he reached the corner of the corridor he stopped and peered around it. He saw no one, but whispering voices were coming from somewhere at the far end.

This was the opulent part of the castle, away from the servant's quarters, and there were long, narrow rugs running down the centre of the corridors. A wide variety of paintings, both portraits and landscapes, were displayed on the walls, and ahead of him Doranei could see a large map of the whole area covering one wall. It had been painted by Countess Derenin, the lady of the house, and was accurate enough that the king had consulted it often in the past few days. The local suzerain's family was an ancient one which had managed to adapt and thrive under King Emin's rule, unlike many who didn't understand the art of compromise and had been eclipsed by the king's ambitious supporters.

Doranei walked silently on the rug until he was almost at the end. There he stopped, feeling horribly exposed, as another deep voice joined in. He heard the words clearly, though there was a thick stone wall between them; the voice echoed in Doranei's head without hindrance or distortion, though it was quiet and sounded strangely far away. It made his teeth ache, and as he winced at the sensation his bruised head increased its throbbing, sending flashes of pain down across his eyes.

'You ask me to put myself in the power of others.'

Doranei covered his ears, but it made no difference – the voice was not loud, only penetrating, and his hands felt as insubstantial as the walls. He could hear nothing but the words – no cadence or accent to place the speaker.

'What did you think would happen?'

He recognised that voice; it was Lord Isak, more focused than he had been earlier that day. Whoever – *whatever*, Doranei realised – Isak was talking to, they had made him forget his pain, for a little while at least.

'*It cannot be permitted.*'

'It must,' whispered a third person – Mihn – urgently, 'there is no other way.'

'*Find another.*'

'No,' said Isak. 'You cannot command me; that much I know.'

The white-eye sounded strange to Doranei and after a moment he realised it was the lack of antagonism in his voice. The spark of aggression, that fire within all white-eyes, had been extinguished within him.

'*You invite catastrophe – you do not understand the forces you play with.*'

Isak laughed, although it was more a strangled wheeze. 'I have nothing but the scars of understanding. I was born to command, born to change.'

'This will be done,' Mihn added, 'and you *must* play your part.'

There was a long period of silence, and Doranei waited with his fists clenched tight in anticipation of the echoing voice in his head.

At last, '*What of the Ralebrat? They will not heed my call.*'

'They will heed ours,' Isak said.

'*They are not to be trusted.*'

'The service I ask is great. They must be rewarded for their losses. The price is forgiveness, long overdue absolution.'

The voice became no louder, but Doranei felt it press all the harder on his eardrums, an intensity born of outrage. '*You presume too much.*'

'As is my lot,' Isak said, the weight of the Land in his voice. 'This Land shall be made anew, the cruelties of the past left behind.'

Doranei crept closer. Now he could see the door at the end of the corridor was ajar, a faint blue light spilling around its edges and outlining a dark figure. Though he was unable to make out any detail, Doranei still felt terrified, and the air grew thick and heavy around him.

'*Some crimes haunt you still,*' the figure said with cold derision.

Its face was hidden, but Doranei felt the force of its presence like the looming bulk of Blackfang, and for a moment he was sure the figure's words were directed at him, rather than Isak.

'*There is a scent of vampire about these halls. Are you so sure of those around you?*' the figure asked, and Doranei flinched, an icy ball of dread filling his stomach.

He backed off down the corridor and wasted no time in fleeing silently to the furthest corner of the castle, the panicked thump of his heart pounding in his ears.

Knight-Cardinal Certinse looked up from the pile of papers on his desk. The night was well advanced and his head was pounding. The hot summer's day had left his study stuffy and malodorous; the bunches of fragrant lavender and pepper grass hung over the door and windows had done more to add to the heavy atmosphere than relieve it.

His eyes drifted to the door that led to his bedroom; the thought of sleep was enticing, especially compared with tallies of import taxes. Certinse stood, reaching for the candlestick on his desk, but he was stopped by a muffled commotion from somewhere downstairs.

'What now?' he wearily asked the empty room. 'I'm too tired for another late-night chat with High Priest Garash.'

Abruptly the door opened and Captain Perforren entered, a worried expression on his face. 'My apologies, Knight-Cardinal, but a visitor has just arrived.'

'A visitor? There are still Menin soldiers outside the house, aren't there?'

'And men of the Devout Congress inside the door,' his aide added. 'They, ah, they didn't manage to stop your visitor. I think he has them confused.'

'Explain quickly,' Certinse said, hearing boots on the stair.

'He arrived with one of the Jesters! The soldiers don't know what to do; he's a Demi-God, after all.'

Certinse managed a smile at last. 'That'll confuse the bastards sure enough. Is the visitor Luerce?'

'Nope,' said a deep voice from the corridor, 'no one so special.' A tall man entered. A white patchwork cloak didn't do much to disguise his powerful frame. He wore a sword at his hip and held a dagger in his left hand. Certinse blinked a moment before recognising the man, Duchess Escral's bodyguard, Kayel.

'A little late for a social call, isn't it, Sergeant Kayel?'

Kayel raised his right hand, in which was a glass bottle of brandy. 'Never too late for a drink between friends.'

Certinse regarded him for a moment, his face blank, before gesturing for Perforren to leave. 'Your young prince is still looking to be friends then?'

Kayel watched Perforren shut the door behind himself before heading for the glasses on a side-table. He poured a large measure of brandy into each wide-bottomed glass and handed one to the Knight-Cardinal.

He raised his glass in a toast. 'Ruhen stands for peace in this Land,' Kayel said gravely. 'Friends is all he's looking for.'

'Tell that to the priests plaguing me,' Certinse muttered, showing the sergeant to one of the chairs at the far side of the room, set on either side of the empty fireplace. 'I'm amazed some of those fools preaching in Akell got out again without being lynched. Ruhen may have his admirers here, but they're keeping their heads down.'

'Who can blame 'em? It's better than getting 'em chopped off.' Ilumene took a big gulp of brandy. 'Speakin' of your priests, I thought I'd come see how that situation was workin' out.'

Certinse gave him a sour look. 'Is that supposed to be funny?'

'You see me laughin'? It's my concern when Ruhen's Children ain't allowed to spread their beliefs, when they get strung up for the *heresy* of criticisin' priests. An' I b'lieve it's your concern that you, as Knight-Cardinal, ain't in command of your own Order – that you got to answer to a crowd o' fanatics who've forced their way into power.'

'I'm not sure what you're saying here,' Certinse said cautiously. 'Are you asking whether I'm plotting against fellow members of the Knights of the Temples?'

Kayel laughed. 'No! I'm sayin' in your place, I'd likely gettin' ready to murder the whole damn lot of 'em! And, I'm askin' why you ain't done so already – they've robbed you o' your Order, and if you don't take it back soon, it's gone for good.'

The sergeant knocked back the last of his brandy and rose to fetch the bottle. As he turned his back, Certinse inspected the man. His high boots looked scuffed and dirty, dull black rather than polished to a shine, but they looked well-cared-for; Kayel was a man used to walking, he surmised; he obviously knew the value of good boots. He didn't recognise the style of the lines of black stitching, but he did recognise the concealed pommel of a dagger when he saw it.

'The Menin Army's been gone a while now,' Kayel said as he offered Certinse more, 'long enough that the war's likely to be done soon. Whichever way it goes, the Land's goin' to be a different place after.'

'Undeniably,' Certinse agreed, 'but I can't be sure there will be an Order of the Knights of the Temples left to see this new Land.'

'So why ain't you moved? You've hardly made much effort to help out Ruhen's Children, and you know we're happy for you to exploit us that way – don't hurt our cause a shred.'

'Unfortunately the matter is not so simple,' Certinse said. 'My Order is by definition composed of the pious. Our rank and file are all volunteers, and most joined for higher reasons than the stipend.'

'So they'll take their whippings like dogs?' Kayel asked, momentarily surprised, 'they'll cower and whine, all the while shrinking from a raised hand? And never once thinking to bite back?'

'The analogy is accurate,' Certinse agreed. 'They're an army, and properly trained. I have been paying careful attention, as you might imagine, but there are simply not enough men willing to consider insurrection against a body of priests.'

'But no one's likely to complain if it's done for them?'

The Knight-Cardinal smiled. *Interesting*, he thought suddenly, *the man's accent has softened now we're at the meat of the conversation. He's not playing the big simple soldier any more.*

There was something more, something else at the back of his mind trying to grab his attention. *Ah yes, he speaks Farlan well, very well. That's not the casual familiarity of a mercenary.* Certinse had spent more years than he cared to remember in exile, living under King Emin's rule after Lord Bahl's ban on the Knights of the Temples. Over that time he'd noticed a number of common errors in the way people there spoke the Farlan dialect; some were glaring, some subtle enough for most native speakers to not pick up on immediately. Sergeant Kayel had made none of those mistakes, none at all.

'Obviously I couldn't condone any such actions,' he said carefully, mindful of being lured into speaking too openly, 'and on a purely logistical note I would point out that only the Menin have the capability to do such a thing. A covert mission of the scale required would be near-impossible.'

Kayel didn't blink. 'It so happens,' he said cagily, 'that there might be some new arrivals in the Circle City very soon. The call of Ruhen's message has reached further than many might believe, and a few remarkable followers have been attracted to him.'

'Such as the Jesters?'

Kayel shook his head. 'Their losses were considerable in the battle against the Farlan; only half a dozen acolytes remain.'

'I'm intrigued,' Certinse said, guessing he was going to be told no more. 'If they are so remarkable it's a shame I remain under house arrest, unable to receive visitors without the escort of Demi-Gods.'

'A shame indeed. If anything were to happen, however, you would have to step in quickly – no sense giving the opportunists a chance, is there? A symbolic figure would be useful in that instance, I think you'll find; remind the Order of its founding principles.' Kayel gave him a sly look and set aside his glass. As he was making ready to leave he added, 'My view is it'd be sensible to prepare against all eventualities. Either King Emin wins this war and the Circle City's in need of a leader again, or Lord Styrax wins, and he'll be looking for a permanent ruler for each region of his empire. If that happens, I'm sure he'd be glad of strong allies before he heads towards Tirah – especially if one has connections in those parts already.'

Certinse smiled. 'My first obligation must certainly be the stability of the Order, yes – my scholarship has perhaps been neglected in recent years, but it's never too late to refresh one's memory of the Order's founding principles. This current fervour could be far better employed in the pursuit of the Order's greater purpose, I suspect – and never let it be said I am closed to new ideas. Your little prince's message, for example; even an old soldier such as I could be swayed. The Land will soon be tired of war – if it could be ended swiftly the Gods themselves would surely thank us.'

*

For a moment Doranei forgot himself and stopped, staring in wonder: far away over the moor a flock of birds were diving and wheeling in a great cloud against the sky, while closer at hand, swifts darted and swooped, feasting on the insects stirred up by the activity on the moor. He could hear the beating of thousands of wings in unison.

'Not a sight you ever get bored of, eh?' Veil commented from his right.

Doranei nodded dumbly as the flocks swept over a slight rise on the moor and flattened into a swirling cable of birds that arched up into the sky. Further east, orange-edge striations of cloud lay above the horizon and he felt a slight shadow fall over them as the flock veered past.

'Is that supposed to be funny?' snapped the man standing between them. His left arm was resting lightly on Doranei's shoulder.

'What? Hah! No – not a joke,' Veil said, a brief grin flashing across his face.

The third man in their group was a mage from Narkang called Tasseran Holtai, who was generally acknowledged to be the finest scryer in the kingdom. Unfortunately, his years of service had come at a price: he had been completely blind for almost a decade.

'Aye, we only joke with men we like,' Doranei growled while Veil looked skyward in exasperation.

'You impudent peasant!' Holtai spat, swinging his walking stick at Doranei's shins.

The King's Man hopped nimbly away from the blow and stifled a laugh as Veil was jabbed in the ribs with the stick in Doranei's place.

'I don't care what favour the king has for you, I'll have you flogged for your insolence!' he snarled.

'I'm afraid there's already a queue for that pleasure,' Veil said cheerfully, 'so let's get this done first.'

Mage Holtai turned in Veil's direction, far from mollified, but aware the king was waiting. He was a sprightly man of more than seventy winters, his white moustache neatly trimmed and his clothing immaculate, as ever – today he wore a long purple robe edged in gold. His skills had brought him not only considerable personal wealth, but also great political power in Narkang; he was a poor enemy to make, even for the Brotherhood.

473

'Shift yourself then, you wretch,' the mage hissed, grabbing wildly for Doranei's shoulder again.

The King's Man raised his eyebrows and rolled his eyes at Veil, who grinned back. He stepped closer and guided Holtai's hand to his shoulder, but they had gone only a few steps before the old man grabbed him by the collar and wrenched him backwards with more strength than Doranei would have expected from a frail-looking old man.

'Not so fast you damn fool!' the mage snarled.

Doranei bit back his instinctive response and slowed his pace until they were shuffling through the flattened grass towards a raised mound of indeterminate purpose. It was five feet high, and it was encircled by a staked ditch twenty yards out, and a full company of soldiers – fifty men – looking extremely bored.

On the mound itself stood two unmistakable figures: Endine and Cetarn, King Emin's most trusted mages. Tomal Endine, a wiry, rat-like man, sat cross-legged before one of a dozen wooden posts. One hand was pressed against it and trails of white light danced around him. His colleague and friend Shile Cetarn lounged nearby, resting part of his considerable weight on an enormous wooden mallet. As they neared, Doranei was amused to see Endine moving away from the post, then falling backwards in shock as Cetarn wasted no time in taking an almighty swing with the mallet to pound it into the ground.

Doranei grinned, he could just imagine the mage's furious squawks of outrage – and Cetarn shared his sense of humour; before he could take a second swing the white-eye-sized mage had dropped the mallet and doubled over, his roaring bellows of laughter reaching the plodding trio a hundred yards off.

'Doranei, my favourite drunkard!' Cetarn yelled once the trio were within shouting distance. 'Come to swing a hammer for me?'

'Reckon you need the exercise more than me,' Doranei shouted back. 'We're here to test out your work.'

At that Endine began to cough, until Cetarn slapped him hard on the back, laughing again. 'Not that; the boy's a drunk, not mad!'

Doranei and Veil exchanged confused looks, but Cetarn didn't bother to explain himself as he hauled Endine back onto his feet again. 'It's not finished,' Cetarn continued, his round head flushed pinker than normal, 'but it's good enough for your need, and I can always nudge things along.'

'I can manage perfectly well without your help, Shile,' the blind mage said primly. 'I mastered my art long before you were born, young man.'

'Indeed you did, sir,' Cetarn agreed, 'but you will be scrying up to a hundred miles while the adepts of the Hidden Tower attempt to stymie your efforts. The help is yours, whether you like it or not.'

Mage Holtai's face soured as though he'd just swallowed a bug. 'If I need your assistance I will request it,' he said firmly. 'Until that becomes the case your power will only make my efforts all the more noticeable.'

He started to walk a little faster, and tugged impatiently at Doranei's shoulder for him to keep up. As they reached the mound Doranei saw an iron chain half-buried in the earth, running north from one of the posts along the ground. Whatever magic they had planned, Doranei knew he didn't want to be anywhere near the results.

He helped Mage Holtai up onto the mound and looked around from his elevated position. A hundred and fifty yards off, almost half a mile from Moorview Castle itself, was a complicated forward defence post that a thousand men were still working on. Three square towers surrounded by twelve-foot-deep ditches were to be the heart of their defences – though by no means the only line of defence. Two longer ditches were being dug on each flank, forming two sides of a triangle, with the removed earth being used for ramparts behind. Fire-blackened stakes were being hammered into both ramparts and ditches.

The moor was covered with smaller ditches and treacherous holes, as much a way to keep the waiting army busy as to hinder the Menin's advance to battle wherever possible. The battle-hardened Menin heavy infantry needed to close and bring the fight to the Narkang forces. The king intended to make that a costly process.

Doranei looked down at the soldiers all around them. The core of the Narkang army was the Kingsguard, but that was only five legions; five thousand men. There were a similar number of mercenaries from the north and western isles, but the bulk of their troops had been hastily raised and were being drilled right now:

475

advance and retreat, form line, form square, right turn, set spears
... To Doranei's experienced eye, it was all painfully slow.

Unlike the Farlan they had no system of martial obligation among
the nobility, and many of the ennobled veterans from King Emin's
wars of conquest had died since then. They might have gathered
fifty thousand troops, but they amounted to little more than con-
scripts and volunteers, from all walks of life. More were arriving
daily. What they didn't have was the command structure required.
Just getting the new men armed and sorted into legions was proving
taxing enough, for all the king's advance preparations.

'What're all these, symbols of the Gods?' Veil asked Cetarn,
pointing at the wooden posts as the blind mage made himself
comfortable on a rug at the centre of the mound. He peered at the
nearest. 'Yes, the whole Upper Circle, it looks.'

'One aspect of our preparations,' Cetarn declared, 'harnessing
the energies of the Land – but if you think I'm going to waste my
valuable time giving you two dullards an explanation you could
never fully fathom, you're more fools than I thought!'

'Shile,' Holtai said, arranging his robe around him, 'if you don't
mind?'

'Of course, Master Holtai, my apologies.' Cetarn grinned at the
King's Men, grabbed his mallet and retreated off the mound with
Endine. When Doranei started to follow, the big mage motioned
for them to stay where they were, a little behind Mage Holtai,
looking down at the old man's thinning pate while he settled himself
again and began to mumble arcane words.

Mage Holtai sat rigid and upright, facing west, with his eyes
closed, chanting in an unintelligible monotone for ten minutes or
more. Twice the mage's tone altered abruptly, moving up the scale
as he craned his scrawny neck high, before dropping back down
the register again.

The two other mages were watching intently as the old man gave
a sudden exhalation and ended his chant. Doranei and Veil both
advanced and knelt at his side, ready to listen.

'I see a cavalry force, several legions strong,' the mage said in a
strained whisper, 'engaging the enemy.'

'Green scarves?' Doranei asked, and received a nod in reply.
General Daken's troops were obviously still harrying the enemy.

'Smoke in the distance,' he went on, 'another town burns. I see standards, the Fanged Skull, and more: many states. Ismess, Fortinn, two Ruby Towers. The mosaic flag of Tor Salan, even Chetse – some of the Ten Thousand.'

'No Devoted?' Veil asked.

It took him a long time to answer, but when he did it was just to croak 'no'.

'How many Chetse?' Doranei tried.

'Many flags, many legions.'

He scowled. The rumours were true then, the core of the Chetse Army had voluntarily joined Lord Styrax – what was left of it after the slaughter outside the gates of Thotel, anyway. Styrax wouldn't have allowed the Menin troops to be outnumbered if he didn't trust the loyalty of the Chetse.

'What about cavalry?' Veil asked.

'Three legions, not Menin.'

Doranei thought for a moment. 'Can you tell which town it is?'

'A stone bridge crosses the river; upstream is a small fort on an outcrop.'

'Terochay,' the King's Men said together before Doranei continued, 'At the edge of the moor; sixty miles or so. Doubt any of the poor bastards even left the town after we'd stripped it of supplies.'

'Gives us a week?' Veil hazarded.

'Thereabouts.'

'Find the other armies,' he urged the old man.

As the mage recommenced his chant, Doranei rose and continued to survey the moor. It would be a desperate fight, though he still didn't see how Isak could hope to turn the tide. They had picked as good a place to fight as any army could hope for, providing Lord Styrax with the choice of a long route round the forest with dwindling supplies and a hostile force behind, or battle on ground of their choosing. If they were going to win, it wouldn't be because of some broken-down white-eye.

Attacking defended ground was far from ideal, but Styrax wouldn't shrink from the challenge. His shock troops were the finest in the Land, and they'd been getting a lot of practice this past year. Once he pierced the defensive line, chaos would ensue.

It didn't take Mage Holtai long to find the other two army groups advancing on Tairen Moor. They were keeping within a day's march of each other. Soon the mage was recounting details in his rasping voice for the King's Men to commit to memory and report back, and all the time he was speaking, Doranei watched the clouds massing on the northern horizon, preparing to roll over the moor and unleash yet another ferocious storm.

His throat was becoming tight with anticipation. Time had almost run out for them, and for Doranei it couldn't come too soon. The reports of destruction had been horrific: dozens of towns and Gods-knew how many villages razed to the ground. Few had escaped the wholesale slaughter in Aroth, and that city's brutal destruction had set the pattern for the weeks that followed.

The dead numbered not their hundreds, but in tens of thousands. The eastern half of the country had been largely devastated, and though Doranei understood the need for a fighting retreat, he hated it as much as the rest of the army did.

But now King Emin had drawn a line. Win or lose, here they would make their stand in a week's time. Here they would stand or fall, and the Kingdom of Narkang and the Three Cities would stand with them, or fall with them.

CHAPTER 34

Daken slipped off the plundered Menin half-helm and wiped the sweat from his bald head. The morning was well advanced and they had been working hard. He could feel his horse's lungs beneath him, working like steady bellows. He ran a hand down its neck and patted the beast's scarred shoulder. It bore a sheen of sweat, both from the exercise and the warm summer sun. By contrast the wind felt cool on his back and neck.

'Your orders, General?' asked the young nobleman beside him. Marshal Dassai, like his men, was filthy and tired, but they were also proud. They had fought bravely for weeks, following General Daken into the teeth of the enemy with a determination as savage as that of their white-eye commander.

'Hold here,' Daken said, 'and send a company to scout each flank, watch fer surprises. An hour's rest for the others.'

Dassai relayed the order with a smile on his blue-scarred face. Litania, Larat's Trickster Aspect, had been having her fun with Daken's officers. While they slept she had entered their dreams and marked each one differently, with long, elegant sweeps of blue, like stylised flower stems that ended in curious, drooping hooks of flowers.

Strangely, the days of violence had left the men inured to such trifles, and instead of undermining Daken, Litania had succeeded in binding the men to him with an unwavering loyalty.

Daken himself stayed in the saddle, peering out over the moor. There was little to interrupt the view from where they were: he could see the disturbance of the Menin Army in the distance: three distinct columns of marching men with supporting divisions of cavalry interspersed between them. On the right, two or three miles away, was the long granite tor the locals called the Moor Dragon.

It was featureless, and largely useless, as it was near-impossible to scale.

'They're keeping tight,' he commented at last.

Marshal Dassai nodded and passed him up a waterskin. 'Their scryers tell the same story as ours, no doubt: half a day's march to Moorview, and they could attack this evening if they wished.' He rubbed his cropped hair, still finding it strange.

Dassai had inherited his title at nine winters, but he'd grown up the image of his father, a noted soldier. It had near broken his heart that he'd been powerless to help his people, even to flee. As they'd retreated through his own lands, he'd had to leave his twin sister the task of packing their valuables and escaping before the Menin arrived to raze their home. Now, his home almost certainly destroyed, the tenants who farmed his lands slaughtered or driven off, his sister missing, presumed dead, he had nothing. He was only a soldier, with no time for anything except the defeat of the Menin bastards.

'The scryers are the only ones who'll want to go now,' Daken said darkly, watching the nearest enemy divisions with a malevolent eye. 'Rest of 'em will want to rest.'

Dassai turned towards Moorview Castle, which nestled in an indentation in the forest, too distant for him to make out. The hill it stood on was as unimpressive as this nameless mound, and there was almost nothing in between except enough open flat ground that the two armies would get a good look at each other long before they clashed.

'Let them come,' Dassai replied fiercely. 'I've no problem with the enemy being tired by the time they reach our defences.'

'Makes my skin itch, is what it does,' Daken muttered. 'Don't expect most o' the king's infantry'll be much use, but I still don't like jus' sittin' here waiting for 'em.'

'What? We shouldn't allow an undefeated general a choice in how he attacks?' Dassai said with a wry smile. 'You may have a point, but we don't have much option there.'

'That we don't.'

Daken looked at the other two legions under his command. They had taken up position on the southwest flank of the hill, ready to continue back towards Moorview when the command came.

'Might manage one last strike before we give up, though. Ain't killed misself a Litse yet, and I reckon they're still with that advance guard.'

'How?'

'We send the other legions in a long line to skirt the enemy, makin' it look like we're all there. They follow them 'round that damned dragon lump there, they'll be slow to react to us.'

'And we keep one legion here, concealed?' Dassai frowned. 'But then what? There are more than four legions in that advance guard. They just need to advance into us and we have to turn. If they do follow, there's no one to hit them as we retreat.'

'Exactly,' Daken said with a sudden gleam in his eye, 'no one in their right mind would try it!'

Dassai laughed, realising what Daken had in mind, and ran to give the orders.

There was barely a grumble from the soldiers as they changed positions, despite the hardships Daken had already put them through. They knew the end was in sight, and one final victory under the gaze of King Emin and his troops, that'd be a good note to go out on.

An hour later and the smile was gone from Dassai's face. Even Daken looked tense as the two men and a scout lay on their bellies on the hill's southern side. Each had a green scarf tied around his neck, the nearest to uniform they possessed.

'How close do you want them?' Dassai asked through the steel grille of his visor.

'Close,' Daken growled, refusing to be any more specific. Less than a mile away three legions were heading straight for them, following the easiest path as they led the way for the rest of the army. They hadn't sent scouts any further ahead – Daken had weaned them off that particular habit several weeks back by leaving a dozen of his best archers in his wake at every obstacle. Now the Menin only marched en masse now, despite the slower pace.

'That looks close to me, General,' the scout said cautiously. He knew Daken wasn't a stickler for protocol, but his bouts of good humour and informality never fully masked the fact that he was a white-eye and dangerous to predict.

'Me too,' Daken declared, his voice husky at the prospect of the violence to come. 'Far enough to think, close enough not to think so hard.'

They wriggled back until they were out of sight, then leapt to their feet and joined the remaining legion. There were more than a thousand men, and Daken could see they were ready: unafraid, and as keen to shed Menin blood as he. The white-eye stood in his stirrups, raised his axe, and gave the signal, leading them down to the lower edges of the hill, where the slope was shallow enough to keep their formation, but still gave them some protection.

When they caught sight of the enemy, the troops gave an unprompted roar of defiance – one that was repeated as Daken raised his blood-streaked axe above his head and added his own voice.

The troops stared at each other, no more than three hundred yards apart, and close enough that Daken could make out the colours on their flags. One was white, the other two black: a Litse and two Menin light cavalry legions. The main bulk of the army was further back, almost a mile behind the advance guard.

'Looks like you were right, General,' Dassai commented, 'the main body has slowed down: our decoy legions have won us some space to work with.'

'Aye, fucking genius I am,' Daken muttered, watching the nearer legions intently.

The enemy clattered to a ragged halt while their commander decided what to do. Their lines were tight; no doubt to keep them ordered and under control, but it wouldn't help them with what Daken had planned.

'Get us close enough, then give 'em a volley, let's see if we can help 'em make up their minds,' he told the marshal, who yelled the command.

The legion advanced slowly, arrows notched, bolts loaded and ready to fire. To the enemy it must have appeared they were still trying to induce a pursuit, moving cautiously enough to flee at a moment's notice. They stood their ground and watched the Narkang cavalry approach, content to wait for them to get too close.

Dassai looked askance at Daken; the white-eye was sitting hunched in his saddle, fingers tight around the stained leather grip of his axe. As he gave the order to fire he saw Daken taking deep breaths, and his face slowly broke out into a manic grin. The arrows struck and he saw several men fall from their horses, and a few of the beasts themselves reared and kicked out in pain.

'One more volley,' Daken growled through bared teeth. He slipped the half-helm onto his head and watched as the horses continued walking forward all the while, closing the ground slowly and steadily.

Dassai gave the order, wondering idly whether his general would remember to give the order, or if he would just charge out all alone – that was perfectly possible, after all. The second volley killed more, and the reply from the Litse horsemen fell short, the angle of the slope and the wind against them.

'Move, you lazy fuckers,' someone commented from Dassai's left, 'maybe you'll get close enough to hit something smaller than a hill.' As Daken laughed out loud the marshal turned to see the speaker was a squadron captain, probably the most experienced man in the entire legion.

As bidden, the Litse began to edge closer, one block of cavalry on the left flank moving forward to a better position. Dassai felt a surge of anticipation as he saw the Litse advance, the slope taking them away from their allies.

'Fuckers just dog-legged themselves!' Daken announced loudly. 'That's enough fer me; charge, you mad bastards!' The white-eye spurred his horse hard and the beast leaped forward as Daken raised his axe.

Marshal Dassai's own mount followed out of instinct, as did those around him, and even before he'd had a chance to repeat the order hundreds were already charging.

Following the general's lead, the young marshal urged his horse faster, a javelin held ready. With the slope on their side the distance dwindled with shocking speed and as Dassai hurled his javelin, closely followed by those around him, he saw the shock their charge had already caused. The Litse left flank was still trying to advance, while the right flank was trying to turn and withdraw to the safety of the main body of men, but as he pulled his sabre free, Dassai could see it was too late, there would be no avoiding their charge.

Daken barrelled directly into the exposed right wing of the Litse, screaming unintelligible curses. An arrow caught him in the upper arm, but he barely had time to notice before his horse had ploughed straight into the pale ranks of the enemy. An extended crash followed moments later as the rest of the troops arrived, but Daken was lost to his blood-rage. His horse battered a path through the first rank, and as its padded chest smashed against the first, throwing the rider from his saddle, Daken's axe missed the man by a whisker. The white-eye whirled around and hacked down at the next, his axe shattering the soldier's small shield and continuing through his chest.

Daken wrenched the weapon back and struck right as his horse pushed deeper into the Litse ranks. The next was felled as easily as the first, then he felt a horse smash against his own beast and before he could turn, an arm grabbed at his, nearly pulling him from the saddle. The white-eye, screaming curses, hauled back and the moment he felt the man's grip give he jabbed over-arm with the butt of his axe and shattered the man's cheekbone.

He raised the weapon again and saw a moment of pure terror on the face of the Litse before the curved blade chopped down into the side of his head and blood exploded everywhere, soaking Daken's face. The white-eye swore and shook his head, trusting his men to protect him as he blinked the gore away.

Dassai, seeing his commander in need, moved in to cover him, but as his sabre glanced off a Litse's shield, he realised it wasn't even necessary – the Litse were barely even trying to fight back. He looked around and realised it was the same everywhere; they were struggling against their own in a frantic bid to escape. Half of the Narkang men had already pushed through the gap as the wing collapsed under their assault and were wheeling around to hit the centre Menin legion in their flank.

He stood tall in his stirrups, but still couldn't see much more than a chaotic swirl of figures as the black livery and flashes of green tore deeper into the enemy ranks.

'Watch your back!' roared a voice beside him, and as Dassai turned the head of an enemy soldier was snapped backwards as Daken lunged and caught him in the throat with the spike of his axe.

He didn't wait to thank the white-eye but went for the next Litse himself, slashing the man's shoulder and tipping him from the saddle. He felt a spear bite the wooden shield held close to his body and slammed it against his ribs, but he managed to deflect the weapon and dislodge it from its owner's grip by battering the shaft with his sabre. Before the man could grab his own sword, Dassai had made up the ground and cut across his exposed face, throwing him back in a spray of blood.

As the injured man reeled away it seemed to Dassai that was the breaking point. Like a herd of cattle, the Litse suddenly turned and bolted, abandoning their weapons and fleeing from the savage assault. A great cheer went up as the Litse broke, but the Narkang fighters wasted no time in exploiting the gap and turned to support those who'd already pushed through and hit the exposed centre legion. Seeing the first legion run, the Menin cavalry wilted under the assault and tried to scatter in all directions.

Seeing the confusion up ahead Daken roared, 'Dismount!' at the top of his voice.

As the marshal repeated the order he saw more than a hundred had done so already, anticipating the order. He too slipped from his saddle and followed Daken as the white-eye ran towards the Menin cavalry, knowing from experience it would be impossible to order their lines in time. A man on horseback normally had the advantage, but cavalry in disarray couldn't properly fight off a concerted assault.

Panicked shouts came from the enemy line as the Narkang soldiers streamed towards them. They were only a hundred yards off, tightly packed and boxed in by the fleeing Litse. In the time it had taken Daken's men to charge and butcher a significant number of Litse, the Menin cavalry's attempt to turn and attack had failed miserably, a disordered mess made worse by some of the Litse actually running between squadrons of Menin in panic. Now many soldiers were milling about in confusion while dozens of voices yelled conflicting orders, warnings and curses.

One Menin squadron took the initiative and lowered spears, but as they began to advance, their officers called them back and they faltered in confusion.

Daken ignored everything but his target, an officer in the Menin front rank. A pair of horsemen saw him closing in and galloped to stop him, but before they could run him down, a ghostly figure darted forward in a blaze of smoky blue light. The horses shied away as Litania clawed at their eyes and left long bloody trails torn into their heads. One panicked entirely and ran across the path of other Menin trying to meet the onrush.

The other rider, shouting in alarm, wrenched his horse away

from the Aspect's clawed fingers and wheeled it in a circle as he tried to get the beast back under control, but Daken reached the man before the circle was complete and hammered his axe into the man's back. The Menin arched in pain and fell, but Daken had already moved on, blood-splattered and roaring his defiance. Again the enemy shrank back as more of Daken's legion arrived, lunging up with their spears and pulling men from the saddle. Without a cohesive line to defend, the closest Menin tried to turn away, obstructing their comrades who, not realising the danger, continued to press forward.

Dassai found Daken again as he was carving a bloody circle through the air, swinging two-handed through the panicked Menin. Dassai had his sabre in one hand and snatched up a discarded spear in the other, using them to carve a path through the chaos. He got as close to Daken as he dared, knowing the Menin would be fighting alone, vulnerable to the Narkang men acting in unison.

Ahead of him Daken screamed, and foamed bloodily at the mouth where he'd bitten his own tongue. He gave no thought to tactics as he threw himself at one Menin after the next, determined to massacre his way through the enemy ranks. The young marshal was forced to keep back or be cut down himself as he followed in Daken's wake, running through those men who wheeled away from the dervish hacking madly in all directions.

The Menin didn't stay to fight. Within minutes they were sounding the retreat, trying to batter a path through their comrades. The Narkang had discovered over the last few weeks the Menin light cavalry hated close-quarters fighting, and without space to move, their height advantage meant nothing. Men lay screaming all around, many with the spears that had driven them from their saddles still lodged in their bellies.

Just as he began to see daylight through the thinning crowd of Menin, Dassai slipped on a bloody tuft of grass, and by the time he recovered his balance, the bulk of the Menin were throwing their weapons away and fleeing after their reluctant Litse allies. A few Narkang soldiers pursued, but they were on foot and soon gave up the chase, panting and bellowing Daken's name as they ran back to their colleagues.

'Back to the horses!' Dassai shouted at the top of his voice. Fatigue meant the first few words were lost on the bulk of their men, but once again, they were expecting the order. The rest of the Menin would not be far away, and if they didn't escape now they'd be the ones on the receiving end of a charge.

'Run, you fuckers!' Daken roared, staring after the fleeing cavalry, 'run and tell your lord I'll do the same ta him!'

'General!' Dassai yelled.

Daken whirled around, and for a moment his eyes were filled with blind fury, then it subsided and the white-eye gave him a bloody grin, sweat and blood running from his bald head. There was still a stub of arrow protruding from his left arm and a shallow cut running along his cheek.

'Dassai,' he laughed, raising his axe, 'first blood to us!'

'It's who gets the last I'm worried about,' Dassai said, only half-joking as he watched the advancing Menin.

'Oh, piss on you, that was the best fun I'll have all year,' the general said, slapping Dassai on the shoulder as he passed. Daken paused and leaned close to Dassai's ear. 'Now shift yourself, ya bastard!' he roared at the top of his voice, and with that, the white-eye set off towards the abandoned horses, laughing mightily all the way.

Dassai spared one last look at the rest of the Menin Army, looming large on the moor ahead.

That's the last we'll run, he promised them silently. *Next time, it's to the death.*

CHAPTER 35

Doranei watched the grainy light of dawn creep over Tairen Moor, his hand never leaving his sword. The Menin were out there, a dark smear in the distance – both nebulous and threatening. He couldn't help wondering if the fears of the many had come true and they truly were an unstoppable force led by an invincible warrior.

He tried to find the fear inside him, but it wouldn't come. The King's Man looked down at the discarded jug of wine at his feet. The contents spilled red, soaking into the earth and wood of the rampart. The wine had tasted like ashes in his mouth – like the pyres of Scree, or the shattered streets of Byora where Sebe had died. He didn't crave alcohol, not this morning. The feeling thrumming through his bones was something else, an angry impatience.

'This is another man's war,' he said dully, nudging the jug with his toe. 'Let them come, and quickly.'

'It's our war now,' Veil reminded Doranei as he drank from a waterskin. 'It weren't the Farlan brought this plague upon the kingdom; it were coming sure enough anyway.'

Doranei didn't reply. He didn't want to speak what was on his mind, to hand the burden on to his friend, but it was there at the back of his mind. He was tired of this all, tired of the years of struggle and seeing precious little victory from it.

Maybe all that drinking's finally paid off, he thought sourly, *it's finally managed to numb what's inside.*

The Menin had made camp a few miles away, not close enough to contain the Narkang Army, but still a threat. General Daken had arrived mid-afternoon with the news of one final engagement: one little piece of hurt delivered for the thousands murdered in their advance. His scouts had confirmed the scryers' intelligence: their baggage train was small and their supplies were dwindling.

Doranei leaned forward over the rampart wall, looking past the fire-dampening charms inscribed on the outside and down to the ditch below it. In a few hours he would be killing men at this very spot, spilling their blood and battering them back into the ditch. This was the heart of the army's defences; a fortress of earth and fresh-cut logs a hundred yards across, intended to meet the crashing wave of Menin infantry and hold firm.

Behind him was the mound of earth where Endine and Cetarn had been hammering stakes into the ground. Only Isak and Mihn went there now, sometimes accompanied by the witch of Llehden or Legana, but Doranei couldn't imagine what they were up to. The company of guards was still stationed there, to keep all others away, but he'd never seen the three do anything remotely of interest. Isak had stood there for several hours yesterday, just staring into the distance as the ghost hour came and went.

He turned and looked past the squat central tower of the fort. Cetarn had inexplicably chained the mound to the ground, which was now the centre point of a dozen or so buried tendrils, each one a hundred feet or more in length. It was dark now, but Doranei could make out the tattered grey cloak Isak wore. He elbowed Veil and pointed.

'Aye, back there again,' Veil said. 'Harnessing the energies o' the Land – isn't that what Cetarn called it?'

The white-eye was a strange figure within the massive army camp. Almost everyone else wore armour, but Isak still shuffled about in ragged clothes, and used his tattered cloak to hide his scars from the rest of the Land. Doranei didn't know whether Isak even owned any armour any more – although surely the king's armourers could have beaten something out for him by now.

'You reckon he's drawing power from that heap of dirt?' Doranei's voice dropped to a whisper so the Kingsguard soldiers manning the wall couldn't hear. 'I got to say, I don't think he's the man we once knew.'

'That doesn't surprise me,' Veil said. He grimaced at the thought of what Isak might have endured.

'What if the king's gambling on it though?' Doranei said. 'Why's this all so secret? Not sure he'll be calling down the storm any time soon these days.'

'You rein that in,' Veil said sharply. 'I don't give a damn what's goin' on in your head these days, there can't be talk like that just before a battle!'

'I didn't mean it like that,' Doranei protested grumpily, knowing he was in the wrong, 'just not used to surprises, and now there's a plan I ain't party to.'

'Well you're the one walked away, and you ain't a general; we ain't soldiers. This ain't our world, so our skills aren't in demand here.' Veil gave him a hard look. 'Now shut the fuck up and don't let me hear another word. No joke, Brother; you sounded like Ilumene for a moment there – Coran hears that shit and he'll break you in pieces.'

Doranei gave a start, his mouth dropping open in surprise. As he replayed Veil's words in his head he realised he'd been right. Doranei found himself recoiling from the realisation: Ilumene's betrayal had been preceded by increasing resentment towards the king, and the assumption that his advice should always be sought, no matter what the situation.

The King's Men were supposed to be faceless and silent, removed from politics and power, personal ambitions and desires foresworn ... Only Ilumene hadn't been able to accept his place, one he'd embraced until he decided he stood above the rest.

Doranei found himself half a pace removed from the Brotherhood, and his thoughts had followed the same track – and Veil was right; Coran would kill him for taking even a step down that path. The more he thought about it, the more Doranei realised he wouldn't be able to blame the white-eye for it. Doranei had personally cut down one of the Brothers killed by Ilumene during his bloody defection. He hadn't just murdered the man, he'd pinned the bastard to a wall using eight shortswords, then ritually disembowelled him and fed his heart to the man's own dogs.

'Sorry,' he muttered, abashed. 'You're right.'

'I know,' Veil said airily, 'and after this, you'n'me are going to get your shit in order, y'hear? Should be Sebe doin' it, I know, but that's not going to happen and he was my friend too. He'd want me in his stead to see the job done and I'll be proud t'do it.'

Sebe, Doranei thought glumly, *this life's harder without you here. Maybe that's what I'm impatient for. This war I can manage, been living with horror for too long as it is. Zhia I can handle, or survive her, at least.*

But do this all without the Brother I leaned on most of all? That's harder than I'd realised.

'I hear you,' Doranei said in a quiet voice. He resumed his position, staring out toward the Menin, willing them on.

See you when the killing's done, Brother.

Kastan Styrax walked out of his tent and stopped as the Bloodsworn knights who had camped around him in a protective ring raised their weapons and roared, their wordless fervour booming out all around and echoed back by the tens of thousands beyond.

He faced them silently, looking around at the cheering soldiers and matching their gaze. Wearing the black whorled armour of Koezh Vukotic he stood with his head uncovered and accepted their adulation. The thick black curls of his hair were tied back in the manner of a Menin nobleman, neatly, without frippery or adornment, while the ghost of a beard lay upon his cheeks. It was unusual for Lord Styrax not to be clean-shaven, but if anything he looked more Menin as a result.

Strapped to his back was the fanged broadsword he'd prised from the dead fingers of Lord Akass, his predecessor: the first great feat of many, and the one that had set him on this path. All those years ago – centuries, now – Kastan had realised it was true, that he was like no other mortal. His time in the Reavers had been not only for training and preparation, it had been a refuge against the weight of expectation placed on his shoulders when he had turned sixteen. That day he had been offered a glimpse of his true potential, the weapon the Gods intended him to be.

Even for a white-eye, it was almost too much to bear, Styrax thought as he let the waves of cheering crash over him. *Even when I saw the Reavers were lesser kin, it was too much to ask of a boy.*

Lord Styrax smiled, and with a deliberately slow movement he reached behind his head and drew the enormous black broadsword. The cheers became deafening and the élite Bloodsworn dropped to one knee, weapons touching the ground as their lord raised Kobra's split tip to the sky and added his own booming voice to the tumult.

'We go to war!' Styrax roared as the thousands raised their own weapons. He turned slowly, watching the faces around him fill with fierce pride.

'This long march has been hard,' he called, pausing to give them all time to remember the stories of the tribe's past, 'and it is more than the weak who have fallen along the path!'

Deverk Grast had marched the Menin away from the West and ordered that the weak be allowed to fall at the wayside. Once the greatest of the seven tribes, the Menin had endured horrors in the Waste as they travelled to the Ring of Fire; they had nearly been broken as they tried to carve a new home in the wilderness. There were many sects within the tribe who saw this invasion as a return to glory; the rightful return to their place as the foremost of the tribes of man.

'The pain has been the same for us all, the loss and the suffering shared among proud brothers!'

Styrax felt his face tighten. In his mind's eye he saw Kohrad exchanging blows with Lord Isak, matching the silver-blurred stokes of the Farlan with all the fire and ferocity he'd possessed. He saw Kohrad struck and stagger, the emerald hilt of Eolis blazing through the storm of magic as he pitched backwards and fell.

'The end is not yet in sight,' he shouted, 'but the reckoning has come. We have beaten all in our path, and when Narkang falls the spine of the West will be broken!

'The Chetse we defeated, and they honoured us by joining our cause!

'The Farlan we defeated, and they ran for home!'

Whistles and catcalls came from all around, then laughter. Styrax waited for the noise to abate, then went on, 'The Farlan ran, and they will run again – but first we take down this *self-anointed* – a man too afraid to let his rabble of an army past their ditches to face us like men.

'Show them how men fight, brothers; call the names of our fallen and show them the price of cowardice. We go to war!'

His last words were barely heard as the soldiers yelled in frenzied abandon. General Gaur signalled the drummers to beat to orders, but even the heavy thump of the huge wardrums was swallowed by the clamour. Only when the great curling horns of the Chetse legions sounded and the Menin drums repeated the command did it die down and order resume.

Styrax turned to Gaur and the beastman bowed awkwardly. General Vrill appeared behind him.

'The legions have their orders?' Styrax asked.

'They have, my Lord,' Vrill called, also bowing. The duke was ready for battle, the ribbons fixed to his white armour trembling in the dull morning light. 'My infantry are moving out as I speak.'

'Good. I'll be counting on you to stir up a little confusion and panic.'

'While you assault a fixed position,' Vrill said pointedly. 'While we *both* assault fixed positions, with our forces nicely divided.'

Styrax gave the small white-eye a sharp look and sheathed Kobra again. 'Vrill, you may lecture me about dwindling supplies and lines of communication, or you may remind me of Erialave's tenets of the field. You may not, however, do both.'

Vrill bowed, lower this time. 'Apologies, my Lord. I remain yours to command. My concerns are for your safety, not my own.'

'We've overswept his land and killed half his people – still think *King* Emin is going to conjure up a surprise we can't handle?' Styrax said with a slightly forced smile.

He knew Vrill was right about much, but they simply couldn't wait to devise something intricate, nor could they evade the Narkang force – and he did not want to. Supplies were running dangerously low, and they needed a decisive victory, or they would begin to starve within the week. He'd given the order that there was to be no guard left with the baggage. One way or another, this day would be decisive. Styrax was certain his armies would show their worth.

'I think a surprise doesn't need to be your equal if it truly is a surprise – he possesses a Crystal Skull, according to Major Amber and—'

'And I have several!' Styrax growled, 'to say nothing of the fact none of his mages are my equal, nor Lord Larim's nor, most likely, half of Larim's acolytes.'

Vrill opened his mouth to argue, then shut it again with a snap. The decision was made and the most likely result of arguing further would be a swift death. 'As you command, my Lord,' he said in a tight, controlled voice. 'Do you have final orders for me before I go to my command?'

Styrax, his hands balled into fists, made himself calm down. After a moment, he said, 'Take your time. They'll not come to you, so once you've cleared away the skirmishers you can negotiate the advance ditches slowly. Keep your formation and keep close to the tree-line. If they have cavalry hidden there they'll run long before you reach them, for fear of being pinned down.'

Vrill looked up at the sky. It was still early and there was a blanket of thin cloud overhead. 'A good thing they want to keep your wyvern on the ground,' he commented. 'There's a lot of marching to do today; hot sun's the last thing we'll need.'

Styrax nodded. 'With any luck they'll keep the clouds there for us so I won't have to.' He offered a hand to his general who looked startled for a moment before remembering himself and taking it. 'Good hunting – if you break their line or draw them out, don't hesitate. Keep a mage close and send me a message if they're weakening; I'll get their attention while you win the battle.'

Vrill couldn't help but grin at the prospect, a flush of animation crossing his usually composed face. Lord Styrax was not a man who shared victory easily, but this he meant. Duke Vrill had the right flank; he had ten legions to march to the tree-line and in through the narrow channel King Emin had left on the edge of the forest: two thousand cavalry to protect his flank and eight thousand infantry to throw against the enemy line.

Once past the defensive ditches of the Narkang Army it would become brutal, bloody sword-work. With a breach, the quality of the Menin heavy infantry and the savagery of the Chetse élite axemen would come into their own.

'Good luck to you too, my Lord,' Vrill said with meaning.

The bulk of the army, double the number at Vrill's command, would be directly assaulting the fort at the heart of the Narkang defences, marching straight towards the enemy on ground of the enemy's choosing. A further six legions protected their left flank and rear, where the Narkang cavalry would be trying to make their greater numbers count.

They would be assailed on two sides, barely able to fight back until they breached the fort's walls: it would be the greatest test the Menin Army had ever faced. Their enemy was ruthlessly inventive and had had weeks to prepare for battle; that made it a horrific prospect – but Lord Styrax himself would be leading them, and that was enough for the army.

Styrax watched Vrill go, then raised an armour-clad arm and struck it against General Gaur's. The two had no need for parting words. Gaur had devised the plan with his lord, and he knew his part well enough; everything else was understood. He left without a word.

Styrax looked out towards the enemy lines, visualising what he'd scouted from wyvernback the previous evening: two great defensive ditches, each running for more than half a mile, reached out from the castle called Moorview in a diamond shape, with a wooden fort at the nearest point and Moorview at its rear. The castle was set in an indent of the forest, although there was open ground on its right flank. His scouts reported smaller, staggered defences set beyond each of the great ditches.

The Narkang cavalry would be concentrated on the open ground on Styrax's left, which gave them space to manoeuvre. The bulk of King Emin's army would be behind the ditches, probably concentrated at cither end, and he guessed their orders would be simple enough: stay put, and resist assault. Doing anything so complicated as advancing would leave inexperienced troops vulnerable – and they were inexperienced; six months before they'd all been farmers and ploughboys! – so it was unlikely the Menin would be able to tempt them out. Still, Vrill had a few hundred captives to execute in plain view, just in case he could torture them into forgetting their orders.

'Sound the advance,' Styrax called, 'and let's show them what they're all afraid of.'

The Bloodsworn around him turned to march to their positions – on foot, fighting as his bodyguard – but two lingered, staring straight at Styrax, barely ten yards away. He felt a prickle of magic tremble through the air and was drawing his sword before he'd had time to think.

As the man on the left ran forward, the Bloodsworn armour started to disintegrate, pieces cascading from its body as it moved with impossible speed. It had covered the ground between them in a heartbeat, bringing up a shimmering sword, ready to strike. Styrax threw himself back, but his attacker followed, blindingly fast, his sword distorting the air as they parried and broke, and moved again, and again.

Styrax blocked with desperation, the weapons moving too fast for a normal human to clearly see. His armour turned a glancing blow in a shower of sparks and Styrax went briefly onto the attack with a volley of blows that would have felled any normal man –

but each was met and blocked, and the ring of their blades came so fast it sounded like shattering glass.

Distantly he felt a flicker of apprehension as he finally recognised the figure attacking. The armour now was identical to his own, and the sword seemed to tear at the air it passed. Styrax found secure footing and drew on his Crystal Skulls. The magical artefacts pulsed at his command, tendrils of spitting light lashing out, burning furrows through the earth and scorching the moorland grass.

Koezh Vukotic pressed his advantage. Staying light on his feet, he dipped and weaved his way between the savage streams of magic, cutting through the storm with his rage-filled sword. Koezh forced Styrax to turn, deflecting his sword up and catching the Menin lord a glancing blow across the ribs. It didn't pierce the metal, but even as Styrax slashed at his opponent's head, Koezh had moved and cut across Styrax's cuirass, nicking the edge of the monogram plate bearing Koezh's own initials.

Styrax hurled himself forward, using his greater bulk as a battering ram to drive Koezh back, but the vampire rode the blow and turned it to his advantage, nearly managing to thrust his sword point into the back of Styrax's knee, then smashing the pommel of his sword into Styrax's chest. The white-eye saw the blow coming and slashed crossways, forcing Koezh to retreat or be decapitated. He won himself an instant to breath—

—and a second figure flew forward while flames erupted from the ground all around them, and Styrax twisted with unnatural grace, parrying the blow and filling his sword with magic to score a blistering trail down the other attacker's thigh – but his blow was turned by the same whorled armour, and his attacker had already pivoted and kicked out at him. Styrax dropped to a half-crouch, pinning the armoured foot under his arm and punching with his left hand into the side of Zhia's knee. He didn't wait to see if he'd caused any damage, but rolled his body through the air, moving around Zhia to use her as a shield against Koezh's follow-up.

Styrax caught a glint of red light in the air and summoned a grey dome of energy to deflect the bloody fire lashing down at his head. He released Zhia, but kept her between himself and Koezh, knowing her to be the weaker fighter. White swirls danced around her body, exploding into sunbursts of sparks as his sword hit them. She retreated, keeping her sword close to her body as she waited for a chance to get inside his guard. He obliged; smashing an elbow forward as she stepped into a thrust and snapping her head back.

With both fists around his grip Styrax punched her in the chest, putting all his power into the blow. It smashed her backwards, driving Zhia through the air, but before she'd even hit the ground Styrax was moving, striking out as Koezh came at his other side. The blow was parried and he dropped low to slash at the vampire's legs, but it was deflected into the ground even as Koezh hacked at his neck and was stopped by a grey bar of magic.

Koezh made a twisting gesture with his hand and Styrax felt his feet wrenched sideways. He turned into the movement, flinging himself around, and as he dropped, he lashed out wildly, as Koezh turned the blows with practised ease.

One-handed, Styrax turned his first two blows, and stepped into the third, casting forward a corkscrew of raw energy, and somehow the vampire managed to both drive himself backwards while at the same time twisting so one arm pierced the centre of the spiral. With one hand, Koezh grasped the stream of magic itself and savagely ripped it away.

With the energy dissipated, he cut upwards at Styrax, but the white-eye had already retreated and he smashed Kobra down, nearly catching Koezh on the upswing– but the vampire sprang away, sliding backwards across the magic-scorched grass.

Styrax braced himself and unleashed the full force of the Skulls at Koezh, but the twisting cable of uncontrolled magic unravelled, spraying wildly all around while the Skull fixed to Koezh's own armour blazed bright white.

Zhia appeared in Styrax's periphery. The whorled pattern on her cuirass was distorted and buckled, but it didn't hamper her as she raced back into the fray. Styrax stepped away from her charge, taking a glancing blow from her sword on his pauldron as he extended his sword and felt it pierce the flexible mesh covering her armpit. He drove forward, and as Kobra's fangs skewered her flesh he dragged and her side around and lifted his weapon, pulling her on to her tiptoes.

Then, sensing Koezh behind him he tugged Kobra out of Zhia's armpit and slashing left-handed as he moved to the left, away from the vampire's onrush. Koezh anticipated the move and a grey bar of energy caught Styrax's sword before it could cover his body.

The vampire cut up at his exposed wrist; Styrax had to lean forward to take the blow on his vambrace instead, but still he felt the sword pierce the metal and a hot burst of pain flowered in his arm.

He dived forward frantically, evading the next crippling blow, and rolled close to the perimeter of flames that was keeping his soldiers away. He felt the sizzle of acid on his flesh: Koezh's sword had scarred his skin again. Now he placed both hands on his own sword and flooded his body with magic to wash away the pain before leaping to his feet and immediately dodging to strike inside Koezh's follow-up blow.

The vampire moved even faster now, aware his sister was injured and the fight was all his own. They struck and blocked and parried in turn, until they locked swords, pulling each other to within a few inches. Each tried to shove the other off-balance in the split-second before retreating, but their unnatural strength was equally matched.

Styrax stepped back first, cutting up at Koezh's hands, checking the blow and lunging at his face. Koezh, the smaller man, dodged with astonishing speed, diverting the thrust upwards with the guard of his sword and turning it into a thrust of his own. Styrax stepped into the blow, catching it on his chest before Koezh could get any force behind it, then slamming an elbow down onto Koezh's shoulder and at last getting him off balance.

Side-on to his enemy, Styrax swung down as he moved clear; trying to chop into the vampire's throat, but Koezh dropped flat on his back and the blow caught only thin air. As Styrax stabbed down, Kobra's fangs met a flat grey disc. With his full strength behind the blow, the weapon penetrated, but the impact juddered right through Styrax's body and the fangs were stopped by Koezh's cuirass – and Styrax had to hop gracelessly back to save his ankles.

Koezh was already striking as he leaped to his feet and caught Styrax's blade as they both moved into the attack, locking weapons again. Styrax, catching a movement out of the corner of his eye, threw himself backwards as Zhia arrived. He gave ground right up to the encircling flames, desperate for space to evade her – only to watch in astonishment as Zhia's slender sword ran straight and true into the seam of the black cuirass, driving deep inside.

Her brother faltered, driven sideways by the unexpected impact, but before he could react, Zhia forced her sword further into Koezh's guts. A gasp of pain escaped his lips as she retracted the weapon and stepped back. Her brother staggered and dropped to one knee, his hand going to his side as a spurt of black blood spilled out.

Styrax didn't hesitate, advancing and smashing Koezh's sword aside. With the vampire defenceless, he cut at his opponent's neck and felt Kobra tear through the armour. Koezh fell, limp before he hit the ground and a sudden silence descended.

'I'm sorry, brother,' Zhia whispered, her voice strained, 'but it must be this way.'

She turned to Styrax, who faced her with his weapon raised warily, but the Vukotic princess shook her head and sheathed her weapon.

'You will have to enjoy your battle alone, Lord Styrax – I am done for the day.' Her right arm went to the armpit where he'd injured her. He could hear from her laboured voice that the wound was severe.

Do I kill her now, while I have the chance?

'You could kill me,' she said, correctly guessing his thoughts, 'but that would deny you an ally for the future – one who could be of use to a collector.'

With a gesture she dismissed the flames crackling all around them and the true Bloodsworn rushed forward, stopping dead as Styrax raised a hand. He thought for a moment, panting to get his breath back after the furious exchange, barely able to string a coherent thought together.

'Go then,' he said eventually, 'go with my blessing and remember this debt.'

'My debt to you? How very male,' Zhia gasped, her arm drawn tight up to her chest. 'I suppose that's all the thanks I'll get for persuading Koezh our chances would be better without the Legion of the Damned.'

She looked down at the corpse of her brother, lying at Styrax's feet. A faint mist was building over it as his body started to decay and disintegrate.

'As you wish,' she said finally. 'Until we meet again.'

She turned and faced the wall of soldiers. They didn't move, and she looked back at Styrax, who gestured, parting the Bloodsworn for her. Once a path was clear, the vampire left without looking back once.

Styrax looked down at the putrefying armoured corpse at his feet. Koezh's Crystal Skull was still attached to the cuirass, and he quickly tugged it free. The armour was already soft and malleable, decaying with Koezh's body; the metal would melt into nothingness unless it was removed with alacrity, as Styrax had the first time they fought. If not, it would slowly reform with Koezh's body in the crypt beneath the Castle of Silence, far to the east. Koezh's sword was similarly indistinct within the mist, and as he watched, it sank into the moorland beneath it, unclaimed yet again.

He looked up at the assembled troops surrounding him. With an effort he smiled. 'First blood to us,' he announced hoarsely. The responding cheer was deafening.

'Enemy's advancing,' Veil said, pointing.

King Emin looked up. 'So it begins,' he muttered. 'How about the left flank?'

Veil squinted at where the smaller Menin force had formed up, by the tree-line. 'Looks like it – I'd need a mage to be sure.'

'Where are the damn mages?' Emin growled, seeing nothing but soldiers. The fort contained more than a thousand men, as closely packed in as could be managed without causing complete chaos.

'There's the runt,' Coran said, indicating the diminutive form of Tomal Endine, who was weaving a path towards them, through the Kingsguard and the catapult platforms that stood between the central tower and Emin's position on the rampart.

The mage laboured up the wooden ramp towards King Emin, and Coran reached down to drag the small man the last yard while he gasped for breath. The King's bodyguard stood out from the crowd by more than size now – his cuirass and helm were painted a bright bloody red, in contrast to the green and gold livery that surrounded him. The rest of the Brotherhood wore black-painted armour, punctuating the crowd of resplendent Kingsguard like needles secreted in a haystack.

'Piss and daemons,' Doranei said, 'man's exhausted and the battle's not started yet!'

Endine gave Doranei an unfriendly look and sparks crackled momentarily across his knuckles.

'Your Majesty, Mage Holtai reports both sections of the enemy are advancing. Two lines of heavy infantry are moving directly here, with archers and cavalry protecting them, while a mixed force of infantry and cavalry are stationed on their left flank. The smaller force is keeping tight to the forest and they too are protected on their left flank by cavalry.'

King Emin nodded and turned to face his army, the bulk of which was lined up behind the long ditches. They stood in long lines that would be vulnerable on the open field, but these great defensive works would massively reduce the force of any infantry charge.

'There is more, your Majesty,' Endine said urgently, 'I sensed magic used in the enemy camp – not a spell in progress, but energies shaped quickly, with violence meant.'

'Which means?'

'That I don't know, but most likely Lord Styrax fought someone of great power – perhaps he even gave Larat's Chosen a Crystal Skull to use in battle and had it turned against him.'

King Emin frowned. 'I doubt that; he will assume he has the advantage there without help from doubtful sources.'

'I can see no other explanation – the magic expended was considerable—'

'And without a Crystal Skull,' Emin finished for him, 'what fool would bother?' He forced a smile. 'It'll do us no good speculating. If the enemy is divided, they'll be less enthusiastic about throwing themselves on our stake-points!' The king gestured towards the long lines of raised stakes surrounding the fort and provoked a cheer from those nearby.

'Endine, return to your post,' King Emin said once the noise had abated, 'when I need Cetarn signalled I'll send a runner. In the meantime, keep us safe!'

The sickly mage bowed and scuttled back to the tower in the centre of the fort where the scryer, Mage Holtai, sat watching the enemy's movements, and three battle-mages waited for the coming assault.

'Will Cetarn be enough?' Doranei asked quietly. 'He's no white-eye, no matter what they've cooked up on that chained mound.'

'Cetarn will play his part,' Emin replied distantly, 'as must we all.'

'Is that why you're here, your Majesty?'

Emin gave him a sharp look. 'Your meaning?'

Doranei edged forward, keeping his voice as low as possible and ignoring the fact that Coran also stepped closer, just in case. 'The fort is vulnerable; you must see that.'

'Must I?'

'Yes,' Doranei said firmly, 'the ditches aren't long enough to be certain we won't be cut off, yet here's where you make your stand. Wouldn't it be better if you moved further back, where the whole army can see your standard and take heart?'

King Emin gave him a more genuine smile than he had Endine. 'No, my friend, it is best I'm here, on that you must trust me – as I trust you and Coran to keep me safe.'

'Are you intentionally putting yourself in a dangerous position?' Doranei asked quietly.

'Remember this – we are all in mortal danger today,' Emin said, 'and it will do the men good to see that I take the same risks they do. In the context of a battle plan, my significance should not be overstated. If Kastan Styrax wishes me dead, he will achieve that goal wherever I stand. My death may be a blow, but the Menin know they must do more than that to win the day.'

'It'd be a bloody good start though,' Doranei hissed, prompting a bellow of unexpected laughter from King Emin.

'Hah, you could be right there! So let's give them something more pressing to think about, eh?'

King Emin clapped him on the shoulder and turned back to the Menin Army. Their progress was difficult to discern, but they were still well outside the range markers the Narkang troops had installed on the moor.

The ground dead ahead was clear and open, but on both left and right were sets of ditches, staggered so six divisions of archers could hurt the enemy before they came anywhere near the Narkang Army. Working in concert with each other and with squadrons of cavalry supporting them, the archers would engage in a fighting retreat, with little fear of being caught in the open.

'Signal the cavalry to advance,' he called aloud, and a sergeant below him took up the order and it started repeating at a roar. On the tower, a red flag was run up the pole.

'That's not going to be enough, however much we outnumber 'em.'

'I know,' King Emin said distantly, 'but they may yet make a mistake in the heat of the moment. If nothing else, it will give them pause for thought while they attempt to charge through us.' He started towards a ballistae station on their right, where the rampart walkway bulged to allow easy movement, but before he reached it, the voices within the fort were dropping and faces began to turn his way.

The king faced his men, then swept off his flamboyant hat so his face was visible to all. He gave them a moment to remember the stories, the legend of a king to rival any the Land had yet seen. He had as commanding a presence as any white-eye, and his quiet assurance and cold eyes gave no reason to doubt the reputed genius of his intellect, nor the ruthless ambition that had driven his own conquest two decades previously.

'Brothers,' King Emin called in a loud, clear voice, 'our time of reckoning has come.'

Doranei watched the effect of the king's piercing ice-blue gaze sweeping over his troops, as the men stood a shade more upright under that imperious stare.

'The so-called "first tribes" have marched on our lands,' King Emin announced, raising his arms as though to embrace the army, 'intent on destroying all we have built and all we hold dear.'

He looked around, catching people's eyes, so every man thought he spoke directly to him. 'In their envy,' he cried, 'they come to kill us, to murder this dream we share. They see the twilight of their own kind and for that they fear us.'

He raised his voice, little by little, as he went on, 'They fear our great kingdom, because it stands for an end to the ways of the past – an end to the ties of tradition and ancient prejudice. An end to the dream that they are better than we.

'Twenty years ago I realised the truth, one I see realised in the faces all around me: I believed that we were equal of any of the seven tribes – but now I see we are greater still!'

He paused, waiting and watching, until the watching soldiers were breathless with anticipation.

'When the White Circle attacked Narkang, many of you fought alongside me, fought as equals alongside Lord Isak himself, and when the breach came it was his actions that saved the day, and yet – and yet he did not claim the title of hero that day, though he was more than entitled.'

Doranei could feel the expectation building like a tidal wave inside them all.

'Young as he was, Isak knew his God would protect him as he called the storm down, and secure in that knowledge, he sought to close the breach alone.'

King Emin paused again. The faces were rapt, every man holding his breath until the king slowly raised a finger. Doranei felt the murmurs building from the crowd.

'But . . . but in that breach he was not alone—'

He got no further as a roar of approval crashed out around the fort, drowning out all other sounds. The king waited for the tumult to die down again, knowing their pride would eclipse any thing else he might now say. Many of those present had fought on the walls of the White Palace; many friends had died beside them, and they had all known their lives were hanging in the balance when Lord Isak of the Farlan had stayed alone to defend the wall.

'—yes, brothers, there was another – one who was neither white-eye, nor favoured of the Gods. Commander Brandt was a man, no different to you or me, and yet he was *a hero*! He was not even a soldier – the City Watch was his mistress, and he served it faithfully, man and boy.

'When the time came, this simple watchman sacrificed himself for the city he loved, for his wife and children, and to protect this dream we share! And he did so gladly.

'He stood, back to back with a figure from myth – back to back and unafraid!'

King Emin turned to the advancing Menin Army, then back to his men, a mocking smile on his lips as he made a dismissive gesture.

'*Equal* to the Seven Tribes? No – not that day, nor for ever more! They come to kill us; they come to conquer us, *because they fear us*! Without the patronage of Gods here we stand, as strong as any of them, and solely through our own endeavour. Even now they dare not face us alone, but with reluctant, fearful allies.'

The king gestured at the faces arrayed below him. 'The blessed of the War God march on us, yet I see no fear on your faces. They have hurt us, they have razed our towns and murdered our countrymen, yet still I do not see fear. Instead I see a people of one mind, a people of one unstoppable resolve!

'Together, brothers, we will show them the quality they fear, the true strength of the nation that eclipses them! This day I leave the field as King of Narkang, or not at all, and as a watchman once laid his life down for his wife and children, so shall I, if the Gods demand it!

'We are steel, tempered in the flames of their disdain. On steel, their ancient bronze will break. Tomorrow we will pity them, for their time is done, but today we will show them only our rage!

'Rage for the innocents they have slain. Rage for the threat to those we hold dear. Face them, my brothers – face them and show them the strength of free men!'

CHAPTER 36

'Where is that novice-fucking cripple?' bellowed a voice from some-where behind. 'Osh! Where are you, you cockless relic?'

Hambalay Osh stifled a smile and turned stiffly. He had pos-itioned himself on a small rise, the better to view the troops under his command, and from there he could see a figure forcing its way through the crowd of soldiers. The Mystic of Karkarn was today dressed in a long red robe with bronze-coloured braiding, and a bronze helm covered the grey stubble on his head and cheeks. A long shield rested against his left side, partially hiding the metal brace that encased his leg.

'Daken!' he called as the white-eye barged through the assembled soldiers, knocking one infantryman to the ground in the process.

'That's fucking General Daken to you,' the man roared cheer-fully, grinning in anticipation of the battle to come. He grabbed the ageing mystic in a bearhug, chuckling madly. 'Still upright, then?'

Osh gestured to his ruined knee – after escaping the Ruby Tower in Byora, with a little help from the Brotherhood, the mage, Tomal Endine, had healed the injury as best he could, but Osh still need the brace to stop the knee collapsing underneath him. 'Until you give me a good shove anyway.'

Daken did just that, thumping Osh hard on the chest and doub-ling over with laughter as he fell backwards onto his rump. The mystic gave a wheezing cough, trying to recover his breath while Osh's aides helped him up.

'I suppose,' Osh puffed, 'I asked for that.'

'Sounded like'n invitation to me,' Daken agreed, beaming. The white-eye general wore a battered breastplate and a plundered Menin helm, but the cloak around his neck was pristine: white, with a red border. Osh tilted his head to get a better look at the design on it: a massive curved axe.

'Fate's eyes,' Osh breathed, 'he really has ennobled you?'

'Aye, but he made me a marshal too!' Daken said, grinning. 'Likes a man who carries out orders well, does King Emin.'

Osh turned and looked towards the defensive lines ten yards away. 'So you're here commanding this flank?' They were near the tree-line, and the smaller of the two Menin forces was closing in, now only four hundred yards away.

Daken nodded. 'He wants my axe here, help hold the line. I command this flank, General Lopir's got the cavalry, and Suzerain Tenber has the right, for all the good he can do there.'

'The reserve?'

'Yours to call when you want 'em, half o' Tenber's infantry are moving this way already.' Daken's face twisted in scorn. 'Fer some reason he's given command of the reserve to a bunch o' Raylin there – some local crone and that blind bitch who smells like a Demi-God and is pretty enough to be the next thing I ask the king fer!'

A tall soldier in Canar Fell colours interrupted them. 'Sir, the first line of skirmishers are withdrawing.'

The pair looked over the heads of the blue-liveried infantry and watched the furthest division of archers scramble back towards the Narkang lines. They were pursued by two regiments of light cavalry, but without enthusiasm as a second division of bowmen positioned behind the next staggered ditch had already started firing.

'Hurry up, ya bastards!' Daken called out to the enemy army, 'we're gettin' bored back here!'

Osh smiled, watching the effect one white-eye's belligerence could have on a unit of men. This was why Daken had been removed from the cavalry: to stiffen the resolve of nervous troops in the face of an undefeated enemy.

More enemy cavalry were out ahead of the advancing legions. Those not engaged in trying to clear the skirmishers lingered on the edge of bowshot, but Osh knew they wouldn't stay there long: Before the heavy infantry caught them up they'd start to strafe the Narkang line, see if they could draw out a pursuit. If anyone followed they'd quickly be surrounded and wiped out, so every single officer had had the same order drummed into them: if they allowed anyone to leave the line without a clear order from the king or a general, they would be executed.

Not long after, the beat of drums drifted over the moor and the sound prompted a sudden jerk from the cavalry and a grin from Daken.

'Here they come,' he yelled triumphantly, 'now hold the line, all o' you!' He beckoned over one of Osh's aides. 'Archers ready, fire on my word.'

The man saluted and gestured to a major commanding the archers on the right.

Daken watched the Menin follow the tree-line, aiming to slant across the line of pikemen holding the open ground at the end of the ditch. 'Rear legion,' he called, turning to face the officer waiting for his order, 'five volleys, fifty yards in from the trees – furthest range: Fore legions, *fire at will!*'

Osh resisted the urge to duck as he heard the dull thrum of bowstrings ring out and a cloud of black arrows flashed over their heads, arching down towards the attacking cavalry, and before the second volley was loosed, the first of the enemy were tumbling from their horses.

The cavalry pressed on, unable to do anything but close the ground and throw their javelins at the infantry; attacking an ordered line head-on would be suicide, and even their efforts to ride down the line cost them dearly as archers were positioned there specifically to pick them off.

'Hold the line!' an officer shouted from within the press of infantry, and his call was quickly taken up by the rest as the cavalry swept past and turned away.

Once they moved away Osh could see the heavy infantry behind: armoured Menin troops with fat, oval shields and long spears, advancing steadily in two wide blocks. They appeared oblivious to the streams of arrows raining in on their flank from archers behind the ditch.

'Rear legions, another five volleys, furthest range,' Osh called to the officer behind him, 'then keep firing just beyond our line.'

'What're we missin' here?' Daken muttered as the officer spread the order. 'Those heavy infantry ain't goin' to push their way through eight ranks o' pikes, not unless they got another few legions behind.'

'Scryer said eight of them, but they don't look like they're all engaging yet,' said the mystic, scratching his cheek. He looked up suddenly. ''Ware incoming arrows!' Osh called loudly. They watched the missiles fall with a strange detachment, knowing they could do nothing – most fell short, but a few found their mark and the screaming started.

As the Menin closed they heard shouts from their left, at the tree-line. A fierce grin appeared on Daken's face as a youth ran out from the trees, one of the division of volunteer infantry stationed there.

'Chetse!' the youth shouted again and again in a high, panicked voice, 'Chetse in the trees!'

It took Osh a moment to place his uniform, then the mystic realised he'd last seen it on the streets of Narkang: this division was comprised of City Watchmen, who'd arrived unannounced a few days before, inspired by the sacrifice of Commander Brandt, in Narkang the previous year. They'd been assigned to the forest, as their weapons were barely suited to an open battlefield.

Daken moved with surprising speed. The youth running towards them, still shouting, barely had time to look surprised before Daken clouted him around the head hard enough to knock him down.

Osh looked at the rear rank of the pikemen; the white-eye had been right to do so; they were looking panicked at the thought of Chetse axemen appearing behind them.

'I heard ya the first time,' Daken growled, standing over the young watchman, 'now: get up!'

The youth was still sprawled on his back, dazed by the blow. He was wearing a peaked iron helm and a leather coat and carried a wooden shield; not much protection against the Menin, but good for anyone trying to negotiate the dense forest. At the white-eye's words he pulled himself to his feet and saluted clumsily.

Daken unsheathed his axe and brandished it above his head. 'First reserve division to me,' he shouted, heading towards the tree-line and dragging the youth with him.

Five hundred men broke to run after him as their officers bellowed the order, awkwardly forming a shield wall in five uneven ranks no more than thirty yards from the first tree of the forest. Ahead of them walked the white-eye general, into the gloom of the forest. Seeing nothing, he shoved the young watchman forward.

'Go keep a watch out for 'em,' he roared.

The youth, still shaking, headed back into the forest to find the enemy, while Daken started barking orders.

He's enjoying himself, the mystic realised. *He's looking forward to facing axemen as mad as he is. Reckon he's the only one.*

'Damn you, Cetarn,' King Emin hissed, 'what in the name of the Dark Place are you waiting for?'

The Menin were marching ever closer, hunkered down behind their shields under a barrage of arrows and ballistae bolts. Their own archers were massed in loose order ahead of the infantry, doing their best to limit the effectiveness of the Narkang bowmen. The main front line was made up of alternating Menin heavy infantry and troops from the Chetse élite Ten Thousand.

Doranei looked back at the central tower where Endine was standing with Fei Ebarn and the scowling mercenary, Wentersorn, the two battle-mages who'd been part of the assault on the Ruby Tower. Camba Firnin, the illusionist, was down by one of the catapults, filling the bowl with something horrific. Doranei waved madly until Endine noticed him, but the scrawny mage just gestured for them to wait.

The main line of Menin was a hundred yards away now. Doranei drew his sword and felt a rush of power tingle up his arm as Aracnan's weapon seemed to drink in the summer sunlight. It was most likely even more ancient than Doranei's vampire lover, and there was something about it he disliked, but it was worth its weight in battle: it was frighteningly swift, and could cleave both an enemy's weapon and his helm in one stroke.

Under Hambalay Osh's tuition Doranei had been learning a new style of fighting, one more akin to the ritualistic combat used by warrior-monks. Mystics of Karkarn and the like eschewed armour, concentrating instead on technique and clean, controlled strikes rather than the fury required on a battlefield, where blows had to batter through a man's defences.

'Now we'll see something,' Veil commented as Ebarn stepped back from the catapult. The crew wasted no time in firing the weapon and half a dozen clay balls the size of baby's heads were hurled over the wall. Doranei kept one eye on Ebarn, having seen her magic work before; the mage was standing perfectly still, her eyes closed. The balls spread unevenly in the air and had barely started to drop by the time they reached the front rank.

When they were still at least twenty yards off the ground Ebarn clapped her hands together once, then made as she were flinging the contents before her, and Doranei heard the crump of igniting flames. A sheet of fire tore through the air above the Menin and flopped down on top of them, sloping down off their raised shields onto the men below. Screams echoed across the moor, followed by cheers from the fort, but the Menin faltered only a moment, and a roar of defiance was their response when a ballista bolt tore deeper into the blackened ranks. They were ten legions of élite troops; it would take more than one mage to turn them back.

When the Menin were eighty yards away Doranei felt a tremor run through the earth rampart of the fort. Behind them he could just make out the oversized shape of Cetarn on the circular earthen platform they had built. The air above him was shuddering as though it were being assailed and the iron chains running from the mound into the ground lifted, taking the slack as cracking loops of energy ran through them.

'Piss and daemons,' Doranei breathed, watching the tortured air crackling. With a final flourish Cetarn dropped to one knee and slammed both hands to the ground and a great crash reverberated as a burst of energy surged towards the enemy lines and into a Chetse legion.

Half of the first rank were thrown from their feet, but they were the lucky ones. A boom like distant thunder rumbled out, and the rear ranks on one side of the legion disappeared in a great cloud of dust. Doranei gaped as he realised the ground had opened up underneath them, swallowing several hundred men.

'Karkarn's horn,' Veil breathed, 'I didn't know the old bugger had it in him!'

'He didn't,' the king said grimly. He was now wearing a steel helm detailed in gold – for the first time. His flamboyant feathered hat he'd tossed over the rampart, declaring to the amusement of all that he'd fetch it later.

'What—?' Doranei hesitated. 'He has a Skull? You've ordered him to sacrifice himself?'

'I've done what I must,' the king said sharply, 'Endine and Cetarn as are much of the Brotherhood as you or Sebe and they know their duty just as well. Cetarn may be the only mage here capable of this, he knows it, and he volunteered for the task.'

Doranei ducked his head in acknowledgement. He'd blurted it out without thinking; not out of a desire to question the king's decision. 'Of course – I just realised why Cetarn made a point of toasting the Brotherhood two nights past. Wish I'd known.'

'Aye,' said the king, 'normal men aren't built for channelling so much power. He knows he'll either burn himself out with the Skull, or he'll become Styrax's principal target.'

'Is that why—?' Doranei looked back at Cetarn and the troops guarding him. 'Never mind – it'll just make my head hurt.'

The king smiled briefly at him, a flash of teeth showing behind the steel grille visor. 'There's a lot doing that right now – let's just try to survive the day.'

'Here they come,' Coran growled from behind the king, his huge mace in one hand, a spear in the other. He circled his shoulders, stretched his arms, and got ready to drive his spear all the way through the first man to reach him.

The Menin were fifty yards off.

Doranei heard the order to charge, followed by a roar of hatred from the thousands massing and almost immediately the Chetse moved ahead of the more-disciplined Menin infantry. The King's Man raised his sword and looked down at the rampart. A spiked ditch at the base of an earth wall, propped by wood. Their climb would be difficult, but far from impossible.

The first Chetse berserker raced up to them and threw himself across the ditch, stabbing a dagger into the earth wall to brace himself as he swung his axe.

The blow was never finished. Coran leaned forward, teeth bared in fury, and drove his spear into the man before the closest defender could move. In his ferocity the white-eye spitted the wild-haired Chetse in the side, ramming the spear deep into his ribs. The Chetse was thrown back into the ditch below as Coran wrenched the weapon back out, his snarl of bloodlust drowned out by the shouts of the men around him. Then the rest arrived like a breaking wave and Doranei saw only the shrieking horde. He lunged and felt his blade bite the first.

*

Daken hammered the butt of his axe into the Chetse's face and felt bone shatter. The impact left blood spurting over his face as the soldier fell, but another was immediately in his place, aiming a hefty overhead swing at Daken's skull. He reached up with his axe and caught the descending shaft before it had built up speed, then kicked his attacker square in the midriff. The Chetse was bowled over by the force of the kick and Daken stepped into the gap, growling like an animal and hacking left and right into the unprotected flanks of those on either side.

'Daken, back in line!' Osh roared from somewhere behind. It was the second time he'd needed reminding and with a hiss of frustration the Mad Axe stepped back between the spear-points of his comrades.

The Chetse were charging raggedly from the trees, any semblance of order gone as they pushed their way through the thick forest. One group had barrelled straight into the side of the pikemen, but a company of Kingsguard had rushed to cut them down. Osh had sent a division to bolster the tree-end of the main defensive line, and lend their shoulders to the press.

The Menin heavy infantry had reached their line now and were battering away at the longer pikes, desperate to make a hole they could exploit. Thus far only a few men had got through, and they had been dispatched relatively easily, but the closer they got the more were able to evade the twelve-foot weapons.

'More of 'em!' Daken shouted joyfully as another hundred Chetse raced from the trees, screaming murderously.

The first few slammed bodily into Daken's defensive line. One rebounded and was thrown off his feet, others were impaled on the lowered spears, but two managed to slip through the line and hack down into the blue-painted wooden shields. Daken saw one chopped in half, and the man holding it fell screaming as the axe bit into his arm. Suddenly there was a terrific roar from the forest and the sound of something crashing against the trees. The roar was joined by a second: deep animal calls that, given the enemy, could mean only one thing.

Daken felt a shudder of fear run through his troops and sneered in disgust. A pair of Chetse saw him and came directly for him, one, bearing a massive circular shield, charged straight on to smash the spears out of the way, but the white-eye jumped forward and swung his axe like a club, catching the flat steel boss on the edge with such force he heard the man's arm snap. The blow knocked the shield aside, into the other soldier, and caused them both to stumble. Daken felled one with a blow to the neck and was about to run the other through when he was beaten to it by one of his men.

The trees ahead shook and in the darkness Daken saw a massive shape looming. Behind it came a second, an enormous club in its grip. The minotaurs caught sight of him and scrambled forward, ducking under branches and bellowing furiously.

'Shift yourself, bitch!' Daken shouted, thumping a fist against his own chest.

A dozen bluish wisps, faint in the daylight, flashed out from his body like misty tentacles. They raced forward and merged into a figure gliding at head-height through the air: a slender female figure with long hair that danced like snakes.

Litania, the Trickster was on the loose.

The first minotaur swiped at the Aspect of Larat, but its crudely shaped axe parted only air. The beast turned to follow the movement, confused by the ghostly shape, and Daken, following Litania's path, reached the minotaur in a few paces.

The beast was still tracking Litania and didn't notice Daken until the white-eye braced himself and threw his whole weight behind his axe. The weapon bit deep into the minotaur's knee, crunching into bone and causing it to howl with agony. It swiped one enormous fist towards Daken, but he'd already thrown himself clear and as it took a step forward the injured leg buckled.

Daken rolled to his feet and charged on, trusting the infantry to deal with the fallen one. He could hear Litania's high, girlish laugh as she danced in the air before the face of the second minotaur. The beast tried to grab at her, its clumsy fingers grasping wildly, and failed. Litania laughed and darted back, rising high above the minotaur's head, and it lurched forward, trying to follow—

—until it was suddenly jerked back by the head, almost losing its footing entirely. The minotaur had somehow managed to hook one of its curling horns on a low branch, and while Litania giggled in malicious delight, Daken stabbed the beast through the armpit. The spike went all the way in, driving towards the creature's lung, but he didn't hang around to see if the blow was mortal; he tugged out the weapon and chopped at its ribs, gashing through the minotaur's thick flank.

The monster reeled from the impact, wrenching its head violently enough to splinter the thick branch, but still unable to disentangle itself. Blood poured from its wounds; Daken realised they were both grave, but the beast was not yet dead. One spearman got too close, and it smashed him in the back so hard his spine crumpled.

Daken moved further around the minotaur, glancing over his shoulder to check there were no Chetse waiting to do the same to him, then raised his axe high above his head and stabbed the spike into the beast's neck. It grunted and squealed in pain, ripping the branch from the tree trunk, but as it turned on him it got three spears almost simultaneously in the back.

Daken hoisted his axe again and hacked furiously at the minotaur's face, cleaving it open. The beast arched its back and as it began to fall, Daken threw himself bodily at the toppling beast and delivered another enormous blow to its face before its shoulders hit the ground.

He looked up to discover he was standing on the minotaur's shuddering stomach, now slick with blood, while the beast heaved its last breath and his soldiers watched in horror.

'What's wrong with you lot?' he rasped, throat tight as the bloodlust coursed through his body. 'Not enjoying yerselves yet?'

Doranei punched forward with his shield, not even seeing what he caught, and swung his black broadsword blindly. He felt it part armour and continue through flesh, followed by a cry of pain as he yanked the sword back and felt the attacker fall away. He paused to gulp air, while the Land seemed to recede from around him. Cocooned by screams and the clash of metal, Doranei found his eyes drawn to the neat arcs of spattered blood on the inside of his shield, each one curving around his closed fist but leaving his glove unstained.

The King's Man was still staring at his fist when something smashed into the side of his head and black stars burst before his eyes. Doranei crashed sideways and collided with someone's legs, bringing them down too. He flailed drunkenly at the figure lying across him, unable to see through the blur in his eyes. He dropped his sword, got one arm underneath the man and pushed up. His vision cleared as the weight was lifted from his chest and he recognised, Daratin, a young Brother, who'd fallen on him.

Daratin had barely got to his feet when a Menin spear slammed into his chest, straight through his armour, and Doranei watched in horror as his mouth fell open as he was driven back. The scream was cut short as Daratin's knees gave way and he collapsed. Still holding the spear, the Menin soldier heaved his way into view, shield raised high to ward off a blow from Veil. Doranei scrabbled on the ground for his sword, but Coran was already leaping to his rescue.

The big white-eye charged past Veil, roaring like an enraged lion, and smashed his mace down onto the Menin's shield. The man crumpled under the terrific impact, his arm and shoulder shattered, and fell at Coran's feet. The white-eye stamped down on his spine and Doranei heard a wet crunch as he struggled up, pushing himself forward to protect Coran's side as the white-eye raised his mace once again.

Completely indefatigable, Coran hammered his mace onto another Menin head and Doranei saw the neck snap under the force of the blow, but such was the white-eye's speed he struck the next Menin barely a second later, and felled him too.

Doranei looked over the rampart. It was a chaotic mess beyond their lines, the Menin and Chetse enemy advancing steadily behind their large shields, through a rain of arrows and blows. He chanced a second pause to check on the king, and saw his monarch was striking and dodging with the deftness of a duellist, red sparks bursting from the impact whenever his enchanted axe met steel. On his other side was Suzerain Derenin, the burly lord of Moorview Castle, and the veterans in his service, all fighting furiously for the families who'd refused to be sent away and now waited to tend the injured.

As Coran backed off to return to his place in King Emin's lee, Doranei punched at a Chetse with his shield, catching the man a glancing blow on his shoulder and knocking him off-balance. A second Chetse saw the opportunity and jumped up, one foot on his comrade's back and the other against the gouged earth rampart. Doranei swung at the man but missed and had to turn his sword horizontal to take the impact of the man's axe. The magical weapon

516

met force with force, cutting into the axe-head and absorbing most of the blow.

Doranei didn't waste time being surprised, he wrenched the sword back and tugged the axe from the Chetse's hands; his second strike across the man's face cut bronze helm, flesh and bone with equal ease.

From overhead a pair of steel grapples dropped down right in front of him, catching on the logs supporting the rampart; he cut through the rope of one quickly enough, but before he could get to the other, one end of the log was dislodged in an explosion of earth and tugged towards the Menin lines.

He watched a small trail of soil patter down onto his boots, and it momentarily increased as the ground shook beneath him. Doranei sensed everyone hesitate, and for a half-second silence fell as a heavy reverberation ran forward across the moor. On both sides the men of the Brotherhood recovered quickest and ran through their opponents, but most eyes were on the tremor shuddering through the Menin ranks. A great tearing sound rang out as a circle of ground thirty yards across dropped suddenly away beneath a tightly packed Menin legion, taking a hundred or more men with it.

Doranei blinked. A great cloud of dust had been thrown up, and in the middle, a sudden blazing light erupted and through the swirl he saw a tall figure in brightly coloured robes, standing with arms outstretched where there was no ground to stand on. Spinning bands of light raced from each hand to the air underneath him and with a flourish the mage started moving backwards. He staggered slightly as he reached firm ground again, but he was otherwise unharmed.

'That fat bastard better step up the pace!' Coran growled as he smashed through yet another shield.

Doranei didn't waste time agreeing. The battle hadn't been raging for long, barely a quarter of an hour, he'd guess, but that was only Coran's second attempt, and they were badly outnumbered here. Whatever their advantages of position, their losses weren't so easily replaced on the line.

The sudden heavy beat of drums from the back of the Menin line sparked a flicker of hope in his heart. At first nothing happened, but then the call was taken up and the attackers edged backwards, away from the reach of the Narkang weapons. Once disengaged, they wasted little time in turning and heading for the gaps between the men of the second rank.

'Hold the line,' King Emin shouted hoarsely, Suzerain Derenin repeated it more loudly, and immediately the order was shouted from all sides. Doranei looked at the men standing with him as someone dragged dead Brother Daratin out of the way. No one showed much inclination to pursue the enemy; the sight of Narkang bolts taking them down as they fled was enough for most. The battle was far from won, but they all knew a pursuit could mean it lost soon enough.

'Enjoy it, brothers!' King Emin shouted after a mouthful of water. 'Enjoy the sight. They're not used to this! You're the first to drive them back – and that won't be the last lesson we teach Lord Styrax today!'

Despite himself Doranei raised his sword and cheered with the rest of them. There'd be little enough to cheer come the end of the day. But as he shouted with the others, he found his body didn't want to stop. Tired though he was, that sudden rush, feeling alive as he yelled himself hoarse, was hard to let go of. Then Veil tossed him a flask of brandy and he felt something better.

Standing with one foot on the artillery's marker stone, Lord Styrax watched his first wave fall back without comment. He started to turn to his right, and stopped when he realised no one was there. Under his enclosed black helm his expression darkened: he still expected to find Kohrad in his lee. The young white-eye had been slow to learn restraint, so he'd kept him close, to teach him the skills he'd need when he inherited his father's empire.

Styrax's hand tightened into a fist. There would be no inheritance now. He could nominate a successor – a man he respected, and trusted with the future of his empire – but there would be no swelling of the heart as he watched his son find his own path to greatness. Kohrad's mother, Selar, had poisoned her own womb when she saw how he worshipped his father; Kohrad's betrayal had broken her heart.

'Captain Hain,' he called brusquely. 'What is the state of the cavalry?'

The officer hurried up and saluted. What was left of his troops had been temporarily reassigned, and Hain attached to Styrax's own command staff. 'It's good, my Lord. General Gaur continues to shadow the enemy, to ensure they cannot outflank us, so their horsemen are effectively negated.'

'I am glad to hear it,' Styrax said, still staring towards the fort. 'What are the casualties from that first tunnelling spell?'

'Severe: at least a regiment incapacitated, probably the best part of two. We must assume the second strike has had the same effect.'

The huge white-eye was silent for a moment. 'Tell me, Captain Hain,' he said eventually, 'if you were King Emin, how would you approach this battle?'

'I—Ah, I'd expect it to be my last, sir. A lord's importance to his army is immense, especially when inexperienced troops make up the majority.'

The white-eye nodded. 'So you would expect me to kill you as swiftly as I can. Why then would you place yourself in a crucial position?'

'Because my presence would inspire them to fight hardest. If the position falls, then my life is likely lost, no matter where I am. Casualties in the first wave look heavy; it'll cost thousands to take for sure.'

Styrax raised a hand to stop him. 'Or you could place yourself there as a lure, to keep me occupied while the weapon you hope will win the battle does just that.'

Hain shrugged and tugged the strap holding his axe in place. 'Didn't hear what we did at Tor Salan, then. It's a desperate thing to trust your whole nation to.'

'But if you fear there is no other option?'

'Then I'd defend that weapon with everything I have. Make sure no one gets through, no matter the cost, and aye, risk my own life to drawn the attack away.'

Lord Styrax turned and looked back at the cavalry. It was hard to make much out as they were spread out to prevent enemy incursions. There had been dozens of small engagements, testing the enemy and probing for weaknesses but Gaur would see they remained inconclusive. The enemy had the advantage of numbers, but the beastman had two heavy infantry legions to hold his centre. If the Narkang cavalry tried to pin Gaur down or swamp him, they'd find themselves blunted on his shield wall, then butchered.

He looked further, to the seven legions of the reserve, three of which were Menin heavy infantry. They remained in formation directly behind Styrax, ready to exploit any opening.

'Send the second wave to attack the fort and a rider to inform General Gaur I'm committing the reserve. I want the Bloodsworn, Reavers and remaining minotaurs on the right flank of the fort with the Menin reserve, and Lord Larim to take the other flank with the rest, together with Gaur's infantry. Gaur is to keep tight to the first wave of troops once they've reformed and use them as he seems fit.'

'Like pulling the head off a sentinel lizard,' Captain Hain commented as he saluted to acknowledge the orders.

'Exactly – I'll deal with this weapon myself and leave King Emin stranded. He'll learn the hard way that no defence is absolute.' Styrax stared at the fort, where the king was commanding its defence. 'But of course, full honours to any man taking the king's head before they surrender, Menin or otherwise. Ensure the men know.'

The fighting along the tree-line was growing increasingly desperate. Daken prowled behind the lines of troops like a hunting lion, all the while bellowing orders and cursing. Osh watched him, blood-stained and battered after the desperate fight with the Chetse but as unrelenting as winter. Intentionally or not, Daken was performing exactly the role King Emin had intended for him: the raging, indefatigable white-eye hero. He was egomaniacal by nature and blood-crazed in battle; it was impossible not to take heart from the Mad Axe's presence. Daken's legend was mixed, but Osh could see Daken's past crimes meant little here.

Large numbers of Chetse had got lost in the tangled forest, trying to skirt the troops stationed there, making little headway as they'd attacked piecemeal. Now the men were gathering up the several hundred Menin dead and piling them up as makeshift barricades – they wouldn't stop anyone attacking, but it channelled the remaining forays to ground of Osh's choosing as well as keeping the troops busy.

The Menin had withdrawn to regroup after half an hour of brutal hand-to-hand combat, the sobbing cries of the injured filling the air as they were dragged back from the front line. The grass at their feet was stained by the blood and loosened bowels, and Osh could see from the faces of those left that the full horror of the battle was settling in. The only thing he could do about it was to keep the men busy, bringing up the next line of troops and withdrawing the battered legion that had borne the brunt of the first assault.

Counting the dead was difficult amidst all the bustle and chaos. The open ground was a hundred yards across, and the dead lay strewn across it. The enemy had brought makeshift walkways to cross the fifteen-foot-deep ditch and used their archers to pin the down the defenders while they got enough troops across to take them down. Their attack plan had nearly succeeded.

Shouts suddenly rang out from the front rank of troops. Osh scanned the ground, at first thinking the Menin were advancing already, but he could see nothing. When he listened more carefully he realised it was anger, not alarm, that he was hearing.

He sent one of the young officers attending him to investigate while he checked behind him: an old man's battlefield paranoia never died. Troops behind stood in neat blocks; a division of five hundred spearmen was heading over to bolster his numbers. Companies of fifty were stationed all around, watching for surprises from the rear. They'd had to deal with a second pair of minotaurs, but now all was quiet; it appeared they'd weathered the worst of the flanking attack. He doubted they'd try to surprise them again from the forest – it was impossible to maintain any form of order there, and a piecemeal assault wasn't going to be enough.

'Sir,' called the lieutenant as he returned, face pale, 'sir, they've got captives out on their line – they're torturing them.' The young man was barely old enough to join the army – seventeen winters if that, and most likely a year into some commission promised before his parents had known what was coming.

'Tell our archers to fire on them,' Osh ordered.

'But they're women and children, sir!' the youth exclaimed in dismay.

Osh lurched forward and grabbed him by the throat with one powerful hand. 'Sonny, they're going to die, no matter what – so you'd wish them something slow and agonising, or the peace of a swift death?'

'No, sir – yes, sir,' the lieutenant spluttered.

Osh released him. 'Exactly. So give the order.'

He watched, his teeth gritted, as the first few arrows were fired. Despite the deaths they'd just seen, the slaughter of hundreds whose blood now stained their boots, shooting at captives was clearly a reminder of things they'd pushed to the back of their minds. Osh knew men faced battle in different ways, but none wanted to dwell on thoughts of family and loved ones: that sucked the fire from a man's belly, and sure as anything would see him face-down in the mud before long.

And now I'm at it, Osh chided himself, *Gods, man – you are getting old!*

'No time for all that,' he said aloud, ignoring the questioning looks he got from his remaining aides, 'what are the bastards going to try next?'

'Ah, Reavers, sir?' opined the boldest of his aides, a tall olive-skinned youth who has been one of Osh's pupils until war had broken out, when he had begged to join his teacher's staff.

'Let's hope not,' Osh laughed. 'Last thing we need's more bloody white-eyes here! But you're right – it'll be something to disrupt us. Maybe mages, something to give them a step forward, at least. They won't win the ground easily, there's too many of us to push back, so they'll need to chop a path through.'

'Shall I send another division to support? Increase the number of ranks?'

Osh frowned at the lines of fresh infantry, their pike-heads glinting in a rare shaft of sunlight. The men were eight ranks deep and tightly packed. He shook his head. 'No, it's sufficient. Bring the reserves up in regiment blocks with free ground around them. I want them to be able to react when the unexpected is thrown at us.'

'Tachrenn Lecha,' General Vrill said slowly, as he watched the last of the captives discarded after having their throats cut.

The Chetse commander turned to face the white-eye, screwing his eyes up slightly as the Menin's enchanted armour fluttered in a breeze that Lecha could not feel, the air around it appearing to constantly dance and twist.

'General,' Lecha said dully, letting the head of his axe fall to the ground. The tall Chetse's skin had turned almost bronze in the summer sun, a similar hue to his polished armour. He tugged his helm from his head and tucked it under his arm as he waited for Vrill to speak. He had little time for most Menin officers, despite acknowledging Lord Styrax as a man capable of leading them all to glory.

'Your troops are ready?'

'For what?' Lecha spat. 'Another suicide mission? It looks to me as though most of the Flamestone Legion aren't coming back out of that damn forest.'

'For the decisive action,' Vrill growled, swinging abruptly around towards Lecha and forcing the smaller man to step back. 'Your legion is the Caraper Guard, is it not? And is that not a powerful, armoured predator?'

'It is,' Lecha said warily.

'Well, emulate it then.' Vrill pointed at the left flank of the open ground, where the ranks of enemy abutted the long defensive ditch. 'We've heard enough of the strength of Chetse warriors; now it's time to prove it. Reform your legion, forty ranks deep, and punch through the enemy. Add whatever remains of the Flamestone Legion to extend your front ranks and conceal your depth.'

'Just us?'

'Not alone.' Vrill assessed the two Menin heavy infantry legions briefly. 'The Second Tocar Legion on your right flank, the First behind you. We'll move up the line to widen the breach.' He gestured towards a hairless mage with unnaturally pale skin hovering nearby. 'Lord Styrax intends to penetrate the line behind the fort – let us show him how it's done.'

Tachrenn Lecha bared his teeth and jerked his axe up into his hands. Heading back towards his men the Chetse called back to Vrill, not caring who else could hear, 'Tsatach's chosen people will show you all.'

CHAPTER 37

Osh watched a line of shadow sweep from the north over the Narkang lines as a bank of cloud drew in. The late morning sun was again hidden as the king's mages kept the threat of a storm close to dissuade Lord Styrax from employing his wyvern.

'Enemy advancing,' called one of his aides, hurrying up from his position at the ditch, 'Menin legion in deep order on the left. Chetse legion tight to them, and more Menin approaching the ditch directly.'

Osh hissed a curse as he turned to wave forward more troops. 'Major, take your troops and brace the left flank – shoulders in their backs, man.' He pointed to where he wanted them, and didn't wait to watch them go. He walked to the aide's station at the ditch: there was a division of archers on the right of the Chetse, then a gap of fifty yards before two legions of infantry in Byoran colours. He could see they carried more bridges to throw across the ditch; many of their front rank were using them as shields against the continuous arrow-fire.

Daken appeared at his side, clapping a massive hand on the ageing warrior's shoulder. 'Not getting enough action at the back, eh?'

'I'm trying to work out if they've got anything more up their sleeves than brute force.'

'Force works fer me. Strongest man wins, that's the way o' things,' Daken declared.

They watched the enemy approach at a steady tramp. They wouldn't want to be running more than two hundred yards in heavy armour, however quickly they wanted to cover the ground. The Menin approached with spears ready to be levelled, hunched down behind their shields, while the Chetse carried shields only in their front ranks, to protect the majority while they closed for the kill.

At seventy yards, Osh suddenly felt a cold ball of dread appear in his stomach. The Chetse legion had angled unexpectedly, just as they were readying to charge, moving ahead of the slower Menin. Suddenly the right hand side of their line faltered and Osh realised what they were up to: the Chetse were in deep formation, massed on one side behind a standard front rank. The effect of the men of the right halting slanted the legion's advance so when the charge was sounded, they were coming at an angle.

'Merciful Gods,' Osh breathed.

For once Daken had nothing to add. He pointed with his axe to the alarmed aides behind them. 'Summon the reserves, everyone you can – now!'

There was little time for anything more. A great roar came from the Chetse legion as they gathered pace, their shield line intact and closing. Osh felt the rumble of their feet through the ground: fifty yards, now thirty . . . The pikemen lowered their weapons to present a spiked wall, but now the pikes weren't pointing directly at the enemy.

Osh looked around as enemy arrows began to fall and the Byoran troops marched steadily towards him. He stood only twenty yards from the end of the ditch and felt as much as heard the impact as the Chetse collided with their line. It rang out like a long peal of thunder, distantly building before crashing against his ears.

The ranks shuddered visibly, and a dozen men in the final rank were thrown from their feet as the force was transmitted back through the press of bodies. Any screams were drowned out by the clatter of weapons and the bloodthirsty bellows of the Chetse . . . then it went suddenly and terribly quiet. Normally the front line would hunker down behind their shields and let the heavy axes do their horrific work, but not this time. Osh found himself frozen, unable to move as the line of conflict paused, held in the balance, before the Chetse drove forward as one.

The concentrated mass of troops was too much to bear and more fell at the back of the legion and were trampled as several hundred men were physically shoved backwards a step, then another. The front rank was hidden from him but Osh could picture it easily enough, his troops pressed further up against each other, able to do little beyond keep their pikes level while the Chetse drove harder and harder into them. However many Chetse were dead at the front, those at the back would know nothing of casualties, only that they could not stop pushing at any cost.

On the left he heard the Menin crunch into the supported side of the line with another terrific crash, though without the momentum of the Chetse charge. Directly ahead Osh saw the remaining infantry, lighter-armed spearmen, running forward amidst a hail of arrows from all directions. He flinched when one thwacked into his helm, but it glanced away harmlessly.

The spearmen threw down more than a dozen bridges and walkways, some six feet or more wide; the defending regiments ran to meet their attackers, and a savage struggle for each began, as they battered each other to death in the restricted space. One bridge was thrown down barely ten yards from where they stood, and Daken forced a path to the head of it and stood with one foot on the wooden platform as he waited for the attack.

He smashed at their shields with his great axe, pitching one after another down into the ditch through his sheer strength. After four men had fallen, the enemy hesitated, stunned by the raging white-eye with glowing blue tattoos, and the defenders had enough time to chop away at the end of the bridge and shatter the wood until that too dropped into the ditch below.

The Narkang pikemen were not faring so well. The Chetse continued to heave forward with practised skill. Their long two-handed axes decimated heads and pike-shafts alike, and Osh saw the line weaken further and started to buckle. Men started thinking only about survival, and began to give way to the pressure as they were forced further back. With each step the Chetse gave a triumphal shout, driving forward with one will, and after barely a minute their greater strength told and the line of pikemen parted and split.

Some scrambled madly backwards as the front ranks collapsed, only to be trampled in the onrush, while the right flank disintegrated, dozens pushed by their terrified comrades into the open end of the defensive ditch. Others found themselves colliding with the line of defenders behind the ditch.

Icy fear filled Osh's gut as the first of the Chetse shields burst through. 'Where are the reserves?' he croaked. 'Daken!'

The white-eye looked over and saw the danger. The Chetse were still advancing in close order, towards the archers strung behind the main line, who panicked and fled, most heading directly into the forest. Beside them was a division of pikemen, the troops who had held the line in the first assault.

Leaving his own position Daken brandished his axe to wave the reserve troops forward. 'Charge, you bastards!' he hollered, and without waiting, the white-eye followed his own orders, heading straight for the exposed flank for the Chetse, his axe raised. As he ran, a long tendril of bluish light darted out from his body and snagged the ankles of several soldiers, who stumbled and fell, sprawling under the feet of their comrades and causing a moment of confusion just as Daken arrived to decapitate the nearest. He wasn't alone for long as the pikemen followed their white-eye general's lead. They all knew what would happen if the Menin gained a foothold inside the Narkang lines, and that knowledge overrode their fear.

Daken battered away at the nearest Chetse, hacking furiously at the smaller soldiers, whilst being careful not to cut a path into their ranks and find himself surrounded. The flank of the legion ground to a halt as the soldiers turned to face the new assault, and their tight formation stretched, becoming ragged as the rest continued to advance on through then a chorus of whoops and shouts came from the forest side and a disordered crowd of soldiers raced out from the trees into the Chetse's other flank. The Narkang Watchmen had arrived.

Finally the Chetse stopped and prepared to defend themselves. The reserve pikemen were advancing towards their short front rank and the mass of Watchmen, bolstered by some of those archers who'd just fled into the trees, slammed into the side of the Chetse, attacking furiously.

Osh took a moment to look back along the ditch and saw they were holding – but only barely.

'Sen, get that messenger to summon more troops from the reserve, as many as he can!' Osh yelled, grabbing his former pupil by the arm and shoving him towards a horseman stationed behind the advancing pikemen. 'Is the ditch breached?'

'No, sir,' answered another aide, looking down the defensive line, 'only one bridge has gained ground and there's a company already surrounding the incursion.'

The Mystic of Karkarn turned back to the Chetse. They may have been under assault on three sides, but they were by far the most ferocious of the troops involved. Making a decision, he yelled at a squad of pikemen standing ready to see off the next bridging attempt and beckoned to include his own small command staff too, 'All of you; come with me!' With that, Osh started limping towards Daken's small group attacking the left flank of the Chetse, but before they arrived he could see the Chetse line had relaxed and lost its tight formation, the better to surround and slaughter their attackers.

'But, sir, look!' said his young lieutenant, the fear evident in his voice as he pointed to a second block of troops following in the path of the Chetse.

'I know that,' Osh growled, grabbing the youth by the arm and dragging him a few steps along, 'but you don't get to choose every fight – the longer we hold 'em, the better chance the rest have.' He released the lieutenant and drew his scimitar. 'Form up on me, you coddled girlies! It's time to see if any o' you had a teacher worth a damn!' And he headed straight for the few dozen Chetse who'd broken away from their line, intent on surrounding and destroying Daken's men. Under his breath he muttered a prayer, one he'd never spoken before; it was reserved for moments such as this: '*Karkarn aid me, for these offerings with my blade. Karkarn welcome me, for this day I die.*'

Lord Styrax watched the second wave march within bowshot of the fort and raised his own sword. All around him the heavy infantry roared with one voice, thumping the butts of their spears against the ground. The beat of the war drums behind cut through the noise and they set off, marching in time towards the open stretch of ground between the wooden fort and the defensive ditch. With only seventy yards of ground to work with he'd stood two legions side by side, fifty men in each tight rank, and he'd placed himself in the centre.

Since the Cheme Third Legion had been decimated, the Second was on his right, the Arohat Fourth on his left and the more manoeuvrable Cheme First in front, already closing on the defensive ditch. The archers there started firing as soon as they were past the marker, but Styrax's attention was on the solid line of defenders ahead. There were at least three legions packed into one solid line – it was impossible to judge how many, but it looked like the commander had pushed as many troops as he could into that gap. No doubt there were several legions of archers behind.

'My Lord?' said a cultured voice behind him, 'my coterie-brother has contacted me.' Mage Esetar sounded animated for a change, the prospect of marching into battle and being surrounded by death apparently exciting the Adept of Larat. It didn't surprise Styrax; Esetar epitomised everything that folk hated about his kind: he was sadistically cruel, and dispassionate about almost everything. Only power and death could spark some life in his washed-out, almost reptilian face.

'He reports Duke Vrill has breached the line, but they are defending it vigorously.'

'Hear that, Hain? The enemy are vigorous,' Styrax said, not taking his eyes off the enemy for a moment.

Captain Hain glanced at his lord. 'Aye, sir.' His face was grave behind his half-helm; his humour had died with the bulk of his legion.

'Have the men step lively, then,' the Lord of the Menin ordered, 'Vrill will be insufferable if he wins this battle – I may have to kill him.'

'Advance pace, sir, aye,' Hain said, and repeated the order at the top of his voice to the drummer. The command was beaten out, and on the final note the two legions broke into a jog, ignoring the arrows that started whistling down almost immediately. Styrax could see the men of the First Legion were getting a harder time of it, out ahead of the main body and lacking the heavy armour of their comrades in the Second.

One hundred yards from the enemy line the hail of arrows intensified as the fort too turned its weapons on them; now black ballista bolts of varying sizes were slamming into the side of the Arohat Fourth, and a name was shouted out by someone in the front rank of the Cheme legion, calling the first blood. As he looked over he felt the solid impact of an arrow on his pauldron, pounding his shoulder back, but he was lucky: the head had failed to punch through his armour.

'Esetar,' Styrax called over the clamour of the dead soldier's name, 'signal the Reavers.' The élite white-eye regiment was in its customary place, stationed behind the advance troops, ready to be thrown by mages directly into the fighting. His remaining minotaurs, more than a dozen of the monsters, trailed behind the Cheme First, screened from the worst of the artillery fire until they were within leaping distance of the ditch.

Fifty yards. A new drum beat crashed out, a frantic heavy hammering readying the men for the charge. Styrax added his deep voice to those around him bellowing out the name of the first man lost. The infantry hefted their spears. The drumming intensified, and with a roar they were off, surging forward like a tidal wave.

Styrax put his free hand to the Skulls on his chest and felt the vast power inside them kick like a mule. With energies crackling around his unarmoured left hand, racing along the lines of scar tissue, he reached out towards the enemy.

The Narkang troops lacked the armour of his heavy infantry, most were wearing only studded leather tunics and peaked helms. As Styrax ran he yelled arcane words that caused the mage behind him to squawk with surprise. The words seemed to flow from his mouth like jagged shards of ice, sharp edges brushing over his tongue to meet the raging power held in his hand. A cold cloud filled with murderous slivers of energy roiled over the ground, glints and winks of steel reflecting the jagged clumps of grass underneath.

The vaporous mass started rolling now, swift and savage, leaving the grass ripped up as it went scything over the moor until it gusted through the enemy soldiers like a bank of darkly glittering smoke. Styrax watched men staggering and falling as their unprotected legs were slashed to ribbons, dropping their pikes, or throwing them away as the murderous magic sliced its way through the Narkang defence. The front ranks crumpled, just as the Menin charged, first one line of men then a second, and a third, falling to their knees across a twenty-yard stretch.

Styrax grinned maniacally at the sound of the high screams of men in agony before his own troops drowned them out with shouts of brutal intent. Distantly he heard the minotaurs joining in the savage cry, but in the next moment the gap between them had closed to nothing and he shouted even louder as his infantry smashed into the still-reeling enemy. With shields high and spears back they drove in, stamping down on the shrieking fallen, bludgeoning the pikes with their heavy shields, then stabbing forward with broadsword and longsword, scimitar and sabre.

The Menin exploited the gap left by the magic-struck pikemen, savagely attacking the disordered and poorly armoured defenders, while Captain Hain led the next ranks of Menin onwards. A shriek of fury cut through the cacophony as the Reavers arrived on their blade-edged shields to fall upon the assailed enemy. Even their warcries were drowned out by the roaring minotaurs as the monsters joined the battle. Styrax beamed as he saw the ripple of fear run visibly through the besieged pikemen.

With Kobra drawn he started pushing forward to get to the heart of the fighting, but he was stopped in his tracks as another great tremor ran through the ground. Suddenly the air was full of crashing and confusion, and they heard the groan of the earth tearing open. Styrax followed the sound and turned – just as four ranks of the Cheme Legion disappeared in a cloud of dust, dropping like stones into the hole beneath them.

We must—The thought didn't get any further as he sensed something else blossom on the battlefield, magic as vast and weighty as the Narkang weapon, but still distant. Surprise turned into astonishment, then anxiety as a presence shimmered into being like a beacon igniting into a blaze . . .

Except the presence wasn't ahead of him, it was behind.

He turned, even as he realised who it was, though he couldn't see anything past the Bloodsworn behind him. But there was no mistaking that scent; he knew it only too well . . . and the knowledge sparked something akin to fear in his belly. The air behind his troops seemed to judder, and a haze of dust appeared.

The presence was not alone.

Not alone, no, he'd not come alone, Styrax thought, desperately trying to work out what this would mean, whether he needed to pull back from the fight, go and deal with the new threat first. The cries of injured men from the crater behind put paid to that thought; he couldn't leave this weapon alone, or it would devastate his army.

The time has come, he realised. *King Emin's made my choice for me – I must destroy this weapon, and hold nothing back to do so. We live and die on this strike of the sword. Would I have it any other way?*

Lord Styrax ignored the presence and turned back to the fight, barging his way forward to bring his formidable skills to bear. Even before he reached the defenders he could see their eyes widen in fear as they saw just how huge he was.

You will have to wait, Mortal-Aspect, he thought as his obsidian-black sword tore into the first Narkang soldier. The blade greedily absorbed the spilt blood. *But never fear; I have strength enough to teach both King Emin and Karkarn a lesson they'll never forget ... if they even live that long.*

The lance drifted down in a smooth, practised arc, timed to perfection, and the steel tip drove into the nearest enemy's unprotected throat. His head snapped backwards under the force of the blow and blood sprayed into the air. Momentum carried Vesna's hunter on into the dead man's horse and its armoured shoulder smashed the smaller steed away. Vesna reached for his sword as the crash of similar impacts all around him sounded: the Farlan had arrived.

The cavalry were completely unprepared for the Farlan assault, and panic ensued as those who tried to flee got caught up with those trying to stand their ground. The scarlet-liveried Ruby Tower Guards had recognised their black-and-white-clad attackers well enough; they were reluctant allies of the Menin, and few wanted to face the charge of the Ghosts. They knew they weren't strong enough to face the heavy cavalry of the Farlan, and they barely tried. As Vesna fought his way through, the Byorans struck back weakly, more interested in getting out of his way. Many never even raised their weapons as he chopped a bloody path through.

The air was filled with the stink of blood and shit and sweat, and all Vesna could hear was the clash of steel and the screams of the dead and dying, a symphony of pain that made his divine half soar. His heart hammered loud in his chest, suddenly alive, and beating with more power than ever before. He struck again and again, blindingly fast, already moving, ready for the next blow, while men fell like wheat before him.

A Byoran braver than most of them lunged at him with his spear, and Vesna was forced to twist in his saddle to deflect it. The press of men behind him was pushing his horse away, out of reach, but Vesna swept his sword low, then up, stretching his arm and slicing towards the man's face – and felt the weapon jar and bite into flesh, but his hunter carried him on, and he didn't see if he had killed the man.

Instead, he found himself face to face with the Byoran standard bearer, who went at him with a long sabre, which Vesna caught on his shield, raising sparks off the embossed lion's head. Sweeping upwards with his own weapon he sheared through the standard's pole, and brought the sword back down to chop through the Byoran's wrist on the downwards swing. The man fell screaming, and the standard fluttered as it toppled after him.

And what remained of the Byoran resistance collapsed.

They ran blindly from the black-and-white-liveried soldiers and colourfully dressed nobles, all of whom were hacking around themselves with equal savagery. The swords and war-hammers and axes took a terrible toll, despite halting their chase after no more than twenty yards, pulling back into formation, ready for the next challenge.

Vesna saw General Lahk's legion advancing to their left flank. The Chetse had spotted them and an infantry division was approaching quickly – but in their fervour, they had underestimated the distance between the forces. Vesna turned the other way to check on Suzerain Torl's more lightly armed legion of black-clad Brethren – more than a match for anything the Menin could call on. Vesna couldn't see their one force of heavy cavalry, the Bloodsworn, which was conspicuously absent, but he wasn't complaining. As much as the Iron General side of him might have wanted to test his Ghosts against the fanatical Menin élite, the human side overruled it.

Battles are there to be won; glory can take care of itself: the sentiment came unbidden, the memory of his first weapons-tutor, Shab. Like many young nobles, Vesna had been interested only in glory and elegance at first, and using a shield as an offensive weapon had offended that sensibility, until Shab had proved otherwise – the hard way.

He smiled grimly to himself. 'And this lot don't stand a chance,' he muttered.

'Nope,' replied Swordmaster Pettir beside him, 'we'll be sending the whole damn lot to the Herald's Hall soon enough – they're buggered.'

'But not quickly,' broke in a hesitant voice. Legion Chaplain Cerrat was standing a few feet away, and his bright white robes were splattered with mud and gore. 'King Emin could fall by the time we reach him.'

The young man looked stunned by his first battle, but he'd clearly given good account of himself. His robe had been sliced open, revealing the armour underneath, and the gibbous blade of his moon-glaive was stained with blood.

'Not quickly, no,' Vesna admitted, scanning the troops ahead of them. The infantry looked ragged to his practised eye, but there was still the greater part of five legions of heavy infantry between them and the king, enough to swamp Vesna's three thousand cavalry. 'But that's not our concern right now; the king will just have to stand.'

A hunting horn rang out over the moor and the three men watched General Lahk lead a wedge of Ghosts into the centre of the advancing Chetse legion, who were lacking both the heavy armour and the spears of the Menin infantry. With any luck they would be as brutally – and speedily – dealt with as the Byoran Guardsmen. In the distance he could see a massive engagement going on at the furthest fortification: thousands of soldiers were swarming over all sides of it in what he guessed was a pincer movement. On the left the Narkang cavalry were massed, apparently waiting for the enemy to react to the Farlan shock troops before committing themselves.

'*Did we arrive too late?*' Vesna asked as he signalled for his legion to close on Lahk's. The Dark Monks had already moved up, approaching the Chetse's other flank, and they were also preparing to charge. It was too late to countermand that order, Vesna thought; they would have to let this move play out before he could strike at the rear of Styrax's main force.

'Advance at the canter,' he called. Ahead were two stationary cavalry legions and one of Menin infantry, both close enough to come to the Chetse's rescue, perhaps – but showing no inclination to do so. They had a massive cavalry force on their other flank, and no apparent intention of moving, or breaking their formation, any more than they already had.

'That's it, you worry about your own skins,' Vesna said with forced cheer, causing Pettir to laugh coarsely. 'We'll keep you boxed in there, and cut your lord's hamstrings while you watch.'

'Can you sense Styrax?'

Vesna pointed towards the wooden fort. 'He's up there, right in the thick of it all.'

'He's committed then. If you can sense him, he must know we're back here.'

Vesna laughed. 'Trust me on that – I made quite sure of it. He knows he's running out of time. Might be we can force him into something desperate.'

Lord Styrax lashed out, feeling the blood patter onto his armour as he sliced through flesh and bone. A falling body thumped against his leg and he turned on instinct, cutting up, but catching only air. He moved into the gap, and continued to hew a path through the Narkang defenders, hearing the clatter of armour in his wake as the Cheme men surged up to support him. Over their heads he could see the minotaurs had leaped over the ditch and were battering the enemy – they'd already torn a hole in the line and the enemy were looking hard-pressed to fill it.

More and more of his soldiers poured over the ditches, eagerly charging in the wake of the minotaurs – then a great shaking ran through the ground again. Styrax hissed his defiance and pushed on, not waiting to watch as the Narkang mage ripped another bloody great hole in the ground underneath his monstrous shock-troops. He answered with lances of darkness and flame that gouged furrows through the ground and ripped soldiers in half. The defenders were definitely buckling under the assault, unable to resist the pressure being exerted by his minotaurs and Reavers.

The Menin white-eyes had congregated near the rear of the enemy line, not far from where Styrax himself was standing. They were fighting back to back, leaping forward to kill with axe and shield before withdrawing, howling maniacally all the while. The white-eyes moved with such speed and aggression the Narkang could barely get close enough to bring their pikes to bear. The Cheme infantry were pressing further and further forward, and Styrax cast darting spirals of slicing magic into the supporting troops. They were inching closer to the mage's platform.

There was a crash beside him as the soldier on Styrax's left vanished and a heartrending scream rang out. When he turned, he saw the soldier's body lying behind him. A ballista bolt had turned him into a bloody, shrieking mess. Captain Hain took one look and dropped his axe into the injured man's neck, saving him a last few seconds or minutes of pain before moving to take his place. Styrax, furious, flicked his free hand towards the ballista and shouted arcane words over the clamour, and the air around it burst into flame, engulfing both engine and crew.

The white-eye, seeing an enemy commander ahead of him, struck out, but missed as the red-helmed nobleman jumped back and out of the way. Styrax moved with breathtaking speed, kicking the man in the chest and knocking him flying, then swiftly dispatching the hurscal next to him. He fought on, his upward blow taking out the man in front of him, the downward sweep taking care of the man behind him. He stepped into the gap they left, lunged right to impale a soldier, sweeping his leg out to kick the feet from underneath another, then trampling him to his death and he moved on another foot.

He moved so quickly that the next figure to loom into view was almost decapitated before he'd seen them; Styrax checked his blow just in time and Kobra's fanged swordpoint glanced harmlessly off the Reaver's cheek-guard. The smaller white-eye was shaking with bloodlust and euphoria; at Kobra's touch the Reaver reared backwards in surprise, but wasted no time in throwing himself at Styrax. The Menin lord sidestepped the maddened Reaver and dodged his axe, twisting as the Reaver's momentum carried him past and cracking him on the back of the head. The blow dropped the white-eye instantly, and the Cheme soldiers behind him jumped the felled man without stopping.

Their goal was in sight.

Seeing the defenders' line torn open, Styrax allowed himself a moment of quiet satisfaction. A rabble of frantic soldiers stood between him and the mage's platform, but behind him he could hear his Bloodsworn and the remaining Reavers making their presence felt. And away over the moor he could feel the Mortal-Aspect of Karkarn coming closer, the beat of his hooves echoing in Styrax's mind. He ran forward, crackling bands of energy wrapping his sword, eager to be unleashed at the mage ahead.

As though in response, the ground began to rumble again, faster and more urgent this time, and above him the air roiled, tinted red – by blood, or magic? Styrax couldn't tell; the air was suffused with both. All he could see around him was frantic movement and swirling dust, the chaos of war – and he its beating heart. He screamed, and pushed them on, one last drive to the heart of the enemy's defences, to break them before Karkarn's Mortal-Aspect could get to them.

Daken rolled in the blood-spattered dirt, his fingers stiff around the handle of his axe. The sky turned from pink to black as he forced himself onto his back and discovered his left arm was broken. He couldn't feel the fingers of that hand – couldn't see if he even still had his hand in the butcher's mess surrounding him. His ribs felt like they were on fire, and the memory of a steel-bound shield being smashed into his side flashed across his mind. The Land was silent around him, other than a constant, dull note that rang in his ears, filling his head.

Daken looked up at the sky. Dark clouds were rolling high above; he felt their cool touch on his skin. The pain in his side receded as a voice drifted closer. He didn't know the words, but the voice was girlish. Daken blinked, not comprehending, as the voice gradually drew closer, until she was whispering into his ear. He felt her fingers on his skin, and when he flinched, he felt a fresh searing pain down his ribs.

'It is time,' the girl whispered, her voice laden with breathy, seductive promise. 'Strike now, my precious.'

Daken felt her hands underneath him, lifting him up until his feet were underneath him once more. Shapes blurred across his vision, all meaningless, until he suddenly saw a face, one like his own, who stared at Daken in surprise, frozen in the moment of lifting his helm from his head, spilling black-red hair onto his shoulders.

Daken felt a beast snarl in his belly and his fingers tightened about his axe. He wrenched it forward, dragging the heavy weapon up from the ground one last time to hold it high above his head. The other white-eye let his helm fall again, and it was as if both men moved in slow motion as Daken let his axe fall, inexorably, and it slammed down high on the side of the man's helm, and the steel crumpled like tin under the enormous force of the blow.

Daken felt the shock of impact in his arm as the white-eye's head snapped downward; he was dead before he hit the ground. Daken stumbled forward, his feet falling from underneath him, then the girl's hands were under him again and he felt her pulling his body past the dead white-eye, over the bloody earth until the ground disappeared beneath his feet and he was falling into darkness . . .

'Coran, go!' the king yelled at the top of his voice, startling Doranei. The Menin in front of him tripped on a corpse underfoot and he dropped his guard to catch himself. Doranei cracked his shield into the man's temple with such force it shattered what was left of the frame. He shook the useless pieces from his arm and looked around for Coran.

The big white-eye had dropped from the rampart and was heading for the reserve division of Kingsguard, standing ready in the centre of the fort.

'Your Majesty,' Doranei shouted, 'where's he going?'

'Styrax has broken the line,' the king replied, standing still for a heartbeat as he assessed the assaulting troops once more. 'Someone must try to cut him off from his troops.'

The fort was a scene of horror, no scrap of ground untouched by the gore of mutilated men, and the screams of the dead and dying rose and fell in fearful cacophony. Doranei grabbed a discarded shield from the ground, only to discard it again when he saw an arm still snagged in the handles. As a Chetse warrior struggled up what remained of the ripped-apart rampart wall, even that élite warrior looked drained by the effort. Doranei flicked the shield, arm still attached, at the Chetse to slow him, then stabbed the man in his face, slicing a bloody furrow through his cheek.

A moment later Doranei felt his foot go from underneath him. He skidded on a blood-slicked log and crashed heavily on the ground. The king, seeing him fall, moved to cover him – and stepped into an arrow that caught him high in the shoulder, pitching him backwards onto the ramp to the ground.

Doranei gave a shout of horror and forced himself upright, realising the effect such a sight would have on the defenders, but Veil had seen too, and beat him to it. The King's Man pulled the ensorcelled axe from Emin's unresisting grip, snapped the shaft of the arrow, and helped him over to a standard pole he could use to support his weight.

Three Chetse, emboldened by the sight, surged over the rampart wall, but Doranei was ready and charged into them, his sword cutting a dark path through the stinking air. Two were killed cleanly; he caught the down-swing of the third Chetse's axe on his sword and kneed him in the balls, following that up with an elbow that knocked him over, and swiftly finished him off.

'Keep the king safe!' Veil yelled as he took up position beside Doranei. Blood was flowing freely down the side of his face. 'If he falls they'll crumble,' he said more quietly.

Over the clatter and crash of battle Doranei heard a roar from the reserve Kingsguard as Coran led them out into a slaughter every bit as bad as the one they'd just left. Veil nudged him and pointed at what looked like a cavalry battle, and both men felt a sudden surge of hope: it looked like General Lopir had got around and was tearing through the light Menin cavalry.

A gust of cool wind blew across the ramparts, and Doranei felt a few spots of rain. Strangely, the patter of water seemed to wash away his fears, and he felt a swell of elation. On his left, Suzerain Derenin, the Lord of Moorview, cleaved into a man's neck. The nobleman was caked in blood and filth, and his arm sagged under the weight of his notched, broken-tipped sword, but from somewhere he found the strength to lift it again and meet the next attacker.

Doranei checked his monarch was still standing, then, shouting incoherently, he threw himself back into the fray with renewed strength. He dropped to one knee to slash across a Chetse's belly, catching him under the breastplate, and the man fell, staring down in disbelief as his guts spilled into the churned-up mud – until Veil clouted him across the face and sent him tumbling down the gouged slope.

Behind them one of the battle-mages cast another lance of fire into the crowd of attackers, but they were exhausted and the fire barely sizzled as it hit.

Doranei felt a fine mist of rain on the exposed parts of his face, and unbidden, a memory rose in his mind: the scent of the ocean, rolling in over Narkang's streets, and in that moment he felt the strength of the nation behind him as King Emin's words blossomed to life in his heart.

One way or another, he realised, *it ends now.*

Coran raced ahead of the Kingsguard, ignoring the nearest Menin as he pounded towards the heart of the Bloodsworn regiments. A flood of green and gold followed him as five hundred Narkang élite, fresh to the battle, sprinted to keep up. The few Menin trying to work their way around to the fighting on the other side were cut down in moments, and the disordered flank of the Bloodsworn disintegrated as the Narkang soldiers smashed into it.

Coran was still ahead, battering a path through the enemy, swinging his mace about his head, letting its great weight crush armour and skulls alike. He was less encumbered than the Bloodsworn, and strong enough to fell a man with every blow, despite their heavy armour. Those few who managed to strike back at him found their swords glancing off his armour as Coran twisted and turned, never staying still, never giving them more than a glimpse of any vulnerable part of his body.

The Kingsguard caught him up and drove like a cavalry wedge into the slower-moving knights, knocking them aside, even wrestling them to the ground to get them out of their way as Coran led the charge to the Cheme infantry. The enemy were reeling from the speed and ferocity of their assault, Coran's wordless rage echoing in their ears as the Kingsguard followed him joyously into the teeth of the battle.

The white-eye plunged the spiked tip of his mace down into a man's neck and felt the armour over the collar-bone snap and buckle. The mace snagged on the armour as he tried to withdraw it, distracting him for long enough for an axe to crash into his shoulder. He grunted at the pain as the black-iron was unable to withstand the full force of the blow, spun around and used the vambrace on his left arm to bludgeon the knight in the side of the head, knocking the man into a Kingsguard, who finished him.

A flash of agony lanced through his injured shoulder as Coran hauled back on his mace, still trying to free it, but a Bloodsworn lashed out at him and he was forced to dodge to the side. Swearing furiously, the huge white-eye kicked at the head of his mace in frustration, and it flew up from the corpse in a spray of blood – just as a Menin knight took advantage of his momentary lack of concentration.

But Coran was faster than the Bloodsworn, and he lunged forward before the knight could strike again and punched right through his cuirass.

Something struck him on the side of the head, and Coran wheeled and swung out blindly. He hit something, but couldn't see what, then he felt a burst of pain in his ankle and toppled like a tree, crashing onto his back. He lay there a moment, stunned, waiting for the final blow – then he saw movement surging past: the Kings-guard had overrun him.

Someone grabbed his arm and helped Coran up, and he shouted thanks without looking to see who it was, hobbling forward as fast as he could, anxious to rejoin the fight. A bright light exploded through the air, splitting through two Kingsguard in a fountain of blood, and finally Coran saw the one he'd been seeking. The pain faded away, now a distant memory, as something stirred deep within him. He tasted the air, and felt his teeth bare in a savage grin at the stink of blood and guts all around. He'd been born and bred for war, but now the bloodlust receded in Coran's mind and he recognised the moment he had been waiting for all his adult life. This eclipsed Ilumene, and any other unfinished business. *This* was what he'd been created for.

He absentmindedly jabbed the butt of his mace into a soldier who appeared in front of him, knocking the man flying, just as Lord Styrax dismissively turned away from him and raised a misty-grey shield just in time to stop a white ball of fire from Cetarn on his earthen platform. Coran reversed his mace and stabbed the spike down into the soldier's head, his eyes still firmly fixed on Styrax, while a low growl built in his throat.

A short Menin clutching an axe jumped between them and aimed for Coran's ribs, but the white-eye swayed out of the way. At last he tore his eyes from the huge white-eye lord. He wrenched his mace up and caught the short Menin soldier a glancing blow on his shoulder, which knocked the man off-balance. Coran kicked his near leg out from under him, dropping the Menin. A tall soldier ran to save his officer, but Coran swung at his face, smashing away both helm and jaw in a burst of blood. The short Menin took advantage of the death of his trooper to stab Coran in the thigh with the spike of his own axe, while the white-eye was fending off blows from elsewhere.

Coran howled and staggered away, and the Menin, still grimly clutching onto his axe, found himself pulled to his feet. Coran grabbed the man's arm and yanked him closer before he punched him in the face with the mace. The Menin's head snapped back, falling limp, and Coran shoved the man into his next attacker, but not in time to prevent an axe hitting his injured arm. He lurched sideways, only to be caught from the other side. This time stars burst before his eyes. He was drunk with pain, remaining on his feet through sheer force of will as he fended off blows from all sides. A white-visored Bloodsworn ran in for the kill, and after stabbing him in the groin, Coran picked him up and tipped him onto a pair of infantrymen, knocking them to the ground. He let the momentum of his blow carry him around, barely seeing the next soldier as he caught him in the chest, throwing him backwards and into the man behind. Coran stabbed him in the face as a spear drove deep into his side, and he turned, screaming and swinging his mace down in one last killing stroke.

The weapon slipped from his grip and agony ripped up his spine. His left leg buckled as he reached for the next Menin and he slipped to one knee. His vision was already blurring as something struck him in the back of the head. He never saw the axe swinging up to meet his falling neck.

Styrax sensed the troops behind him being driven back, but still he didn't turn. Riotous energies were turning the air scorching hot – the mage had a Skull, that was clear, and whoever it was, he knew he would not survive the day; he was letting the power within the Skull run rampant, and channelling such a vast stream of energy meant he was burning out his own brain at the same time.

The sensation sparked incandescent fury in Styrax's belly. He'd felt this before, when the Farlan bastard had killed his son. He marched on, head down as he kept his defences up, barely seeing his men around him being torn apart by the blistering rage in the air. Styrax tightened his grip on his sword. He was unable to counter-attack without weakening his shields or scorching his own mind. He fought for every step, like fighting a swift current, but step by step he closed on the hillock. The air screamed and ripped before his eyes, burst white and gold like the heart of a star, until suddenly he was there, taking the sloped side of the platform in one stride.

The energies winked out, vanishing instantaneously, and for a breathless moment the gigantic white-eye and the mage faced each other. The mage was a big man himself, the size of a normal white-eye, but his face was withered, the veins in his neck bulged out, and his skin was as white as his hair. As Styrax met the man's tortured gaze, the mage's hair crumbled to ash. The Lord of the

Menin raised Kobra high, and with an almighty effort, he cleaved the mage's body in two, from left shoulder to right hip.

Styrax felt the Land slow about him, a hush descending over the slaughter. The mage's Crystal Skull hovered before him, waiting for the white-eye to claim his prize. He turned about to face the fort, which was being slowly engulfed by his soldiers. At the foot of the platform Reavers and Bloodsworn – the few dozen men left – were desperately trying to resist the Kingsguard, while the greater bulk of the Cheme legion on his left were readying themselves for a counter-attack.

Lightning split the sky as his fingers closed about the Skull, and a sense of victory descended upon him. Up above, the heavens roared their approval, and underfoot the ground shook, echoing the vast, looming power of the clouds. Through the Skull he could feel trails of energy running through the moor, great iron chains drawing power to him through the earth. He turned lazily towards the beleaguered fort and the mages at its heart, sensing their presence like campfires in the dark.

It ends now, Styrax thought with grim finality.

The Land exploded underneath him. Everything went white.

ENDGAME

With his hand flat against the ground, Isak watched lightning strike the chains around the earthen platform. A haze of white fire encircled it, leaping up from the iron links and between the steel-capped stakes set in the surrounding ditch. Great chunks of soil flew up into the air as great thick-limbed figures of earth and stone rose up on all sides. The figures moved slowly, but with strange grace, reaching to the sky as they ascended from the churned ground between platform and ditch.

Their inhuman faces were serene as they advanced on the black-armoured white-eye, quite unlike other elementals Isak had seen before. But these were Ralebrat; they were a breed apart from the rest – and they had the chance for atonement for their deeds during the Great War within their grasp. Some looked carved from stone, others were made of pebbles and dirt, like a statue without its skin. As the fire all around intensified, they attacked.

Isak stood, letting the cloak slip away from his shoulders. Underneath, he was shirtless, displaying the heart rune engraved on his chest, and as faces turned his way, he felt their gaze like needles, pricking into the long swathes of twisted tissue that covered most of his body. One hand covered his belly and the jagged scar that ran up his stomach. That wound he'd not received in Ghenna. That memory the witch had not been able to erase.

Isak watched Styrax's blade, remembering its presence in his own gut – the white-hot pain, the way it jerked through flesh and bone, how it ripped out his guts ... and he remembered his own high-pitched screaming. At that moment he'd smelled the hot, foetid breeze and he'd heard the chittering voices as darkness fell like acid eating his vision, and the emptiness of the grave swept over him.

Isak pulled his body straight as he faced the man who had killed him. On his chest the heart rune blazed hot and fierce on his skin, but *this* pain was welcome.

Styrax didn't see him at first. He moved with dazzling speed, wielding Kobra with strength and precision, hewing a space in the centre of the platform, even as more Ralebrat rose to ward off the assault of the Menin bodyguard. As he moved, the white-eye lord weaved a skein of magic about him, a net of light spun from his sword to tangle the Ralebrat as they closed in on him. Already a dozen lay on the ground, looking like shattered monuments as the injured elementals struggled to escape the broken forms they had taken.

Then he caught sight of Isak, and Isak felt the look like a blow. It took all his strength not to shy away from Styrax, to lift his eyes and match the gaze of the one to whom his life and death had been bound, long before Isak was even born.

Styrax hesitated too, and the Ralebrat pulled back, keeping just beyond range of the fanged sword. On the other side of the ditch that encircled the earthen mound, the battle was still raging fiercely. Within the defensive boundary, there was a moment of unearthly calm.

'I killed you,' Styrax cried. 'I saw you fall into Ghenna.'

Isak felt the words like a punch in the gut. Above him, as the sky was torn by lightning he cringed from the brightness, raising his left hand to shield his eyes. The thick lines of shadowy scarring on his left arm were vivid against his pale skin.

'I know,' Isak said in barely more than a whisper, slowly lowering his arm again. 'You killed me. And here I stand.'

'How?' Styrax asked.

Isak gave him a broken smile, though his damaged lips and missing teeth made it more a grimace. 'Your arrogance – your rage – they showed me the way. We are all slaves to our birth.' He brought his right hand from behind his back and in it was Eolis, shining unnaturally bright against the storm-darkened moor.

'You want to fight me again?' Styrax laughed coldly.

Isak shook his head, though the damage to his neck and shoulder made it almost impossible for him to turn to the left now. 'The Gods made you to be peerless in combat,' he said. 'I cannot beat you. No single mortal could beat you. And now no God would dare try.'

Styrax was silent a moment, then he removed his helm, and Isak saw his face properly for the first time. In his dreams it had always been covered, and the day Styrax had killed him, pain had blurred his vision. To his surprise, it was an unremarkable face, neither ugly nor handsome. Lord Bahl had looked rough and unfinished, but that was not the case with Kastan Styrax: his face was simply a canvas upon which power and strength had been painted. It was with the set of his jaw and the look in his eye that made Lord Styrax arresting to behold.

'Then why are you here?'

Isak saw his finger brush the Crystal Skull fused to his sword-hilt, summoning the wyvern. The Menin Lord knew a trap when he saw it, but he was content to talk while his wyvern braved the lightning-lit sky to get to him.

'To judge you,' Isak said simply. 'Look at the Skull in your hand.'

Styrax stared at the shining object for a few moments. 'This is not the one King Emin took from Scree?'

'It is Dreams,' Isak confirmed, and held Eolis awkwardly out before him. The sword bore another Skull. Behind him three figures were slowly approaching. Legana and the witch of Llehden flanked him, one on either side. Their part in this was played. Mihn stood behind, in his master's shadow. They watched in silence, bearing witness to the consequences of their actions.

'This one is Ruling, first among the Crystal Skulls,' Isak said.

He stabbed the sword down into the ground and unleashed the power of the Skull. White cracks appeared in the ground, racing through the trampled grass towards the mage's platform.

Styrax immediately raised his defences and a cocoon of energy burst into life all around him before the shining cracks could reach him – but the shimmering power raced around the platform, well clear of the Menin lord.

Once again the tortured air roiled under the magical assault. Isak felt the scars on his skin come alive with pain, but still he continued, guiding the force through the Skull and into the sword.

Now, for the first time, he raised his voice, crying out, 'Obey me – come forth!'

Colours burst all around and lightning lashed the ground between them, ripping the air apart to reveal a swirling column of darkness behind.

'Come!'

The darkness writhed, coils of energy spreading to encircle the platform. Jagged lightning forked across the sky, again and again, striking all around the perimeter of the earthen platform. The Ralebrat reeled and cowered, some dying even as they supplicated themselves.

Isak pulled Eolis from the ground and levelled it towards the darkness, and the column wrenched around so violently the air itself ignited, burning white-hot. Death stepped out of the dark and raised His golden sceptre and all around the platform the Gods of the Upper Circle of the Pantheon stepped forward, obeying Isak's call.

The Skull of Ruling was tied to Death, the Chief of the Gods, and it was the most powerful, and the most perilous to use. Aryn Bwr had seen that, and known that possession conferred the strength of rule, but Death's place was at the very centre of the Land, and that was too much for even a king to bear long.

At the sight of the Gods who'd abandoned them in punishment millennia ago, the Ralebrat attacked once more, throwing themselves with abandon at the Lord of the Menin. His protective cocoon burst blindingly as they destroyed themselves upon it, but still they did not stop.

'Peerless you were made, and unmatched you will die!' Isak shouted over the wind that churned around them.

The Gods of the Upper Circle knelt, arms outstretched in the torrent of magic that was whirling, faster and faster, around the platform, all focused on Lord Styrax – save for Nartis, whose blank, midnight-blue face watched Isak.

'But death is not the only defeat. You taught me that.'

An incantation tolled through the fractured air, the sonorous voices of Gods drawing such a torrent of magic down from the sky that the very clouds above were dragged down.

Styrax didn't wait to hear more, but started to fight his way towards the platform's edge, but the Ralebrat continued to bar his way. They didn't make any attempt to fight their preternaturally swift opponent, just threw their stone bodies in his path to slow him as the energies surrounding the Gods and Isak struck at everything within the circle, battering elementals and mortal alike. The Ralebrat were shattered, but the white-eye was only driven back a step

547

or two as the Crystal Skulls on his armour pierced the blistering hurricane of magic, flaring as bright as the sun.

'They gave you power,' Isak cried, feeling the sparks of energy burst from his white eyes and race across his skin. 'In their fear they gave you more power than any mortal should possess, and with it came pride, and arrogance: an understanding that nothing was beyond your skills. That no being – mortal or God – was your better.'

Isak took hold of Eolis in both hands, letting the blade cut deep into one palm. The blood seemed to boil on its surface and some droplets were scattered by the wind, but there was enough of the viscous liquid to run the length of its edge.

His voice dropped to a whisper, but it resonated around the moor like the heartbeat of the Land itself. It shuddered through earth, flesh and God alike. Somewhere far away he heard Mihn cry out.

'And so I curse you,' Isak gasped, both with the pain running through his body and the memories of Styrax's vengeance.

Up above, the Menin's wyvern was a dark shape in the sky, compelled by its master's call despite the lighting. Styrax reached out with his sword and turned in a full circle, casting a burning trail of light that drove even the Gods back, but he could not stop their chant as Isak continued, 'They made you to be untouched by God or mortal. As I cannot kill you, so I curse you, not with death but life,' he choked. Limbs shaking and bile rising in his throat, he deflected the vast raw power Styrax was throwing in all directions.

The wyvern dropped closer, close enough for the Menin to reach its claws, but it was too late and they both felt it.

'I curse you – with the pain of ten thousand days in the Dark Place, with the life's blood of a mage's sacrifice, with Death's authority held in my hands.'

He felt it then, the cold fingers in his mind, and on Styrax's face he saw the icy claws reached even deeper in.

'I curse you, and I strike your name from history,' Isak howled in agony and grief, 'stripped of arrogance and pride, empty of the self you once knew, gutted of all you are. I take your name and all you have won by the strength of your hand. I curse you for eternity, to find only darkness where once you knew your own face.'

He could not speak any longer as the chill touch of the curse entered his mind, questing through the brutalised corners of his head for a name and ripping it away forever. Isak felt the words fade like a whisper on the wind, a curl of smoke whose shape hung on the breeze and was then gone – vanished.

The man on the platform screamed, his hands clasped to his head, his fingers digging so deeply in that blood welled up. Skull and sword discarded, he fell to his knees as the claws tore into his brain. The Skulls fused to his cuirass dropped from the armour, then the first of the black whorled plates slipped off his body and clattered to the ground. The man was oblivious; convulsing, he collapsed to the floor.

Isak heard shouts from all around as the curse spread, reaching out through friend and enemy alike to steal a name from all of them before rippling further out and across the Land. He felt the power of the Gods, fed by the Skulls in their midst, waxing strong, even as the effort drained them.

The man on the platform writhed and shrieked as the claws reached the last recesses of his soul, shredding memories and excising even the smallest remnants of the man he had once been. He tried to fight, beating at his head and ripping his clothes, but to no avail. The curse bit deep, as he scratched bloody shreds of cloth from his body. Somehow he fought his way upright, muscles straining against the weight of the Land, but all the while he was howling at what was being taken from him.

And then it was over. The gale subsided, the magic of the Gods dissipated, and the man fell, exhausted, mewling, to his knees. Isak took a hesitant step forward, barely able to stay upright himself.

'And I dub you the Ragged Man,' he whispered, blood trickling from his nose and mouth as he spoke.

He reached Death and the cowled figure turned to face him. The air smelled of age and fatigue, of a temple drained of its majesty and power.

'It is done,' Death intoned. He made a dismissive gesture at the Ragged Man, and a pair of Ralebrat grasped the whimpering figure by each arm and dragged him into the ground, moving through the earth as easily as a bird ducking below the surface of a lake.

'They will take him far from here.'

'There is a cottage by a lake,' Isak said hoarsely. 'There is a place for him there.'

Death inclined His head. The God's presence was less awe-inspiring now – the curse had required so much power that the Upper Circle were winking out of existence, back to their distant palace. Only Karkarn, Nartis and Death remained.

'You know what you have done,' Nartis called.

Isak felt a great tremor of pain run through his body as he nodded, and in the next moment Mihn was there, slipping underneath him and taking some of Isak's great weight on his shoulders.

'We have weakened you,' the witch of Llehden stated, advancing just past Isak as he wilted under the strain.

'We have made a choice,' Legana added, resting heavily on her staff. The Gods-touched woman faced Death without flinching, her emerald eyes shining through the unnatural gloom. 'A choice that was ours to make.'

'You have weakened us,' Death said slowly, looking from one to the other. 'For what is to come, the Gods will not be able to intervene.'

'Good,' said Legana firmly. 'It is our fate as much as yours. The choice should be ours this time.'

'It is our time,' Isak agreed wearily. 'This was the only way, and now—Now the Land will be remade.'

'By whom?'

The scarred white-eye tried to smile, but it hurt too much. He started to turn away, but caught sight of one half of Cetarn's charred corpse, and his gaze lingered there.

It was the witch who answered, speaking for them all. 'By those of us willing to sacrifice everything.'

The story is concluded in

THE DUSK WATCHMAN

DRAMATIS PERSONAE

Akass, Lord Paden – Deceased Lord of the Menin and Chosen of Karkarn, predecessor of Kastan Styrax

Aladorn, General Dall – Retired soldier from Narkang who helped mastermind King Emin's conquest of the Three Cities

Alterr – Goddess of the Night Sky and Greater Moon, a member of the Upper Circle of the Pantheon

Amanas, Quitin – Keymaster of the Heraldic Library of Tirah

Amavoq – Goddess of the Forest, patron of the Yeetatchen; a member of the Upper Circle of the Pantheon

Amber – A Menin major in the Cheme Third Legion

Antern, Count Opess – Narkang nobleman and advisor to King Emin

Anviss – God of Woods, consort and Aspect of Amavoq, Goddess of the Forest

Aracnan – Immortal mercenary of unknown origin

Ardela – Farlan devotee of the Lady, Legana's companion

Aryn Bwr – Battle name of the last Elven king, who led their rebellion against the Gods. His true name has been excised from history

Asenn – Goddess of Rain and Snow, daughter of Lliot, deceased God of All Waters

Ashar (The Lady of Hidden Paths) – Aspect of Anviss, God of Woods, local to Llehden

Azaer – A shadow

Bahl – Deceased Lord of the Farlan and Chosen of Nartis before Lord Isak

Belarannar – Goddess of the Earth, a member of the Upper Circle of the Pantheon, once patron of the Vukotic tribe

Beyn, Ignas – Member of the Brotherhood

Bolla – Mercenary-turned-penitent of Ushull in the Circle City

Brandt, Commander (Brandt Toquin) – Commander of the Narkang City Watch who died in the defence of the White Palace, younger brother of Suzerain Toquin

Burning Man, the – One of the five Aspects of Death known as the Reapers

Capan (ab Kert ab Coas) – A Harlequin

Carasay, Sir Cerse – Colonel of the Tirah Palace Guard Legions

Carel (Carelfolden), Marshal Betyn – Farlan nobleman, mentor, friend and former commander of Lord Isak's Personal Guard

Cedei, Herred – Member of the Brotherhood

Celao, Lord – Litse white-eye, Chosen of Ilit and ruler of the Ismess quarter of the Circle City

Cerdin – God of Thieves

Cerrat, Jeco – Farlan cleric and Legion Chaplain of the Tirah Palace Guard

Cerrun – God of Gamblers

Certinse, Sir Dirass – Deceased knight and captain in the Palace Guard, third son of Suzerain Tildek

Certinse, Knight–Cardinal Horel – Commander of the Knights of the Temples, younger brother of Suzerain Tildek, Farlan by birth

Certinse, High Cardinal Varn – Farlan cleric. Third son of the Tildek Suzerainty, younger brother of Suzerain Tildek, Knight-Cardinal Certinse and Duchess Lomin

Certinse, Duke Karlat – Deceased Farlan nobleman, ruler of Lomin, nephew of Suzerain Tildek

Cetarn, Shile – A mage in the employ of King Emin

Chade – A Menin huntsman in the service of General Gaur

Chaist, Duke – Ruler of Embere, Member of the Knights of the Temples

Chalat – Deceased former Lord of the Chetse

Charr – Chosen of Tsatach, Krann to Lord Chalat, Lord of the Chetse, who died in the Menin invasion

Chera – A young girl from Llehden

Chirialt, Dermeness – A Farlan mage

Cober – White-eye from Aroth, bodyguard to Count Pellisorn

Coran – White-eye bodyguard of King Emin Thonal of Narkang

Corl – Farlan assassin, a devotee of Kassalain

Corlyn – The traditional name adopted by the head of the Farlan's priest branch of the Cult of Nartis, God of Storms

Cosep, Swordmaster Harle – Farlan soldier

Cuder, Sir Creyl – Knight of Narkang, founding member and Commander of the Brotherhood

Dace (Sir Dace Yoren) – Farlan nobleman, and Count Vesna's best friend; former member of the Palace Guard

Daima – A witch of Llehden

Dainiss – Devotee of the Lady from Canar Fell

Daken (The Mad Axe) – White-eye mercenary from Canar Fell, aligned to Litania the Trickster, an Aspect of Larat, God of Magic

Dapplin, Captain Sontoran – Arothan soldier

Daratin, Kap – Recent recruit to the Brotherhood

Darn, Major Ferek – Menin major in the Cheme Third Legion

Dashain – Second-in-command of the Brotherhood

Dassai, Marshal Canerin – Narkang nobleman

Death – Chief of the Gods and head of the Upper Circle of the Pantheon

Deebek, Sergeant – Menin soldier in the Cheme Third Legion

Derager, Gavai – Wife of a Byoran wine merchant, a Farlan agent

Derager, Lell – Wine merchant from Byora and Farlan agent

Derenin, Suzerain – Narkang nobleman, lord of Moorview Castle

Dirr – Mercenary and thief from Tio He

Disten, Cardinal Fesin – Farlan cleric, once a Legion Chaplain

Doranei, Ashin – A member of the Brotherhood

Doren, Abbot – Deceased abbot of an island monastery and High Priest of Vellern, God of Birds

Dors, Unmen Echail – Farlan priest of Nartis, God of Storms

Ebarn, Fei – Battle-mage from Narkang

Ehla – The name Lord Isak is permitted to use for the witch of Llehden

Eleil, Cardinal Luth – Priest of Ilit, God of the Wind, from Ismess, member of the Knights of the Temples, former head of the Serian in the Circle City, now deputy of the Devout Congress

Eliane – Ruhen's true mother, originally named Haipar, until she lost her memory in Scree

Elshaim – Necromancer from Verech who became a prophet, noted for painting a series of images charting his impending descent into Ghenna

Endine, Tomal – Narkang mage in the employ of King Emin

Enkin (The Hounds of Jaishen) – Daemons that roam the Land hunting Aryn Bwr's soul

Eraliave, General – Elven general who predated the Wars of the Houses and wrote the treatise *Principles of Warfare*

Escral, Duchess Natai – Ruler of Byora, a quarter of the Circle City

Escral, Duke Ganas – Deceased husband of Natai Escral

Esetar, Lakal – Menin mage, Adept of Larat, God of Magic, and part of Larim's coterie

Etesia – Goddess of Lust, one of the three linked Goddesses – with Triena, Goddess of Romantic Love, and Kantay, Goddess of Longing – who together cover love in all its aspects

Etharain, Suzerain Hape – Nobleman from Aroth

Evaole (the Water Bearer) – Aspect of Vasle, God of Rivers

Farlan, Prince Kasi – Farlan prince during the Great War, in whose image white-eyes were created and after whom the lesser moon was named

Fate – Deceased Goddess of Luck, also known as the Lady, killed by Aracnan

Feers, Count Lerail – Farlan nobleman from Tirah

Fernal – Demi-God from Llehden, son of Nartis, the Storm God, and nominated by Isak to be his successor as Lord of the Farlan

Firnin, Camba – Specialist mage from Narkang

Fynner, Chaplain – Priest of Nartis from Lomin and chaplain of the Knights of the Temples

Garash, High Priest Kel – Priest of Belarannar, Goddess of the Earth, from Narkang, member of the Knights of the Temples and head of the Devout Congress

Gaur, General – Beastman warrior from the Waste, Lord Styrax's most trusted general

Genedel – A dragon

Gesh – Litse white-eye and First Guardian of the Library of Seasons

Grast, Deverk – Infamous former Lord of the Menin

Great Wolf, the – One of the five Aspects of Death known as the Reapers

Grepel of the Hearths – Aspect of Tsatach, God of Fire

Grisat – Mercenary-turned-penitent of Ushull in the Circle City

Hain, Captain Gess – Menin officer in the Cheme Third Legion

Haipar the shapeshifter – Raylin mercenary of the Deneli tribe from the Elven Waste, known as Eliane after she loses her memory

Halis, Anversis – Narkang academic, King Emin's uncle

Hastars, Torosay – Arothan mage

Headsman, the – One of the five Aspects of Death known as the Reapers

Herald of Death – Aspect of Death who ushers the dead to their Last Judgement

Herotay, Swordmaster Gal – Deceased Farlan soldier, former Commander of the Swordmasters and Knight-Defender of Tirah

Holtai, Tasseran – Narkang mage and scryer

Horle – Member of the Brotherhood

Hulf – Puppy, now belonging to Isak

Ilit – God of the Wind, patron of the Litse tribe and member of the Upper Circle of the Pantheon

Ilumene – A former member of the Brotherhood, now disciple of Azaer

Introl, Anad – Farlan politician; Gatekeeper of Tirah, member of the City Council; Tila's father

Introl, Tila – Lord Isak's advisor; Count Vesna's fiancée

Isak – Deceased white-eye, former Lord of the Farlan, Duke of Tirah and Chosen of Nartis

Isen – Farlan blade-for-hire

Jachen, (Major Jachen Ansayl) – Commander of Lord Isak's Personal Guard, former mercenary

Jackdaw (Prior Corci) – Former monk of Vellern, God of Birds

Jailer of the Dark – A dragon that fought the Gods during the Age of Myths and lost. Too powerful for them to completely kill, it was chained to the doorway to Death's throne room on the lower slope of Ghain

Jarrage, Major Fenter – Member of the Knights of the Temples from Sautin

Jato, Steward – Steward of the Ruby Tower in Byora

Jesters, the – Four brothers, sons of Death, all Demi-Gods and Raylin mercenaries

Kail (ab Torn ab Venn) – A Harlequin

Kanasis – Aspect of Vrest, God of Beasts

Kantay – Goddess of Longing, sometimes referred to as Queen of the Unrequited. One of the linked Goddesses – with Etesia, Goddess of Lust and Triena, Goddess of Romantic Love – who together cover all the aspects of love

Kao – Berserker Aspect of Karkarn, God of War

Karkarn – God of War, patron of the Menin tribe and member of the Upper Circle of the Pantheon

Kasai, Nanter – Innkeeper's wife from Kamfer's Ford

Kassalain – Goddess of Murder, patron of assassins

Kayel, Sergeant Hener – The alias used by Ilumene in the Circle City

Kenanai the Mother – Aspect of Death, first of the Mercies on the slopes of Ghain

Keness of the Spear – Minor Aspect of Karkarn, God of War

Kerek, Brother – Farlan cleric, secretary to Cardinal Certinse

Kerin, Swordmaster Orayn – Deceased Farlan soldier, Commander of the Swordmasters and Knight-Defender of Tirah

Kiallas – Litse white-eye

Kinna, Lady Ilail – Byoran advisor to Duchess Escral

Kirl, Horsemistress Lay – Menin auxiliary, attached to the Cheme Third Legion

Kitar – Goddess of Harvest and Fertility, member of the Upper Circle of the Pantheon

Kiyer (of the Deluge) – Aspect of Ushull, Goddess of the Mountains, local to the Circle City

Kobel – A veteran Harlequin

Koteer – Demi-God and eldest brother of the Jesters, a son of Death

Kurrest, Captain Jaim – Farlan solider, officer of the Tirah Palace Guard

Lahk, General – Farlan white-eye, commander of the forces in Tirah and a marshal of the Tirah-Tebran border district

Larat – God of Magic & Manipulation, member of the Upper Circle of the Pantheon

Larim, Lord Shotein – Menin white-eye mage, Lord of the Hidden Tower and Chosen of Larat

Latiar, Captain Pinnail – Officer of the Ruby Tower Guard and noted duellist

Lecha, Tachrenn Erach – Chetse legion-commander of the Ten Thousand

Legana – Farlan Mortal-Aspect, formerly devotee, of the Lady, Goddess of Luck, and former agent of Chief Steward Lesarl

Lesarl, Chief Steward Fordan – Principal advisor to the Lord of the Farlan

Leshi – Farlan Ascetite soldier, attached to Lord Isak's Personal Guard

Litania (the Trickster) – Aspect of Larat, God of Magic & Manipulation

Lliot – Deceased God of All Waters and member of the Upper Circle of the Pantheon, whose domain was divided up among his five children: Inoth, Turist, Shoso, Vasle and Asenn

Lokan, Duke Shorin – Farlan nobleman and ruler of Merlat

Lomin, Duchess Feya – Deceased Farlan noblewoman, wife of Koren Lomin, mother to Duke Karlat Certinse, sister to Cardinal Certinse, Knight-Cardinal Certinse and Suzerain Tildek

Lomin, Duke Belir Ankremer – Farlan nobleman, bastard son of the previous Duke of Lomin

Lopir, General – Narkang general

Luerce – Inhabitant of Byora and follower of Azaer

Malich, Cordein – Deceased necromancer from Embere

Marad, Private – Farlan soldier in the Palace Guard, and member of Lord Isak's Personal Guard

Maram Boatman – The mysterious entity who patrols the River Maram between Ghain and Ghenna, the home of daemons

Marn (ab Codor ab Veir) – A Harlequin

Mayel – A novice from Abbot Doren's monastery, native of Scree

Mihn (ab Netren ab Felith) –Failed Harlequin, once Lord Isak's bodyguard and dubbed the Grave Thief by the witch of Llehden

Mikiss, Koden – Deceased Menin army messenger, turned to vampirism by Zhia Vukotic

Mochyd, High Chaplain – Farlan cleric. High Chaplain of the Farlan, head of the chaplain branch of the Cult of Nartis, God of Storms

Morghien – A drifter of Embere descent, known as the man of many spirits

Nai – Former acolyte to the deceased necromancer Isherin Purn

Nartis – God of the Night, Storms and Hunters. Patron of the Farlan tribe and member of the Upper Circle of the Pantheon

Orolay – Farlan blade-for-hire

Osh, Hambalay – Mystic of Karkarn from Canar Fell, known as Brother Penitence

Paen (ab Esor ab Finn) – Priestess of Death from the Harlequin clans

Pellisorn, Count – Nobleman from Aroth, head of the Arothan Honour Council

Perforren, Captain Halier – Farlan officer of the Knights of the Temples, aide to the Knight-Cardinal

Pettir, Swordmaster Korpel – Farlan soldier who succeeded Swordmaster Kerin as Commander of the Swordmasters and Knight-Defender of Tirah

Poisonblade, Arlal – Elven assassin, a true Elf, untouched by the Gods-imposed curse that warps their bodies

Poller, Unmen Ast – Resident priest in Kamfer's Ford, aligned to Death

Purn, Isherin – Deceased Menin necromancer, killed in Scree; once apprenticed to the necromancer Cordein Malich

Ralen, Sergeant Kyn – Farlan soldier in the Palace Guard, member of Lord Isak's Personal Guard

Ranah, Suzerain – Farlan nobleman

Ranah, Scion Ventale – Farlan nobleman

Reshar, Count Eterai – Narkang nobleman

Rojak – Deceased minstrel originally from Embere who died in Scree, first among Azaer's disciples

Ruhen – The name taken by Azaer as a mortal

Sapex, Heten – Menin soldier in the Cheme Third Legion

Saroc, Suzerain Fir – Farlan nobleman and member of the Brethren of the Sacred Teachings

Sebe (Sebetin) – Deceased member of the Brotherhood

Seliasei – Minor Aspect of Vasle, God of Rivers, who now inhabits Morghien

Selsetin, Suzerain Pelan – Deceased Farlan nobleman, believed a follower of Malich Cordein

Semar – Deceased Lord of the Farlan who designed and built the Tower of Semar

Sempes, Duke Faran – Farlan nobleman and ruler of Perlir

Sen, Terolen – Narkang Army lieutenant and pupil of Hambalay Osh

Shaberale, Sergeant-at-Arms Sotonay (Shab) – Deceased Farlan soldier and weaponsmaster who trained Count Vesna

Shalstik – Elven prophet who predicted the return of the Last King

Shanas – Young devotee of the Lady, Goddess of Luck, from south of Aroth

Shanatin, Witchfinder Otei – Member of the Knights of the Temples from Akell, servant of Azaer

Sheredal, Spreader of the Frost – Aspect of Asenn, Goddess of Rain and Snow

Shim (the Bastard) – A man from Canar Thritt who, being partially immune to magic, can kill mages with a touch

Shinir – Farlan Ascetite agent attached to Lord Isak's Personal Guard

Shotir – God of Healing and Forgiveness.

Soldier, the – One of the five Aspects of Death known as the Reapers

Styrax, Scion Kohrad – Deceased Menin white-eye, son of Lord Styrax

Styrax, Duke Kastan – White-eye Lord of the Menin

Tebran, Lady Anatay – Daughter of Suzerain Tebran

Tebran, Suzerain Kehed – Farlan nobleman

Tebran, Scion Pannar – Deceased Farlan nobleman, son of Kehed Tebran

Telasin Daemon-Touch (Captain Peragad Telasin) – former Knight of the Temples who is now partially possessed, by both a daemon and by an Aspect of Vrest, God of Beasts

Telles, Unmen Atay – Deceased Farlan priestess of Death

Tenber, Suzerain – Narkang nobleman

Thonal, King Emin – King of Narkang and the Three Cities

Thonal, Gennay – Deceased elder sister of King Emin

Thonal, Queen Oterness – Queen of Narkang and the Three Cities, a new mother

Timonas, Sergeant – Witchfinder of the Knights of the Temples from Akell

Tiniq – Farlan ranger, General Lahk's twin brother, member of Lord Isak's Personal Guard

Torl, Suzerain Karn – Farlan nobleman and member of the Brethren of the Sacred Teachings

Triena – Goddess of Romantic Love and Fidelity, one of the three linked Goddesses – with Etesia, Goddess of Lust and Kantay, Goddess of Longing – who together cover all love's aspects

Tsatach – God of Fire and the Sun, patron of the Chetse tribe and member of the Upper Circle of the Pantheon

Uresh, Colonel – Menin officer, Commander of the Cheme Third Legion

Ushull – Goddess of the Mountains, Aspect of Belarannar

Vasle – God of Rivers and Inland Seas

Veck, Cardinal – Farlan cleric, second only to the High Cardinal in the cult of Nartis

Veil, Arin – Member of the Brotherhood

Vellern – God of Birds

Vener, General Telith – Member of the Knights of the Temples and ruler of Raland

Venn (ab Teier ab Pirc) – Former Harlequin, now servant of Azaer

Veren – Deceased God of the Beasts and once Member of the Upper Circle of the Pantheon, killed during the Great War

Verliq, Arasay – Celebrated mage and academic, killed by Lord Styrax

Vesna, Count Evanelial – Farlan nobleman, celebrated soldier and Mortal-Aspect of Karkarn, one of Lord Isak's closest friends, affianced to Tila Introl

Vrest – God of the Beasts and member of the Upper Circle of the Pantheon, formerly an Aspect of Veren before Veren's death

Vrill, Duke Anote – Menin white-eye general

Vukotic, Prince Koezh – Ruler of the Vukotic tribe, cursed with vampirism after the Last Battle

Vukotic, Prince Vorizh – Younger brother of Koezh, cursed with vampirism after the Last Battle and subsequently driven insane

Vukotic, Princess Zhia – Youngest of the Vukotic family, cursed with vampirism after the Last Battle

Wentersorn, Edelay – Mercenary battle-mage from Akell

Whisper – Farlan merchant and member of Chief Steward Lesarl's coterie of secret advisors

Wither Queen, the – One of the five Aspects of Death known as the Reapers

Xeliath – Yeetatchen white-eye; the Skull of Dreams is fused to her hand

Yeren, Colonel/Senior Penitent – Mercenary from Canar Thrit in the employ of Cardinal Certinse

Yetah, Suzerain Kollen – Farlan nobleman